SHATTERED

by

Petra Thompson

The Pieces Series: Book One

Published by Thompson Publishers

Thompson Publishers
thompsonpublishers.com

Shattered
Copyright © 2019 by Petra Thompson

Requests for information should be addressed to:
Thompson Publishers, PO Box 2605, Cleveland TN 37320-2605

ISBN: 978-1-64407-006-2 [softcover]

Scripture taken from the New King James Version®. Copyright © 1982 by Thomas Nelson. Used by permission. All rights reserved.

Cover design Craig Thompson © 2019.

Printed in the USA.
First printing.

"Words don't leave bruises on the outside,
but they leave scars on the inside that no one can see,
scars that can leave a person shattered for life."
- Brie

Contents

Introduction

The book you are about to read is a true story -- sort of. It's also a fiction novel -- sort of. Let me explain. When my children turn 13 years old, I give them an unique gift. I set up an appointment each week with a different mentor for the next year of their life. Over the course of 52 weeks, they meet with a wide variety of women (or men, in the case of my sons) from diverse economic, social, ethnic and educational backgrounds. Some are business owners. Some are leaders. Some are retired. In the process, my children get to learn the combined wisdom and insights into life, business, skills and relationships which these men and women are willing to share.

Petra has taken her experiences from her 14th year of life and woven them into a story with a fictional lead character. In some chapters, the names of the women have been changed per their request for privacy or due to security concerns. But the experiences, stories and many of the essential details of the time Petra spent with 52 different women have been recorded. The benefit to you, the reader, is that you can learn along with Petra from the lives and wisdom of these women.

Our fourth child is now going through his mentoring year. Because of the incredible benefits I've seen from this program in the lives of my children, I have written a number of books and resources designed to help families who want to see their own children impacted in positive ways. I also have books for the adults who serve as mentors and the youth who meet with them. Additionally, we have a curriculum developed for churches or community groups to enable volunteers to run a mentoring program locally. I also have a coaching program to help parents or leaders navigate the steps of getting a mentoring program started for a child or group of youth. My desire is to see more people do what I have done. It's worth the time, the energy and the hassle because our children are valuable.

If you want to learn more about the mentoring resources available, contact me at craig@walkwithgod.com or visit https://walkwithgod.com/mentoring for more details.

Craig Thompson

Prologue

I'm an atheist. Well, I haven't always been one. I used to be a Christian. Back when my family was together, and happy, or so it seemed. Back before we found out that my dad was a druggie after he purposefully took an overdose and died. Then my mom got addicted to alcohol and started abusing us kids. So, don't I have a good reason for thinking that if there were a God, then He would've taken better care of me? See, I was raised a Christian because my mom and dad were raised as Christians. They got saved at an early age and went to church; but when I was about six, they decided that they could do better on their own, so they left the church and forgot about God. That was right after I had gotten saved. But then they kept doing these terrible things, and I figured, well, if they can do those things and call themselves Christians, then I don't want to be one.

There are three of us kids. There's my older brother, Jackson, who left home at fifteen because he was tired of being kicked around. Some role model. Next, there's my older sister, Kimberly, who's still around but takes out all her problems on me. She has a bunch of friends and is super popular—and loves taunting me about it. She's not an atheist, but she's definitely not a Christian. Then there's me. Brown hair and brown eyes, I look like an average, normal girl with a normal family. That's all lies. I'm like a book. You can look at my cover and assume so much, and unless you start to read me, I appear normal to all who look at me.

I live in a small house, in a small neighborhood, near the middle of town. The house may be considered decent-sized to some, but it's too crowded for me. In it, there's my mom, my sister, my cat, and my grandmother, Eileen Morgan, who just moved in with us, making the house seem even smaller. Plus, she's been a so-called Christian practically from the womb, so I get sermons from her all the time. "Go to church, stop sinning, you shouldn't hang out with those people, they're bad influences…" Blah, blah, blah. She's such a hypocrite. She doesn't even go to church. Sometimes I wish I could just run away. But, if I had, I wouldn't have met that one girl, on that one day, and had that one conversation.

I was at a Christian summer camp one day, forced to go by my grandmother, and was trying to eat my nasty lunch. I had to eat the cafeteria food because there was no other option—other than starving to death. I recognized some people from school, mostly people I didn't hang out with. At school, I hang out with almost all the groups: the jocks, the pops, the nerds, the normals, and even a few of the bads—though very few of them are actually my friends. I hang out with every group but the Christians. Or the "Jesus jerks," as I like to call them.

So it caught me off guard when one of them, Tina Lankford, came up to me while I was finishing eating and said, "Can we talk? God's got something to say to you."

I was dumbfounded. I didn't believe that there was Someone up there, much less Someone who would want to talk to me. I didn't want to listen to her, but I couldn't help myself. I was super curious to find out what this girl thought a non-existent God was "saying to me." She led me out of the cafeteria to a picnic table and sat down.

"I'm going to get right to the point," she said. "God told me last night to talk some sense into you, and I'm gonna do it. You have been away from God too long. You know, deep down, that there is a God up there, but you have told yourself lies for so long that they have infested your heart and mind. The message God said to tell you is this: 'I am here. You can't see me, and you don't try to listen to me or feel me. You are blinded by fear and hatred. Seek me. Find me through others until you are ready to accept me again yourself.

I have been standing at your door knocking for years, but you have drowned me out. I am finally going to make Myself heard. Stop blaming your mother, your dad, your brother, your sister, and your grandmother. Open the door.'"

In shocked silence, I felt my eyes water. I didn't even know this girl, but the message she gave me was directly for me, and it hit home.

"I thought about this all night," she continued. "I think God wants you to go on a mission to find godly women. Women who seek Him. Women who want to share their story so you can find yours. Women who will talk to you and listen to you. Women who will be your friend. So I challenge you today to find one godly woman every week for the next year. Ask them questions to find out for yourself if there is a God. Will you take the challenge?"

I stared, mutely watching her eager face. Then, hardly realizing it, nodded. "I will," I said.

She smiled, a joy that I couldn't explain lighting up her countenance. "I know you won't regret this!"

I got up from the table and left, feeling warmth inside that I hadn't felt in years. It was like a drop of water on my parched lips.

So that's how I got stuck with this crazy "mission" that I have committed myself to for the next year. I don't know what I was thinking when I agreed to it. But, at least I'll have a good excuse to get out of the house more often. I may give up after a few weeks, but who knows? Perhaps by the end, my cover will have changed, and my story, too.

Chapter One

A frustrated sigh filled the space in my drab, colorless room. I'm supposed to be meeting with a godly woman this week, and the week is almost over. I groaned as I remembered my conversation with Tina. I racked my brain, trying to imagine someone I could meet with. If only Tina had suggested someone then. As I mentally went through, for the millionth time, the limited list of godly women I knew, a light flashed before my eyes. In annoyance, I glared at the now burned-out bulb and then stomped down the stairs to grab a new one for the ceiling fan.

After finding the bulb underneath the bathroom sink, I stopped outside the bathroom to look at the photos on the wall and stared blankly at the picture of our smiling family. It's amazing how much looks can be deceiving. Two participants of the picture have left. My dad left permanently, and my brother left indefinitely. Just then, my grandmother yelled from the living room.

"Brie, please get me a glass of water with four cubes of ice, no straw, and a slice of lemon. I have a headache and getting up will only make it worse."

I rolled my eyes as I clumped over to the yellowed cupboards in the kitchen to grab a glass and fill it up, tempted to tell her that if she could yell that well with a headache, then she ought to get it herself. I was always fetching this or that for her. That's me. Brie Thompson, the family's servant. My actual name's Hazel, but when I was three I snuck out of my bed at night and went into the kitchen to get a snack. The only thing I could reach in the fridge was some Brie cheese, so I pulled it out and began to eat it; however, my family heard me and came into the kitchen to see what the commotion was about. When they found me sitting on the floor eating an enormous amount of cheese, they called me Brie, and the nickname has stuck. I don't even bother introducing myself as Hazel because people have called me Brie most of my life. I've sort of adopted it as my real name. Even some of my teachers call me Brie. Whenever someone calls me Hazel, they normally have to say it twice because I'm not used to being called that.

Upon delivering the requested item to my lazy family relative, I paused as I left the room. An idea was forming, and I could feel it coming up fast. I looked at my grandmother once more, and it popped into my head. I could see if my dad's mom could meet with me. I knew she was Christian, and I figured she would be the best choice to start out with, especially since I hadn't seen her in ages. When Dad died, everyone on his side of the family was ignored, and my mom constantly declined invitations from them until they gave up trying. I didn't agree with my family's decision at the time, but as I grew older, I just accepted the fact that I could do nothing to change anyone's mind on this. I grew bolder with the idea and decided to contact her, looking through an old address book for her number.

When I hesitantly called her, I expected her to hang up on me; however, that wasn't what happened. I was rather shocked when she greeted me with surprise and cordiality. Once I told her the purpose of my call, half expecting her to laugh as if I were a crazy dodo, she readily agreed, telling me that she had been praying for an open door to communicate with my family. After we had formulated to meet the next day, I hung up and went to tell the shocking news to my mother.

I gingerly creeped into her dark bedroom, stepping around piles of dirty clothes, shoes, and empty bottles. I tiptoed over to her bed and shook her cautiously. When she finally woke up, she groggily glared at me and demanded the purpose of this disturbance of her beauty rest. I could tell she was still suffering from a hangover and mumbled that I was meeting with my grandmother tomorrow and wondered if she could take me. She rolled her eyes.

"Your grandmother is in the next room. Why do you need someone to walk you over there tomorrow? You could just talk to her now." I was getting nervous about where this was heading.

"Not your mom," I said in a timid voice. "Dad's mom." She stared wide-eyed at me before bursting into laughter.

"You actually talked to that woman? Have you been drinking?" She erupted into another peal of laughter. I glared at her, wishing she would magically understand.

"I just talked to her on the phone. She wants to meet with me tomorrow." Mom stopped laughing and cocked a sassy eyebrow at me.

"So regardless of my explicit restrictions, you purposefully decided to override my authority and communicate with his family. You, my dear troublemaker, are quite the audacious one. You actually thought that someone related to your father would stick true to her word and actually see you? That would be a first."

I had tilted my chin up higher and higher as she kept talking; however, once she insulted my grandmother, I had had enough. "Pardon me for breathing, but I do believe that as her granddaughter, I have an obvious right to visit her, whether you say so or not. And, contrary to popular belief, she will indeed stay true to her word, if I have any say in this unfair matter." I gazed boldly into her taunting eyes and cocked my own sassy eyebrow right back at her.

"Fine. I will prove to your ignorant soul that she will not do as she promised. I will personally drive the forty-five minutes down to her house just so I can watch the expression of defeat on your face when you realize the cold, hard truth."

I smirked, knowing that she had just talked herself into a trap. Feeling victorious, I gracefully turned on my heels and glided out of the room to replace the light bulb.

The next day, I was genuinely surprised to see that my mom actually followed through with her promise to take me. I lightly bounced into the passenger seat and sat waiting for my mom to turn on the ignition. She was silent on the way down, either from going over the ways she could rub it in my face if I were proven wrong or from the realization that she was talked into a trap by a few simple words and a challenge from a so-called rebellious teenager. I gloated on the fact that she would have to drive away without me once we got to the house.

Once we arrived at the white, ranch-style house, I got out nervously. What if my mom was right? I timidly knocked on the door and clasped my hands behind my back. The door opened and before me, in the flesh, stood the woman I hadn't seen in years.

"Hello, Grandmother."

"Brie?" She paused. "Do you still go by that, or have you changed it back to Hazel?"

"It's still Brie," I said.

"Alright then, Brie." She gave me a bear hug and welcomed me inside. Before heading into the house, I triumphantly looked over my shoulder at my mom as she backed out of the graveled driveway. I couldn't see her expression, which was probably a good thing. Grandmother inquired if I were thirsty—which I was—and she offered me a seat on the couch. She came back from the kitchen with a glass of orange juice and sat down on a chair opposite me.

"You have no idea how happy I am to be meeting with you today! I haven't seen you in forever!"

I smiled sheepishly and couldn't think of anything to say. She wasn't at all like my mom made her appear to be. In fact, she was quite the opposite.

"I was trying to figure out what to do with you today, and I wondered if you would like to do a flannelgraph story from the Bible, since you used to love those as a kid. I don't know if you still love them because I'm not quite familiar with your recent interests." She added the latter part with a knowing look followed by an understanding smile. "But I know that isn't all your fault."

I was shocked. Was someone actually not blaming me for something? Everyone always blames me and makes it seem like it's always my fault. I quickly hid my shocked expression and quickly chose the story of the ten plagues from Exodus because I was most familiar with it. I hadn't been to church in years, but I figured that I would remember it well enough.

"When you tell a flannelgraph story," she began, "you have to orderly prepare the pieces and set up all the backgrounds." We went into the room where she kept her materials, and we started going through the pieces. I never knew how hard it was to set up a flannelgraph story. We had to get all the plagues, all the people, all the props and food, and all the scenery, even if we were showing the piece for only a split second.

As I was looking at the flannelgraph pieces, I suddenly had a flashback to when I was a little kid, sitting on a tiny carpet circle in children's church, listening to Grandmother teach the story of the crucifixion with flannelgraph. I was already a Christian at the time, and I sat there with tears streaming down my face as I listened intently to what they had done to Jesus. Grandmother was such a wonderful teacher that I felt like I was actually there. I'm surprised that I remember that snippet of my history, since I laid to rest the faith issue long ago. Yet, I also remember that that was the story that made the children's director mad because showing "gory" pictures to children was not acceptable, so he forbade Grandmother to show the pictures of the crucifixion. As a result, Grandmother stopped teaching there. I didn't understand why he thought it was such a big deal. Even as a young kid, I had already seen plenty of movies with death scenes in them, and I know that other kids had, as well. The flannelgraph pictures were nothing compared to that!

"There's a little book on the dining room table from which you can read the story of the plagues," she remarked, drawing me back to the present, as she set up the easel I would be using for the story. "It tells you the order of the plagues and the background of the story."

I read it to refresh my memory so I wasn't babbling the whole time. I was amazed at what the Egyptians went through during the plagues, and I could see tidbits of the story that had never caught my eye before. For example, the people stayed in the same place for three day during the plague of darkness—although I didn't think that they sat in the same exact spot for three days. That would be a little tough on the rear end. I set up the background for the story and began. I was a bit shaky at first but became more comfortable as I neared the end. The longer I told the story, the more respect I had for my grandmother—how she had to prepare for each story in advance then set up all the pieces every week for the Bible story at church for children who likely had no clue how much time and effort it took her. I know I sure didn't.

"That was wonderful!" Grandmother said as I finished the story. "You were very good." I was startled at the praise. I rarely heard anything complimentary from anyone, so to hear that I was actually good at something was a mind-boggling affair.

Once the story was over, we put all the flannelgraph away.

"Would you like to get some fresh air?" Grandmother said. "I would love to show you my flowers." I nodded, and she smiled wide as she led me out the door to her flower garden. She showed me her rhododendrons and geraniums. As I walked through the roses and wildflowers, her two favorite flowers, my sock caught on one of the many thorns from her rosebush. As I knelt down to free my foot she laughed and remarked,

"Growing up, my sister and I weren't allowed to wear socks because they were too 'worldly.' We had to wear nasty pantyhose." I looked at her in incredulity. Socks were considered worldly? Drinking, drugs, and R-rated movies maybe. But socks?

She wasn't finished. "And on top of that, we weren't supposed to go to baseball games or the theater. The first movie I ever saw in the theater was an army flick that my aunt convinced my parents to let my sister and me go see. My uncle was in the army at the time, so my aunt said that we might see him in it. We didn't, but I was able to see my first movie in the theaters."

"I had no idea that the church was so strict back then!" I exclaimed. "Nowadays people go to see movies all the time!"

"Yes, church was pretty strict in my days. Things have changed a lot over the past few decades, however, and that's why you see people doing things that wouldn't have been acceptable at all in my time." We walked back inside and sat down in the living room to continue talking.

"Well, I guess the best place to start," Grandmother began, "if I were telling you my story, is with my name. On my birth certificate, my name is Daisy Naomi Ruth Ridgeway, but when I got my driver's license, I dropped my first name and went by Naomi."

"That's cool that you just up and changed your name," I commented. "Kind of like me. Isn't that a Bible name?"

"Yes! It comes from the Book of Ruth, where Naomi leaves her homeland because of famine, her husband and sons die in the foreign land, and then she returns to Israel with her daughter-in-law Ruth. I was a lot like my namesake growing up. I was born in Buford, GA but then moved all over Georgia. Being a pastor's kid, I didn't stay in one place for a long time."

"I remember," she continued, "the time my dad was pastoring a church in Lafayette, GA. We didn't really like living there, but we had to stay. One night, my dad had a dream that we had moved to Fitzgerald, GA. When he shared it with us the next morning, we didn't believe him; we figured the dream was merely a product of his desire to leave. However, after breakfast, he got a phone call from a leader of the denomination that he was being sent to pastor in Fitzgerald. We were pretty shocked."

I was skeptical. God gave him a dream that he would move? God giving people dreams was only for biblical people like Jacob or Joseph or Paul, not ordinary, modern people. I sighed inwardly. I had figured that I would probably get a sermon while meeting with Grandmother. At least she seemed legit and not a hypocrite, like all the other people I knew.

"When I was seven," she went on, "my church was having a revival, and it was summertime in Georgia so the doors were wide open in the church. When the altar call came, I was ready to walk to the front and get saved, but the devil told me that I shouldn't go up because I didn't have any shoes on and people would laugh at me. Well, I didn't go up, and so I didn't get saved. Four years later, two women, Ms. Peacock and Ms. Roach, were speaking in tongues, and the interpretation of it was that the shades of darkness were falling and that Jesus was coming back. Well, that scared me good because it was nighttime, and it was dark outside, making it all the more real. I went down to the altar and didn't leave until I was saved and started speaking in tongues."

"After I got saved, other Christian kids and I would have prayer meetings at the church. We would meet to pray and read the Bible. Becoming saved was one of the most important decisions I've ever made."

The most important decision ever? I was surprised.

"An important lesson I learned growing up," Grandmother continued, "was that you don't mess with the Lord's business. A neighbor that went to the same church as us came over one day and asked my mom if the church could have one of our chickens for the chicken dinner they were hosting to raise money. My mom didn't want the church to kill one of her laying hens, so she said no. Later that day, she went outside to check on the hens and found one of them dead. That's when I learned that you should never mess with the Lord's business."

I couldn't imagine why her God would want to kill one of her hens! I mean, couldn't He just have found another chicken somewhere else? That seemed very vindictive and controlling. Feeling like Grandmother was starting to talk too much about God, I decided to shift the conversation to a safer topic. "What did you like to do when you were my age?"

"I loved to play on the swings, as well as play house, hide and seek, tag, hopscotch, and dolls. I still have a doll from my childhood that's over seventy-five years old!"

I looked at her in surprise. She would keep a doll for that long? I couldn't think of anything that I still have that I played with when I was young—and that wasn't too long ago.

"What do you like to do?" Grandmother asked me.

Her question took me aback. She seemed genuinely interested in me. My brain raced as I tried to think of something I liked to do.

"Well, I love to read books. I always have quite a bit of free time on my hands, since I'm not on a sports team or anything. I can't wait until I'm old enough to get a job and make my own money. Then I'll not only have money to spend on things I think are important but I'll also fill up that time slot with something productive instead of being made to do menial chores because 'idle hands are the devil's work,' as my grandmother so fondly puts it."

"Well, if you grew up in my time, you wouldn't have to wait very long to get a job," Grandmother inserted. "My first job was in a department store at age thirteen. It didn't pay as much as young kids get paid today, but the money went further. The first time I earned what I thought was a lot of money was when my dad said that he would give me five bucks if I could learn a song on the piano. To you, five bucks might not be much, but back then, it was a lot of money. I wanted that money, so I learned a song to play at church. Once on stage, I sat down and promptly forgot where to put my hands to start the song! My brother had to come up on stage and show me where to put my hands, and then I was able to play the song. I bought a jacket with the money I earned from that." I smiled somewhat ruefully, thinking that I would probably forget how to play in front of everyone as well. Just then, I looked at my watch and gasped in horror.

"My mom is going to be here in four minutes," I said, in a slightly worried tone. Mom had probably been fuming when she saw that not only was I spending the day with Naomi (because she did, in fact, stick to her promise) but that she would have to spend time in town finding things to do before coming back to get me because she was wrong about my Grandmother. I doubted that she would be happy, so I was dreading the trip home. It would be almost an hour of either her shrieking made-up lectures to save face or deadly silent rage, like an ominous fog that covers a ghost town, and you don't know what's in it or what will emerge. I shuddered.

Grandmother stood up. "I'm so glad that you were able to come, darling. It was fun seeing my precious granddaughter today. You've made my day shine."

I warmed at the compliment and dropped my head shyly. "Thanks. It was enjoyable being able to spend time with you because I was expecting a somewhat different reception, since my mom always pushed you all away."

"Well, if I didn't love God and put God first, then who knows how I might have received you? Those are the qualities of a godly woman, you know." I bobbed my head up and down for lack of words.

"Other qualities of a godly woman are knowing and loving the Lord, knowing the Word and practicing it, giving of herself and her time, dressing to honor the Lord, and exhibiting the fruit of the Spirit in her life."

Just then, my mom arrived. I peeked hesitantly out the window to the car and did a weather evaluation. An ominous fog look was upon her face, and I knew it would be a long forty-five minutes. I gave Grandmother a big hug and walked out the door. The trip home was anything but pleasant, and I seriously considered jumping out the window and walking home.

I talked with Tina the next day and told her whom I had met with and how it went. She told me that it was good to start with family members first before looking for other options. She said that if I needed suggestions, she had a few ladies in mind she could set me up with. I thanked her, still a little uneasy about my promise but willing to give it a shot.

As I lay in bed that night, I thought about how strange it was that I didn't remember how nice my grandmother was. I guess time can make people forget many things. Anyway, one down, fifty-one more to go. I don't know what will be at the end of my journey or what my perspective will be, but I know that it will be a challenge week by week; and by the end, I will at least have met fifty-two new women who hopefully will have given me tons of different views about life.

Chapter Two

One afternoon, my grandmother called up to me to clean out my junk drawer. I had been sitting on my bed, reading the latest novel in a series I was going through, and eating a nasty store-bought cinnamon roll, when it was all interrupted. I didn't know why my dresser drawer mattered to her, but I wasn't going to argue. She was always telling me to clean something. Grumbling, I put down the book—right at the climax of suspense— and stomped over to my dresser to begin the monotonous task of sorting through old cards and junk. I heaved the drawer over to my bed and unceremoniously dumped the entire contents onto my drab comforter. A few cards slid off the mattress and ended up beneath the bed, but I ignored them as I stared at the large mountain of mementos. I began organizing old trinkets, cards, papers, and a random collection of seashells.

After a boring hour and a half, I stretched the cramp in my neck as I sighed. At least the mountain was now down to well-organized molehills. I bent down to pick up the cards that had fallen to the floor when suddenly I came across a birthday card that was signed by an "Aunt Carolyn." I squinted, not recognizing the name. So, bolstering up my courage, I went into my sister's perfect royal domain and asked her who the woman was—after the mandatory tasks of knocking on her door, politely asking if I might come in, and bowing low as I walked into the room. (I have never actually done the last one before, but I have been very tempted to do so on occasion.) Reluctantly, and with a great deal of haughtiness to my "ever so humble question," she replied that it was our dad's aunt who had occasionally invited our family over for meals, but we hadn't been since Dad's death because Mom kept declining her invitations. As Kimberly kept describing her, it all came back to me, and I left her room. I remembered that when I was a kid, Aunt Carolyn made the best cinnamon rolls, and I loved to eat them whenever we went to her house.

Glancing back at the card, I noticed that she had penned a Bible verse, John 3:16, and the words, "God bless you and keep you safe throughout your journey in life." Why I didn't remember that she was a Christian, I don't know. Maybe it was because she never hit me black and blue with Bible verses and off-the-wall theology. Suddenly, I had an urge to get to know this relative whom all I remember about her was that she had made amazing cinnamon rolls. As I fingered the card, I noticed something written on the back: "If you ever need a voice of encouragement, give me a call at this number." Perhaps she could be the woman for my next meeting; however, would she even want to meet with me? I figured there was no harm in trying. I called the number written on the card, and, after the fourth ring, I was about to dejectedly hang up the phone when she picked up. She was ecstatic to hear from me and told me to come over the very next day morning.

My sister was completely adamant about not driving me, seeing how she had set her heart on chilling on the couch with a bag of cookies and Captain America 3, but my grandmother made her take me because, as she put it, "You need the fresh air." So, peeling her thin form off the couch and out the door, she flopped into the tiny minivan and angrily turned on the ignition. Half an hour later, we arrived at the massive house, where she dropped me off, book in hand. She smirked when she peeled out of the driveway, yelling, "Don't let her see the book, or she'll think you're strange, like everyone else at school does!"

I glared at her, partly because she was right and partly because she was so annoying at all times. But just in case, I tucked the book behind my back as I slowly walked up the long walkway until I halted in front of the ginormous dark oak double doors framed with stained glass windows. Nervously I lifted the lion doorknocker, which fell with a loud boom, and waited. When Aunt Carolyn opened the door with a large smile on her face, I lost most of my butterflies. She looked like I remembered her: brown hair, a warm expression, and glasses over her brown eyes. She spotted the book immediately, and after warmly greeting me and inviting me in, she inquired about it.

Shamefacedly, I told her the book title, expecting the natural following of a smirk as well as an eye roll. I got neither. Instead, she told me she loved novels, especially historical ones. One she recommended to me was Girl With Seven Names. I was elated that I finally had someone with which to share my passion for books—the nerds at school didn't count. She led me up the spiral staircase to the tippy-top floor, where there were plush chairs and a coffee table with a tray of hot cinnamon rolls on its smooth surface. I gingerly sank into a chair, feeling the warmth surrounding me, and immediately reached for one of the gooey pastries after Aunt Carolyn asked if I wanted one. They were as scrumptious as I had remembered. As I sat licking my fingers and reaching for a napkin, Aunt Carolyn gracefully sat down and began to share in a melodious voice a little about herself.

"You probably don't remember much about me; you were so young the last time we really spent time together. Yet even then," she said with a twinkle in her eye, "you couldn't keep away from my cinnamon rolls," as I reached for yet another bun. Quickly, I pulled my hand back, but the sparkle in her eye and the smile on her lips let me know that it was all right.

She began telling me about herself in depth. "I was born in Dayton, OH, as Carolyn Lytle. My family then moved to Richmond, IN," and here she began ticking them off on her fingers. "Then to Coalmont, IN, where I actually ate coal as a child, then to Ashland, OH, then to Norwood, OH, then to Uhrichsville, OH, where I attended Shaker Heights University, then to Cleveland, TN, where I attended Lee College, then to Nashville, TN, where I attended Peabody College, and finally to Springfield, OH." She paused to catch her breath. "I was a pastor's daughter; I moved a lot."

When she said this, I tuned her out for a reality check. She was a pastor's kid? Huh. I knew a PK once named Brittany. She was as spoiled as mayo left out in the sun for three days. Brittany the Brat. She would bully me so much and then still claim to be a Christian. Another hypocrite. And my aunt was a PK? I know their type too well. Who cares if she can make amazing cinnamon rolls! Maybe meeting with her was a mistake.

As I was silently criticizing her, I heard her mention skiing. I went skiing as a kid, and I fell in love with it; but ever since my dad died, I have never gotten to go again because we never had the money and no one else in my family shared the same passion. That word drew my attention back to what she was saying.

"Skiing has been a deep passion of mine, especially on the Rockies. But with fun also comes misfortune. Once when I was skiing, I tripped on my skis and went flying towards a tree, but thankfully my hand went between my head and the tree. This broke the bones in my hand, but it also saved me from likely death." Rotating her hand around, she said, "I believe God definitely healed my hand because I have absolutely no arthritis in it to this day." I was skeptical about that, because if a so-called God could "heal" her hand, then why didn't He heal my dad from his drug addiction?

"So what do you do now when you aren't skiing?" I asked, as I reached for my third cinnamon roll.

"My husband, Gene Clifton, is a dentist, and I work as the office manager for his dental business. But," she added, leaning slightly forward as if to share an important secret, "my real job is with the kids who come into the office. All my life I've wanted to help struggling kids, and I even got my Masters degree at Ohio State in helping the neurologically handicapped. Now, I can do what I believe God wants me to do with my life in helping children. A saying that I love states, 'I didn't follow the path that I thought I would, but I believe I have ended up where I need to be.'"

I felt something strange as she said that. Something I hadn't felt in a while. Could it be that little, worn down, pathetic me actually felt like I could amount to something from just one crazy saying? Preposterous. It was probably too many cinnamon rolls.

She paused, asking if I would like a glass of milk. I was pretty thirsty after three rolls, but I could only nod because I had taken yet another roll and had chewed off a bite larger than normal, and I didn't want to mumble out a response. As she went down to the kitchen to grab two glasses of milk, I reflected on her earlier statement, that she was doing what God wanted her to do. If there were a God, sitting way up high on His throne, would He really care what insignificant people were doing? Would He care what I was doing? He must care a little because supposedly He sent Tina with a straightforward message for me. Yet, it doesn't seem like He cared what my dad did nor what my brother's doing, not having heard from him in years; however, Aunt Carolyn seems to truly believe that God directs what we do with our lives, and it seems like she is in the right place. I remember having gone to their dentist office when I was really young to get my tooth pulled, and although I was in pain for a while, I received a cool souvenir, a tooth holder, that brought a smile to my face. Soon she returned with two tall, pretty glasses of cold milk. I immediately downed almost half of mine, resulting in an unsightly milk mustache. She laughed outright, and after being made aware of the reason, I joined her.

After taking a sip of milk, she continued. "Something else I do, when I'm not skiing or working in the dental office, is traveling the world. I have visited between forty and fifty countries throughout my life, most of them with my husband."

My ears perked up at that because I've always wanted to travel, but we've never had the money. With my luck, I'd probably end up going two steps from my house before I got called back in to do some chore. Intently, I listened as she talked about swimming off the coast of her favorite location, Antarctica, and eating fish (one of her favorite foods) in Japan, and even seeing the dirty streets of Shanghai.

"I feel very blessed to have seen so much of our amazing world and its beautiful scenery. I also have enjoyed meeting so many different people and cultures. My favorite part about seeing the world is being in a culture and learning about its different cults and religions to see where they came from. And I have noticed that even though I may believe in a different God than most of the people I saw, that doesn't stop me from loving and accepting them. That's what people want: love and acceptance. I believe that sharing your life is sharing your faith. Let your life show Jesus."

"So, if a stranger showed up on your doorstep one day," I asked her, "not knowing you or the God you believe in, then what would be one word you would say to tell your story and the story of God?"

"Grace," she quickly responded. "I also believe that having gratitude is important and that honor is imperative. I honored my parents so much that even when I didn't agree with them, I didn't want to do anything that would bring disgrace to them. I think that it is essential to be open with your parents."

Honor my parents? How in the world could anyone honor a man who was a hypocrite, not to mention the fact that he left my alcoholic mom to take care of three children because he committed suicide? And then there's my mom, who doesn't give a rip about what happens to us kids. If I were stupid enough to follow my dad's footsteps, or my mom's, for that matter, she probably wouldn't even notice. I would never be able to honor them. I didn't say anything, though.

Since Tina would probably get onto me if I didn't find out her favorite part of the Bible, I somewhat hesitantly asked her that question.

"My favorite chapter is Proverbs 31," she responded, "which describes a woman of noble character. To me, the qualities of a noble, godly woman are patience, love, kindness, generosity, meekness, gentleness, forgiveness, and a gentle strength."

What a list! What flesh and blood woman could have a few of these qualities, much less all of them? Well, at least now I have a list that I can compare women to who claim to be Christians. Right then, I received a text from Kimberly letting me know that she had arrived.

I told Aunt Carolyn, so we stood up, gathered up the napkins, glasses, and the now empty tray of cinnamon rolls, and headed down the stairs. She gave me a hug as she said goodbye.

"I hope to see you again, sweet girl. I hope your family will accept my invitation to come over for dinner sometime." I thanked her and walked out the door. My sister was waiting impatiently for me in the car and barely waited until I had climbed into the car before rocketing out of the long driveway.

As we drove home, one word came to mind that described Carolyn Clifton: respectful. I didn't run into too many people who honored and respected their parents like Carolyn did. Even though I got to know my great aunt better, it didn't settle my conflict with the whole Christian-thing. I'm still not sure if Christians are godly people, since all of the ones I know are hypocrites. I shook my head. Not all of them. Naomi Thompson didn't seem to be a hypocrite, and Aunt Carolyn seemed genuine. Maybe they just have better qualities than others, and it really isn't that they believe in a so-called God. I've worked way too hard building up my walls against anything good anyone tries to do or say to me to tear those walls down now. I've been burned one too many times to try again.

Chapter Three

One bright morning I was relaxing on my bed when my phone rang. I picked it up and frowned. I didn't recognize the number. Regardless, I answered it.

"Hello?"

"I just had this great idea about whom you should meet with for your challenge!"

I rolled my eyes. Of course it would be Tina. Who else would sound so incredibly enthusiastic and high-pitched? "How did you get my number?"

She cleared her throat. "I sort of texted a bunch of people at school until one finally gave me your number."

What a stalker. I sighed as I remembered what she had said. "So what's your great idea?"

"There's an older woman that goes to my church that I was talking with on Sunday. She seemed a little lonely, and I thought that maybe you could spend some time with her this week. When I mentioned you to her, she seemed interested in your challenge and said she'd love to meet with you. You would be able to meet with a godly woman, and I think you would have a lot of fun."

I contemplated it. It sounded like a good idea, and I didn't have anything planned, so I agreed. "Alright, I'll do it. When will I be meeting with her?"

She squealed. "Great! The meeting will be on Thursday for about four hours. I'll send you the address. Oh! Her name's Naomi Deans."

I said goodbye and hung up. Sighing, I stood up and stretched. I didn't think I would ever get used to Tina.

Two days later, I stood in front of Naomi's apartment door, too scared to knock. I had forgotten to ask Tina what she was like, so I didn't know if I was getting myself into something I couldn't fix. Timidly, I knocked on her door, and when the door finally creaked open, I found myself face-to-face with Naomi Deans. She wasn't at all like I had expected. A kind smile greeted me from a welcoming face.

I smiled back. "Hi, I'm Brie."

"Come in, come in! When Tina said you were coming, I couldn't wait!"

With a large smile, she ushered me in and gave me a tour of her beautiful apartment. It was very homey and artistic, with beautiful pillows on the soft couches with quilts thrown over the back. She then took me into her kitchen and started to talk. "I don't know about you, but I love to bake, so we will be making different desserts today." My expectancy of boredom soon began to give way to excitement. She pointed to the faucet. "The first thing we will do is wash our hands." I walked over to the sink and lathered up my hands.

"I'm going to show you how to make individual servings of yummy dirt cake," she said as she pulled out a can of cherry pie filling from the pantry. "We're going to eat it for lunch." Eat dirt cake? I used to make mud pies as a kid. I sure hoped this was better than those pies—they were gritty and nasty!

She put a handful of Oreo cookies in a bag and crushed them with a rolling pin. She then took a spoon and scooped some of the crumbs and shook them into the bottom of two clear plastic cups. She added a layer of cherry pie filling and finally sprayed some Redi-Whip onto those color-contrasting ingredients. She repeated the process until the cup was full. I watched her go through the steps with my mouth watering. I could hardly wait for lunch. To top off the amazing desert with a flourish, she plopped a cherry in the middle of a pile of whipped cream. She carefully set the two cups in the fridge and turned around.

"Now, we'll start prepping for chocolate peanut clusters and peppermint bark." I licked my lips in delight, scarcely containing a squeal. I was actually going to make something useful! In the microwave, we melted broken pieces of dark chocolate in a large measuring cup. After stirring it smooth, we poured the salty peanuts into it. They looked like little people floating in the rich darkness. We then took spoonfuls of the mixture and plopped them in clusters on a pan before putting them in the fridge to harden.

Next, we turned our attention to the peppermint bark. We melted both dark and white chocolate in separate bowls. We spread the dark chocolate on a jellyroll pan and gingerly placed it in the fridge flat until it was hardened. Once it was solid, we poured the white chocolate on top of it and then sprinkled crushed peppermint candies (which we had crushed in a food processor) onto the white layer before putting it back in the fridge. We wiped off the countertop, put the few remaining dirty dishes in the sink, and washed our hands, looking proudly at the now clean kitchen. About ten minutes later, the clusters and peppermint bark were cold, so we placed them into individual bags. She looked at me with a kind smile.

"I'm going to let you take all of them home with you today." I looked at her in amazement. She was going to just give them to me? No strings attached?

I started stuttering out my gratitude. "Thank you so much, ma'am! I don't know how to repay you!" She waved a hand at me, as if I were talking nonsense.

"It's a gift. No payment necessary." I smiled gratefully, amazed at her kindness.

Next, she led me to the dining room table. "I enjoy making craft items, and I thought about sharing my hobby with you." Wow. She can bake great desserts and make crafts?

She inserted a short, wooden stick in a one-inch foam ball. She glued the stick in a small votive candleholder filled with beads. Then we took ribbons and bows, and shaped and pinned them onto the foam to eventually form what looked like to be a beribboned topiary tree. Once done, she draped a string of pearls across the ribbons. It was beautiful. She got up to show me a few others that she had made in the past. They were masterfully done. At this point, she sat down again in one of the dining chairs and began talking.

"How would this arrangement work out? I'll tell you some about me, and then you'll tell me some about you. Deal?"

I nodded my head, grateful that she had made the suggestion. I was still new at meeting with godly women, and this was the first person I had met with that wasn't a family member.

She began. "My full name is Naomi Ruby Deans, and I was born 85 years ago in Middlesex, NC, where I lived for twelve years before moving to various cities in North Carolina. Eventually, we went to Washington D.C., where I got my first job at a naval gun factory." She leaned close, as if to tell an important secret. Out of curiosity, I leaned in as well. "I also worked with the FBI for a time."

I leaned back in amazement. She had worked with the highest detective agency in the country? She sure didn't look like a spy. She kept right on talking, however, so I didn't press her for information.

"I returned to Middlesex and went from working at a gun factory to working at the North Carolina Church of God State Offices. Now there's a shift in occupation—from killing to saving!" she said with a wink. "After thirteen years, my saving occupation shifted from people to money: I started working at a bank. Eventually, I worked at Wells Fargo. When I was applying for the job there, I didn't know that it was for the secretary to the vice president of the bank! Because of that job, I was able to win a cruise." My eyes widened as I pictured a giant boat on sparkling waters with champagne and chocolate.

"I love traveling," she continued, "and I've been to many places during my lifetime. I've visited Europe four times, and I have been to Germany, England, Switzerland, Belgium, Hawaii, Austria, San Juan, St. Thomas, and Israel. The most exciting time in my life was when I went to England for the first time with my sister and her family. Now, I think I've shared more than enough so far. Your turn!"

She grinned at me, and I had to grin back. I had just met her, and I now knew more about her than I could have hoped. But I was sucked back to the present when I realized that I, in turn, had to talk about myself now.

"Well, I've never traveled out of the country before, so I don't have much experience there. I was born and raised here. I have a cat named Thunder, a sister named Kimberly and a brother named Jackson." As I mentioned my siblings' names, I felt a stab of anger. Why was I bothering telling her about them? They definitely didn't deserve it. I masked these feeling, however, and kept talking. "I love to read, and I love the color blue."

She smiled. "I like the color lavender, and I also enjoy reading. My favorite author is Grace Livingston Hill."

She paused for a moment, as if deciding what we could do next. "Why don't we make a tater tot bag?" she suggested.

I nodded, grateful that I wouldn't have to talk about my family anymore, although I had no idea what a tater tot bag was. We walked into her sewing room and retrieved the necessary materials for the craft. As she sewed the material together on the sewing machine, she explained what a tater tot bag was: a cloth bag in which you put a potato, and then stick it in the microwave, and presto! You have a toasty, cooked potato, ready to eat. She showed me how to work the sewing machine, and let me work on it some. When the bag was finished, I was amazed at the final result.

"Once again, you have made something beautiful out of nothing," I said in admiration.

"A long time ago," Naomi explained, "I resolved that I would keep myself busy rather than stay idle, as Ecclesiastes states. That's why I'm always trying to fill my time with something productive."

"What happened when you were idle? Did you get in a lot of trouble as a kid if you weren't doing something?"

She shook her head. "Things were super strict back then, so there wasn't much that I could get in trouble with. We had to wear garters to church every Sunday, and on top of that, I didn't participate in any of the school activities because of the church's regulations. Since my dad was a pastor, I really had to obey all the rules to the letter."

I felt a stab of disappointment. She was a PK as well? I couldn't believe it. The first three people I have met with have all been pastors' kids. Why do I always keep running into these kinds of people?

"So what was the worst trouble you got into as a kid?" I asked skeptically, not believing that she did anything worse than singing off-key in the choir. "I bet it wasn't anything too bad, given your strict circumstances."

She chuckled. "The worst trouble I ever got into, as a child, was when I stole plums from my uncle's tree." At the surprised look on my face, she continued. "I didn't think it was wrong since I was only taking the ones from the ground, but I got in trouble when my parents found out because I was still stealing."

I was bemused. She stole? I guess she wasn't a perfect PK. But then, who was? Aside from Brittany the Brat, I remembered a girl when I was younger that was a PK, and she was as spoiled as the plums that fell on the ground from Naomi's uncle's tree. Millie the Monster. She was a little brat that got her way in everything. I remember the time that she was going to sing "Amazing Grace" on stage for church, and instead, she burst out singing the latest pop song, which was completely inappropriate. All her dad said to her was, "You know you shouldn't sing so loud in church, honey. It may make Deacon Gilder ask the church directory board for a new hearing aid." And I can't forget the time that she snuck up behind poor old Miss Herring and screamed, "There's a spider on your hand!" right in her ear, causing her to spill her coffee all over her dress. She was in therapy for seven months. Of course, there was no spider, even though Millie claimed there was. So if Naomi said she was a PK, then I can't fathom what she might've done and believed it to be righteous.

At this point, our time together was almost over. I thanked her for her time and teaching me how to work a sewing machine.

"My pleasure! Working reminds me of my favorite Bible verse, Romans 8:28, which says, 'And we know that all things work together for good to those who love God, to those who are called according to his purpose.' I'm so thankful that God is taking care of me. He always looks out for us, you know."

I smiled weakly. Maybe in her case, she could believe that; but in my case, there wasn't a chance that He looked out for me. But, I pondered, do I love God, as the verse requires? How can I expect a promise to be fulfilled if I don't do the requirements?

She kept talking. "Jesus is the greatest friend anyone can have. But to be a godly woman, serving Him, you have to be true to God's Word." I was instantly alert. Did she just say godly woman? I hadn't even told her about my mission. I wrote that down in the corner of my brain, hoping that when Tina quizzed me later, she would be satisfied. As the clock struck 2:00, I got up, gave her a hug, and left. I walked outside and felt the fresh air around me as I sighed. I wished this were easier.

I reflected on my time with Naomi as I waited outside for my grandmother to pick me up. I thought of two words that described Naomi Deans. Creative and hard working. It amazed me how hard she could work and how talented she was at everything. I even learned a few things. A tater tot bag might not be a wedding dress with a ten-foot train, but at least I learned how to work a sewing machine, a skill that was more interesting than my talents of tanning well and speed texting with my thumbs. My day definitely wasn't what I had expected, but at least I didn't sit around doing nothing!

In talking with Tina later about my time with Naomi, she mentioned that she knew of a woman whom she would love for me to meet next. I didn't say no, so she'll probably arrange the meeting, even though I didn't say yes. I'd better be more careful with letting Tina handle my meetings. If I let her do whatever she thinks would be cool, then one day I'll be meeting with some cuckoo psycho-path and be in serious trouble, all because Tina thought she was godly.

Chapter Four

It was the perfect day outside. The sun was glistening off our swimming pool, the wind was blowing a wispy spider web, and the weather was perfect. But I was stuck in my room, a jumble of nerves. Tina had arranged for me to meet a woman she knew, which was going to take place in exactly twenty-three minutes and fifteen seconds. Not that I was nervous or anything… I just didn't want it to turn out wrong.

For the thirteenth time, I anxiously checked my reflection in the mirror. I looked the same as I did two seconds ago: same dull, lifeless brown hair and panicked brown eyes. I looked at my carefully-picked outfit: a blue shirt with jeans and sandals. I hoped it wouldn't be too classy or too casual. I became annoyed with all my fretting. Why was I like this? I jumped up from my bed and paced on the already worn path on my carpet. I had already met with three women; I should be over this hump! But I'm not, and that bothers me. I will do this, I decided resolutely. I have to conquer this or else I'll never finish. So, even though I was tempted to make a run for the hills, I grabbed my purse and walked determinedly down the stairs. At the foot of the staircase, I paused. Doubts flooded my mind like a river of worry. I tilted my chin up firmly. I would do this if it killed me. I still have that pepper spray, if the time comes to use it.

Suddenly, I heard a sound and looked out the window. A white BMW pulled into the driveway. I gulped, and shuffled outside, wanting to get it over with. I walked over to the car, hoping that the driver would be nice and not an over-the-top Christian—or the complete opposite and a crazed woman with a pointy hat. In one split second, all my fears were put to rest as the woman got out of the car. She wasn't any of the descriptions I had worried about, as far as I could tell. She had brown hair that was highlighted with blond streaks. She was gorgeous and definitely not an old woman. She walked over to me with a dazzling smile and gave me a hug.

"I'm Arlyne VanHook. I've heard so much about you from Tina. I'm very glad you've agreed to meet with me!" I could only dazedly nod like a bobble head doll before getting into her car with most of my fretful feelings flying out the window as we drove away from my house. She smiled at me.

"Are you hungry? I haven't eaten since 7:30."

"I had a late breakfast," I responded shyly. "I'm pretty hungry, though." She smiled exuberantly.

"Great! There's a wonderful restaurant located downtown called Café Roma that I want to take you to." I had no objection, so we made the drive to the restaurant.

She looked over at me as we drove along. "So how has your 'mission' been going?" Startled, I whipped my head toward her and looked super surprised.

She gave me a strange look. "Tina said that you had some sort of challenge with God going on that was somehow connected with me meeting with you."

I nodded, wary. "Long story short, I was, in a moment of weakness, compelled into agreeing to a crazy proposition of which I am now tied to meeting with fifty-two different women and talking to them about their experiences."

She grinned. "So I'm part of this 'crazy proposition'?"

Flustered, I quickly changed my words. "Well, it's not like I don't want to meet with you, or anything. It's just I was tricked into doing this."

She laughed outright. "I'm just teasing you. I won't take anything offensively."

I laughed, relieved. It was fun, feeling like we were old friends, even though we had just met.

We arrived at the restaurant, parked next to the building, and went around to the entrance. As I walked in, I was amazed at the beauty inside. It felt so homey and comfortable, yet it didn't feel too encroaching. We were seated at a small table, and I marveled at the ease and grace that was just oozing from the workers. After ordering water and an appetizer of sweet potato fries, Arlyne dove into the conversation.

"First off, let me say that I am so glad that we are meeting today! Tina speaks very highly of you."

I didn't know why. I haven't exactly been a good influence on her.

"I'll start off talking about the basics of my life," she continued. "My name is Irene Arlyne VanHook. You're probably wondering why I have a name that rhymes. My mom wanted her baby's name to be Arlyne Santos. No middle name. But when she told the nurse, the nurse heard wrong and wrote 'Irene.' So, I have had to live with the burden of telling people to call me Arlyne even though my name technically is Irene. This was especially hard when I had to change schools because our family moved. I was born in Oakland, CA, and then I moved to Puerto Rico when I was three. When I was eight, my family and I moved back to California, and when I was nineteen, I moved to Cleveland, TN to attend Lee University." She paused as the waiter brought our sweet potato fries. I mentally tried to organize all the information she had just given me; it was a lot to take in.

"Moving to Cleveland," she continued, "has been the best decision I've ever made. I had to take a leap of faith to do that, not knowing what it was like or whether I would like it, but I believe that I did the right thing." I nodded as I grabbed a fry from the large pile on the plate. I felt a twinge of disappointment when she mentioned faith, but decided to get over it because I wasn't going to let a little word stop me from getting to know her. Her next question surprised me.

"What about you? Tell me about yourself. It can be random facts; I don't care." I glanced nervously at her and sipped some water to moisten my dry throat.

"Okay, um, I like to read, ski, and listen to music. I also own a gray cat named Thunder who loves to sleep on my bed, even though he's technically not allowed to. I also do a little photography when I can." I had been given a small digital camera a few years ago that I liked to use.

Her eyes lit up. "I'm a photographer as well. I even own a photography business! And music is a passion of mine. I lead worship at my church, and I play the flute, violin, and guitar. Do you play an instrument?"

I shook my head sadly. "I don't have any musical talent. In fact, I was so bad on the recorder in elementary school that I would hide in the bathroom during music class so no one would hear how terrible I was. I got in a lot of trouble when my parents found out I was cutting class."

"I remember a day when I cut class," Arlyne said with a painful smile as she munched thoughtfully on one of the last remaining fries. "When I was a kid in seventh grade, a group of about twenty kids talked me into cutting school with them. Some of them had friends that drove, and so we all drove together an hour away down to a boardwalk at Santa Cruz that had rollercoasters, stands, and games. We had a lot of innocent fun, but we got in trouble because we got caught in traffic on the way back, making us late to get to school before our parents arrived. That was the worst trouble I've ever gotten in." I laughed, trying to imagine a person like her skipping school. She just looked too sweet.

By this time, our main course had arrived. We had both ordered caprese, which is tomatoes covered in fresh mozzarella, as well as bisque. The food was amazing! For dessert, we ordered their delicious chocolate cherry homemade ice cream and poured espresso on top. It was scrumptious. We walked outside into the warm air and as we got into her car, she clued me in to the schedule for the day.

"So the game plan is this: I'm going to show you how to take still life photos from a professional photographer's point of view. Then we're going to do a photoshoot with you and my daughter. In order for that to happen, I'm going to swing by Target and get you a sundress."

I blinked, hardly believing what I was hearing. I was going to learn how to take professional pictures? And get a new dress? I was immediately suspicious. "What do I have to do to pay it off? I don't have much money to my name."

She tilted her head and looked at me square in the eye. "It's a gift. I don't expect anything from you except your cooperation in the photoshoot."

I couldn't fathom that. Someone was willing to spend her hard-earned money to pay for a sundress for an unimportant child? I didn't understand it. Maybe some people actually did do things out of the goodness of their heart. Who knew? Yet I was still skeptical.

"So why should it matter to you whether I have a new dress or not? I mean, I really do appreciate it, but I need to know why you would do this."

She looked at me kindly. "I'm buying you this dress not only because I want to but also because I want to show you love. If I am to have the qualities of a godly woman, then I need to have obedience to the Lord as well as humility, honesty, patience, and a teachable spirit. That all leads back to love. To be honest, like the quality I mentioned earlier, it's hard to reach out to someone who doesn't want to be reached, so I thought that if I bought you the new dress, you might be more open to what I have to say. Sometimes that's what God does to us. In order to reach our spirits, He will give us gifts to make us want to be with Him more, even if our motives are selfish. He can still make good out of selfish motives."

I looked at her with a surprised yet pained expression. She had to be bluffing. How did she know? I didn't want to be reached, but I had never told anyone. To cover up the fact that she had touched a sore spot, I thought back to her list of godly women qualities and cynically asked, "How do you know if those are the qualities of a godly woman?"

"Being a godly woman," she began, "is reflecting God. So, if you describe the qualities of God, then you just need to apply those qualities to yourself."

I silently snorted. She actually believed there was a God and that the qualities of a godly woman came from Him? Whew, I think she needs to take a break from all this holy stuff before she starts believing something even crazier. With that in mind, I steered the conversation away from Christianity.

"So, do you have any kids?" I noticed that she hadn't mentioned much about her family except that she had a daughter.

"Yes. I have a son named Logan and a daughter named Maddy. I love them a lot."

"What are your methods of rearing them?" I bet it was nothing like how I was reared.

"In rearing my kids, I don't want to enforce super strict ways upon them; instead, my husband Jason and I help them stay on the right path without pressing on them to follow tons of church rules, because we don't want them to hate church."

I sighed quietly. Once again, the conversation shifted to churchy topics. I had already done one subject change, and I didn't want to offend her by changing again; she was doing so much for me already, so I decided to play along.

"So when did you become a Christian?" I hadn't expected to say that; it just popped out before I could stop it.

She seemed just as surprised as I was as that I had said it, but responded fairly quickly. "Between the ages of seven and ten, I received Jesus into my life and got filled with the

Holy Spirit. My dad was a minister, and now I'm the worship leader at a Methodist church."

At that, I stared at her in surprise. I thought she would be in some sort of Pentecostal church, being filled with the Holy Spirit at such a young age and all. I was raised Pentecostal before we left the church and seemed to remember learning that Methodists don't typically speak in tongues. So why is she at a Methodist church?

She wasn't finished, however. "My favorite part of being in the music ministry position is being able to lead people to a place where they're in the presence of God. The flip side of that, though, is when I don't see them reacting to the songs in the way I thought they would, I feel disappointed. Yet, many times those are the days that people come up to me after service and tell me that they felt the presence of God so strongly that they began to cry during the songs."

"I haven't always worked in music ministry," she continued. "At our previous church, I was helping out in the children's department. I loved that church. It was an old, well-established Pentecostal church, and I felt at home there. However, after some changes in the music ministry, we felt that we should leave. I felt sad, but I trusted God to lead us exactly where He wanted us. We found ourselves at the front doors of a Methodist church. I went in with high hopes of 'reforming them,' but I soon found out that they truly loved God, even though the majority of the congregation didn't speak in tongues. I realized that you don't have to have the ability to speak in tongues to be able to love God with your whole heart. You can still talk to Him with love and worship, even if it isn't in the Pentecostal way of worshipping. I realized that even if I'm up on stage leading worship and not everyone is reacting with craziness and shouts, God is still there. He is in the crazy, and He is in the still. It all depends on the person and how they talk to God and react to God. A few people in the church speak in tongues, but they use it in a different way than Pentecostals; they use it as their personal prayer language with God."

I looked at her in amazement. I had never thought of it in that light before. When I used to believe in a so-called God, I always believed that Methodists didn't know God, but it appears to me that I've been judging them by their cover instead of trying to get to know them. Just like people look at me and judge me by my cover.

At that point, we arrived at Target and headed to the clothing department, where we started going through dresses until Arlyne found a dress that was perfect. It was light lavender in color with different shades of purple through it. It even had gorgeous brass buttons lined up the front. It fit perfectly. Arlyne immediately went up to the front to buy it. I was astounded at the price, but when I tried to protest, she waved it away.

"Nonsense, you need something extra special for today."

We then drove to Food City, where we bought gourmet cheese, flowers, potatoes, and other necessities for the photoshoot she was going to do on still life. Once we reached her large, two-story home, we put the food in the fridge, and she showed me how to set up still life photography. It was amazing to be able to watch her in her element. She let me do my own cheese board with different types of food on it, and she had an old table that she set the board on. She said she loved using natural lighting, so she had the table by a window that had light streaming in through the clear glass panes.

Then, with a flourish, she handed me her camera so I could start taking pictures. I was shocked that she would trust me with such a valuable piece of equipment. I suddenly became so nervous that I would drop it, break it somehow, or delete all the other photos already on it. My hands were clammy as I tried to adjust the focus. As Arlyne coached me and encouraged me, though, I settled down and became more comfortable with the camera. I moved around, trying out different angles. The light was coming in just right to land delicately on the captivating food.

After taking pictures for a good long while, I changed into my new dress and prepared for the modeling photoshoot. Arlyne's daughter, Maddy, was going to come along with us so I could learn how to take pictures of other people, not just cheese. Arlyne drove us to a hill near their house. It was super lush and green. She had me start posing, and I was really nervous at first, never having done this before, but my confidence grew little by little until at the end, I felt like a pro. She then showed me the basics of what to do when taking pictures of a person, her daughter being her example. Unfortunately, it started sprinkling, and I was worried we would have to stop the photoshoot. Thankfully, Arlyne had an umbrella, and after ten minutes, the rain had passed. Maddy posed in different positions while I zoomed in and out to try and capture the best picture. Soon we left the hill and drove to an old, rustic barn that was built out of different types of wood. Maddy had brought her ukulele—which she could even play while holding it behind her head—and I was able to take some pictures of her before Arlyne retrieved the camera and took pictures of me posing against the side of the barn.

After the photoshoot, we went back to the house, where we ate a delicious dinner of salad and German pasties—essentially meat pie—with chocolate chip skillet cake for dessert. I had never tasted anything like it. It was amazing!

It was getting dark, and my time with Arlyne was coming to an end. I reluctantly gathered up my stuff. She drove me back to my drab house, where I had only boredom awaiting me. The day with her gave me a picture of what a happy family was supposed to be like, one that had each other as friends rather than having a friendship with a cat, like I did. Arlyne was so graceful, patient, thoughtful, and very enjoyable company. I lamented not being able to have that kind of happy family. However, her joy had brightened my day. She definitely didn't have a big sharp nose, and her teeth were perfectly straight; and the only broom she owns is for sweeping the kitchen. I would love to meet with her again, even if it's only for a casual rendezvous. Like getting Starbucks.

Chapter Five

My mom had been really annoyed with me lately—first it was one thing and then another. Finally, my mom had had enough. To punish me, she decided to use the most torturous method she could think of: make me go to a church and hang out with a Christian woman, Laura Allen, while helping her in her office. More like hang myself while in the office. A church? No amount of begging, wheedling, or life-or-death pleading made her change her mind. I had no clue why she was acquainted with a Christian. She hadn't been to church in years, so I was surprised that she remembered this item of torture for her "beloved" daughter.

I desperately didn't want to spend my day at a church, of all places. What if any kids I knew saw me go into a church? I would never live it down. So in order to try my best to stay home, I faked a fever. But Mom made it clear that even if I had Ebola, she wouldn't care; she had already scheduled it, and I was going to do it.

She literally dragged me out of bed by my hair and threw some clothes in my face, telling me that if I wasn't dressed and in the car in ten minutes, I would have a lot worse to face than just meeting with a Christian for a day. I was in the car before the ten minutes were up. For the entire ride to the church, I sat in a dismal silence. I was doomed to be executed, either socially by any of my friends that happened to see me or physically by my mother.

At the church property, she dropped me off at the side door and expectantly waited for me to go in.

"Don't even think of not spending the whole morning here, missy," she growled. "I've already told Laura that you will be with her until lunch."

My shoulders slumped. I had considered that, but now that hope of escape was dashed to pieces. I walked up to the door but couldn't seem to open it. If I went in, I had a future of taunting and shunning for the rest of my life from people I knew; but if I didn't go in, then "the rest of my life" would be shortened drastically because of one big, mean monster waiting impatiently for me to willingly go inside my grave. I knew I really didn't have a choice. Slowly, I creaked open the door and slipped inside, a scowl plastered on my face. I was ready to just get it over with.

A woman sitting in an office located by the door greeted me. "Hello there! You must be Penny's daughter, Brie. She told me you were coming to help me around the office." She ushered me into her office, and I dejectedly plopped in a brown chair. I had been hoping to just tell her that I was being forced to come, but she seemed so happy that I didn't want to ruin her mood, nor did I want my mom on my back for revealing my true feelings.

As I was sitting there, a thought bounced off the walls of my brain a few times before I could finally read it: maybe I could make her one of my 52 godly women. That way, if one of my friends inevitably asked why I was at a church, I could say that I was doing something for Tina. That technically was true because she did want me to do this challenge, although it wasn't completely accurate. So in a moment of decision, I completely changed my bored demeanor to a cheerful face and asked what I could do to help.

"Well, I'm willing to bet that your mom didn't exactly speak the truth when she said you would 'willingly help around the office for thirty hours if I wanted you to, all with a cheerful smile on your sweet face.'"

I gagged. She had gone that far? I thought she had just told Laura that I was coming, not all those completely inaccurate details about me. But hey, she said I had a sweet face, even though I knew she didn't believe it, so I will just hold on to that for later use. The woman, whatever her name was, took one look at my incredulous face and knew there were two sides to this story.

"What did you do to end up here?" At the shocked look on my face from her having guessed why I was there, she added, "I've heard you're an atheist, so I can imagine that coming into a church wouldn't exactly be your place of amusement."

"Well, I've been getting on her nerves at the house, so she decided that the only way to get me to stop annoying her would be to punish me in a way I would never forget."

She laughed. "I can understand this being a punishment for you. See, I wasn't always a Christian. In fact, my dad was an alcoholic and my parents divorced when I was six."

I was shocked. She didn't come from a perfect family? I felt a connection click between us because I knew what it was like to be on the opposite end of a drunkard. So how did she end up working in a church?

As if reading my mind, she continued. "I was saved and filled with the Holy Spirit at age thirteen, but that was because of my mom's best friend, not my mom. She would take me to Sunday school every week, and I enjoyed the atmosphere of the church because there I felt safe and loved."

Connection broken. She actually enjoyed the atmosphere of a church? I slumped further down in my chair. She wasn't finished, though.

"I had always considered myself a Christian, but until I was thirteen, I never really felt truly saved."

Truly saved? What's that supposed to mean? That she believed more in a non-existent God? I scoffed. I didn't even know this woman's name, and I made the decision to make her one of my godly women? What was I thinking? Nevertheless, I sat still as a pole in my chair and waited for her to continue to other topics. She shifted the subject slightly, thankfully, and I was able to relax a little.

"Even though I wasn't raised a Christian, I have discovered through the years that God can still use people who didn't know Him all their lives. Take my life, for example. I was born in Pittsburgh, PA, and I was a cheerleader in middle school until I turned thirteen." I looked at her admiringly. She had the courage to be in front of people while doing flips, scary stunts, and cheers for sweating football players? That took guts.

"At the age of 13, my mom and I moved to Tampa, FL," Laura continued, "where I played volleyball instead of cheering. I found a church to attend and became involved with the church youth choir, where God used me to spread His gospel through song. It was pretty hot there, but I liked it."

"After graduating from high school, I moved to Cleveland, TN, to attend Lee College, which was very strict at the time. One of the rules Lee had was that unless it was thirty degrees or below, girls had to wear skirts; and in the cafeteria, girls always had to wear skirts, no matter the weather. I grew up in a home where I could wear pants and shorts, so I couldn't understand why they had such crazy rules."

"One winter day, it was under thirty degrees, and school was cancelled. My friends and I wanted to eat in the cafeteria, since we didn't own a car to drive to a restaurant off-campus; however, we didn't want to put on skirts and freeze our legs off. We decided to trick the cafeteria workers. We put on jeans and a shirt, pulled on tall boots, and wore a long overcoat. We went to the cafeteria and the worker there scanned our passes and waved us through, thinking that we were wearing skirts under our coats. We were feeling triumphant as we picked up our food. The next day's classes were cancelled as well, so we tried the same thing; but the worker became suspicious and told us to open our coats. We couldn't hide the truth any longer, and we were sent back to the dorm to put skirts on."

I laughed. I couldn't believe that they almost avoided trouble twice! She was my sort of person. It's funny to see how much things have changed since then. Nowadays, girls are wearing tiny little shorts, and no one really has strict rules against it. "So was that the worst trouble you were ever in?" I asked.

"No, the worst was back in middle school in Pennsylvania. Since it was so cold in the winter, the school had a rule that if the buses were fifteen minutes late picking you up, you could go home and not have to go to school that day. One day, my friends and I had been standing there for what we thought was fifteen minutes, and so even though we saw the bus coming, we went to a friend's house to play for the rest of the day. I was in a lot of trouble with my mom for skipping school."

I nodded. "I've skipped school before, and my mom was not happy."

"I know how hard it is to fight the temptation of skipping school, but because I stuck to it and never skipped again, when I attended college, I was able to join Lee Singers and travel all over the world to places like Austria, Romania, Russia, and throughout the United States."

"So what was your favorite place?" I asked. I wanted to travel when I grew up, so if I collected people's opinions while I was young, then when I could finally travel, I'd know just where to go.

"Probably Austria," she responded. "It was really pretty."

I smiled. Even the name sounded pretty. "After you graduated from Lee, did you stay in Tennessee permanently?" I asked.

"No," she said. "I worked at Life Care for a while until I married my husband, Steve, and then we moved to Tampa, FL. After living in Tampa for 8½ years, my husband and I decided to move back to Cleveland to work at Westmore Church of God in the music department, where we've worked for seventeen years."

My mouth fell open. "I can't imagine working in the same place for that long. I admire you for being able to stick it out. So out of the 17 years, what would be your favorite and least favorite parts of working at this church?"

"My favorite part of working here is God using me to help people; that really makes me feel fulfilled. I also love the people I work with. My least favorite part is that I hate my office." She laughed at this. "It's super ugly, and I don't like having to see it all day long."

As I looked around, she explained her dislike. "Before I came," she began, "they had wallpapered the office, but instead of taking down the wallpaper when I arrived, they painted over it, and now the wallpaper is ripping, making it look dirty and old." I saw where she was pointing and completely understood her misery.

"I want to take it all down," she confessed, "and paint it a different color, but it would take a lot of time and effort. I wouldn't really mind the work, but I would just have to find the time to do it."

I understood that. It would be terrible to have to come to work every day knowing that it could be different but not being able to change it because you didn't have the time. Just then, she checked her phone.

"Oh no! Steve needs a photocopy of a paper in five minutes! I'm going to run to the printer down the hall. Be right back!"

I smiled at her as she rushed out the door. In a few minutes, she was back.

"Sorry about that. He relies on me to help him with the papers for the choir and orchestra. In fact, we relied on each other a lot when we were first married." She sat down in a chair.

"At the beginning of our marriage," she began, "we weren't able to have children, and so for three years I prayed for children. One day at a camp meeting, a man came up to me with what I call 'crazy eyes' and said that God was telling me that I needed to 'accept my healing.' So that day, I fell on my knees and gave everything completely to God. Some time later after a church service, a woman in the congregation came up to me and said nonchalantly, 'While you were singing today, I saw an angel holding three babies over your head.' I thanked her but thought that she must be mistaken and didn't know that I couldn't have children. However, three months later, after returning home from the doctor's office for a checkup, I received a call from the nurse who rattled off a bunch of numbers about my blood work. Having no clue what the numbers meant, I asked if something was wrong. She informed me that I was pregnant. I was elated; yet part of me didn't want to believe it. To confirm the report, I went to the doctor and found out that I had twins."

I was amazed. This was something that could only be explained as miraculous. I couldn't push it away. Only a God, such as the one she believed in, could have done this. She went on with her story. "One week later, I went in for yet another checkup, and I found out that I had triplets. Steve and I went to a specialist to get his advice, and he told us that we should abort two of the babies because I would be in danger with triplets and either the babies or I could die. I told the doctor that if God gave me these babies, then they were in His hands. If they died or if I died, then it would be His decision; but I would not take the lives of the babies."

Did she seriously take the risk of dying so lightly that she basically laughed in its face? She had her life to think about, not some unborn babies'.

"The doctor was angry with me," she continued, "but when the time came for me to deliver, he was one of the doctors present. He said later that if he hadn't witnessed it for himself, he never would've believed that it was possible for a woman of my size and strength to successfully deliver three babies and live. So now, whenever I'm struggling, I remember my miracle babies and have so much more faith in God because of them."

I was astounded. It was such a testimony that could only point to a God. Could I say that my thoughts on her God were misguided? Oh, what was I thinking? Of course there was no one in the great big sky, especially not Someone who would be powerful enough to do this. Yet there was no other explanation.

"If anyone were to ask me what the biggest adventure in my life was," she said, "I would tell him that it was rearing my triplets."

I happened to glance at the time and realized that my mom would be here any minute to pick me up. I told that to Laura, and she smiled.

"Alright. Well, if you take anything away from what I've said today, take away this: if you live by example, not just by words, and aren't ashamed to talk about Jesus openly, then you demonstrate the qualities of a godly woman."

I looked at her closely. How did she know that I was just about to ask her opinion on what the qualities of a godly woman were? It was really coincidental. I shook it off and stood up, thanked her for her time and then left her office.

My mom was waiting outside, and I climbed into the car, where she gave me a look as if to say, "Will you ever purposefully get on my nerves again after knowing what I can do?" I gave her a smile, to her evident surprise, and contemplated the morning. My spontaneous meeting with Laura Allen wasn't exactly what I would call normal, but I still learned many things, like what a self-giving person looked like. Laura was willing to give up her life for her three unborn sons, and she had to go through many troubles and challenges to be where she is now: working for a church while being a mom to triplet sons that could've died. I don't know if I could do that. Seems like no matter who you are, to be a godly woman calls for a lot of trouble. Trouble that I don't know if I would be willing to go through.

Chapter Six

I collapsed into bed, exhausted. I had just finished walking the neighbor's dog for the thirteenth time in the past five days. They were on vacation and didn't want to take their demon Chihuahua, Chi-Chi, with them; so they asked me to take care of him while they were gone. I accepted only because they would be paying me a fairly large sum of money to do it. They seemed to think that because he's a Chee-huahua, they had to name him Chi-Chi. So original. So thirteen walks, seventeen pooper-scooper pickups, a new pair of shoes (which that evil munchkin decided to destroy), and countless hours of incessant barking in my ears later, I was done. I had contemplated multiple malicious plans for him, such as dognapping him and shipping him off to Moscow, giving him a sleeping potion and shoving him in the closet until the owners come back, or arranging some sort of deal with the Asian restaurant down the road. All I had thought of was in vain because there was absolutely no conceivable way to follow through with those gruesome, devilish considerations.

I had had a minimal amount of patience today, and that vermin had taken my patience numbers into the negative thousands, which caused me do something extreme while watching him at the neighbor's house. I have to admit, I'm still laughing at the look on the dog's face when I took the muzzle I had found amongst a pile of Chi-Chi's things and, when the unremitting racket of his unlimited vocal chords was at its climax of shrillness, quickly put it on. Chi-Chi's mouth closed, and he quickly discovered that he could no longer hinge open his jaw to finish his famous song from his band, The Psychotic Muffin Shredders. He made a muffled noise, one I could only label as a yelp. I started guffawing until I literally thought my mucus membranes would drip out my eyes. It was painfully comical.

Once I regained control of myself, however, I realized that he wasn't moving. In fact, while I had been rejoicing in my brilliance at the creative, what I called harmless, way to silence his annoying yowling, he had fallen to the floor with his eyes rolled back in his head, not breathing. In panicked desperation, I took the muzzle off and started shoving my fingers down his tiny throat in the hope that I might make contact with the blockage. I couldn't fathom what I would conjure up to explain this tragedy to his faithful owners. Suddenly, he coughed up a small object. I shrieked in horror, expecting it to be some sort of internal article from his stomach. I gingerly picked it up, hoping it wasn't anything important. Instead, what it was made me growl in frustration and shoot bullet eyes at the sheepish mutt. It just so happened to be the pearl earring I had lost just a few minutes earlier, the one that I had gotten for twelve bucks at Claire's. And now I have ascertained that this monster had eaten it, choked on it, and caused me to plunge my fingers down his sticky gullet! It was too much. I locked him up in his cage and stormed home.

So now I'm lying on my bed, wishing that I had never agreed to the preposterous idea of taking care of a dog for five days. And to make matters worse, I got a text from the owners this morning, reminding me to take him today to his monthly appointment with the hairdresser, which is an entire afternoon affair. Whatever hair they even see on that bald rat is beyond my imagination. With a sigh, I heaved myself up from my comfortable, horizontal posture and prepared to take him to his "appointment." I gathered my purse and Chi-Chi and got in the car. My grandmother had some errands to do in town, so she offered to take me to the beast's beautician.

After she dropped us off in front of Tootsie's Tresses, she informed me that there was a book fair going on across the street, if I wanted to go while the dog was at his appointment.

At the mention of books, my ears immediately perked up, and already I was imagining all the books I would look through and maybe even read curled up in a corner somewhere. At my excited response, she gave me money for some books and for the entrance fee before driving away. I was slightly suspicious because she usually only gives me money if she knows I'm not going to spend it, but I shrugged it off. Maybe she was just being nice. At any rate, Chi-Chi was straining at the leash to enter the brightly colored salon, and his excitement only escalated as I entered and spent an insurmountable amount of time signing him in.

Letting out a sigh of relief, I left the fake, too-cheery colors of the building behind and walked across the street to the gigantic warehouse. After paying for my ticket in the foyer, I entered the main room and nearly had my breath taken from me as I gazed at the unfathomable number of books—aisles and aisles of books stacked neatly on tables or shelved orderly on bookshelves. I felt like I was in a dream as I slowly walked down the aisles, dazedly looking from one side to the other at the colorfully decorated booths and the smiling staff, but mostly at the beautiful books.

I decided to force myself to walk through the whole fair before cracking open even one book, just to see what was available. It was as I was walking down aisle four and seeing my tenth sign about a homeschool curriculum special that it dawned on me that this wasn't an ordinary book fair. It was a curriculum fair for homeschoolers! I stood in the middle of the aisle in shock for several seconds. I could not believe this. I was actually in the same building that homeschoolers visit to get their schoolbooks!

I had met a homeschooler one time at a youth camp, and that time was one too many. Her name was Charity Faith, and she had braces, glasses, no eyebrows, and sounded like a Webster's dictionary. That alone should've clued me in to pivot on my heels and run away as if Godzilla himself were chasing me. But no, like a brainless bird, I stayed and introduced myself because she was the camp director's daughter and got free canteen cards that she would give out to her "friends." Since I decided to introduce myself, however, I thereby unknowingly gave her permission to follow me around for the rest of camp talking in a foreign language called Webster-ese and telling everyone that we were best friends.

I hinted countless times to her to stay away from me and go bother someone else, but either she was deaf, or she was determined to make me look like a fool, with her goody-two-shoes sayings, poor fashion choices, and her holy way of living. To make matters worse, she prayed before every single meal and made me bow my head with her every time. But because of the canteen cards, I kept acting like her "best friend." By the end of camp, though, I was done. After she suggested that we become pen pals (since she didn't have a phone) to keep in touch until next year, I gave up the act and told her how I felt. In the aftermath of the exposition of my true colors, she prayed for me! In front of the entire camp! I was humiliated for life. So it was an unpleasant shock for me to be at a homeschool fair where homeschool parents get curriculum because they can't just enroll their children into a normal school where they wouldn't be unsocial, walking Webster dictionaries.

After the initial shock wore off, I comforted myself that it still had books, and I was itching to get my hands on some to look through. Maybe the first one would be the book on how to train your Chihuahua that I had seen on aisle five, and I could give it to my neighbors as a not-so-subtle hint.

I was walking down the last aisle when I came to a booth tucked in the corner called Educating For Success. The two women there smiled at me. As if my legs had a mind of their own, I walked over to their booth and absentmindedly looked through their pamphlet. One of the women, whose nametag read "Rhea Perry," came up to me and started promoting her Home Educators Conference, telling me the details of it and how God had given her favor with so many millionaires.

"I don't believe in God. I'm an atheist." I cocked an eyebrow and lifted my chin to ready myself for the onslaught that was sure to follow that kind of remark at a homeschool conference.

"Oh really?" Rhea said, not batting an eye. "I used to be an atheist."

Stunned at what I had just heard, I stood there speechless. An atheist? Here? At this homeschool (and very Christian-emphasized) fair? No way! Wait a minute... She said "used to." So what religion is she now? My curiosity just wouldn't let it rest.

"So if you used to be an atheist, what are you now?" I asked in a voice mixed with haughtiness, frustration, and inquisitiveness.

"I'm a Christian now. I used to be an atheist, not because I hated God but because I had never really been told about Him. And because I wasn't exposed to all that God stuff, I also believed in evolution. I remember having friends who would set me up with college theology students to argue about evolution. I would spew out arguments that I personally didn't believe, just so they would get mad." Here, she stopped and laughed at the memory of how riled they would become.

After wiping her eyes, she continued. "See, atheists believe that Christians make up their God so that they can use Him as a crutch to support their failures and to blame for their mistakes. But my atheist days were about to be over. I had been dating a boy in college whose mom had given me a Bible; but on March 23, 1975, he dumped me, and I was devastated. I opened the Bible and read Matthew 6:33, which says, 'But seek first the kingdom of God and His righteousness, and all these things shall be added to you.' Right then and there, I had a come-to-Jesus meeting and gave my heart to the Lord. After I told my friends what had happened, I asked them where to start reading the Bible. 'Start at the beginning,' they said, after getting over the initial shock. So, I read the first verse of Genesis, something I had never done before in my entire life, and do you know what?" I shook my head. "I became a Creationist right then."

I was incredulous. "How did you suddenly become a Creationist after reading the first verse of Genesis? I mean, if you believed in evolution for such a long time, what would change your entire mindset in a blink of an eye?"

"Genesis 1:1 clearly states that in the beginning, God created the heavens and the earth. I was an evolutionist because I believed in nothing, so when I read that verse, after believing in the God of that verse, I knew Genesis 1:1 was true."

"After coming to believe in God," she continued, "many things didn't matter anymore. I was in a college sorority, but I abandoned the club because it didn't matter anymore how people perceived me or the crowd I hung around."

Her words pierced my heart. That is what I was trying to do—find a group of kids who thought I was great and wanted to hang around me. So, this Christian thing took away her desire to be popular and well-liked? That's crazy!

"I also was studying to be an architect," Rhea continued, "but after giving my heart to Jesus, I even didn't care about that anymore."

"So you gave up being an architect," I stated, "just because you became a Christian?"

"I just wasn't interested in it anymore," she answered, "regardless of the fact that I had spent two years on it already. But God started talking to me, and He told me, through a person at the college, that I should run for the Vice Presidency of the School of Education. I thought that no one would vote for me, so instead I ran for Senator of the Hill and lost. I told God the next year that if He wanted me to be Vice President, then I needed some help. I went over to the sign-up sheet and put my name on it. No one else signed up.

Needless to say, I won the Vice Presidency." Our discussion had to stop then because she had a seminar to present; however, she invited me to sit in on the workshop—maybe I would learn something interesting.

In the curtained, closed-off seminar area, Rhea began by talking about creativity. "You don't learn to think creatively by following the rules. You learn by trying and failing a lot. As homeschoolers, we have the freedom to be creative in how we teach. If your students can't focus on a textbook, then get them a different type of book, or think of a creative way for them to learn the subject matter: maybe through hands-on projects, field trips, animals, or music. For example, when I was in Girl Scouts at the age of fifteen, some of us were dropped off on the Suwannee River for seven days in a canoe, floating down the river during the day and sleeping on the banks at night until we met up with the rest of the group. It took a lot of creativity to come up with ideas to survive on the river, but we did it. Some of your ideas may fail, but you just might find one that turns your student onto learning."

Failure. That's my nemesis. If I'm not absolutely sure of success, I don't even start something. Enough people have told me in my life that I'm a failure, so why should I do something and prove it? Yet, when was the last time I thought creatively? Racking my brain, I couldn't come up with a single incident—unless it was this morning with the muzzle. I smiled just thinking about it. But that had almost failed, too, with the almost death of Chi-Chi. But it didn't, and the creativity felt so good that I almost didn't feel like a failure at the time. Maybe Rhea is correct. Trying and possibly failing can teach creativity. My mind was pulled back to the seminar by a family story Rhea was sharing.

"My eldest son, Drew, now owns two trucking companies and a car lot, but he didn't start out that big. He started out making money when we saw a truck of bunnies parked in the sun. The truck driver was going to kill them because they seemed sick and ready to die. Drew bought them all for fifty cents each and then, from another person, bought cages for them. He transported them home where he revived them, and then he took them to the flea market where he sold the bunnies with their cages for five dollars a piece. He sold almost every single bunny that day and came home with more money in his pocket than he had spent on them, because he saw an opportunity and invested in it."

As I exited the seminar with the rest of the audience, I thought about the different ways she had talked about how to make money. I was still mulling it over when we arrived back at the Educating For Success booth. I asked her the question that I couldn't seem to get out of my head.

"What inspired you to make more money?"

"Actually, being poor inspired me to make more money," she began. "I got tired of not having enough money to do anything, like eating out, taking trips, or helping people financially. When my mom got very sick in Florida and the doctor told me I needed to come right away, I couldn't see any way to go because we didn't have enough money for the trip. I hated being told that something was impossible because 'no' isn't in my vocabulary. Eventually, I was able to go and see her before she passed away. Even though her death was a bad experience for me, I believe that every bad thing that's happened to me has caused something good to happen to me. Good things can come out of bad if God is in control."

"Our church leadership said that you shouldn't make a so-called 'unfair deal' with other people—that's what they said Drew had done with the bunnies—but I began to wonder if that wasn't the case. I began searching through the Bible and found a ton of verses about making money. I started teaching about it, and people started listening to me. I had conferences where I would have millionaires and multi-millionaires up on my stage sharing how they made their fortunes. So that's what inspired me to make more money. Being poor."

I understood fully wanting to do something so badly—like ski or travel—and not being able to because I didn't have the money. I would love to make more money, but could a mere teenager become an entrepreneur? Would I be willing to risk multiple failures for the chance to perhaps succeed? I wanted to stop having to be financially dependent on other people for the things I wanted and found important, but I had no clue how.

"So what could I do to make money?" I asked anxiously.

"Well, do you play an instrument? I used to play the trumpet in a band for ribbon cutting ceremonies. You could, perhaps go a musical route."

I shook my head regretfully. "I have no talent in the music industry. But maybe I could learn the trumpet like you. My friends keep pressuring me to join the band anyway."

She gave me a sympathetic smile and shook her head. "Something I discovered when I was first learning about God was that I can't try to be something I'm not. I just need to keep reading the Bible, and if God wants me to change, then He'll change me Himself. So don't try to change based on what other people want you to do, even if it seems like you should. God created you the way you are, and if He wants you to change, then in His timing, He will change you. Look at me! I used to be an atheist. But God changed me. I used to be an alcoholic, but God changed that, too."

I was struck speechless. She used to be an alcoholic? And now she's a Christian? If only her God, if He's real, would change my mom and release her from the curse of that trash. Yet, Rhea's words in the seminar were so powerful that it seemed like she wished everyone would change to become entrepreneurs and discover their creativity.

"I love it when I talk to someone about ideas," she had said, "and the light in their eyes comes on, and they later come back and tell me how they put the plan into action. I love putting plans into action, but I despise the details. I'm a big picture person who wants to put a plan into action immediately, but my detail friends tell me all the details that have to happen before it can be done. So I patiently—or sometimes not so patiently—wait, and eventually, perhaps after a few failures and setbacks, the plan succeeds. See, you must have vision."

I nodded my head, understanding the disappointment of immediately wanting to do something but can't until all the little things are taken care of. Looking at my watch, I realized with a sigh that one little thing I needed to take care of was to pick up Chi-Chi from Tootsie's Tresses. Once I told Rhea that I needed to pick up the dog I was watching, she remarked that pet-sitting was a fantastic way for me to make money and that she was sure that I would find other creative ways to make extra cash. As I gave her a hug, she told me, "I hope you find more people who will speak into your life, especially godly women—women who are loving, happy, joyful, and peaceful. It is a godly woman who makes a happy house."

I now had even more proof that no one in my house was godly. Speaking of the women in my house, I needed to find out why my grandmother would deliberately send me over to a homeschool fair, knowing how I despised homeschoolers.

I headed over to the salon to pick up my responsibility. As I snapped on his heavy leash, I began to realize that as annoying as this dog may be, he was a creative opportunity for cash. I walked to the curb, just as my grandmother drove up in front of the salon. After putting the dog in his cage and climbing into the car, I launched into giving her an earful of where I had conveniently ended up. She acted way too innocent, and I came to the conclusion that she had definitely known where she was sending me from the triumphant look on her face. I figured she hadn't wanted me to spend her money on books, so I felt some sense of victory when I told her that I had indeed bought a book, Creating Comradeship With Your Chihuahua.

I also told her that I met a woman named Rhea Perry and how she was so vision minded that she didn't care if no one had ever devised the idea before; she would look ahead to the future and plan today based on the effects it would have tomorrow. My grandmother absentmindedly nodded her head, and I realized that I was actually being positive about the day. Upon realizing my optimism, I quickly changed my tuned and continued with my accusations, even though in the back of my mind I realized that Rhea had unintentionally been the godly woman I needed to meet with for the week.

As soon as I arrived home, I took the dog back to his kennel where he promptly licked my hand. I snatched it back as if he had just bitten it. Who knows what kind of diseases he could be carrying? I waited impatiently for his owners' return. When they finally arrived, I grabbed my money, shoved the book into their hands, accepted their thanks with a combination of a low guttural growl and panicked hysteria, and sprinted home. Dashing inside, I received orders from my grandmother that she wanted me to go to church the next day, orders which I promptly talked my way out of.

I flopped onto my bed, still exhausted but not as emotionally drained as before. From the delighted reactions of Chi-Chi's owners when I gave them the book, they'll probably ask me to dog-sit for them again—and that rabies-carrying monster will probably also start preaching to me just like my grandmother! Everyone else seemed to feel the need to evangelize me. If I need spirituality, I'll let them know. It can be so frustrating! Maybe I should meet with a Mongolian next time, so I won't be able to understand her. It's a thought.

Chapter Seven

I sank slowly, feeling the coolness of the water envelop me in its chilly grasp. My lungs started tightening slightly, and I used both feet to push off the bottom of the pool toward the surface. As I broke through the water, the night sky looked down on me with foreboding. I knew I wasn't supposed to be out at that hour, or in the pool at all, without permission after I had let Chi-Chi swim in the pool one day. He tore several holes in the liner with his claws while he was trying to climb out; my Mom was not a happy camper, to say the least. However, I couldn't sleep because of the heat, and I knew it was useless to thrash around in bed for hours, so I decided to take a quick night swim. When we bought this tiny house, it already had the pool, which was a deciding factor in us buying it. The pool has its pros and cons, and one of the pros is that on nights like this, it invites you to come slip into the smooth waters to cool off. Like I was doing, unsupervised and unauthorized. After an undetermined amount of time, I stepped out of the relaxing water into the humid night air. As I dried off, a noise startled me, and I spun around. My mom stood on the back porch, livid. I gulped and stared at my mom with the look of a deer in the headlights.

"M-m-mom! What are you d-d-doing out here on this f-f-fine night?"

She sneered at the guilty look on my face as she took a swig from her beer can. "Me? Oh, I just thought I would get a little fresh air, seeing how it's only three in the morning, and all. The night's still young!"

I chuckled nervously, wishing that she would disappear. "Well, the weather is definitely pretty great. But like you said, it's three in the morning, so I had better get back to bed."

She pouted mockingly. "What? This early? I insist; you must stay up a little longer. In fact, why don't you, while you're already up, go clean the kitchen? Also, I noticed that my bathroom is pretty nasty, so to clean it efficiently, you may want to use your toothbrush. And now that I think of it, I have a friend who needs some help tomorrow around the office. I was going to decline, but I know you would just love to go. In fact, I'm surprised you're not begging me to go. I know I'm doing you a favor, so don't thank me. In fact, you can write an essay about your time with her once you get back so I know you weren't sleeping." She shrugged in her oversized pajama shirt with a contented sigh. "Well, I guess I'd better be getting to bed. When I wake up, I can't wait to see how clean both the kitchen and bathroom are! And get this, my precious little doll," at this point, she lost the happy-go-lucky act and narrowed her eyes at me. "If they aren't spotless by the time I wake up, then you will be scrubbing the floor of my bathroom with your tongue for the next five years." She then smiled sweetly, pivoted on her blue slippers, and strolled into the house.

I stood there shivering, as I mentally calculated how long it would be before I was able to collapse in my bed. After concluding that I would get very little sleep tonight, I shuffled into the kitchen, still dripping, and began the monotonous task, and then shuffled into my mom's bathroom, careful not to wake her up, and began to clean it. Three and a half hours later, I sank gratefully into bed and was asleep before my head touched the pillow. Way too soon, I awoke to my mom shaking me hard enough to cause an earthquake in California.

"Get up," she hissed. "You have twenty minutes before I leave to take you to help my friend around the office. If you are late, you will be sentenced to the worst punishment you can imagine for the rest of your life." I got up. In nineteen minutes, just for triumph's sake, I sat in the car with my manipulative mother as she backed out of the driveway and pulled onto the road. Ten minutes later we arrived at our destination. I knew nothing of this woman and was contemplating making a run for it when my mom grabbed my arm and shoved me toward a woman coming out the front door of the large, fancy building. A sign announced that this was The Church of God of Prophecy International Offices. She gave my mom a hug and then turned toward me with a hug as well.

"Well, hello there. This a pleasant surprise!" She gave my mom an inquisitive glance and my mom explained.

"She has, out of the graciousness of her heart, willingly volunteered to come today and help! Isn't she just so sweet?" She gave me a warning look as she fondly—or not so fondly—gave my chin a little pat to close my gaping mouth. I forced a smile as my eye involuntarily twitched. A small movement, but the woman saw it and gave me a knowing wink.

To me, she said, "Why don't we head inside?" To my mom, she said, "You can pick her up at twelve. That is, unless she's driven to madness by me." She chuckled at that as she ushered me inside to sign in. I didn't know if the chuckle was a good sign or a bad sign.

"So what did you do for her to bring you here today?" I stared at her wide-eyed. How did she know?

"I kind of went swimming at three in the morning last night, which she wasn't very pleased about."

She laughed. "Well, I hope you won't find this much of a punishment."

I grimaced ruefully. "I hope you don't take it like that," I said apologetically. "This isn't my punishment. It's just my mom wanting time off. My actual punishment was cleaning the kitchen and bathroom until about 6:30 this morning. The punishment is not hanging out with you; it's giving her a report on my time here once I get back so she knows I didn't sleep the whole time." She laughed outright, and then she gave me a sympathetic look.

"I hope I won't put you to sleep. I'll try to give you enough information so you can give a good report. I'm Cathy, by the way."

Through my sleep-deprived head, a thought rang out. What if I took this opportunity to make her one of my godly women? She works in the church's headquarters and she smiles a lot, so she must be a Christian. I quickly decided that, yes, she would be a good choice. Biting my lip, I told her about my challenge and asked if she would like to be one of my fifty-two godly women.

Smiling from ear to ear, she nodded exuberantly. "It would be an honor!" I sighed, relieved.

She led me up the stairs to the second level where she showed me around the offices. We headed to the conference room for a devotional time that they apparently have every morning. I was puzzled when she told me about the devotional. First off, the whole idea of business people having a devotional every morning was beyond me. I didn't know why they would bother to take time out of their day to study—I gagged inwardly—the Bible. Second, why is it that everywhere I go, I seem to run into a Christian activity? I'm just on this mission because I agreed to it in a moment of weakness. I don't want to be changed by Christianity and its holy ways. As Rhea Perry said, wait for God to change me, and if He wants me to, then He will. And since He doesn't exist, I won't have to worry about changing. I smirked. I probably took that way out of context, but the meaning stays the same, right?

I hate being unsure, and I've been feeling way too unsure these past few weeks. The only thing that keeps me from throwing in the towel is the fact that I would feel terrible leaving something unfinished. I need everything to be perfectly in order for me to feel accomplished, and if something is left unfinished, or I fail at something, then I feel worthless and feel that I don't live up to everyone's expectations. So I keep on, through the evangelizing and the taunts from my family and the nagging in the back of my mind which throws me off balance, just to finish this.

The devotion was about Elijah and how God sent a fire, an earthquake, and a great wind, but He wasn't in any of them. I grinned inwardly at this point because, obviously, if He wasn't in any of that, He doesn't exist. But the chapter went on to say that God sent a quiet whisper, and He was in that. I dropped the grin. I didn't want to hear this at all. All these false words and lies trying to sneak into people's lives and ruin them for life. I tuned the noise out until they were done.

"In a few minutes, prayer will begin in the chapel," Cathy told me cheerfully. I stifled an eye roll. Prayer? They expect me to pray with them? I tilted my head sideways and stated what I had been trying not to say for the past few minutes.

"Sorry I didn't mention it earlier, but I'm an atheist." I stared at her, waiting for a change in her face. Seeing none, I added, "But I can come to prayer if you want." This time I couldn't help it. I sighed, and my shoulders slumped.

She looked inquisitively at me and nodded. "Okay, I understand, but it would be great if you came in just to observe what we do."

I slowly followed her into the room across the hall where a bunch of chairs were set up and music was playing softly. I walked in behind her and uncertainly took my seat. A man walked in and started listing off people and places that needed prayer. I didn't know any of the people he mentioned, so there was no way I was going to be involved in the actual praying. People started getting up and turning to kneel in front of their seats. Cathy did that as well, and I followed suit, not wanting to stick out like a sore thumb. She began to pray, and I knelt next to her, unsure of what to do. Not having any other thoughts, I began to focus on the music in the background. I recognized some of the songs, vaguely remembering them from my childhood. After ten minutes, Cathy and I left the room and strode down the hallway to her office. I surveyed the room, wondering how I was supposed to help her.

"So where do I start?" I inquired.

Smiling, she motioned to a brown, leather chair and said, "Let's get acquainted first. Helping can wait."

Relieved, I quickly flopped into the chair before she could change her mind. I started talking. "Since I don't exactly know you—actually, I've never met you before in my life—I'm going to first ask you some foundational questions; then you can have the reins and tell me things you would like to share. Question one: what's your name?"

She smiled at my straightforward method of getting to know unfamiliar people. "Catherine Grace Harris Payne," she said. "Harris was my maiden name, and Payne is my married name."

"What are things you love to do?" I inquired.

"I love going to the beach. I love to swim and walk, to read and write. I love to eat Mexican food and salty stuff."

"You mentioned reading. What's your favorite book?"

"The Bible definitely," but at the sight of my pained expression, she added, "I also love Piercing The Darkness." I was glad that she mentioned something other than the Bible. I've had enough of the Bible this morning to last me for a good long while.

"So what do you do here?"

She gave me a questioning look. "Didn't your mom tell you anything about me?"

I shook my head. She rolled her eyes playfully and grinned. "I'm a minister, and my mom was a minister before me. I got saved at an early age, but at the age of eight I actually and fully understood the meaning of giving my heart to God. It was at that time that I got filled with the Holy Spirit. Because of my ministerial work, I've been to 108 nations around the globe, and I've been to Africa 22 times." I looked at her, fascinated. I would love to travel, but I wouldn't enjoy having to go into—ugh—ministry just to travel. Aunt Carolyn travels, and she isn't a minister. Maybe there's hope.

She continued. "Ministry does come with its costs, however, as does everything. One time I was praying for people, and a woman began shouting profanities. She became so irate that she tackled me to the ground, giving me several injuries." I winced aloud, imagining the crushing blow. Cathy didn't look to be the football type.

"Praying there must have been the worst decision you've ever made!" I exclaimed.

She paused only a moment and, shaking her head, said, "No. The worst decision I've ever made is wasting time. It's inevitable to waste time during your lifetime. However, if you're doing something that isn't using your time wisely, at least make it something that brings you joy. For example, if I waste time reading a book instead of preparing for a trip, the book at least gives me joy and laughter, rather than actually wasting my time with, say, sitting around and doing something that does nothing to better my physical or mental state." I was surprised at her response, to be honest. I expected something random and very spiritual, but this was something that could relate to any person about anything, not just to spiritually bad decisions. I was impressed, so I decided to let her talk, to see what else she had to say.

"You can have the reins of the conversation now."

"Thank you. I'm going to start out by telling you my story. I was born in Norfolk, VA, and I got off to a rocky start. Because of complications during the pregnancy, I was born with my face crushed into my shoulder and my feet were bent so my toes touched my shin. I had no nose bone, and, in general, I was deformed. The doctor said I would never walk and that there was extensive brain damage."

I was surprised. She had been born deformed?

"My mom cried and cried, praying over me for weeks. She would massage my feet and face, trying to bring them back to their normal positions. My older sister was very jealous of me because she was young at the time and didn't understand why I needed to have so much attention. One day when my mom was praying for me, she felt the presence of the Lord in the room and, as a sign of faith, she reached out to touch the hem of His robe, like the woman in the Bible from Matthew 9:20-22. Immediately, she felt a release of faith. She told Jesus, 'I give this child to you.' A few weeks later, she saw a change in my face. My face started filling in, my head started shifting to its proper position, and the missing nose bone started growing. In a few more weeks, I was completely healed."

I sat there astonished. Her God actually healed her completely from deformity! I studied her intently. There were no scars or marks anywhere that I could see. How could a God so powerful not care at all for anyone related to me? Did He care only about ministers?

Cathy continued. "When I was in the first grade, my mom got a call to come to the school. When she met with my teacher, my teacher asked her if she knew her daughter was different. My mom asked her in what way was I different, remembering that the doctor had said I had extensive brain damage. My teacher said that I had an understanding that couldn't be explained. She would teach something, and I would understand it the first time she explained it. I would then get bored with class because she would have to teach it several more times to the other students. My teacher wanted me to be moved up two grades because I was so incredibly intelligent. My mom, however, didn't want me to pass my older sister, so she declined."

What a shame. I would love to be smart enough to be in a higher grade than my sister.

"This intelligence wasn't only relegated to academics. I was also so gifted in my biblical astuteness that I was appointed as a youth pastor at the age of twelve, teaching people at least twice my age! Another spiritual gift that operates through me is the gift of healing. God can heal people through me. One time I was praying for a woman with a deadly cancer and felt a supernatural surge of fire while praying for her. She was healed. Another time, I was praying for a woman with a brain tumor. I put my hand upon her head and the tumor left immediately. I believe I am a product of my mom's supernatural faith, and because of that, I am able to be used supernaturally."

I had an inner struggle then. How could anyone heal a deadly brain tumor? And what was that whole thing about a surge of fire? Did she feel like she was burning? And if so, why would God make a person suffer through that? I kept these questions to myself, however. No need to make a scene. She kept talking.

"There was a rough time in my family, though. My dad always said he was saved, but he may have never really known the Lord. My dad lost hope at some point in his life and spent the next forty years in rebellion against the Lord. He drank some, and he hit my mom twice. The second time he hit her, she packed her bags and got ready to leave; but he begged her to stay. She told him that she would stay; but if he ever hit her again, she would leave without saying anything, and he would never see her again."

I understood everything in that statement. My mom has abused us kids for years with her words. Words don't leave bruises on the outside, but they leave scars on the inside that no one can see, scars that can leave a person shattered for life.

"I've never felt in danger as a kid, but I did feel in danger when I was flying to Cuba on a mission trip. While in the air, the plane started spiraling to the ground; people were screaming and crying. I sat there smiling because my life literally flashed before my eyes—I saw my husband, my son, and my ministry. I thought, 'Wow, how cool is this? I'm going to die taking the gospel to Cuba. What an amazing thing to put in the history books!' Obviously I didn't die," she said, grinning. "The plane leveled off and shakily flew to a nearby airport in the Bahamas. The EMTs had to come on the plane and pry a lady's hands off her seat because she was hysterically crying. When I remember this incident, Romans 8:28 comes to mind. It says, 'And we know that all things work together for good to those who love God, to those who are the called according to His purpose.' This is the Bible verse that has impacted my life the most. Thankfully, God spared everyone's lives that day. But everyone must die someday, as my dad found out." She paused a moment, collecting herself.

"My dad was in the hospital, dying because of cancer. I was there, as was my mom, regardless of what he had done to us in the past. I called my sister, telling her that she should come, and she refused, saying that he was going to be fine, like the other times. After I hung up, I could tell that my dad was seeing something. I followed his eyes and saw that he was watching something out of the window. I told my mom, but initially she didn't think he had seen anything; however, once she watched his eyes, she knew he had. He followed it into the room until it was at the foot of his bed. At that point, my mom could see it: it was the angel of death that had come for my father. He died, but I know my dad went in peace, believing, because I felt the presence of God in the room. I just have to have faith that I'll see him again."

I was very upset at this point. It was just too close to home: a father who dies and leaves his wife and two girls. How could Cathy trust that a non-existent God would allow her father to go to heaven, a father that had mistreated her and her mom? Either she's crazy, or her God is actually real. Cathy didn't look to be the crazy type. I couldn't understand it.

"Life is an adventure," she stated, drawing me back into the conversation, "but the biggest adventure in a person's life is his or her godly journey towards the Lord. If you want to become a godly woman, her qualities can be found in Proverbs 31." I nodded as if I knew precisely what Proverbs 31 said, even though I didn't have the slightest clue.

At that instant, I looked down at my watch and realized in growing dread that it was two past twelve. "My mom will be here any minute, and I haven't helped you at all!" I couldn't fathom what my mom would do to me if she found out.

She consoled me with a hug. "Don't worry. I'll tell her that you gave me ideas for the book I'm writing."

I smiled, relieved. I walked down the stairs to where my mom was impatiently waiting for me in the lobby. She glared at me as I got in the car, as if it were my fault I wasn't out by twelve exactly. Once we got home, I went inside and ran up to my room where I fell on my bed, exhausted, and lay there reflecting on the day. Cathy Payne was so devoted to God and to being His servant. I'm stuck with being devoted to seeing this challenge through, even though it is hard work. At least my mom didn't make me "help" with someone super mean or boring. I shook off all other thoughts as I drifted off into dreamland, even though it was barely past noon. I was exhausted from the day but glad I got to meet with Cathy and hear her amazing stories.

Chapter Eight

I needed cash badly. My current tennis racket, which had five strings missing and a grip that was made out of duct tape, finally snapped in two yesterday after years of my poor attempts at tennis. I really wanted to buy a brand new racket. I went around the neighborhood asking people for jobs that might be manageable for a thirteen-year-old girl. After half an hour of searching, I finally came across a job that I thought I could handle. Apparently, the Johnsons in the ginormous mansion on the next block wanted a willing, able person to babysit their sweet little seven-year-old angel, Arianna, that evening. I jumped at the chance, scarcely believing my good fortune. I ran home to tell my grandmother where I was going to be for the evening, so she wouldn't call the police to report a "missing child." She had always had a flair for the dramatic. Upon my return, Arianna's parents left with the promise to be back at 10:00 that evening, four and a half hours from their departure. I turned toward the little pixie but was surprised to find that she was scowling at me.

"Arianna, sweetie, what would you like to play?" She curled her little lip at me. I was stunned. It looked so out of place that I wondered if she was conscious of doing it.

She replied tartly. "You won't be playing anything with me today. It's okay though," she said, as she tapped her chin. "You can be my waitress and serve me some cherry tarts from the tall cabinet, as well as a glass of grape juice. I'll be up in my royal domain awaiting you." She turned and haughtily strutted out of the room like some celebrity and pranced up the stairs. Halfway up, she slowly turned around and narrowed her saucy eyes at me.

"Oh, I forgot to mention. Be snappy about it." With that, she continued her arrogant stroll up the stairs. My eyes were bigger than Saturn itself, I'm sure, and my jaw dangled precariously about three feet below where it was supposed to be. Dazedly, I walked into the kitchen, all the while slapping myself for the fact that I was so gullible to be coaxed into babysitting a royal brat. And now I was stuck with her for the next four hours, twenty-six minutes, and fourteen seconds—but it wasn't like I was counting or anything.

Reluctantly, I gathered up the demanded items and slowly clumped up the stairs to her "domain." Upon opening the dark oak double doors, complete with a brass knocker, my jaw completely unhinged and came crashing to the ground. She was correct when she called it her "royal domain." It could have been Queen Victoria's room! It was larger than all the rooms in my house put together. For a seven-year-old! I surveyed the luxurious sitting room carpeted with pink, plush shag. One wall proudly displayed two ceiling-to-floor bookshelves full of picture books. A forty-inch flat screen television hung on another wall amidst portraits of herself. Stylishly positioned was a hot pink fluffy couch and a small wooden table covered with bowls of sweets, tarts, and delicacies. I noticed, with much annoyance, that there was a plate piled high with cherry tarts, as well as two glasses of grape juice.

I continued to gape as I walked into the bedroom. One wall displayed a giant stained glass picture window of an angel that looked out on a gorgeous view of their property. The sunshine filtered in and landed on her fluffy, king-sized bed with seven stuffed animals, thirteen different-sized pillows, and a soft, pink comforter. My eyes wandered over the rest of her room and were not surprised to see another flat screen television, a top-quality kitchen complete with a juice bar, another couch, a baby grand piano, a fireplace, and a small waterfall cascading over beautiful marble tiles into a pit of assorted rocks and goldfish. A crystal chandelier hung proudly from the tall ceiling, and twin jeweled lamps were stationed on either side of her bed. A gorgeous dresser sat in the corner with jewelry boxes on it.

I stared in astonishment at all the furnishings as I continued the visual tour. I walked over to a closed door and stealthily opened it and walked inside. What I saw was fit for a queen. Clothes lined the sides, and shoes were racked on pink shelves. Accessories, such as hats, sunglasses, and scarves, filled one shelf near the back. As I walked out, I was startled by a loud and exaggerated "A-hem." I jerked my head around to find Arianna staring at me with beady little eyes and a suspicious look on her angry face.

"Deciding we would develop a habit for sticky fingers while we were here, eh?"

I glared at her in astonishment. "I was only looking, your highness. I have no inkling about taking anything."

She smirked. "Can't take a bit of teasing, huh? Well, where's my food?"

I plopped the tray down on a nearby glass table, making her cock an eyebrow of arrogance.

"You couldn't have brought a napkin?" At my low guttural growl, she quickly made amends. "Very well, this will have to do for now. Just grab a towel from the bathroom, in case I spill something on this beautiful carpet. Although," she added as a second thought, "I'm too perfect to make a mess."

I struggled to keep my fingers clutched behind my back to avoid scratching her little eyes out. I stomped into the bathroom and stopped in utter amazement. It was massive. A jacuzzi was in one corner, with a small door in it so children could easily enter and exit. A shower was in the next corner, complete with marble tile and a gorgeous faucet that would cascade water onto the lovely tiles below. I could only gape—I hate to admit it—in jealousy. How is it fair that a spoiled seven-year old could have all of this while I couldn't afford a tennis racket? I wanted more than anything for this day to be over. Arianna strutted into the bathroom with an incredulous look on her face.

"Are you blind? The towels are literally right in front of your face!" I blinked. She was correct. There was a shelf of terry cloth towels right in front of my nose. I methodically picked one up, handed it to her, and walked out of the luxurious room.

Four painful hours later, her parents returned. They had wide smiles from the relaxing evening, and I, not wanting to tell them the truth about their little "angel" and spoil their night, asked for my pay. My eyes widened until I thought they were going to pop out of my skull: they put a fifty-dollar bill in my bare palm. I stuttered out my gratitude, hoping I wasn't dreaming, and raced out their front door, down their lengthy driveway, and all the way home.

The next day, I beamed with satisfaction as I heard the blissful sound of the receipt gliding out of the cash register at the sporting goods store. The moment I had been waiting for all night long was here. I grasped my new, blue tennis racket with glee. I could finally learn how to play tennis correctly, instead of having to change my swing so I wouldn't break a string. The icing on the cake was that Tina texted me earlier this morning telling me that she had contacted a tennis friend about giving me a lesson, and this friend had agreed. I was going to meet with a real tennis player to get a lesson. I couldn't wait!

When I returned home, I quickly changed into my tennis clothes, and then my mom drove me to the tennis courts, where I anxiously anticipated the tennis player's arrival. Since there was a court that was open, I decided to practice everything I possibly knew about tennis. In the middle of my 14th serve, I saw a woman approaching my court wearing tennis shorts, a tank top, and a visor. I became so flustered that I served the ball into the adjoining court. Fuming, I inwardly kicked myself at the horrible first impression I had just made. Nonetheless, I walked over to her and introduced myself.

"Hi, I'm Brie."

"Hey there," she said. "My name's Gayle. I've heard a lot about you from Tina."

I smiled, although inwardly I wondered what Tina had told her—probably that I was a terrible tennis player; and now she had proof to back up Tina's assessment.

But Gayle was still smiling at me. "Are you ready to begin the lesson?" she asked. Boy was I ever!

She started going over the basics. I was filled with happiness as I was finally able to learn from a pro the right way to play tennis. She guided me through the motions and encouraged me the entire time. If I hit it over the fence for the millionth time because my weight wasn't on my front foot, she would build my confidence back up and throw me another ball. While we were taking a water break on the bench, she started sharing with me about rest and recreation.

"Rest and recreation are very important to a person's body. You can rest by going to sleep, but you can also rest by putting away distractions and being okay with the quiet. Christ is our rest, and He injects us with rest; we just have to be quiet. When we give a little more to Him, He in return gives us more back." The second she started talking about God, I became suspicious. So that's why Tina wanted me to meet with this person so badly! She was my next godly woman. Why would Tina purposefully trick me? Of course, she probably knew that I would've been stuck all day today wondering whom to meet with on this last day of the week (I really shouldn't keep putting these things off until the last possible moment) so she had this genius idea to have me meet with Gayle. I came back to reality when Gayle turned and faced me.

"See, we have three important things in our life: our body, our mind, and our spirit. If one is not rested, then the other two will suffer."

We finished our short break and headed back out to the courts. We played tennis for another half hour; and all the while she kept coaching me, and I kept slowly progressing. Finally, she looked at the time. "We had better get off the courts; we are past our time. I sure wouldn't want to get in trouble. Trouble has a way of finding me in the strangest places."

I was instantly curious. "What happened?" I asked, grabbing some balls as I headed off the court.

"In my senior year of high school, at the end of the year, I was laughing in class and my teacher got mad because he had had a bad day, I suppose. Anyway, he said that I was banished from the classroom. I didn't know what to do, but the day was almost over, so I decided I would just go home. The next day at school, I was talking with the Assistant Principal and mentioned that I had left school. He was so shocked. He told me that students were never, ever allowed to leave the grounds without permission. He could have caused me more trouble than I had already experienced with my teacher." I was listening, amused. It sounded super fun to be able to get away with breaking the rules.

"Would you like to get some lunch," she asked, "before returning home?"

"Lunch would be great," I responded enthusiastically. "I'm starving!"

We quickly loaded up her Hummer with the tennis equipment and hopped into her SUV.

"So tell me about yourself," she remarked to me as she drove out of the parking lot. I shrugged, uncomfortable.

"There's not much to tell. I'm just an average girl going to an average school." At her look of dissatisfaction, I hurriedly continued.

"Um, well, I like to ski, and I like to play tennis, as you can tell. I love to read, and I am allergic to cilantro."

She laughed. "Well, at least I'll know what's wrong if you pass out at the restaurant." I smiled hesitantly. I hoped that she was joking, for my sake.

"Now that you've spilled your side, I'll tell you a few random facts about myself. My name is Gayle Galloway Cobb. A while ago, I dropped my first name and went by my middle name, Gayle, then used my maiden name, Galloway, as my middle name. I was born in Louisville, KY, I've broken my tailbone riding a bike, my favorite song is 'Revelation Song' by Kari Jobe, and I love chips." I was out of my reserved mood by now, enjoying her company. We pulled up to the mall and headed inside. There was a nice Mexican restaurant right inside the entrance that had an outdoor patio. We walked in and ordered. While we waited for our meal, I asked her to tell me more about herself, explaining my challenge.

"Certainly!" She said with no hesitation.

"I have to warn you, however," I said reluctantly. "I'm an atheist, so I may be a little iffy on some subjects. If you see me wrinkle my nose, don't take it personally."

She laughed outright. "I won't. And don't worry; Tina has already informed me of your faith status. Here goes. I'm going to get the religious stuff out of the way so you won't feel uncomfortable the entire time."

"I was saved at age nine at a Kentucky Youth Camp," she began, "and I was filled with the Holy Spirit at age sixteen at a Perry Stone revival."

At this point her eyes took on an excited glimmer. "I have been reading Ecclesiastes the past few weeks, and it has been eye opening! It was written by King Solomon, and it discusses how he went on a search for the meaning of life. He had wealth and wisdom, but he wanted to know the meaning of life."

I definitely didn't have wealth, and wisdom was definitely out of the question. In fact, I used to think that if I swallowed a seed, dirt, and water, then I could grow a plant in my stomach!

Our food came then. I had ordered a fajita, and it was sizzling hot. She looked at me over her fajita side dish with expectant eyes.

"Now, what do you want me to tell you?" she asked.

I scrambled to think of something. "So what would be one of your fondest memories?"

She smiled, remembering. "I was at a women's retreat a few years ago, and that night as I was praying, a woman named Ginger Robinson approached me and told me she had a message for me from God."

I groaned silently. Another so-called message? It's the same old story I've heard over and over again in my challenge. Yet, all the women have come from such diverse backgrounds. How can they have the same story? Could it be that this God-thing is for real?

"The message was this," she continued. "'Forget about the past and look to the future. Open your eyes.' I didn't know what it meant until later that night, when my roommate at the retreat, Karen Young, helped me come to an understanding of it. I had felt in the past like it was too late for me to be used by God, that I had missed my chance. However, I was to forget about that and look to the future." She put a bite of refried beans in her mouth and then continued speaking of her memories.

"I know that there is a God because of this next story I'm going to tell you." I slumped in my seat. Not another story about God! Seeming not to notice, Gayle continued. "I have a niece who, when she was six years old, was diagnosed with a liver disease. I watched her slowly die for six years. When she reached twelve, the medical personnel finally deemed her sick enough to get on the liver transplant list. Her parents were told not to go 50 miles away from the hospital, so that they could be called at a moment's notice. It could take weeks, months, or years before a liver would be available, but we kept hoping and praying. Three days after being on the list, they got a phone call at 12:01 in the morning from the hospital, telling them to come to the hospital because a liver was ready for a transplant. Her parents took her there, and waited and waited for the surgery to begin. She was yellow and thin, barely surviving. Finally, she was called to the surgery room, and later that day we went in to see her. Already she was functioning properly. Color was back in her cheeks, and she was smiling. It was a miracle."

That last statement shook me good and hard. A miraculous God? He hadn't done anything miraculous in my life. How could He exist? Yet, how can I deny what happened to Cathy Payne or Laura Allen or this niece? I didn't want to think about it right now. The niece was just saved because a person gave her a liver. Nothing more. I not-so-discreetly steered the conversation from spirituality.

"So, do you have any children?"

She stared at me inquisitively, as if wondering what brought on this topic. She nodded slowly. "Yes. I have two daughters. My eldest, Sarah, graduated this year, and Rachel is going to be a senior this coming semester."

"So what school do they go to?"

"They've been homeschooled all their lives. In fact, it was the best decision of my life. When Rachel was four, my husband, David, suggested homeschooling them, and I firmly declined. There was no way I would homeschool my children. But it must have been God's will because when Sarah was in kindergarten, I was looking at her playing, and I had a 180-degree turn around of my heart. It's been the hardest, but happiest, choice of my life." I stared at her, astonishment creeping all over my face. She homeschooled her kids? Here I was, talking with a mom who homeschooled! I had no clue. She didn't seem like the stereotypical homeschool mom at all. She stood up then and grabbed her stuff.

"Let's get you home, shall we?" I nodded. We went out to her car and piled in. On our way back to my house, she asked me a question.

"So what is the one question you want to know from me? I can see it in your eyes that you have one."

I smiled. She missed nothing. I didn't beat around the bush but instead got straight to the point. "What are the qualities of a godly woman?"

Her eyes widened. "Ah, good question. I think to be a godly woman, you need to invest your time and energy into getting to know the God you serve. And I'm not talking about a tennis serve," she said with a wink. And with that, she drove up to my house, where I jumped out of the car, grabbing my new blue racket as I went, and walked to the other side to give her a hug.

"Thanks for the lesson!" I said. She tilted her head, probably curious of which lesson I meant, the tennis lesson or the life lesson. But she smiled back.

"You're welcome! I would love to do this again, if you have time." I nodded my affirmation and ran inside. I took the steps two at a time to get to my room. Proudly, I placed my racket by my dresser and stepped back to get a good look at it. It was barely worn after today's playing, and I could still smell the newness. It had taken a lot to get this racket, having to babysit a torturous monster for most of last night, but in the end, it was well worth it. And I didn't have to worry about meeting with someone today because Tina had planned it all out for me. I sighed. School would be starting next week, and it would get a lot harder to find women to meet with, so I hoped that Tina would continue to give me ideas and suggestions. I plopped down in my green chair and blew out a breath. Eight down, forty-four more to go. I just hope I don't give up before the end.

Chapter Nine

Today in school, Tina came up to me with a face full of hope and excitement, but it quickly turned into a worried look before she began talking in a hesitant voice.

"I have a question for you," she began uncertainly, "but you have to be honest with me when I ask your input, okay?" I nodded, wondering where she was going with this.

"I have a Christian friend here at school whom I told about your mission. She in turn told her mom, who would love to meet with you. Now, you have to be honest and tell me if you are actually interested." She raised an eyebrow, as if expecting me to talk my way out of it, which wouldn't be a bad idea.

"Well, what's she like? I mean, if she's super Christian-y and expects me to be perfect, she'll have something else coming to her."

Tina rolled her blue eyes. "No, nothing like that. In fact, you will probably get along with her very well."

I sighed. I knew that whether I wanted to or not, I was going to be meeting with this mystery person. I nodded.

Tina squealed happily and gave me a big hug, a hug I quickly tried to pull away from. "You won't regret this, I promise!" She nearly shouted.

In a gloomy voice, I muttered, "One can only hope." In a worried voice, I continued. "Can you give me any details about her? For example, is she blond or brunette? Green eyes or blue? Shy or audacious..." Tina cut me off in mid-sentence.

"She has brown hair, brown eyes, somewhere in the middle, and you don't need to worry about her because, like I just said, you will get along with her perfectly—I hope." The latter bit she added in an undertone, but not too quietly for my bat-ears to hear that she wasn't telling me something.

I gave her a suspicious look. "What did you say?"

She quickly jerked her head around, as if looking for a place to escape. "Nothing too important. I only said that you would get along with her perfectly because she's not a dope."

I narrowed my eyes into hyphens. I was about to find out why she would be muttering under her breath when to my startled dismay, she suddenly sprinted away from me. Over her shoulder, she shouted back. "I'll be late for my next class if we continue this lively discussion! See you on Monday! The woman will pick you up today at your lunchtime. She has permission from the school to take you out for the rest of the day."

I grumbled all the way to my next class. "She wasn't asking for my permission; she was making sure I knew I was going to the gallows. I can't believe I let her trick me into signing my own death warrant! That sneaky little fox is going to get what she has coming to her." All through class, I worried about my meeting. Would I be tortured with the thirteen thousand ways to punish a non-believer until she converts? Would I have to lead a prayer meeting? Did this woman know that I was an atheist? Did she care? For crying out loud, I didn't even know her name! I was so caught up in my own thoughts that my math teacher had to call my name three times before I dazedly answered.

Finally, it was lunchtime. With beads of sweat on my upper lip and nervousness crawling up my spine, I made my way to the principal's office. I was directed into his large office by his secretary, and there sat a woman I had never seen before in my life. She had red hair, green eyes, and probably kept Sephora in business with the amount of makeup she was wearing. She didn't look at all like the description Tina gave me, but she could have dyed her hair recently without Tina knowing about it as well as bought colored contacts.

Desperate to make a good impression, I walked over to her and stuck out my hand. She stared at me silently and quizzically for a long, heart-pounding moment, clearly not sure of what to do.

With growing dread, I began concocting a horrible story in my mind about how she contracted a vocal cord infection as a baby and now isn't able to talk. That was probably what Tina was worried about! I swallowed and started talking. "Hi there. What will we be doing today?"

At her blank stare, I gave a wild-eyed look to the door. Was she deaf as well? Tina was going to get it. I started talking to her in what little sign language I knew. She stared with a startled look at my bumbling fingers trying to spell hello. I realized that this meeting was going to be harder than I thought.

I started shouting slowly. "Hel-lo. Wh-at are w-ee doing too-day?" The corners of her mouth tilted up ever so slightly. I mimicked the action, hoping she would understand that I could communicate with her in whatever way she was most familiar. "Wh-at is y-our nay-me?" Her shoulders moved up and down, and I wondered if she didn't have a name. I started copying her movements when I suddenly realized that she was laughing. She turned in her chair toward the desk and opened her lipstick-coated mouth.

"You were right, Dave. It looks like I should take that counseling job after all. You definitely have some weirdos at this school. Well, it was nice talking to you. I'd better get back to my house. My Labrador is calling my name."

I just then noticed the principal sitting at his desk with a baffled expression. She turned and looked at the disbelief on my face. I started stuttering. "B-b-but I thought you were d-deaf and couldn't t-talk!"

She burst out laughing. "No, sweetie. I can hear and talk just fine. I have no clue whom you mistook me to be, but I've never seen you before in my life; however, I probably will after this little, how do I put it, enlightening episode. You see, I will be your school's new counselor!"

I stared at her blankly. What had I gotten myself into? "Aren't you taking me out to lunch today to hang out?" Shaking her head bemusedly, she gave me an I-will-be-seeing-you-more-than-once-in-my-office-because-you-are-psycho look, and then she briskly walked out the door. I swallowed my obvious humiliation and turned to the principal.

"If she's not meeting with me, who is? I was told to go to your office because I was meeting with someone today at this time."

From behind me, a voice rang out. "You're not meeting with her, but with me. And I promise you, I'm not deaf or dumb." A chuckle followed.

I turned and saw a brunette woman in the doorway staring at me with a mischievous smile lurking on her lips and a gleam in her brown eyes.

"Actually, I'm glad that you're not going home with that lady," the mystery woman said, chortling. "I don't know much about her, but I do know that she used to be in a traveling circus as a tightrope walker—which explains the makeup. Who knows? She may have had you balancing on a string thirty feet in the air. That totally contradicts my plans for you today. See, I'm the one who will be taking you out for lunch and spending the day with you."

My mouth hung open like a puffer fish. "Were you standing there the whole time?"

She started laughing. "Yes, and I apologize for not saying anything sooner, but it was very funny to watch. I'm Jennifer Browning, by the way."

I nodded mutely. Tina is now on my hit list. I can't believe I'm going to be meeting with a woman who had seen the whole thing and didn't step in to save my honor. At least I know nothing else can go wrong with her. I hope.

We exited the shameful office and headed to her black vehicle that was parked in a visitor's parking spot. We climbed in, and she started the engine. She drove downtown and began looking for a place to park.

Glancing over at me, she said, "We will be eating at Café Roma, if that's alright with you."

"That's great!" I said. I had been there before with Arlyne VanHook, and I loved it. I definitely wouldn't mind going again. We walked in and I was yet again surrounded by the elegance of the restaurant. The place was practically empty, so we were quickly seated at a corner table. As I sat down, I noticed a lady seated on the opposite end of the restaurant. She looked to be in her seventies. She was wearing a grey raincoat, strange for this heat, and her expression was very intriguing. She looked completely peaceful, and her face almost seemed to light up, even while in the dark restaurant. Shaking my head, I turned to the one-page menu and began perusing through it. I decided on the same thing I had had with Arlyne, the tomato bisque and caprese. As we ate, Jennifer started talking.

"As soon as my daughter Abby told me about you and your mission, I knew I had to meet you." She paused as she took a drink of water to wash down the grilled cheese wrap she was eating. "I had the hardest time trying to figure out what to do with you today because I didn't know what you atheists enjoy doing."

In my mind, I groaned. I figured she would probably be a Bible-blabbing Christian. I braced myself for whatever scripture would be thrown my way.

"You may be wondering," she continued, "how I am able to take you out to eat during the time that people like me would normally be working, right?" I nodded. I had vaguely thought about that.

"Well, on August 25, 2016, God told me to stop working. I had been a realtor for a long time (there's a story behind that), and to just give it up at the drop of a hat was very risky." I bobbed my head. I'll say!

"Nevertheless, God told me to do it, so I started going through the process of retiring my position." I felt my mouth drop open. She gave up her job just because God said so? She was getting crazier and crazier.

"On September 30, my position as a realtor was completely inactive. I then had a ton of free time on my hands that I wasn't used to. To fill my time, I started having personal Bible studies every morning, and then I would try to encourage people throughout the day. If I knew someone was going through a hard time, I would send them a text every now and then during the day to build up their spirits."

I stared at her. Encourage people? She would take time out of her day just to help people not be sad? In my opinion, let them be sad. Why bother taking time to get them out of their funk? They'll just get right back into it as soon as they don't feel amazing. Believe me, I know from experience.

"Why would you do that?" I asked, puzzled.

"Even though it doesn't matter that much what we say in life—because our actions are more important—right voices equal right choices. That's my favorite saying and a great reminder to keep in check the voices that come into my life so I can make good choices. If I let a person tell me lies about myself, then, first of all, why am I even acquainted with that person? They will eventually rot my brain with their twisted ways of thinking until I go jump off a bridge with the rest of them. I had these kinds of friends as a teenager, and they affected me in more ways than I could count. See, when I was young, I always felt like I needed to conform to whatever situation I was in. For example, if I were at church, I would be in the church mold. If I were at school with art people, I would be in the art mold. I would change my personality based on my surroundings. In fact, the worst decision I've ever made was being peer pressured to do things that normally I wouldn't have done, just so I could be accepted. It wasn't until I became a Christian at the age of 18 that I decided to accept who I was and not change for anyone. That was the best decision I've ever made." She paused to take a bite of food and motioned for me to talk some.

Hesitantly I began. "As you know, I go to Keaton Middle School. I've never had an actual job, unless dog sitting and babysitting counts. Unlike most people, I love strange foods. Radishes, quesadillas, and jellybeans are on my top five favorites list." I waited for a grimace at the mention of those very contrasting foods, but instead she gave an interested nod.

"Well, I can't exactly relate, but I do enjoy salmon." I gave her a puzzled look, but shrugged it off. She was absolutely not what I had expected, thanks to Tina's descriptions of her—or lack of them.

We finished up our food and headed out of the building. Instead of heading to her car, however, we walked down the sidewalk and entered a shop called Free to Fly. It was adorable. There were earrings, purses, bracelets, and other items in the eclectic mix—and all of it was handmade! She told me what the store was about as she picked out a pair of earrings.

"This store is a place where women who have no place to stay, with no money and no hope, are taught how to make all these items; they learn a trade."

I was impressed. I never knew that my town had a store that cared about women like that. As I walked around, some hand lotion caught my eye. A sign next to them said, "Goat Milk Creams, $13." Intrigued, I walked over to the little table and picked up a medium-sized bottle. It was cucumber melon body lotion by Udder Joy. I smiled brightly as I read the cute pun. I showed it to Jenn and she, to my surprise, said that she was going to buy it for me. I thanked her kindly, surprised at her generosity.

As we walked back to her car, I asked her what the story was behind her becoming a realtor.

"When my eldest daughter, Ansley, was young," Jennifer began, "my husband and I were having a hard time paying the bills while living in Florida. I decided that I needed to find a job. A man in our church needed a loan processor, so I volunteered, even though I had absolutely no idea what that was." I was shocked. She would volunteer to do something that she had no clue about? She could fail and then be blacklisted! What was she thinking?

"I learned the job by making mistakes and by asking other people," she said, as if reading my thoughts. "I became a loan processor for four other people, as well. I realized after a while that mortgage brokers made more money than loan processors, so I became a mortgage broker. After that, our family moved to Cleveland, TN where I switched from being a mortgage broker to a real estate agent. By now we had another daughter, Abby, whom you know from school. I became a very successful realtor, and it all started from me being willing to do something that I had absolutely no clue about. Like Philippians 1:6 says, if God begins a good work in you, He'll carry through with it. But you can't be afraid of failure."

That last comment hit home. My biggest fear is failure, and she's telling me not to be afraid of it? That's absurd!

"See, a godly woman is obedient to what God says about her life, so by becoming a loan processor, I was fulfilling that. As a reward, I was able to eventually have an amazing profession as a realtor and make money for our family. Other traits of a godly woman are working hard and speaking life to people. I was listening to a song the other day called

'How Great is Your Love' by Vaughn Thompson, and it spoke life to me. It's my favorite song. In fact, I'd love for you to listen to it."

I looked at her warily. Was she just trying to preach a sermon to me by "letting" me listen to a song? I love music, and she may be just trying to get me to listen to a Christian song so I wouldn't get angry, like I would if she just told me the words of the song.

After I hesitantly nodded, she pulled the song up on her phone and pushed play. Immediately, piano notes filled the car. I listened intently as a man's voice rang out through the speakers. It was a beautiful song, but too much about God's love and all those other lies. As soon as the song was over, I immediately changed the subject. "What's an embarrassing story from your childhood that you don't like remembering?"

She gave me an exasperated look. "Let me get this straight. You want me to remember an embarrassing story I don't want to remember?"

I gave her a sheepish grin. "When you put it that way, it does sound a bit strange, but yes."

She laughed as she pulled into her driveway. "Okay, here goes. I'm going to tell you about the worst trouble I ever found myself in. But, as a disclaimer, it was all because I was in the wrong place at the wrong time." She paused here as we exited the car and walked inside the house. Once we were seated in the kitchen, she continued. "It all began when I went to the movies with some friends one Saturday night. Because it was Saturday, I couldn't sleep over at someone else's house because my parents wanted me to go to church the next day."

I stifled an eye-roll. What is it with parents and not wanting kids to have fun?

"Since the movie theater was about forty-five minutes away from my house," she continued, "we decided to meet at a friend's house and carpool to the theater."

"Everything was going according to plan until after the movie. I was ready to ride back home, but some of the girls who had driven down had boyfriends in the area, and they were going to stay for a while and hang out with them. They suggested I get a ride home with Andy, who had come to see the movie—and who just happened to be my ex-boyfriend. I sure wasn't very happy about the arrangement, but it was my only chance to return home at a decent hour. I walked over to Andy and asked him if I could catch a ride home with him, since he was about to leave; and he consented."

"I stepped up into his truck, thinking he would just hop in and we would go, but I had to wait a very long time before he finally climbed in and started the engine. As we drove toward home, I thought to myself, 'This is so awkward. I'm sitting here with my ex-boyfriend who hasn't said a word to me since he entered the car, and we have another half hour drive.' Since I wasn't saying anything either, we were driving in complete silence down a nearly deserted road. Suddenly, Andy turned onto a dirt road that led into the woods, which puzzled me. After he stopped the truck, he bounded out and disappeared into the woods. Apparently, he had to use the men's outdoor restroom. Relieved, he climbed back into the truck and drove toward the main road. As soon as we turned onto the main road, we saw police cars flashing their lights up ahead. The policemen had pulled someone over and were surrounding the car. As cars would pass them, they would shine their flashlights into the passing vehicles. As we slowly drove by, a policemen shone his light at Andy and immediately held up his hands, motioning for us to stop."

"Now I was really perplexed. Why would the policeman stop us? He opened Andy's door and, as soon as he saw Andy's eyes, asked him to get out of the vehicle. I watched as he made Andy walk around and then led him away from the truck. I sat there, apprehension mounting, waiting for Andy to return. I was startled by a knock on my window. I turned and there stood a cop, motioning for me to get out of the car. I obliged, wondering what was happening. They made me walk around, smelled my breath, and asked me questions. I told them the situation and that I was just waiting for Andy to return so I could get home. They looked at me as if I were crazy. 'You won't be going anywhere with him tonight,' one cop said, pointing to Andy who, handcuffed, was climbing into the back of the police car. I gasped as I actually looked at him for the first time that night. He was stone drunk."

I sucked my breath in sharply. I hadn't been expecting that.

"That explained why he never talked—he was completely drunk! I had just thought that he didn't want to make it awkward. Just then, a policeman walked over to me. I groaned. It was my dad's best friend, Mr. Danny. He asked me what I was doing with Andy, and I told him, head hanging. He told me to get into his squad car."

"I walked over to the car," Jennifer said as she shifted her position on her chair, "and dejectedly sat in the back. When he came over, he told me to sit in the front because I wasn't in trouble. Before we left, he called my parents, letting them know that he was bringing me home. That really made them worry—a cop bringing their already-very-late daughter home. All the way home, Mr. Danny gave me lots of good advice, to which I carefully listened. As soon as we drove up in front of my house, my dad came running out and gave me a big hug. Although I was in a lot of trouble, my dad didn't lecture me until he knew that I was all right. I know that God saved me that night by putting those three policemen on the road because if they hadn't been checking the cars that passed, I could've gotten killed with Andy being so drunk."

I sighed inwardly, disappointed. Why does everything always have to have some sort of God-thing connected to it? Why not just keep talking and forget about the whole Bible thing? Things have been a whole lot better ever since I stopped believing in that wishy-washy stuff. Hasn't it? Let's see, my dad's dead. My mom's always drunk. My brother's who knows where. And, as the cherry on top of that beautiful dessert, my grandmother is a Bible-thumping hypocrite. Maybe things haven't been as good as I wanted to believe.

Jennifer was talking again with a smile on her face, which told me she had something good to say. "An amazing miracle that took place in my life was when my youngest daughter, Ava, was really young."

Never mind. Not something good. A miracle? Seriously? I don't want to hear another thing that impacted her, and she believed it to be God. Nevertheless, I had enough sense not to voice my thoughts, so Jennifer just kept on talking.

"My husband Jason was throwing a football one day, and it shattered the window of our Kia Soul. We didn't have enough money to pay for it or get a new car, so I was praying and praying for us to somehow get the money to fix it. God said to me, 'It will all be paid off by the end of the year.'"

Hold up. God told you this? Wow. So He's going to provide the money for the car He allowed to be ruined in the first place.

"One day, Jason was driving along listening to the radio, and the radio host said that if you called in to the station, you could be entered into a sports contest. He was one of the few callers who were chosen for the contest. He made it through the basketball rounds to the final round: he had to throw a Nerf football from the thirty-yard line of a football field into the window of a Kia Soul sitting at the back of the end zone. He was one of three people to go and attempt it."

I was on the edge of my seat to see what happened next. Miracle or not, this was interesting.

"On that day, I was at home with my three daughters, anxiously waiting for the results. I was in my kitchen, waiting and wishing I had someone to pray with about this. God told me right then that I did have someone to pray with: my three daughters. I walked over to them, and we started praying that their daddy would be like David from the Bible and slay this giant of our financial problem. Later he called. He had done it."

My eyes grew wide. I couldn't believe it! He had actually thrown the football through the tiny window of that car! It was absolutely ridiculous. As if she read my mind, she pulled out her phone and showed me the video from YouTube. I watched it and could clearly see the football sailing into the window. "Did you win anything?" I asked.

She smiled. "We won the car the football sailed through! It was a financial miracle!" Boy, it sure sounded like a modern-day David and Goliath story, but instead of a rock, it was a Nerf football that defeated their financial giant.

I looked at the clock and realized our time was technically finished. I gathered my stuff before we piled into her car again. When she dropped me off, I gave her a hug and told her goodbye.

I walked inside and headed upstairs to my room. Thanks to Tina, today had had its ups and downs. I bet she knew that that circus clown would be in the principal's office and that I would make a fool of myself. She is going to get an earful on Monday! However, I'm not at all upset that I met with Jennifer Browning. She's very fun-loving and generous. In fact, maybe I should try and connect with her daughter, Abby. I've only talked to her twice, and both times were brief, but she does seem nice. Maybe I can connect with her next week at lunch.

Chapter Ten

I huffed in aggravation. It was Friday, and I needed someone to meet with. I had already met with nine women, some related, some not. I stood up suddenly from my comfortable position on my soft, green chair in my bedroom. Related! I could meet with a family member! Only who? I was definitely not meeting with my mom or my sister. I could try and branch out by meeting with an extended member just like I had with my grandmother and great aunt. Now that I had narrowed it down to my first, second, third, fourth cousins, great aunts, and aunts, I could pick someone. I had better make a rule that she has to be at least over eighteen. That took out most of the second, third, and fourth cousins. Also, I needed to make sure that she wasn't over a two-hour drive so my grandmother wouldn't freak out about me being so far away and tell my mom that I was gone—if I didn't run into my mom on the way out.

My mom doesn't even know about my mission, and I don't plan on telling her anytime soon. She would probably have a hissy fit and forbid me. Since that would mean that I couldn't finish what I started, I doubt she will know before I finish, if at all. My method to explain all these meetings has been somewhat easy, seeing how, with the exception of a few, she had planned them unknowingly or I had met with people who fit into my scheduled activities, such as tennis players, school projects, "book" fair workers, and so on. The few that have been hard to get past her without her becoming suspicious have mostly been family members, and I took care of those myself rather nicely, if I do say so myself. How can I explain meeting with this woman—whoever she will be—to my mom?

The answer became very clear when I entered her darkened room to get the scrapbook full of extended family photos from years back. Mom was lying supine on her bed, out cold, with an empty bottle of alcohol sitting on her nightstand. I tried not to grin too hard, as it might wake her up—joy was so seldom in her room that the breakthrough of the happiness might jolt her senses awake. I tiptoed over to the small bookcase and gingerly pulled out the large, blue binder. Once the book was safely lodged in a death grip between my sweaty palms, I silently crept out the door and victoriously scampered up the steps to my room.

The minute I was in the safety of my room, I sank into the same green chair and cracked open the dusty cover. I gazed, mesmerized, at the faded pages. It was filled with comical pictures and memories I had forgotten. I grew sad as I remembered all the fun things we used to do before we became a dysfunctional family. Although it was slightly depressing, my spirits rose when I spotted a woman in one of the large group pictures whom I had almost forgotten. She was my first cousin but about fifteen years my senior. I remembered her as fun-loving and easy-going, but for the life of me, I couldn't seem to remember her name. I looked at other pictures, hoping to find her face again, which I did multiple times. I finally discovered her name when I absentmindedly flipped over one of the photos and found that someone had taken the liberty to write down the names of the people in the photo. Her name was Hannah. Finally, I thought, I can contact her!

I started looking through the contacts on my phone. As a child, I had wanted a phone with a burning passion, so while I waited for it, I had collected the phone numbers of everyone I knew and wrote them in a file. Although I didn't obtain my phone until after we had stopped communicating with the extended relatives, I had still entered into my phone all the numbers I had collected. Or so I thought. I scrolled through every single contact and still didn't find her phone number. I was incredulous. I growled at my electronic device and wished I could magically put a number into it that I didn't know.

Just then, an idea struck me. I bet my paternal grandmother would have Hannah's number. I anxiously sent her a quick text, to which she responded only a few nail-chewing, agonizing minutes later. She had it and sent it to me. After thanking her profusely, and with a triumphant smile, I punched in the numbers to call Hannah's phone. As I waited for the satisfying click of the opposite end picking up, I paced. I was becoming very good at this procedure because this is what happened with nearly every woman—I would get nervous and pace, fret, or worry.

Finally, I heard her voice on the other end of the line. "Hello?"

I felt relief flood over me. I quickly told her who I was, what I wanted, and why I was doing it. She readily agreed and told me that she was super excited to see me again. We agreed to meet the next day, on Saturday, and she would come and pick me up from my house. I thought that might prove to be a slight problem, as I would have to do some fast explaining to my mom. But, to my great delight, she slept in late Saturday morning, and Hannah, with her two children, was able to pick me up without any problems.

When we arrived at her house, we hopped out of the car and went through the front door. Immediately, I was overcome with nervousness. What was I thinking? She had two kids to take care of, and here I was, another burden placed upon her for the day. I resolved right then that I wouldn't be an annoyance, but instead I would be a big help with watching the kids and doing whatever it took to not make her dislike me. We went into her very cute living room, complete with a television cabinet full of movies, and sat down on the comfortable couches. She picked up her one-and-a-half-year-old girl, Callie, and sat her down on her lap while her three-year-old boy, Jase, played with some toys on the rug.

"I am so excited about today!" Hannah began. "I haven't seen you in forever, so we have a lot of catching up to do." I nodded. Seeing how I hadn't seen her since I was a child, we could be here all day reminiscing about old times and sharing the latest stories.

"After you told me that you were doing this challenge, I was super enthused. I love what you're doing! It is so special, and I think that by the end, you will have noticed a giant difference in your life."

I smiled weakly at her before saying something I was starting to dread, for whatever reason. "I'm an atheist. I'm only doing this challenge because a girl at school practically forced me to."

She gave a shocked look at my statement but recovered. "Okay, I can understand that. I'll try to remember that so I don't say something wrong and make you never want to come see me again." She chuckled at this as she set Callie on the floor to play.

I shook my head. "It would probably be the other way around. I'm always sticking my foot in my mouth."

She looked at me with a pained expression. "It probably wouldn't be as bad as the time I made that one decision." She paused at this point, as if wondering whether to tell me or not. She evidently decided I could handle it because she began talking. "The worst decision I have ever made cost me a lot throughout multiple years of my life. When I was in high school, I decided, for whatever reason, that I was going to be rebellious; I had always been so good, I decided that a little bad wouldn't hurt me." She paused and looked me in the eye. "It was all a trick from the devil. He pulled me into the depths of sin. I thought I would be able to get out of the trap at any given time, but I was dead wrong. I was saved in elementary school and was even filled with the Holy Spirit at the age of twelve, but it was as if I had forgotten all of it as soon as I started believing the devil's lies. Because I didn't have a dad (he died when I was three), I started seeking out boys. I thought that it wasn't a big deal, and I believed Satan's lies, thinking that it wouldn't affect me. The years when you are 14 until 17 are a spiritual warfare battle. In my life, I was so ensnared during that time that I found myself in the worst trouble I had ever gotten into: I kissed a boy in front of the school, and my mom saw me."

I stared at her in disbelief. Her mom saw her kissing a boy? That must have been super awkward having to face her mom that day after school. My mom probably wouldn't care if I did that, but my grandmother definitely would.

"Would you change all of that from your past?" I asked.

She shook her head firmly. "No." At my surprised look, she added. "God has used a ton of things in my life, even if they were bad, for good in my life. The harder the times have been, the more it is evident that He is so good."

I thought about this. She actually seemed like she believed what she was saying. "So if you wouldn't change anything about your past, would you change anything about you?" I didn't see anything outwardly that needed to be changed; she was gorgeous! To my amazement, she nodded.

"I wouldn't struggle with being so anxious. I don't like it, and it's not good for me."

I nodded. I could definitely relate. That was my life every day.

Just then, Callie came over to her and started whimpering. Hannah hoisted her up on her lap and asked. "Are you hungry?" At her fussy reply, Hannah then looked at me.

"What about you? Are you hungry?"

I nodded exuberantly. All this talking had given me a ravenous desire for food. We gathered up our stuff and climbed into her black vehicle where we immediately headed for Jimmy John's, which is like Subway. We ordered our sandwiches in the drive-thru, where I ordered a turkey and bacon sandwich. After that, we drove to Chick-fil-A to pick up chicken nuggets for Callie.

While we waited at a red light outside of the restaurant, I asked Hannah what her current job was. She gave me a smile. "Actually, that was the hardest and biggest decision of my life." I waited for her to go on.

"I quit my job at Lectrus to be a stay-at-home mom." I was surprised. She went on. "My husband, Jarrod, is a police officer, and he has to work night shifts, which results in him sleeping until the afternoon. I knew that if I worked, I would never see him. Having a good relationship with him was more important than having a job."

I was baffled. No one does that nowadays. Every woman I know always wants a job to make more money, whether it pulls time away from her family or not. Yet, Hannah gave up her job just so she could stay home with her family.

"That must have been super hard," I said, with a sympathetic look.

She nodded. "It was, but because I made that decision, I've been able to see my husband every day."

As soon as the light turned green, she gunned the engine and headed toward a plaza located across from Chick-fil-A.

"I thought we could stop in at Target and get you something."

I thanked her enthusiastically, wondering vaguely if I looked like a poor, homeless hobo—it seemed like most of the women I'd met with wanted to buy me something. We walked into the store and headed for the clothing department, where I found a charcoal sweater that was more comfortable than anything I owned. I thanked her again and again as she paid for it at the register.

On the way to the car, I said with satisfaction, "This sweater is wonderful! I can finally own something cuter than my sister's clothes."

She looked at me quizzically for a moment, and then, when we had climbed back into her car and were on the road again, she said, "I'm an only child, but I'm sure that if you have siblings, it's easy to compare yourself to them; however, you should never compare yourself to them. God made you specifically for your own personal story, and it doesn't make you any less by not being a clone of your siblings."

I groaned inwardly. I knew I shouldn't have mentioned that. Now I was getting a sermon; however, something in me made me listen, for whatever reason. So, despite my best efforts, I found myself listening to her.

"All your weaknesses and strengths are purposeful. Don't compare yourself to anyone else's dreams. Be who you are, and be who you want to be. God will use you for greater things than you could ever have imagined about your life if you will be who He created you to be. See, I had small dreams growing up because I thought I wouldn't ever amount to anything. When I was in a public school, I was getting A's, but when I transferred to a private school, I began making D's. The devil kept telling me that I was super dumb and that I wouldn't amount to anything. Yet, when I worked for Lectrus, I was head over all the payrolls. All the devil said was lies, lies I shouldn't have believed, lies you shouldn't believe either."

She continued talking. "I think the hardest part of being a godly woman is not being distracted by the lies that Satan whispers to us. A godly woman should seek God first in everything and let Him be a part of every area of her life, putting aside her desires in order to further the kingdom in whatever way God says for her to do it. A woman sets the tone of the home, and Satan can upset the cart if can keep the woman from being godly." That explained why our family was doing so badly.

"Just as Jeremiah 29:13 says," she went on, "'you will seek me and find me when you search for me with all your heart.' We have to seek Him with all our hearts if we want Him to fully occupy our hearts. In reality, though, God is waiting right outside our hearts for us to open the door, so we really don't have to go very far to try and find Him. There's a song that goes along with that called 'Reckless Love.' It talks about how there's nothing that God won't tear down just to chase after us, to try and gain us back." She paused, which put emphasis on her next words. "His grace and love are bigger than you could ever imagine."

I looked intensely at her. Did she really believe that, or was she just quoting something she had heard all her life?

As if reading my mind, she looked at me and said, "If it weren't for the grace and love of God, He would not have placed on my mom's heart to pray for me while I was making those terrible decisions in high school. This was her prayer day in and day out: that I would submit myself before God. Her prayers pulled me through. When I finally realized that I was in too deep, I completely humbled myself before the Lord and asked Him to get me out of the mess. And do you know what? He did."

"I learned a lot from that experience," she explained, "but coming out of it was a very slow process. The more counsel I sought, the better off I became. To this day, I still go to a counselor occasionally, because I have seen it as a very beneficial tool of wisdom from a source other than my family."

I could see that if you didn't want to talk to your family about something but still needed to get it off your chest, talking to a counselor would be a good idea. However, I for one wouldn't want to go to my school's counselor. My run-in with her just last week was enough for me!

By now, we were almost to her house, and Jase, who was sitting in the back seat, was being loud. I asked him if we could play the quiet game. Obviously, he did not want to play because he continued to be loud. So Hannah said in a joking tone, "Oh well, I guess she gets to eat your sandwich since she won."

He looked at me and then at his mom and then said, "I'm being quiet now." He was instantly silent for three whole seconds, and, in a low, dangerous tone, he said to me, "Don't eat my sandwich." Hannah looked at me, and we burst out laughing.

As I wiped the tears from my eyes, I realized that I was having a good time. Maybe it was possible to have fun with a challenge I was forced into; and even though I received a sermon, somehow I didn't seem to mind it as much.

We climbed out of the car and walked into Hannah's house, where we ate our lunch and Hannah put the kids down for a nap. Once she came out of Jase's room, we sat on her couch with fuzzy blankets and ice cream and watched a hilarious Don Knotts movie. It was a lot of fun.

Sadly, though, our time had to come to a close. We climbed yet again into her car, and she started the engine. She drove me back to my house, where I reluctantly climbed out of the car. She hopped out of the car as well and came over to my side of the car where she gave me a hug.

"I had a lot of fun with you today," she told me. "If you ever want to come again to hang out, let me know. I would love to do this again."

"Definitely! Thank you so much for meeting with me!" I walked inside and headed up to my room. Thankfully, my mom seemed to still be asleep, so I didn't have to run into her. My meeting with Hannah wasn't at all like I had expected; it was full of laughter and fun. And even the "sermons" were interesting. One thing I can say about Hannah is that she is passionate about what she believes. She almost got me interested in her God. Almost.

Chapter Eleven

It was officially the worst day of my life. My friends had been wondering why I was cutting band class, a class that they coerced into signing up for. These "friends" told me that I could play a super simple instrument, but I was afraid that I wouldn't be good at it, and ended up just cutting class so I wouldn't have to embarrass myself in front of everyone. I might have accidentally told them some huge whoppers about why I was cutting class just to get them off my back, such as I was helping a teacher clean up her classroom; or my frail, elderly grandmother needed me to run some errands at the store, and I had received permission from the school to help her almost every day. On the days I didn't have the so-called permission, I was comforting sick girls who were throwing up in the bathroom, helping nerve-racked students to study because they weren't prepared for an exam the next class period, or other extremely caring activities.

In general, I came across as a helpful, thoughtful, good student who loved band and had a wonderful talent for it but was never able to participate in class because of helpful activities, to my feigned disappointment. I now know not to tell whoppers as big as the ones I told my fellow band members. Okay, I now know not to tell whoppers whatsoever because they can come back and bite you, like I was soon to find out.

It was just another boring day at school when I heard my name called over the PA system during lunch. The voice was saying that I was to report to the band room immediately. I was super baffled, but I knew that I had to go or else I would have to go to the principal's office, where my mom would have to come and pay my bail to free me, and I would be free once more from the icy clutches of the office's low air conditioning but still in the grip of my mom's wrath. Needless to say, I didn't want to have to go through all of that trouble, so, with a sigh, I slowly stood up and made my way to the band room as I tried to figure out what they would be concerned about.

Whenever I would skip class, I would normally smooth things over with Ms. Applebee with some sort of peace offering, like a bouquet of flowers I picked from the garden next door or a box of uneaten Valentine chocolates. It didn't do me any harm either that I just happened to be her boyfriend's second cousin, so I would put in a good word for her every now and then with him, as well as give her information about him that she may not have known—like how as a kid, he could spew orange juice out his nose without even barely trying. Therefore, it didn't make sense that she would turn me in now. I did notice, however, that as I left the lunch table, a bunch of my fellow band members were sharing unreadable looks with each other. By now, I had reached the band door and was debating whether or not to actually go through with this. I did, though (to my later regret) and walked cautiously into the semi-dark room where a few people sat at a table. I recognized Ms. Applebee as one of them, who wore an unexplainable smile on her face. One of the men there motioned for me to take a seat, which I did nervously.

He began, "We have received information from a couple of students that you would be interested in playing in our orchestra for our upcoming concert."

My mouth dropped open. Was he loony? I never said that! I was about to tell him the truth when he continued. "They said that you were too nervous to try out at the auditions we had a couple weeks ago, even though you are apparently fantastic at the piano."

I shoved every notion of telling the truth out the window. I vaguely remembered telling some classmates that little white lie—as well as other not-so-little-or-white ones. If I said that I wasn't completely honest about that, then I would get in more trouble with my classmates, with the principal (since he would find out about all the skipped days), and eventually with my mom. I clamped my mouth shut and tried to think of a way out of this. Eventually, I opened it and asked as innocently as I could, "What does this have to do with me?"

The man smiled at me. "Our pianist just moved to Nebraska, and since your friends said that you had told them that you were too scared to audition but still wanted to be in it, we," here he pointed at the other people around him, "have decided to let you be the orchestra pianist, even though you didn't try out."

I looked at him in sheer terror. I would have to play the piano in front of billions and billions of people without even knowing how? Sounded like a nightmare. I had absolutely no way of getting out of this, except tell the truth, which I obviously wasn't going to do. I racked my brain, but I still couldn't find any way to get out of this mess.

"I guess it's all settled then. Thank you very much for accepting the position." The man smiled at me once more before heading out the door.

I looked at his back as he sailed out the door. I never said that I had accepted it! How dare he? I just wanted to spit! The other participants of the room followed him out, all except Ms. Applebee. She looked at me with an unreadable expression.

"Darling," she began, "I didn't tell them about the fact that you have skipped almost every day of band since this year started, so they don't realize that you aren't able to play the piano, like you told your friends." She gave me a hard look here. "But I know that you will think of something. It's high time you learned an instrument, anyway. I believe you would be very good at the piano. You have potential." I stared at her with unbelieving eyes. Potential? Yeah, right. There was no alternative for me, though, other than hiring a professional to do an overdub.

I walked slowly back to the lunchroom, where the kids were just finishing up. My "friends" smiled at me as I plodded over to their table. "No need to thank us," they said. "We just did it out of the goodness of our hearts." If only they knew. I couldn't accuse them, however, unless I wanted to be socially killed by all. I grimaced at them and hoped it looked like a grateful smile.

"I don't know what to say," I said through tightly gritted teeth. They gave me a sympathetic look, as if to say, "We knew you would love it! You will now forever be in our debt for this courageous act of unselfish ambition." Little did they know, I would have vengeance for this.

After arriving home from school, I plotted. What could I do to either get myself out of this mess or learn how to play the piano well enough to be seen in front of my friends, who must think I'm a concert pianist, and the rest of the audience? Since a solid hour of thinking took me nowhere with how to get out of this without telling the truth, I decided I'd have to go the route of figuring out a way to learn how to play the piano and the song in the next two weeks. I would have to find a teacher willing to teach me for free and able to teach me well enough to play in an orchestra in the short span of two weeks. I searched through my contacts for a good long while before deciding that I did not know any piano players. I had one option. Two rings later, Tina answered her phone.

"Do you know any piano teachers who would teach me daily—for free—how to play a song I don't even know on a piano I know even less about in two weeks?"

She didn't even ask why. "Yep. In fact, I will give her a call right now and see if she would be willing to teach you." With that, she hung up to call the woman. I did the only thing I could at the moment. I paced. Within a few minutes, Tina called me back. "She said she would love to give you free lessons as long as you, in return, give her a free ticket to the performance. You will be meeting with her tomorrow afternoon after school. She will pick you up at 3:45." I thanked her profusely. Wondering what I would have done if I hadn't known Tina, I gratefully sank into a chair.

The next day, I made it through school without too many mishaps. And by that I mean no one had found out that I couldn't play the piano. I did go to the band room to get the music from my "lovely" teacher. She gave me a sympathetic smile.

"How's everything working out?" I gave her the low-down about getting a piano teacher for the next two weeks. She seemed enthusiastic about it, and I wondered if she had led the group in the decision to "let" me join the orchestra. At 3:45, I waited outside the school building for this mysterious woman. A few minutes later, a van drove up beside me. A woman climbed out, who looked to be in her mid-sixties, and walked over to where I was standing.

"Hello, are you my new piano student?" she asked pleasantly. I nodded. She must be my teacher.

"I'm Charlene McCullough. We'll be going back to my house to have the lesson." We climbed into her car and buckled up. As she pulled out of the parking lot, she asked, "So why do you need to learn how to play the piano in two weeks?" I told her the basic gist of it, and she gave me an understanding look.

"I hope to be able to teach you well enough that you will be able to play in two weeks. But if not, then you will at least know the basics, so you could fake it while a professional recording is actually playing." I gave her a surprised look. That was one of my options, but I didn't think that she would have thought of that.

We arrived at her large house and walked inside. I was immediately surrounded with magnificence. It was beautiful. I hesitantly peered into the sitting room and saw a gorgeous black grand piano. When she walked into the room, I complemented her on her house. She thanked me with a little smile, and we walked over to the instrument. First, she taught me a C scale, which I caught onto surprisingly quickly. Then she taught me some other scales as well as arpeggios. I was seriously shocked that I learned the former and latter so well and fast. Charlene was apparently just as surprised.

"You're telling me that you've never played the piano before?" Charlene asked incredulously.

At my nod, she acted as though I were a child prodigy. I never thought I would be good at the piano since I was so bad at the recorder in elementary school; I had just given up any hope of being musically talented. That was apparently wrong, though, as I went through scale after scale, my fingers properly curving to play. Soon, I had perfected them to the limit, and we were still left with an hour of time.

She looked at me with a smile. "You have real talent, dear. Since you learned what I was going to teach you in half an hour, instead of an hour and a half as I had thought, why don't we have a little chat? I would love to know more about you."

I was agreeable to that, and she asked me how I knew Tina. Now I was in a rough spot. If I told the truth, what if she made fun of me? But judging from the fact that she had encouraged me through my progress on the piano, I decided to give it a try. I quickly explained the mission I was on, and suddenly it hit me. Tina! My goodness, that girl was tricky! No wonder she had found a piano teacher so quickly! This woman probably went to her church, and Tina knew that I would get along with her so well that I would just happen to make her one of my 52 godly women! Tina did have a knack, though, for finding amazing women. I could only hope that her record wouldn't change. In a guarded tone, I asked Charlene the question: "Would you be one of my 52 godly women?"

"Yes, yes, and a thousand times, yes! It would be an honor. I hope I won't disappoint you with the stories I would love to share with you about my life."

I didn't think that would be possible, judging from what I could see around me, so I settled into a chair next to the piano as she began.

"You already know my name, so I'll dispose of the pleasantries and get to the heart of my journey. I have had two husbands in my life, although both have died. My first husband, Neil, already had three boys when I married him. We then had three more children: a girl and two boys. He was a missionary, and he traveled all over the world with his mission work until the day he was injured on the mission field. The mission team had run out of water because they had been in the area longer than they had expected. Neil's brain became dehydrated, and he had a stroke. When he returned home, he was in a wheelchair and couldn't walk or talk. I was so upset at God." I froze. She didn't always love God? Here was someone talking my language.

"I was so upset," she continued, "because I didn't know why God would allow him to have a stroke after he had willingly served Him since the age of 18." She paused, and I wondered the same thing. She looked off into the distance, as if remembering something.

"Come to think of it, that's just what Neil's mom did when her husband, Neil's father, died. She questioned God, asking Him why he would take her husband after he had just recently become a Christian. She received the answer: her husband wouldn't have been ready to go later on, so He had to take him while he still believed in God." Wait. God actually talked to her? Yeah, right. Who in their right mind would believe that whopper? I shifted in my chair, feeling a bit high and mighty, knowing that He never would've actually talked to her.

"Anyway, back to Neil. He eventually developed cancer, and we had to drive to a treatment facility in Rochester, Minnesota. The building had a piano in the large sitting room that had a sign on it: 'If anyone wants to play the piano, feel free to.' Even though I knew how to play, I didn't want to because I was sure that there were so many other people who could play better than I could. We were in Rochester for quite a while, and every day my husband would ask me to play the piano, but I wouldn't because by now, I had heard many people play, and they were all extremely good."

She paused as she walked into the kitchen to grab some water for us. When she came back I took a long sip, grateful for the cool liquid.

"Yet, every day my husband kept begging me to play. Finally, I gave in and, to content my husband, sat down to play. I started playing 'Great is Thy Faithfulness' because out of all the people I had heard play the piano, not one had played a Christian song. Just as I hit the final note, ready to get up from the bench and be done with the ordeal, a woman came running out of one of the nearby rooms with tears in her eyes. She told me that she had just found out that she had cancer and had called her pastor to pray for her. He told her to focus only on the faithfulness of God. She said that the minute he stopped talking, I started playing that song. She gave me a hug, and I felt truly blessed to have helped someone in that way." I was puzzled. How could people think of God's "faithfulness" when He had just made her have cancer? It was crazy what some people believed.

"While Neil was in the hospital during his fight against cancer," Charlene continued, "he roomed with a cussing, evil man. This man was never satisfied with anything. His pillow wasn't fluffed enough, the food was always terrible, so on and so forth. It went on and on. One day, a couple came to sing for Neil, and as they walked in, I warned them about the man. He was currently sleeping, and I didn't want him to wake up. They said they would be quiet, and so we began to sing. After a while, the noise grew as we became more passionate with the songs. After a wonderful time of singing, the couple left, and I began talking with Neil. Suddenly, I heard someone calling my name; it was the roommate. He told me that he heard us singing. I immediately apologized, expecting a chew-out, but instead, he cut me off and said that the songs about Jesus made him cry. He said that he realized that he needed to be saved. I was so happy about his decision to follow Jesus that I even bought him a Bible to help him learn more about God. He eventually was elected to the board of deacons at our church. I realized then that if Neil hadn't had that stroke, then that man wouldn't have been saved. I told God that if Neil needed to have a stroke just so his roommate could receive Christ, then it was worth it."

What?? She would believe that, even though her husband was slowly dying? Surely one evil man's soul wasn't worth the life of a good man, right? My brain was getting more confused by the minute.

As if reading my thoughts, Charlene said, "That wasn't the only person Neil was able to guide to salvation. One time on the mission field, Neil was in serious trouble. A group of people, carrying machetes, entered his village and tried to kill him."

I gasped. I wasn't expecting the story to take such a drastic turn.

"God wouldn't allow them to slaughter him, though. Instead, He had a plan."

He had a plan. So cliché. That's like the motto of every church ever. However, I admitted to myself that the story had grabbed my attention.

"The evil men grabbed Neil's Bible and took it out to the field, where they began violently attacking it with their machetes."

Talk about some anger issues! I bet they kept all the counselors in their village in business.

"However, God was guiding their blades. They were cutting the Bible directly down the middle. At that moment, God sent a sharp wind that blew all the pages all over the village. The men were triumphant, thinking that they had destroyed something of the Christians. They were totally wrong. Like always, God turned something terrible into a beautiful work. The pages that blew all over the village fell in places where people would see them and read them. They were confused about who this God was, so they came to the mission station to ask Neil about God, and once there, many got saved."

I felt my jaw dropping. Usually I would say that it was just a coincidence, but it seemed impossible that the machetes would cut the Bible exactly down the spine and that the wind would just happen to whip up at that very moment and blow the pages where they could be seen. It seemed like I had been hearing a lot of miracles recently. Like Jennifer, for example, with the whole football thing. Or Cathy, with her transformation from a disfigured baby to a beautiful woman. It seemed really strange that they all had these crazy stories about miracles.

She gave me a happy smile. "As for the three men who were trying to kill my husband, God had a plan in mind for even them. One of the three came back to the mission station and became saved!"

I was astonished. The missionaries would accept him after he had wanted to kill Neil? What forgiveness! "What about the other two?" I asked.

She looked less happy. "They were in a fight with a stranger and were chopped into pieces with a machete."

I felt like I needed to regurgitate. That was a hard picture to get out of my mind; I was sorry I had asked. Yet, I was still amazed that the same action they had tried to do to a missionary of "God" would be their own death, and not too long after they had attempted the deadly plan.

"When were you saved?" I asked, figuring that she must have been a churchgoer all her life to marry a missionary.

"I was saved at age eight at an altar in a Jacksonville church. It was not until I was in college in Birmingham, Alabama that I was filled with the Holy Spirit. One night, the church I attended in Birmingham was having a prayer meeting, so some friends drove me to the service. The leader gave an invitation for people to come to the altar to receive the Holy Spirit. I went down and was filled, continuing to pray until midnight. When I arrived back on campus, however, there was a slight problem. My dorm had a curfew, which was way before midnight, and, thus, the doors were locked. I went to the resident director's room and asked her if she could unlock the doors. She was very surprised to see me out so late, since I was normally always in by curfew. When she asked what I was doing out so late, I replied that I was at a prayer meeting. I stood there waiting for my punishment for breaking curfew, but she completely waved it off, since I was at a prayer meeting. I wish I had been as fortunate that other time I was in trouble." I waited impatiently for her to go on. She had me intrigued.

"Things that are acceptable today were not always acceptable years ago."

I nodded. I had heard similar stories from different people I had already met with about strict rules from their childhood.

She continued. "I wasn't allowed to go to the movies, but one day I decided that I wanted to go badly enough to sneak out with a few friends. My mom had a rule that I had to call her after ten o'clock if I wasn't back at the house by that time. Since the movie went past ten o'clock, I called her while at the drive-in movie theater. She heard a bunch of noise in the background, and later, when I arrived home, she asked if I was at a theater. I told her no, but she kept asking me until I finally told her the truth. I found myself in the most trouble I had ever been in in my life."

I could relate. I had lied about my piano skills, and now I was in a heap of trouble, even though I found out I actually could play the piano.

"However, I believe that the reason God allows bad things to happen to us is because He lets us see how well we are standing on the Rock. It's a true test of a godly woman. If you can stay on the Rock during the bad times, you pass the test."

Hold up. Did she just say godly woman? Perfect time for my question. "What are the qualities of a godly woman then?"

She gave me a smile. "The qualities of a godly woman are these: to live her belief in Jesus during the good times and the bad, to love God with all her heart, and to live like she talks."

Ooh. That last one stung. It was an obvious jab at me, since I wasn't living like I talked at all. I had told so many lies I could write a book about them. The funny thing about it was that I could still remember every single one that I told, as if they were eternally seared into my brain; and I remembered the bad feeling I had when telling each one. It shouldn't really matter to me, though. I'm not some sort of righteous person. In fact, I'm far from it. Why, then, did I always feel remorse after telling one?

I shook off the feeling and asked, "What's your favorite saying?"

"'A synonym for Jesus is love. If you can see love, then you can see Jesus.' This ties right in with my favorite Bible verse, John 3:16."

Wow, that's pretty deep. She even threw in some scripture to "gnaw on."

"The last story I have to offer you is my son David's story. My husband and I raised our kids in church. Our son David liked a girl down the street during his last years of high school, but she and some of her friends drank with their parents because they didn't believe it was wrong. David wasn't allowed to because we believed it was wrong. All the girls in high school adored him." She leaned towards me. "I know I shouldn't brag, but David was very easy on the eyes." She leaned back in her chair and continued. "The girls who liked him, however, went to the country club, and since he wasn't allowed to go, he couldn't really 'have fun' like they did."

"David was taking a class on existentialism, and one day he came home with some shocking news. He said that the church thing may be fine with us, but he didn't want any more of it."

Atta boy, David! He finally realized the truth. This story seemed super Christian at first, but it's getting better by the second. Someone finally agreed with me.

"On top of that solid blow to the stomach, he also said he didn't want to be a part of the family anymore."

Ooh. That hurt. Man, I wish I had brought popcorn! It would've been perfect with this story!

"He was eighteen by now, and he was about to go to college, so even though we tried talking to him, he left with bitterness and hatred, especially hatred toward his dad. Neil had been away a lot doing missionary work, and even when he was home he had a weak body so he could never really play with the kids, especially David. David had begun to get angrier and angrier, particularly when he wasn't able to go to any of the "fun" places, such as the country club. While he was at college, he would call and talk to me, but he would refuse to talk to his dad. Neil was so upset, but he started praying for David."

Oh, boy. You had better watch out, David; he's praying! Like that will actually do any good.

"For at least two hours every day, Neil would go in his prayer room and start praying fervently, so fervently, in fact, that the rest of the family could hear him groaning. I told him to stop praying because David was lost and may never come back and Neil was ignoring the other kids to pray for a wayward one. He told me that he didn't have a child to lose. I tried to tell him that it was killing him, but he wouldn't listen."

"David soon met a Baptist girl named Tracy, who read the Bible and went to church; and, to my surprise, he married her. He never participated in these activities with her, but at least she was an influence to him. One day, after fifteen years of separating himself from the family, David called me out of the blue."

I couldn't wait. Was it that he was sick, or was he going to drop another bomb?

"He couldn't sleep."

Wow. What a letdown.

"He told me that he would wake up in the middle of the night and hear voices, but no one was there."

I totally take that back. This is like a horror movie! Creepy, invisible voices in the dead of night.

"He couldn't really pick up on what they were saying, but he could never go to sleep after that. A few years later, he called me again, saying that the voices hadn't stopped and that he slept very little. I told him that God was trying to get him back and that he needed to get on his knees and ask God to show Himself."

He probably didn't listen to that, seeing how he hadn't listened to anything else she had tried to say for the past who-knows-how-long.

"Tracy called me a little while later, asking what I had said to him. She said that she had come in and found him crying. I knew he wasn't saved yet, but at least he was listening to me."

Aw, I was expecting a better ending. I was surprised that he actually took her suggestion and used it. Apparently, Charlene wasn't finished.

"There was a guy at David's work named Thomas who was seven years his junior, even though he was in a higher position than David. David hated him. He despised having to go to him to ask what something was or to get permission for something. During lunch one day, David saw him reading a Bible and started hooting. He told all the other guys there what Thomas was doing. Thomas merely shrugged it off, saying that he chose to read the Bible in his free time. About this time, something life-changing occurred."

I sat, clutching the edge of my seat. What could be more exciting than what she had already shared?

"Neil was in the hospital for cancer treatments, and his roommate had gotten saved, and that's when it happened."

Don't leave me in suspense! There are too many cliffhangers in this story.

"David was at home sick, and Tracy was away from the house."

Man, that must've been rough. No one to give you comfort, or massage your tired feet, or make you chicken noodle soup.

"While he was lying in bed, he heard those voices again, and this time, he could clearly hear what they were saying to him."

What did they say?? Who were these mysterious voices? Why was he even hearing them in the first place?

"They said, 'David, you have made a fool out of your life. You should just end your life right now. Go into the kitchen and get a butcher knife and cut your throat.'"

I stared at her, aghast. This was way scarier than any horror movie I had seen. Unseen voices telling you to kill yourself? And telling you how to do it? I would've been dead by now, scared to death. She wasn't finished.

"At his refusal, an invisible force starting yanking him out of bed."

Oh. My. Goodness. That would have been the most terrifying thing in the world. Worse than having to swim through a pool full of sharks while you're bleeding openly from a wound you obtained from a goliath tarantula during your less-than-pleasant visit to South America where you were attacked by a tribe of bullet ants, almost eaten by a gator, and terrorized to insanity by a talking macaw. Talk about heart stopping. Literally.

"He became so scared. He needed someone in the house with him, but he didn't know whom to call since I was in Hawaii and Joe was at a meeting. He had only one option. He called Thomas. Once he answered, David pleaded for Thomas to come to his house and help him. Thomas said that he couldn't since he was at work. After inquiring what was wrong with David, however, Thomas immediately asked him if he wanted to be saved. David agreed on the spot. Thomas led him through a short but life-changing prayer. Once the prayer was over, Thomas told him that there were no more demons living in him anymore because Jesus now ruled his heart. He warned David, however, that they would come back and try to again gain admittance into his mind to convince him that he should kill himself. Thomas urged him to plead the blood of Jesus to save him, and once he did that, they would flee."

"As soon as David hung up the phone, he realized that he needed to talk to his dad. He rushed to the hospital and walked inside, still sick. He hesitantly entered the hospital room and then ran to his dad. His brother Joe, who had finished his meeting, looked up in surprise from where he was sitting next to his dad. David told his dad what had happened to him. Since Neil was still recovering from the stroke, David had to repeat himself several times until his dad understood. Once he did, tears of joy slid down his face. David was 38 when he finally gave his life back to the Lord."

He was away from God for 20 years? Yikes.

"David started a prayer group with a few of his mountain biker friends. He used to bike some of the tallest mountains in the world until an accident caused him to see with a blue tint for the rest of his life. They made shirts that said 'Cycling to the Son' on them. I finally had the privilege of meeting Thomas at a party we threw for David after his baptism. I told him how thankful I was for him and what he had done for David. Well, that pretty much sums up David's story."

I was speechless. I couldn't understand how all that had happened to only one person.

Charlene then looked at the clock and shook her head in amazement. "My, my, how the time does get away from us! We've gone on for two hours, and there I was thinking it was only a few minutes. I had better get you home before your mom begins to worry where you are." I was about to tell her that my mom could care less if I were gone forever, but I decided not to.

We climbed into her car, and she started the engine as I told her the directions to my house. She dropped me off at my doorstep, and I waved goodbye as she slowly pulled out of the driveway.

As I walked inside, I realized two things. One, I hadn't told her that I was an atheist, and two, I was actually good at an instrument! I clumped up the steps to my room, where homework awaited me—similar to an executioner waiting for a prisoner, or bug spray waiting for a cockroach, or better yet, a rainy day waiting for a birthday party. As I walked into my room, I wondered what would be a good adjective for Charlene. She could fit the title of almost any, but I think that wise would be a good one. She knew a lot and had experienced so much. Maybe we could talk more during tomorrow's piano lesson. And the next day's lesson. And the next day's lesson. And the next day's lesson. Hopefully, she will be able to turn me into Beethoven by the end of two weeks.

Chapter Twelve

My cat is a blessing and a burden. Poor little Thunder is probably confused from being both screeched at and serenaded. He is an inside cat that rarely causes trouble, sleeps on a little bed in my room, and only requires food once a day; and he is very good at comforting me when I'm upset; however, he's not always perfect.

This particular day, however, he decided, out of the blue, that he liked a fast-moving pace better than the easy-going one he was used to. And what a fast-moving pace it was! I was sitting on my bed, digging through my giant continent of homework in my backpack in an attempt to find the pencil I had just lost in the Amazon Rainforest called math, science, and history, when I heard a swish. I looked up with sweat gushing down my face from excavating in the world's darkest cave and was extremely startled to see that Thunder was no longer on his mat, peacefully snoozing in the shaft of sunlight pouring in from a window close by. Instead, as I stumbled up out of the black, depressing mineshaft, I caught a glimpse of his gray tail rounding the corner of the stairwell as he bounded down the steps.

In panicked desperation, I started scurrying after him like an intoxicated chicken trying to catch a juicy little beetle. My knees were so weak after sitting on the bed for such a long time that when I ran, my feet flopped up at weird angles, and my elbows swung jointly from side to side, giving the image of a sad rooster airing out his armpits. Consequently, I was a pitiful sight, and to make matters worse, Thunder had already run out the door that my sister had just coincidently opened. I screeched angrily at her as I scuttled out the door, still chasing my cat. She yelled back an equally angry response that bounced off my ears as I barreled after my escaping feline.

He streaked through the streets of my neighborhood, passing the Johnson's mansion on the next block, until we were far from our house and in a neighborhood I didn't recognize. Running out of steam, I screeched to a halt and tried to regain some form of oxygen. He, too, seemed to realize that it had been about 72 miles since he had taken a rest, so he stopped. Seizing the opportunity, I slunk closer to him and was just about to snatch him up when he was up like a shot and careered down the road. I yelled futilely at him to stop, then hoisted myself up and continued my pursuit of my putrid, provoking pet.

He had been running on the road in a fairly straight line so far, but suddenly he took a sharp turn to the right. Puzzled, I did likewise, never taking my eyes off him, and ran right into a telephone pole. I should have recorded what I saw because I had a clear sight of the entire galaxy, including all the stars, black holes, and UFOs. Dazed, I staggered after him, hoping that I was going in the right direction. By now, I knew that all the neighbors had seen me and had probably called the police. This very second, my picture could be up in post offices all across America as the psycho who was chasing an innocent cat, yelling threats, and running into objects of society. I was the perfect image of insanity. Just then, I heard it: the slow, high-pitched whine of a police car's siren. My nightmare had become reality. I turned my head around as I continued sprinting down the street. It wasn't in sight yet, so I could possibly hide until it drove past me and then continue the search for my cat that had, by now, disappeared from sight.

Frantically, I scanned the horizon, and off in the distance I saw a gray form that suddenly cut across a lawn, a lawn that was extremely well manicured, to say the very least. There were what seemed like billions of flowers, trees, and to top it off, a waterfall cascading down rocks into a pool with a mini bridge crossing over it. It was beautiful, and my cat just ran right through it. I was scared now. Not only did I have the FBI after me, my cat just ran across what I was sure was the most expensive lawn in this entire neighborhood, and that's saying a lot, because I'm pretty sure I saw Bill Gates back there having tea with Prince William.

Surreptitiously—which meant that every single person in the radius of ten miles noticed me—I started creeping across the lawn, looking everywhere for my cat. Translation: I galumphed through the grass like an overweight elephant pulling a plow through a field while screaming my cat's name at the top of my lung capacity. Out of the corner of my eye, I saw a flash of gray. I veered to the northeast and started chasing it. I dodged the neatly kept beds of flowers, the artistically designed pots of plants, and the white steppingstones—all with dirty shoes.

I turned a corner, noticing the beautiful swimming pool as I ran, and stopped short. There, on the mini bridge I had seen earlier, was my cat. I could scarcely believe my luck. He was only ten feet away, and if I played it right, I could calm him down to give me time to grab him. I started coaxing him to come to me; he looked like he would rather be drowned in a pool of sewer water than come to me. I started tempting him with promises of sweets, his favorite chew toy, and much more, if he would just come home. He looked like he would rather be on a diet of carrots and turnips for the next two years than come home.

At this point, I was fed up. I had to get my cat before the owners of the house, whoever they were, found out that a wanted criminal was on their property, ruining their lawns and failing to get an animal off their expensive bridge overlooking an expensive waterfall surrounded by expensive beauty, all of which would be ruined if my cat wouldn't come to me. I was now begging my cat to come to me, literally on my hands and knees, with my hands clasped together like it was a matter of life or death—which it would be if my mom found out. Let's just say that it would be worse than the time Chi-Chi tore a hole in our swimming pool liner. In other words, certain death awaited me.

Thunder was getting restless, and I knew that he would probably bolt at any moment. I slowly started to creep towards him. Despite my best attempts of being sneaky, he knew I was trying to get him. He looked around for an escape route, and his expression turned to a look of pure horror as he stared in dismay at the water on both sides of him, and a crazy owner before him. Luck was with me that he didn't look behind him and see the open pathway to freedom. Suddenly, a look of determination crossed his facial features. He slowly yet determinedly raised both paws in the air. I gave him a funny look. What was he doing? He squinted his little eyes, puffed his furry cheeks full of air, and stood on his hind legs, wobbling his hips slowly. I blinked in disbelief. Surely I was seeing things. Why was my cat acting like an emotional rumba dancer? Was this just a trick to try and get me to let him run away again? Resembling a skeptical goat, I wasn't going to let him trick me again.

He gave one last look up at the sky before shutting his eyes, and, as if imitating an Olympic high dive champion, he plummeted through the crisp air and plunged into the depths below. I watched, transfixed, as he had bravely—or not so bravely—spiraled off the bridge to meet his doom. I suddenly snapped out of my trance, realizing that even though he was the reason I was being chased by the SWAT team, he was still my kitty. Knowing that, I, being the ever-noble one, screamed and leapt off the bridge after him. Not headfirst, because I still had some sense in me, although obviously not enough because I still jumped off a bridge into a seven-foot pool to attempt to save an animal.

I felt the water surround me as I splashed into the liquid. I popped my head out of the water to take a breath and try and locate my cat. As I screamed his name over and over again, while treading water, my leg brushed against a furry object. By brushed, I mean

I accidentally cracked his skull with my log of a leg, and if he weren't already dead, he probably would be by now. I gasped a big breath of air and dove beneath the surface. Once I had grabbed him, I swam up and over to the edge of the pool. He was limp in my hands, and I started pumping his chest, patting him on the back, and yelling his name, trying whatever I could to get him to breathe again. After a terrible minute, he sputtered. He was alive!

He started hacking, and I quickly stepped aside out of the way of his oncoming stream of phlegm. When he had regained some semblance of sanity, he looked at me in terror. I was too scared for his life to scold him for the moment, but once we were safe and dry at home, he would get a full chewing-out. However, I'm not sure if we will make it home without 1. The police catching me, 2. Getting caught by the owners, or 3. Him running away again. I quickly grabbed him in order to prevent the last one from occurring. He looked at me, startled, and then seeming to remember what he had done, drooped his bushy eyebrows as if he were about to be led to the chopping block. I stood up, wringing out my shirt as I did, and started squishing my way back to the main road. About ten steps from the pool, I heard a noise behind me.

Startled, I spun around, and as I was rotating, my already wet shoe caught on a wet patch of grass, and I went down like a hippo falling from an airplane. To make matters worse, I forgot that I was still holding a cat, and I landed right on top of Thunder. He was not happy, whatsoever. Hissing and scratching, he clawed me off. With blood on my face, I slowly turned around to confront this mystery person. It turned out to be a middle-aged woman with blond hair, and she eyed me from head to toe, obviously startled to find a drenched girl now trying to calm an equally drenched cat in her backyard. She opened her mouth, and I braced myself, expecting a barrage of accusations that would inevitably end me up in jail. Surprisingly, what she said to me were the last words I thought I would hear from her.

"I didn't expect you here in my backyard with a soaking cat, but you scheduled this, so I guess you can just get cleaned up inside." She turned to go back indoors then paused, as if remembering something. "Your cat will be taken care of as well, so when we go inside, you can just hand your pet to one of the servants."

Dude. She had servants? More importantly, why wasn't she mad? And why was she expecting me? I had never seen this woman in my life. Confused, I followed her through the French doors into a large room with a pool table in the middle of it. The table was absolutely gorgeous. The wood was as smooth as silk, and the pool sticks were very ornate. A woman walked into the room and took my cat from me and handed me a towel. I let her do it without a protest. They will most likely take better care of him than I ever could. Then this woman led me into yet another room that was just overflowing with elegance. She sat down in a chair by a wooden table and motioned for me to sit as well. I sat down on the towel and was about to tell her who I really was when she started talking.

"Buenos Días! I'm Bonnie Hathcock; you must be Juanita Sanchez."

Back the truck up! I'm who? I don't even know a Juanita, and I'm definitely not Hispanic. I know I'm relatively tan, but, seriously, do I look Hispanic? And I have no idea what she just said. She wasn't finished, however, with all the misunderstandings.

"You called me a few days ago, saying that you wanted to meet me for a coaching session."

Hold up. I never called this woman, much less scheduled an appointment for soccer lessons!

"I had expected you today, but not soaking wet, and definitely not with a cat. But surprises aren't meant to be predictable. I guess we'll get started, since we only have a few hours to discuss identity."

Discuss what? I decided to nip it in the bud before it got anymore confusing. "Excuse me?" I asked timidly.

She gave me a little smile. "Yes? Feel free to speak your mind."

"First off, I appreciate what you've done to help me, not calling the cops and all, but I'm not who you think I am."

She gave me a sympathetic nod. "I know you're going to want to feel guilty about things you've done in the past, but you shouldn't feel bad. I'm not going to judge you."

Wait, what? She thought I felt guilty? "No, that's not what I meant. I'm not Juanita Sanchez, or whomever you were expecting."

Now she was confused, just like I was. "You're not? Why were you on my lawn then?"

Oh boy, once I told her, I would end up with the fate I was destined to when my cat jumped off the bridge, and I, always the crowd-follower, jumped off after him. In as few words as possible, I quickly told her about my day. Instead of ringing up the police department, like I had expected, she gave me a funny look.

"Are you a Christian?"

Now where had that come from? I was expecting a strange comment, yes, but that was way off topic. "Um, no," I responded, "I'm not. I'm actually an atheist."

She did a little "hmm" to herself before saying, "I already had this time slot open for a coaching session, and since I shouldn't waste precious time, I'm just going to let you fill the spot instead."

Wait, I was going to be a student? Part of me was just thankful I wasn't behind bars, yet the other part knew that she was going to try and convert me somehow. I've survived people trying to Christianize me so far, but I've never been behind bars, so the obvious solution here was to participate in whatever she said, and once done, go home and never speak of this again. So, based on that knowledge, I let her know that I would be willing.

She went out of the room to grab some papers and pens, and when she returned, a woman was behind her, the same woman who had taken my cat earlier. This time, however, she was carrying coffee, water, and some mouth-watering cookies. I licked my chops, wondering when I would be able to satisfy my hunger on this fine feast. She set them down on the table before us and then left the room. Bonnie sat down and handed me a stack of papers. I rifled through them and was surprised that they had nothing to do with sports. I voiced my question.

"Why are we doing paperwork? I thought I was going to learn how to kick a soccer ball."

She started laughing, a realization spreading across her face. "Oh no, I'm not a sports coach; I'm a self-image coach." At my confused look, she explained. "I help people through struggles, and I help them come to better grips with themselves. For example, I help them understand that they're unconditionally worthy."

Unconditionally worthy? That sort of stuff isn't meant for me. I'm so not unconditionally worthy. Those sort of wonderful, hopeful things aren't for people like me who haven't done a thing in their life to deserve it. It's going to be hard to get through, what did she say? A few hours? She'll probably talk about stuff that doesn't relate to me, like that whole mess about being unconditionally worthy. She must have caught on to what I was thinking, though, because she gave me a strange look.

"Let's start on the first exercise. I want you to take this list of adjectives and put a check by the ones you are, and put a double check by the ones you aspire to be."

O-kay, that's not too hard, right? Just check the ones I'm positive I am, without bragging, and double check a few I may want to be when I'm forty or something. As I looked down at the sheet of paper, however, I realized that it wasn't going to be that easy. There were almost a hundred adjectives listed here! This could take a while. I began looking through them and checked off quite a few on the first page—which made me nervous because if that were how it went the entire time, it would seem like I was amazing. Then I got to the second page. There were considerably less checks on that page, and the number dwindled down to practically nothing by the time I reached the last page. Now for what I aspire to be. That number was basically a little less than what I was, and there were still a lot of adjectives left. I decided to just tell her I was done and see what her reaction would be. She had been reading some papers while I did this activity, and I put the pen down and leaned back in my chair to signify that I was done. The movement wasn't done in vain because she looked up and smiled at me.

"Are you done?" she asked.

I nodded, so she held out her hand for the papers of adjectives. I gave them to her, looking for a sign of disapproval. She had no change in facial features but simply wrote them down on her paper. Once she was done, she asked me to pick out my top ten adjectives that I had checked off.

"It doesn't matter whether you are them or whether you aspire to be them; I just want you to write down your top ten." She handed me my papers back.

I obeyed readily. It wasn't hard to find the top ten out of, what, thirty? It wasn't really that pitiful of a number, but it seemed like it. Once I had given her the ten, she made me go to five. And when I had picked out five, she began talking about them. For my top five, I had picked "involved" and "thoughtful" as ones I am, and "secure," "honorable," and "calm" as ones I want to be. For the ones I am, though, I might as well put those under the category of aspire to be. I wasn't exactly involved or thoughtful; I just put them as my top five because I want to be them. I also didn't want a sermon on how precious I was, and how I shouldn't think any less of myself. That's the main reason why I didn't just put all the adjectives as aspire to be but instead put some under a not-completely-true category. Thankfully, she didn't seem to catch on to what I had done. Or maybe she did, but didn't say anything other than they were good choices before moving on to a different activity. I was so silent at this point she knew something was wrong.

"I have a feeling that you don't feel worthy. Am I right, or is my tactic for reading people's minds outdated?"

I gaped at her. How did she know? I decided to go along with what she said and see where she took this topic of conversation. She handed me a sheet of paper and asked me to write "unworthy" and "worthy" at the top, separated by a line down the middle. I fulfilled her request.

"Now, what I want you to do is tell me this: how do you feel when you walk into a room?"

What kind of a question is that? With an incredulous look at her, I thought about it carefully before responding.

"I suppose that I'm not very good at walking into a room, especially by myself, confidently. I tend to slip in unnoticed until I find my group of friends."

Her eyes lit up. "Do you feel awkward at times, walking into a room?" At my nod, she spoke. "Aha! At the top of your paper, on the side that says 'unworthy,' write 'awkward.'"

I did so, not knowing where this was going.

She kept right on with that topic. "I'm going to go out on a limb here and guess that you also feel vulnerable and afraid, am I right?" I nodded again. She was good at guessing.

"Write those down on the left column as well."

I quickly jotted down on the unworthy side those two words, words that made me think hard. I really did feel awkward, afraid, and vulnerable.

"Now, you mentioned that you always look for your friends. How do you feel when you don't immediately see them? Do you feel alone or that you don't belong?"

"Yes to both of those," I said, in a voice that was seriously worried. My list was getting really long, and I didn't have a thing on the "worthy" side. This just confirmed my suspicions that I wasn't good enough. I wrote down the latest two with a heavy heart.

"When you don't see them, or if they're not there at all, how does it make you feel?"

"Anxious for them to get there, and somewhat upset that they aren't there already." Even I was surprised that had come out of my mouth. I wasn't meaning to be that honest. She seemed to take it in stride, though.

"Do you feel judgmental, since they weren't there already?" I bobbed my head. "And I'm going to guess that you become disconnected from everything going on around you."

Again, I nodded. She was spot on! I now had a ton of feelings that screamed unworthy, and none that said I was even the least bit worthy.

"Now, what we're going to do is this: for every word you have written on the left column, we are going to use the opposite of it and write that word down in the right column, the one that says 'worthy.' What's the first word on your list?" She glanced over at my paper. "'Awkward?' Okay, so on the right side, write 'graceful.'"

I stifled a snort. Me, graceful? I don't think so. I trip over my feet so much that when I don't trip more than three times a day, I get asked by fellow students if I was finally cured of my clumsiness. I wrote it down anyway, halfway curious as to what she would put down for the other ones. I still didn't understand how that made me worthy, especially if it were untrue.

"The next words," she said, glancing yet again at my paper, "are 'vulnerable' and 'afraid.' For 'vulnerable,' write 'secure;' and for 'afraid,' write 'excited.'"

What? Let's see, secure and excited. Am I either? Hmm, let me think... Nope! I wrote them down anyways.

"The next words are 'alone,' and 'don't belong.' For them, write 'connected' and 'belong' respectively."

My pen was gliding smoothly over the paper. She was getting down to the bottom of the list.

"'Anxious,' 'judgmental,' and 'disconnected' are the last three, and for those the words will be 'peaceful,' 'accepting,' and 'connected' in that order."

We had finished going through the list, and I had written down a word for everything but didn't feel any different.

"My challenge for you is to practice going from the left column to the right. As soon as you feel vulnerable or alone, remember that you are secure and connected. What you repeat often enough, you will begin to believe. And when you believe it, you will see a change. It takes practice, though, so practice a lot."

"Another suggestion is to gravitate to your gifts. If you know what your gifts are, then you can be more natural and more confident in what you do. You can then look for jobs that go hand in hand with your talents, and if you love your job, you'll never work a day in your life."

"This is very good advice," I commented. "You seem like you have done this for a long time."

"Thank you. I've not always been like this, though." At my skeptical look, she continued, "My dad left when I was three, my mom was always working trying to make enough money to support us, and my younger brother was abused by my older cousin when we lived with them in their tiny apartment." I was shocked. I assumed that she had grown up rich and famous, seeing how she was in this gorgeous house.

"And to put the icing on the cake, I had to be rescued from a sewer drain by my dear aunt." Wow. She had been through a lot.

"I wrote a book about my journey from the sewer drain to the boardroom. It's called Lilac Dreams; I can give you a copy if you like."

"Yes, I'd love to read it! Reading is one of the things I love to do."

"There were two things that got me to the boardroom: determination and grit. Determination will get you there, and grit will keep you there. At the top of the corporate ladder, there's no one to pass off the hard problems to, so you have to deal with them yourself. That's one of the main reasons you need grit. When you're in a pickle, it's necessary to remember the qualities of a godly woman: kindness, humility, acceptance, and ego strength not ego need. In life, you are like a pinball machine. People will try to pull your levers and push your buttons, and if you aren't grounded in who you are, then you will explode with different balls of emotions."

I smiled at her. She had helped me so much, even though this meeting was impromptu. She looked at the time right then.

"Oh my. Time completely got away from me. We are two minutes from when this is scheduled to end." She stood, and I followed her. She led me into a room where she signed the inside cover of a book and handed it to me. It was Lilac Dreams, her book. I thanked her again as we made our way to the door.

"This book is an example of Jeremiah 29:11. It shows that God really does have a plan for each and every person."

Just then, the woman who had brought the cookies and had taken my cat walked in the room carrying the said cat. She handed him to me with a smile. I gratefully placed him in my arms and walked out the door Bonnie was holding open, wishing her a good day and thanking her for her generous schedule change. Once outside, I began the walk home. Thunder seemed very content in my arms, probably still recovering from his little swim in the pond. On the way home, I realized that I could count Bonnie as the godly woman for the week. I'm sure Tina didn't care that I hadn't officially asked her.

After about thirty minutes, I saw our house in the distance. When we finally collapsed on the front steps, Thunder was feeling better. He scampered out of my arms and started pawing the door, trying to get in. I slowly creaked my joints until I was standing so I could open the door for him. As soon as the door was ajar, he bolted inside and ran up the stairs. I just shook my head at him as I followed at a much slower pace. Finally, in the safety of my room, I crashed onto my bed, still piled high with homework, and mulled over what Bonnie had said today. It was all terrific advice, but it would take a lot of practice to make it become a habit. I couldn't wait to read her book, though. If she had such a life-impacting story and ended up where she is now, then maybe there's hope for me, too.

Chapter Thirteen

One bright Wednesday afternoon, I was leisurely reading in a soft, comfortable chair when I realized, with dread, that Friday was a friend's ballet performance, and I had promised not only to go to it but I had also dropped hints that I was going to get her something special if she, in return, would come to my upcoming band performance. (I now was fantastic at playing the piano—for a beginner, I mean.) Since she obviously was going to come to the concert, I had to figure out what to get her. I ran a couple of ideas through my head before finally deciding on flowers, since it seemed like that was what all ballerinas received after a performance. The only question was where would I get flowers that were cheap enough for me to buy, would stay fresh until Friday, and looked amazing? My schedule was full the next day, so I couldn't go then. Concerning the money issue, I decided to see if I could sweet-talk my grandmother into contributing some, since she wouldn't be spending money on me but on someone else.

I clomped down the stairs and headed for the living room, where she would inevitably be. I was right, and I asked my question before I got cold feet. She gave a little "humph," obviously trying to decide if I was being serious. She evidently believed me and, to my surprise, reached into her pocket and pulled out a twenty-dollar bill.

"You can't get flowers cheap these days. Be sure they smell nice, aren't wilted, and that they come with extra plant food, in case you have to keep them for longer than expected."

I thanked her and walked out of the room, doing a victory dance once out of sight. I struck a cowboy pose with a finger gun and pretended to blow the smoke off the top of it. I was planning on spending ten to fifteen bucks of my own, so with our money combined, I could probably get something nicer than a bouquet from Walmart.

With the money in my pocket, I climbed into the car. My "chivalrous" sister was going to "graciously" give me a ride to a flower shop. Translation: she pitched a fit when she found out she would have to chauffeur me "all the way" to Georgia to a flower shop before going to meet up with her friends near the shop anyways. She fumed—more like pouted—all the way to the floral shop. I decided on this particular shop because it was my paternal aunt's floral shop, who was also the mother of Hannah, my cousin.

Before we had left, I had given my aunt a call, letting her know I was coming down to buy some flowers. She not only expressed her excitement at seeing me but she also suggested that I hang out with her while Kimberly was with her friends. I had also asked if she would be one of my 52 godly women—I might as well kill two birds with one stone. She had heard about my challenge from Hannah and readily agreed. I was thrilled to see yet another family member that I hadn't seen in ages.

When we finally arrived, I hopped out and walked to the front door of the flower shop. I had only been here once, and all I remembered was the name: AnnOther Flower Shop. Her name wasn't Ann, though. It was Cheryl McGee. She had bought the shop from a woman named Ann and never changed the name. The bell jangled as I opened the front door. A voice called out from the back that she would be just a minute, so I started looking around. It was a beautiful shop, and I was enjoying myself immensely when I was startled by a voice behind me. I turned around and was grabbed into a bear hug by my aunt.

"I can't believe it! If someone had told me that I would be meeting with you today for a godly challenge, I honestly wouldn't have believed her. The last thing I heard about you was that you were an atheist. Is that correct?"

I nodded and then clarified. "I still am an atheist. I'm only doing this because a girl from school coerced me into it."

She looked disappointed, but then brightened. "At least you're still doing it! But enough about this, I need to get your order for the flowers, and then we can hang out." She gave me a sheepish look before telling me news that made me groan silently.

"I thought you were a Christian, so I planned on you helping my husband and me with the bus ministry tonight for our church."

What? I didn't know anything about helping out on a bus. I didn't even know what a bus ministry was. Nevertheless, I had to do it because I couldn't be by myself in Georgia at night. Reluctantly, I nodded my head and told her that I would help. She smiled broadly and gave me a hug. She then led me to the back of the store and asked me what I wanted for my order. I decided on a dozen pink roses and explained how much money I had. She told me that the amount was perfect. While she put together the roses, I asked if I could do anything to help out. She gladly accepted the offer, asking if I would be willing to help out with folder work.

"I'm not sure how to do that, but I'll give it my best shot," I said in a hesitant yet determined tone.

"It's pretty easy. All you have to do is write down what I tell you to."

It sounded simple enough, so I sat on a stool next to the worktable and reached for a pen. She gave me a stack of large nametags and pulled out a crate of folders. She looked at a customer's folder and if the customer had bought within the last year, she put it in a stack by me. I, in turn, would write down the customer's name, address, and phone number onto the nametag and then move on to the next folder. We were moving along at quite a clip, and about an hour and many folders later, I noticed that she was limping. Concerned, I asked what had happened. She winced as she sat down.

"On my birthday, I rolled my ankle. It hasn't gotten much better, so it really hurts, especially when I walk."

I expressed my sympathy and asked if I could do anything for her, seeing as we were taking a break from doing folders.

"If you'll promise me to be careful, I would love for you to collect the mail for me. If you walk a ways down the sidewalk, you'll be able to cross the street to pick it up from the post office." At my puzzled look, she added. "I don't want you to cross as soon as you go out the back door because the road curves there, and cars come barreling around there very dangerously. I don't want you to get hit by a car."

I was slightly baffled; she was looking out for my safety. It was such a new prospect that I wasn't able to grasp the fact that someone actually cared whether I lived or not. She gave me the post office box key as well as directions on how to find it. I walked out into the brisk air and walked a ways down the sidewalk, as she had said. Once I was certain that no cars were coming close enough to make me a hood ornament, I sprinted across the street as if there were a pack of wolves chasing me. I didn't stop running until I yanked open the door of the post office. I found her mailbox pretty easily, and I grabbed the mail inside it before running back outside. I had to stand in the same spot for about seven minutes, wiggling incessantly, because so many cars were coming in such a consistent way that I couldn't run back across the street. Eventually, though, I was able to make it to the other side—like the proverbial chicken. After entering the shop, I handed her the mail and collapsed into a chair, exhausted from my Usain Bolt imitation.

"Thanks!" she said. "Good to see you back safe and sound."

I nodded vaguely. That was an experience I would never forget. I slowly got up from the chair and stretched. I was a bit hungry, but I didn't want to inconvenience my aunt and uncle. If they didn't normally eat dinner until six or seven o'clock, then I would be hurrying them, seeing how it wasn't even five o'clock yet.

I walked back over to the worktable and started writing nametags again from the tall stack of folders waiting for me. I actually enjoyed it, to my surprise. Aunt Cheryl came over and started sorting through folders again before she eventually decided to put me on the phone with my grandmother, her mom. I had known subconsciously that she worked part-time with my aunt, but it hadn't clicked until then that I was working in the place that my grandmother did. We came up with a nice system. I would tell Grandmother a name, and she would look up that name in her computer database at home. If the person had bought within the year, I would put the folder in the "yes" pile for me to later write down the customer's information. If he hadn't, I would put the file in the "no" pile and never worry about it again. It was a very efficient way of handling the files, and once we had gone through all the files from A-T, Aunt Cheryl suggested we take a break. I agreed, so we stopped what we were doing. Aunt Cheryl went to get us some water, and when she came back, she looked at me quizzically.

I wanted to know why. "Penny for your thoughts?" I inquired.

"Are you going to ask me any questions?" At my confused look, she went on. "For example, is this like an interview, or do you just hang out with me?"

Ohhhh, she meant the 52 godly women thing. I guess I could ask her some questions while we took a break.

"Did you always want to own your own business and be a floral designer?"

She laughed. "No! Not at all. I was born into a Christian, loving family, and my only goals were to be married, be a stay-at-home mom, and have three kids. I got saved as a young child, went to church all the time while growing up, was a people pleaser, and wasn't rebellious. All in all, I was a pretty good person. I even went to Lee College for three years before coming back home. And that's when my world shook—I met Andy Parris."

A love story? How sweet! I couldn't wait to hear it.

"There weren't many guys I knew that loved Jesus, but Andy did, so I was impressed. We dated some before I married him on September 8, 1984. Five years into the marriage, however, I found out things about Andy."

What kind of things? Did he have an allergy to Cheetos or something?

"He was addicted to pornography, he was unfaithful as a husband, and he was a homosexual."

Oh man. Not good. Can't even compare that to a Cheetos allergy. How again did she not know this when she met him?

As if reading my mind, she answered my question. "I thought he was good, but I was raised naïvely. I didn't think a person could have all that bad stuff and still "love Jesus" or pretend to. Our marriage was very rocky. He would make me believe that he had put everything behind him, but in reality, he hadn't. In 1989, Hannah was born, and that completely shifted my perspective. I now had a child to rear. In 1991, we were so much in debt that we had to find another means of income. That is when we bought this flower shop. Before we borrowed the money to buy the shop, Andy wanted to do an AIDS test. I personally thought he was just worried, since he was a worrier. In June, the test came back negative. He didn't have AIDS"

I breathed a sigh of relief. That would have been pretty sad if it had come back positive. Even though he was a bad man, he was still her husband.

"We bought the business, and Andy did the designing, being the creative one, and I did the book work, being the not-very-creative one. Things were moving along rather well and by May, we bought a house and were able to move out of our mobile home. Yet,

Andy, being the hypochondriac that he was, thought something was still wrong with him; and this time, I also believed that something really was wrong with him. He scheduled an appointment with the doctor for a physical; however, while awaiting the results, he had a dream that when he came out of the office with the results, his family was crying. To keep the dream from coming true, he went to get the results by himself. I was at work when he called me. He had AIDS"

Oh no. That's an automatic death sentence!

"To tell the truth, I was pretty upset with God."

Wait. My church-going aunt was upset with the "Creator of the universe?" How dare she? It apparently didn't last very long, though, as she continued.

"God gave me a scripture, and it made me stop arguing. The scripture was Isaiah 45:9, which basically says not to quarrel with God."

So some lies from a beat-up book made you stop arguing with a pretend character even though that same pretend character made your husband have an impending doom?

"On September 19, Andy was admitted into the hospital with pneumonia. I prayed for him and the church prayed. Some friends sat down with me and told me to trust God's sovereignty and give it to Him. Andy should have died right then, but God raised him up. Over the next few months, Andy seemed to slowly recover; and during that time, we found out how much he had jeopardized our lives from his promiscuity. However, God allowed him to live to give him time to repent, to set things straight with us, and to get his will made. God taught me a lot as I prayed and cried. I didn't know how to run this business or make a living, but I learned how to run the business while he was at home dying."

My heart was weeping. How sad is that? You have to daily work a business you don't know anything about while your husband is dying at home.

"I spent a lot of time praying to be able to learn the ropes of being an owner of a flower shop. God taught me so much. Eventually, the shop turned into a really good source of income. In February, God gave me a verse out of Ruth and told me that He was my source. I asked God if Andy was going to live or die; God told me that he was going to die."

No! What a terrible answer. If God can do anything, why couldn't He save him?

"Andy went to the hospital and came home with hospice. He died on April 10, 1994. Hannah was almost five when he died, about to start kindergarten."

Wow, that's hard. I know what it's like to be young and fatherless.

"A few years later, God gave me another scripture, Jeremiah 33:11, which mentions marriage."

Why would her God want to rub it in her face that she lost her marriage? I'm sure she was well aware that she wasn't still married.

"He told me that I would have another husband."

Oh. That's different. Why didn't she say so in the first place?

"I thought He meant soon, and I was always on the lookout for a husband. Years passed. I learned that God wanted to teach me how to wait. Like Joseph, He was testing me. I waited for a long time. However, during my singleness, God did a work in me. He taught me to look to Him as my Provider, my Protector, and my Husband. I also changed how I looked. Growing up, I would dress to please my parents, and when I was married, I dressed to please my husband. Now that I was single, I could dress how I wanted. I could change my outward appearance to be the best me I could be. I was pretty happy with myself. Different guys came along who wanted to date me. Because I didn't trust my ability to pick a husband—seeing how I picked a man like Andy the first time—I told God to pick the right man for me and confirm it to me over and over. I attended the singles class at church, but

I went on less than five dates in fourteen years."

No "right" men? I think she just had super high standards for a husband.

"Any time a guy walked into my life, I prayed that if he wasn't the right one, God would take him out of my life. You don't know how many guys just kept disappearing! One even ended up in Washington State—practically the farthest the guy could go in the continental U.S. to drop out of my life! In February 2008, a woman called me to consider dating a man named Eddie McGee, whose wife had died two years earlier and whom I knew vaguely from church. By now, however, I had so many walls around my heart against men that I scared most men off. Imagine my surprise when Ed walked into my shop one day and asked me out on a date!"

I, for one, would have likely fainted. I've never been asked out on an actual date before, just asked to school dances by guys who were incredibly desperate. I've always declined, though.

"I was still praying my if-he's-not-the-right-man-send-him-away prayer, but he wasn't going away. After some time, we saw that it was a God-thing. God brought much healing to me through Ed. He is such a godly man who has cherished me, something I didn't experience with Andy. Ed's just another example of how, when you wait on the Lord, He blesses you."

As in when you sneeze? Pretty weird. I remembered then that she mentioned practically nothing about Hannah. Raising a five-year-old without a husband must have been extremely hard. I asked her that question, and I got my answer.

"It was, indeed, hard. I had to pray for wisdom a lot. I purposely put Hannah around godly men who would speak into her life. Whenever Hannah did something wrong, I couldn't just say, 'Wait until your father gets home'—for obvious reasons. I had to deal with it, and I wasn't going to let her off the hook without the consequences of her wrong behavior. I answered to God whenever I would discipline Hannah, and if Hannah didn't like my consequences, I would tell her to take it up with God because I was answering to Him. Despite all that, we were very close."

I smiled. Having heard Hannah's story, I was able to begin connecting the dots. All but one. She never told me when she and Ed married.

"We married not too long after he asked me out on that first date. Since we knew it was a God-thing, why wait?" She chuckled at this.

Right then, she looked at her watch.

"Oh my, we need to get ready for the bus ministry."

I gulped, not knowing what to expect. What would these kids be like?

I found out soon enough. We went to her house, where she changed her clothes and got her stuff. Uncle Ed joined us as we drove to the church they attend, Redemption to the Nations. Once we arrived, we walked up the steps into a giant, white bus. I grabbed a broom and started sweeping the aisle, per my aunt's request, and my uncle was working on the mechanical side of things. After I finished sweeping, I hopped down the steps of the bus to climb back into the car to ride with Aunt Cheryl to a store to buy candy for the kids. After we had purchased five large bags of candy—which weren't all for that night, as she informed me later—we returned to the church and boarded the bus.

Uncle Ed began driving around the inner city, passing one house after another. We finally came to a stop in front of one particular house, and a few kids came out and climbed onto the bus, pausing a few seconds for Aunt Cheryl to give them nametags. This went on for an hour or more. We would stop at houses and pick up kids, occasionally getting papers from the parents which were permission slips for their children to ride the bus. That way, if something happened to the kid, they couldn't press charges against the church because they had agreed to let their kid ride. Once all the kids had been picked up, we started driving back to the church.

While I sat on the first row of the bus, a little boy came to sit next to me. He was the sweetest thing, and I instantly fell in love with him. He had such cool ideas and was a great listener. The ride to the church passed quickly. Once we dropped the kids off to go to their respective classes, Aunt Cheryl and I drove to Chick-fil-A to get food. I happily chomped on some fries as we made our way back to the church. After we, as well as Uncle Ed, had eaten, we prepared to do the route all over again.

As the children came out of the church building and walked towards the bus, I noticed that they didn't seem very attentive to what their parents had taught them about manners—unless their parents hadn't taught them any. I felt sympathy for them. They acted as if they were independent, which made me wonder how many of the kids actually had parents looking after them. Eventually, they were all loaded up on the bus, and we were off. On the way to their houses, I stood near the back of the bus to help keep the kids quiet. It was very loud, to say the least. I was very busy, telling kids to sit, comforting kids, hushing kids, so on and so forth. We had lots of adult help on the way back, though, which I was very thankful for. When we dwindled down to the last few kids on the bus, the workers—including me—were able to relax and chat with the kids.

Soon, all the kids were dropped off at the proper houses, and only the workers remained on the bus. There was some candy left over, so we treated ourselves to a stream of sugar as the bus rolled toward the church.

After disembarking, I realized how drained I was, but I was also so thankful to have been a part of the bus ministry. I learned a lot from it, and I would definitely think twice before complaining about my little annoyances again. These kids had so little, and they were pushing through it, most of them with smiles on their faces. It was incredible how brave they were. They were able to laugh and play even though their families were falling apart, or they hadn't had a good meal in a while, or bad things were going on at home. I felt a connection with the kids, although they had a worse life than I did.

As I walked slowly over to my sister's car, I ran through the day's events in my head. Aunt Cheryl was a remarkable woman, a very godly woman—which, according to her, meant that a woman was faithful to God, honest, and a never-ending pursuer of the Lord. I realized that I wanted to spend more time with her. When this challenge started out, I was not exactly happy with it and had no idea where to find godly women. Now I'm realizing that I haven't had to go to Tina for advice about a woman in quite a few weeks. Sure, she had set a bunch up without my knowledge, but they had turned out better than alright. Maybe by the end, I will take it all on my shoulders; however, taking ownership of this challenge does not mean that my views on Christianity will change. That's the only thing I can count on to stay the same.

Chapter Fourteen

A swift breeze picked up as I briskly bicycled down the sidewalk on a mission. I had walked into Dunkin' Donuts that morning to grab a donut, since I didn't live too far from Dunkin' Donuts and school had canceled due to a burst pipe. I had spotted my college friend Bailey working behind the counter. She had just gotten a call from a woman she knew to see if she could drop off some donuts for her. Bailey didn't have the time to go out there, but the woman was a family friend, and she didn't want to disappoint her. In her distress, she pleaded with me to drop them off for her—and I would even be able to keep whatever tips the woman gave me. This woman had already pre-paid for the donuts, and my job was just to take a form with me that said she received them.

That was how I ended up pedaling my beat-up bicycle around Lee University, looking very lost as I tried to find one particular building. It's no wonder that most students are late for class. I bet they just get lost in this giant place. That and no parking. I'm glad I'm not driving because, if I were, I would never get these delectable desserts delivered without earning a parking ticket by parking someplace definitely illegal, like by a fire hydrant or in a handicapped parking spot.

I needed to keep my mind on the present, however. The donuts were precariously balanced on the tiny basket my bicycle wore proudly like an old shoe. It wasn't pretty, to say the least. I had gotten the bicycle a year and a half ago, so not only was it too small for me but also the person who bought it for me, who shall remain unnamed, thought I still liked Disney princesses. So here I was, riding a Cinderella bicycle with a dilapidated flowery basket three times too small for the giant box of donuts on top of it.

As I slowed to a stop to try and find my bearings, my worst nightmare came true. As I hit a rut, the box of donuts sailed through the air in slow motion. Also in slow motion, I gasped and jumped off my bike, extending my arms as fast as I could—which isn't very fast if you're moving in slow motion—to tightly grasp the corners of the box and pull it safely to my chest. Then time sped back to normal, and I went down like a freight train onto the cold concrete below, still holding the donuts beneath me. I groaned in frustration. I was barely wounded, except for my pride, of course, little though it was.

I slowly picked myself up from the ground and inspected the box of donuts. The top was barely crushed. By barely, I mean a walrus could have belly-flopped onto it, and it wouldn't have been any worse than it already was. Inside, the donuts were not too bad, all things considered. Three donuts were barely edible, but eight were only slightly mushed, the icing smeared across the top of the box. The last one, a chocolate donut with multi-colored sprinkles, was the only reason I didn't just crawl into a hole right then. It was perfect. The icing hadn't been touched, and the sprinkles were beautifully intact. It was like looking at a sparkly unicorn sprinkling pixie dust in a fairy tale, while the rest of the donuts looked like an overweight, beached whale crusted with day-old kelp.

I had a few options, all of which might end badly for me. Option number one: fix everything the best I could and still deliver, hoping that the perfect donut would make the woman forget the fact that the other donuts looked as pitiful as wilted lettuce. Option number two: eat all the donuts and pretend that the woman hadn't ordered any, which would be hard to do, since I still had that form that needed to be signed by her. Option number three: tell the woman what happened and hope my friend wouldn't be too mad at me. The last option I didn't particularly like, and realizing that I wouldn't be able to eat the donuts fast enough for someone not to see me, I opted for option number one.

I straightened the box back to its original shape and started fixing the donuts. I arranged them so when the woman opened the box, she saw the better ones first, including the perfect donut, and the bad donuts I put sporadically throughout the mix. Once I had scraped the icing off the lid and plunked it artistically on the donuts (meaning that it looked like a Picasso painting), I closed the box, put it carefully on the basket again, and pulled out the sheet of directions. It said that I was supposed to turn right at a certain building, but I didn't know how to get to that building from where I was.

I followed street signs and the feeling in my gut until I finally saw the landmark up ahead. Once I turned right, I spotted the destination of the not-so-delectable-anymore desserts. I slowly bicycled towards it, the precious cargo wobbling only slightly. As I cruised to a stop, I carefully swung my leg off the bike and picked up the box of donuts. I walked to the big metal door leading into the building and pushed. It didn't budge. Frowning, I pushed again. Still no effect. I set the donuts on a safe ledge and then grunted and heaved with all I was worth, but that door wasn't going anywhere. In one last desperate attempt to get in, I took three steps back. Breathing in and out like a hyperventilating rhino, I mustered every amount of energy I had left and charged to the door. The result was another trip to the ground—for the second time that day—and a giant bruise on my shoulder. I slowly picked myself and turned around. A woman was staring at me, looking at me from head to toe as her mouth twitched with a held-back guffaw.

"You have to pull," she said, motioning to a sign on the door.

Dumbly, I followed her pointing finger to where there was, indeed, a sign on the door that stated in large, bold letters, "Pull." Now completely humiliated beyond imagination, I tried to make amends.

"I, ah, I definitely knew that. I was, um, just practicing for the football team."

Now the corners of her mouth were twitching full time. "Football team?"

"Yep. It's a very special team, only girls, and I'm the double quarterbacker." As soon as the words left my mouth, I wished I could snatch them back in. What was I thinking?

By now, her shoulders were vibrating uncontrollably, and she was clamping her tongue between her teeth. "Double—," she paused as a laugh slipped out. "Quarterbacker? What do you, um, do?"

"I wrestle people to the ground while my teammates score."

She was laughing even harder now. I was shamed for life. I picked up the box of donuts and slowly pulled the door open. I could hear her laughter echoing throughout the halls as I walked down a corridor and towards an open door that had voices coming from within the room. I peeked in to try and find the woman who had made the order, Carolyn Dirksen. My eyes swept across the reception room and landed on a sweet lady with glasses whom I was drawn to because of her authoritative air. I walked over to her and asked if she knew a woman named Carolyn Dirksen.

"I am she," the woman said daintily. She took the box of donuts and set them on a table. She entered one of the offices, and I hoped she would bring back a nice tip before signing the paper. After a good long while, though, she still hadn't come out. I decided to see what was going on, so I walked to the office where she had disappeared and peeked in. She was sitting at a desk, sorting through papers as she talked to someone on the phone. I cleared my throat. She looked up, startled. She motioned for me to have a seat. I gingerly sat down and looked around. She had plaques on the walls for different accomplishments. Apparently, from what I could see, she was an English teacher at this college and was on the Church of God World Missions board. When she hung up the phone, she turned in her chair to face me.

"May I help you?"

I sat there a little confused. Did she forget, in such a short span of time, about the donuts?

Just then, her eyes grew wide. "Oh my. Are you Penny's daughter?"

I started. How did she know my mom? Cautiously, I answered her. "Yes, do you know her?"

She chuckled. "Know her? She took my English class back when she was in college. She was one of a kind, that's for sure. I can't believe you're her daughter. Did she send you?"

She did seem to have forgotten about the donuts. I shook my head. "No, I'm here because I delivered the donuts. Speaking of which, I need you to sign here saying that you received them." I sat there, slightly dazed at what she had just said. My mom took English in college? That's why I always felt like a Webster dictionary was chewing me up whenever she yelled at me.

She widened her eyes slightly. "I'm so sorry; I completely forgot about them!" She leaned over and signed it, then handed me a five. "Thank you for bringing them."

"You're welcome!" I stood up to leave when she held out a hand.

"Could you tell me how your family's doing? I haven't heard a thing from Penny in years. I did hear about Jared. I'm very sorry."

I ignored the feelings of sadness when she mentioned my dad and instead smiled slightly, an idea rushing into my mind before my 'crazy idea police' censored it. What if I made her one of my 52 godly women? She seemed to be a Christian, working at a Christian college and being on a missions board and all. She could be part of my challenge, but it also meant that I would have to tell her about my dysfunctional family, who take all the "fun" out of dysfunctional until it's just dysctional. I decided it was worth it and told her about my challenge and asked if she would be a part of it. After she agreed to my proposal, I began telling her what our family was doing currently.

"We live in a small house with a pool." As I shared some details, my mind wandered, remembering all the adventures I have had in that house in the past three months since starting my challenge. It was hard to believe I had already met with thirteen women. "I own a sweet cat named Thunder," I ended, "and he's the only pet I've ever had." As I glanced at the wall clock, I was surprised that I had been talking for a solid ten minutes.

Carolyn gave me a smile. "Is your mother still keeping up her reputation for talking like a dictionary?"

I nodded. I wondered if she also knew that she did most of the talking while drunk. I felt like I had done enough talking, so I started asking her some questions in return.

"Yes, as long as I can ask you spontaneous questions now and then."

"How long have you been teaching English?"

"Fifty years. I've seen lots of changes in students and in the university itself."

"Congratulations! What made you stay at the same school for so long?"

She smiled. "I've always liked working in a Christian environment, and I have also received various promotions as the years have gone by. I worked for fourteen years as a faculty member, teaching full time. When Paul Conn became president of the college, I became the department chair. With everything changing, I enjoyed having the privilege of being at the table when decisions were made so I could voice my opinion. Then I became the Dean of the College of Arts and Sciences for two years when the college became a university. After that, I was the Vice President for Academics for fourteen years before I became a teacher to teachers—teaching teachers how to become better teachers."

I chuckled at this. She was a teacher who was teaching teachers how to teach students better?

"Plus, Lee has changed so much over the last fifty years that it has felt like I was working at different schools. That's why I was able to stay so long at Lee."

She paused as the phone rang. She looked at me apologetically then picked it up. I did another scan of her office as she finished up her conversation.

"What would be your favorite part of working here?"

She smiled. "I like talking with the faculty about how to be better teachers. That was why we ordered donuts this morning."

Ah. It was strange how I always seemed to meet my next godly woman in the most random places, in the craziest places.

"Would you say that this would be the best time in your life?" I asked.

"No. The best time was when my daughter was young and my mom was still alive."

"Is she your only child?"

She smiled, remembering. "No. When I was thirty, my husband and I adopted three orphaned siblings who were 9, 11, and 12 at the time. Their parents had been alcoholics before they died, so the kids had behavioral issues growing up because of things that had happened to them when they were young."

I knew what that was like. I had experienced both the alcoholic parent side of things, and the dead parent side of things.

"However," Carolyn continued, "about five years ago, our youngest adopted daughter was diagnosed with inoperable cancer. She got sick and eventually died. She had a thirteen-year-old son whom we took care of until he married.

"Did you want to reach out to more kids after that experience?"

"I did get involved in more children's projects, especially the Phebe Gray Orphanage in Liberia. I was even able to visit that orphanage. It had 104 kids, no running water, no electricity, and a school for their orphans plus 100 kids from other places. They needed so much, and many people gave. Thirty computers were donated to the orphanage for the computer lab. One thousand books were donated to the library, and people gave linens, medicine, mosquito netting, food, and school materials. As well, since there was an 85% unemployment rate in Liberia, World Missions even raised the money needed for the orphans' college tuition after they graduated from the orphanage school."

"Have you been to other countries besides Liberia?"

"Let's see...I've been to Zambia, Kenya, Mongolia, Vietnam, Ukraine, South Africa, China, and North Korea."

I was impressed. "That's a lot. How do you manage to go to all of them and still teach English?"

"I go to a country in the summer and come home for the rest of the year."

"Which country do you think you accomplished the most in?"

"In 1984, my husband and I went to China. There were practically no foreigners in the country at the time, since the ban on foreigners had just been lifted, so we were virtually the only strangers in the country. We went into the country as English teachers for a college, but we were also able to share Christianity. The students knew we were Christians, and they were interested in Christianity since their country had banned people from coming in to preach a different religion, including Christianity. We shared as much as we could, within the boundaries set by the government, and even incorporated Christian books into our classes, like Pilgrim's Progress."

I inwardly scoffed. I can't believe those students would actually believe all that nonsense about God.

"We went to China for one year, then came here for one year, then back to China. The first year in China was the biggest adventure in my life."

"Did you ever feel scared in any of the countries you went to?"

"In North Korea, yes. But I knew that with God, everything turns out okay in the end because He mentions in Ephesians 2:10 that we are His workmanship created for good works. So if God has created me to do good works, I doubt anything can happen that won't go along with His plan."

Ugh. Why does everything have to point back to God? But that reminded me, I had to ask her what her take on godly women was. When I voiced my question, she spoke the following: "A godly woman has a direct connection to God, has a sense of God's presence, and lives like Christ in the community."

Just then, I looked at the clock. "Oh no! I told Bailey that I would be back by 11:00 so she could get this signed form."

She smiled. "It was a pleasure meeting you, and I wish you all the best. Tell your mother hello for me!" She showed me to the door, and I thanked her for her time as I hightailed it out of there. I ran down the hallway and stopped at the door. I heard a noise behind me and turned. The same woman who had witnessed my embarrassing scene earlier was standing there, grinning.

I was frustrated. "What? Did you expect me to forget how to open this door in the time I was here?" She hid a smile—no small feat since that grin could have been a clone to a watermelon slice. My frustration grew. "Well, let me prove it to you that I'm not a mindless Martian." I reached for the door and put one hand on it, giving her a wide-eyed look as if explaining to a child. "See, I have to pull it open." And with that, I pulled it with all I had in me. Nothing happened. I could feel color rising in my cheeks about the color of a ripe raspberry. She was, of course, already gasping out laughter. "Sweetie, this door is like any other door. You pull it one direction, and push it the other. So, you have to push it from this side."

I mumbled an unintelligible response and pushed it open. Daylight hit me in the face, and I staggered out into the bright sunlight, all with her watching me with her shoulders shaking like a pneumatic drill. I walked over to my bicycle, grumbling about how a college should have bigger signs so you don't make a fool out of yourself when you try to open a door. I started to climb on my bicycle when I saw it. A parking ticket was sitting on my handlebars. In anguish, I looked at where I had parked my bicycle. Surely I couldn't have taken someone's spot! But, as I had predicted earlier, I had done what I thought I would never do. I had parked so haphazardly that my bicycle's kickstand had given out, and my bike had fallen against a fire hydrant. I must've been in such a hurry to get the delivery over with that I didn't realize where I had parked my bike. I shook my head as I looked at the ticket. I could understand a ticket for a car, but a bike? Really? This day was as rotten as fermented llama hair.

As I slowly pedaled away from the building, however, I began to see that it did have some good points in it, such as the fact that I was able to meet Carolyn Dirksen and that I wasn't chewed out for the donuts—if she noticed. She was a remarkable woman and very perseverant. You had to have perseverance if you worked at a college for 50 years!

Chapter Fifteen

I was tired, annoyed, and hungry. A beautiful combination that equals a grumpy teenager about to visit a construction site. My family had decided—without my input, I might add—to drive all the way up to Kentucky to visit my mom's brother for the weekend. He was into construction and promised to give us a tour while we were there. I don't know what got into my mom. Just out of the blue, she brought up the subject about a week ago, and, naturally, my grandmother agreed, seeing how she would be able to see both of her children together. I didn't know this uncle at all and didn't plan on getting too attached to him in the three days we were up there.

We had been in the van for over two hours without taking a stop, and I was getting restless. My sister, of course, had the privilege of sitting in the backseat by herself, meaning she had legroom, a place to take a nap, and the farthest spot from my mom. My grandmother was driving, and my mom was in the passenger seat, which meant if she wanted to start nagging me, she easily could. I looked out the window to try and gauge where we were. A sign about ten miles back read that we were in Rogersville, TN. I had no clue where that was, but it looked like one of those sweet towns that you read about in books. We passed multiple farms and barns, houses with cute trim, and even lakes—or ponds, to be exact. I pulled out my phone to see if I had any cellular coverage. Surprisingly, my phone found a connection within two minutes. I logged on to the Internet and searched for food places in this town. Of course, there was a McDonald's, a Burger King, and other fast food restaurants, but I wanted something unique. I had been complaining so much during the trip that my grandmother, to keep me quiet, told me that I could pick where we stopped to eat on the way up to Kentucky. I was pacified.

To make them suffer, I was going to choose the most expensive place to eat at with the longest wait time. I wanted to show them that when they forced me into a trip I didn't want to go on, there were consequences. As I was scrolling through places to eat, I finally decided on a grill place farther away from town. They were reluctant to eat there, but they had to stay true to their word. We turned onto the road that led to the restaurant and drove about 3 miles when suddenly the car sputtered, jerked, and promptly stopped. Of course, I was blamed. As if I had planned for the car to fail when we were finally going to get something to eat!

Since I was "the reason we had no way of making it to Kentucky before nightfall" and since our cell phones weren't getting a signal at the location where we were stranded, I was chosen to hike all the way back to town and get someone to help us. Needless to say, I didn't like their choice of gopher. I walked and walked, and two excruciating miles later, after not having passed a single gas station, I pulled out my phone and turned on locations, hoping that my phone could find a signal. Immediately, results popped up of multiple businesses around me—though where, I wasn't sure, since nothing around me resembled a store. Apparently, I was only three minutes from a cake shop! I quickened my pace, knowing that if I went there, I could get help for our car and maybe even order something sweet. I glanced at my phone occasionally as I drew closer to what appeared to be the place. There was a sign outside of a house that said, "Faith Baked Cakes." Just my luck. Running into a Christian way up here in Rogersville. With reluctance, I knocked on the screened door. A woman opened it up.

"May I help you?"

I nodded. "Hi, I'm Brie. My family's car broke down, and we need someone to help us get it started again. Also, what kind of desserts do you bake?"

She laughed at my sudden change of topic. "I do all sorts. And as for your car, I can call a guy to help you. He's a whiz with vehicles." She paused, considering something. "Why don't you come in and sit a spell while I call him? It may take a bit of time, depending on where he's at."

"Thank you," I said gratefully. "It would be lovely to rest my tired feet."

I stumbled through the doorway and found myself in something like a large kitchen. There were shelves lining the walls, multiple ovens, and all sorts of cake and cookie equipment and ingredients. She motioned for me to sit on a stool, which I did with a tired smile.

"I'm Shona House, by the way. Where are you headed?"

Without going into too much detail, I explained what had happened, finishing with, "And now they will hate me even more than normal because our 'vacation' was shortened a few hours."

She gave me a sympathetic look. "I'm sorry you're in this situation. On the bright side, though, God always makes good out of a bad situation!"

No. Please don't start preaching. I have just spent two hours with my grandmother in a closed vehicle. I have had all the preaching I need to last me a lifetime. "So you must be a Christian," I said with little enthusiasm.

"Yes, I am. Without God, I wouldn't own this shop, I wouldn't be where I am right now, and I might even be dead!"

Now I was definitely intrigued, despite my better judgment. "Why did you start the shop?"

She laughed outright. "Honey, are you sure you have time? We could be here for hours."

I checked the clock hanging on the wall, knew my family couldn't get any madder at me than they already were, and nodded. "If you're willing, I would love to hear it." Then I told her about my challenge and asked if she would be a part of it. I knew I was making a rash decision, but the week was about to end, and I sure wasn't going to find any Christians at my uncle's house! What's the worst that could happen? To my delight, she was more than willing to be one of my 52 godly women.

"Let me first go make that call to the mechanic," she said, "and then I will pour you something to drink. We may be here a while, and it's too hot in here to not have something to sip on."

When she returned, she was not only carrying a tall glass of homemade lemonade but also a mouth-watering grilled cheese sandwich. I thanked her profusely and dug in once she had said the blessing.

"I called the mechanic, and he is on his way to look at your car. Now we can talk. Let me start at the beginning. I knew I wanted to make cakes at the age of ten after one night's bingo game."

What in the world do bingo and cake have in common?

"While my family and I were playing bingo," she began, "a man walked out through a set of doors with the door prize of the night: a giant, five-tiered wedding cake. I was absolutely fascinated. Right then and there, I knew that was what I wanted to do. As a young child, I loved to go outdoors and make mud pies. As I got older, my siblings, cousins, and I would play restaurant, and I was always the chef. I think God placed those seeds in me at that early age because He knew the occupational path I would take."

God placed seeds in her? Was He a gardener? Did He also plant onions and tomatoes? I wanted to snort, but I knew that would be ungracious.

"As a 16 year old, I had my first opportunity to make a specialty cake. My maternal grandma, who was getting remarried after being widowed for several years, asked me if I would like to make her wedding cake. I was honored but also nervous because I had never done a wedding cake before. I asked the home economics director at my high school if she could teach me how to make a cake. With her guidance, I made a simple wedding cake: a white butter cake with blue roses."

So she now has experience. Okay, that's cool, but I figured the story would be a bit longer. I was right.

"Years passed. I had just married my husband, Eric, when I started gathering a lot of information on being a pastry chef. I wanted to attend baking classes in Chicago, but we didn't have the money for it. Because I really wanted to attend, I sold my car for $800, bought a ticket to Chicago, and spent three weeks learning master cake decorating and candy making. I was up at five in the morning and went to bed exhausted at eleven each night. Nevertheless, despite the crazy hours, I came home full of ideas. I was so excited that I started a cake shop downtown that had a constant flow of customers. I did that for two and a half years until my first son, Landon, was born, after which I became a stay-at-home mom. Twenty-two months later, Justin was born. I would do occasional cake jobs, but in general, I didn't do much baking to sell—not with two rambunctious boys to keep up with."

She took a sip of lemonade to quench her parched throat and then continued with her story. "Fast forward about fourteen years. Landon was in high school, and Eric had just been laid off his job as a supervisor at a glass plant. We started praying that God would give him the right job. One day, my family went to a get-together, and a guy randomly walked up to us and said that he knew someone who wanted to talk to Eric about a job offer. We prayed about it, and I felt that Eric would get the job."

Of course, that's the answer to every bad situation. Just pray about it, and your problems are magically solved. "So did he?" I questioned.

"He did. He was accepted as second-in-command at a glass plant in Laurinburg, North Carolina. He didn't even have a college education, but they took his experience over education. He lived in a camper in Laurinburg and drove back and forth for two years to visit and to see the kids' football games. The boys and I were going to move to North Carolina as soon as we saved the needed money, so I started making cakes again."

"About one month before Landon's graduation and our move to North Carolina, the guidance counselor at the boys' school had a dream about me—actually it was more like a vision. She told me, 'I dreamt you built a shop on the side of your house, and in it you baked cakes. You prayed for the people who ordered and received the cakes, and you put Bible verses on the boxes. You even had a person working for you. The name of the shop was Faith Baked Cakes.' I thanked her for sharing it with me and told her that I might do it when I moved to North Carolina. Finally, it was time for Landon's graduation and our move to North Carolina. The morning before the graduation, the school hosted a breakfast for the graduates and their families. Afterwards, Landon left for his graduation practice, and Eric, Justin, and I headed home on the highway, laughing and cutting up as we all sat buckled on the front bench seat of our truck. As we started passing a concrete truck, an elderly couple pulled out in front of the said truck."

Oh no. This didn't sound good.

"The truck driver slammed on his brakes and swerved, cutting us off. Eric veered our truck out of the way; and when the concrete truck returned to its own lane, I suggested we quickly pass the truck so it wouldn't hit us. I remember looking at the elderly couple as we also passed their vehicle, thinking that they could have been killed."

That was close. Three different vehicles and their occupants had been in serious danger.

Apparently Shona wasn't finished, though. "As we were switching lanes, our car began to fishtail. We began heading off the road where there was an embankment with fence posts on it. I remember thinking that we were going to mess up Eric's truck and take out the row of fence posts. I started to lean in to Justin to brace for the impact. I heard a big boom, and then there was silence."

Oh. My. Goodness. I don't know how her God will turn this bad situation into a good one, like she stated earlier that He would do.

"After that boom, there was another boom, and I was knocked silly. The first boom was our truck crashing into the fence post. The second boom was the truck landing on its top. Something had hit me hard in the face, but I wasn't knocked out. When I looked around me, it wasn't a pretty picture. Justin, unconscious, was hanging upside down by his seatbelt out the front of the truck. All I could see of Eric was his arm and leg. In front of me was the engine, pinning me in. Since I was the only one conscious, getting help rested on me. I started praying out loud, telling God that I needed help and that I needed the engine off me."

Like He's actually going to help you. Why would He help since He was the One who made you wreck in the first place? I shifted my position on the stool.

"I don't know how I escaped, but the next thing I knew, I was standing outside the truck. I immediately started hollering to Justin and Eric, trying to get a response from them. Neither would answer me. Saying a prayer for Justin and Eric, I ran towards the highway, trying to find help. I saw two women running towards me. The first woman was a school bus driver—same as I was—and the other woman was her daughter. I borrowed the woman's cell phone to call my mom and my brother-in-law, who was our youth pastor, to start the prayer chain. Apparently, I also called Landon and left a voicemail about the accident, although I don't remember calling him."

"The woman's daughter had already called an ambulance, which had arrived, so I went back to the site of the accident. The paramedics firmly grabbed me and forced me to sit down because I was messed up more than I knew. I was just running on adrenaline and God. Since they wouldn't let me up, I started praying. I probably sounded like a crazy woman, praying loudly and fighting all the help they tried to give me. Something in my heart said that Eric was gone, but I felt like I needed to pray for Justin. As I sat there praying, my vision suddenly started to leave. That really scared me, so I told God to please send someone I knew to help me. It wasn't two seconds later when I felt a tap on my shoulder. It was a friend whose extremely southern drawl was unmistakable."

Wow. I wish my life were that easy. Just snap my fingers and get whatever I wanted.

"The paramedics lifted me onto a stretcher and wheeled me into an ambulance to await one of the three helicopters that would transport us to the hospital. I kept asking about Justin and someone finally came up to me and said that Justin was moving. When I asked about Eric, though, no one would say anything other than that they were working on him. I kept praying and yelling and talking so much until the paramedic, fed up with my caterwauling, said, 'If you don't be quiet, I'm going to give you a shot to knock you out.' I was furious. I said, 'You're not going to give me a shot, and you're not going to knock me out. Instead, if I can climb out of this bed, I will find that shot and give that shot to you. I need to know about my family!'"

You tell them, Shona! I would want to know about my family, too, if I were in her position. That is, if I had a family I actually cared about.

"That kept him quiet for a while. However, as I was lying there, I heard them call off one of the helicopters. That was when I knew Eric was dead."

Oh man. I feel so badly for her, and her kids. I could relate to the death of a dad. Going through loss will forever have a grip on your soul. I took a slow, somber sip of my lemonade. The glass was almost empty.

"Despite my sadness, I was still praying for Justin as they wheeled me out to the helicopter. Being a mother, I wouldn't get in until Justin's helicopter took off. I braced my arms against the sides of the helicopter, not wanting to get in. They hit my arms until I had giant bruises on them. Finally, they were so mad at me that they gave me the knockout shot they had threatened me with earlier."

"I woke up in the hospital with my mom sitting next to me. She gave me an update on the accident, but she wouldn't say anything about Eric. About that time, a man wearing a turban-like hat walked over to me and said with a heavy accent, 'Can I pray for you?' I remember looking at him with a funny expression, and, under heavy medication, exclaimed, 'No! You can't pray for me because I don't pray to Allah.'"

I started laughing so hard. She did what? Shona joined in on the laughter.

"Afterwards, my pastor came in, and I immediately asked him about Eric. When he wouldn't tell me anything, I said, 'Look, I just want to know if he's okay—whether he's okay here or whether he's okay up in heaven. I can handle it.' He said Eric had passed away. I cried some, then asked about Justin. Just then, a doctor friend came in and said that he had taken over as Justin's doctor and that they were doing everything they could for Justin. However, Justin only had an 8% chance of survival. I prayed and prayed."

That's not going to help this time. You should have figured that out, seeing how God allowed your husband to die.

"By now, Landon had arrived at the hospital. He was doing okay—considering how his family had just been in a car accident, his dad was dead, his brother may die, and all the day before his graduation. Not to mention I was being stubborn and wouldn't let them operate or scan me until I saw Justin. Seeing how I was set in my ways, they put me in a wheelchair and took me to him. Justin looked horrible. There were tubes running out of him, and there was blood all over the place. His lungs and kidneys were punctured, he had ruptured his spleen, and there were 390 stitches all over him. If he hadn't had braces on, he would've lost his teeth. The doctors said he shouldn't have lived, but because Eric's elbow had hit Justin's head during the accident, Justin went unconscious, making him go limp and thus decreasing his injuries. I went to his bedside. I told everybody to pray. We started begging God to save him. By the time I said, 'Amen,' Justin was moving."

No way. That's absolutely impossible! But one look at her face told me that she was telling the truth. It was incredible.

"I said that was all I needed to do, so the nurse wheeled me back to my room and the doctors prepared to examine me to see what injuries I had. The next morning I awoke to comforting news: Justin had made it through the night. With my fears settled, I told Landon it was time for him to graduate. Landon said that he was not going to his graduation, but I told him that he was most assuredly going to his graduation and that I was going, too. Of course, everyone was opposed to the idea. They said that all sorts of stuff could be wrong with me. I reassured them that I would return and that they could finish all their tests. They still were adamant that I couldn't go. Angrily, I exclaimed, 'I'm going. I have to see my son graduate.' They had no choice but to let me go."

"A friend drove Landon to the graduation, and my sister came to take me to the graduation. As I was leaving, the doctors gave me scrubs and shoe cover-ups to wear because my clothes were covered in blood. I urged my sister to drive as fast as she could—Landon was graduating in fifteen minutes and we were forty minutes away. I called the school to move Landon to the end of the line so I could see him graduate. As I was wheeled into the gymnasium, Landon was about to walk across the stage. I sat there proud of Landon as his name was called."

Just in time, huh?

"Then something amazing happened. Everybody in the gym stood up and started clapping for him as he received his diploma. So many people were crying—even the principal was crying. After Landon walked across the stage, I gave him a giant hug. We had just showed the whole town that it doesn't matter what happens in life. God will never leave us. He still has a plan and is in control of everything. God is real."

Maybe to you. I know He isn't to me. I used to hold onto that false hope, but I learned the hard way that some things aren't meant to be.

"I returned to the hospital, like I had promised. While I was gone, Justin had woken up and had pulled the tube out of his throat—he was a lot like me. He wanted to know where everyone was. They had to give him a shot to make him calm down. We had to postpone the funeral because Justin was still unstable, but then one week later, he came home. A week! He had an eight percent chance of living, and he came home after one week in the hospital. If that wasn't the Lord, then I don't know what it was."

There has to be a reasonable explanation for it besides the supernatural. My guess is a really good hospital staff.

"Once Justin was home, we started planning for Eric's funeral. I said that we weren't going to have a depressing, sad, weepy funeral. When a Christian dies, you know where they go. God isn't some made up, mysterious person sitting in the clouds somewhere. He's real."

Will she stop the "He's real" business? You can't see Him or touch Him or hear Him, so how can He be real?

"My brother-in-law officiated the funeral, and it wasn't that sad, considering everything—we even sang 'Happy Song Hymn.' People came from everywhere for his funeral. Eric's entire shift from the North Carolina glass plant came. It took over 6 hours for the people to walk through the receiving line. Despite the circumstances, I still believed that nothing bad happens without God turning it into something great."

"The next week I was at home, not knowing what I was going to do. I thought, 'I'm about to lose the house. We're going to have to live in a tent, and we will have to hunt and fish.' So I prayed, talking to God like I would anybody else. As I prayed, I heard these words, 'Remember the dream.' I told God, 'The dream was meant for North Carolina, and we never went.' He said, 'Remember the dream.' I told God, 'I have no money to build a cake shop onto the side of my house.' He said, 'Remember the dream.' I was pretty frustrated."

I understood. I have had to deal with the same sort of repetition, only it was from my grandmother.

"Then one day I was sitting at the dining room table feeling sorry for myself, when my father-in-law came in crying. I froze; I couldn't handle any more bad news. But it was just the opposite. He had received a letter from Eric's workplace informing him that Eric had had life insurance. I couldn't believe it. He wasn't there long enough to even have life insurance. It dawned on me that God was taking care of us. I ran up to the cemetery where Eric was buried and praised God. When I came back, I thought about what to do with the money. I ended up paying off the house and the cars and then put money aside for Justin and Landon to attend college. There was still $23,000 left. And, of course, I kept hearing, 'Remember the dream.' So I said to God, 'Tell me how to do it. There is not enough money left to build a shop, buy equipment, and purchase ingredients. Yet, what I have left, I will give to you.'"

"I stepped out in faith. I paid a company to dig the footers and lay the foundation. Then people started showing up from all over the place, people I hardly knew, to volunteer their labor. People also donated things—like windows and doors. Finally, the shop was built, with about $5,000 still left. I didn't install air conditioning or heat because that would've taken most of the remaining money. Instead, my three sisters-in-law bought me a window air conditioning unit, and I bought a small heater."

"Now I had to get all the equipment. I asked God how I was going to get really good-quality equipment for $5,000—a good freezer alone costs $40,000. Just then, my sister called. She had a friend who owned a catering shop who was going out of business. She wanted to give me a deal, so I needed to drive up and meet her. I told my sister that I wasn't going to meet her because it was still going to be way too expensive for me to afford."

Sure it was. No one would just give away good equipment.

"She became so frustrated with me. She said, 'Shona, you need to put on your big girl panties and get up here!' Feeling sorry for myself, I went. The friend had a lot of expensive equipment that she was getting rid of, but it was highly unlikely that she would sell it all for under $35,000. To my amazement, she said that the Lord had told her to give me a deal. Still having a bad attitude, I mockingly asked what the Lord had said to sell it to me for. She said, 'The Lord said to sell all of this to you for $1,500.' You could've knocked me down with a feather. I started writing that check as fast as I could make my hand move before she changed her mind. Then I thanked the Lord. As always, He was taking care of me despite my doubts."

Hmm. I'm still skeptical. I bet the woman just used God's name so she could attach a giant string to the deal and have Shona forever indebted to her.

"After that, my faith starting growing, with John 14:1-6 really reminding me that God was the Way, not me. I had the majority of the equipment that I needed except for the ovens, so I asked the Lord for a bunch of ovens. Just then, I heard a knock on the door. Standing there were three friends that said they each wanted to buy an oven in Eric's memory. It was truly a blessing. Now I had everything ready for the health inspector. He didn't like the fact that I didn't have a bathroom in the shop, even though I had a bathroom three feet from the shop inside my house."

Yep. You have to have everything to the letter or else you're in big trouble.

"He talked to someone over the phone, however, and they decided that I could open up. I was ecstatic. It was all falling into place! I went to the courthouse and bought my license. When questioned about the name, I answered, 'Faith Baked Cakes'—I couldn't name it anything but what was in the dream. Since opening my shop seven years ago, I have met all sorts of people, talked in churches, and have been on food shows. I'm also able to share Jesus with others because of it. When I have food left over from an order, I'll take it to the sick. When people order a cake for a sick child, I'll do it for free. I want to give back with this business since God has given me so much. He has given me encouragement, physical items, and lots of ideas. He also gave me a worker, like the dream indicated. It was a friend named Lee who caught the cake-making fever one morning at 2:30 as he graciously helped me fill orders. He was the one who also encouraged me to take the University of Tennessee 12-week culinary program, and because of that program, I'm able to include catering in the services I provide."

Lee seems like a good friend to her. Wonder what it feels like. "Your shop seems to be doing exceptionally well, despite the trauma you went through," I commented. "How have your boys done since the accident?"

"Both boys attended college and were cheerleaders."

"Cheerleaders?" I exclaimed. "I sure didn't expect that!"

Laughing, Shona explained. "When the boys were born, I had a friend who taught tumbling at the same place I taught baton twirling. I had been a majorette in college, so I used my skill to provide some income. Remember, any talent you have you can use to provide some income. Anyway, the boys would go with me sometimes and watch the tumbling class. One morning while Eric was at work, Landon, who was five years old at the time, ran down the steps and told me to watch him. As I stood there, he jumped and did a perfect back tuck."

Whoa. That's really impressive. A five-year-old boy doing a back tuck?

"I told him to do it again. He did it again and again. I asked him who taught him to do that. He said that no one did; he just watched the cheerleaders doing it and then copied them. I showed Sarah, the tumbling coach, and she was so excited that she asked if the boys could be on the cheer team. I said, 'Uh, my boys aren't going to be cheerleaders. Eric won't allow it.' She said that all they would do would be the tumbling. If I would let the boys be on the team, there would be no charge for lessons."

"As I predicted, Eric was completely against it. I asked him if we could just watch one of the competitions, and he agreed to that. At the competition, we were both blown away with the kids doing flips all over the place. After seeing that, Eric agreed that they could tumble, and they tumbled from then on."

"When Landon applied to the University of Tennessee, he decided to try out for their cheerleading squad. Not only did he make it, but he also received a full ride to UT for cheerleading. Justin received a full ride to Emory and Henry, but it was for football. However, Justin didn't like the college because it went against his values, so he decided to transfer to UT. I told him that he was about to throw away a full ride, but he countered my protests with, 'Don't you always tell us to do what we feel God is telling us to do?'"

Ooh. Turning the words right back around at her.

"Justin filled out the application forms for UT but then learned that they were full. So we started praying. One week later, he received a letter that said he had been accepted at UT. He also tried out for and made the cheerleading squad, receiving almost a full ride. Landon graduated in 2015, and Justin graduated May 2017. They now work as event coordinators for cheer squads, and they can do any kind of flip you could think of. We all don't have the same talents—I bake, my sons flip, and my friend can fix any car. God has a purpose for each one of our lives, and He puts ideas in our minds for a reason. If you want to be a godly woman, you need to stay close to God and honor God first before taking care of your husband and family. Many things come our way in life that we have no clue about, and it's best to be as close to God as possible."

Uh-huh. I've heard all this purpose talk before. It's strange, though, to think that she would still believe in her God after all He put her through. I happened to glance at the clock above her head.

"Oh no! My family is going to kill me! It's been almost two hours."

She stood up quickly and threw me a worried look. "I hope you won't be in too much trouble. Let me send some cookies with you; maybe your family will forgive you easier."

"Thank you so much! I enjoyed hearing your story."

She smiled and held the door open for me so I could carry the cookies out. "You are welcome to come back any time." I waved at her as I walked down her gravel driveway. Shona House was a remarkable woman. She had been through so much and was still very encouraging and happy. I thought about her as I walked toward where the car had broken down. When I finally saw it in the distance, I noticed a mechanic shutting the hood of our car and wiping his greasy hands on an already greasy rag. I breathed a sigh of relief. Just in time. I held up the cookies with a fake smile, hoping they would forget that I had been gone way too long when they tasted these scrumptious treats. They did seem to soften at the sight of them. Whatever punishment I received, though, would be worth my meeting with Shona. She was really outspoken about her God and all the things He had done for her. It did seem like many of her prayers had been answered, but perhaps that was because God only listens to saintly people. I think I will be able to endure Kentucky a bit better because of meeting with Shona. Just a bit, though. I'm definitely not coming home with any grass, blue or otherwise.

Chapter Sixteen

"I want you to come! If you say no, you'll hurt my feelings," Tina said with a slight pout. It was a Wednesday morning, and already I was feeling like I had been run over by a train. A train named Tina, who had begged me all week to go with her to some Christian event tonight called Fields of Faith, hosted by Fellowship of Christian Athletes. Fields of Faith—what a perfect name for an event where you meet at a high school football stadium and talk about God. How cliché.

"I already gave you my answer, Tina. I'm not going to waste my time listening to some preacher."

Tina frowned. "He isn't 'some preacher.' He has spoken all over the country in schools and in other places."

I sighed and started walking towards class. "There won't be anything in it for me, though. I'll just have to sit there as he rambles on about stuff I've already heard from my 52 godly women."

Tina smiled slyly. "Speaking of that, whom did you meet with this week?"

I rolled my eyes. "No one yet. But don't worry. I'm sure I will have found someone by the end of the week."

She laughed knowingly. "Maybe so, but I can guarantee that you could meet with someone today and get it over with, if you go to the convention."

Now she had my attention, which I'm sure was her plan all along. "How? Did you set up another meeting for me?"

She found the tops of her shoes very interesting all of a sudden.

"You did, didn't you? Well, let me tell you something; you'll have to cancel. I'm. Not. Going." With that, I flounced away to class. She needed to learn to keep her nose where it belonged. Out of my business. I'm sure I will find a woman to meet with this week. Don't I always?

After school, I was waiting for the school bus when I heard someone behind me calling my name. It was Tina, again.

"Just hear me out. I know you don't want to go, but I know you won't regret it if you do. This woman is in charge of running tonight's event, so if you meet with her, you'd get a behind-the-scenes peek at running a big event."

"Why do you want me to go so much? I'm an atheist. I'm not going to be 'reformed' or anything, and you know that. Why would you try so hard to get me to go to some random event I wouldn't like?"

She shrugged. "I guess I figured you would like to meet this woman. She's amazing and funny. Have I ever set you up with someone terrible?"

I had to admit that she had me there. I didn't want to do this at all, but it would be better than waiting until Saturday to hook up with someone. With a huge sigh, I looked at her. "I'll do it." She started squealing, but I cut her off. "However, you owe me big time."

She sort of waved it away. "I know, I know. I can send you a batch of cookies or something later."

Cookies, my foot—I knew as well as she did that I wouldn't get any cookies from her.

As I walked into my house, I regretted having sigreed to go tonight. At least Tina had the sense to tell me the woman's name, Teresa Green. I didn't know what she looked like though. I was supposed to meet her downtown, so lots of things could go wrong—like being kidnapped by someone I thought was Teresa Green but really wasn't. Or what if she didn't really want to meet with me, and her half-hearted, "Yes," was over-exaggerated by Tina when she told me, "She is looking forward to meeting you with great joy." I'm always so nervous whenever I don't plan the meeting. I changed into a presentable outfit and made sure my phone was 100% charged—I might need it to block out all the false and crazy ideas that would inevitably be proposed tonight.

Once I was ready, I walked down the stairs into the living room and asked my grandmother for a ride downtown. Of course, she was instantly suspicious of why, and I told her—discreetly, of course—that I was going to help out at Fields of Faith. She sort of sniffed at me, obviously disappointed that I wasn't trying to get into trouble. She didn't seem excited at all that I was "reforming." Just another example of how she doesn't really care about me after all; however, I had figured that out many years ago the moment I met her. She was too consumed with Kimberly to notice little me. Even now, she has a hard time realizing that she does, in fact, have another granddaughter.

She grumpily pushed herself off the couch and pulled on some shoes. I walked out to the car and hopped inside. I was rather happy to be escaping the house for most of the night. My grandmother drove the fifteen minutes into town, where she dropped me off in front of a large building. She smiled patronizingly at me.

"I will pick you up whenever you call. If you're out too late, though, I will have retired, and you will need to call your sister to come pick you up."

Ha. Like I would do that. Even if I were in Chicago at midnight, not knowing a soul, and the only phone number I had was my sister's, I wouldn't call her. If I did, she would pick me up and then lecture me all the way home about all the things she could have been doing instead of having to drive her poor sister from her unfortunate situation. Then she would turn around and tell all her friends about how she graciously helped me out. Not to mention the fact that she would never let me forget it and would always use it as blackmail. Nope. I'd rather walk home if the event went too long.

I waved goodbye to my grandmother, turned around, and walked toward the large building that was supposedly Teresa's workplace. I hesitantly walked through the glass double doors. My eyes adjusted to the light inside, and I looked around at the sweet, charming place. However, I had no clue where to go. Just then, I heard footsteps coming. I cringed slightly, hoping I wasn't in trouble. A woman rounded the corner in front of me and smiled.

"Are you Tina's friend?

"Yes ma'am, I am. Would you happen to be Teresa Green?" I asked gingerly, remembering the time I thought the school counselor was Jennifer Browning. That was such an awkward moment, and I didn't want to repeat it.

"That would be me. When Tina told me about your challenge and asked if I would be a part of it, I was ecstatic! I couldn't wait to meet you." She looked at me carefully. "Tina said you are an atheist. Is that right?"

I nodded. I couldn't figure out why Tina kept telling people I was an atheist when she knew it bothered me. Yet, why did it bother me so much to admit that I didn't believe in their "precious" faith? Why should I care if people look down on me for not believing there's a God?

"That's correct. Sometimes I wonder why I ever let her talk me into this challenge."

She smiled. "Well, Tina has her ways. She could talk a hard-lucked fellow into giving her his last penny. She just has the right words at the right time, and before you know it, you have just agreed to something you never in a million years would've thought you'd be doing."

I had to laugh. She was completely correct. Teresa then motioned for me to follow her as she punched in a security number into a box next to a door that led to a staircase. Once it opened, we walked up the flight of stairs to the second level. As we climbed, she gave me some background about the building.

"This used to be the Princess Theater. It was a beautiful spot in Cleveland where people from all over the area would come to see movies." We opened the door to the next level and walked through a reception area of couch clusters and small tables. She then took me past a few offices before stopping in front of a large picture. It was of Jimmy Stewart standing in front of a very cute theater. On closer inspection, I realized that it was the Princess Theater. We moved from the picture to her office, where I noticed an FCA emblem on her door as I accepted one of the chairs offered to me.

"I am not very familiar with your challenge," Teresa said as she sat behind her desk. "Could you fill me in on it?"

I silently groaned. Please no. I didn't want to talk about me right now. Regardless, I started explaining about it. I finished by saying that the woman I meet with tells me a lot about herself, hinting that she could talk now.

She took the bait and started. "Well, let me tell you a bit about myself and my husband. I love serving people, and my husband and I were youth pastors for most of our marriage."

"When did you get married?" I asked. The real question was, "How long have you had to suffer through the torture of preaching to kids?" I didn't say the latter out loud, of course.

"I married Robert Green when I turned 18. My mom was a prayer warrior, and she prayed for us all the time. I learned a phrase from her that I have carried throughout my life: 'Take what you have and turn it into something you need or want.' People are usually not content with what they have, so whenever I don't like what I have, I try to remember that phrase and be resourceful with what I have. We moved to Cleveland twenty years ago, first living in an apartment and then later moving into a house. I was discontented with the house. I had to remember that phrase a lot, and eventually I turned my house into what I wanted it to look like. It now has an Irish theme because I visited Ireland a while ago and absolutely loved it."

"Have you been to any other countries?" I asked.

She smiled. "Lots. I've been to Canada, Brazil, Paraguay, Mexico, Dominican Republic, Bahamas, and Honduras. When Robert went to Honduras one year, he met a little two-year-old named Junior that he fell in love with. When he first met the boy, Junior was wearing a Florida Gators shirt. Robert is a huge fan of the Gators, and he was drawn to the kid. The next year, he went back to Honduras and saw the kid again. We decided to sponsor him and his brother because even though he was only two when he met Robert, he still remembered him a year later."

"That's cool. I've always wanted to travel. Maybe I can hide in your trunk when you go on your next trip." I smiled nervously, hoping she would think it was funny.

To my relief, she laughed. "That would be cool. However, I think that the security guards would catch you before you were carted into the belly of the plane."

She was right, of course. "So was Robert a youth pastor when you got married?"

"No. For the first six months of our marriage, Robert had a secular job; however, he wasn't happy there so he went into the ministry."

Willingly? He left a perfectly good job to tell people about a pretend character? What sort of a person would do that? It's not like ministers make a lot of money.

"Robert and I moved to Florida in 1988 and started evangelizing. We were offered a youth pastorate in Marianna, FL, so we moved there. After two years, we went to Winterhaven, FL, to be youth pastors for the next four years. Both our daughters were born there, and I became a stay-at-home mom for the next thirteen years. Despite the joy of having two beautiful daughters, the church was having some problems. A stranger had come to our church, and with his corrupt talk and ideas, he destroyed the church in six months. We were so upset that we left, going to Pensacola for a six-month job offer that turned into two years. But we were restless, so we started looking for new opportunities, and we came across a job opening in Tennessee for the North Cleveland Church of God. While we were there for the job interview, my mom, who lived in Cleveland, found out that she had breast cancer. I was so glad we got the job because I was able to spend the extra time with her. She died soon afterwards."

I gasped. At least she was in the area so she could be with her mom before she passed away. I don't know what I would've done if I had been out of town when my dad died.

"I was upset, but Psalm 139 reminded me that God knows when I sit and when I rise. He knows my thoughts before I know them, and He follows me wherever I go. We kept youth pastoring at North Cleveland until we found a spot open at Westmore Church of God. We took the position and stayed there for 13 years. God really blessed our efforts as we taught those teenagers to love the Lord, love the Word, and pray, qualities that I believe signify a godly person. The result was that the youth group increased from 75 to 300."

That many kids wanted to go to church? Who raised them, Martin Luther? I couldn't imagine ever wanting to go to church, having to sit for hours listening to some man yell fire and brimstone at you. It's definitely not my cup of tea.

"Has it always been easy pastoring?" I asked. If she worked with kids, it couldn't have been that hard. I know that I'm not too hard to deal with.

"Definitely not."

Whoa. Wasn't expecting that.

"I made some terrible decisions during the middle of my life. When Robert and I were working at Westmore as youth pastors, I had an affair with the children's pastor. It was a horrible time, but I am a better person today because of what happened, so I wouldn't change it. We had to step down from our position as youth pastors; however, despite the hurt that it caused, I decided that I wouldn't let one bad year out of 39 define who I was. I learned an important lesson during that time: your friends may stay with you through the good times, but the only one who will stay with you through the good and bad times is Jesus. My husband and I never divorced; he chose to stay with me despite the choices I had made and through the terrible times that ensued. As a result, Robert and I renewed our marriage vows on our 20th wedding anniversary."

What a way to show that no matter what your spouse does to you, your love overpowers everything else! What unconditional love.

She continued speaking. "One thing I learned through the ordeal is that a church should require all its staff members and their spouses to attend marriage counseling to make sure their marriage is doing well. Just because people have a position in a church does not mean that their marriage is absolutely perfect. I would also like the same requirements to be implemented here for the FCA staff."

Just then, she glanced at her phone. "Oh boy, we'd better get moving if we want to start setting up for Fields of Faith."

I silently prepared myself. I had no clue what would happen tonight, but I was going to bear it all with a smile. She handed me a box of pens and asked if I would go through them and make sure they all worked.

"At the end of service, we will have an altar call for people to either accept Christ or rededicate their lives to Him. We will have papers on which they can write which decision they've made."

These people are crazy! Why would they rededicate themselves to a fake person? Why not just un-dedicate? That would be what I would do if I were in their shoes. Despite my thoughts, I started sorting through the pens. She had given me a piece of paper to write on, so I checked the pens on it before tossing them in either the good pile or the bad pile.

Once that was done, we gathered together all the items she would need tonight and headed to her car. She drove to Bradley High School and parked the car by the football stadium. We then unloaded most of the items. We left a "Fields of Faith" sign in the trunk that needed to be put up as well as boxes of foam hands. My job was to write "FCA" on all the hands. There were five boxes of them, but I wasn't discouraged. I was glad for the simple job; I had expected something harder. By the time I got done, more and more kids were being dropped off and some pavilions were being set up. I started walking around to see what people were advertising, and I wanted to see if I recognized any kids from school—so I could steer clear of them. No way did I want word to get out that the adamant atheist was at a Christian event. I had walked about ten steps when someone came rushing up behind me. Startled, I turned around and saw Tina.

"I can't believe you're actually here," she squealed. "I thought it was a dream when you agreed to meet with Teresa today!"

"So did I," I muttered as she skipped away. "So did I." I walked around a little more before returning to Teresa's car. I had seen a few people I knew from school, but most of the students were strangers. Fortunately, she was still there, talking to some important-looking people.

She turned to me. "I will be down on the field for most of the night, so you can sit with one of your friends, and then afterwards I will meet you here to take you home."

Good. That solves the problem about calling my grandmother. Wait, what friends? Did she seriously assume that I, an atheist, would have friends at this Christian event? Oh yeah. Tina, the one who coordinated my meeting with Teresa. Likely, though, I won't be able to find her in this crowd. The dilemma was solved when Tina came running up behind me and asked if I would sit with her. I agreed because I would be lost in the sea of people if she wasn't with me. She led me to a section in the bleachers where I saw some people from school, like Jennifer Browning's daughter Abby. I could tell that most of them were shocked that I was there. I knew this would be the talk of school tomorrow. I was going to have to lie low. Maybe I could fake bronchitis. Averting my eyes from all those staring at me, I looked down on the field and saw a makeshift stage on the fifty-yard line. I wondered how well I would be able to see. Not that it mattered.

Just then, the service started. Of course, they played songs that I didn't know, but they were all essentially the same with the same cliché Christian lyrics. "Your love is so mighty, your grace is so marvelous," so on and so forth. I was bored halfway through song number one. The people around me seemed to be taking it in, though. There were a bunch of them raising their hands. I wanted to escape. Finally, and not a moment too soon, the songs ended, and a guy walked on the stage. He started talking, and I sort of halfway listened. He had apparently spoken at a lot of schools before tonight, and most of the kids seemed to really connect with what he was saying. Me? I was ready to go. There were a few things that caught my attention, such as the fact that his mom was an alcoholic as well. The rest of what he said was just the expected Christian lies like, "God is real," "He'll never leave you," and "He is a good God." Unbelievable things like that.

A while later, he ended his message and had an altar call—the one that I helped prepare for. A few of the people around me went down to the field. It shocked me the number of kids who actually cared enough about a pretense God to risk public humiliation. After they prayed, the speaker told everyone to come down to the field to pray. Everyone didn't include me, did it? However, I didn't have a choice in the matter as Tina, sensing my hesitation, grabbed my arm tightly and led me down to the field with her. I was fuming. No one should be bossing me around. I had a right to either go down or not. It's a free country! A minute later, I was on the field and everyone was grabbing hands. I was reluctant to hold anybody's hand, but I had to. After he prayed, everyone started dispersing. I got out of there as fast as my legs would take me. I arrived breathlessly at Teresa's car, and ten minutes or so later, Teresa met me there.

"What did you think?" She looked expectant.

I didn't want to burst her bubble, but I also didn't want to lie while at a Christian convention—I think Christians can sniff out deception a mile away.

Then a light came on in her eyes. "Oh, I forgot that you're an atheist. Well, we'd better get in the car if you want to make it home by 9:00."

I looked at my phone. Surprised that it was so late, I grabbed my things and jumped in her car. The trip back to my house was fairly pleasant. She made small talk, not referring to the event again. In my mind, she went up in rank because she didn't try to beat me over the head with a Bible or try to find out what convicted me tonight. I was mostly just relieved that the day was over. When she dropped me off, I thanked her for a great day and walked inside.

Once in my bedroom, I collapsed into my chair. The day had been tiring but fun. Teresa didn't shove her religion down my throat, and I had a great time learning the ropes. I was glad Tina had set us up—though I would never admit that to Tina. No need for her to get on her high horse. For the next woman I meet with, I want to do it on my own terms. I know that Tina tried to get me to that event tonight just so maybe I would "convert." She should have known better.

Chapter Seventeen

I had promised myself last week that I would find my next 52 godly woman, but so far I was getting nowhere. I had gotten a lead on one, but when I contacted her, she wasn't available. I had brainstormed for hours but hadn't thought of anyone else. I was desperate. To try and clear my head, I decided to go for a walk. Making sure that Thunder didn't follow me, so we wouldn't have a cat-astrophe like last time, I opened the door slightly and stepped out into the cool air, quickly shutting the door behind me. It was nearly fall, and the leaves were starting to drop from the trees. I had worn a t-shirt today, and I had forgotten to bring a coat, so I was freezing my tail off already. After walking for three minutes with icicles hanging off my nose and no ideas, I heard a car behind me. I moved further off the side of the road so it could pass, but to my surprise it slowed down until it was coasting beside me. The window rolled down, and a woman in the driver's seat smiled at me worriedly.

"Sweetie, do you need a ride somewhere? You don't have a coat in this cool weather, and I don't want you to freeze."

I smiled, touched that this stranger would be considerate enough to offer a ride to a random girl. She couldn't do anything about me freezing, though. I was already a snowman. I almost said no, then something inside said I should take the offered ride. I thanked the woman and asked if she could take me to a friend's house that was located next to Walmart. The friend, of course, was Tina, and I had reluctantly decided to ask her for suggestions about whom to meet with next, seeing how I wasn't very productive with ideas.

The woman made small talk with me as we rode along. Once we got to where Tina lived, however, she stared at me. "You know Tina?"

I said, "Yes ma'am."

Her eyes widened slightly. "Are you an atheist?"

I said, "Yes ma'am."

Her eyes widened even more. "Do you go to KMS?"

I said, "Yes ma'am."

Her eyes were very wide now. "You're Brie, aren't you? The one doing the challenge!"

Tina! That girl thought she could tell every living stranger about what I was doing. When would she learn not to give out information to people? I slowly nodded.

She smiled at me. "I heard about it from Tina and absolutely loved the idea!"

Suddenly I got an idea. "Would you be one of my godly women for this?" I assumed since Tina told her about the challenge, she must be a Christian.

She smiled wide. "I would be honored if I could be a part of it! I'm Ashley Waldrop, by the way. I'm the youth pastor's wife at the church Tina attends."

Ah. What a coincidence. Who would have thought that I would just happen to be taking a walk at the same time Tina's youth pastor's wife would be driving in my neighborhood. We decided that after she dropped me off at home and I grabbed a few things—like a coat—she would pick me up later and take me to lunch so we could talk. Lunch was an hour away, however, so I had time to gather my thoughts. As crazy as it might seem, it was almost as if Tina had planned all this. What are the chances of something like this happening? Very slim, I can tell you that.

When Ashley came back to pick me up, I had on much warmer clothes and was mentally prepared. I didn't know what to expect from a youth pastor's wife. Would I be preached at or loved? She drove to Dos Bros and parked. I noticed she had some sort of package with her. Of course, I was curious. Was she taking me to a birthday party?

When we walked through the doors of the restaurant, there were very few people eating in the dining area, and I didn't recognize anyone, so I decided that it wasn't a birthday party. Once we had ordered, we filled our glasses with beverages: hers with tea, mine with a soda suicide. As we waited for our number to be called for our food, I asked her about herself.

"I guess I'll just start at the beginning. As I told you, I'm a youth pastor's wife. My job, though, is being my husband Jared's helpmate in youth pastoring—I'm not hired by the church to work for them, but I help all I can."

Just then, our food came. I stared hungrily at the delicious quesadilla placed before me. Ashley said a prayer, and then we started digging into our food. The food was absolutely amazing.

"I love Mexican food," I said. "I've always wanted to know who was the first person to invent it. By doing that, I'd probably need a time machine, though, which doesn't exist. If you had a time machine, where would you go in history?"

"I would travel back to biblical times and talk to Esther because Esther had great courage. I would also like to talk to the woman described in John chapter 8 who was caught in the very act of adultery. The religious leaders wanted to stone her, but Jesus told them that he who was without sin should cast the first stone. Of course, they were all sinners, so they couldn't stone her. Jesus was the only one without sin, but He didn't condemn her. Instead, He told her to go and sin no more. She was shown grace and mercy by Jesus."

What? Jesus was "without sin" and had the power to tell people to leave a sinner alone? That reminds me of what the speaker talked about at Fields of Faith, how Jesus didn't have any sin. He didn't cheat on tests, say any little white lies, or even use His sleeve to wipe His nose! Well, the speaker didn't say all that, but I got the point. What would it be like to have never done anything wrong, or like the woman in John 8, to be freed from guilt over wrongs you have done? Hold up. What am I thinking? This is taking me down a road I wasn't wanting or planning.

She didn't seem to see that I was struggling inwardly. Instead, she went back to the topic we were discussing before she talked about a "sinless" Jesus. "That's who I would talk to, but if I could go to see any place in history, I would choose to see the time of the Revolutionary War because I love old history like that."

By now, we were both full but not quite finished with our food so we requested doggy bags for our leftovers. She seemed to be thinking about something and then determinedly reached under the mahogany-colored table. Confused, I started to look under the table to see if she had dropped something. Smiling mysteriously, she placed on the table the pink gift bag I had seen earlier in the car.

"I wanted to get you this. I saw it in the store the other day and knew it would be perfect to help someone remember important qualities."

I was too shocked to respond. I had just met this woman and she bought me a present? What sort of person would do that? A kind-hearted one, I can tell you that. I pulled the white tissue paper off the top of the bag and peered inside. I put my hand inside and brought out a beautiful necklace and a journal. Speechless, I just looked at it. The necklace had a rectangular pendant hanging from it that had words on each of the four sides: "I am loved," "I am strong," "I am worthy," "I am enough." Also hanging from the necklace was a small, purple butterfly and a circular, golden pendant which read, "Beautiful." I stared at her.

"I cannot believe you did this for me. This is incredible. Thank you so much!"

She just smiled. "The journal is so you can write your thoughts on paper to sort them out. It's like venting to a friend, but it won't take things personally or tell anyone." She chuckled.

I immediately unclasped the necklace and put it around my neck. It felt like it belonged there. I knew I would wear it all the time. I still couldn't get over the fact that she had bought me something so beautiful.

We stood up and threw our trash away. I refilled my drink, and we exited the restaurant, with leftovers in tow, to climb into her car. She turned on the car and looked at me.

"Do you paint?"

I stared blankly at her. "I'm not an artist, but I can at least hold a paintbrush the correct way. I think."

She laughed. "Great. I thought about taking you to a local art place to paint. The woman who owns it has pottery and canvases that you can paint on."

This was too much. "Why would you do these generous things? I have no way of repaying your kindness."

She shook her head. "It's a gift. If I want to be a godly woman, I have to have the right qualities. And to me, the qualities of a godly woman are being meek, having security in the Lord, knowing who I am in the Lord, and having the fruit of the Spirit. In order to have the fruit of the Spirit, I must practice them daily. So this is my way of showing love, kindness, and goodness, three of the fruits of the Spirit."

We rode to the art shop in a comfortable silence. When we pulled into the parking lot, I saw what it was called—The Clayful Artist. If it were as adorable as its name, it was bound to be a cute shop. We walked into the shop and were greeted by a woman wearing a smock.

"Hello, my name's Nikki. What would you like to paint today? We have canvas sizes and prices on this wall,"—here she gestured to a wall beside her—"and pottery on this wall." Now she turned to point at shelves with white pottery. "Once you have decided what to paint, I want to explain some basic directions for the paint, okay?"

We agreed, so she went to the back of the shop and left us to look around. I decided to do a piece of pottery because I knew I would be better at painting if I had some guidelines to paint on. As I examined the pieces, I realized how hard it was going to be to pick out a piece of pottery. She had so many diverse, adorable options. Fifteen minutes later, I finally decided on a vase. Ashley chose a Christmas spoon rest, and we called for Nikki. She gave us a little talk about what the paint would look like once it came out of the kiln, which I learned was like an oven for pottery to make it smooth and shiny.

We started painting. It was very relaxing and soothing to the soul. I was subconsciously listening to the music in the background when a song came on that started talking about trouble and how trouble is resolved. Ashley, seeming to know the song, started singing. I said, "I bet you never got in trouble, being a pastor's wife and all."

"Actually, I once got into a lot of trouble. When I was in high school, living in a small town outside of Charlotte, North Carolina, my dad was a full-time pastor. Two weeks before my birthday, he was chosen to be the state youth director. That was a hard time for me because my identity had been in being a pastor's daughter and attending youth group all the time. After his job change, however, he travelled all the time to preach, and we had to travel with him. I no longer had a home church or a youth group to call my own. In tenth grade, struggling with who I was, I hung out with the wrong people who didn't make good choices. I began talking like them, and I eventually strayed from the Lord."

That doesn't seem too bad. Finally coming to her senses about God, making friends with people who weren't exactly perfect, and not talking quite as holy? Not the worst that she could have done. Did her parents actually punish her for that?

"Despite my choices, God still shielded me from making decisions that could've ruined me. That didn't mean I never made any bad choices. One time, my girl friends and I lied to our parents about being at a friend's house, when actually we were hanging out with some really bad people. I was caught because my parents ended up calling the friend's parents to see if I was really there. Although it sounds bad, it was the best thing that could've happened to me."

How? You were caught, and now you were going to get in trouble.

"It was in the middle of the night when I was discovered, and by the time I had returned home, I had been grounded for the whole summer. Because I couldn't do anything all summer, I went to church and plugged in to the youth group. My mom decided that we wouldn't go anymore with my dad when he traveled so I could really become involved with our church. I also stopped hanging out with my previous friends and cut off all communication with them. Even though I had made some horrible decisions and had walked away from the Lord, God called me into ministry during my last year of high school. I really felt Romans 8:28 speaking to me, which says, 'And we know that all things work together for good to them that love God, to them who are the called according to His purpose.' I was called, even though I didn't think I could have a second chance, and I was given grace, just like the woman in John who was about to be stoned."

I still didn't see how that was the best thing that could've happened to her. I wondered aloud who influenced her the most in her life: her friends or other people.

"The best influences in my life were my parents. They have been married for 39 years, and they raised my sister and me the right way."

Huh. I would have thought it would've been her friends, seeing how they were serious influences in her life. Maybe not the best influences, though.

We painted for a while more before finishing up. My vase was a turquoise color with a vine circling down it. We gave Nikki our slightly wet pottery and headed out the door. I thanked Ashley for such a wonderful day and climbed in the car. On the ride to my house, she looked over at me and said, "I want to tell you what was the most important lesson I learned growing up. I feel as if you need to hear it. It's this: to speak out in love, and live your life with an open heart to others. It hasn't always been easy for me because I can be very fearful at times, but I just have to remember that God is with me at all times, so I don't have to be afraid."

What words of wisdom! I felt truly touched by them, surprising myself. I didn't expect to get so sentimental over a statement, and I managed to refrain from bursting into tears, but it still rocked my world. Live my life with an open heart? Does that mean that I have to be open to Christian thoughts and ways, too? I guess it would only be fair to give Christians a chance to express their opinions, just like I express my opinions. The polite thing to do would be at least to listen to them. Besides, it's not like I would become a Christian just because I listened, right?

I couldn't dwell on that long, however, because right then we pulled up in front of my house. We both climbed out and walked to the door. She surprised me by hugging me. What surprised me even more was that I hugged her back.

She smiled and said, "A word of advice I would give to you is this: find your voice and gain confidence. Use your words in a good way, and live your life openly, all in God's name." With that, she turned around and walked back to her car, waving to me as she backed out of the driveway.

I walked inside and up the stairs to my room. The day had been full of surprises, and I was ready to call it a night and hit the hay early. As I pulled on my pajamas, I realized that I should really pay attention to my next few godly women, just so that they won't think I'm narrow-minded, not wanting to hear them out or anything. Maybe I could learn a few more tips to help me out in life. I snuggled down on my bed and reminisced about my day with Ashley. I still couldn't get over the fact that she would buy me things and treat me nice, despite the fact that she had just met me. What unconditional kindness! I have met a few people who were similar to her—like Tina and a few of my godly women. Maybe somehow their religion is making them love like that.

Chapter Eighteen

Why in the world was everyone so frustrated with me? Ok, that was a rhetorical question. I knew the answer, for the most part, but it was so painful for me to admit it. A few days ago, I decided to listen to the school choir practice. It made me laugh so hard that I fell off my chair in the corner of the choir room. They sounded awful—like a grater scraping against violin strings while four baby mice squealed in a closet. Awful. So how could I help it if I giggled? Well, I actually laughed as loudly as I could, much to my later regret. Then, I proceeded to snort out mocking sounds of my version of what they sounded like. It was not exactly appreciated. In fact, my friends who sang in the choir came barreling towards me as soon as practice let out and hissed insults at me. It was like being attacked by snakes. I escaped as soon as I could and hoped they would forget it all by the next day.

I was not in luck, however. Not only had they not forgotten it, they had told the entire school about it. Some kids were on my side—mostly the ones who had heard the choir before—but most of the students were mad at me. I thought that my cold shoulder punishment would have been over in a few days, but my "friends" decided to take it a step further. I walked through the doors of school one morning and knew immediately that something was wrong. My friends were mysterious, the teachers were acting strange, and no one was talking to me. It reminded me of the time when my "friends" set me up with the band, but the atmosphere was more menacing this time. I soon found out what was wrong. After math class, my name was called over the intercom. I reported to the band room, like last time, only this time, I wasn't greeted with smiles from the few teachers there. Rather, they looked very annoyed that they had to waste their time with me.

I sat in a cold, metal chair and prepared myself for the onslaught of insults that were sure to come. Instead, the choir director—a balding, middle-aged man—stood and smiled at me, the first smile I'd seen all day—unless you count the smile Thunder always gives me before I leave in the morning. I told you he was a great cat.

The man spoke. "I understand that you were very, um, interested in choir the other day."

Interested wouldn't be my word of choice. Perhaps humorously entertained, because it was the funniest thing that I had seen in a long time. It was even funnier than the time I saw my elderly neighbor in her partially see-through nightgown at six in the morning, singing and dancing for her plants. When you see an 87-year-old woman in a silk bed sheet singing Christmas music in April, all the while performing her version of Swan Lake for the rhododendrons, all you can do is laugh. Anyway, where were we? Ah, yes, choir.

"Yes, sir, I do admit that it captured my undivided attention."

He seemed impressed with my expanse of vocabulary and manners. The other teachers there, however, were not moved. They glared at me. I held their stare, daring them to drop first. They shifted their eyes a split second later. I always win staring contests.

I decided to play the apology card to swing some people back on my side. "I have taken into consideration my actions of last week, and I want to profusely apologize for my inconsiderate, thoughtless ridicule. I hope you will be able to find it in your hearts," your cold, cruel, calloused hearts, I added silently, "to forgive me." Immediately, two of the teachers shared a glance and then smiled at me, assuring me silently that all was forgiven. The other one, though, wasn't touched by my completely fake performance. To be honest, I was surprised that the other teachers had bought it.

The choir director smiled a fatherly smile. "Of course you're forgiven. But I didn't bring you in here to make you apologize."

Wait, what? Why was I wasting my time then?

He continued. "I wanted to inform you that we have decided to recruit new members for the choir."

What does this have to do with me? I'm not exactly a professional marketer who specializes in recruiting kids to join a choir of mice.

He gestured to the people around him. "We have come to the conclusion that you would make a lovely asset to our singing group!" He literally beamed at me. As if I were just yearning to join a group of chattering squirrels.

I was about to tell him, 'Thanks, but no thanks, partner,' and skedaddle, when he tilted his head and added, in a somewhat threatening tone, "You will join, right? We need more students who have a ready desire to use their vocal cords for more than just talking, and I was under the impression from some of your friends that you are a great singer."

What have they done? This is the second time in less than a semester that my "friends" have set me up with activities that I wanted nothing to do with. I learned how to play the piano enough to get by for the concert, but singing is an entirely different story. I had felt sorry the past few days for what I had done because of the treatment I was getting, but now I was really sorry.

"Sir, I hope you don't think it rude of me, but—"

He cut me off. "I am so happy you are willing to be a part of our lovely choir. I hope you have a pleasant experience. The principal's secretary will give you your new schedule. Good day!" With that, he exited the room, the other teachers close at his heels. They obviously didn't want to be around when I exploded.

I was still pacing in the room, muttering threats under my breath, when Tina walked in.

"Hey," she said, very tentatively. "I hope you don't hold this against them forever."

I spun around, panting like a mad dog. "Forever?" I gave a bitter laugh. "Not forever, just long enough to get them back. I will have revenge, no matter how long it takes me!"

She frowned disapprovingly, and I sensed I was about to get a sermon. "Romans 12:19 says, 'Beloved, do not avenge yourselves, but rather give place to wrath; for it is written, "Vengeance is Mine, I will repay," says the Lord.'"

First off, I'm not beloved; second, vengeance isn't the Lord's; third, "the Lord" isn't real, and therefore He can't have revenge anyway. I was about to spout all this at her when a thought occurred to me. What if I used the tips Ashley gave me, to use my words in a profitable way. In that vein, I told Tina I appreciated her advice but didn't think it applied to me. She was, as I suspected, very surprised when I didn't storm off because she gave me a sermon. But, as I also suspected, she had more to say.

"It does apply to you because you are loved by God, whether you believe in Him or not. He doesn't want you to use anger to take revenge. I think that if you just let this go, without getting back at them, you will feel better in the end. Plus, they would just get you back for whatever you decide to do to them, and that would start an ongoing war."

It made sense, but I didn't want it to make sense. Instead, I changed the subject. "Do you know any singing teachers?" Tina stared at me quizzically. "I can't sing to save my life, and I want to make the choir better, not worse." She grinned, and I mentally slapped myself. I had unknowingly chosen to go the peaceful route. I'm not sure why, but it felt, well, more peaceful.

"In answer to your question," Tina said, "I do know someone who teaches voice lessons at Lee University. She is a Christian as well." Tina grinned widely, showing off all her sparkling teeth. "In case you're wondering, that was a hint."

I smiled condescendingly at her. "I'm sure I will find my own godly woman this week, thank you very much."

She hid a disbelieving smirk with her hand. "You're very welcome. I hope you have fun, uh, finding your mentor for this week!" And with that, she strolled away through the door, as if she hadn't a care in the world. Which, she probably hadn't. I sighed and was about to walk out of the band room and hope it was all a dream when I received a text on my phone. It was from Tina. She had sent me the contact information of the voice teacher, whose name was Debbie Sheeks. Under the contact information, she also sent a smiley face with the words, "She will agree to be your godly woman for this week if you use my name. I know her." She added, "Don't forget, tomorrow we have the day off because it's some sort of holiday! Perfect timing, right?" I rolled my eyes. Tina always had to have the last word. I had forgotten that school was out tomorrow. Well, I definitely wasn't going to let her coerce me into meeting this woman if I didn't want to.

Exactly two hours, three minutes, and twenty-four seconds later, I sat in the chair in my bedroom and groaned.

"No ideas! Weak, pitiful, useless brain!" I punctuated each insult with a head bang against the wall. I came to the conclusion that Tina must be a hypnotist. Every time she wanted me to meet with somebody I didn't want to, I ended up obeying her and meeting with the woman. I could think of no one else. It was Thursday already, and Tina knew that. She figured that most people would have plans for the weekend, so I had five days in the week to schedule an appointment and get it over with. It was also late in the day, and I had no hope of scheduling anything with anyone, so it would have to be tomorrow, which meant I had to contact them today, so on and so forth. In short, I would be meeting with Debbie Sheeks tomorrow, if she would agree to meet with tone-deaf old me.

The next morning, I walked into the doors of the Lee music building. They hurt. I gingerly swung open the door and limped up the stairs located next to the door, following signs as I went. Soon I arrived at the top of the stairs, only panting slightly. A long hallway lay before my eyes, and I had to choose whether to go right or left. I was about to go with the reliable eenie-meenie-miney-mo factor, when I heard a voice to my right.

"Hello! Are you Tina's friend Brie?"

I turned to where a woman was walking down the hallway towards me. "Yes, ma'am. I'm here for the voice lesson and the meeting."

She smiled. "I can't wait to get to know you! Tina has told me so much about you!"

She has, has she? I wonder what about? The fact that I don't sing and can't sing, or the fact that I don't want to do the challenge and can't do the challenge? Well, I technically can do the challenge—it's just usually not very high on my priority list until the end of the week.

We went down the hallway and into a room. It had a piano, a desk, two chairs, and a bookcase. She motioned for me to sit in one of the chairs. I did as instructed and opened my mouth to begin talking when she started talking, relieving me of striking up a conversation.

"I'm not familiar with your challenge, but I scheduled our day based on what I thought you might be comfortable with. Tina said you were very laid back."

Really? I had better schedule a meeting for Tina with Tina's pastor. She needs to learn the importance of not lying. I've already learned that lesson, and I'm not even a Christian!

She continued. "I have a student scheduled for a voice lesson in a few minutes. Then we can talk and do your lesson. After that, we will head to lunch and I will take you to your house, or wherever you want me to drop you off."

"Sounds good!" I was grateful she was going to be feeding me. As for dropping me off,

I wanted to talk with Tina anyway, so I texted her and asked if I could spend the night. A few minutes later, after probably restarting her heart after realizing that I still wanted to spend time with her, she sent back an enthusiastic, "Yes!" with multiple emojis. I smiled at her enthusiasm.

Just then, I heard a knock on the door. Debbie opened it and ushered a young woman into the room. I could tell she looked slightly nervous at me being there, and I moved to a different chair so she could sit next to the piano.

Debbie explained that I wasn't a music judge; I was simply shadowing her for the day. The woman looked very relieved. They began the voice lesson. It consisted of scales and exercises with the vocal cords that I would never be able to do. Once that was done, Debbie pulled out some music and began to play accompaniment with the singer. The song was titled, 'To a Wild Rose,' and it was beautiful. I would never be able to hit the high notes that were being sung, but if I could sing it an octave lower—if I could sing it at all—it would be heart breaking. They worked on some more songs and then said goodbye.

We were once again by ourselves. "You are a wonderful singer and a thorough teacher," I commented enthusiastically. "Do you enjoy helping your students improve their singing?" Her fervent "Yes!" made me laugh.

"Did you graduate from Lee or just decide to come here out of the blue?"

"Yes, I did graduate from here with a major in music. I dated my husband, Randy, who's a year older than I am, my sophomore year, and we were married the day after I graduated."

"Where were you married?" I always love hearing people's romance stories.

"We were married on a Sunday at Westmore Church of God, the church I currently attend."

Well, I was hoping for something besides a church—maybe an outdoor setting by a lake. My parents married in a church and look where they ended up. I bet her parents probably married in a church, too. If so, did her parents end up like mine?

I voiced the question and received a sad response. "My mom died when she was only 26 and I was three. When my mom died, I, as well as my two older brothers, went to live with my grandpa and my creative and amazing grandma, whom I learned to look up to all throughout my growing up years. When I lived with my grandparents, I was always at church because my grandpa was a pastor. I grew up playing the piano for church, and I have sung in church since I was three years old."

Wow. I would get stage fright, most likely. I felt an invisible bond connecting us somehow. One of her parents died when she was young, just like me. She also grew up in church and was around her grandmother a lot, just like me. Unlike me, however, I saw the light and moved away from "the light." It was a very practical decision, one that everyone should make. But obviously Debbie didn't. I couldn't understand why not. We both had felt loss with ones we loved, but she hadn't come to the realization I had, that God isn't real.

Just then, she clasped her hands together and said, "I think we have time for a voice lesson before we head off to lunch."

I swallowed. Right. The lesson. "I want to warn you before we begin: I can't sing at all. I don't even attempt to sing in the shower because I know my bathroom mirror would shatter at some of my song renditions."

She laughed. "Don't talk like that, or you'll believe it. You need to have confidence in yourself. Let's start with some scales. I want to test your range."

Range? Like a firing range? Oh boy, I was done for. She began playing on the piano, and I followed along the best I could. It turned out that my voice didn't sound like a burping baby after all. Instead, it was more like a chirping cricket.

She kept encouraging me through it all, though. She gave me useful pointers to control my voice, like, "Keep your mouth wide open when you sing so the note can come out better." To my utter surprise, I slowly began to improve. I found out that I could sing pretty high. She started playing a song from The Sound of Music, and I sang along. It was the most fun I had had with singing in a long time.

Right as we were about to launch into another song, though, the clock struck 12:00. It was almost like Cinderella, the way we got our stuff together and headed off to lunch so quickly. We briskly walked through the campus to the cafeteria. She gave the woman at the door lunch tickets, and we placed our personal items on a table. We walked to the different food areas and looked to see what was available. It all looked delicious, and I had a hard time deciding. Eventually, though, I chose a salad, some chicken, and bread sticks. We began eating. She had said a short prayer before we ate, but I tried not to think about it. If she wanted to believe in that stuff, fine. If not, also fine. I wasn't going to judge. At least, I didn't think so.

As I continued to eat, she suddenly surprised me with a question. "What are your opinions about Christianity?"

Wait. Normally people ask if I'm a Christian; they don't ask about my views on it. I felt respect for her for being able to ask that. "Actually, I'm an atheist. I used to be a Christian until I realized that there wasn't a God."

She peered at me. "If you don't mind my asking, what happened that made you change so suddenly?"

I chewed for a minute. I had never gone too in depth about the change, but I decided it wouldn't hurt to tell her. She may even consider becoming an atheist, too.

"My parents left the church when I was young. I had just become a Christian, and I didn't understand why they would do that. Then, after a few years, I became used to not hearing about God or talking to God. My siblings were already adjusted to the change, and my parents were completely fine with it. I decided to make everyone happy and stop talking about a God who loved me." I had to swallow a few tears. I had forgotten how sad I had been and how alone I had felt when I realized that there wasn't a God who loved me.

"Then the real blow came when my dad was found dead in his bedroom with a suicide note in his hand. He had a drug overdose." At this point, I was crying. I regretted opening up like that because I was making a scene, but it felt good to get it out in the open. "I was the one who found him. He was the only one who cared for me, laughed with me, and spent time with me; and he had just died. On purpose, too, even though he knew I would be left alone to suffer through the hate my family feels for me." I attempted a smile. "That is why I know there is no God. If someone with the power to save really existed, then why wouldn't He save my dad? I don't want to have any false hope, thinking that my life will magically change for the better when my dad isn't coming back."

She was silent for a long time. "First of all, I want to apologize for bringing that up. That is a very sensitive subject for anyone to discuss, much less a girl your age. Second, I want to tell you a few things I learned growing up. You see, I was lonely in school, but I knew I was special because I was God's. I can't imagine ever going through life without God. I grew up with a strong awareness of eternity, even when I was young. I knew there was a God. The most important thing I learned in life was to be consistent and faithful in what I did, and to be stable in my emotions. I was able to do that because I knew who I was in the Lord. I know you're probably thinking that what I'm saying isn't helping whatsoever, but if you will make even a small place in your heart for Jesus, like it says in Isaiah 40:3, your life will be changed, and you will experience great stability as well." She smiled. "These qualities of stability and consistency should be portrayed in godly women, as well as selflessness and humility. I will be praying for you, regardless of whatever you decide to do."

I was still swiping away my tears. "Thank you." If her God really was real and if someone was praying to Him for me, I was in a pretty good situation.

We were finished with our food now, and we threw away our trash and walked outside. She looked at me. "To lighten the mood, can I tell you about the time I got in trouble here at Lee?" Immediately I perked up and nodded. I loved a good story of people getting into trouble.

"It was the worst trouble I ever got in, to be exact. I was at the music building and Randy was there, as well as the Dean of Students, Paul Duncan. I was wearing a short skirt, which was against school policy, so he told me to go change it. I felt annoyed that he should reprimand me for it because I wasn't the only girl on campus wearing a skirt shorter than I was supposed to. As soon as I thought he had left, I immediately turned to my friends and started ranting about how strict he was. Then I turned around. He was still standing there and had heard everything I had just spouted off to my friends. I got in big trouble, but I learned not to mouth off—especially when the person you're mouthing off about is right behind you!"

I laughed, bad feelings almost completely forgotten. I wish I could've seen the look on her face when she turned around and saw him standing there. Must've been priceless.

We soon arrived at the music building. She set a few things back in her office and then we climbed in her car. When we arrived at Tina's house, she reminded me that she would be praying for me and to not forget what she had said. I promised I wouldn't, then climbed out of the car and knocked on Tina's door. As I watched her car drive off, I realized that she was the first person I had really told about my dad. I even cried in front of her. I knew that my journey in life had just taken a drastic turn, but I couldn't ruminate on that right now because Tina swung the door open and ushered me in, asking all about my voice lesson and my meeting with Debbie. She peppered me with questions over dinner and until we fell asleep. I only answered some. If she knew everything that had happened, she would probably use it to convert me. And I can't have that happen.

Chapter Nineteen

It was finally fall break, the week every student looks forward to from the beginning of August because the majority of those students took a vacation for that week. I wasn't so fortunate. Since it was already Thursday and I hadn't done anything for most of the week except laze around and sleep, I decided to find something productive to do for the last couple of days of fall break. I flopped down on my bed to think. My eyes roamed around my room and landed on a book I was borrowing from the library for my journalism course.

I had decided to take an online course in journalism for at least a semester to prepare myself for high school. I liked to write, and one of my many goals in life was to be the editor of the high school newspaper. The class was hard work, but I wanted to be prepared for high school, which was coming up way too quickly; however, I felt like the online course wasn't preparing me enough to be the newspaper editor. I sat straight up in bed, an idea forming. Maybe I could find someone who ran a magazine or a newspaper, then I could find out what it was like to keep people informed with all the comings and goings of the city. The first step to meeting a writer was finding a writer, and I had no clue how to find one, so I did what I always did when I was puzzled: I called Tina.

Of course she had an answer to my problem. "I know someone who owns a magazine! And she's a Christian, so you could meet with her for your challenge! I'll give you her number."

Oh great. Why again did I ask Tina? All I wanted to do was meet with a magazine owner, not meet with a Christian for my challenge. "Thanks, but no thanks."

Even though Tina was with her family in Nevada, I knew she was probably frowning. "You couldn't see an opportunity if it hit you in the face!"

I wasn't budging. If I said yes, Tina would feel as if she knew yet another person I didn't. On the other hand, no one else knew anybody I could meet with, so I needed to grab this chance. But, on the other hand, Tina would hold it against me in the future. However, on the third hand, which I didn't have, she wouldn't do that anyway because she's too Christian. Since I was running out of hands and good reasons not to let Tina set me up with this mysterious magazine owner, I glared at the ceiling and said, "Fine. You can tell her she can meet with me, but if this is all a flop, you will pay."

She simply laughed. "Yeah, yeah. I'll text her first and let her know who you are, but I want you to text her and figure out a time to meet. Her name's Bethany Ruckman."

I hung up and then sat down in my green chair. After a couple of minutes, Tina sent me her contact info, and I texted Bethany. While I waited for her to respond, I went downstairs and poured myself some water. When she responded, she said that she would love to meet with me, and that she was free for dinner if that would work with me. We decided on a time and place, and then I told my grandmother that I would be gone for the evening. I explained what it was for, and she nodded absentmindedly, barely looking up from her book. I sighed and went back upstairs to get ready. When will she ever realize that I exist? I shook my head and then thought about Bethany. I've considered running a magazine as a career, but I would need a lot of advice first—which is why I didn't stress too much over the meeting as 5:00 quickly approached. In fact, I almost had a sense of peace, if you could call not biting my nails or chewing my hair or pacing my bedroom floor peace. I changed into a comfortable yet fashionable outfit, brushed my hair, and waited.

She arrived promptly at 5:00. I walked outside and introduced myself before she could knock on our door and see what a mess our house was in. She was very sweet from the start so I couldn't understand why Tina apologized. Once I climbed into her van and she started talking, however, I understood. "I am so very glad I'm able to be a part of your challenge! It sounds so exciting. I wish I could have more time with you today!"

"Me, too," I said. I couldn't wait to get to know her.

On our way to Panera, Bethany said, "To kick things off, I wanted to tell you what God put on my heart to say to you: pride always gets in the way of grace. Also, I feel as though you need to find your inner circle because that's very important while you're growing up."

Inner circle? Well, I have friends, but I don't really have super close friends whom I know I could count on no matter what, but I guess that's okay. People don't really needs a "best friend for life," do they? I don't know. Maybe I should start looking for someone to become closer with.

She looked thoughtful for a moment as she pulled into a parking spot at the restaurant. "What are some questions you normally ask the women you meet with?"

I shrugged. "There are only a few that I ask every woman, and one of them is this: 'What are the qualities of a godly woman?'"

As she walked into the building, she said, "That's a hard question to answer correctly, if there really is a correct answer. My view on it is this: if you lead everyone around you to Christ, then you, in my opinion, are a godly woman because when you do that, you need other godly qualities to do that. So if your ultimate goal is to lead everyone to Jesus, then you will have a lot more qualities in you than just that one."

That was very thought provoking. If you were a Christian, that is. I decided to move on to the next question before I could think about why I was actually intrigued by her thought-provoking answer. As she ordered our food, I asked her, "What is your favorite Bible verse?"

She looked very indecisive for a moment before answering. "I love the book of James, which is filled with wonderfully deep verses, so I won't be able to pick my favorite; however, I think that James 1:19-20 is a great daily reminder, which basically says to be quick to hear, slow to speak, and slow to anger because anger does not produce the righteousness of God."

The first part of that saying is very good to remember, Christian or not: be quick to hear, slow to speak, and slow to anger. Good moral saying.

Our food came just then. I had ordered a salad and some potato soup; it smelled amazing. She prayed over our food, and then we dug in. As I chewed, I realized that she hadn't said anything about her magazine yet.

"Tell me about your magazine. What is it called?"

"GoodNews Magazine. My family and I run it."

I figured it would probably have a Christian name. "Are all the articles about God?"

She laughed. "No. We have lots of variety in our magazine, such as recipes, how to handle money, local business advertising, and all kinds of interesting tidbits to pull the readers in."

I took a bite of food before asking, "How do you find people to write the articles for your magazine?"

"At the beginning, we asked people in our church whom we knew were writers. Now, we have people from all over the community send us emails if they want to write something for our magazine."

"How do you pay for the magazine to keep running?"

She took a sip of her drink. "Local businesses pay us to advertise in our magazine."

"Has it been easy running a magazine?"

She started laughing so hard that I began to look for a carpet to crawl under. "How about I tell you the story of how it all started? That may clear things up a bit. Before the magazine started, I was at nursing school, my husband Matt was working full time, and our kids were in a public school for most of the day. We were content with our life—at least, we were until God laid on my heart the feeling that we weren't supposed to be so disconnected and that Matt needed to work from home."

Disconnected? I can see why she'd think that: her attending nursing school and Matt with his job didn't exactly give them quality time with each other or their kids, especially when, in the evenings, their kids had homework and they were tired. At my house, I rarely see my family members; however, I don't see why you would give up a full time job just because the family wasn't all connected at the hip.

"I shared the idea with Matt, but he did not like it in the least. We were doing very well financially, and he didn't see why he should give up his job just because I felt that he should. We fought about it for a year and a half; it was very troubling. I knew God wanted us to do something different, but Matt didn't feel the same way. One day, however, everything changed."

"Matt's job was in medical sales, so he would go to hospitals to talk to doctors. He was in the waiting room of a hospital one day when a woman walked in. His job was done, and he was about to leave when she said, 'I feel like you need to preach the gospel.' He was very rocked by that statement. A month later, he had such a strong feeling to tell people about Jesus that he called his boss and told him that he couldn't work anymore. His boss wasn't happy with that and pleaded for him to stay, but Matt quit."

That makes no sense. Why would he give up his great paying job, even when his boss pleaded for him not to?

"He then came home and told me what had happened. I was partially relieved that he was agreeing with me, but I was also frustrated that he had taken so long! Now that we were on the same page, we needed to figure out what exactly we were going to do to spread the gospel. Matt's mom owned a Christian newspaper, and we thought about doing that, but we liked the idea of a magazine better. We took a serious leap of faith, but it has been worth it."

You took a leap of faith? Wait, so you believed that God would pull you through and He did? You must have a close connection with Him because I believed in Him and what happened? Oh, yeah, I found the only human being who ever loved me dead on the floor.

She finished up her story as we finished up our food. "After I graduated from nursing school, and thus had much more free time on my hands, we were able to start GoodNews Magazine. Matt started advertising for a magazine we didn't yet have, but people were really excited about it. In the first month, we broke even. It was a miracle! And the publication has constantly grown over the last five years. We decided that God wanted us to be even more together as a family, so we took our kids out of public school and started homeschooling them."

"That's quite a story," I stated after taking my last swig of soda. "It hasn't been all happiness and laughter, but it sounds like it all worked out in the end."

She smiled. "You're correct." We grabbed our stuff and walked to her car. Once we buckled in, she said, "Before we call it a day, I want to take you to an adorable art place in town. That is, if you like art."

I smiled broadly. "I love art. Thank you so much!"

When we got closer to the art place, I saw that it was familiar. She had chosen The Clayful Artist as my surprise. We walked through the door and chose our pottery to paint. Since I had been there before, I had a better idea of what to do. We made small talk as we painted, but mostly we were in a comfortable silence. About an hour later, we were done.

As she drove me home, I thanked her profusely for such a wonderful day. Not only had I gotten input from someone who owned a magazine, but I also met with an incredible woman!

When I walked into the house, I saw my grandmother still in the living room reading a book. She didn't acknowledge me at all. I blew out a breath and slowly walked upstairs. I didn't understand why I cared that she didn't notice me; it meant that she wouldn't be constantly nagging me, but everyone wants to be loved. Everyone has a deep longing for love from another person. I never like admitting that I want someone to love me; it makes me feel weak to need something from someone else. Yet, I can never completely shake off the emptiness I feel inside, the jealousy I feel when I see other kids with their families, kids who are cherished. I'm just a nobody, just a nameless face, just another heart that's been shattered by too many people.

Chapter Twenty

I plopped down on my chair in my room and tried to regain my breath. Unbelievable. I read the letter again, wondering if it were even real. Apparently, I had been doing so well in school recently that private schools were starting to take notice. I set down the letter from the third private school that week and smiled. I couldn't believe it. I, the dummy of all classes at school and the recipient of the "Most Times to The Office" award, now have three different scholarships to three different private schools! Somebody had better pinch me. I couldn't wait to tell my mom, my sister, and my grandmother—just to rub it in, of course. This news was meant for one purpose: to show off.

Each letter had wonderful remarks about me that I knew would make both my mom and Kimberly mad, although my grandmother would probably be fine with them. My mom would be mad because I would actually have a bright future, and she would realize that she wouldn't be able to call me a failure anymore without me bringing this up. Kimberly would be mad because she knew that I would rub it in her face that I was smarter than she. She would pretend not to be affected by it but then try and kill me later, even if my "righteous" grandmother was watching. We both knew that if she did something terrible, Grandmother would likely overlook it, still calling her the "perfect" child. With me, on the other hand, it's the opposite. If my toe crosses the line one millimeter, she's on me like a bloodhound, slobbering out Scripture about how judgment will come for me and my soul will rot because I'm such a failure. I know life isn't fair—obviously, seeing how much has happened to me—but if my grandmother really does believe in God, then why doesn't she give me some of the grace I hear about from Tina all the time?

Sometimes I feel myself wondering what it would be like to open myself back up to God, but then I realize that if I "follow Jesus," then I might end up like my grandmother, fussy, grumpy, and irritating. That's when I know that I shouldn't even bother with Christianity. My one goal in life is to never end up like my grandmother, and I aim to keep that goal, which means not becoming a hypocritical Christian. In fact, I don't aim to become a Christian at all.

I shook off those thoughts and walked across the hall to Kimberly's room. I knocked twice and opened the door. She immediately looked up from her phone and glared at me as if I had just decided to kill all the baby koalas in Australia.

"You know the rule. You can't just walk in without asking first. Now go back out." She tossed her blond hair and pursed her lips together.

I lifted an annoyed eyebrow and frowned. What a jerk. I slowly exited the room backwards and lifted my hand to the doorframe. I deliberately knocked again and asked, "Can I come in now, your Excellency?"

She growled. "Whatever."

I smirked and walked in. "I just wanted to share my good news with you."

She pursed her lips. "Unless it's that you failed every class today, you don't have good news. You're too bad to have anything good happen to you."

Chuckling at her ignorance, I sat down in one of her overstuffed chairs that my grandmother had purchased for her "so she could be more comfortable as she studied for her classes."

"I just received three letters this week from three different private schools." I waited to see what her response would be.

As I expected, she wasn't impressed. Narrowing her green eyes, she said, "What did they say: 'We want you in our juvenile delinquent program?'"

I shook my head. "No, I found out that I'm so smart that three different schools offered me a scholarship to be a part of each of their schools."

Since I was looking for it, I could momentarily enjoy the look of shock that came over her face. But it disappeared as quickly as it had come.

"Obviously, the letters were addressed to me. But since you can barely read, you thought they were to you." She frowned sympathetically. "Better luck next time."

I had expected that. In one swift motion I pulled out a piece of paper and showed it to her. "If you can't see my name on it, then you're the one who can't read."

She growled and snatched the letter from my hands. "Impossible. No one in their right mind would ever want you to come to their school. This must be a mistake." And with that she ripped the letter in half, then quarters, then eighths, until it was a pile of confetti on her floor. She smiled in evil satisfaction. "Oops, I must have slipped. Guess you should've known better than to think that you were good enough for anything."

I smirked as I walked out of the room. "And that, my dear sister, is why you always make a copy," I said, pulling out the real letter and waving it at her before ducking out of her room.

Leaving my sister speechless, I fairly skipped into my own room and sank onto my bed, delighted in knowing that no longer could she say that I wasn't smart. I reread one of the letters again—for the thirteenth time—and noticed that at the bottom it stated that I could schedule a tour of the school to learn more about it. None of the others mentioned that, so I decided that if they cared enough about their prospective students to give them a tour and allow them to talk with the teachers, it must be a school worth going to. With their letter in hand, I hung the other two letters on my corkboard and stepped back to admire them. I realized that the women I had been meeting with for my challenge actually were having a positive influence on me—my grades had greatly improved and I wasn't getting into as much trouble at school. But that's where the influence ended. I am no closer to believing in all that Christianity stuff than I was at the beginning—at least I don't think I am.

As I sat down and mulled over my challenge, I realized that I needed to schedule a tour of the private school I had picked—Tennessee Christian Preparatory School. I noticed a number at the bottom of the letter, so I decided to text it. The name located next to the number, Ginger Robinson, sounded familiar. After racking my brain for a few minutes, it hit me that it was the woman who had given Gayle Cobb (the woman I met with three months ago) the message from God. Small world. I shot off a quick text to her, telling her who I was and letting her know that I would like a tour of the school. In a few minutes, she responded and told me that I could come in tomorrow if I could get out of school. I quickly texted one of my teachers and explained the situation to her. She told me that I could use one of my sick day passes. I then prepared for the next day, gathering as much information on the school that I could so I would be able to impress them with my knowledge of the school. By the time I fell asleep, I was mentally exhausted, ready to shoot the next person who said "school" and realizing that I had most likely wasted two hours of my life cramming my head with useless pieces of information.

The next morning, I woke up and noticed three things: I had twenty-four minutes to make it to TCPS, I was starving, and I had a bad cold. Not the best combination to wake up to when you have an important meeting. I quickly leaped out of bed, pulled on the outfit that I had chosen the night before, and ran downstairs. As I stuffed a banana in my mouth, I glanced at the clock hanging on the wall—I had sixteen minutes. I ran to my grandmother's room and burst through without knocking. Big mistake.

"Thtop! Thlam that thing! I need privathy!"

I quickly slammed the door and ran to the bathroom, where I promptly started scrubbing my eyes with water. Something about seeing your grandmother without her false teeth, in a pink Disney princess nightgown, with her hair in curlers and wearing a green face mask to try and help her wrinkly skin is very disturbing to the eyes, especially since I knew none of these facts until this moment.

I groaned as I realized that not only was I scarred for life but I had also wasted precious minutes. Slowly and cautiously, I went back to her bedroom and knocked on the door, loud and hard.

"What do you want?" she asked grumpily through the door.

I swallowed. "I have an important meeting this morning in fourteen minutes, and I was wondering if you could drive me to it."

She screeched out a laugh. "You actually think I would drive you to a meeting this early?"

I frowned. It was time to pull out the big guns. "It's not that far away, and it's at a private school. They want me to come and tour the school so I could possibly come to it."

There was silence behind the door. I knew I had gotten her. Finally, the door cracked open, and she stared at me—thankfully she had put her teeth in and had taken the mask off.

"Why in the world does a private school want you at their school? It's not like you're smart or anything."

Okay, ouch. That well-placed barb found its mark. "Contrary to popular belief, I have been making more A's in the past few months than I have in the past few years. And, in answer to your previous question, I don't know why they picked me. I don't know anyone at that school, so no one put in a good word for me or bribed the teachers, as you might think."

I was close to ripping my grandmother's hair out—with my teeth. She didn't love me— love was out of the question—but she still delighted in making me feel absolutely useless and a burden to everyone around me. Yet, despite her abhorrence of me, I didn't hate her. I didn't love her, either. It was a twisted type of tolerance. She pushed my limits at times, such as now, but she was still my flesh and blood and didn't have any addictions—unlike some people I knew. I didn't know why I didn't hate her, but I just couldn't.

I knew that she lashed out at me only because she was hurting. Her son-in-law had had a serious issue which she wasn't able to protect her daughter from, her daughter currently has a serious issue, and her grandson is gone. She doesn't know how to fix any of it, so instead, she lashes out to make others hurt as she does. Usually, I simply try to ignore it, but at times like this, it becomes difficult to act decently to an immature fuddy-duddy. I inhaled slowly and counted to ten. Then twenty. Then thirty. Finally, after forty long seconds, I could look at her again without having ill intentions crowding my brain.

She seemed to sense that I had control of my feelings but could explode at any moment, so she agreed to drive me, shutting the door so she could put some actual clothes on. I thought she should have kept on the Cinderella nightgown—it was such a good look for her. Not.

We finally made it out the door, into the car, and to the school with just enough time to spare—barely. I walked into what I assumed was the main building of the school and found myself in a hallway with doors lining either side of it. It looked like a normal school, so I decided that one of these doors should lead me to a teacher. Scanning the nameplates on the doors, I found the one that read "Ginger Robinson." I opened the door and saw a woman sitting behind her desk.

"Hi, I'm Brie, the student you offered a scholarship to. Are you Ginger Robinson?"

She smiled broadly. "Yes, I am. It's so good to meet Tina's friend."

No. You have got to be joking. Tina wouldn't. Or would she? Would she, a Christian—not to mention a serious goody-two-shoes—send me forged letters just so I could meet with a godly woman? It seemed too scheming to be Tina, so I asked if the school really wanted me to come.

"Yes. We believe that you would be a great asset to our journalism team, not to mention your musical talent and your excellent grades."

Aha. I always knew that one day all my hard work would pay off. "How is Tina involved, then?"

She chuckled. "I have been trying to get Tina to come to TCPS for several years now, but she always has an excuse. When I called to inform her of another opening in our school and to ask her to reconsider coming, she immediately cut me off and told me all about you, saying what a wonderful student and person you would be for our program. I had to agree once I saw your school records."

I felt proud that she liked my grades, but to get all the attention off of me, I asked her if she could show me around the school. She agreed.

After a brief tour, I realized what a fun person Ginger was. She didn't make me feel intimidated, didn't load me up with useless facts about the school—which I would have already known anyway—and she made me feel at home. She told me about some of the classes that she taught at the school, and one of them was a Bible class.

"In the Bible class," she began, "I have two exchange students who, when they first came here, knew nothing about God. They hadn't heard anything about Him. It has been very hard trying to introduce them to Christianity."

I'm reconsidering going here. Do I have a choice about going to this Bible class? I don't want to be forced into Christianity, just so I can get a good grade. As we returned to her office, she shut the door and sat down behind her light brown desk. "How do you like the school so far?"

I smiled wide. "I love it. However, there is one problem. How much will it cost?"

She looked at me and said, "I'm going to be honest with you. It's going to be a lot of money, despite the scholarship. You may want to pray about it before coming. But remember, we need to pray so that our hearts and minds will be changed, not God's. If He wants you here, He'll show you."

I grimaced. Prayer. Yeah, right. "I'm an atheist. I don't think I will be doing much praying about this, other than to my grandmother to ask for money."

She looked surprised at first, and then became curious as she leaned across her desk. "Then how do you know Tina, if not from her church?"

"From school. She approached me one day and told me God had something to say to me, that He apparently wanted me to start meeting with godly women." I rolled my eyes. As if He really had told Tina that. "After that, we were 'kindred spirits,'" I said in a sarcastic voice.

She tilted her head. "Well, I wasn't expecting that, to be honest. What is this meeting with godly women about?"

I had predicted that. "It's where I meet with a godly woman once a week for a year. Tina makes sure I do it every week, and I just try not to be rude to all the Christians I meet with. But it can become frustrating when everyone tries to convert me, whether they know it or not." Suddenly I had an idea. A brilliant, masterful, genius thought conception. I leaned forward in my plush seat. "Would you like to be one of my godly women? Basically what happens is the woman just tells me things she's learned in life, and what she believes the qualities of a godly woman are."

She thought for a minute, contemplating her options. "Will you listen to what I have to say or is this a checklist of something you have to get done this week?"

I colored beet-red. "I'll try my best to listen to you. I can't promise I will believe it, though."

"Then yes, I would like to share with you the lessons I have learned in life."

I grinned. "Fantastic!"

"Let's start with the qualities and get them out of the way," she said with a slight laugh. "It will take me a lot longer to share my life lessons. For me, the qualities of a godly woman are these: one who has a heart for God and who chooses to respond to every situation by making conscientious decisions rather than having kneejerk reactions. Remember, you can have good qualities in you and still not be godly. The godly part comes from having a relationship with God."

I had never thought of that. I had always figured that if you were a kind soul, you were a Christian. That's an interesting piece of meat to gnaw on later. "When you're not at school, what do you do for fun?"

She chuckled as she leaned back in her chair. "I run—which is hilarious because I used to despise running. One day, about three years ago, I thought I heard God tell me to run, but I figured I was imagining it because I knew that God knew that I hated running. For two to three weeks this went on: I would hear God telling me to run, but since I didn't want to, I would chalk it up to something else."

She paused for a moment. "Finally, I gave up. I slipped my running shoes on and started running. I was so out of shape that I couldn't run very far, but I found out why God wanted me to run. He wanted some quiet time with me. So, for the past three years, I have run every single day except for two, when I was physically unable to. I was going through extreme hardship, and if I hadn't run every day, I would've fallen apart; but I knew that if I kept running and having my quiet time with God, then He would give me strength. I realized that I should obey Him no matter what He says—even if it's something I hate to do—because He's the only one who knows my future, and obedience means my future will be what He wants. If we knew what God knows, we would make the decisions that He is wanting us to make; but we don't know the future, so we must rely on God."

Wow. Make decisions based on what someone else wants for you that ultimately you would choose anyway if you knew the big picture? What a strange idea. Something she said sparked a question. "What hardship were you going through that you needed strength for?"

She looked at the clock and then at me. "That's a long story that I can tell you over lunch, if you would like. It's currently my lunch break."

I readily agreed to the proposition, so we climbed into her car, and she drove us to Olive Garden. Once we had ordered our food, she began.

"In July 2013, Jeremy (my husband), Madray and Mallory (my two daughters), and I were all going from Illinois to Washington, D.C. for a family vacation. Jeremy wasn't feeling well during our vacation, but we all wrote it off, thinking the pain would subside. Rather than subsiding, however, his stomach pain became excruciating. Thinking it was a kidney stone, I rushed him to a nearby hospital. We didn't think it would actually be anything serious, so we weren't very worried as the two girls and I sat in the waiting room. When the doctor walked in, we expected him to tell us that Jeremy was fine and that we could continue our vacation."

I had a bad feeling about this.

"Instead, he said that Jeremy had a large mass on one of his kidneys and that we needed to go home immediately so Jeremy could see his regular physician and find out what

116

needed to be done with him. After the doctor left, I began reading the Bible for scriptures to comfort me and give me strength. As I was flipping through the pages, the Lord said to me, 'I am your Rock and your Strong Tower.' That gave me such peace."

Huh. It's strange that she would feel peace because of a few words.

"We left the hospital in a much different mood than we had walked into it with. After we had climbed into the car, Jeremy grabbed my hand and started praying. 'O Lord, You are my Rock and my Strong Tower.' I was stunned. That was exactly what the Lord had said to me in the waiting room."

Just an enormous coincidence.

She took a sip of water before continuing. "We flew to St. Louis and took a train from there to a motel. Since we thought we were going to be gone for two weeks, we had packed a lot of luggage; now we had to cart it with us as we were trying to board the train. I say trying because none of our tickets would scan except for Mallory's, my eleven-year-old daughter. She boarded the train because she thought we were right behind her, but we weren't. The buzzer signaled that the train was about to leave, so I started screaming for Mallory to get off the train. Suddenly, our tickets were accepted, so we rushed to board the train; however, Mallory wasn't on the train because, being the obedient girl that she was, she had disembarked. I started yelling for her to get back on the train, and she jumped on just as it started pulling away from the station."

Oh man, that was a lucky escape. What if they had been separated? I took a bite of a breadstick. It was delicious, but I barely tasted it, I was so involved in the story.

"People were staring at us, and I apologized for making such a disruption. 'I'm so sorry. We don't like to make a scene.' As soon as I said that, Jeremy collapsed."

I inhaled sharply. This story isn't turning out the way I had expected. If she believes so strongly in her God, then why would He let her husband be so sick, if He really cared?

"As the train sped along, we called the hospital to let them know we were coming. The tumor had broken from his kidney and had traveled up in three pieces through his inferior vena cave (the large vein that carries the blood from the lower body to the heart) and through his heart; however, one piece remained in his heart, blocking it. He had just enough blood flowing through his body to keep him alive. When we arrived at the hospital, he had open-heart surgery and kidney surgery. The girls and I told him goodbye before the surgery because we didn't expect him to survive. The surgeries were supposed to take fourteen hours total, but they only took four. Jeremy recovered from the surgeries, and I began to become more hopeful."

Yes! That's what I'm talking about. I victoriously took a sip of my strawberry lemonade.

"However, in January, the doctor discovered a brain tumor plus new cancerous tissue. I was so upset. It was always bad news and never good news. He died a few weeks later on January 26, 2014. However, since then, I have come to realize that even though God may give big 'noes,' He also gives small 'yeses.'"

What? Her husband just died, and yet she's still not mad at God for letting him die? How could she only focus on the positive? He gave such a huge "no" to her serious prayer that little "yeses" shouldn't even matter!

She kept talking. "Sometimes we focus so much on the big 'no' that we neglect to notice the 'yeses' that He gives us. I prayed that God would heal Jeremy, but He said, 'No'. He answered my prayer, just not in the way I had expected."

Sounds familiar. I had prayed so hard that my daddy would open his brown eyes back up and talk to me when I found him in his room. But it was all to no avail. He never woke up. I had done everything I knew possible to make God change His mind about taking my dad, but He didn't answer! Not one single word from Him for years. I knew then that there was no such thing as a good God, or any God for that matter. If there were a good God, then He would have saved my dad.

She kept talking. "Yet even though my husband was dying before my eyes, I found peace from God. Because I was so close to God, I knew without a shadow of a doubt that God was with me."

How is it fair that we both had lost someone we loved, yet she still has hope to hang on to? I stabbed a forkful of salad and put it in my mouth.

She was still talking, unaware that I was on the verge of a mental meltdown. "On top of the fact that He was with me, God had been preparing me for Jeremy's death without my knowledge. Jeremy was the pastor of our church, and I led a small group there. A few months before we left on our vacation and I found out he was sick, I was talking to my group about security. I told them that if my security was in being a pastor's wife, then what if Jeremy wasn't the pastor anymore? What would I do then? I then asked what if my security was in being Jeremy's wife? If Jeremy died, I wouldn't have security anymore. I told them that if my security was in earthly things, I was in trouble."

Huh. I had never thought of that. I guess I have a little security in some things, but for the most part, I normally don't feel secure.

"What God said to me that made me so at peace was this: 'Sometimes it will be clear, other times it won't be; but don't worry, for I am with you.'"

To me, He would have said: "I will never make it clear for you, it will always be foggy, and you will spend the rest of your life worried, depressed, and hurt. And by the way, I was never with you and never will be." That's my life in a nutshell.

We finished the remainder of our food and stood. As we headed to her car, she said, "My favorite Bible verse is Psalm 40:11 which says, 'Do not withhold your tender mercies from me, O Lord; let your lovingkindness and your truth continually preserve me.'"

Lovingkindness? I was amazed that she could still quote scripture and be happy with her husband dead. Just then, I had a memory of when I was a little girl. The Sunday school teacher had told us the story of a man named Job. He had lost his children, his property, and had painful boils all over his body because he was holy and upright, and the devil wanted him to curse God. Yet, through it all, he praised God. Ginger was a lot like Job. She was holy and upright, so the devil wanted her to suffer. Yet, through it all, Ginger was still praising God.

I didn't think any more on the subject, though, because we arrived at the school. We walked into the building together and went to her office.

Once there, she turned to me and asked, "What do you think about the school? Do you think you will come to it?"

I thought for a minute. I went through a list of pros and cons in my head. On the bright side, it would be great for my college résumé; on the not-so-bright side, I wouldn't see any of my teachers anymore and I wouldn't see Tina. I hadn't realized until then how attached I had become to her. She was the only true friend I had. With that in mind, I turned to Ginger.

"I thank you for the opportunity, but I think that not only would I not be able to afford it, I would also miss out on a chance to become good friends with a great girl."

She nodded, realizing that I was talking about Tina. "I understand. I hope that you will come visit me again soon, though."

I promised I would, and then stood up from the chair. I thanked her for her time and walked out of her office. I called my grandmother to come and pick me up and then sat down on the front steps of the school to wait for her. As I sat there, I ruminated over my day. Ginger really struck me as a strong woman. I admired her ability to love even when times became tough. Even if we didn't agree on her faith, I felt as if we could relate based on the fact that we had both faced death—except she went through her struggles without complaint, and I went through mine feeling sorry for myself. I have a feeling that she is who she is today because of her decision to keep pushing forward and live, rather than simply accepting the pressure and giving up. I, on the other hand, deserve the pressure of the world on my shoulders. Right before my dad killed himself, I was arguing with him about going to the movies with my friends that night. He wanted me to stay home so I could hang out with my family, but I, the selfish child, demanded to be taken to the movies. I told him that if he didn't take me, I didn't want him to be my dad anymore. Then my wish came true later that evening. It's my fault he's dead. That's why I deserve the pressure, and there's no one willing to take my place underneath this pressure so I can be free from it.

Chapter Twenty-One

Dead silence momentarily filled my classroom before excited chatter erupted from every corner. My teacher had just announced that at the end of the week, all the honor students (which included me, since I had been making such good grades) would be traveling to Kentucky to visit the Creation Museum and the Ark Encounter for our big trip of the year. Why, you may ask, was a public school club going to two obviously Christian places? The only reason I could think of was that the sponsor of our honor club was a Christian, and she picked where we would go.

I wasn't happy about the choice of the trip's destination, but it meant no regular school on Friday, and that was a plus. I had no idea what the museum was about, but I was sure Tina would know; and she was in almost every single class I had, which was an incredible coincidence—or was it planned so that she could keep tabs on me at all times? The teacher handed out permission forms for our parents to sign, and as I took mine, I whistled softly at the amount of information—and money—needed. I could fill out everything on here and forge my mom's signature without anyone being the wiser, but I couldn't just randomly ask for this amount of money. I sighed. I was going to have to ask my mom if I could go.

Hearing my sigh, Tina turned around in her seat in front of me and frowned somewhat suspiciously.

"Don't tell me you're considering not going. I've been before, and this is an amazing experience! You just have to go."

I rolled my eyes at her lack of brain cells. "I'm not concerned about whether or not this will be fun. I'm concerned about having to actually speak with my mom or grandmother about the money."

Her eyes slowly got wider as she understood. "Ah. You don't want to rouse the dragon, eh?"

Tina and I call my mother a dragon because she sleeps a lot—like fairy tale dragons— breathes fire upon awakening, and has bad breath. It's a perfect match. I smirked, wondering what she might think if she knew I called her that behind her back. She'd probably spew more fire. I think Tina feels a little bad about calling her that because of the whole Christian love thing, but I constantly reassure her that she wouldn't care. Even though she probably would. It's just a little white lie, though. I'm sure it doesn't really matter.

When I arrived home later that day, I had it all planned out about what to say to my mom about the trip. I had decided to talk with my mom instead of my grandmother since the school needed my guardian's signature on the paper—even though "guardian" would be the last word I would use to describe my mom. I tiptoed to her bedroom door and took a breath, slowly releasing it. I could do this.

"Mom?" I began, knocking on the wooden frame. No answer. I tried calling and knocking again, this time louder and more rapid. As a million thoughts crowded my brain, I suddenly had a flashback to when the same thing happened when my dad died. I had gone to knock on his bedroom door chad he never answered. Of course, I had to be the one who found him lying there. And now the same scenario was happening here. I was frantic. It's not like I have a great bond with my mom, to say the least, but I didn't want to be stuck living under the guardianship of my grandmother for the rest of my born days. In desperation,

I finally burst into her room. She wasn't there. I tried the bathroom, but she wasn't there either. Relieved that she wasn't dead, but still panicked as to where she was, I ran into the living room to ask my grandmother.

Instead of seeing an old lady sitting haughtily in her rocker, I saw my mom.

"What are you doing?" I asked, quite puzzled. My mom's schedule each day is to sleep until eleven, have a muffin and coffee, and then go into town where she's a part-time cashier at Walmart. She then comes home and continues to sleep, unless she goes to the bar after work. Besides her Walmart job, she also has a job correcting English papers for college students by email, which she mostly does in her bedroom. She doesn't feel compelled to make much money because Grandmother was left quite an inheritance by my grandfather, and she also gets retirement funds from the government. That's why Mom doesn't feel the need to work at anything harder than beeping cartons of milk and fixing grammar mistakes. That's why it's abnormal to ever see her sitting in the living room.

"What are you doing up?" I asked again, completely baffled.

She looked at me, feigning surprise. "Why wouldn't I be up? It's only 4:47, and the sun hasn't even gone down yet."

I rolled my eyes. I could think of about one million reasons why she shouldn't be up, all of them given to me by her when I have questioned her about her sleep schedule in days past. But I decided to let this pass until later so I could seize the opportunity to talk to her while she was still awake. "The school is taking all the honor students on a trip to Kentucky on Friday, and I was wondering if I could go. It's to a museum, it's only $80 for all the expenses, and best of all, it's a two-day trip, so you will be rid of me for two whole days." The last part had a bite, and I knew she heard it.

"First off, what museum is it? Second, where will you be staying? And third, why aren't you asking your grandmother? She could've easily said yes, which would've saved me the trouble of having to listen to you."

I winced. Her words always hit me in the back like a knife, some twisting the knife deeper, others barely poking, but it hurt all the same. "I need your signature on the paper, or they won't let me go."

She raised her eyebrows and widened her green eyes. "Aha. I knew you wouldn't talk to me without having a pressing reason. Only Kim and my mother will actually have a conversation with me nowadays. Your father was always too soft on you when it came to teaching you proper manners."

I bristled. Through gritted teeth, I hissed, "You can attack me all you want, but I won't let you disrespect the dead, especially since it's my dad you're talking about."

She smirked sardonically as she played with a strand of her blond hair. "Apparently I've finally found your weak spot. So you really did love your father, even though he was a fool?"

I nearly pulled her hair out. "My dad was a better parent than you ever were or ever will be. He actually treated me like a human being who has feelings, rather than a mangy dog. I thought mothers were supposed to be caring and kind to their own children. I wish I never had you for a mother!"

I stormed out of the living room and slammed the front door behind me. Thoughts rampaged through my head. That conversation was even more proof that no one loved me, not even my own mother. I started walking down the street. Little voices screamed in my head. There was no one who loved me. Everyone acted as if I were invisible. If no one loved me, it wouldn't make a difference if I decided to just up and leave this wretched world, would it? It's not like they would notice. The more I thought about it, the more appealing it sounded. Leave the pain and worry behind. I could just find a simple, painless way to kill myself and then it would all be over. I wouldn't have to deal with anyone any longer, and they wouldn't have to deal with me. Right as I was about to turn around and go back to the house to figure out the quickest way to kill myself, something stopped me. I felt a strange, peaceful sensation, as if something or someone were calling out to me, trying to get me to listen. I turned around. Standing less than five feet away was that strange lady in the grey raincoat. What was up with that? She looked deep into my eyes.

"Don't be like your father. Choose to live." As suddenly as she had appeared, she walked away until I couldn't see her anymore. I scrunched up my eyebrows. Weirdo. What was she talking about? Why would I be like my father, unless...oh.

I knew. This must have been what Dad thought before he took the drug overdose. That no one loved him, that he would never do anything purposeful, and that it would be easier for everyone if he just died. How wrong he was. I cared. I loved him. I needed him. It wasn't easier after he died. What if people felt that way about me if I died? Voices were battling in my head, trying to take control. The loud voice said that no one would notice or care if I died, but the little voice said that Tina would care. The women I've met with would care. Ms. Applebee would care. Suddenly, I didn't feel completely unloved. Even if only one person loved me, I didn't want them to feel like I did when Dad died. I didn't want them to wonder what they had done to make me kill myself. The loud voice took control again and started reminding me of all the things my mother had ever said about me, playing them over and over again in my head. I almost cracked under the pressure, but I felt a stirring in my heart, a calling to something greater.

I knew right then that I needed to talk to Tina. I slumped against a tree as I dialed her cell phone number. When she picked up, I told her what had happened and what I had almost done. I heard her gasp over the phone.

"Oh my goodness, I'm so thankful you're alive!" I heard her praying on the other end, praying for me. "Would you be open to meeting with a counselor about it?"

I frowned. Would I? I already felt better knowing for sure that Tina cared about whether I lived or died. But meeting with a stranger to talk about my personal life? I wasn't sure, but because Tina thought it was a good idea, I decided to go for it. "Sure. If you think that's the best thing to do, I'll do it. Also, my mom wasn't exactly excited about me going on the trip because she would have to spend more on me than she likes to. What should I do?"

"I know a woman who works there."

Why did that not surprise me? But I didn't understand what that had to do with me.

She continued. "If I can talk her into meeting with you for 52 godly women, then you could go and interview her. I'm not able to spend the night because I have an event the next day and need to get back home, so you could just ride home with me after your interview. I'm only going because I love the Creation Museum."

I was incredibly confused but tried to unscramble what she said. "So what you're saying is that I will ride up to Kentucky on the bus, interview this woman, then ride back home with you the same day. Will I be able to visit the museum?"

"I don't know. If you wanted to see it, you would have to pay for a ticket. The total price you would give to the school would be less, since you wouldn't need a hotel room, but it still may be more than you want to spend. I just thought you might want a day away from your family to clear your head."

She was right about that. "That's actually an incredible idea! I'm not particularly interested in seeing Christian exhibits, anyway. I was just going so I could get away from my family. This would hit two birds with one stone: I'd get to clear my head and get my weekly challenge out of the way." Then I paused. "If my mom agrees."

Tina sighed. "I know it's a struggle to talk with your mom, so maybe your grandmother would be fine with signing as your guardian instead."

I thanked her for her ideas and hung up. When I walked back inside the house, I wasn't surprised to see that my mom wasn't in the living room anymore. I spent about twenty seconds looking for my grandmother before I found her in the kitchen drinking grapefruit juice—no wonder she's always so sour-faced. I talked to her about what I would be doing in Kentucky, leaving out the fact that it was for my challenge, and assured her that it wouldn't cost nearly as much as the paper listed. Surprisingly, she agreed to let me go and to pay for it.

"Sometimes I disagree with your mother's ways of raising you kids. I think it would be a great learning experience to interview a scientist. And just think, the school picked you out of all people to interview her!"

I smiled weakly. I sort of lied about that, but it was the only thing I could think of to have it make sense. I'm sure it will be fine.

The next day, I proudly took the signed form to my teacher after class. I let her know about how I wouldn't be staying the whole time and that I would be interviewing a scientist. She was impressed that I knew a scientist there and told me that I would only have to pay $20 for the trip, since gas still costs money. I was surprised I didn't have to pay more. I guess the combo ticket really was the majority of the cost. When I told Tina that I could go, she squealed and grabbed me into a bear hug. After awkwardly patting her on the back, I quickly untangled myself. I'm not the hugging type.

When the bus left for Kentucky that Friday, I was proud to be on it. I had finally done something I hadn't done in a long time: I stood up to my mom instead of sniveling into a corner. As a result, I was able to go on this trip. On the ride up, I thought about the lady in that crazy grey raincoat. If she hadn't been there with me, I might have actually killed myself. I owed her a lot. I slapped myself on the head. I forgot to ask her her name. Oh, well. I probably wouldn't see her again, so it didn't really matter that much.

After several long hours on the bus, which mostly consisted of me listening to music as an attempt to block out my classmates' noise, I felt a tug on my sleeve. Tina, who had taken the liberty of sitting by me—without asking—was trying to get me to sit up.

"What? I was about to fall asleep." I felt miffed at the fact that just when I was finally on the point of dreamland, I was aroused from bliss.

She smiled sympathetically. "Sorry, but I needed to tell you something important. I remembered that you probably know nothing about what the scientist does, and since you're set up for an hour and a half long interview, I took the liberty of compiling a list of science-related questions you could ask her. I may have overstepped my bounds, but you can still ask other questions. I just didn't want you to feel awkward about not being prepared. By the way, the scientist is actually a molecular geneticist, so I thought I might want to warn you that she isn't just an average scientist."

I took the sheet of paper she handed me and smiled. "Thanks. I hadn't thought of that, and I'm glad you did." I was a little hurt that she thought I didn't know enough science to properly interview a molecular geneticist, but she was kind in going the extra mile to help me. "By the way, what's the molecular geneticist's name?"

"Her name's Dana. Dana Atley."

Just at that moment, a voice was heard from the front of the bus, letting us know we had just a few minutes before we arrived at the museum. When we finally pulled into the parking lot of an enormous building, I felt a thrill. Being an honor student was fun—even though I wouldn't be able to tour the museum. I'm sure Tina will tell me all about it on the way home.

Our group walked inside and stood in a line for about twenty minutes before we could get our tickets. When it came my turn, I told the woman that I wasn't touring the museum but that I was meeting with one of the scientists here. She looked skeptical but shrugged and let me go on with the group.

Just a few minutes later, our group started to walk down a hallway to start the tour. Tina stayed behind with me for a few minutes until a woman called her name. She turned, smiled, and introduced me to Dr. Atley. She then said a quick farewell and ran to catch up with the rest of the group.

Dana looked at me and smiled. "Brie, is it? I'm glad to meet you. Why don't we go to my office to start the interview?"

I agreed, and we soon found ourselves sitting in her office. I decided to start it off in a rapid-fire style with questions I already knew. "What are the qualities of a godly woman?"

She looked thoughtful for a moment before replying. "Prioritizing life appropriately."

"What scripture has helped you most in life?"

"It's a toss up between 1 Peter 3:13, which says, 'And who is he who will harm you if you become followers of what is good?' and 2 Chronicles 20:17, which says, 'You will not need to fight in this battle. Position yourselves, stand still and see the salvation of the LORD, who is with you, O Judah and Jerusalem. Do not fear or be dismayed; tomorrow go out against them, for the LORD is with you.'"

That was it for my questions, so I brought out Tina's list of questions and read the first one. "What's the coolest fossil you've ever seen or heard about?"

"It would have to be an Ichthyosaur found in Germany. It was giving birth when it fossilized."

Wow, that's something you don't hear about every day. I went to the next question. "What has been the most rewarding part in adopting Sadie?" She adopted a child? Neat!

"Probably being able to raise a new generation of believers to spread the gospel. It's hard to raise a child, but it's important. The impact you make on your children makes you want to be a better person because they're constantly watching you and mimicking you."

I wish she had told my mom and my dad that. Moving on. "What contribution to medicine can stem cell research make?" Wow. Tina must be some crazy smart person to even know to ask these questions.

"Adult stem cell research has many benefits, but it's still a work in progress. Concerning embryonic stem cell research, however, I am completely against it."

Hmm. Interesting. So she must be against abortion. Not too many scientists are outspoken on their views about that. I went to the next question, which tied into what she had just said. "How can Christians support good medical stem cell research without supporting the unethical research of embryonic stem cells?" Oh my goodness. Why did Tina put in Christian questions? I didn't know that she had, or I may have gone through and crossed them out.

"You just have to be careful about what you give your money to. You have to make sure you completely understand what the organization supports before financially backing it."

Good answer. "What are the unique things you have seen in the design of human or animal cells which have led you to believe more strongly in a Creator rather than in evolution?" Was Tina trying to send me a message here? She knew I believed in evolution, so why would she have me ask questions about the flaws in evolution?

"Cells are so highly organized in the body, it's like a little city. I wonder why anyone can look at all the cells in a human body and still believe in evolution. It's like a watch. If I took the back off the watch and saw all the little parts inside, I'd have to realize that someone put that together."

That's a neat answer. She tied in her belief to something I could relate to, a watch. Wait a minute. She was talking about how cells show there is a God, and I definitely didn't agree with that. I moved on before I went into a mental shutdown.

"Most molecular biologists believe that animals and humans share a common ancestor," I read. "Why do you think this is a common view among biologists, and what is the evidence for this point of view? How do you look at the same data they're looking at and come to different conclusions?" Apparently Tina was trying her best to make me think.

She thought for a moment before answering. "It's a common view because it's what has been taught. Unless you go to a Christian college, you won't be taught about any other point of view. Because it's a common thought, most people never think to question it. They assume it's true, even though there's no evidence to back it up."

Wait, no evidence? Out of all the scientists in the world, not a single one could come up with evidence, and yet I've believed it this whole time?

She continued. "Biologists who believe that animals and humans share a common ancestor say that time is the key, and that if something is given enough time, anything can happen. However, time is not the key; even if you were given trillions of years, nothing would happen. The key is you have to have a mechanism, a genetic mechanism. That's what allows change from one kind into another kind, and there is no mechanism in that theory. They see that genetic mechanism can cause variation and speciation, like among finches, so they extrapolate it."

What? Even with trillions of years, nothing would happen? Mind. Blown. I moved on to a different question, one I felt safe asking. "What is your role here at Answers in Genesis, and how did you come to work here?"

"I'm the ministry content administrator. About 90% of my job is reviewing all content Answers in Genesis makes—books, videos, etc. I speak, write, and am a media representative, which basically means if journalists want an interview, they interview me. I taught college residentially for six years. Before I started my sixth year, though, I really wanted to do something in the area of creation/evolution, and I told God that if He opened the door for me, I would walk through it. A guy from Answers in Genesis went to my church, and our friendship eventually led him to bring me here for an interview."

That's one nice friend. "Why is it dangerous for churches to compromise the history in Genesis?" What is Tina getting at?

"It's the foundation of the gospel. Some Christians believe that God created everything but then stepped out of it, the big bang happened, and then evolution 'took its course.' The problem with that is that most of those Christians don't believe in Adam and Eve; and if they don't believe in Adam and Eve, they don't believe in the Fall or sin, which means Jesus wouldn't need to redeem us."

Ah. That's what Tina wanted me to hear. Humph. Next question. "Do you believe God created dangerous animals and poisonous viruses, or do you believe these are results of the Fall?" I should have read that one first. Tina actually had me use God's name as if I believed in Him? How dare she push my beliefs aside as if they don't matter!

"I believe that dangerous animals are the result of the Fall, but let me clarify. A spider, for example, still had its web and its ways of catching creatures in it before the Fall, but it just never used those things in a bad way until after the Fall. As for viruses and bacteria, it's a little trickier. I would say that they have probably accumulated mutations to the point that they are now dangerous. Most microbes are good, outweighing the bad, but because of the Fall, mutations have changed some of them to become bad."

"How do you respond to people who believe mutations with natural selection are able to improve and benefit a species?"

She smirked as she gave her answer. "I say show me the evidence—because they can't. They'll try, but they won't be able to give an official summary."

Wow. I never knew that there were so many things I believed in that had no evidence. I guess it's like she said—if you're taught something, you never think to challenge it. This next question I was actually interested to hear her answer: "Have you ever debated an atheist?"

She leaned back in her chair. "No, not really. Generally, atheists won't debate with others opposed to their beliefs because they say that it's too difficult to present their views in certain settings to convince people. Plus, atheists don't want to debate Christians because they don't want to give their Christian opponent equal time, which would happen in a debate, and perhaps sway some people in the audience toward Christianity. Atheists feel as if it gives us too much publicity."

True. She knew her facts about us. "How do you deal with ridicule that comes your way for believing that the Bible is scientifically true?" Most of that ridicule is well placed; those who actually believe in the baloney that God exists are blind to what goes on around them.

"I don't listen to it. I used to. When I first came here, I Googled my name and started reading all the things people were saying about me, but now I don't. It's not healthy. It used to really bother my daughter when people would say things or write things about me that were mean, but I would tell her that it wasn't me they hated. It was God. What really bothers me, though, is when Christians come up against me and ridicule me. If they really are my brother and sister in Christ, they should act more Christ-like."

Well, I suppose that makes sense. If an atheist came up to me and started making fun of me for what I believed, I would be mad. "What are your views on atheists? Do you believe they truly believe in their views, or are they in total denial?" What?? Why would Tina put that question in here? I can't believe I actually read that without realizing what I was saying.

She shook her head sadly. "They're in total denial. They don't have the Holy Spirit to help them, so they are totally blind. It's my job to present the truth. It's the Holy Spirit's job to convict them and convince them of that truth. I could show them all the evidence in the world, showing them that their evidence is in no way scientific, and they won't believe it. It's staring them in the face, but they're blinded. But I also believe that the reason they get so riled up when I talk about God is that in the deepest part of their hearts, they know it's true. They just suppress it."

Ha. Yeah, right. What evidence? I'm not blinded; in fact, I have my eyes open to what Christians can't see. I looked down at the list—I just couldn't wait to find out what Tina had for me next. However, to my surprise, there were no questions left. When I looked up, Dr. Atley was glancing at her watch.

"Oh wow, it has already been an hour and a half! How time flies!"

I was shocked that it was already time to end, but Tina had timed it out well because I had no more questions. "Thank you for your time. It was nice meeting you."

"Likewise. I'll walk you back to the exit."

When we came to where I was supposed to meet Tina, I said goodbye and waved as she walked back to her office.

Tina came a minute later. She had broken away from the group so that she could meet me, even though the tour wasn't finished yet. "How was it?"

I glared at her. "It would have been much better if you hadn't put all those questions in about evolution, God, atheism, etc. I felt so awkward sitting there as she talked about everything I didn't believe in!"

She grimaced. "Sorry. When I wrote the list, I forgot you were an atheist and most of those questions I have always wondered what the answer would be from a scientist's point of view."

I could understand that, but there were a little too many questions in there that had to do with me. "Okay, but still, you should've at least warned me about them."

She smirked. "But if I had done that, you wouldn't have asked her those questions because you wouldn't have thought them important. Now, am I right or am I right?"

I rolled my eyes. "You don't exactly give me a choice. Obviously, you're right."

She laughed, and we walked outside together to her mom's car, where her mom was waiting with a smile on her face.

"Hi, girls. Did you have a nice time?"

I said yes, and I meant it. Even though I felt slightly upset about the questions Tina had me ask, I really enjoyed meeting Dana Atley. She made me really think about some of my beliefs. Honestly, I was more than a little shook up about how no scientist has proof for evolution, something I've believed in ever since I stopped believing in God. I just always thought someone, out of all the technological people in the world, would find some sort of way to prove evolution, but it seems that no one can. So if there's no evidence for evolution, then how are we alive today?

Chapter Twenty-Two

Great excitement pervaded the eighth grade class all morning, which was a complete abnormality. We had learned during first period that the school board had decided to give the eighth graders a day off. What was the catch? We were instead going to shadow a businesswoman or a businessman who had graciously offered to let a student spend the day with her or him to "prepare us for the future." The teacher had posted on the bulletin board two lists: one of businesswomen and one of businessmen. She called students up a few at a time to randomly pick a name—the boys choosing a businessman and the girls choosing a businesswoman. I picked a woman named Esmerelda Lee—actually she was the only woman left by the time I was called to the front. The paper noted that she was a marketer. I didn't know a thing about marketing, but I figured I would know something by the end of my time with her.

The exciting part for most of us was not that we were following adults around all day to watch them do their job but that we didn't have to do math, science, history—you know, the whole nine yards. Many of us—including me—thought that the adults would just tell us to sit in a chair as they did paperwork or fiddled around on their computer; and if that were the case, then we would be free to be on our phones the whole day rather than having to listen to a teacher talk about George Washington, linear equations, or how to properly dissect a flea. To my way of thinking, it was going to be a very relaxing day.

I was wrong. The next day, all the eighth graders and their teachers met by the flagpole so we could wait around until our respective adults came to whisk us away to their jobs. One by one, adults came with slips of paper in their hands to find their little assistant for the day. The kids slowly dispersed until there were only about ten kids left, including me.

I began to get nervous. How dumb would I look if I didn't have anyone show up for me? Everyone would think that the person I had chosen didn't like me and decided to back out at the last minute. I would be the talk of the school, and not in a good way. Just when I could've been a loaded gun with all the bullets I was sweating, I heard someone call my name. I turned, and there stood whom I assumed was Esmerelda Lee. I breathed an enormous sigh of relief. As we walked to her car, I sized her up: she had dark skin, gorgeous black hair, and looked very professional in her fashionable clothes. I knew today would be an interesting day, even if I did sit around the whole time.

When we had climbed into her car and buckled our seatbelts, she turned to me and said, "I'm going to give you the low-down of what's happening today. As you know, I'm a marketer, working for a company in Chicago, and I'm over several senior living facilities here in Tennessee. What we will be doing today is going to a facility in Athens to strategize how they can obtain more residents and to help them with any problems they may have."

She included me in that statement. How cute, but how inaccurate. I couldn't market to save my life. Tina would've been a better fit with this person. She talks me into almost every meeting with a godly woman. She could talk a fly into buying insect repellant, she could talk a deer into wearing bright red, and she could even talk a tiger into going vegetarian! Yes, she would have been a great help to this lady. Not me. I can't even convince my cat to stop running away from me! I don't see what I will be able to do to be an asset to her today.

We rode to the facility without saying too much. She asked me questions about myself, but I, of course, answered practically nothing. She probably thought I was either super shy or had some serious issues with moving my mouth. When we finally arrived at the facility and had climbed out of the car, it was raining. I ran as quickly as I could to the building so I could find shelter before I was thoroughly soaked. She followed soon after—though much more lady-like than I had—and we walked into the building only slightly dripping.

She led me into an office where she set her things down on a table and motioned for me to do likewise. She turned to greet a woman who had just walked in and then introduced me. She proceeded to introduce me to several others in the office before taking me down a hallway to where a group of people were having a meeting. I felt slightly awkward standing there as Esmerelda, also standing, listened to what they were saying; I was just a random kid that no one knew and to whom no one paid much attention. So this is what it's like to be the proverbial fly on the wall. Once the meeting was over, everyone sprung out of their chairs and left the room except for a few women who seemed to be in charge of the facility. Esmerelda began asking one of the women about problems with the facility.

"I noticed the rain. Is it flooding again?"

The other woman nodded, clearly annoyed that the rain had come. "There's flooding all down one hallway, and in several of the rooms. We're currently trying to put a fan to it all, but it's not drying as fast as it should. I had the maintenance man use a Shop-Vac to suck up most of the water."

Esmerelda nodded in satisfaction. "That should keep it in check for now, but we need to find the heart of the problem." With that in mind, she determinedly marched down the hallway, with me hot on her heels. She pushed open an exterior door and walked outside. The rain had let up some, but it was still sprinkling as she and I walked past flowerbeds and benches until we came upon a man sitting by a drain-like hole. She asked him if he knew what was causing the flooding, and he told her that there seemed to be a blockage in the drain where the water was supposed to be pouring into; thus, instead of exiting the drain, the water was backing up in the pipes into the facility.

She nodded grimly and thanked the man for finding the problem. We then turned around and went back into the building. I could tell that she wasn't happy that the problem was just now being found out, but she was also glad that they would be able to fix it before the next rain.

We walked down a corridor and came to a room that was empty. Esmerelda immediately got right to work, giving people instructions on what to take out, what to put where, so on and so forth. Apparently, a person in town was interested in moving his sister here, and he was coming by in less than an hour. This was the only room available, and it needed to look great, smell great, and be just what he was looking for. I was put to work hauling buckets of supplies and plumbing items.

In no time at all, the room looked great. I proudly looked around and felt glad that I actually helped with something. Esmerelda and I walked back to the office, and as we were about to sit down, a man walked in the door. She immediately went over to him, introducing herself and making him feel welcome. Apparently, he was the man who was going to take a look at the room. I sat down and watched as Esmerelda led him into another office and introduced him to the woman over the facility. Then she returned and sat down by me.

"I think this is the place he's looking for." She then paused. "I'm sorry; this probably isn't the work day you were thinking of."

I smiled. "Ever since I started meeting with godly women once a week, I'm not surprised by a lot." I almost slapped myself. Where did that come from? Oh, great. What if she took offense to that? What if she thought I was crazy? I should have kept my big mouth shut. I sat there, waiting for her to act as if I were a crazy Christian.

Instead, she looked at me in surprise. "Wow, that's incredible! I've never heard of anyone doing that. What inspired you to do that?"

I was shocked she wasn't offended, which meant she was probably a Christian. Then I remembered that I had seen a Bible lying on her console in the car when I had climbed in. "A friend from school. She told me that 'God' wanted me to meet with godly women for a year, once a week. I didn't take her seriously at first, but it's been very interesting." Talking about it reminded me that I hadn't met with a godly woman this week. Suddenly, I had a brilliant idea. "Would you be interested in being my godly woman for this week?"

She looked flattered. "Me? I would be honored!"

I smiled. She was very excited about it.

Then she looked puzzled. "What do I do?"

I laughed. "Basically I ask you questions, you tell me your life story, and I'm able to learn from it."

"Okay, sounds easy enough." Then she stopped. "I have an idea; why don't we just talk over lunch so we don't get interrupted? If we talk here we may have lots of people going in and out of the room."

"Sure! That sounds great." About ten minutes later, the visiting gentleman came out of the office and left the building. Esmerelda walked in and talked to the head woman. When she came out, she was smiling. "He likes the room, and he signed the papers, saying he wants the room for his sister." When the employees there heard that, they started cheering.

I smiled in spite of myself. These people really loved what they did. Soon, lunch hour came, and I started to get hungry. I didn't want to say anything and make Esmerelda feel bad, in case she was planning on having a late lunch. Despite my best efforts not to complain vocally, though, my stomach decided to make some protests of its own. So while we sat at the table together as she typed on her computer, some very peculiar noises started coming from my stomach. Esmerelda laughed.

"Sounds like you're just as hungry as I am."

I looked at her, face past red and pushing magenta. "Sorry, I didn't mean any offense—"

She stopped me right then. "It's okay, I was starving anyways. Let's get our stuff and leave, shall we?"

I nodded gratefully. In a minute, we were in her car heading towards town. She stopped at Deli Boys. We walked inside and ordered. After we sat down at a table, Esmerelda began talking.

"I grew up in South Africa. My parents were missionaries there and introduced Jesus to many people; yet in spite of that, there was still a lot of racial segregation. There were separate schools and separate shopping centers. But those weren't the only separations in South Africa. When I was thirteen, my family went to the beach. As I entered a hotel located next to the beach, I was told to use the back entrance, and we were given a room that was on the poorly kept side of the hotel because 'whites were better.' When I finally went to the ocean, they had a buoy separating the ocean from blacks and whites. I accidentally crossed into the whites' ocean, and a lifeguard pushed me back to 'my' side."

I was appalled. How could they separate an ocean? Didn't they know that they were in the same water? I guess they wanted to make a point, stupid though it may be.

"I wanted to get out the country because of the incredible amount of hatred and racism. I wanted to come to America. Since I was a high school senior, my dad told me that if I were going to America, I needed to go to Lee College. I applied and they said they would give me a one-year scholarship. At the age of 17, I purchased a one-way ticket to Cleveland, Tennessee, and I was full of hopes and aspirations. Upon finally arriving at the college, however, I found out that there had been a mistake and that they weren't going to give me the scholarship."

Oh no. That must have been awful, knowing that you couldn't go back home but also knowing that you couldn't stay.

"I was stuck in a strange country with strange people with no idea what to do. I talked to anyone in authority at Lee to see if something could be done for me. Finally, a man told me that if I made straight A's and could come up with $1200, he would let me attend for a year. I hastily agreed to his stipulations before he could change his mind, and I started college. I worked all that year while still attending Lee to come up with the required $1200."

I'm so glad she found a way to survive in a strange country. If I ever got stuck in a foreign land with no way home, I probably would have ended up on the streets, begging.

"I went to a friend's house in Georgia during the summer to earn more money, but I was so exhausted, I was ready to quit. One Sunday, I went to a church next to the Kentucky Fried Chicken restaurant where I currently worked and sat down in the back. To my surprise, the pastor called me to the front. He said, 'Don't look back; the Lord has a plan for your life.' It was a message from God."

There are so many "messages from God" nowadays. Tina gets a message from God. Gayle, Shona, and Bethany get a message from God. And now Esmerelda gets a message from God! I don't know what to believe. I used to think that people were just wacko when they told other people things that were "from God." Now, I'm not so sure.

"I was so energized by the word from God that I went back to Lee my second year and became a Resident Assistant, which paid for my dormitory. I was able to receive many scholarships, and, by the time I graduated, I had no student loans. God took care of my finances. It was a complete miracle."

Our food came right then. I was about to dig into my turkey sandwich when she started praying. I awkwardly put down my sandwich, closed my eyes, and folded my hands. When she was done, I picked up my sandwich, for the second time, and started eating while she finished her story.

"Soon after I graduated, I wanted to attend medical school, but I didn't have the money—you had to have $150,000. People encouraged me to apply for loans so I could go, but I didn't want to incur any debt. Instead, I received a partial scholarship to obtain my Masters in public health, and, upon graduation, was hired at Life Care Centers of America."

Wow. What a success story! I wonder if I will ever be like her, able to overcome what her past brands her as and prove them all wrong.

"Sometimes you have to give up on your dreams to have a better future. I had to give up on my dream of going to medical school, but now I have a future I never thought I would have. My favorite Bible verse, Psalm 38:9, says it well: 'Lord, all my desire is before You; and my sighing is not hidden from You.' God knows what we want and what we long for, but sometimes He has something much better for us."

Giving up on dreams is a tough decision to make. Some people never give up on their dreams, even when they know that another path is better. Those are the ones who don't live life to the fullest because they're too busy chasing after a dream that never comes true.

Since she had paused to take a sip of water, I asked my standard question, "What are the qualities of a godly woman?"

She smiled. "The qualities of a godly woman are these: fearing the Lord, loving people whom others don't love, and being productive with her time." Then, as an afterthought, she added, "And humility. But humility is not letting people trample you, but it is putting others above yourself. Many people believe that humility means other people should run your life for you because they seem smarter, wiser, or more capable than you. However, humility isn't thinking less of yourself. It's thinking of yourself less."

And I always thought humility meant being a little wallflower. Apparently, I was wrong.

"However, there are times when you need to let people, especially your parents, lead your life, and that is because they have experienced more of life. For example, a fashion show was being held near my home, and I wanted to model in it; but my parents said no. Despite what they said, I snuck out and went to where the modeling show was being held—at a nightclub—and got ready to model. I thought it was just going to be a fashion show held at a nightclub. As soon as the music started, however, I knew it was going to be nothing but a nightclub. I immediately left the building. Just then, my dad's car slowly drove by the building."

That's pretty random that he would just happen to be driving by the nightclub just as she walked out of the building. I finished the last bite of my sandwich.

"He looked out his window and said, 'Esmerelda, what did you learn?' I told him, 'I don't think that was a place in which the Holy Spirit would have gone.' After that, I always wanted to make my dad proud of me, and I never again wanted to be caught in a place like that."

I wish I still had the opportunity to make my dad proud of me. I remember when we'd go skiing together, and he would teach me something new every time we went. One time I had just learned how to stop. My dad took me up to the top of the bunny hill and told me to go down. I didn't want to and told him I was scared. He said, "I'll always be here to catch you, sweetie. Don't worry." I skied down the slope and was able to stop all by myself. He was so proud of me that he bought ice cream when we got home. Too bad he didn't keep his promise to me, though.

To hide my sudden bout of emotions, I wiped my mouth on my napkin and set it on my plate. We were both done with our food, so we left the restaurant. She looked at her phone and realized it was already two o'clock. The school had told us to spend at least four hours with the person we had picked. I had spent six.

"Oh, wow. Time flies. I guess I had better take you to wherever you need me to drop you off." She looked at me with a question in her eyes.

"If it's not too much trouble, to my house. I can give you directions."

"Of course!"

We shortly arrived at my house, and as I climbed out of the car and shut the door, she stopped me by rolling down the window.

"I wanted you to know that I had fun with you today. Thanks for letting me be a part of your challenge. You're a very special girl."

With that, she waved goodbye and started to drive away. I felt tears coming to my eyes. No one had told me I was special since my dad was alive. It didn't change anything to think of that, though. No amount of what-ifs could bring him back. No amount of tears could fix the hole inside. No one could ever fill his place. I'm fatherless.

Chapter Twenty-Three

If I could think of one word to describe my brain, it would be panicked. Tina was turning fourteen November 18th, and she had invited me to come to her birthday sleepover. That wasn't the reason I was panicked. It was because I didn't know what to purchase for her birthday gift. I paced through Walmart, frantically running my fingers through my tousled hair. She was too old for a Barbie, but other than dolls, I had no clue what to get her. I hadn't been invited to a birthday party in about three years—ever since I gave a girl a pack of chocolate-covered nuts, a stuffed dog, and a soccer ball. How was I supposed to know that she had a major allergy to nuts, her dog had just died, and she had just tried out for the school soccer team and hadn't made it? I was named the worst gift-giver ever, and no one wanted me to come to birthday parties anymore.

So understandably, this was a huge ball of stress to try and not botch this present. I had gone through nearly every aisle in the store and knew it better than my own bedroom without finding a thing. I knew nothing about her likes and dislikes and couldn't bear the thought of getting her something offensive. The only safe present would be to get her a Bible, but I wasn't going anywhere near the Christian stores in town—plus she probably already had five perfectly good ones. As I sadly stood outside the store waiting for my grandmother to come pick me up, an idea hit me. She seemed like the vintage-type girl. What if I got her one of those room decorations that has an inspirational saying on it? Like, "Keep dreaming" or "Smile always" or "Never give up." I'm sure she would appreciate having one in her room. The only problem now was to find some place which carried them for a reasonable price. I couldn't ask Tina for references—for obvious reasons—so I would have to find this one all on my own.

As soon as I was home, I ran upstairs to my computer and started searching for businesses in my area that carried wooden room decorations. There were tons of results, which made my job even harder. How was I supposed to pick a company, a piece, and a saying on it? In case no one's noticed, I'm terrible at making decisions. I had narrowed it down to about five possible companies when I got a text from Tina. Immediately, I turned my computer off before realizing that she couldn't see my computer. I thumped my head at how dim-witted I could be at times! I read her text; she was just reminding me that I needed to meet with a godly woman this week. I rolled my eyes. She had this brilliant idea that she needed to make sure I was continuously meeting with someone, so she sent me a "gentle reminder" each day so I wouldn't "forget." I almost texted her back to please stop sending me texts, when I had an idea. I could kill two birds with one stone if I found a Christian woman who made room decorations who would also meet with me. That made my searching a lot easier, and after twenty minutes, I had found a woman named Serena Roberts, texted her about who I was and what I wanted, and had gotten a reply. I was going to meet with her tomorrow, and she would talk with me while making the gift for Tina—all before I left to go to Tina's party. I couldn't wait to see what was going to happen.

The next morning, I woke up and yawned. I had had a great night's sleep, and I was excited to meet Serena. However, I wasn't supposed to meet with her until eleven. In the meantime, I decided to eat breakfast, get dressed, and pack for Tina's party tonight.

I slurped some slightly soggy cereal as I thought about how much I have changed since doing this challenge. My grades have seriously improved, I have more patience, and I have gained friends in the process. I'm kind of thankful that Tina dragged me into this challenge kicking and screaming—now I only pout and throw a figurative temper tantrum every now and then. Ok, sometimes a literal tantrum, but really, sometimes it's hard not to, what with all I have to deal with at times.

Now, finished with my squishy, sugary shredded wheat, I pulled on some comfortable clothes, brushed my teeth, and started to pack. Once I finished, I sat around and waited for Serena. She came promptly at eleven, and I climbed into her car after she had pulled up.

"Hi, Serena. Thanks for meeting with me. I know Tina will be happy with whatever decoration you make."

She smiled, but then her eyes grew wide. "Wait, is your friend called Tina? Does she go to KMS, always wears her hair down, and has an incredible talent to talk people into anything?"

I chuckled. "That's her. It sounds like you know her pretty well."

"I go to church with her. I didn't know she was turning 14! When you see her, give her my best regards. Now," she said as we pulled up in front of a house, "let's go make her the best birthday gift ever, shall we? Not only that, but I can't wait to be a part of your challenge."

We walked into her house and set our bags on the dining room table. I marveled at the black, intricate design painted on it. "Where did you find a table this detailed? It must have cost a fortune!"

She laughed. "Actually, the table didn't come with the design."

I frowned. "Then how—" I stopped as I noticed her smile. "You? You did this? It's incredible!"

She thanked me. "It took a very long time, but it was worth it. It goes along with my favorite verse, which is 1 Thessalonians 4:11. I especially love the part that talks about working with your hands."

I couldn't believe she had done it. It was so detailed and symmetrical, it must have taken hours to do just a little portion of the table. She walked into a different room and came back carrying six pieces of wood in assorted sizes.

"I didn't know what you'd think of this as a present. Since Thanksgiving is just around the corner, I thought it would be cool if we could make something Thanksgiving-y." I nodded my agreement, so she continued. "It's something I've done before, so I know that it will turn out all right. These six pieces of wood will end up spelling 'Happy Thanksgiving.' That's not all, though. On the back of each piece of wood will be more letters spelling out Merry Christmas."

"That's so cute! Tina will go crazy over it! How do you set up the pieces, though?"

She set up the pieces of wood the way they would be once they were painted. The long piece of wood she set on the bottom. Then, she placed three shorter pieces on top of the long one. Lastly, she set two taller pieces beside the long one, making a stair-step effect. It looked super neat. I couldn't wait to start making it.

She brought out the paint and handed me a paintbrush. I was surprised. "Me? But I have no clue what to do."

She chuckled. "I'll be doing it too, don't worry. I just thought that Tina would love a gift more if she knew you helped make it."

She was right, of course. Tina would go crazy over my gift if she knew I had a hand in making it. Plus, she would also be happy that I had—voluntarily—met with a godly woman. "Well, what are we waiting for? Let's do this thing!"

She agreed and showed me what to do first. "As you can see, I've already done the long part and stained and painted the blocks so we can now put letters on them. I have printed out papers with the letters on them in large font so we can use a special type of rub-off paper to trace the letters on the blocks of woods. Then, we'll remove the paper and the rub-off paper and paint the letters using the trace marks we already put on the wood."

It sounded simple enough, so I started tracing. While we traced, I asked her my standard challenge question. "What are the qualities of a godly woman to you?"

"I think a godly woman should not just know about Jesus but seek to connect with Him. She also makes wise decisions about who or what gets her time. Lastly, she takes care of the things and the talents God has entrusted her with."

That sounded like a really deep answer. She must have been a Christian forever with no problems whatsoever. I put my thoughts into a question but didn't receive the answer I was expecting.

"No. I had a faith crisis when my kids were toddlers. See, when your kids start asking questions about faith, it really makes you think about your faith, especially when you're trying to match your answers with your husband's. Your kids are on their own faith journey. You can be a good example to them, but you can't make them walk your path. Each person needs to find out if Christianity is her own faith or her parents'. Not only did I have a faith crisis, but I have had a lot of struggles in my life."

I became curious as I began to paint a block of wood. "What has been your biggest struggle?"

"The biggest challenge I've had to face is growing up in a dysfunctional family. At church, we seemed like the perfect family, but at home it was the complete opposite. The hardest thing I have ever had to understand was grace. Ever since I was a child, I've always thought that if you made a mistake, you'd be avoided. I had heard about grace, but I never really experienced it. I always hid all my mistakes because I didn't think grace was real, at least not for me. It affected me for years."

Wow. She was almost just like me. I never really believed grace was real, either. I still don't. It's great that she thought it was real and that it helped her, but grace is not for me.

She continued talking. "Jesus has really stayed with me through the years, no matter what. He has dried my tears, provided when I needed provision, and gave me my two boys. Is it okay if I tell you how I came to have twin boys?"

I nodded. I was curious as to what she was talking about.

"Alexander and I had been married for fifteen years, but I wasn't able to have kids. I was crushed. There were some super godly women at my church who would hold prayer meetings every now and then. For whatever reason, they decided to invite me one night. I opened up to them and told them that I wasn't able to have kids. They prayed for me, and one woman had a prophecy about me. She said that I would have twin boys who wouldn't look like each other. One would love music and have blond hair, and the other would have brown hair. When that woman spoke it, I knew it was true."

How could she know it was true? Did the woman wear a handkerchief, hoop earrings, and carry around a crystal ball? Or did Serena just believe that since she was in a church, it must be a "prophecy from God?" She must have been really desperate to go so far as to believe whatever crazy prophecies came her way. To each his own, I guess. I moved onto my third block.

"Two months later, I found out I was carrying twins."

What? I guess it wasn't just a crazy prophecy.

She continued. "I was teaching middle school at the time but had to go on bed rest because at my checkup we couldn't find one of the twin's heartbeat right away. While I was in bed for three months, my husband was busy finishing up his Ph.D. Then, on December 1st, I went into labor and rode to the hospital for a C-section. When I woke up and was finally allowed to hold my babies, I was awestruck with the miracles I was holding in my arms. They were so precious."

She was a lot like Laura Allen.

Serena continued her story. "The boys were able to come home after a couple of extra weeks in the hospital, but they didn't have much time to adjust from the hospital to our home because we soon moved to Connecticut, where Alexander had just gotten a job."

We had finished with the "Happy Thanksgiving" side of the blocks, so we turned them around and started painting the "Merry Christmas" side. "You mentioned earlier that you struggled with accepting grace for a long time. Do you still struggle with it?

She nodded sadly. "Sometimes I still do, but there's a story behind that. When Alexander and I moved to Connecticut with our boys, he was at Yale as a scientist, and I was at home with infant twins, spiraling out of control. Everything I had done wrong in my life was coming to the surface of our marriage. I started going to counseling, but I still didn't think grace was real—and even if it were, I sure didn't deserve it. However, on May the first, I was sitting in the back of a church, and it clicked. I got up from my seat and ran to the altar. I re-asked Jesus into my heart and was baptized soon after. Even though I know I'm forgiven, the devil still tries to get in my head some days and pound me down. But God keeps reassuring me that I am forgiven."

We were done painting the blocks, so after they had dried, Serena carried them outside to spray them with a finish. When the finish had dried, she placed them in a bag and handed it to me.

"I had such a great time with you today!" Serena said, giving me a hug. "I hope what I said impacted you."

I smiled. "Thanks so much for doing this with me! Tina's going to love this. I couldn't have done it without you." I didn't answer her question about her impacting me. She did, but admitting it would have made me confused because I thought I had come to certain conclusions in my life that I didn't want to change.

She showed me out the door, and I waved goodbye. I had arranged for my grandmother to pick me up because I didn't want to trouble Serena with dropping me back off at my house. On the drive home, I looked at the birthday gift for Tina and smiled. She will be so happy I had met with Serena—and on my own, too! Maybe she will stop texting me little reminders about meeting with women because she will be confident enough to realize I can now do it on my own. And maybe cockroaches will take over the planet and terminate us all!

Chapter Twenty-Four

There were exactly three days until Thanksgiving, and I was the only person in my family who was excited about the holidays, not only because it was Thanksgiving, but also because my birthday was the day after Thanksgiving, the 24rd. When I brought up the subject with my family members, they had some interesting answers.

My grandmother: "I don't know why you think we should work our tails off for a meal that we probably won't even eat." She peered at me intensely. "We haven't had a Thanksgiving meal in years. What's got into you that you suddenly think it's important?"

My sister: "What do we have to be thankful for? Anyway, I don't want to have to slave over a hot stove making food the whole day when I could just grab a granola bar and eat it in my room."

Finally, my mom: "You really think we should waste hours of our time cooking, then waste even more time sitting together at the table to talk about what we're thankful for? Why do you care? Thanksgiving is about giving thanks, and unless you're just so happy that you got higher than a D on your science test, you can't sincerely give thanks."

I dejectedly shuffled away, muttering in protest that I had been making A's on all my science tests except one, which was a B. The general idea I got was that my family was—to put it mildly—less enthused about the holiday than I was. I stomped up to my room to figure out what to do. I had thought it would be nice if we could celebrate a holiday like old times, plus it may make certain people in my family less grumpy. I contemplated what to do. I could forget about the whole thing and act like I have for the past few years, skipping over the holiday. I could make everything myself, eat everything myself, but then have to clean everything myself. Or, I could make the meal and talk my family into eating it with me in exchange for them doing the dishes.

I decided to go with the last option. When I asked my family members whether or not they would eat the meal if I cooked it and then would clean the kitchen afterwards, they all grudgingly agreed. My grandmother seemed a little less chilly when she heard she wouldn't have to make it herself. She even offered to pay for all the ingredients. I started making a list of foods we used to eat together on Thanksgiving. After writing down about six different foods, I stopped. I had just realized that even though I knew what the dishes tasted like, I had no clue how to make many of them—especially the turkey. I sighed heavily. Whenever I tried to do something good, it seemed like nothing worked out. I did the only thing I could do at the moment to solve the problem—I called Tina.

"Do you know anyone who can make some incredible Thanksgiving food?" I asked, after letting her know what I was doing. "I can do about four out of the six dishes for the meal, but as for the sweet potatoes and the dessert, I'm lost." I wasn't having turkey because I knew the hassle that went into preparing it. Instead, my grandmother was going to purchase a rotisserie chicken from Walmart. Not exactly a turkey, but at least we would have meat.

Tina was super excited that I was doing this of my own volition. "I know the perfect person! If you're willing, she could also be your godly woman for the week."

I had expected as much. Tina never passed up an opportunity to casually drop not-so-subtle-hints about my challenge when she was asked about things not regarding godly women whatsoever. I sighed loudly, crackling the reception on the phone. "I guess so." I was willing to do almost anything to get the meal done.

She squealed. "Great! I'll text Vanessa and let her know about your dilemma. She will probably want to meet with you the day before Thanksgiving, so she can make the food with you and then just let you take it home. Also, that's the first day of Thanksgiving break."

I wondered why I was going to such trouble over one day, but I decided that this family needed a day to forget everything else. Tina texted me the next day, letting me know that Vanessa, the woman she was going to set me up with, was able to meet with me the day before Thanksgiving. I decided to start planning out my food in the mean time. My grandmother was surprised and pleased that the foods I had chosen were not only family traditions but also had ingredients that weren't expensive. I wasn't sure whether she was happier about the money or the food, but either way, she was at least smiling at me again. My sister was treating me better, too—not much, but at least a little. She actually walked into the same room I was in and didn't make some sort of degrading comment about me. I know, right? Serious improvement. As for my mom, she was still doing her normal schedule and didn't give a rip about what I was doing.

The day I was supposed to meet with Vanessa, I felt frantic. What if, while I was at her house, I put salt in the dessert instead of sugar and ruined the whole thing? I knew I was no Martha Stewart, and I wasn't sure I could ever be good at baking. Despite my misgivings, I found myself at Vanessa's house ready to bake. Right off the bat, I knew that we would have a great time. She was a very encouraging woman with a sweet spirit.

"I'm Vanessa Broxbern. Tina told me about your challenge. I think it's pretty neat. She also told me that you felt a little worried about tomorrow."

I smiled wryly. "To say the least. I know that if I mess up with any of the food, I probably won't have an opportunity like this again until I'm out of the house."

She frowned. "In that case, we need to make the best dessert your family has ever tasted. I have two types of dessert in mind: a rich pumpkin pie and hockey pucks—which are basically peanut butter and crackers covered in chocolate and sprinkles."

I felt like an English bulldog when she described the desserts—drool flying everywhere. "Sounds amazing. When do we start?"

She laughed. "Right now. I won't be making the sweet potatoes with you because of time, but I will give you the recipe. I believe you'll be able to follow it, since it's pretty easy."

Since she thought I could do it, I knew that I would give it my best shot. If it failed, I still would have five other dishes to present to my family. I'm sure Thunder would love burnt sweet potatoes, anyway. He's not very picky.

She led me over to the island in her kitchen, where she had the ingredients already set out. We were going to make the pie first. She verbally took me through each step of the process before we began. She wanted me to do most of the cooking, but, upon my request, she relented to do the hard parts—I didn't trust myself. I poured the ingredients, one at a time, into a bowl, making sure I was doing everything to the letter. When I put in the pumpkin purée, the smell took me back many Thanksgivings ago when I ate pumpkin pie for the first time, relishing the taste.

Once everything was mixed together, she brought out a flaky piecrust, already in an aluminum pie pan. She spooned the thick batter into it and made sure it was even in the pan. Then, she put the already delicious looking pie in the oven. While it was baking into a golden delight, we started on the hockey pucks. First, we sat down and started spreading creamy peanut butter onto buttery, round crackers. When we had completed about 45 peanut butter and cracker sandwiches, Vanessa walked to the fridge and pulled out a container of sweetened chocolate squares. She took several of the chocolate squares, placed them in a bowl, and slid the bowl in the microwave to let the chocolate melt into a gooey pile.

While she was doing that, she had me pull out wax paper from a drawer and spread two sheets out on the countertop. When the chocolate was melted, she set it on the counter by the crackers. Using tongs, she picked up a cracker sandwich and dipped it fully into the divine stickiness. Then, she pulled it out again and placed it on the wax paper. She repeated this process until all the crackers had a thick layer of silky chocolate covering them. She handed me a container of sprinkles.

"Go ahead and start scattering the sprinkles on. I need to take the pie out of the oven."

I gladly did so, making sure there were just enough on each. She pulled the pie out of the oven and I almost collapsed. It looked perfect. The golden shine of the baked pumpkin was exquisite, and the smell—the smell had me wishing Thanksgiving came every day so I could have an excuse to make it more often. She set it on the cooling racks and smiled widely.

"That looks amazing." Then, turning to me, she asked, "Are you finished with the sprinkles? I thought we could do whatever you do for your challenge over lunch. I hope you're okay with egg salad sandwiches. Do you have any allergies?"

Egg salad sandwiches had been one of my favorite lunches growing up. Sadly, though, I rarely had them anymore. "That would be great! The only food allergy I have is to cilantro." I shuddered. "I can't stand it."

She looked flabbergasted. "I can't imagine life without cilantro. It's one of my favorite herbs to put in food."

I laughed. I helped her make the egg salad sandwiches, and then we sat down at the table. She prayed a simple prayer, thanking God for allowing me to spend the day with her and for providing the food. I was surprised she said my name in her prayer. Not many people did that.

After a few bites, I asked her what the qualities of a godly woman were to her.

"A godly woman knows who she's living for, fights to keep her faith, and blesses those around her."

Fights to keep her faith? You mean, if she feels as if God isn't real, she fights to keep believing that He is rather than just accepting that He doesn't exist? Interesting. I asked her what her favorite verse was, wondering if it would be a faith verse.

"Well, I have a favorite chapter because I can't decide on a favorite verse. It's Psalm 136, which talks about how we should always give thanks to the Lord. Throughout the whole chapter, the phrase 'For His mercy endures forever' is repeated in every verse. It's a very uplifting passage of scripture, especially when you need mercy and wonder if He will give you any."

Wait, there's a mercy that lasts forever? There's no such thing. Everybody's grace has a limit, especially when people do bad things to them. So how could Vanessa sit there and believe that God has everlasting mercy?

"Have you ever personally experienced this everlasting mercy?" I asked, as I ate the remains of my sandwich.

"Yes I have. It was during the biggest challenge in my life, when a tornado came and destroyed our house, killed my sister-in-law, and killed our baby son. It was really hard to deal with the grief. But God put people in our lives to help us get back up, and He can do that for anyone. Sometimes we don't know how things will turn out, and those are the hardest times."

Oh, wow. She knows what it's like to lose someone you love—not just one person but two, and at the same time! If her God did this to her, why is she still a Christian? Why has she forgiven Him for doing this to her?

As if reading my mind, she continued. "As you go through life, you must be a forgiver. You can either stay down and be mad when life hits you or you can forgive—both others and yourself. My husband Ferguson has really influenced me in this area. Whenever life hits him down, he gets right back up and runs after God."

That's not what I've been doing. I keep getting smashed to the ground and, taking the hint, I've stayed down. I guess I've been doing a little too much staying down for my own good. Maybe I should change that. But, that means I would have to forgive others and myself, which is something I would really have to work on. Forgiving others means that I'll have to swallow my pride—which is no easy feat, since it's as big as an overweight walrus. As for forgiving myself... well, after further contemplation it's just too hard. If I am the fault of something, why should I be forgiven for it? I need to just take responsibility for my actions. Besides, what if other people see me forgiving myself and think that I shouldn't be forgiven? No, there are some things that just can't be forgiven.

She stood up and walked over to her bookshelf. She brought over a book called Long Way Gone and handed it to me. "I want you to borrow this. Take it home and read it. I feel as if you need to hear the message it gives."

I thanked her, silently wondering why she thought I needed to hear "its message." At least it was a new book I could read. I put it aside and stood up, stretching. A movement out the front windows caught my eye: it was my sister coming to pick me up.

I turned to Vanessa. "My sister just arrived, so I need to go. Thanks so much for your time!"

She saddened at the fact that I would be leaving. She turned to carefully place the desserts in two boxes and then handed me the recipes for the sweet potato dish. "I hope you have a wonderful Thanksgiving tomorrow! When you finish the book, you can just give it to Tina, and she will return it to me."

Nodding my head in agreement, I thanked her again for the lovely time and walked outside to where my sister was waiting in the car.

As I climbed in, Kimberly sniffed and commented, "I thought the food would smell like twelve-day-old ambergris, but it actually smells better than I thought it would." She sniffed again. "Well, maybe seven-day-old ambergris."

I feigned shock. "What? You gave me an actual compliment? I don't think I'm worthy of this, your Eminence." I rolled my eyes. She knew it smelled great; she just didn't want to admit it.

The drive back home was long. I couldn't wait until I finally arrived home so I could put these two, sweet-smelling babies in a safe place, far from my sister's grasp. We pulled into our driveway, and I climbed out of the car as quickly as possible. When I strode inside, I hurriedly entered the kitchen and put the desserts in the back of a cabinet. Satisfied that it was safe for the present, I climbed up the stairs and into my room, where I collapsed on my chair. I pulled out the book from Vanessa, and, seeing as I had nothing better to do, began to read it.

It was a story of a young man who was a preacher's kid and who had an amazing talent on the guitar. However, even though he played for all the tent revivals his dad held, he wanted to sign with a recording company and become famous. His dad knew that all the recording companies only cared about making money, and they didn't give a fig leaf for his son or his son's heart. Realizing this, he told his son not to sign with anyone. Of course, the son was mad that he was being held back from his "true potential," so he ended up leaving, stealing a wad of his dad's money, as well as his dad's precious guitar that his dad played at all the revivals.

Before he could sign with anyone, though, someone robbed him of his guitar, and he was left in a strange place without any way of making money. He knew he couldn't go home since he had run out on his dad, so he started doing odd jobs around town until he eventually got back on his feet, bought another guitar, and finally signed a deal with a recording company. Later on in the book, the man was at a party and saw the guitar that had been stolen from him years earlier. He tried to take it back unnoticed but was caught. At that exact moment, a fire started in the house, and a mysterious stranger rescued him just before he was consumed in the flames.

He woke up in the hospital. When he received the news from the doctors, it was bad. His hands were so scarred that he was told that he would never play the guitar again, his throat was so scarred that he could barely talk, and some of his organs had been damaged. After much perseverance and hard work, he relearned how to play the guitar, but he was never satisfied. He worked hard at a myriad of jobs so that when he returned home, he could repay his dad the money he had stolen from him. Finally, he was so broken and alone that he decided to return home, even though he did not yet have all the money needed to repay his dad.

Sadly, he never saw his dad again. When he returned home, his dad's friend told him that his dad had died from a mysterious illness. The friend told him that his dad never stopping loving him or waiting for his return. His dad would've forgiven him even if he had returned home empty-handed. The son was heartbroken.

As I read the last few pages of the book, where the man becomes famous and dedicates a song to his dad, I swallowed tears. It was very heartrending. I turned to the last page and nearly started weeping. The final words of the book were these: "No gone is ever too far gone." I didn't understand how the man's father could watch and wait for his son to come home even though his son had taken everything from him and had left him abandoned.

Just as I put the book down and wiped my eyes, I heard a strange noise downstairs. It sounded like my grandmother had drawn in a sharp breath and then leaned heavily against the wall. I had heard about heart attacks and knew what to do in the case of one. I careered out of my room and barreled down the stairs. Just as I reached the first level, I saw my grandmother staring at the door. I turned to where the door was open and nearly collapsed. There, in the flesh, was the one person I never thought I would see again and, quite frankly, didn't care if I ever saw again.

The stranger slowly opened his mouth and uttered with a sad looking smile two words that rocked my world: "Hey, Sis."

Chapter Twenty-Five

I felt my mouth go dry, and I had to swallow. "Jackson?" I couldn't believe it. The prodigal son had returned home—but why? He probably needed money. He left without a second thought, so he wouldn't have returned home without a good reason. As my grandmother slowly walked away to her bedroom, I felt the anger of three years building up inside me.

"How could you leave when I needed you most?" I screamed, feeling the tears coursing down my cheeks. "Dad died, Jackson. He died and it seemed I was the only one who cared. I thought you loved him, but you didn't even stay for the funeral! How could you just turn your back on your family and leave when they needed you most?"

His Adam's apple bobbed as he fought back tears. "I'm sorry, Brie. Can you forgive me? I was blind then. I was hurting, and although you were the only person who sympathized with me, I had to leave because everyone else was just so caught up in other things that I couldn't handle it. I needed to clear my head, and I had a lot of soul-searching to do. If I had known how much going away would affect you, I would have reconsidered; but I never would change what has happened to me."

I gave him a puzzled look as I reached for a nearby tissue to blow my nose.

He smiled nervously. "I'm a Christian."

My eyes bugged out. "What? You mean, you would believe and trust a God who took our dad away? I thought that everyone in our family had silently agreed to never speak of Him again!"

He sighed. "I know, and that's the sad part. You see, God's not cruel or unjust. I don't like the fact that Dad died anymore than you do, but God didn't do it to punish us. He did it so we could become closer to Him. Even though you may feel fatherless, you're not. God is your Father, and if you will only allow Him to heal you, you can rise up from the broken places in your life and pursue Him."

I sputtered. "You really expect me to listen to you? You've been out of my life for three years, without so much as a goodbye. Now you come back and expect forgiveness for leaving, and you want to preach a sermon to me?" Shaking my head, I smiled wryly. "Maybe your God works for you, but He and I have never gotten along."

Sadly, he dropped his head. "I figured you might be a little upset about me coming back, but I didn't know you held such a grudge against me. You may not understand, but staying here would have been the death of me. Everything here would've reminded me of Dad, and I would have never forgiven myself or God for what had happened to him."

His words sounded familiar. Then, I remembered that Vanessa had said them just a few hours earlier. I shook those thoughts off. Jackson didn't deserve forgiveness. With that, I stormed past him out the door and down the road. He wanted me to forgive him for leaving me? He wanted me to forgive God, who took away my dad? He wanted too much from me, and I wouldn't budge from my beliefs. In fact, his coming back only intensified the pain of losing Dad. He looked too much like him. I couldn't take it anymore and slumped to my knees next to a tree, sobbing. I began to remember. As kids, Jackson and I were always together. Despite our age differences, he would always look out for me, and I trusted that he would always be there. His leaving had left a hole in my heart, which I had tried to mend with other things.

Now that he was back, I didn't know if I had room in my heart for him anymore. What if I trusted him again, and he left again? I would die. But as I knelt there in the bitter cold, I remembered the book Vanessa had lent me. The prodigal hadn't deserved forgiveness.

In fact, he deserved to be thrown out of his house, but his father still looked for him every day, hoping his son would return. I blew out a breath that clouded in the cold. For the past few months, I had learned many important lessons from the women I had met with. One lesson was to forgive. Maybe I should finally put that into practice because, like the book said, no gone is ever too far gone. I shook my head. Jackson didn't deserve forgiveness. He deserved to be kicked out of the house. As I stood up to do just that, I felt a hand on my arm. I turned around in surprise. I hadn't heard anyone come up behind me. To my utter shock, it was the lady in the grey coat. She smiled that wispy smile.

"If you do not forgive men their sins, neither will your Father forgive your sins. Do not withhold grace from others, when you have been given it. Embrace your brother, and welcome him back home."

With that, she walked away into the woods and soon was out of sight. I shook my head. That was crazy. Not only did she, a complete stranger, somehow know about my brother, but she also knew that I hadn't forgiven him. She was right, though.

I slowly began walking back to my house. When I went inside, I saw my brother sitting at the kitchen table, head in his hands. "Oh, Lord. I've made a mess of things coming back. Please give me peace and guidance to know what to do."

Seeing him sitting there tore my heart. All he wanted was love, and I had brushed him off just because he believed differently than I did. What a jerk and a hypocrite I've been. Tina doesn't ignore me because I'm an atheist and she's not. Instead, she loves me even when I don't deserve it. Couldn't I do that for my own brother? I ran over to him and threw my arms around his neck.

"I'm so sorry, Jackson. I should have forgiven you from the start, but you reminded me too much of Dad; and it was hard to think straight with all the painful memories you were reminding me of. Can you forgive me?"

He looked astonished for a moment and then returned my hug. "Of course I will. I know that you felt more than a little hurt when I left. What made you change your mind to forgive me?"

I thought about my options. One, I could tell him about my challenge and how it has affected me, or, two, I could brush it off and not really answer his question. Since he obviously seemed to truly be a Christian, I decided to tell him about Tina and my challenge. He was surprised at first, seeing how I was an atheist, but then his face lit up with happiness that I had decided to follow through with it.

"I would like to meet this Tina of yours, if you think that would be okay. She appears to be doing the same thing I'm trying to do—reach out in the dark to starving souls and provide light and the Bread of Life." I nodded, unable to say anything. He hugged me again. "I'm so glad you're not mad at me. I look forward to getting to know you better, Brie-brie." The nickname of my nickname brought a smile to my face. I hadn't heard anyone call me that in a long, long time.

The next couple of days passed in a blur. Thanksgiving was rather strange. Mom refused to eat with us because she was mad at Jackson for leaving and then coming back a Christian. Grandmother was happy that her grandson was home and made him feel welcome. As for Kim, I don't really know what she felt like. She ate with us but didn't say more than ten words the whole meal. I was so in shock all weekend that my birthday passed without anyone really remembering. To celebrate, I threw myself a party—a pity party. I shouldn't have pouted so much, though. Tina didn't even know it was my birthday, or else she probably would've called. So I ended up feeling sorry for myself all weekend; however, come Monday, I was feeling happy, until I arrived at school.

One of my friends ran up to me, shock on her face. "Your Christian brother is actually staying in your house? Like, a Jesus jerk?" I slowly nodded. She narrowed her eyes. "And you're not going to do anything about it?" I slowly shook my head. He was my brother and had just as much right to stay there as I did. She lifted her chin. "You know what this means, right?" She smirked as she slowly turned away. "You're one of them now."

I felt like I had been hit in the face by a bucket of water. What did she mean? That if I didn't try to persuade my brother to leave the house, I was going to be contaminated by Christianity and all my friends would isolate me? I quickly learned that she wasn't the only person who had heard about Jackson. Before lunch, I had received ten angry comments, five unsigned notes saying what a goody-two-shoes I was, and a piece of chewed gum in my hair. I stood before the mirror in the bathroom before lunch, trying to get the gum out of my hair when Tina walked in.

She rushed over to me. "I am so sorry for what's being done to you."

I sadly looked at her. "I didn't know people were so mean not only to Christians but also to people who associate with Christians."

"Many Christians and their friends are persecuted big time for what the Christians believe."

I felt sorry for those people, but, at the moment, I mostly felt sorry for myself, that I was in this mess. Apparently, my brother had started a big prayer meeting downtown right in the middle of the mall. All my "friends" saw it and told the whole school once they found out it was my brother.

Lunch was disastrous. Someone not only spit in my food when I went to grab a drink but they also put a ketchup packet on my seat so when I sat down I got a surprise. That was the last straw. I was so fed up, I went to the nurse and pretended to be sick—which I was in a way—so I could go home. I knew I couldn't go back to school the next day, but if I told my brother why, he would feel badly and maybe even leave again. So, I came up with a plan. I would pretend to be interested in TCPS again so I could go there during school; then I would come home and decide not to go there. The next day, I would act as if I had a bad virus so I could stay home from school, and then I would have to figure out what to do for Thursday and Friday.

I contacted Ginger to let her know I was coming, then told a teacher I was going to TCPS to look into their school again. She was fine with it, so I found myself at TCPS the next day. When I saw Ginger, she gave me a hug.

"You said you needed to talk. What's the problem?"

I told her everything. She listened carefully and then smiled sympathetically. "I understand you're having a hard time, but you can't run from the problem. You have to face it, no matter how hard it is." Then she looked at her watch. "Oh, no. I have to teach my class in five minutes." She paused. "I know you don't want to go home yet, and I'm sorry we can't talk anymore, but I do know someone who works here that you could talk with." As an afterthought, she added, "You could also meet with her for your challenge, if you still need to meet with a woman this week."

I figured it would be all right, so I nodded. She led me down the hallway to an office and ushered me inside. "Jenn," she said, "this is Brie, the girl I met with a couple of weeks ago that's doing the challenge. Would you like to be a part of it?"

She swiveled in her chair towards us and smiled broadly. "I would love to." To me, she added, "I'm Jenn Taylor, by the way. I'm the administrative assistant here at the school."

I sat down and began telling her why I was at the school. She nodded sympathetically. Wanting to get the attention off me, I asked her what she would be doing today.

"Today is a very packed day. TCPS is getting ready for Whoville—a fair we do each year to raise money for the school, since TCPS is a non-profit school. The tuition the students pay goes to pay for books and the faculty; but we have to raise money for the other things we need to buy. Vendors from all over pay to set up tables to sell their products, and then people from around the community pay an entry fee to come into the fair to buy the vendors' items as well as concession food. All in all, it's a fun day." She looked at me. "Be sure you love what you do. I'm very busy all the time, so I'm glad I love what I do, or else it would be a terrible day every day."

Good advice. I would have to remember that later when I landed my first job. "Why did you get this job?"

"I applied for this job because I wanted to be around my boys. I have three boys, and I had homeschooled them for a few years before enrolling them here. I didn't want them to grow up not being around me, so I got a job where they went to school—here."

"You homeschooled them? Why did you stop?" Most people who homeschool don't stop homeschooling until their kids graduate from high school.

"We moved to Germany for a year, and homeschooling is illegal there, so the boys had to attend a public school. When we came back, we homeschooled them for a year, but my eldest was about to go into high school, and my husband and I felt like he needed a better academic rigor than what I was able to give him. We didn't want to put them in a public school again, so we placed them in a private school."

Understandable. "Did you like going to Germany?"

She leaned back in her chair. "When I first went to Germany, I wasn't exactly thrilled. In fact, I kept telling myself that it was only a year, just so I could get through each day. Halfway through our time there, I switched mentalities, and I began to enjoy living in Germany. By the ninth month, when we started packing up our bags to return home, I was finally happy with where I was. It was a little bit too late, though. I wish I had been more open when we first arrived. I learned an important lesson that year: do everything with your whole heart and to the best of your abilities so that you can honor God."

Honor a God I don't believe exists? Like I would do that.

She continued. "Germany was a great experience, but it was also very different. I went from homeschooling my boys and constantly being around them to having them be in a public school and hardly ever seeing them. However, I was able to help out at their school by chaperoning on field trips and such. Right before Christmas, I was able to bring a manger scene to their school and tell the students the Christmas story. After that, I continued to return to their school to tell the students more Bible stories. It was a cool way to share the Gospel."

Interesting. She must really love her kids to sacrifice her time to make sure that they received some sort of Christian influence, even while in public school. "Who influenced you the most to inspire you do so much for your kids?"

"The most influential person in my life was my mom. She always had a smile, no matter what. She was also very thoughtful. However, my mom got breast cancer at 58 years old."

Oh no. That's really rough.

"She had a great attitude through it all, though. She went into remission and was cancer-free—for a little while. She was part of the 1% that got Acute Myeloid Leukemia from the drug in chemotherapy. She saw it as a win-win. She said that if she died, she got to be with Jesus; and if she stayed, she got to be with us. I hope that when I face obstacles, I can have the same attitude as my mom."

What an encouraging ending to a sad story. When most people—like my grandmother— have bad things happen to them, they lash out at the people around them; and those people can't comfort them very easily. It's great that Jenn's mom didn't have a bad attitude. As I looked at my phone to check the time, I realized that Jackson had texted me, asking me why I wasn't at school. I had no clue how he found out I wasn't there, but the damage was done. I would have to tell him in person. I told Jenn what was happening, and she smiled.

"Just remember, the truth will always come to the light, so I'm glad you're telling him right now instead of lying and having him find out later."

I was about to leave when I remembered one question I hadn't asked her yet. "Before I go, what are the qualities of a godly woman to you?"

"Kindness, mercy, and hard work. They are all such incredible qualities that a godly woman should have—especially hard work. It's challenging to commit to doing hard work all the time, but when you finish the job, it's definitely worth it."

As I walked out of the school, I thought about what she had just said. Mercy and kindness, huh? My so-called friends sure don't deserve either after how they've been treating me, but I guess that if I've been given it, I should give it.

When I saw my brother later that day, I confessed what had happened. He was immediately upset that people were treating me that way. He looked so despondent that I told him that even though I didn't agree with his views, he was still my brother, and if his faith made him that happy, then so be it. I don't know why I said that, but it was the first thing I could think of to keep him from deciding he didn't belong and leave. As for who told Jackson I wasn't at school, I don't know for sure, but my bet would be on a girl whose name rhymes with Bean-a.

Chapter Twenty-Six

I couldn't believe my ears. Did my brother actually say that he was considering doing mission work? As in, telling people about his God in places where he could get put in jail for it? Or, worse, get killed? I couldn't believe it—not only did he want to leave me again but he also wanted to put his life on the line to tell people a lie.

He sighed as he sank into a chair in the living room. "I never said I would. I'm just saying that it's something I've been considering for a while, and it's also something God has laid on my heart to do. I never meant to scare you."

I was enraged. I started pacing on the carpet. "What I'm hearing is that you would rather listen to a non-existent person in the sky than your own sister! Do you have any idea what missionaries have to face? Persecution, weird food, dangerous diseases, I could go on and on! It's not some fun adventure, Jackson."

"It would be a fun adventure to me, Brie. I love God, and I would do anything He told me to do. If that meant risking my life for Him, I would do it in a heartbeat. He died for you and me, in case you've forgotten your Sunday school lessons, so the least I can do is tell people about Him."

I dug my fingernails into my skin. He was being brainwashed by this religion. "I don't want to argue with you, but if I have to just to keep you from being killed for a made-up God, I will."

With that, I turned on my heels and stormed up to my room, where I continued to pace. What was I going to do? My talking wasn't going to convince him not to leave, so I would have to find a way to show him that missionaries have it tougher than he thinks. But how? I wasn't a missionary, and I didn't know anyone who was a missionary. Suddenly, I got it. Tina would know a missionary! Probably at least five missionaries. As I celebrated my genius brain, though, I realized that if I told Tina why I needed to meet with a missionary, she wouldn't be happy that I was discouraging my brother from doing what she probably would encourage. So I decided to deceive her. I know, Tina didn't deserve to be deceived, but rather deserved the truth; however, if she knew the truth, she might encourage my brother to become a missionary, and then he would leave me, again. No, I concluded, it was better if she didn't know the whole truth just yet.

I sent Tina a text, asking her if she could find a missionary to meet with me this week for my challenge. She responded within a minute, with a large "YES!" and about a billion exclamation points. She probably thought this was a turning point for me, since this was the first time I had asked her specifically to set up a meeting with a godly woman. Oh, well, let her think what she wants. At least now she might stop being so nagging about me meeting with godly women.

The next morning, Tina texted me and told me that she had talked with a missionary named Jessica Gygax who was interested in meeting with me. Tina said that if my schedule was clear, Jessica could meet with me in an hour and keep me for lunch. I agreed instantly. Even though it was a Saturday, I had nothing to do. I figured I could meet with Jessica, ask her my challenge questions (so I could say I did it), and then grill her the rest of the time on every hard thing in mission work so I could then convince Jackson not to leave. Confident in my great plan, I sat in the kitchen and ate my breakfast of Fruit Loops with a smile on my face.

I dressed, brushed my teeth, and hopped in the car. My grandmother needed to run into town for several errands and had graciously allowed me to catch a ride with her. She didn't ask why I needed to go to this person's house, for which I was thankful. I didn't want to have to lie anymore than I had to. When I was dropped off at the house, I walked to the door and knocked.

A moment later it swung open to reveal a woman carrying a young boy. She ushered me in, and we sat down in the living room.

"It's so good to meet you! Tina told me all about you, and I can't wait to help you out with your challenge!"

I smiled. "Great! What normally happens is that I ask the woman some questions, she answers them, and then we hang out doing whatever the woman normally does on a day-to-day basis." I looked at her, wide-eyed. "That doesn't mean we're going to have to eat worms, does it?"

She laughed. "No. For lunch, we will be having Asian stir-fry—bugs not included."

I sighed in relief. For a minute there, I thought we were actually going to do what she would do on the mission field. That reminded me that I didn't know where she was doing mission work.

"I was a missionary in Asia for three years with my husband and two sons, William and Elijah," she said, gesturing to the son she had on her lap and then to another young boy playing on the carpet. "We then moved to Switzerland and have been ministering there for the past several years."

I noticed that she brightened when she spoke of Asia but then lost the enthusiasm while transitioning to Switzerland. "Why didn't you stay in Asia?"

She laughed wryly. "The Lord wanted us to go to Switzerland. I had planned to live in Asia for the rest of my life; however, after three years, God told my husband and me that we were going to move. I was very upset with that, but I knew God had said it. Just to make sure it was from God, Micah and I fasted and prayed separately for three days. On the third day, we told each other what we felt like God was saying. Both of us felt as if God was telling us to move to Switzerland. Moving was extremely hard because I loved the country so much, but it was God's plan for my life, and who was I to argue with that? It just goes to show that we can make plans, but the Lord's will ultimately prevails. This idea is found in my favorite Bible verse, Proverbs 19:21, which says, 'There are many plans in a man's heart; nevertheless, the Lord's counsel—that will stand.'"

She would really give up friends and familiarity just because her God said so? That's pretty sacrificial. I don't think I would be able to do that. Jackson seems to think he can. I sighed inwardly, wondering what I was going to do with him. "What was your favorite thing about Asia?"

"Definitely the people. They would give you the shirt off their back if you asked them, despite the fact that they were very poor. They just wanted to be your friend."

Her friend? That's incredible. If I were poor, I'd probably hang on to whatever clothes I had, rather than giving them to other people. "Was it hard leaving Asia?"

She nodded. "Yes, but even though I was upset that I wasn't able to stay in Asia longer than three years, I was glad I didn't know that before I went. If I had known I was only going to be there for three years, I wouldn't have made the memories I had or made the relationships I did. With that in mind, I realize that if I don't invest myself into the people of Switzerland, I will miss out on beautiful things."

I guess I should start looking around me to make sure I'm not missing out on something beautiful. But enough focusing on me. I needed to find some information to dissuade my brother in becoming a missionary. "What was your least favorite thing about Asia?"

"In Asia, it was very hard to prepare food because of the flies. Driving was a challenge, as well, because no one followed the rules of the road. To them, laws on paper didn't mean as much as a person in authority whom they respected telling them what to do. Also, I had to be careful whom I talked to about God. I could answer any question about God they gave me, but if I started the conversation, it was called 'evangelizing.'"

That's not fair. Haven't they heard of "freedom of speech"? Oh wait, I guess that only applies when you're in America. "What happened if you were caught evangelizing?"

She set her son down on the floor and watched him grab a toy before answering. "Missionaries would be warned to not do it again. If they were caught a second time, they would be sent out of the country, put on a blacklist, and not allowed into the country again. The locals, on the other hand, would be imprisoned and would face much harder challenges. In one country, some people were inviting teenagers from the countryside to a special school where they would teach them different trades. The students would stay at the school until they had learned their trade well enough to go back to their villages. Almost all of the kids weren't Christians when they arrived at the school because they came from hostile villages; but after attending the school, 95% of them became Christians. Once they had their trade mastered, they would return home. Some of them even told their families about Jesus, even though they could go to jail for it—or, worse, disappear because of their beliefs."

"One girl wouldn't return to her family until she was prepared spiritually in the Word of God. She knew that if she went back and tried to tell her family and friends about Jesus, she would easily become shaken in her faith because she wasn't grounded in the Word. So, instead of going home during the holidays, she stayed at the school and read the Bible, delving deeper into it each day."

That's strange. She would rather stay at the school and read her Bible than see her family? What kind of a spell was she under? I mean, sure, if you believe in God, then great, but reading her Bible all day long? That's a little too much, if you ask me.

As she looked at the clock, she stood up. "I believe it's time for a lunch break. What do you say?"

My stomach growled in response, to my dismay. I'm sure my face was beyond red. She simply laughed and headed to the kitchen. She pulled out a cutting board and handed me a knife and some bell peppers. I began to cut them up as she cut up some other vegetables. Once they were all cut, she put some coconut oil in a frying pan and started tossing in different vegetables and some chicken. Before long, it smelled wonderful in the kitchen, and I started setting the table, hardly able to wait for lunch. When the stir-fry was done, we all sat down at the table as Jessica gave thanks to God "for giving us this wonderful meal." I couldn't understand why people felt inclined to do that. It's not like God was here, cooking it for us.

I took a bite of the stir-fry and sighed with delight. It was absolutely amazing. I had it polished off in no time. Once done, I turned to Jessica with one more question to ask her before I had to leave. "What are the qualities of a godly woman?"

She smiled as she wiped her mouth. "The qualities of a godly woman are many, but I believe a key one is to follow what God wants for you, even if you or the people around you don't agree with it—like going to Switzerland when you love Asia."

Well. That completely ruins my argument for Jackson to stay. I had better not tell anyone that, or they'll remind me of it when I try and stop Jackson from leaving.

Once lunch was finished, Jessica gave me a hug. "Thanks for spending time with me. I loved getting to know you!"

I smiled. "Me too. I wish you luck on your mission work!" I received a text just then from my grandmother, telling me that she was outside waiting for me. I said goodbye and left.

Jessica was a great woman, who really seemed to love doing mission work, but I didn't want Jackson to do that. He couldn't leave me. As I reflected on all Jessica had said, however, I realized that the good things outweighed the bad. If I really loved my brother, wouldn't I want the best for him? Jessica made it seem as though it was an adventure, and my brother is all about adventures. It's quite sad that I claim to love him and yet I'm trying to keep him from doing what he loves.

As soon as I got home, I walked inside and found Jackson. "I wanted to tell you that if you really want to do missions, you have my blessing. I shouldn't have the power to keep you from doing something you want to do, even though I've heard some bad things about it."

He looked as if he would explode, he was so happy. "Brie, this is an answer to prayer! I prayed you would see the good in it! Thank you so much."

I was startled. My blessing was an answer to prayer? You mean, he was praying for me? He must really want to do this, if he went so far as to mention me in his prayers. I guess I'll see where this goes.

As if reading my thoughts, he said, "I'm so happy you aren't mad anymore! You won't regret letting me go!"

I frowned as I walked upstairs. I only hoped he was right.

Chapter Twenty-Seven

I could not believe it. I had gotten sucked into playing a game of truth or dare at school with Tina and her friends, and now I was regretting it. One of her friends, Emma Sanders, was a dancer, and she believed that ballet was harder than any other sport. Of course, I wasn't buying that. I used to ski, and I play tennis. Skiing isn't the most active sport, but it's tolling. Tennis, on the other hand, is a very active sport, and I believe it ranks higher than ballet. I mean, honestly, all you do is plié all day, stretch a little, and wear tutus. So when she mentioned that ballet was, by far, the hardest sport, I verbally disagreed, listing all the sports that were harder than ballet, including football. Big mistake. It was her turn to dare someone, and she chose me. Her dare for me was to spend just half a day with one of her dance teachers, Alexis Burleson, to learn what she does on a daily basis, and then take a ballet class with Emma later that evening, so I would know what Emma has to do every day in dance class.

If I refused, I would be listed as a chicken, too scared to take a little ballet class. If I accepted, however, I would have to spend a day doing easy, boring things like stretching, curtsying, and speaking French. The last one would be more of a challenge since I didn't know that much French besides the basics. I decided to accept the dare because, one, I could prove that ballet was easy; two, I could become more flexible by the end of the day; and three, if this teacher happens to be a Christian, I could ask get her to be one of my godly women. Since there was no school the next day because of a possibility of snow, we agreed that would be the day I did the dare. I asked Tina later if she knew whether Alexis was a Christian or not. She immediately knew what I was getting at.

"She is, and I know she would love to be part of your challenge! In fact, I'll text her today and let her know. You have great ideas!"

I smirked. "You're right; I do." She rolled her eyes as I laughed. After school, I went home and made a list of everything I needed for a dance class, according to Emma. I started packing a bag with the following: a leotard Emma was letting me borrow, tights Emma was letting me borrow, a skirt Emma was letting me borrow, ballet shoes Emma was letting me borrow, a bottle of water, a bottle of Gatorade, five protein bars, a bag of trail mix, ten bobby pins, two ponytail holders, a brush, and a guidebook on French. I figured it wouldn't hurt to be prepared. I fell asleep dreaming of the look on Emma's face when I survived her little ballet class and proved her wrong. I mean, really, how hard could ballet really be?

The next morning, I hitched a ride with Jackson to the ballet studio. He was a bit skeptical that I would survive a ballet class, but I figured he just knew nothing about how easy ballet was. As I climbed out of the car, I noticed some light snow falling from the sky. I enjoyed it for a brief moment before I walked in the door and was then greeted by Alexis.

"I hear you're here to prove how easy it is to be a dancer," she said, smiling. "As well as doing your challenge, of course."

I nodded. "That's right. What do we do first?"

She led me outside to her car. "First things first. We're going to Starbucks to have coffee with Jesus."

I was confused. Having coffee with Jesus? What did she mean?

At my baffled look, she explained. "I do my devotions in the morning while drinking coffee, so I like to call it that."

We pulled into the parking lot of Starbucks and climbed out of the car. Once inside, she ordered what she wanted then turned to me, wanting to know what I wanted. Since this was only my second time at Starbucks, I shrugged.

"I don't know coffee well enough to know what to order."

She smiled. "In that case, can I order for you?" I nodded. She turned to the cashier and tried to order me the highest cold caffeine drink they had. Unfortunately, they were out, so she got me the second highest. I couldn't wait to try it. In all the times I had drunk coffee, it had never affected me. I was about to find out if anything could. I decided to put it aside while we did whatever devotion she had planned. We sat down and she opened up a book that said, Letters From Heaven. I wondered what kind of a book would have letters from heaven in it. She told me that it was the book of Ephesians put in simpler words.

I listened as she began to read. After reading a little bit, she looked up from her book.

"I really love Ephesians 1:4, which says, 'Just as He chose us in Him before the foundation of the world, that we should be holy and without blame before Him in love.' Before we were created, God made a plan that He would see us all in an unstained innocence, as holy in His eyes."

What? God's original plan for us was for us to be innocent and holy? Well, I've already messed that up. It's a good thing God doesn't exist, or I would be on His naughty list big time. Why would God, if He actually existed, plan for us to be holy and innocent? There is a big thing called sin in this world that stains all innocence and so-called holiness. If God can see everything, can't He see that, as humans, we couldn't live up to those expectations? That's a pretty tall order, one that no one will be able to fill.

I was so frustrated with all the jumbled thoughts in my head that I decided to do something I had never done before: I asked a theological question. "Why would God demand us to be holy and innocent if He knew we were going to mess up?"

She smiled at me. "Because God has never-ending grace. When Adam and Eve sinned, it wasn't because they were under too much pressure to be good; it was because they had free will. We will always have two choices with every decision we make: God's way or our way. If we choose God's way, it results in us giving up ourselves to Him but ultimately gaining eternal freedom; but if we choose our way, we head down the wrong path, a path the devil wants us to pick which will end in eternal bondage. That doesn't mean that when we mess up, we get no second chances. Instead, if we ask forgiveness from God, He gives us grace and redeems us from our sin. That's how much God loves us."

That was a lot to take in. I had never thought of that. I mean, I knew about Adam and Eve, but I had always thought that if you mess up, you're sunk. No second chances. However, it appears that God has enough grace to go around for everyone. Even for me. I must have looked really confused because she spoke again.

"Have you ever listened to Céline Dion's music?"

I nodded as I took my first sip of the coffee, which was amazing.

She continued. "I adore Céline Dion's love songs because they can be equated to God's love for us."

As my mind scrolled through the list of my top favorite songs by her, I was floored by Alexis' comparison. God loves me that much? That is—as I hastily tried to clear my mind of all these foreign thoughts—if there really is a God at all. I pulled my thoughts back to what Alexis was saying.

"While on the topic of love, I believe a good quality of a godly woman is being intentional about loving people." She then glanced at the time. "We need to get going if we're going to stay on schedule." She stood up and gathered her things together. "Come on. We're going to work out."

I nervously pushed back my chair. What did she just say? Does she mean work out as in lifting heavy metal objects and doing pushups? I'm not so sure that I will enjoy that—or, more specifically, that I will be able to do that. Nevertheless, I stood up as well and followed her out to her car. We drove in comfortable silence until we arrived at the YMCA, where she had a membership. We strolled inside, and, after she signed us both in, we walked into the main workout area where people were running on treadmills, biking on stationary bikes, lifting weights the size of small boulders, and doing pushups as if they couldn't get enough. I swallowed.

"What's first?" I was going to do this. I had to. If I didn't, I would thereby prove my own point wrong—that dancers actually have it harder than I thought. However, the more I thought about it, the more I realized that Alexis wouldn't make me do anything hard, since I was just a kid.

She grinned. "We have to warm up our muscles first. If you work out before doing that, you'll tear something."

She led me through some basic stretching exercises, and I felt as though I was keeping up pretty well. I wasn't the most flexible, but I was only a foot away from getting my right split. My left one, however, was a little less impressive. After that, I expected us to hit the metal right away, but Alexis simply stood up from her previous position on the floor and said, "I'm going to the bathroom."

Before she walked away, however, she looked at me and grinned slyly. "Hold plank till I get back."

I stared at her retreating back in horror. I hoped she wasn't one of those people who liked to read a novel while they're in the bathroom because I could only hold plank for about 12 seconds. Nevertheless, I wasn't daunted by her challenge—too much. I reluctantly got on the floor and proceeded to hold plank. By the time I got to five seconds, I was sweating bullets. At nine, my arms began to shake. I surprised myself by going to thirteen, then fifteen, until I was at thirty whole seconds. By this time, I was sure I was going to pass out. I could barely breathe, and my arms demanded rest. I frantically began looking around for Alexis. Surely it didn't take her thirty whole seconds to go to the bathroom, right? I was about to collapse when she walked over to me and laughed.

"I hope you realize that when you hold plank, you can't keep your knees on the ground. You have to keep all your weight on your arms and use your abs to support you."

Abs? What abs? I burned off so many calories the last time I tried to flex my abs that I had to eat half a container of Oreos just to make up for it. I'm not fat, just less motivated to be chiseled out of stone like some people. I mumbled some sort of response then stood up, face flaming. So what if I couldn't hold plank? I'm not a pirate. I'm sure I can do everything else she throws at me.

I was wrong. She took me over to an area where there were weights stacked on racks. "When you have a plan, you have to be careful that you don't waste time while doing it, whether that's in your mind, body, or spirit. My plan is to get you to the point where you feel confident in working out by yourself."

In that case, we'll be here forever. I don't see that confidence she speaks of in my near future. I took the five-pound weights she handed me and nearly dropped them. She showed me with her own set of weights (which were so heavy they would have killed me if I tried to lift one with both hands) what I was to do with mine: curl to the front eight times, curl to the side eight times, and lift them above my head, clicking them together eight times. I tried doing the front curls eight times, but I was so worn out after two curls, I didn't know if I would be able to continue. She helped me get through it, though. I did sets of eight for all of them. Then I repeated the whole entire process three times. I gasped for water halfway through my last set of lifting above my head. She encouraged me on. My arms struggled as they strained against the extreme force shoving my arms down. I felt as though I were lifting an entire mammoth. Finally, with Alexis lifting my arms to complete the click for me, I was done. I buckled down onto the floor and gasped for breath, sweat gushing out of my pores.

She laughed. "Alright, that's all with the weights. Now we're going to do leg exercises."

I groaned. More? I thought that would be all. I stumbled over to the biking machine Alexis was standing next to and slowly got on. Once I straddled the bike, I started pedaling. Slowly.

She grinned. "You're going so slow that if you were on the road right now, the bike would have toppled over."

I began to pedal faster until I heard the whirring sound of the bike spinning the air. I felt pretty happy that I was actually accomplishing something. That is, until Alexis pushed a lever. Instantly, it was harder to pedal. I began to snort like a rambunctious bull as I strained to push the pedals around and around. I asked her about the lever.

"It controls how hard it is to pedal."

Ah. I could have figured that out myself if it weren't for the fact that half my brain cells were now dead from lack of Oreos. Working out for me equals doing three pushups, taking a small nap, and then eating Oreos to celebrate the pushups. By the time I finished this workout... Well, let's just say that Walmart is going to run out of Oreo cookies in ten minutes flat.

She continued putting on and taking off pressure for the bike until I knew I was going to die if I didn't stop pedaling. Finally, after what seemed like forever, she said, "Okay, I think that's enough for now. I don't know if you'll be warmed up enough for this evening's ballet class, though. Let's go ahead and eat before I take you back to the studio."

Food. The thought made me happy again. I was so hungry I could eat a blue whale. After we climbed into her car, she started driving to Deli Boys. I saw my coffee in her car and reached for it, eager to hydrate my body and give it some extra energy. To start a conversation, I asked, "What's an important life lesson you've learned?"

"A life lesson God has taught me is that I am not a burden or an inconvenience and that He delights in taking care of my needs. A lot of the time, people don't want to ask for help for anything because it makes them feel weak or makes them feel badly that they're making someone go out of their way to do something they need. God delights in taking care of us. We should never stop coming to Him with our problems."

I always thought telling other people your problems and relying on someone else made them upset. I know that if I go to my sister or my mom, they become upset that I didn't just deal with it myself. I took another sip of my coffee and realized my stomach was starting to curdle. I pressed a hand against it as she looked over at me.

"You okay?"

I shook my head. "I don't know what's wrong." Then we both noticed the coffee at the same time. She looked at me with an incredulous expression.

"Please tell me you haven't been drinking caffeine on an empty stomach right after working out."

I groaned miserably. She looked at me sympathetically. "I'm sorry. Once you start eating, it'll pass—eventually," she added in an undertone.

I smiled weakly. "I'm sure I'll be fine. In the meantime, what's another life lesson you've learned?" I knew if she started talking, it would take my mind off my stomach.

"I've learned that it's okay to grieve. When you lose someone you love, whether they move, pass away, or betray you, it's okay to grieve for them. However, if your hope is gone when they leave, it was an unhealthy relationship; and it is better that they left so you can place your hope where it belongs—not in people but in the Lord. When all your hope is in God, you can still mourn for others, but your heart will remain steadfast in Jesus so you won't lose hope and you'll be able to move on in life."

I was guilty on all charges. When Jackson betrayed me by leaving when I needed him most, the part of my heart that I'd given to him went with him. And when my dad died, I felt as though he had taken all my hope with him to his grave. But putting my hope in God? I didn't know. It would be incredible to not have to worry about my hopes and dreams because I have someone to hold on to, but why should I put my hope in God? He never showed up when I needed Him the most.

We pulled into a parking spot for the restaurant, and once inside, I tried not to hurl as I waited for the coffee to settle. I ordered some sort of sandwich—I wasn't really focusing on food at the moment—and went to get my drink. After pouring about eight different healthy, all-organic soft drinks (which sounded like an oxymoron) into my cup to make a suicide, I sat down at the table Alexis had picked for us. I drank and drank until the coffee at least had some friends down there, waiting for the food to come. When the food did arrive, I was relieved to know that I had ordered a turkey sandwich, which I like. If I had unknowingly ordered some vegan, gluten-free, this-is-only-for-an-ultimate-health-freak sandwich, I probably would have hurled all over the table—and all over Alexis. We made quick work of our sandwiches and then hastily returned to her car; she had lead rehearsal at her studio in a few minutes.

"What performance are you preparing for?"

"It's called The Veil. It's basically the story of Creation through dance. I play the role of the Spirit of God who creates everything. Once Adam and Eve are created, there is a temptation scene where the person playing Satan, Anna Thompson, tempts Adam and Eve and eventually convinces them to eat the forbidden fruit, resulting in the Spirit of God separating Himself from all humanity with a veil. Then Jesus, also played by me, comes through the veil in human flesh to redeem humanity from sin. Once the crucifixion is enacted, I am put back behind the veil. A recorded monologue is played, where I talk about how evil is strong but Jesus is stronger. Then, as the music builds, I tear down the veil and the humans are redeemed from their shame."

I blinked, trying to take it all in. "That's pretty incredible." I had never thought of Jesus that way. Sure, He was a real person because there is historical proof, and I have to believe that He died and then came back to life because there's medical proof for that; but there's no proof that He's the Son of God. However, when Alexis described it with such passion and such belief, it would make even the most hard-core atheist question her beliefs—including me.

We arrived at Unity Dance Studios then and climbed out of the car. Once inside, we walked into the main dance studio. I sat down in a chair next to the wall and watched as Alexis greeted the lead dancers. They did a short warm-up, and then they started practicing. I was enjoying watching them because they were really good, and they danced with emotion and passion. After about an hour and a half, they decided to call it quits. Alexis walked over to me and said that the ballet class I would be taking would be starting in about forty-five minutes, so I should probably start getting ready.

Inwardly, I scoffed. It wouldn't take me forty-five minutes to get ready. I decided to do it anyway just so I could prove her wrong.

Thirty minutes later I stood in the bathroom still trying to pull on my tights. I had put on my leotard before realizing that I had forgotten to put the tights on first. Then I had to take off the leotard and put the tights on under it. Then, once I had the tights and leotard on, I realized I had to go to the bathroom. As a result, I was still struggling after half an hour of no progress. Once my leotard and tights were safely on, I put on the skirt and the ballet shoes. Then I started with my hair. I put it up in a high ponytail and began to strategize on how I was going to make a bun because I realized that I had never had any experience with making buns. I eventually decided on braiding the ponytail and then pinning it into a bun. Three bobby pins in, I realized I had lost at least six. So, with the last bobby pin left, I shoved it in and hoped the bun stayed.

Opening the bathroom door, I walked out into the dressing area where I had put my bag. I drank a few sips of Gatorade and ate half of the protein bar. I needed energy if the class was as hard as Emma said it would be—which I sincerely doubted. Other girls of all ages began to arrive and put their stuff away. They already had their ballet clothes on, and they had nice, neat buns that weren't going to fall out halfway through class like I knew mine would. Finally, Emma arrived. When she saw me, she grinned and gave me a hug.

"I can't wait till class starts! This will definitely be an experience you won't forget." She exchanged knowing looks with another dancer.

I shrugged off all my worries and decided that it couldn't be that bad. A young woman with black hair walked out of the studio and announced, "Class is starting!"

At those words, all the dancers rose as one and walked into the studio.

As the dancers brought some barres out from by the wall, Emma whispered to me that the young woman with black hair was Katherine, the teacher of the class. Once everyone had a spot at a barre, Katherine instructed us to lie flat on our backs. I did, wondering what this was all about. She turned some music on and then came to the front of the room and lay on her back as well.

"Crunch front!" I listened in horror as I realized I would have to work out again, for the second time that day. After a solid five minutes of crunches, planks, and pushups, I knew I wouldn't last much longer. Thankfully, though, Katherine said we could get up and stretch out our abs, which I did obligingly. I was glad that the hard stuff was out of the way. Now I could do curtsies and stretch.

I was dead wrong. Katherine did lead us through some stretches, and we did some combinations with pliés in them, but that was it. Everything else we did was mind-challenging combinations with super quick frappés, super slow rond de jambes, super tiring holding your foot in passé for forever, and it went on and on. No matter how hard it was, I wouldn't show any sort of giving up. I was twenty minutes into this hour and a half class. I could and would do this.

Except for adagio. As soon as Katherine began to demonstrate what we would be doing, I couldn't picture myself lasting two seconds. She expected us to keep our leg in front of us at ninety degrees and hold it there. Then move it to the side. Then move it to the back. Then reverse the whole process! Then do it all on relevé! I figured that no one else would be able to do this either, so I felt confident in the dancers' support with my objection when I raised my hand.

She smiled at me. "Yes?"

"Can we not do this one? I know that no one will be able to do this incredibly hard combination, so why don't we just skip it and save us the energy of trying and failing?"

She looked confused. "I don't know what you mean. These dancers are very capable of doing this adagio. In fact, this adagio is one of the easier ones."

What? I looked around me and saw that all the dancers were staring at me as if I had grown a second nose. Oops. I guess they were capable. I was the one who wasn't capable. I shuffled my feet. "Never mind. I think I have enough energy."

She smiled as if I were crazy—which I was—then turned on the music. The first ninety-degree développé I did was okay, considering the fact that my energy level was in the negatives. However, the rest of the développés decreased in degrees until I was doing thirty-degree développés—which was still too high for my feeble knees. Torrents of moist perspiration gushed down my back, saturating my leotard. My bun had already halfway fallen out, and I was shaking like a leaf in the middle of a tornado.

Finally, the music ended, and I collapsed in a pile on the floor, pretending I was stretching. Emma gave me a look, and I knew that she wasn't fooled. I quickly stood up so I wouldn't be called a wimp, although I knew that I would probably fall over again. No one else seemed to be breathing like a locomotive or sweating buckets, so I tried to force myself to hold my head high. For the next thirty minutes, there were combinations that slowly wore me down to the point where I was inhaling water like oxygen, sitting every chance I got, and wishing I had never, ever said that dancing was easy.

When Katherine asked us to put the barres away, I put my hands on the barre and lifted. Nothing happened. I was so incredibly worn out that I couldn't even lift a ten-pound barre. With a smirk, Emma grabbed the barre single-handedly, lifted it up, and carried it all the way to the other side of the room. I watched amazed before crawling to the wall where I drank some water and scarfed down a protein bar. I thought that would be the end of class, but no, we still had to do "center"—whatever that meant.

I soon found out. We first did a "petite allegro," which basically means jumping a lot and killing your calves to the beat of a quick, staccato piano song. A cramp crept its way up my right calf and squeezed tight. It felt like someone had cut through the flesh of my leg and had started sawing my muscles with a serrated knife—it wasn't pleasant, to put it mildly. With a moan of pain, I crumpled onto the floor hugging my leg to my chest. Emma looked at me in alarm.

"Don't bend it! Straighten it out so you can stretch it, and the cramp will go away eventually."

I nodded as if I knew that and did it. Two minutes and seventeen seconds later, it finally left. I sighed in relief and stood up. My calf still felt like someone was wringing it like a dishrag, but at least the sawing pain had gone away. We then did an adagio in center. It was long, it was hard, and I knew if I didn't do something, I would pass out from lack of Oreos. I asked if I could grab something from my bag and then escaped as soon as I was given permission. I ate two more protein bars, drank the rest of my Gatorade, and tried to regain my breath. Once I felt like I wouldn't make a fool of myself, I went back to class.

Katherine was explaining a combination when I entered the studio. I tried to follow along as much as I could, but the French for Dummies book I had read didn't equip me with everything I needed for this class. It just kept me from being completely lost. I eventually figured out that we were supposed to do some sort of tom-bae-potter-boo-ray before doing a peer-ooh-wet—which was basically a spin with your knee up high. You then repeated that all the way across the floor before doing some sort of leap. I figured it was easy enough, so I walked to where a line was starting for the dancers to do the combination.

When it was my turn, I gingerly started across the floor. I hurt so badly and was sweating so much that I was surprised I didn't slip on my own sweat and collapse. I was doing all the tom-baes, twirls, and leaps to the best of my ability—in other words, I probably looked like a gangly giraffe with dislocated knees. When I finished, I turned to the teacher, expecting some sort of kind word, maybe a pat on the back, perhaps even a standing ovation. Instead, she gave me a surprised look then turned to the other dancers who were going across the floor. I shrugged off the look, thinking my talents probably astounded her. When I did the whole combination from the left side, I felt slightly less confident halfway through it, but I still felt like I was doing better than all the other dancers even while breathing like a bull—until I looked into the mirror.

I was so shocked at how horribly I was doing that I just stopped in the middle of the dance floor and stared at myself. As a result, the dancer who was behind me immediately ran into me. I quickly ran off the floor and sat down. I thought I was doing fine, but I really did look like that giraffe—only worse. I had believed I was doing so much better. I guess "fake it till you make it" isn't exactly a good phrase for ballet. Once the music was done, Katherine brought us all out to the middle of the dance floor. She played a soft song as we curtsied—which I could barely do, I hurt so badly. I was about to leave to go eat another protein bar when Katherine began to pray. All the other dancers had their heads bowed and their eyes closed, so I followed suit.

Who would have thought? Praying after a dance class. When she finished, everyone clapped and thanked her for class. They snagged their water bottles and left the room to grab their dance bags. I did the same. Once I had packed all my stuff together, I turned around ready to go, but Emma blocked my path.

"Well? Was it as easy as you had imagined? Did our 'simple exercises' bore you?" Her voice held a note of triumph.

I was about to retort that I had held my own but then realized that I really didn't. I sighed. "It was harder than I expected, I'll give you that. I feel like I've been run over by a train, then had all my muscles stretched to the point of ripping, then was mauled by a bear."

She grinned. "And that's just the easy part. Wait till tomorrow. You won't be able to get out of bed, much less function fully at school."

I groaned. "I guess ballet is harder than all the sports I claimed were harder."

She smiled slyly. "You see, if ballet were easy, they would call it football."

I laughed. She had totally stolen that line from a movie. I left the building and climbed into the car where my brother was waiting for me. I told him what had happened, and he nodded like he was expecting that. On the way home, I realized that my meeting with Alexis went really well, and I enjoyed it—even though every muscle in my body was now torn. Maybe I should see The Veil in February; it could prove to be interesting. In fact, this whole day with Alexis has proved to be interesting. She really made me rethink my thoughts about God, and it seems that I have started to doubt the non-existence of God. Rather than trying to constantly debate whether God's real or not, I've been more intrigued with whether He cares for me or not. If He doesn't care for me, I shouldn't feel compelled to "believe in Him." But what if He does?

Chapter Twenty-Eight

Ah, the life of a broke teenager. I was in quite a pickle at the moment. Seriously, I was toast. My financial circumstances weren't very grape. I desperately needed money for Christmas presents; however, I couldn't ketchup to the amount of dough that I needed. Sighing, I mustard up enough strength to stand from my previous position—lying on my bed—and bemoaned my fate of being that one person who buys everyone a dollar box of candy for Christmas.

I knew I needed to find a job quickly because Christmas was just around the corner. I started pacing, deep in thought. I'd already tried babysitting, and that proved to be a disaster. I also dog sat Chi-Chi, which also proved to be a disaster. But, hey, you have to take what you get. At least I was paid handsomely for both of those jobs. Then I snapped my fingers, an idea forming.

I could walk dogs for people! Dogs seemed to like me well enough, and it wouldn't take too much time out of my day, only about an hour; and if I garnered enough customers, it would be good money. Genius, that's what I am. I immediately started writing down a list of people who owned dogs. Once I had written down about ten or so, I texted them all. While I waited for their responses, I made myself a smoothie. As I blended all the ingredients together, my phone began to buzz with texts. Only two of the people I had texted were interested in having their dogs walked by me. The others claimed they liked doing it themselves. I groaned in disappointment. I had researched on what to charge, and I was only charging ten bucks for every half-hour walk I took them on. It's not like I wanted a million bucks for it! Okay, I wanted it, but I didn't ask for it!

I decided to text Tina to see if she knew any dog owners who needed someone to walk their dog for them. She responded almost instantly—I wonder if she's literally glued to her phone! Tina said a woman had asked her just the other day if she would walk her dog for her; and Tina had already texted her and asked if I could do it instead. That girl must have electric thumbs to text that fast! I thanked Tina and asked for the woman's contact information so I could get ahold of her myself. When she sent me the name and number, I realized that the name, Karen Young, looked vaguely familiar; I just couldn't place where I had heard it. Then, I remembered.

When Gayle Cobb went to a women's retreat and got a message from God, she was rooming with this Karen Young. Small world! I texted Karen, and we worked out the details of when I would come. She wanted me to come tomorrow and then walk her dog for the rest of the week, every day, around dinnertime. I was excited to get started; it was the first meeting I had scheduled in a long time that wasn't with a godly woman—instead, it was with a dog.

Suddenly, I slapped my forehead in consternation. A godly woman meeting! My challenge! I groaned. I had completely forgotten about it. Maybe I could find out if Karen was a Christian, and, if so, see if she would be willing to meet with me for my challenge. That way, I would be able to hit two birds with one stone. After texting her again, I sat down in my green chair and contemplated what my life was going to be like once the challenge was over. I was already halfway done, and my thoughts and beliefs were completely messed up. I don't believe in evolution anymore because it's a lie, but I don't know what to believe. It seems like every time I turn around, somebody proves one of my beliefs wrong and shoves God in its place. Even if God were real—which is a big if—how do I know that He would care for me and love me like He loves others? I don't know. All I know is that if God exists, He had the power to keep my dad from dying, and He didn't. He could've at least let my last time with him be good, but He didn't. No warning, no "message from God," no vision, nothing. I think maybe I should stop trying to prove His inexistence and instead figure out whether He cares about me or not. If He doesn't, then I shouldn't feel obligated to believe in Him or love Him.

The more I think about it, the better of an idea it seems to be. I don't have any substantial proof that God doesn't exist, so why not just do a trial for a few months and really try and see if He loves me? What's the worst that could happen? I mean, really, if there really is a God who loves and cares about me, then it is all the better for me, right? Someone who would watch out for me and take care of me when I get upset. I don't currently have anyone in my life that really does that, anyway.

I tilted my head decidedly. Yes! For the next 6 months, I will forget my previous belief that God doesn't exist and instead try and see if He loves me enough to willingly forgive all the many sins I've accumulated in life. Of course, it's not like I fully believe that He's real, but I won't deny that I've heard some pretty amazing stories these past few months.

I was interrupted from my rumination by a text message. Karen said that she indeed was a Christian and that she would love to meet with me tomorrow as part of my challenge. She also said that if I were free, she could take me out for an early dinner at Kumo to talk before I walked the dog. I agreed, and so it was settled.

The next morning, I prepared myself for the day. I stuffed an extra change of clothes in a bag because if you ever come in contact with an animal, it's always good to be prepared. I definitely did not need to wear my earrings from Claire's, and I wasn't going to wear anything I really liked—even though Karen's dog was probably a harmless Yorkshire Terrier. After school, I was able to catch a ride with Jackson to the Asian restaurant to meet Karen. As I walked inside, I saw a woman sitting alone at a table and assumed it was Karen. I waved and strode over to her.

"Hi! Are you Karen?"

She smiled. "Yes, I am. And you must be my dog walker. Have a seat."

I did so with a smile. A waiter scurried over to take our orders, and I ordered the teriyaki chicken. After ordering, Karen turned to me.

"So what do you normally do when you meet with women for your challenge?"

"I ask them questions, and they basically tell me their life story. Then we spend some time getting to know one another. It's pretty easy."

She looked a little relieved. "Great. How about this? You can ask me questions before our food comes, and then I can tell you my life story while we eat."

"Sounds good! My first question is one I always ask: what are the qualities of a godly woman?"

Karen paused a moment before responding. "I believe the qualities of a godly woman are these: to have a heart for God, to want to do what's right, and to spend time with Him. A godly woman knows that spending time with God and sacrificing everything for Him will be worth it."

How? If you sacrifice everything, how will it be worth it? Sure, you can go to heaven if you "simply believe in Jesus," but that's only if you believe heaven's real. I seem to have more questions that can ever be answered. Speaking of questions, I had better ask one before Karen wondered if I had forgotten how to talk.

"What's your favorite Bible verse?"

"My favorite passage is Proverbs 3:5-7, which says, 'Trust in the Lord with all your heart, and lean not on your own understanding; in all your ways acknowledge Him, and He shall

160

direct your paths. Do not be wise in your own eyes; fear the Lord and depart from evil.' I have to believe God is good, or else I would have been without hope during the hard times in my life."

"What sort of hard times?"

"Well, I'll tell you in a second; our food is coming." Our food was, indeed, coming, and it smelled scrumptious. When my plate was set before me, I gaped at the amount of food on it. There was chicken, vegetables, and rice—all in large quantities. After a short prayer, we dug in. The food was amazing. Karen was also eating with enthusiasm, and after a while, she took a long drink of water and began her story.

"I'm from Alabama, where I lived on Lookout Mountain. When I was 3, my mom and dad divorced. My mom remarried two years later, and my dad moved to Pennsylvania. I lived with my mom, stepdad, and younger brother on a "picture book" family farm that was owned by my grandpa—who had 100 acres. All of my family members lived on the farm. When I was five years old, I began attending a house church that my aunt and uncle had at their house. During one of the meetings, I gave my life to God. I remember feeling that I was a sinner and that I needed God. After becoming saved, I felt lighter. A couple of years later, I started going to a Church of God church, and that is when my spiritual life really began growing."

So her dad was out of the picture for most of her growing-up life, too. The only difference is that she could still visit her dad. I can't. I took a bite of chicken and allowed myself to be lost in its delectableness.

"However, it wasn't all dreams and fairy tales after that. When I turned fourteen, my mom died in a car accident. It was terrible. I stayed involved with the church, but my mom's death shattered my idealistic childhood."

So she does know what it's like to lose a parent. I don't understand why she stayed in church, though. We both lost a parent at a young age, but we made drastically different decisions about the whole Christianity thing.

She drank some more water before continuing. "My mom died on a Saturday. The Wednesday before, the church was having a testimony service. My mom stood up and said that she was ready to die and that if something happened to her, she was ready to meet the Lord. I believe God prompted her to testify that night so I would be reassured when she died. I remember being in complete shock when I found out she had died. That night, I dreamed that my mom was still alive; however, when I woke up, I was slapped with the truth. I felt alone and scared, and it was such a dark time; but I knew that God was with me. I didn't question Him or get mad at Him because I knew, deep down, that I needed Him too much and that if I started doubting Him and His ways, I would fall apart."

I could completely relate with her. I too had been slapped with the truth and had felt alone and scared; but I didn't even try to pretend that God was with me because I knew He wasn't. I did question Him, and I was also mad at Him, and I didn't feel like I needed Him. Yet, where did it leave me at the end of it all? I fell apart academically, socially, and mentally.

We were both finished with our food by now, so we gathered our belongings and stood up. Karen paid the bill, and we left the restaurant. Once we had climbed into her truck, she finished her story.

"My stepdad tried to rear my brother and me after that, but he fell apart. I took on the responsibility of the house, which wasn't our house for much longer. You see, my stepdad and my mom's family never got along, so once my mom died, he didn't want to continue living around them. We then moved to Sand Mountain. It was like starting a whole new life."

That must have been awful. Leaving everyone and everything she knew just as she was about to enter high school.

"After college, I married and had a daughter; and it was during that time that I learned the meaning of true forgiveness. I called up my stepdad and shared with him things that he had done that had hurt me. I didn't accuse him; I just told him so I could then forgive him. The power of forgiveness is underestimated. After I forgave, everything shifted, and I was living a new life."

Maybe all of the women I've met with went to the same school where they learned how to subtly sneak the word forgiveness into their sentences. Out of all the things I've been told, forgiveness has been one of the main themes, especially from women like Shona House, Charlene McCullough, Serena Roberts, and Vanessa Broxbern.

Right then, she pulled into a driveway of what I assumed was her house. We climbed out and walked to the front door, where she unlocked it and ushered me in. Noticing the time, I asked her if she wanted me to walk her dog right then.

"That would be wonderful. I'll just go outside and call Bigfoot to the back stoop. I normally walk him, but I've been needing to do some projects around the house to get ready for Christmas, and I haven't had enough time."

Bigfoot? Like, the fictitious ape that lives in the mountains and scares people? As I changed into my junk clothes and walked out to the back porch, I wondered why she would name her little dog such a big name. Suddenly, I was knocked flat onto my back with the wind pushed out of me. A bulky, coarse tongue began licking my face. I panicked. Was it a cow? Was it a bear? Was it a Martian who had landed in Karen's backyard with the hopes of engulfing me with its nasty tongue? Then, in an instant, it was gone. In a daze, I stood up and searched blindly for something to wipe my face on. I was very thankful that I had changed into my bad clothes before I was so viciously assaulted.

Karen came to the rescue with a towel. "I'm so sorry. Normally Bigfoot isn't this up front with visitors. He's a Great Pyrenees, so his natural instincts are to protect the ones he loves."

You mean, I was attacked by a dog? I cleared my vision and looked at the big ball of white fur that Karen was holding by the collar. At that moment, I understood why he was called Bigfoot. Fido and Walter aren't exactly fitting names for a dog of such size. He eagerly strained to come at me again, so I scurried away from him at least six feet. She laughed apologetically.

"Maybe I should walk with you just for today, until you get used to his pushy ways."

I nodded my agreement—still unsure on whether or not I should be charging more based on size. I gingerly grabbed the leash and started down the road—or rather, was hauled down the road. I pulled on the leash, trying to get Bigfoot to slow down, but to no avail. Karen ran to catch up to me.

"Would you like me to help you with that?"

I grimaced. "I feel so badly. I'm supposed to be walking your dog, but I can't even make him walk. I guess I'm running your dog instead."

She laughed. "It's okay. Bigfoot is a big dog and is pretty hard to control. He'll get used to you."

One can only hope. I allowed her to take the leash, and she yanked hard until Bigfoot had slowed to a canter. I stared at her, wondering how in the world she could have enough strength to control such a colossal monster. I plodded along beside her, wishing I could be talented enough to at least walk dogs. In order to pass the time and get my mind off my challenges, I asked her what her biggest challenge was.

"When my mom died. I know that most people get mad at God when they lose someone they love, but I knew that He had a purpose for doing that."

What purpose? To make you feel alone and scared? To be slapped with the truth over and over again?

"We live in a broken world. God chooses not to control people, so the drunk driver ran my mom off the road. He chose not to save her, but He still has a plan."

He also "chose" not to save my dad. I doubt He has a plan incorporated with that act of cruelty, though. So far I haven't been getting any vibes that God really loves me. It is interesting, however, that Karen would still love God despite the fact that He took away her mom.

She handed me the leash again, and I took it. "Maybe he's used to you by now."

Nope. As soon as he realized that his leash was in a newbie's hands, he took off. I was once again jerked down the road, almost toppling face-first onto the asphalt. Karen once again took the leash and turned the dog around so that we were headed back to the house. After noticing my dejected expression, she said, "Don't worry. Failure is the best teacher. I'm sure tomorrow he will allow you to control him."

Hmm. I wasn't so sure that would be true. Bigfoot was set against me.

When we arrived back at her house, she took the leash off Bigfoot and let him go romping through the yard. We were about to walk inside the house when a car's horn alerted me to my brother's presence. I waved to let him know that I was coming, and then I turned to Karen.

"Thanks so much for meeting with me! I'm sorry I couldn't walk Bigfoot, but tomorrow I will come prepared." With a bulldozer and a grappling hook instead of his leash.

She smiled warmly. "I'm really happy that you've been doing this challenge. Never be afraid to learn from other people. Don't let fear intimidate you from seeking them out." She put some money into my hand. "You weren't able to walk him all by yourself today, but you still tried, and I want you to be able to know that even if you fail, you still tried, and that's important."

I thanked her, said goodbye, and walked to where my brother was waiting. Once I had climbed in, he pulled out of the driveway and headed for home.

"How'd it go?"

I smiled at him. "Well, I was maliciously attacked by a giant ball of fur who was bigger than this van, weighed more than this van, and licked me like a Popsicle. He dragged me all over the neighborhood before Karen came to my rescue. Other than that, it was a great day. The food at Kumo was amazing, and I loved meeting with Karen." I paused. "By the way, thanks for asking." On the drive home, I thought about what Karen had said over lunch about her mom. I still couldn't figure out why she, having gone through the same tragedy of losing a parent, would choose to still love and follow God. I may never know.

Chapter Twenty-Nine

Christmas flew by in a blur of red and green. I made some good money by walking dogs, and because of that, I was able to purchase some not-so-cheap presents for family and friends. For Tina, I bought her a frame with a picture of the two of us eating cake at her birthday party. Cheesy, I know, but she seemed to like it. For my grandmother, I got her a new Disney nightgown. To the rest of the family, it seemed like a joke, and they all laughed. But I knew my grandmother liked it, even though she pretended to dislike it so everyone else wouldn't discover her secret fetish for Disney. For my mom, who actually stayed up for most of the day to celebrate with us, I purchased a necklace—because when all else fails, you can always go with jewelry. For my sister, I bought her a Starbucks gift card. Impersonal, yes, but she at least thanked me for it.

Finally, for Jackson, I got him a new Bible. I had noticed that his was falling apart at the seams, so I risked what little reputation I had left to darken the doors of a Christian bookstore and buy him a journal Bible. I almost opened it to see what the big deal was with this book but then stopped myself. Sure, I might be trying to see if God is for me or not, but that doesn't mean I need to start reading some dusty history book. He was overjoyed with the gift, even though my sister and mom gave it a disdainful glance. I myself received some assorted trinkets, but the one that stood out was the gift from Jackson.

I believe it was spurred on because of what I had told him the week before. I had confessed to him that I was going to forget my former beliefs and try and find out if God cares for me enough for me to "serve" Him. He seemed greatly interested that I was technically no longer an atheist; however, I knew that once the remaining six months of the challenge were over, I would fall back to my normal lifestyle where God meant nothing.

Anyway, when I opened my gift from him, there lay the one book I said I would never read. Jackson had gotten me a Bible. I looked at him in surprise. My family members looked at him in surprise and then at me in surprise. I stared back. Did they honestly think I was a Christian? No, this was just a random gift.

Later, I pulled Jackson aside from the rest of the family and asked, almost accusingly, "Why did you buy me a Bible, of all things?"

He smiled. "I knew you wouldn't exactly be pleased, but think of it this way: if you really are trying to find out for yourself if God loves you, you have to look in all the places, not just in the places you want to look because you know you won't find anything there."

He gave me the look. I shifted my eyes to the floor. He was very right. I didn't want to read anything remotely Christian because I was afraid that I would stumble onto something that would prove God's love for me. Jackson wasn't going to allow me to do that. There were still some problems, however.

"But Jackson, if I start reading that thing, everyone and their brother will think I'm a Christian, and I'm not!"

He sighed. "Since when have you cared what people think of you? Who cares whether they think you're a Christian? In fact, it would be better if they think you are a Christian rather than a trouble-making pagan. Who knows? Even by not being a Christian, you might inspire others to find out more about Christianity if you're even remotely like one."

I rolled my eyes. "I don't want people to become Christians and be hurt in the same way I was. They would blame me, and, once again, I would be the talk of the town. Besides, everyone knows I'm an atheist. If I were seen with a Bible, they would think of me as a hypocrite, pretending to be an atheist when I really was a Christian or the other way around."

With that, I walked away. When I lay in bed that night, unable to fall asleep, I realized that it couldn't hurt to at least read a little, as long as I didn't do it in front of anyone who would take it the wrong way, like Jackson or Tina. They would probably try to lead me through the sinner's prayer right then! I will only read it to try to find evidence to refute what I currently believe: that God doesn't care for sinners like me.

The next morning, I locked my door and went to where the Bible was sitting on my nightstand. Jackson had been sleeping on the couch ever since he came home, and Kim was in her own room, but I knew it could only take a couple of seconds for them to open the door and find me reading a Bible.

I cautiously opened it up. After reading the table of contents, I realized that I had no clue where to start looking for any type of proof nor what kind of proof to look for. I couldn't ask Jackson or Tina for help, and I couldn't ask anyone that I really knew, or else they may "accidentally" tell someone else. The obvious choice would be to ask a pastor or his wife, but seeing how I don't go to church, I don't have a pastor.

Then, I had the perfect idea. My dad's sister, Charissa, had been a pastor's wife back when my dad was still alive. I'm not sure if she is anymore, since I've only recently started seeing that side of the family. If she is, though, I could meet with her for my challenge—so I would have a reason to give Jackson as to why I was meeting with a pastor's wife—then while with her, ask her where to start reading in the Bible.

I quickly texted my paternal grandmother to ask her what my aunt's phone number was. She responded pretty quickly, and I texted the number. I went downstairs and ate a strawberry Pop-Tart with a glass of milk while I waited. I was amazed at how quickly I was going through the challenge. I had already met with 28 women, and, if my aunt agrees, I will have met with 29 women by the end of the week. Pride filled me as I realized that I could've quit multiple times, but I never did.

Just then, Aunt Charissa replied to my text with "YES!" I chuckled. She also said that if I had asked her a week before or after she would have had to say, "No" because she lives out in Colorado. This week, however, she had flown in to visit Grandmother, so she could be able to meet with me the next day if I were available.

We decided to meet halfway at a coffee shop called Wired Coffee Bar, located in Ooltewah. That way, I wouldn't have to catch a ride all the way down to Rossville, and she wouldn't have to drive all the way up to Tennessee. I easily persuaded Jackson to give me a ride down to Ooltewah, since he was all for me meeting with godly women.

Once there, I walked into the coffee shop, my Bible safely tucked away in my purse, out of sight. I spotted my aunt immediately—since there were very few other people in the cafe at the moment, and all of them were old men. I greeted her, and she gave me a hug.

"Would you like anything to eat or drink?" she quickly asked. "They make really good beverages."

I requested hot chocolate and, at her insistence, a muffin. As she went to the counter to buy it, I sat down in a booth. When she returned, I sipped on the drink. It was hot, but delicious. She took the seat across from me and smiled.

"I'm so glad to see you. It's been years, and you've grown up so much." She looked at me pensively. "So, I heard that you're an atheist now. How's that going?"

I nearly spewed my hot chocolate all over her. How did she find that out? Nevertheless, I had to answer. "Well, I was perfectly fine with it until a Christian at school forced me into this challenge. Now, I've decided that there may be a God up there; however, I just want to find out whether He cares for me enough to forgive me and all of my failures and shortcomings. So, I'm no longer an atheist, but I'm definitely not a Christian." I looked at her curiously. "Who told you I was?"

She gave me a puzzled look. "Hannah Justice. You were pretty determined you were an atheist when you met with her. What changed?"

"I met with a scientist who proved that my former belief in evolution was wrong and who created doubts in my mind about the non-existence of God. Which reminds me," I said, as I pulled my Bible out from my purse. "I need help on where to start in this thing. Jackson got it for me for Christmas, but I'm only reading it so I can find proof of whether or not God really loves and cares for heathens like me."

She looked at me as if she couldn't quite understand me, which was reasonable. I couldn't quite understand myself at times, especially now. "I think you should start in John. After reading that, get back to me and I can help you from there."

I nodded. "Okay, thanks."

Sipping her cocoa, she said, "What am I supposed to do for this challenge? Do I ask you questions, or the other way around? I did prepare something to talk to you about, if you want to hear it."

"Normally," I said, "I have a few standard questions to ask, but then the woman I meet with shares whatever she wants to."

She pulled out a computer. "Sounds good. Why don't you ask your questions first, and then you can eat your muffin while I talk?"

"My first question is this: what are the key qualities of a godly woman?"

She took a sip of her cocoa before answering. "I believe that one of the most important qualities in a godly woman is servanthood."

Hmm... Servanthood. That was a touchy subject with me. It's not like I won't hold open the door for someone if they need help, but become a slave to everyone around me? I looked at her, barely concealing my surprise. No one I had met with had said that yet. I was expecting love, peace, or patience—you know, the fruit of the Spirit. This must mean that she lives out servanthood daily, or else she wouldn't have thought of that right off the top of her head. "Does your favorite Bible verse also go along with servanthood?" I asked, a little flippantly.

"In fact, it does," she said, smiling. "My favorite verse is Colossians 3:23-24, which says, 'And whatever you do, do it heartily, as to the Lord and not to men, knowing that from the Lord you will receive the reward of the inheritance; for you serve the Lord Christ.'"

That's strange that both her favorite verse and her opinion of what a godly woman should be are both about servanthood. But maybe it was just a fluke—everything she says today couldn't possibly be about servanthood. Oh, snicker doodle. I just jinxed it. Anxious to hear whether my prediction would come true, I cut my questions short. "That's all. You can talk now."

She nodded. "Okay, I'll do that. What I really wanted to talk to you about today is," she paused slightly, "servanthood."

I totally called that.

"We are servants of the King; so, when we serve others, we are also serving Christ, just like Colossians says. Jesus is the ultimate example for servanthood. Matthew 20:28 says, 'Just as the Son of Man did not come to be served, but to serve, and to give His life a ransom for many.' Jesus spent His last few hours before he died serving His disciples by washing their feet."

Wow. That's pretty gross. I probably could never wash someone's feet, and yet that act of servitude was one of the last things Jesus did before He died.

"Christ's unconditional love is our motivation for serving others. Philippians 2:5-8 says, 'Let this mind be in you which was also in Christ Jesus, who, being in the form of God, did not consider it robbery to be equal with God, but made Himself of no reputation, taking the form of a bondservant, and coming in the likeness of men. And being found in appearance as a man, He humbled Himself and became obedient to the point of death, even the death of the cross.'"

I had never heard this before. I knew the whole "Jesus died for your sins" story, but this put a whole new twist to it. Let's do some pretending for a moment. If I were someone immensely famous and rich, I wouldn't want to leave all that and go live in some shack like a slave, with no reputation, and obey a master even to the point of dying, if that is what he wanted.

She continued, "Nothing disciplines our flesh as much as serving because there is no task that is below you when you're a servant."

Aw, man. That means that you have to take all the jobs no one wants. It's like at school when you can choose to either be a teacher's aide or clean the classroom. No one picks the classroom. But she's saying that if you're a servant, you take the cleaning job?

Who would do that? But, on the other hand, if Jesus would, instead of partying or going on a cruise, wash His disciples' feet in His last hours on earth, then shouldn't we at least do something close to that? It has been proven that Jesus did exist, and even if He's not the Son of God, He's still a really good role model to follow.

She wasn't done. "You shouldn't wait until you feel an obvious push from God to serve, but instead, do it when you know it needs to be done, no matter whether God wrote it in black and white for you or not. And while being a servant, you can't just sit on a shelf and look pretty. You have to get sweaty and dirty while still having a good attitude. You have to be durable, not dainty. Bill Hybels puts it this way: 'I would never want to reach out someday with a soft, non-calloused hand—a hand never dirtied by serving—and shake the nail-pierced hand of Jesus.' In 2 Timothy 2:20 it says, 'But in a great house there are not only vessels of gold and silver but also of wood and clay, some for honor and some for dishonor.' You need to be like a clean mug ready for use, rather than like a dainty china teacup or a Christmas dish which rarely are used."

So what she's saying is that we need to be ready to serve, that no matter where we are or who we're with, the people around us will know they can count on us to be a servant. That would be pretty cool to have that kind of reputation, but that would also mean I would have to start serving everyone in every situation.

She looked back at her computer. "Here's a story I heard about a taxicab driver that you might find interesting. Listen to these words he wrote. 'Because I drive the night shift, my cab often becomes a moving confessional. Passengers climb in, sit behind me in total anonymity, and tell me about their lives. I encounter people whose lives amaze me, ennoble me, make me laugh, and sometimes weep. But none touched me more than a woman I picked up late one August night. Responding to a call from a small, brick, four-plex in a quiet part of town, I assumed I was being sent to pick up some partiers, or someone who had just had a fight with a lover, or a worker heading to an early shift at a factory in the industrial part of town. When I arrived at 2:30 a.m., the building was dark except for a single light in a ground floor window. Under these circumstances, many drivers would have just honked once or twice and then driven away, but I had seen too many impoverished people who depended on taxis as their only means of transportation.'"

I would suppose so. If you don't own a car or a bicycle, you can't get around town any other way unless you walk—or ride a donkey.

"'Unless a situation smelled of danger, I always went to the door. This passenger might be someone who needs my assistance, I reasoned to myself. So I walked to the door and knocked.'"

"'"Just a minute," a frail, elderly voice answered. After a long pause, the door opened. A small woman who looked to be eighty stood before me. The apartment looked as if no one had lived in it for years. All the furniture was covered with sheets, there were no clocks on the walls, and no knickknacks or utensils on the counters. In the corner was a cardboard box filled with photos and glassware. She asked me to carry her bag out to the cab. I took the bag and then turned to assist her. She kept thanking me for my kindness as we walked to the cab.'"

"'Once in the cab, she gave me an address, then asked, "Could you drive through downtown?" I told her it wasn't the shortest way. "Oh, I don't mind," she said. "I'm in no hurry. I'm on my way to hospice." Her eyes glistened. "I don't have any family left, and the doctor says I don't have very long." I quietly reached over and shut off the meter.'"

Enthralled, I took a sip of hot cocoa, barely even registering how it tasted.

Aunt Charissa continued the story. "'For the next two hours, we drove through the city. She showed me the building where she had once worked as an elevator operator. We drove through different neighborhoods where she had lived and stopped in front of buildings that brought back sweet memories for her.'"

"'As the first hint of the sun was cresting the horizon, she suddenly said, "I'm tired. Let's go now." I drove to the address she had given me. Two orderlies came out to the cab as soon as we pulled up. I opened up the trunk and took the small suitcase to the door. The woman was already seated in a wheelchair.'"

"'"How much do I owe you?" she asked, reaching for her purse.'"

"'"Nothing," I said. She told me that I had to make a living, but I said that there would be other passengers.'"

"'I bent and gave her a hug. She held onto me tightly. "You gave an old woman a little moment of joy," she said. "Thank you." I squeezed her hand and then walked into the dim morning light.'"

I discreetly wiped my eye, pretending I had a loose eyelash. I felt compassion for the old lady, knowing that no one would care whether she lived or died.

"'Behind me, a door shut. It was the sound of the closing of a life. I didn't pick up any more passengers that shift. For the rest of that day, I could hardly talk. What if that woman had gotten an angry driver, or one who was impatient to end his shift? What if I had only honked once, and then driven away? I don't think that I have done anything more important in my life than picking up that frail woman. We're conditioned to thinking that our lives revolve around great moments. But great moments often catch us unaware—beautifully wrapped in what others may consider a small one.' That was written by Melvin Newland."

I froze, my cup of cocoa halfway to my mouth. Do I focus only on big moments and miss important moments hiding in what I see as only small, insignificant ones?

Aunt Charissa expounded on what Melvin had to say. "If we serve, we can find some great moments, like making a person's day or finding true friends because of how we act."

Just then, I received a text from Jackson, telling me that he was outside waiting for me. I relayed the information to Aunt Charissa, who stood up and gathered her things, saying, "I loved meeting with you. I hope you gained information that you can use as you continue in life."

I gave her a quick hug, thanked her, and walked outside. Jackson had gotten out of the car to say hello to her. Once we were both in the vehicle, he drove us back to our house. On the way, I ruminated on what she had said. Basically, if you believe in God, being a servant is a way to give back to Him for giving you everything. But even if you don't believe in Him, serving is still a good trait in people. What was it that the taxi driver had said? Oh, yeah, that he didn't think he had ever done anything more important than serving that old lady. Being a servant, huh? I guess I could give it a shot. However, I'm not so sure that I will automatically jump into servant mode. It might take a while. Nevertheless, I will try—which is more than I would have done a few months ago. I guess this challenge has been changing me for the better after all.

Chapter Thirty

I haven't found an ounce of proof that God loves me. I can sort of acknowledge the fact that God might be real, so I wouldn't consider myself an atheist anymore, per se, but I'm not a Christian. I don't believe that "Jesus died for me and that if I give my life to Him, I will go to heaven" because I can't find any proof that Jesus loves me unconditionally and died for me. If I only had some proof, I could maybe start opening up a little more. Maybe there is a God, but if that same God took away my dad, then I don't want Him. If He loves me, He would know that I loved my dad more than anyone else in the world. To take him away was to strip me of my own heart.

I haven't tried Aunt Charissa's suggestion yet—reading John—because I haven't worked up enough courage to open up the Bible. I'm afraid that I will find evidence that God is mad at for pushing Him away all these years, for spitting in His face and then running far, far away. I couldn't imagine that someone would love me enough to keep running after me even when I've kept running away, but I wish there was someone like that. I don't believe He would want me to be one of His followers because even though I followed Him when I was little, I quit.

What am I going to do? Most everyone around me thinks I'm a rock-solid atheist. Tina still thinks I'm an atheist whom she thinks she can change. Jackson thinks I'm uncertain on my beliefs, which is true. What do I think? I don't even know now. I guess I'm a no-religionist. Sometimes I think that I'm so close to finding hope again, but then suddenly it's yanked from in front of me. I try to find where I can find hope again, but then I get doubts and hesitations on whether I'm going in the right direction. Yet, does anyone know what the "right" direction actually is? Everyone has his own viewpoint; I'm just trying to find which one is the best for me.

I arose from the green chair in my room and started one of my favorite pastimes—pacing. Let's say I do decide that Christianity is right for me. If what people say is true, then I would have some really good pros: heaven, hope, faith, a best friend, and an eternity with Jesus. But what about the cons? There have to be some negative things about it, and if I'm going to plunge into this, I want to know the worst that could happen.

I stopped pacing and turned to the Bible, still on my nightstand. I lifted my chin. I knew what I was going to do. For the rest of the women I met with, I would pay very close attention and listen to the cons of Christianity. I would also listen to the pros, but if I searched for the cons and found more pros than cons, then I would know that it's the right religion for me. If I found a ton of cons, then I wouldn't feel pressured to consider that as an option.

First things first; I had to schedule an appointment with my next godly woman. The big three-o. I would want it to be someone who has had a lot of cons in her life so I could start on my next mission—finding out what I should believe. Since I wasn't a pro at finding women on purpose—they normally just happened to show up in the weirdest places—I decided to text the only person who would know the person I should meet with next.

Tina answered, as usual, within 3.5 seconds, and said she knew just the woman—Jeni Turner. She said that Jeni had been through some tough times and that I should hear her story. Tina gave me Jeni's number, and I texted her as soon as I received it. When Jeni responded, she said she would love to meet with me. We decided to meet at my house the next day at 7 p.m., and then she would drive me to a coffee shop, and then she would bring me home afterwards. I knew that she could come to my house and pick me up and no one would notice. My mom would be in her room or not even home, my grandmother would be in her room watching either Wheel of Fortune or Jeopardy, depending on how she was feeling, and my sister would be in her room on her phone. Jackson I didn't have to worry about because he already knew what I was doing and why.

The next day, I lounged about, doing practically nothing. School was still out for Christmas break, thankfully, so the amount of things I had to do was the wonderful number of zero. When the time came for Jeni to arrive, I got ready and mentally prepped myself so I would remember to look for Christianity cons.

She arrived in a van and, once I had climbed in, pulled out of my driveway and headed into town. She properly introduced herself and said that she looked forward to getting to know me better.

Before arriving at the coffee shop, Jeni drove me into a neighborhood.

"I wanted to show you the place in which I grew up and tell you some stories of what happened here."

Okay, no cons there. In fact, she hasn't mentioned anything about Christianity or her faith—yet.

"Growing up, I can't remember ever not having a knowledge of Jesus."

Ah, here we go.

"I was a pastor's kid, and I wanted to represent Jesus in a way that made people want Him; however, because of my representation, I was bullied in middle school—something that made me broken and weary."

Hmm. So she tried to represent Jesus and was bullied. Definite con there.

"I felt unpopular all through my school years, even when I was voted homecoming queen; however, the Lord has loved me exceptionally even when no one else has. I can't think of anything I've done to make God love me so much, but He still does. That was my faith foundation—knowing that I was loved unconditionally."

That's a pro. So far, it's one to one. It's interesting that she said exactly what I was reminiscing about earlier—whether I could ever be loved unconditionally. She can, but I don't know about me.

She continued. "I had some very tragic moments growing up. When I was twelve, I had a best friend who was a guy. We always played together, and it was a blast around him. However, on his thirteenth birthday, he and his family went to their houseboat on the lake, and, while there, he died."

Oh man. At such a young age, too.

"I was out playing when my mom came running down the street, screaming my name. I knew something was wrong. She told me that my best friend was dead. I remember his parents wailing day after day. I can recall thinking how hopeless they were because they didn't have Jesus to comfort them. They weren't Christians."

I sat up straight in my seat. What? She's actually saying that you can be completely hopeless if you don't have Jesus? This could be the answer I was looking for. Maybe that's why I was so hopeless and upset when my dad died; however, it could be that even if I had had "Jesus in my heart," I would have still felt hopeless and sad. But who knows? I can't go back and change it, but I can change the decisions I make in the future.

"Another tragedy that happened was that when I was in my senior year of high school, my youth pastor was diagnosed with leukemia. He died a few years after that. It was very painful for me."

She has some serious cons in her story.

"My dad always told me that when you face hard times you will either run to Jesus or away from Him."

Wow. I guess I ran away from Him. Wait, what am I saying? Here I am, actually thinking in spiritual terms? What am I doing? I shook my head to clear any more crazy thoughts and went back into no-religion mode. By doing that, I decided to change the subject—majorly. "What's the worst trouble you ever found yourself in?"

She looked momentarily surprised, since my question was way out in left field, but then answered, smiling. "I think the worst trouble I've ever gotten into was when my friends and I used to TP houses. The funny thing is, though, my mom would drive us there. She knew we were doing it, and she was fine with it. Someone finally caught us, including my mom. It was an embarrassing situation."

I laughed. Who would have thought? I wish my mom would do things like that with me.

Just then, she pulled into Inman Coffee. When we walked inside, she told me to get whatever I wanted. I ordered a fruit smoothie. I know, I know, I had a menu of coffee to pick from, and I ordered a smoothie. It was a good smoothie, though. We sat down on one of the couches there, and she turned to me.

"I've been talking for most of tonight. Do you want to ask me any questions?"

I smiled. "I have a few. What are the qualities of a godly woman?"

She leaned back in her chair. "I think that the qualities of a godly woman are to be real, to be self-aware, to be able to know and realize your temptations so you can counteract them, to be able to discern the different voices in your head, and to be able to follow God's voice even when it's not easy—or popular."

Ouch. That's a toughie. Following God's voice even when it's not easy? Isn't that what Jessica did with her move to Switzerland? And what about discerning the different voices in your head? What's that even supposed to mean? Oh, well. I bet it's not important, anyway.

"What's your favorite verse?"

"My favorite verse is Zephaniah 3:17, which says, 'The Lord your God in your midst, The Mighty One, will save; He will rejoice over you with gladness, He will quiet you with His love, He will rejoice over you with singing.'"

She smiled, as if remembering old memories. "One of my favorite songs to listen to while in the UAE was 'Great I Am.'"

I interrupted her. "You went to the UAE? Why?"

"My family and I were missionaries there. We were there for three years. It was a great experience for all of us."

So she's a missionary, as well.

"When I was diagnosed with cancer, I loved the song 'In Over My Head.' I knew as I was listening to the song that I was going to have to walk through this cancer, even though everyone was saying that they were believing for healing. I knew God wanted me to have cancer. In order to really know the Lord and His attributes, you must face hardship."

This was all coming too fast. She had cancer? "What kind of cancer did you have?"

She took a sip of her smoothie. "Breast cancer."

Oh, man. That's terrible. Wait, she said that even though people believed that she could be healed, she knew that God wanted her to have cancer? Does that mean that even if you believe and have faith, bad things can still happen? I thought that if bad things happened to you, it must mean that God's not with you anymore. Obviously, Jeni doesn't believe that.

She smiled. "However, God healed me. I went to the doctor one day and was told that there wasn't a sign of it."

My jaw fell to the floor. "That's amazing! I can't believe it!" I shook my head, flabbergasted.

She rose. "It's getting late. I'm going to do something with you in the car, and then I'll take you home so you don't have to be up late tonight."

We climbed into her car, and she turned to me. "I want to do a discernment exercise with you."

That was cool with me. I didn't have a clue what discernment was, so whatever I learned couldn't hurt me, right?

"Take this sheet of paper and this pen." She handed them to me. "Now take your phone and use the camera so it's like a mirror." I did so. "Now for the next few minutes I want you to look at yourself and write down on the paper everything you think about yourself. No matter whether they're good or bad, I want you to write them down."

I looked at myself and began writing. All the thoughts that came pouring from my head and onto the page made me feel insecure to the point where I almost started crying.

- Ugly
- Stupid
- Not good enough
- Unworthy
- A failure
- Alone
- Forgotten
- Unloved
- A disappointment
- Unwanted

I stopped writing. I couldn't do it anymore. She must have been watching my face because she said I had done enough.

"I'm not going to ask you what you put down on that paper, but I will tell you this: there are two voices in your head. One is Jesus, who is trying to tell you that you are beautiful, smart, good enough, worthy, an achiever, never alone, the first thought on His mind, loved, a pleasure, and wanted. The other is Satan, who will try and tell you things to make you feel awful about yourself, to bring you to tears, and to make you want to go hide somewhere. Satan loves to hit you when you're down so you feel like you can never get back up. I feel like he has hit you down and that every time you try to stand, you get hit right back down again. I want to encourage you to get back up. Listen to the quiet voice that you may not hear at all times. Let Jesus speak to you and let you know that you are unconditionally loved."

I felt moisture gather in my eyes. Was I crying? Me? The tough girl? The one who could do anything on her own? I guess those words could bring even a grown man to tears.

She reached behind her and pulled out a gift bag. "I want you to have this."

I opened it up and found a journal at the bottom and a package of Crayola markers. On the front of the journal were the words from Jeremiah 29: 11, "For I know the thoughts that I think toward you, says the Lord, thoughts of peace and not of evil, to give you a future and a hope." I stared at it. This was the proof I was looking for. It says it right here. God's plan for me isn't to harm me but to give me a future and to give me hope.

She spoke. "The markers are because your thoughts should be colorful and alive."

I thanked her repeatedly, opening up the journal. For each page, there was a Bible verse at the bottom. She silently turned on the car and began driving back to my house as I gazed at the gift.

Once we arrived at my house, I reached over and gave her a hug. "Thank you so much! To be honest, I met with you so I could find out the flaws in Christianity; however, I believe you completely changed my beliefs forever."

She looked honored. "You're completely welcome. I hope to meet with you again some day, yes?"

I nodded. "Yes."

I climbed out of her car and walked inside, still shaken. If what Jeni said tonight is true, then I don't have to spend six months looking for the proof that Christianity is right for me. I have it already.

Chapter Thirty-One

Once I was safely in the privacy of my bedroom, I went straight to my nightstand and reverently picked up my Bible. By looking at the table of contents, I was able to go straight to the page John started on. However, I wasn't sure if I was reading the right one. There were four different books of John in the Bible! John, 1st John, 2nd John, and 3rd John! I picked the first one and hoped it was the right one. I began reading. "In the beginning was the Word, and the Word was with God, and the Word was God…"

Ten minutes later, I knew. I realized after reading John 3:16, that what the apostle John was saying had to be true. Tina had said that during the New Testament times, Christians were persecuted for their faith; so why would John risk persecution if what he said were a lie? I shut my eyes, appalled at how blind I had been. The evidence really had been right in front of me; I was just too blind to see it.

I have no clue what to do next. I believe that Jesus is the Son of God, and that God really is real; but I don't know what to do about that knowledge. Suddenly, I remembered getting saved when I was a little girl after someone led me through some sort of prayer. I sank to my knees, bowed my head, and began. "Jesus, I know you're real. After years of denying it, I've finally been slapped with the truth—hard. I'm sorry for pushing you away all these years, and I pray you will forgive me for it." I choked back tears. "Help me to be able to discern the voices in my head. I pray you would come into my heart and live through me." Then, as an afterthought, I added, "And Jesus, please don't let Tina freak out too much when I tell her this. Amen."

As I arose, I felt like I could just keep rising until I touched heaven. I felt so light, as if a million elephants had been taken off my shoulders. I could feel goose bumps rising all over my body. I was confused, though. Where were the fireworks? Or the loud explosion? I guess I had always assumed that whenever someone became a Christian, big bangs boomed. But all I felt was utter peace. Peace I hadn't felt since I was little. A peace that enveloped me, gave me security, and told me everything would be all right. At long last, I was finally at peace with God. Then, something inside me wanted to praise God and let Him know how much I loved Him. I did just that. Halfway through my declarations of praise, I was startled to realize I wasn't speaking English anymore. In fact, I didn't even know what language I was speaking in. I just knew it was praise, and it felt wonderful.

Half an hour later, I collapsed in my green chair. I felt as light as a feather. I no longer was worried about what people would think if I became a Christian. Instead, I wanted to declare it to the world. But first, I had to tell a few special people.

I walked downstairs and found Jackson in the kitchen, eating a late night snack.

"Can I talk to you outside?"

He looked a little bewildered but consented. We walked out the back door and sat down in the chairs by the pool.

"What's up?" he questioned

I swallowed. I really, really, really hoped that he wouldn't say, "I told you so." I lifted my chin courageously and began. "As you know, I've been an atheist for the past few years now." He nodded. "However, it wasn't until just recently that I realized I had absolutely no proof on that belief." His eyebrows lifted slightly. I could tell he had no clue where I was going with this. "I began searching for answers, answers to whether God was real, and whether He cared enough for me to forgive me. Then if I found no proof for that either, I would continue being an atheist." I swallowed. Here goes nothing. "An hour ago, I found the proof I was looking for."

He squinted, confused. "Wait, proof for which belief?"

I smiled shakily. "God is real."

His mouth dropped completely open. "What? You mean...you're a Christian now?"

I nodded. "I gave my heart to Jesus before I came to talk to you."

He threw his arms around me. "You have no clue how much this means to me! I prayed for so long that God would reveal Himself to you, and He did!"

"I'm so sorry, Jackson. I should've listened to you when you first told me that you were a believer, but I was so blind." I began crying, and soon we were both crying as we hugged each other.

When we wiped our eyes, we laughed. Jackson spoke first. "This is incredible! Who knows about it yet?"

"No one but you. I thought you should be the first to know."

He smiled. "Wow, thanks. I'm honored. I'm so happy for you."

We both stood up and walked back inside. I went upstairs and collapsed into bed. It was rather late at night, and I was tired. Thinking about what Jackson said, I fell asleep with a smile on my face.

The next day was a Sunday, and I knew Tina would be in church, so I waited until around lunchtime to text her. I asked her if she would be able to meet me at a park in town soon. I said it was important. She immediately texted back and said she could be there in ten minutes.

I had Jackson drive me there. He smiled and waved when he saw Tina, and I wondered what was up between them. He seemed to light up whenever I mentioned Tina's name. Despite their age difference, I knew anything could happen. I would have to keep my eyes open.

Anyway, I had more important matters to deal with at the moment. As a chilly wind picked up, Tina and I chose a bench to sit down on, and she began.

"Look, I'm sorry. I know I should have told you about it before, but I knew she would be a great person for you to meet with. I had hoped you would be happy. She really looks forward to meeting with you."

I was confused. "Who? What are you talking about?"

She widened her eyes and turned bright red. "Ahhh, um, no one you need to be concerned about. Really, you shouldn't worry. Everything's fine."

I was so close to rolling my eyes I could feel a blood vessel burst because of how hard I was restraining them. "Yeah, right. You've always been a horrible liar. Did you set me up with another woman?"

Biting her lip, she nodded. Then she rushed on to explain. "You see, Jackson was talking to me the other day about how he remembered how you guys had a second cousin whom he really missed seeing. When I asked him about her, he kept going on and on about her qualities. I realized what a great person she would be for you to meet with. He helped me set it up. I hope you aren't mad."

I was still stuck on the fact that she and Jackson had been talking the other day. Jackson doesn't just "talk" to my friends, and I don't know why they were suddenly collaborating to find women for me to meet with. However, I wanted to play it cool and find out what I could about them on the sly before interrogating them. "I honestly don't mind that much. It releases me from the pressure of trying to find a woman to meet with this week. Thanks."

She stared at me, eyes as big as saucers. "All right, who are you, and what have you done with the touchy atheist I know so well?"

Finally, I could tell her. "Actually, you'll never be able to use that title on me again."

She frowned. "Touchy? I'm sorry, I didn't mean to imply—"

I cut her off. "No, silly. Atheist." As I waited for the implication of my words to sink in, I sat there with a watermelon smile.

I was right. She freaked out. "WHAT!!! You're a Christian?" I nodded. She became even more freaked out. "I can not believe this! This is absolutely incredible!" She grabbed me in a bear hug and squeezed with enough force to turn my face red and have me gasping for air.

Still struggling to regain oxygen in my lungs, I choked out, "I still have one question: when I was praying, I started talking in a language that wasn't English, and I only know English—fluently at least. I know hello and goodbye in other languages but not the amount I was saying. What was that?"

She smiled broadly. "That just means you were filled with the Holy Spirit, and you were speaking in tongues, as preachers call it."

Ohhhh. When I was younger, I had heard people talk about "being filled", but I had no clue what it meant. I just figured they had gone to an all-you-can-eat buffet. I never made the connection between the two. I was raised Pentecostal, but no one really explained it all to me since I was so young.

I then remembered that she had said something about her setting up a meeting for me. "Who's the woman I'm going to meet with?"

"Germaine Davis. She's your second cousin, on your dad's side. She lives in Georgia. In fact, Jackson was about to drive you down today when you texted me."

She and Jackson really had covered all their bases. "Can I still make it in time?"

Tina nodded vigorously. "Oh, yeah. She said to come whenever and stay until whenever."

I glanced over to where Jackson sat in the car, reading a book. He would drive me all the way down to Georgia in a heartbeat just because Tina asked him to? I filed that away into my brain, in the spot I had reserved for information about Jackson and Tina. Coming back to the present, though, I decided it was high time to reconnect with my second cousin. "Okay, I'll do it." Tina squealed. "Only, I have one question."

She smiled. "Yes?"

I looked her dead in the eye. "Why were you and Jackson planning meetings for me together? You barely know each other."

She looked like a startled rabbit. "What? Well, we just ran into each other at the mall the other day, and he happened to mention your challenge. One thing led to another until we had it all planned out."

I nodded, pretending to understand her completely as I said goodbye and walked to the car. Nevertheless, I didn't believe that it really happened exactly that way. Jackson didn't just go to stores for fun, especially the mall. He was not a shopper, and to just happen to be at the mall the same time Tina was there was strange. Something was up, and I was determined to find out what.

"Hey, Jackson. Would you mind driving me down to Georgia today?"

He smiled. "So you found out, huh? Of course I will."

Within a minute, we were on the road heading down to Georgia. During the trip, I chattered on about a variety of things, keeping the topics bouncing off one another until I finally led the conversation to the Tina topic. I said some nice things about her, to start with, and then turned to him.

"So, what do you think about Tina?"

He looked me with an eyebrow raised. "She's a nice girl, I guess. I don't really know her that well."

I gave him a skeptical look. "That's very accurate, Jackson, which poses the question of why you would go to a mall to hang out with someone you hardly know?"

Jackson blushed. Blushed! Like a little schoolgirl! "I just, well, you know, I had some… things to get done, and it was, well, the convenient location, so…"

I smiled smugly. He was stuttering, blushing, and wouldn't look at me. My suspicions were right. Nevertheless, I decided to just drop the subject and talk to Tina before talking with Jackson again.

I leaned over and flipped on the radio, and we rode the rest of the way listening to some Christian music. I had to admit it was a whole lot better to listen to Christian music than secular music—you didn't have to mute it every other word.

On the way down, I texted Germaine to let her know we were coming. Jackson had found her number from somebody—probably Dad's mom. When we arrived, an older woman came out of the house and hugged us both.

"Welcome! I'm so glad to see you both. You two have grown so much! Come on in!"

We followed her into her house and were ushered into the living room and invited to sit on the sofa.

To me, she said, "I can't wait to begin this challenge of yours." To Jackson, "Feel free to prop your feet up. Andy will be here shortly, and you two can talk it up as much as you want."

I assumed Andy was her husband. I was right. Within moments, a man walked into the living room.

"My goodness, you two have grown. It's been years since I've seen you."

He then turned to Jackson and began talking to him about history, specifically, the Civil War. I could tell he was a history buff. Germaine put her hand on my arm and motioned for me to follow her into the next room. I found myself in a room with two pianos, a dining table, and another couch. My fingers itched to play the pianos. Ever since my lesson with Charlene, I try to keep a sharp eye out for pianos so I can play them. Instead, we sat down at the table.

"Naomi told me what you had done with her," Germaine began. "I thought that today we could chat for a while and then have lunch. After that, I wondered if you would be interested in writing a song with me. I'm a piano teacher to 31 students, and I've written songs on the piano before, but I wasn't sure if you played piano or not."

My mouth dropped open. "Me? I'd love to! I do play the piano. I'm not very good, but—"

She cut me off. "Don't sell yourself short. If you start talking badly about yourself before people can ever find out for themselves about you, you've already put it in their heads what you will act like, sound like, or be like."

I nodded. "Okay, I won't."

She smiled. "Alrighty. What sort of things do you chat about during your challenge meeting?"

"Life, qualities found in godly women, favorite Bible verses—things like that."

After pausing for a moment, she said, "I believe a godly woman must personally know Jesus and be willing to take a stand for Him whenever the need arises. My favorite Bible verse is either John 3:16, which I'm sure you know, or 1 Corinthians 13:13, which basically says that out of faith, hope, and love, the greatest one is love. Both verses are very wonderful."

"What's one lesson you've learned throughout your life?"

"Believing that prayers can be answered. I used to think that my answered prayers were a coincidence because I wasn't sure if it was from God or not, but I know that God does answer prayer, even if it may not be the answer you want." She paused momentarily, deep in thought. "In fact, I have a story that ties right in with that. There was a woman who died and went to heaven for 28 minutes. She went to the throne room. While there, she saw laser beams of light coming from Earth. The beams of light were prayers. She saw angels dispatching answers from God. One of the beams of light startled her. It was her dad, in her hospital room. He said one word—'Jesus'—and immediately she began to descend into her earthly body."

Whoa. That's too cool. That answers so much. That means that even if I feel like the prayers I've prayed in the past went unanswered, they didn't. God just gave me an answer I wasn't wanting, so because I wasn't looking for that answer, I didn't see it as an answer.

I turned to Germaine and stated, "I guess a challenge in being a Christian is looking for God's answers to prayer when you're afraid that His answer won't be the one you want. What's the biggest challenge you've had to face?"

"The biggest challenge I've had to face is to be a caregiver. When my mom and my mother-in-law were sick, I took care of them. You have to completely give yourself up. When you take care of baby, you see growth as reward. When taking care of an older person, you know they won't get better. It's depressing at times, and you have to be completely selfless; but you will receive your reward from God."

She continued. "That's not all the challenges I've had to face. When my grandmother died after a five-year battle with cancer, I was mad at God for making a good, godly woman suffer. That Sunday, my pastor preached on 1 Corinthians 13. He told us that we didn't have to understand all the mysteries of God, but someday we would. After that, God told me to have faith like a child. That's when I really learned to trust God. My grandmother's death was an eye-opener for me, and I learned through it that even though bad things may happen, it can teach us lessons we never would've learned otherwise."

Wow. That sums it all up. Maybe my dad's death wasn't to punish me for something I did wrong, but maybe God wanted to use it to wake me up again. If dad hadn't died, Jackson might have never left and become a Christian; and I might have never done the challenge and, as a result, become a Christian. It's incredible how one thing can play such a big part in your life later on down the road.

Jackson entered the room and interrupted me from my train of thought. He wanted to know if Germaine had a power supply for his phone that he could borrow.

Once she had given him the needed power supply, she turned to me. "This is a perfect example of what I wanted to share with you. Make sure you always connect with God. Imagine you're a computer or another electrical device, and God is your power supply. You have to plug in to Him through prayer, worship, and scripture reading to become restored and recharged."

Germaine then excused herself to ask Jackson and Andy if they were hungry yet. I know I certainly was. She came back into the room and told me that they were both hungry and that we could go to Burger King, if I wanted to. If I wanted to? There's no if with this girl when it comes to hamburgers. We all put on our coats, piled into their car, and Andy drove us to the restaurant. As we walked from the car to inside the restaurant, I hugged my coat tighter around myself; I didn't like the cold.

I ordered a hamburger and fries, like normal, and sat down in a booth with everyone else while we waited for our food. When a server brought our food, she complimented Germaine on her necklace. Germaine thanked her politely. When the server left, Germaine turned to me.

"Here's another lesson to be learned: don't let compliments swell your head. Instead, let them make you humble. God puts you in that spot so you could receive that compliment.

Praise Him, and let Him receive the compliment."

I nodded. I realized how much more I was understanding now that I had become a Christian. Before, half of everything I was told was just going over my head. We ate our food, enjoying every bite. Once done, we made the cold trip back to the car and climbed in. Andy drove us back to their house, and when we walked inside, Germaine steered me into the dining area once again.

"Now, let's write a song, shall we?" she said, her expression bright with anticipation.

I nodded enthusiastically. I walked over to the piano and sat on the bench while she grabbed some blank sheet music.

"First, we figure out what you want the song to be about, and then we put notes to the words."

We spent about ten minutes writing down song ideas on a scrap sheet of paper. Then, we had to come up with words to the song, which Germaine wrote onto the sheet music in professional form. Finally it was starting to look like a real piece of music. We just needed notes.

She had me fiddle around on the piano until I figured out a tune to the words. Once she had written the notes on the paper, we were done. I felt so proud I could burst. I immediately called Jackson in so he could listen to it. I fumbled a bit, but all in all it was pretty good, if I do say so myself. I know it was better than how I did at the band concert. The concert wasn't as bad as I thought it would be, but I knew that I had definitely improved from then. He applauded when I was done and gave me a hug.

"Great job, Sis! That sounded great!"

Just then, Jackson realized the time. "We'd better head on out." To Andy and Germaine he said, "Thanks so much for having us! I had a blast."

I nodded my agreement. "So did I."

With parting hugs and well wishes, we were off. On the way back, I pondered on everything Germaine had said. It was incredible how much more I was taking in now that I had become a Christian. Tina really freaked out. I'm sure everyone else will freak out, too, when they find out. I have to tell them. Like Germaine said today, you have to take a personal stand for Jesus. If I don't even have the guts to tell my family that I'm a Christian, how then will I have the guts to tell kids at school? When we arrived home, I walked upstairs into my bedroom and got ready for bed. School would be starting tomorrow, and I was excited but nervous. As I lay in bed, I said a quick prayer, thanking Jesus for the day and asking for strength to face tomorrow. And for the first time, I knew without a shadow of a doubt that He heard me.

Chapter Thirty-Two

One week later, I was awoken from my beauty rest at too-early o'clock by my phone alerting me to the fact that I had a text message. I was puzzled because no one I knew would text me at this unseemly hour on a Monday morning except for early birds like… Aha. I knew exactly who it was, and I wasn't going to give her the pleasure of responding. Right before I dozed back into dreamland, however, she decided she wasn't going to give me the pleasure of sleeping and called me. I regretted choosing such a perky song for her ringtone. I rolled over, grabbed my phone, and answered.

"Tina! Are you in a different time zone? What in the world is that important that you would wake me up at eight-thirty in the morning! Unlike crazy people like you, I like to sleep in on Martin Luther King Jr. Day."

Tina waited patiently on the other end until I was done. "Our family is hosting a missionary family for the next two days, and I was wondering if you would be interested in meeting with the mom for your challenge. She's an incredible woman, and I know you'd enjoy meeting her."

I sighed loudly. "This couldn't have waited an hour longer?"

She laughed. "Nope. I've been up since 6:45 and have given you this long to sleep. It's been killing me to be patient."

I shuddered. "Since 6:45? You are a crazy person." I gave her question some brief consideration before coming to a conclusion. "Yes, I will meet with this mystery woman. What time and where?"

I could picture her delighted grin through the phone. "Today, in half an hour. She'll pick you up from your house and take you to Lee University, where she and her husband are speaking to a computer class. She'll provide you with lunch and then take you back to your house. And, by the way, her name's Dorinda Beeley."

I thumped my head. I'd been had. "Tina, why do you ask me if I want to meet with these women if you've already scheduled our day together?"

"Oops. Bad connection. Gotta go!"

"Wait, Tina!" But it was too late. She had already hung up. The scoundrel.

Sighing heavily, I rolled out of bed, muttering all the while. Sure, I wanted to meet with Dorinda, but I didn't want to be tricked into meeting with her. If Tina had only asked me, say, yesterday, I would've agreed. Instead, she tricked me into it.

I got dressed and ate a quick breakfast before Dorinda arrived. As I walked outside and greeted her, I noticed that it had started snowing.

She ushered me into the car, where her husband and her son were already waiting, and introduced me. "This is my husband, Greg, and my son, Nathaniel. On the way to Lee, I'll give you a rundown of everything happening today."

I climbed into the car and buckled up. I smiled a hello to Nathaniel, and he shyly waved. I would guess his age to be about two.

She began. "Our company is called LightSys Technology Services. Basically, we do computer work for missionaries and mission organizations for free."

That's admirable. I bet the missionaries really appreciate their help. I know that when my computer acts up, it would be nice to have someone know how to fix it permanently. Instead, I have to reboot it and hope that it will work when I turn it back on.

"Today, when we get to Lee, Greg and I will be speaking to a computer class about using their talent for computers for missions work and about perhaps even joining our company. After class, we'll buy some pizza and set it up on a table. Around lunchtime, when students are getting out of their classes, they'll walk by our table, smell our pizza, and stop. While they eat free pizza, we'll be able to talk to them about our work and encourage them to use their gifts and talents on the mission field, just like we encouraged the students in our classroom."

I laughed. "Pretty clever. You lure them in with the smell of pizza, then try and get them to join your group when they're susceptible."

She nodded and smiled. "Yeah, pretty much."

By this time, we were at our destination. That's when Dorinda started looking for parking. Emphasis on looking, and not on finding. Every time someone would pull out of a parking spot, you'd have five cars veering towards the spot, trying to be the first in. You'd see dance battles occurring over who should get the parking spot. It was incredible that someone didn't get killed. I shook my head, wondering why Lee didn't just build a parking garage.

Finally, Dorinda was able to slip into a parking spot, much to the chagrin of several other drivers. We climbed out of the car, and, going to the other side of the vehicle, I held out my arms for her to pile stuff onto. She had a lot to carry in, and I knew she couldn't do it all by herself, even with her husband helping. As we walked towards the building, I shivered, feeling the icy arms of winter envelop me in their frozen grasp.

Once inside, we walked up the stairs to the computer class. Some students were already there, so we quietly began setting up—except for Nathaniel, who didn't seem to get the memo. If his mom wasn't holding him, he wasn't happy. It was that simple. When the class started, Dorinda had to pick him up and carry him around as she talked. Through all the distractions, however, I was intrigued by what she and Greg were saying.

They said that only one percent of missionaries go to the 10/40 Window. I was confused at first by the term "10/40 Window," but they soon explained that the 10/40 Window is an area of the world from the tenth to the fortieth latitude north, and from the Atlantic Ocean eastward to the Pacific Ocean. This area, which includes North Africa, the Middle East, Asia, and India, contains the least number of Christians in the world. In Asia alone, 29 million people die every year without hearing the name of Jesus.

I couldn't believe it. That many? That's so sad to think that none of those people will go to heaven, unless they changed their hearts at the last minute. And these are the kind of people that Jackson wants to share the gospel with.

I was interrupted from my ponderings when her son started crying. Dorinda had put him down for the moment, and he wasn't happy. Seeing an opportunity to serve, I walked over and picked him up. He still wasn't happy, so I took him outside the classroom. Once he couldn't see his mom, he promptly forgot why he was sad. I smiled to myself. Success! After about half an hour of playing with Nathaniel, Dorinda and Greg came out of the room.

"Thanks so much! We were able to finish up the session. Let's go pick up the pizza and set up the table."

I followed her out to the car. She took him from me and placed him in his car seat. Once he was safely buckled in, we both climbed in and drove to the nearest pizza place. I waited in the car with her adorable son, who had fallen asleep by now, and she shortly returned wielding three boxes of pizza. As she climbed into the driver's seat and started the engine, she handed me the pizzas. I was immediately overcome with the powerful smell, and I sighed dreamily. I couldn't wait to eat these babies.

When we got back to the computer class, we met up with Greg and found a table to put the pizzas on. Then, we went back to the car and grabbed posters, flyers, and signs. Dorinda and Greg set that up while I checked on Nathaniel. Once everything was ready for the students, Dorinda motioned me over to the table.

"Now that the crazy stuff is out of the way, we can talk. Tina said that for your challenge you talk to the women you meet with. What do you want to know?"

I sat down in a nearby chair and selected a slice of pizza, putting it on my plate. "What do you believe the qualities of a godly woman are?"

"I believe that one of the main qualities of a godly woman is to be willing to listen to the Holy Spirit. You have to be willing to listen to God if you want to really do what He wants."

I nodded. Seeing my nod, she continued with that train of thought.

"When a lake flows into a river, the lake isn't just trying and trying to push the water into the river. It happens naturally. It's the same way with the Holy Spirit. He will flow through you naturally if only you will let Him. If there's a dam separating the lake from the river, the water can't flow into the river. In the same way, if you have a dam separating your heart and mind from the Holy Spirit, then He won't flow. It's not like some people believe, that if it's meant for you, it will happen. You have to let the Spirit flow through you."

Wow. I guess when I got saved, I was finally so open and willing that the Holy Spirit just began His natural process of flowing through me.

"What's your favorite scripture?" I asked, taking another bite of pizza. I washed the mouthful down with a sip of Mountain Dew.

She smiled. "My favorite verse would have to be Psalm 119:165, which says, 'Great peace have those who love Your law, and nothing causes them to stumble.'"

Nothing? So, if you love God's law, then you will have incredible peace and won't stumble? That's amazing! "Have you ever stumbled by not going according to His law?"

She nodded. "Yes, as I found out my senior year of high school."

I motioned for her to go on, intrigued.

"I decided I didn't want to do any homework—or work at all. I created false computer files that looked like they were from the school so that whenever my parents wanted to see my work, I would show them the files. I went through all the loopholes and didn't do any work for two semesters; however, I was caught in May, right before I graduated."

My eyes bugged out in astonishment. "What?" I laughed. "I guess people looked at you differently after that, didn't they?"

She nodded, almost sadly. "That's for sure, but even then they didn't see who I really was. You see, there are so many people who look normal, but they have so much hurt inside that you don't know about. I struggled with anxiety and suicide, but no one would have ever guessed just by looking at me. If you judge someone before you ever really talk to them, then you can be horribly wrong. You must try to hear the multiple sides to every story to truly understand a person."

I sat back in my chair, bewildered. She was right. If she hadn't told me that, I would never have guessed that about her.

"Part of the anxiety I dealt with growing up had to do with a key phrase in my house: 'Sorry isn't good enough.' My parents said that sentence because they wanted to see a change in my actions, not just hear 'I'm sorry' all the time. As a child, however, I didn't understand that, so I struggled with self-harm because I thought that if sorry wasn't good enough, what was?"

I nodded, my brow creasing. That's rough to have to go through that as a kid. I know. I have dealt with the same thing.

"I've come to realize," Dorinda continued, "that people in this world, even Christians, judge people so harshly without ever knowing the other side of the story. It's sad how the consequences of people being judgmental are so effective."

That's for sure. I could think of a couple of "Christians" who have judged me numerous times, thus proving my theory back when I was an atheist that I shouldn't become like them.

"Here's an example. I know a Hispanic woman named Kimberly. She was trying to find a home church for her, her African-American husband, and her little kids. When she came to one church, a woman told her that if she hadn't been on drugs when she was pregnant with her son, he wouldn't be autistic. She was shocked and hurt and tried another church. Someone at the next church told her that if her kids had their parents together, they would be more stable—even though she had never divorced, and her family was very stable. Because of those completely critical statements, she now thinks Christians are all super judgmental. Due to her encounters with those people, Kimberly is now agnostic and doesn't like Christians at all."

"That's awful!" I said. "I wish Christians would be a little more loving and accepting, like they're supposed to be. It's human nature to automatically judge; but if you're constantly remembering Jesus, it shouldn't be too hard to realize that the only Judge is God."

She nodded. "That's right; however, not everyone realizes that. Christians have degraded my work; but, if I'm looking to further God's kingdom, I don't have to always be offended by what people say or do because it doesn't matter. I just have to remember that when people act like jerks to me, it's not because their sole purpose in life is to try to make me miserable. It's because they have pain in their past. They were hurt, so they think that the whole world is a jerk; consequently, they, in turn, act like a jerk to the world."

Before I could respond to that, a student walked up to the table.

"Is this pizza free?"

Dorinda smiled. "Yes, as long as you'll talk with us for a second."

He complied, and they began to talk about his major, what he was interested in doing after college, that sort of thing. I wandered off to check on Nathaniel, and when I returned, the student was gone. Dorinda turned to me and smiled.

"Three other students came by while you were gone. Some were interested, some weren't. But I'm not too concerned. We'll be doing this same thing at more colleges in the next few weeks."

I smiled. It sounded like she had her work cut out for her. She began to pack up. On our first trip out to the car, we were putting the items in the trunk when she frowned. I turned to see what she was frowning at and let out a small gasp. The rear tire was flat. She brightened, though.

"I'm glad I know how to change a tire, and, in the process, I can teach you how to change one, as well." She paused. "Unless you already know how."

I shook my head. Not at all. She brought out a towel from the back of the van and set it on the snow-covered ground. She then brought out the spare tire and the jack. She verbally gave me a step-by-step process of what we were going to do. Then, she handed me the jack. I looked at her, aghast.

"Here," she said. "I want you to try. I'll still coach you, but you'll do most of it. I believe this is something every girl needs to learn."

Reluctantly, I took the jack and began. Half an hour later, I was finished. She gave me a hug.

"Great job! You did fantastic!"

By this time, Greg had finished loading up the back of the van. We climbed in and began the trip back to my house. When they dropped me off, I thanked Dorinda for taking time out of her day to spend it with me. Then, I walked inside, waving goodbye as I did so. I knew that I wasn't going to forget the Beeleys anytime soon, especially Dorinda. She has such a selflessness to be devoted to doing mission work all the time. I wish I could learn how to sacrifice myself as Dorinda has, but part of me is scared that even if I had the time and willingness, I wouldn't be of any use to help the Kingdom of God. I'm not incredibly talented or amazing at any one thing. In fact, I'm pretty normal, especially when compared to someone like Tina or my brother. I sighed. Why would God need me to help Him? How am I going to be of use to Him? I hope one day I'll find out that answer.

Chapter Thirty-Three

The next week, I talked with Tina and thanked her for suggesting the meeting with Dorinda. Of course, I said suggesting, even though Tina had set up the whole thing! She was pleased I'd liked her. Tina then must have thought that was a hint to set me up with another godly woman because she suggested several I should meet with. One in particular caught my attention, a woman who had been a missionary for a very long time and had traveled around the world doing mission work. I stopped Tina's spouting of different godly women and told her I wanted to meet with the missionary. My dream to travel the world hadn't diminished, and I was still anxious to discover the best places to travel to so I wouldn't go somewhere and then discover all the cons about it; I would like to be warned ahead of time.

Tina told me that her name was Dorothy Qualls, although she preferred to be called Dot. Tina promised to get back to me with the details regarding our meeting, and she did so during one of our breaks between classes. Dot wanted to meet with me on Thursday for an early dinner.

The next couple of days passed quickly. I was able to practice being a Christian as I reconnected with all my friends I had lost touch with over break. Almost all of them don't rank in the "friend" category now, though, since they disowned me once they learned I was—insert dramatic gasp here—a Christian; but I've made some new ones, mostly those who were friends with Tina. You know, the ones I'd called "Jesus jerks" for years.

Thursday morning came, and I arose happy. I looked forward to meeting Dot all day during school. After school, Jackson drove me home so I could get ready for the meeting until it was time for Dot to show up, which she did, right on time. I walked out to her car and slid in.

"Hi," she said. "Tina's told me so much about you. Where would you like to eat today?"

I thought about it for a minute. "I like Chinese and Japanese food. Whatever restaurant can accommodate that, I'm fine with."

Dot decided on Kumo, which pleased me immensely. After eating there with Karen, I had been longing to go back. When we arrived, we ordered our food—I had the teriyaki chicken again.

Dot turned to me while we waited for our food. "Tina said that you'd have some questions for me. Feel free to ask them whenever."

I smiled. Good ol' Tina, never forgetting a single detail. "Yes. In fact, I'll go ahead and begin right now, since we have some time on our hands before our food comes. What do you believe are the qualities of a godly woman?"

"Learning to hear the voice of God and having a close relationship with Him," she replied.

"How has that applied to your life?"

She paused. "Well, I guess to really answer that, I'll need to tell you my full story. Many, many years ago, I felt called to teach at a Bible school in Fresno, California, so I went. While there, a student my age was at the school. We quickly became friends. When she left to attend seminary and receive her Master's degree, I followed her. After we both finished there, we felt as though we should go into mission work together. It was difficult for me to actually follow through with it because I had a contract with the school I had been teaching at. I would have to drop the contract to go, and there was no guarantee that I was going to get it back. Yet, I did it. Despite the fact that I gave up my job and my income, God never let us go hungry."

Provider. That's another quality I can add to my growing list of God's attributes.

"My ministry partner, Faye Whitten, had a small handicap, so I made sure that I always did the manual labor so all she had to do was pray and study the Bible. She was the evangelist, not me. I didn't like being in the spotlight, which is why I did most of the background work."

She smiled. "So, in answer to your question, I applied that to my life by listening to God's voice that one day at the Bible school and acting on it. If I hadn't have listened to God then, I may never have followed His leading."

Some people never realize how much they miss by not acting on things they're told to do, whether by God or people. At that moment, our food arrived, steaming and amazing-smelling; and I sure didn't want to put off eating that! I bowed my head as Dot said a quick prayer, blessing our food. As I took my first bite, I sighed in pleasure. I couldn't understand why people did so many health diets just for fun. You'd miss out on this! I quickly took a sip of water, clearing my mouth so I could ask another question. "What's a scripture that has impacted your life the most?"

"Proverbs 3:5-6, which says, 'Trust in the Lord with all your heart, and lean not on your own understanding; in all your ways acknowledge Him, and He shall direct your paths.'"

After taking a bite of food and chewing it thoughtfully, she continued. "You really need to fully allow God to direct your paths if you want to be a tool, ready for use. When God puts something in our hearts, we immediately think it will be soon, but it could happen ten to twenty years down the road. It's important not to get ahead of God. Let Him direct you on what to say and do, in His timing." She paused momentarily. "Here's an example. One day, I found out that some missionaries in Ghana were setting up a school. I knew that they were probably going to ask Faye and me to come help out, but I knew we couldn't afford to go. Sure enough, one of the missionaries called and asked. As I was about to decline, God told me that we should go; so I said yes instead. He provided for Faye and me to live there three years. It was His timing for us to go, so He provided a way for us to be there."

That's amazing. Once again, another example of God being a Provider. "Are there other stories you could share about the places you've been?"

She thought for a moment before answering. "One of the strangest experiences I've had with all my traveling was in Nigeria. While leaving the airport area, our car broke down. The driver had to go back into town for help. While he was gone, I saw two kids walking past the car carrying sacks of grain on their heads. Wanting to take their picture, I asked for their permission and they granted it; however, while taking the picture, a man drove by and yelled at me for taking the picture. He then called the police to arrest me, which they did."

I gasped, almost choking on my rice.

"The police eventually let me go," she continued, "but it was a very harrowing experience."

"Out of all the countries you've been to, what's been your favorite country?"

"Ooh, that's a tough one. I think my favorite would be either Ghana or the Philippines."

As I scraped my plate, I asked, "Did you always want to be a missionary, or did you just decide later on in life?"

"When I was in middle school, I used to watch cars drive by and wish that I could travel. Now I'm a missionary who's been to twelve different countries. You never know what the Lord has in store for you. So I guess I didn't always strive to be a missionary; I just had a hunger in me to travel, a hunger the Lord used to further His kingdom."

I became excited. I've always wanted to travel. Did that mean that God could use me in furthering His kingdom? Then, something triggered in my mind about Dot. Tina said that she was still a missionary. I wondered why she didn't just retire. I'm sure she could, if she wanted to. "Why are you still involved in mission work, knowing that you could just retire and support missions with funds instead of doing the work yourself?"

She smiled, eating the last of her food. "I told God last summer that I'm still in good health and that I wanted Him to use me all that He could. Right after that, I got a call from a woman named Teresa Kimbrell, who is a missionary in Zambia. She wanted me to come and help out there for a little bit. When I went, I was also able to visit Victoria Falls, located not too far from there. I was the oldest female to visit Devil's Pool there." At my confused look, she added, "Basically, it's a small pool located at the top of the waterfall. It's for daredevils."

"Whoa. That sounds pretty scary."

She laughed. "It really wasn't as bad as it sounds."

I regarded her with suspicion. "I never would've guessed that you have done something that impulsive. Were you ever that impulsive when you were younger?"

She laughed out loud. "You bet I was. To be quite frank, I was a prankster, and I made my sister miserable. I also made some students miserable when I was a dean for girls at a Bible school."

I raised my eyebrows, intrigued, then motioned for her to continue.

"You see, I had heard some girls talking together about getting their boyfriends to meet them behind the chapel that night just so they could talk and hang out. They didn't know I'd heard them. One girl wasn't sure whether she should do it, so I talked to her later and convinced her to go through with it. Later that night, I waited until all the girls and their boyfriends were behind the chapel talking before doing my part. I strode around the corner of the chapel and scared them all to death. They all tried their best to explain and make excuses. They even took me to dinner to try and butter me up. They didn't know that I wouldn't turn them in, but I still let them sweat all night before telling them that I wasn't going to turn them in. What did I get out of the deal? I not only enjoyed a dinner that wasn't necessary but I also got to see them sweat for hours."

She laughed, long and hard. I joined in her merriment.

"I did another prank when I was at college. You see, a friend was going to come home with me for the summer, but my family had never met her. I told my whole family that she was hard of hearing, so they needed to talk loudly around her. And talk loudly, they did." She started laughing. "It was so funny when they realized she could hear them perfectly."

I giggled. What a prankster. I never would've guessed just by looking at her. She then looked at her watch. "Wow, it's been three hours. I guess time really does fly when you're having fun."

I nodded in agreement. I quickly texted Jackson, letting him know that I was done. He had agreed to pick me up from our meeting. Within a minute, he responded that he was on his way. When he arrived, Dot and I both stood up. Once she had paid for our meal, she gathered me into a hug.

"I hope you have a wonderful evening! I'd like to see you again sometime."

I nodded. "I agree. Thank you so much for meeting with me, and God bless!"

Hearing those words coming out of my mouth sounded strange, but good. I wanted God to bless her, and I was glad that I wasn't fighting Him all the time. Peace felt good.

Chapter Thirty-Four

"Tina, how do you know so many godly women?" It was lunchtime at KMS, and I was digging into my PB&J with fervor. I was still mulling over my meeting with Dot the day before.

She swallowed her mouthful of beef, or at least, I think it was beef. You could never really tell with cafeteria food. "I go to a big church; therefore, I know a lot of people. Also, it has to do with the fact that I actively seek godly mentors for my life."

"Are all the women at your church like the ones I met with—so unique?"

She nodded. "Yeah, pretty much. It's incredible how people from different backgrounds and cultures can unite in worshiping God."

"I really want to come to your church sometime. I know Jackson probably would, too. We've been trying to find a church that we can start attending regularly."

She brightened. "That would be awesome! I can give you directions to where it's located."

Just then, one of my old friends walked by our lunch table and paused, turning to me with a sneer on her face as she flipped her red hair. "I see you've finally become a loser, just like Tina. I always knew you were."

I smiled at her, even though everything in me wanted to see if she'd still be talking like that after I slapped that look off her face. Tina seemed to sense that my blood was becoming a little heated, so she put a hand on my arm. I took a deep breath.

"Hi, Kelsey. Tina was just inviting me to her church. Do you want to come with us?"

Her mask slipped. Just for a millisecond, but it was enough for me to see that underneath all the mean words and jeers, she was human and hurting. I knew she wasn't expecting me to say that. Neither was I, to tell the truth, nor was Tina, for that matter. Kelsey looked around nervously, probably making sure she wasn't seen conversing with the "Jesus jerks," before narrowing her green-eyed gaze suspiciously at us.

"Why?"

I had to think about that one. Why was I inviting her to church? I prayed a quick prayer that God would give me an answer and then opened my mouth.

"Because it's what Jesus would do. He would be nice to everyone, even if they mocked Him or laughed at Him. He came to save the tax collectors and harlots, the thieves and the murderers."

She scowled. "You're comparing me with those people?"

I backtracked quickly. I was treading on thin ice here. "I'm not saying you are those people; I'm just saying that those people didn't have Jesus and neither do you. And if you don't receive Jesus, then you'll have the same fate as the thieves and murderers who don't accept Jesus."

She seemed to think on that. I snuck a glance at Tina. She had her eyes closed, praying. I smiled. She always knew what to do.

Kelsey looked at me with fear in her eyes. "So what you're saying is that if I don't believe in Jesus, I'm going to go to hell?"

I was surprised she believed in hell. When I was an atheist, I didn't believe in anything other than the world I lived in. I nodded. "But you don't have to go to hell if you accept Jesus into your heart. If you simply ask Him to forgive you, and if you accept Him as your Lord, then you will go to heaven."

She seemed to consider that. I knew she was still battling on the inside, so I spoke again,

"I know what it's like to not have God. You feel like you have no meaning, you'll never amount to anything, and that you will always stay a scared, shattered girl."

She sank into the seat beside me and nodded, tears clouding her eyes. I kept going. "Even though you might feel like that now, if you allow Jesus to come you're your heart, then He will be with you and comfort you and give you rest."

She looked up at me. "What do I do?"

I closed my eyes briefly, silently thanking Jesus, before leading her in a simple prayer. I didn't know a lot about the perfect words to say, so I just made it up on the spot.

Once she had finished praying, she started crying. "I'm so sorry that I've been a jerk to you guys, whereas you've been so nice to me, regardless."

I gave her a hug, and Tina patted her arm. "It's okay, Kelsey. All's forgiven."

She looked up at us, red-eyed but happy. "Is Christianity really that easy?"

I thought about that. "It's not easy; it's simple. You believe in Jesus; you go to heaven. Nevertheless, you're going to face hardships because you're now a Christian, but that's because the devil knows what an impact you're going to make for God. The devil will try to stop you from doing God's work, but you have to keep going."

She nodded, taking it all in. "I feel so happy. I feel like a million—"

"Elephants are off your shoulders?" I interrupted.

She nodded. "That's exactly it!"

Just then, the bell rang, signaling that lunch was over. We stood up and grabbed our backpacks and our trash. Kelsey wiped her eyes and smiled faintly. "Thank you again." To Tina, she said, "I'll try to come to your church this Sunday. See you guys later!"

With that, we went our separate ways to our classes. All throughout the day, I wondered what would've happened had I responded in anger to Kelsey's comment. She probably still wouldn't be a Christian, and she'd probably dislike me even more. I silently promised myself that I would forevermore think before speaking. You never know how much your words could mean to someone.

That Sunday, I showed up at Tina's church with Jackson. I was a bit surprised at first that the church Tina attended, Westmore, was the same one that my family used to go to a long, long time ago. I could tell that Jackson was remembering that, too, by the way he looked around and mentioned different memories he had. I spotted Tina immediately, since she was frantically waving at us from a pew.

"Hi! I'm so glad you two could finally come!" She grabbed me in a bear hug and then turned to Jackson. She stared at him for a second before sticking out her hand. He quirked an eyebrow and then, instead of shaking it, bowed over it.

"M'lady."

I stood there, laughing, as I watched the interaction. Obviously, Tina didn't want to hug Jackson because he was a guy, but she didn't want to exclude him from her greeting. He, on the other hand, was a big goofball who wouldn't just shake her hand like a normal person. I felt a tap on my shoulder.

"Kelsey!" I shrieked.

She stood there grinning. "I made it! I can't wait for church to start. I really thought about what you and Tina said. Right after school, I asked my mom to take me by the store to buy a Bible. My mom thought I was crazy, but she took me there anyway; however, when my dad found out..." She slowly shook her head. "Imagine how stubborn-headed you were when you were an atheist. He is twice as bad. I thought he was going to kick me out of the house. Thankfully, though, he didn't." She brightened just a little bit. "Now that I have a Bible, I can show my younger brother some of the scriptures about Jesus and try to talk to him about God."

I smiled at her. "That's great, Kels." Her ten-year-old brother was hopefully still young enough that atheism hadn't gripped his brain. There was still hope for him, and even hope for her dad, too. I mean, if God could reach me and change my life, then He can do it for anyone!

Tina—who was so enthralled with whatever Jackson was saying to her that she just noticed that Kelsey stood there—came and gave her a hug similar to the one she gave me. "Let me introduce you guys to some people around the church. We still have some time before the service starts."

She led us around and introduced us to "Brother Benton," and "Sister Smith," and people whose names got mixed up in my head. I was just about to ask Tina if we could sit down when I felt a hand on my shoulder.

"Oh my goodness, is it really you?"

I turned and found Laura Allen staring at me in amazement. I smiled. "Yes, I've definitely changed since you met with me. I'm a Christian now."

Her eyes widened, and she threw her arms around me. "That's amazing! I'm so happy for you!"

I was about to say more when Tina called me. "I want you to meet someone."

I scurried over to where Tina stood and saw a woman next to her talking with Jackson and Kelsey. "This is Petra Setlich, a good friend of mine. She's from Germany and came to America when she married Lonnie, her husband." A man standing behind her smiled and waved.

I shook hands with both of them. "Nice to meet you."

Tina looked at me and smiled. "I was just telling them about your challenge. Petra thinks it's fantastic." She gave me a meaningful look. I caught on immediately.

"I've met with 33 women so far, all of them unique and amazing. Would you be interested in being number 34?"

She gave me a surprised smile. "I would love to! What do you normally do with the women you meet with?"

I laughed. "Anything and everything. It's whatever the woman wants to do."

She thought for a moment. "Are you interested in musicals?"

I nodded eagerly. "I love them."

"Cinderella is being performed this afternoon at the Tivoli Theater in Chattanooga. Would you be interested in watching it with me? I have an extra ticket."

"That would be amazing!"

I saw Tina watching the exchange with a smile on her face. Obviously, she had known that Petra would say yes to meeting with me.

The five-minute countdown to service started right then, and Tina grabbed Jackson, Kelsey, and me so we could find seats before it started.

Service was amazing. The music was invigorating, the sermon engaging, and the presence of God powerful. I felt at home. Afterwards, Tina asked me how I liked it.

"I didn't."

She knit her brow. "You didn't?"

I shook my head. "I loved it!"

She laughed. She always fell for that. Out of all my friends, she was definitely the most gullible. That's not saying a lot, though, seeing how I didn't have that many friends now; but maybe Kelsey and I could become closer, now that she didn't hate me anymore.

I smiled. Who would have thought? Kelsey and I both hated the "Jesus jerks" with a passion, and now we were both Christians. God definitely has a sense of humor. Petra walked up to me just then, and I gave her a smile.

"Are you ready to go?"

I nodded. "Sure. Let me tell my brother that I'm leaving." I walked over to Jackson and told him I was going with Petra. He gave me a hug and said he'd see me back at home this evening. I then said goodbye to Kelsey and Tina before walking back over to Petra.

We exited through the doors of the church. As we walked to her car, she told me the itinerary for the day. "We're going to stop by the drive through at Wendy's for lunch on the way down to Chattanooga. After watching the musical at the Tivoli, we will return to Cleveland and eat at whatever restaurant you choose."

"Sounds great!"

We arrived at her car and climbed in. There was a Wendy's conveniently located next to the church, so we just skipped on over there and ordered some hamburgers and fries before hitting the road.

I started off the conversation. "What do you think are the qualities of a godly woman?"

She smiled. "That's a tough one. There are definitely many qualities that godly women have, but I think I can narrow it down to this: no matter what happens, you're never rocked in your faith. If you put God first, you will always have the strength to overcome whenever you feel like you are starting to shake a bit in your faith."

"What is a verse that you love?"

"A verse that has impacted my life is Jeremiah 33:3, which says, 'Call to Me, and I will answer you, and show you great and mighty things, which you do not know.' This has definitely been true in my life."

"How?"

"Lonnie and I used to own 32 apartments, but during a hailstorm, they were damaged, and the cost to repair them was $160,000. A man from the insurance company came and informed us that the insurance policy had changed, so, instead of having insurance cover all the costs, we had to pay $1,680 per building. We had never been informed of this change, or we would have done something about it. We didn't have that kind of money, so we did the only thing we could: we prayed. We told God that we were tithers, and in Malachi 3:10, it says that He would rebuke the devourer if we tithed. We prayed that He would deliver us from this situation."

If I were a betting person, I'd bet five bucks that this was going to end miraculously.

"Three months later, the insurance company called. They said that they checked, and they had no record of informing us about the insurance change. They said that we would only be charged $1,000 for the whole project."

Boom! I was right! Jesus. Is. Amazing. "That's incredible! God definitely did show you 'great and mighty things.'"

"Here's another example. I know a woman whose husband had died. She was a widow and didn't have anyone to take care of her, so she told God that He would have to be her husband now and take care of her like her husband would have. God did. He sent people to take care of things that needed repaired around her house, even though she had never told them she needed help. One time, her driveway was deteriorating. God sent a truckload of asphalt to her, and she didn't have to pay for it. It just shows God's great provision for His people."

As she spoke, I noticed that we were suddenly in Chattanooga. She pulled into a parking garage and parked the car. We exited the vehicle and began walking towards the Tivoli. Once inside the lobby, Petra gave the man our tickets. We went into the theater and sat down in our seats. After about fifteen minutes, the lights dimmed, and the show began.

It was absolutely incredible. From scene to scene, I was enchanted. Even though I knew the story of Cinderella like the back of my hand, I wasn't bored. There was never a dull moment. I was laughing, gasping, and near-crying. (I wouldn't actually cry just because of a musical.) At the end, I stood up with the rest of the audience and applauded. That was, by far, the best live musical I had ever seen.

Petra and I talked about it all the way back to her car, saying our favorite parts and mentioning how detailed it was in both the stage set up and the costumes. On the way home, we got to know one another better. I told her what school I went to, what I liked to do, what I didn't like to do, and my biggest fears.

"I absolutely, one hundred percent, cannot stand snakes. Cliché, I know, but still, they're so slimy, scaly, and dangerous that it gives me the heebie-jeebies. And I normally don't tell people that after what one friend did to me after he found out I hated them." I shuddered, remembering it all. "It was during elementary school. He owned a garter snake at the time I mentioned my fear to him, so he decided to see how scared of them I really was. During lunch at school, I opened my brown paper bag and found, not a sandwich, but a snake. Apparently, when I wasn't looking, my 'friend' had switched my bag with his. I screamed, threw the bag up in the air and slid under the table. Of course, the bag—and the snake— came right back down and landed on the floor next to me. The snake slithered out and came straight towards me, obviously angry. I screamed again and jumped onto a chair and then onto the table, trying my best to get as far away as possible. By this time, the teachers had come over to see what the commotion was about and found a snake and a hysterical girl. My friend got suspended for a few days, and I was scarred for life."

We pulled into the Chinese buffet where I wanted to eat, and as Petra climbed out of the car, she said, "That's awful that he would do something like that! I just hate it when people scare their friends. I don't wish fear on anyone because fear is an enemy."

I nodded, glad she agreed with me. Normally, most people would just laugh at me. I really liked Petra Setlich. When we had gotten our food and had found a table, I asked. "What's a tip you can give me for life?"

"You need to marry someone of like faith, someone who has the same strength in the Lord as you do."

"Like you and Lonnie?"

She smiled. "Yes, but it wasn't always that way. We weren't Christians until much later in our lives." She paused. "Let's pray before we get into that."

She said a quick prayer, and then we dug in.

After swallowing a mouthful of crispy shrimp, I asked, "How did you and Lonnie meet?"

"I met my husband in a bar at 2 in the morning."

Eyebrows lifted, I motioned for her to go on.

"In Germany, before I was saved, I worked as a bartender. After my work was done, a friend and I went to get some drinks. The bar we went to was so packed that we had to share a table with some men from the Air Force. Lonnie was one of them. We dated for two years before he proposed. He wanted to get married, but I wasn't sure about going to America. Needless to say, we did get married. After the wedding, which was in Germany, Lonnie was notified that his father had cancer. So, three days after the wedding, he left for America. I followed shortly after. I think the biggest challenge in my life was adjusting to America."

I know it would be difficult for me to just pack up and move to, say, Lithuania. I drank some water and waited for her to continue.

"I was born in Germany, as you know. I grew up in a heathen home and didn't get saved until I was thirty."

"How were you saved?"

"It was after I had come to America. Lonnie and I weren't Christians, and we lived like it.

One day, one of our children went to this church in town and came home full of joy. Both my husband and I were very confused at what had happened. Pretty soon, both of our children were going to this church and kept trying to tell us about this Jesus. Since Lonnie didn't want to see what it was all about, he had me visit the church. As soon as I walked through the doors of the church, I felt this unexplainable peace, and tears started to rise to the surface. I began blinking hard, having no clue why I was on the verge of tears. All during the service, I cried. I cried during the music. I cried while the pastor preached his message. I cried when I went to the altar and got saved. When I returned home, Lonnie asked me how it went, and I told him. The next week, he went with me, and he got saved, as well. We began diving into the Bible to find out all we could about God. And everything we read, we believed."

Everything? That's incredible faith. I have difficulty in believing some of the things in the Bible. "How did your belief in everything you read in the Bible help you with your walk of faith?"

She laughed. "I have a lot of stories. Would you like to hear some of them?"

Intrigued, I nodded. "That'd be great!" At this point, we were almost finished with our food.

"Well, let me start with this one. My daughter had a fever one day, and I had just read the story of Jesus healing Peter's mother-in-law. With that in mind, I rebuked the fever and five minutes later my daughter was healed."

My jaw dropped. I couldn't help it. I had had a fever many times, and it wasn't fun. Nor was recovery that quick. To have a fever leave within five minutes was definitely a work of God.

"Another time, my son had skin lesions. We took him to the doctor, but the medicine was expensive. I went to a gospel meeting shortly after that, and the strangest thing happened. The pastor suddenly said, 'There's someone here who has skin problems.' Now, my son wasn't there, but I prayed and asked the Lord if He would do long-distance healing like He had done with the centurion's servant."

I nodded. I had just read that story the other day.

"The next day, our family went to the lake, and my son wanted to wade in the water. I started to roll up his pant legs but then suddenly stopped. The lesions were gone."

I shook my head, amazed. This was definitely building my faith.

"Lonnie broke his arm one day. I immediately put him in bed and wrapped a wet, thick towel around his broken arm. I called the pastor, and we started praying. Suddenly, as we were praying, Lonnie's arm straightened by itself, the towel became hot, and he was completely healed."

I could really see the hand of God upon her family. These miracles were so mind-blowing that I was just sitting there with a smile on my face.

"Yet another time, I was carrying a pot of boiling water next to my daughter. The pot slipped, and scalding hot water poured all over her. Immediately, third degree burns came up all over her exposed skin. I instantly called my husband in, and we began praying. My daughter fell fast asleep, and every single blister and burn reversed and closed up, all except three scabs."

She smiled. "That's how my belief in everything the Bible says has helped me in my walk of faith."

Our food done, we stood up and walked out to her car. I was still trying to process all she had told me. If God could do all those miracles for her, a person who'd been a heathen for thirty years, then He could also do them for me.

She drove me back to my house, and I thought about how blessed I was that I had gotten to meet her. Just by looking at her, I wouldn't have guessed that she hadn't been a Christian all her life. I should stop looking at the cover of people and assuming things about them. I need to learn and understand their story before coming to conclusions.

When we arrived at my house, I gave her a hug and said goodbye. I had had a lot of fun with her, and I knew I would look for her smiling face whenever I went to church.

The rest of the week passed quickly. Since I didn't have to worry about who I was to meet with, I was able to concentrate on my schooling more, which made the days better when I began acing my tests. The next Sunday, I did see her, and we talked some before and after church. I could tell Tina was happy that we were hanging out.

After church, I went home and into my room. As I sank onto my bed, I checked my phone and noticed a text from the Beta Club teacher. Groaning, I slapped my forehead and lay back on my pillow. I had procrastinated and hadn't completed all my service hours for Beta Club. My grades (and attitude) had improved so much that I was able to be in Beta Club at school; however, that required service hours, and procrastination is my middle name. She had given me until the end of the week to complete the service hours, or else I would be kicked out of the club. Thankfully, though, I had until Friday, and it was only five hours, so I could start now and think of ways to complete service hours. It wasn't going to be easy, but at least it was possible; and that's all that mattered.

Chapter Thirty-Five

Still trying to figure out someway to get my service hours in, I talked to Tina the next day. I had already done the ten required hours with the Beta Club throughout the school year, which was easy because they had set it up and I just had to show up. I now needed to figure out five whole hours worth of service hours, and I had no clue what to do. I wasn't very creative in that department, and the only person I could think of who would help me willingly was Tina.

"I know of a few things you could do," Tina said, "but let me check on it. You have to have the hours in by this Friday, correct?"

I nodded. "And, unless I do all the service hours at night, I will have to find a way out of school."

Later that day, Tina came back to me. "I found a few activities you can volunteer at this week; here are the details for them," she said, handing me a list. "There's a dinner for a charity organization that needs volunteers. It's at night and will probably last an hour and a half to two hours." She paused. "The other activity isn't at night, which means you'd have to get out of school for it. It's working at The Caring Place here in town."

I scrunched my eyebrows together. "What's that?"

"The Caring Place is a place where people who are down on their luck can go and receive free clothes and food once to twice a month, depending on how big their families are. You'd be volunteering at the food part of The Caring Place, probably this Thursday." She peered at me for a moment. "You haven't met with a godly woman this week, have you?"

I shook my head. "I haven't, and yes I would be willing to volunteer there this week." Helping out sounded like something Jesus would do, so I decided to go for it. I had just read the story in John chapter 13 where Jesus washed His disciples' feet. Jesus is the ultimate example of servanthood, just like Aunt Charissa had said.

I spoke with my Beta Club teacher about missing school for one day, and she was nice enough to agree.

Tina sent me some paperwork that I had to fill out and that my mom had to sign. Even though it took a long while to fill out the papers, my mom willingly signed them without complaint; so I was happy. My grandmother helped me with all the other information I didn't know. It was strange; my grandmother had been in much better spirits ever since Jackson came home and I became a Christian. I don't know which one really made her happy, but she had been nicer to me and not as grumpy or as salty.

Tuesday night, I helped at the dinner for the charity and had a lot of fun, to my surprise. I thought that community service would be draining, but it really wasn't.

On Thursday, I put on a thick sweatshirt and some jeans. I had looked up the weather the day before and saw that it was going to be very windy and cold. Sure enough, when Jackson drove me to The Caring Place, the wind was whistling, and it was cold enough to freeze a fire. I waved goodbye to Jackson and walked towards the building as he drove away. The Caring Place was in a very secluded part of town, and I didn't think I had ever seen it before. As I looked around for where I should enter the warehouse-like building, a door swung open on the side of the building. An older woman waved me over.

"Hello! Are you Brie?"

I nodded. "Yes, I am."

She smiled. "I'm Patricia Kinston. I'm so excited to be a part of your challenge, and I'm also excited to have you here with me today!"

I raised my eyebrows slightly. Obviously, Tina had told Patricia about my challenge, and I wasn't one to ruin her fun, especially since Patricia was so excited to be doing it with me. I followed her inside the building and was immediately introduced to Sheila McElhaney, the manager over the food warehouse. She said a quick hello before scurrying off to check on something. I could tell she was very busy. I noticed several people working in the warehouse. Some of them were in a small room packing food into brown paper bags while others were unfolding empty cardboard boxes and stacking them in a pile. Patricia grabbed a cart of dairy products and led me through a door to what appeared to be the front, where she began unloading the products onto a shelf in front of the counter. I started helping her. There was a shelf for dairy, a cart for bread, a shelf for odds and ends, and a place for vegetables.

Once we finished stacking the dairy, she brought me back to the large room and introduced me to everybody. Everyone gave me a warm welcome before going back to their jobs. We returned to the front room, where Patricia brought me behind the counter. On the shelves were dozens and dozens of large brown paper bags crammed with food.

"When people come to The Caring Place, they first go to the building up on the hill beside us. That's where they sign in and show their yearly income to be able to receive food and clothes from us. They pick out a set amount of clothing from that building and are given a slip of paper showing how much food they can receive. In this building, they pick up the amount of food allotted to them, such as one of the brown bags as well as a bag of meat and fruit, which varies based on what we have." She then pointed to the other side of the counter. "They can then get some dairy products, bread, vegetables, and odds and ends. For example, today, since we have a lot of bread, they are able to get three different bread products."

I nodded, taking it all in. "What am I going to be doing today?"

"You'll be helping me here behind the counter."

"Okay, sounds great!" I looked around. "But where are the people?"

She smiled. "We open thirty minutes after the building on the hill does, so we have a few more minutes."

"In the meantime, could you answer some questions for me?"

She nodded. "Sure!"

I thought it was great that God had thought of all the details. He not only gave me a woman to meet with this week, but He also provided little increments of time to talk to her. "Alright, first question. What's your favorite verse?"

"John 3:16. I know that a lot of people probably say that, but it's just an amazing verse. If the gospel had to be narrowed down to one verse, that would explain everything best."

"What are the qualities of a godly woman?"

She pondered that for a moment. "I believe that the qualities of a godly woman are to serve the Lord, pray, read the Bible, and to love your husband and family."

"Has it been easy to do those things?"

She shook her head. "Not all the time. In fact, the hardest challenge I've had to face is marriage. My husband was raised in a divorced family. Because of that, he never saw how to have a good marriage, so he wasn't able to apply that to our marriage."

I gave her a sympathetic look. "I'm sorry." Honestly, I didn't know if I ever wanted to get married. I mean, my parents obviously didn't love each other that much, since my mom turned to the bottle and my dad to the pills. I don't see many good marriages anymore, which makes me scared that I won't have one. I think parents don't realize how much their marriage affects their kids. If their marriage isn't good, then the kids won't know how to have a good marriage when they get married; thus, the cycle continues unless someone has the guts and willpower to make a conscious effort to not be like their parents. Or the kids will be like me and will be afraid of getting married because of what they saw growing up.

Just then, the door opened, and a woman walked in. Immediately, Patricia greeted her with a smile and asked for her slip of paper. After receiving it, she wrote her name down on a clipboard and had me grab one of the brown paper bags. I gave it to the woman with a smile, along with an empty grocery bag. The woman placed in the grocery bag some of the items on the other side of the counter. After she was done, she thanked us and left.

I smiled. It was a lot easier than I thought it would be. As if sensing my happiness, Patricia turned to me.

"The job may be easy with just one person, but we normally have about 80 people come in within a few hours."

My jaw dropped. I didn't know there were that many down-on-their-luck people in Cleveland. I guess I had envisioned everyone having a cozy house with two kids and a dog. How wrong I was.

Over the next hour, I was kept busy with people coming in and out of the doors. I was sent to the back of the warehouse multiple times when there were empty cardboard boxes needing to be torn down or when I needed to get some more bread. I was also the delivery girl: when people had a lot of bags to carry, I would step in and help carry the bags out to their cars for them.

In between people coming and going, I kept up the stream of questions for Patricia. "What's your favorite thing about working here?"

"My favorite thing about working here is that there's never a dull moment."

I laughed. It was so true.

She continued. "I love to be busy, so this is my kind of job."

I gave another person a bag. "Why The Caring Place?"

She wrote something down on her clipboard. "God led my here. I prayed that I would be able to have an opportunity to help people. One night I was at a local church at a Bible study. The women there told me that I should attend the women's retreat they were having soon. I didn't think I could, but one woman told me that she would pay for me to go because God told her that He wanted me to go. Needless to say, I ended up going to the retreat. While there, I was able to meet Sheila McElhaney, the manager over the food warehouse here. Sheila asked for my help here. It was an answer to prayer. I accepted and have been working here for nine months."

That's so neat. "What was it like to start working here?"

She smiled, remembering. "On my first day at The Caring Place, I wondered if I was going to be smart enough to think of everything I needed to do and if I would be able to do it right."

I didn't think her fears were necessary. She had been doing a wonderful job as far as I could tell. Before I could say that, though, I was sent to the back again to get more bread.

It was that way for the rest of the morning: giving bags, grabbing supplies from the back, and talking to Patricia through it all. Every time I went to the back, one of the volunteers would smile at me. It felt good to know that I was needed here.

When I went back to Patricia, I mentioned how nice all the volunteers here were.

She agreed with me. "I love the volunteers here because they want to work here; therefore, they never complain or are grumpy while doing their jobs."

As twelve o'clock neared, the amount of people coming in grew less and less until we only had about one person coming in every couple of minutes. Patricia looked at the clock.

"In just a few minutes, we should be able to close up and head out."

After hearing that, I texted Jackson to let him know. He was currently job-hunting in town, so it wouldn't take him too long to get over here. Sure enough, ten minutes later Jackson pulled up. Almost all the volunteers had left by this point, so it was just Sheila, Patricia, and me who finished locking up and making sure everything was in order.

When Jackson came in, I said goodbye and walked out to the car. I'd had a lot of fun volunteering there. If I needed service hours in the future, I wouldn't hesitate to go there again. On the drive home, I asked Jackson how his job-hunting had gone. He beamed.

"Amazing. I got a job!"

I squealed. "Congratulations! Where is it at?"

"Cracker Barrel. I'm serving tables."

I nodded appreciatively. "Very nice. Do family members of the workers get discounts?"

He laughed. "No."

I frowned. "Rats. I mean, what's the point of getting a job if you can't give your family free things?"

He cocked an eyebrow. "Uhhhh, maybe because you get paid?" He shook his head. "Duh."

I laughed. We were almost home, and I was ready to fall into bed and enjoy a nice nap. My service hours were finally completed, and I felt very happy. Serving others gave me a happiness that came from deep within. Watching all those people receive those bags of food and knowing that I was helping them feed their kids was a life-changer for me.

Chapter Thirty-Six

I had barely completed my service hours before the deadline, but I had done it. My Beta Club teacher was very relieved that I had done it in time. She didn't want to dismiss me from the club, but she did have to make sure rules were enforced. I breathed a huge sigh of relief over the weekend as I got to relax and take a break from stress—until Monday came around.

As soon as I walked through the doors of the school, Tina ran up to me, grabbed me by the arm, and hauled me down the hall.

I struggled to get free. "What are you doing?"

She gave me a worried look. "No time. Just follow me."

I gave her a puzzled look. What could she possibly mean by 'no time'? No time for what?

She pulled me all the way down the hallway until we were in my math classroom. I inhaled sharply. The room was trashed. Papers were chopped up and thrown about the room like confetti, desks and chairs were overturned, and there was glue smeared all over the teacher's brand-new swivel chair she had purchased because she didn't like the other one.

I turned to Tina. "When did this happen?"

She shook her head. "Friday night before the school was locked, but no one knows who it was because the culprits were wearing masks."

"Does the teacher know?"

Again, she shook her head. "Mrs. Goldwyn is apparently sick today, so she's not coming in, but the principal knows, and he's steaming mad."

I stared at her, confused. "Why does this involve me, though?"

She pointed across the room, a grim look on her face. "Look."

I followed her finger and let out a gasp. There, plastered to the wall was a giant sign that said, "Math is just like Mrs. Goldwyn; completely boring." Of course, their choice of verbiage was a lot more colorful. I then went to my desk to sit down and think about who might have done this when I saw a piece of paper crammed inside my desk. It read, "You're a hypocritical jerk. Stop trying to be the teacher's pet or else worse will happen. If you show this note to anyone, you'll be in big trouble." I stared in shock.

I turned to Tina, who was looking over my shoulder with a solemn look on her face. "What in the world! I'm going to get blamed for this because I was in here last on Friday!" I was the teacher's pet, and Mrs. Goldwyn loved me. Every Friday, I stayed in her room after school for about an hour doing homework and helping her clean up. Last Friday she had to leave earlier than normal and asked me to make sure everything was put back where it belonged. She even gave me the key to lock up, provided I turn it in to the office, which I did. The principal was there when I gave it back, so he knows I didn't keep the key; however, he might not believe that I didn't wreck the room before giving him the key. If I showed him this note, the troublemakers might do something worse. If I didn't, I might get in big trouble.

I gave Tina a pitiful look. "I don't know what to do. Why would they target me? They must have known that I would be blamed if they did it Friday night."

She shrugged, confused. "I can't make anything out of it. I guess Kelsey becoming a Christian because of you confirmed to everyone that you're really a Christian, and they aren't happy about it. I think they mostly feel betrayed."

I looked at her, bewilderment all over my face. "Betrayed? I didn't betray them!"

She shook her head. "They think you did. You used to hate Christians and now you are a Christian. They think that you lied to them about hating Christians, since you are one. They feel betrayed because now people are looking at them and thinking that they will also become Christians because if you became one, then they might become one, as well."

I blinked. Slowly. "Surely they aren't lashing out just because of that. I didn't even say anything about them! All this," I gestured around me, "is because of what other people are saying about them?" I shook my head incredulously. "Unbelievable."

Tina gave me a wry smile. "You might have done something similar a couple of months ago."

As I started to deny it, I realized that she was right. If, say, Kelsey had become a Christian when I still hated God, then I probably would've felt betrayed. Nonetheless, I never would've gone this far. "Should I show the principal the note?"

Tina shrugged. "I don't know. I had a talk with the principal before you came and he said the security cameras don't show anybody recognizable, just two people in dark clothes and masks. The room was wrecked about twenty minutes before the school was locked Friday night. Clearly they had thought this through very well. He wanted to believe you didn't do it, but all the evidence is pointing towards you. If you want to try and convince him you aren't to blame, I think you should show him the note. Plus, there were two culprits. Naturally, they thought you and I would be blamed since we hang out, but I have an alibi; I left as soon as school was out with my family to go to a concert all night. I didn't even get home until 11. You don't really hang out with anyone else, so it couldn't have been you and a close friend."

I marched down to the office, note in hand. Once Tina and I were allowed in to see the principal, I showed him the note. "I know it looks like I wrecked the math room, but I promise you I didn't. I love Mrs. Goldwyn and would never break her trust like this. You know I gave you the key."

He nodded as he read the note. "This helps your case a lot. Of course, I'll have to find out whose handwriting this is, but I know you turned the key in. Are you sure you locked the classroom?"

"I think so." I scrunched my eyebrows together. "Actually, I'm not sure. I was just finishing up and was about to leave when a girl named Gracie Roberts walked by the classroom and tripped, spilling her stuff everywhere. I went to help her pick it all up and then closed the door. I can't remember if I locked it, though." I frowned. "I don't know why Gracie would've tripped there. There was nothing in the hallway to trip over."

He matched my frown with one of his own. "Why don't we check out the security footage?" We all gathered around a monitor as he rewound it to Friday, right before I went to the office. We watched as a girl walked down the hallway and looked around. I could see myself in the math room, picking up trash. The girl peeked in the door and then just fell. Straight up fell—on purpose. I looked on as I rushed out of the classroom and helped her up. I then closed the door and went down the hallway the opposite direction. Gracie didn't move. She looked both ways and then checked the math door. It was unlocked. Through the grainy footage, I could see a smile of triumph on her face as she began running down the hallway towards the girls' bathroom. He switched camera views and we watched as she went into the bathroom. She didn't come out for a while, so he fast-forwarded it until the door opened. Gracie, clad in black, walked out. By that time it was twenty minutes before the school was locked. She looked both ways again and then ran down the hall. Coming to the math room, Gracie met up with another figure in black. They walked in, and then we watched as the classroom was destroyed.

He shut it all off. "I'm glad you told me about the incident you had before giving me the key."

"Am I free to go?"

He shook his head. "You're not entirely off the hook because we can't see who the other figure was, but I think that if I bring Ms. Roberts in here for a little chat, she'll come clean. You should be in the clear by this afternoon. It would be helpful, though, if you could clean the classroom instead of going to your first class. I'll let your teachers know, but I think that the less people who know about this, the better."

We agreed to do that. Tina and I went back to the classroom and began to clean up. She looked at me. "Hey, who are you meeting with this week?"

"No one yet. I haven't really thought about it because I figured you probably had someone in mind."

She laughed. "You know me too well. You're right. I wanted to know if you would be interested in meeting with Tracie Shellhouse, the CEO of New Hope Pregnancy Center."

"What's that?"

"It's a center for pregnant women who are thinking about getting an abortion."

I looked at her in horror. "You want me to meet with someone who encourages abortion?"

She snorted. "Tracie is one of the most opposed people to abortion that I've ever met. The center helps persuade women to not get an abortion, but I'll let her talk to you about that when you meet with her."

I laughed. "When? It sounds like you knew I'd say yes."

She giggled. "I did."

I shook my head. "One day that's not going to work. You'll plan something out, and I won't be able to do it. Then you'll be in a real mess."

Tina and I kept cleaning. I first tore down the sign and threw it away. I shuddered as I turned away from the trashcan. To what lengths would these people go to get me to change my beliefs? I didn't want to deny Jesus, especially since I had just read in the Bible today that if I denied Jesus, He would deny me; however, I didn't want to spend all semester cleaning classrooms just because of my beliefs.

I moved on to the next thing that needed my attention: all the papers on the ground. Tina was busily scrubbing the teacher's chair as I scurried to pick up the papers.

Standing up with a groan, Tina said, "I think I've gotten most of it out. How's the paperwork going?"

I laughed at her attempt of humor in this grim situation. "Almost all of it's up. I think we'll be done in a few minutes."

Sure enough, in less than ten minutes, the classroom was spic and span, and the only evidence of the mess was the bulging pile of papers in the trashcan. We left the classroom and went to the principal's office, where we updated him on the situation.

He nodded in approval. "Good work, both of you. Go ahead to your next class, and I'll keep you both informed with what I find out from Gracie."

We continued throughout the rest of the school day without any major events happening. I paid close attention during math and tried to see if anyone was surprised that the mess was cleaned up, but everyone had indifferent expressions, even Gracie. She was a good actress.

After school, I pulled Tina aside. "When will I be meeting with Tracie?"

"Tomorrow."

I nodded. "Okay. What will I be doing?"

"It'll be after school, so she'll probably show you around the center and tell you her story."

"Sounds great!"

The next day, I had Jackson drive me to the center after school. As I climbed out of the car, I looked around. I was glad that this center was in a secluded part of town because I didn't want to have to explain to anyone why I was going into a pregnancy center with my brother. Jackson walked me inside.

I told the receptionist that I was here to meet Tracie Shellhouse. She nodded with a confused expression on her face. I just let her stare. A minute later, a woman walked into the sitting room where I was standing.

She smiled broadly. "Hi, there! I'm Tracie. Are you Brie? The girl doing the challenge?"

I nodded. "That's me."

Before she led me through the door connected to the waiting room, I waved to Jackson as he exited through the main doors. As we walked down the corridor, I asked her how she came to work here.

"I started out as a volunteer at a local clinic while being a stay-at-home mom. While working here, God told me to get my résumé together. I didn't want to because my youngest child was only two years old; however, God wouldn't let me get a peaceful night's sleep until I did so. I was very skeptical about getting a CEO job, the only job I applied for, because there are only about 2,300 crisis pregnancy centers in North America, and most of the positions for a CEO would be filled. The chances of me actually getting a job as a CEO were slim; however, God doesn't work based on chance. Five months later, I had a job offer in Houston, Texas. I took it. During my time there, I would frequently vacation here to Cleveland because God would lead me here."

Here? God would tell her to spend her vacation in Cleveland, and she would do it? That shows faith. I probably would've chosen Florida, thinking I was just imagining that God wanted me to go to Tennessee for my vacations.

We entered a room that appeared to be her office, since the sign said, "Tracie Shellhouse, CEO." Once we had sat down, her behind her desk and I in a cushioned chair opposite her, I spoke. "What are some stories you could tell me about your time in Houston?"

She leaned back in her chair and thought for a minute. "There was one girl who came to the pregnancy center planning on getting an abortion. Once I had talked to her, she knew she couldn't have an abortion, but she also knew that her mom would kick her out of the house when she discovered that she was pregnant. After some encouragement from me, she went home and told her mom. As she anticipated, her mom kicked her out that night. Weeping, she arrived at the pregnancy center, and I let her stay there for the night. The next morning, I called around to see if there was a maternity home anywhere nearby. There was, and I drove her there. The people there welcomed her in like she was family."

What incredible acceptance. If I were ever in the girl's position, my mom definitely would kick me out, or, if she wasn't sober enough to do so, my grandmother would. To find a home with strangers who would welcome you like family would be amazing. I propped my head on one hand and kept listening.

"Anyway, after all my vacations here to Cleveland, I was able to land the job as the CEO here at New Hope. Being the CEO is a big job, and it's been very stressful at times, especially when we've needed money we didn't have."

"What are some examples of times you needed money?"

"We have to raise $400,000 a year to run this clinic. We do free pregnancy tests and free ultrasounds, even though they aren't cheap."

I frowned. "Wait. Why would you provide these free services if they're not cheap and you need to save money?"

"People are more likely to come to our clinic if they see that we do the same things other clinics and hospitals do but for no cost. Then, when they come in and see their baby on the ultrasound, that's when their thoughts about abortion begin to change. They go from calling their baby 'it' to 'my baby.'"

"How do you get the money to offer these services?"

She stacked some papers on her desk. "We have several ways. We have sponsors and churches who donate to our cause, we hold banquets to try and gain sponsors, and we have a Walk For Life every year."

"What's Walk For Life?" I asked, even though I was pretty sure it had something to do with walking.

"It's when people sign up sponsors to give them money for walking 1.5 miles; however, the amount of money raised in the past years hasn't been very good. Before the Walk for Life this past fall, I prayed that God would send the money. He told me, 'I'm going to do something no man can orchestrate. When people see it, they will know it's from Me.' The Walk for Life only brought in $3,600, but the letters we sent out to donors and people from the community brought in $25,000."

I smiled, amazed. "That's incredible!"

She nodded. "Yes, but that's not all God's done for this clinic. I received a call one day about a piece of property. The woman on the phone said her company couldn't use it and that the company would give it to me if I used it for the needy. Well, I decided to sell that property and give the profits to New Hope. After going to the property and looking at it, the realtor told me that the property was only worth about $19,000. I knew I needed to get $40,000 from the property to meet a goal at New Hope. I talked to the realtor later and was surprised to find out that the realtor was putting the property on the market for $40,000—the exact amount I needed, unbeknownst to the realtor."

I shook my head. God is, in fact, awesome, and He shows it in so many ways.

"Anyway, the realtor put a 'For Sale' sign on the property, and the very next day we had 13 offers. That property had sat there for 6 months without a single offer, and the day after we put it up for sale at $40,000 we got thirteen offers. Within three days, I had a check for $38,000. God had taken the value of the property and had doubled it."

"That's amazing!"

She nodded. "Yes, it is. God has really been blessing us. In America, pregnancy clinics versus abortion clinics are now 3 to 1. In 2016, this clinic saved 5 babies. In 2017, we saved 29 babies, which is a 480% increase."

I couldn't believe it. What these people were doing was absolutely incredible, and I prayed right then and there that God would bless them for being so giving of their time and money for babies they might never meet.

At that moment, there was a knock on the closed office door. Tracie strode over to open it, and two college students entered the room and sat down in the two remaining chairs. After introducing me to them, Tracie said that they were helping around the clinic, especially with the banquet that was coming up. My ears perked.

"Banquet?"

She nodded. "Yes. I told you that New Hope does a banquet every year as one of the ways it gets income. That's what they're working on. They call people who have attended the banquet in the past and ask them if they want to buy tickets."

"What happens at this banquet?" I inquired.

"People buy tickets to have a seat at a table. The ticket includes a large dinner, unlimited refills, and a Christian comedian who speaks that night. It's about a two-hour event. During the night, a video is played about one of our clients who decided not to have an abortion.

Also, I say a short spiel about our company and entreat them to donate money. Most people think that their $40 ticket is enough and give very little if anything; however, that's not the truth. We need more money than just $40 per person if we want to keep New Hope afloat. In fact, one of the main reasons this banquet is able to happen is because of volunteers like these two amazing people." She pointed to the two college students.

I was immensely interested. "Do you have volunteers serving the tables?"

She nodded, surprised. "Yes. Are you interested in helping?"

I smiled widely. "I am! When is it?"

She checked a paper on her desk. "It's next month, March 22."

I glanced at the calendar on my phone and then smiled even wider. "Great! I'll be able to do it."

The two college students quickly gave her an update of their progress and then stood to leave the room. "Thanks for stopping by!" Tracie called after them.

When she faced me again, she tilted her head. "So what do you normally do when meeting with women for this challenge?"

"I talk with the women, ask a few standard questions, and spend some time learning what they've learned in life."

"What are some questions you ask each woman?"

"Well, for starters, what's your favorite Bible verse?"

"My favorite verse is Jeremiah 29:11, which says, '"For I know the thoughts that I think toward you, says the Lord, thoughts of peace and not of evil, to give you a future and a hope."'"

"That ties in nicely with everything you stand for here at the center. My next question is this: what are the qualities of a godly woman?"

She thought for a moment. "I believe the qualities of a godly woman are these: humility, patience, and a love that surpasses your feelings—whether you like a person or not, or whether you have to do something you don't want to do." She paused only a second before continuing. "It's just like what I deal with every day. Abortion is life ending, and all you have is regret. Adoption is life giving, and you do it out of love."

I tilted my head. "Adoption is giving up your child. How do you give up a child and call it love?"

"Adoption isn't giving up. Abortion is giving up a child—for good. Adoption is giving love. To give your baby the best chance at life by giving him or her to someone more prepared at life than you are is the greatest love you could give your child. Plus, some families will allow the birth mother to stay in touch with her child, so unless she wants out of her child's life, she can still watch her child grow."

I leaned forward in my seat, noticing how she became animated whenever she talked about abortion versus adoption. "What are some more opinions you have regarding abortion?"

She thought for a minute. "Here's one. There are two premises in abortion. The major premise is that to kill an innocent human is wrong. The minor premise is that abortion kills human beings. Thus, the conclusion is that abortion is wrong. People agree with the major premise, and the minor premise is obvious; but people won't get in the middle of the argument about the conclusion because they think it's political due to what people around them say."

I shook my head. How could anyone think killing an innocent person is okay? Unless, of course, they don't think the baby is a person. "What if people say that the baby isn't really a baby?"

"When Mary spoke to Elizabeth, John was aware, since he 'leaped in the womb.'

Therefore, any baby in the womb has awareness and, thus, shouldn't be killed by anyone in their right mind."

"Well, that's simple, unless people aren't Christians and don't care about killing another human. Christians aren't for abortion, right?"

She shook her head sadly. "Actually, you're very wrong. While most Christians are pro-life, some of them aren't. I always have a question for Christians who are for abortion. I ask them if they believe that God is the creator of mankind. They say yes, and then I ask, 'So you think you can kill something He made because you believe He messed up?'"

I raised my eyebrows. That was very true. By killing a baby, not only are you committing murder but you're also saying that you don't want the gift God is giving you: the gift of a precious life. "What's the most common argument that people give you when you try to convince them not to get an abortion?"

"The typical defense is, 'It's my body; I can do what I want!'" Tracie huffed out a breath. "It's not their body! It's an entirely different body in them!"

She was pretty worked up about this, so I decided to bring the conversation back to a less-agitating subject. "Are there any more stories you can tell me about your experiences here at the clinic?"

She pondered that for a moment and then brightened. "A pregnant woman recently came in here with a fifteen-month-old boy. Two years earlier, she had visited the clinic while pregnant and had become a Christian, thus not getting an abortion—of which the toddler was proof. She told me that she and her husband were too poor now to afford any more children. They had an enormous debt to pay off, so their wages were being garnished. They were living in a trailer without power or running water so that they could buy diapers for her son. She had an abortion appointment planned for the next day. I convinced her to get an ultrasound before she left. She transformed once she saw her baby." Tracie paused, a frown on her face. "However, she never said whether she was going through with the abortion or not. Seven months later, that same woman walked into our clinic with another baby, a girl this time. She told me that if I hadn't been there that day, the baby girl wouldn't be in her arms at that moment. On top of that, she told me that two weeks before giving birth, their enormous debt had been completely erased."

My jaw dropped. "That's fantastic! I bet you were glad that you were working that day so that you could save her baby." I paused. "So why did you start volunteering at a crisis pregnancy center anyway?"

"The reason I really wanted to come work at a pregnancy crisis center is because I've been on the other side."

I looked at her, surprised.

"I got pregnant out of wedlock and found myself sitting in a crisis pregnancy center as a client. I eventually married and eight years later started volunteering at a crisis pregnancy center. I've now been married twenty-two years to a phenomenal man and have four kids."

I didn't know what to say. I definitely never would've guessed just by looking at her. "I bet the women coming in here feel more comfortable when they realize that you've been where they are."

She nodded. "Yes, they do." Then she stood up abruptly and motioned for me to do so, as well. "It's nearing the end of our time, and I wanted to give you a tour before you leave."

"Sounds good to me."

She led me back down the corridor to the front desk. She introduced me to a couple of people and then began the tour. First, we stopped in a room filled with filing cabinets and supplies. Then, we went to an examination room with an ultrasound machine, an examination table, and a computer desk.

"This is where the patients can have their ultrasounds done," Tracie said.

She continued showing me rooms: a bathroom, some offices, a boardroom, and a few counseling rooms. Then she brought me through a set of doors to a room that immediately brought a smile to her face.

"This room is very special not only to the clinic but also to me. When we were finishing this clinic and getting all the rooms ready, I was looking at a blueprint of it and noticed that there was one room that we hadn't done anything with. It was smack dab in the middle of the clinic. As I was thinking about what I should do with the room, I felt the Lord asking me what the heart and center of New Hope really was. Immediately, I thought, 'Prayer.' We turned it into our prayer room."

I smiled. Praying was very important, especially when dealing with the lives of babies. Right then, my phone buzzed, and I saw Jackson's face on the screen. Apologizing to Tracie, I answered the phone.

"Give me just a minute." I then answered it. "Hello?"

"Hey, Brie. I'm out front whenever you're ready."

"Okay, I'll be right out."

I hung up the phone and turned to Tracie. "I have to leave. Thank you so much for spending time with me today!"

She gave me a hug. "No problem! I had a blast."

As we went back to her office so I could get my stuff, I noticed a picture hanging in her office. It was two hands shaping clay, and the clay was a baby. I smiled at it. Of course. The Potter shaping the clay, and the clay is a baby. I thought it was intriguing and took a picture of it with my phone.

We walked to the front entrance, and Tracie saw me out the door. As I climbed into the car and Jackson began pulling away from the building, I waved to her through the window. On the way home, I stared at the passing scenery but didn't really see it. What would it be like to know that you were saving people's lives? To really make a difference and to stop murder? I decided that whenever I could, I would speak out against abortion. Who knows what might happen if I only just spoke the truth?

Chapter Thirty-Seven

I breathed a sigh of relief Tuesday morning when I peeked into the math classroom before my first class and saw that it wasn't trashed again. We were off school Monday for Presidents Day, so I had more time to recuperate from the incident, especially when I found out who did it. After Principal Gordon talked with Gracie, she admitted to wrecking the room once she realized he had security footage. She even told him who did it with her: Rebecca Franklin, a girl who used to be my friend before I became a Christian. Principal Gordon suspended both of them for three days because of the incident.

All throughout the day, I felt awful that they would mess up a classroom just because of my beliefs. I hadn't said anything to them, and I hadn't done anything mean, so why would they just randomly attack me?

I shrugged, my Abercrombie sweater bunching up on my shoulders. Some people are just mean and unpredictable. Part of me wants to get back at the culprits for what they did, but the other part says that it wouldn't be the right thing to do. It's hard to choose the last one, though. I mean, all I want to do is a small prank, something that wouldn't hurt anyone—at least not too badly. Maybe TP-ing their houses, switching out their lunches for something gross, or taking their clothes while they're in the showers.

I shook my head. I needed to regain control of my thoughts and start thinking about good things, like Philippians 4:8 says, the verse I had read that morning. If Tina knew what I was thinking, she'd probably be shocked.

I snorted. Yeah, right. She'd probably expect it from me. Speaking of Tina, she was heading my direction.

"Hey! What's up?" I said.

"The ceiling," she replied, and then doubled over in laughter.

I lifted an un-amused eyebrow. She honestly thought I hadn't heard that one before? I tapped my foot impatiently as her giggles slowly subsided. I rolled my eyes.

"Honestly, you act so crazy sometimes. How's your day been going?"

She stood back up and caught her breath before responding. "Meh. Classes have been monotonous, people annoying, and the food awful. Just another regular day at Keaton Middle School." She paused. "I can't wait for high school. Just think, only a few more months before we're freshmen!"

I nibbled my lower lip. "I don't know. I'm a bit nervous. Just think, all the seniors are going to be towering over us, we'll have harder classes, and there'll be stricter teachers!"

She tilted her head to one side, letting her blond hair splash onto her cheek. I always thought it looked whimsical when that happened. Tina, however, didn't really like it. She said she'd much rather cut her hair short so it brushed her shoulders, instead of cascading down her back, but everyone persuaded her not to. "I think that the teachers would be the same, but it is a little threatening to think of all those seniors." She giggled. "Unless it's your brother."

I frowned. Tina only giggled when she was feeling shy or was trying to hide a full-out laugh. "What's going on with you? It's not like my brother is some superhero or anything."

Jackson had told me after returning home that when he had left home, he backpacked across much of the country, occasionally hitchhiking, until he met a family one summer who were really nice to him. After hearing his story, they took him in. They were the ones who brought him back to Christ, and he stayed with them for a year and a half before he felt the need to return home. They homeschooled their two young children, and they enrolled Jackson in online classes. He said he learned so much from his online classes that he wondered why more people didn't homeschool their kids. Sometimes I wonder how eight hours pass without learning hardly anything. Jackson had continued his online classes ever since he got back at Thanksgiving, and he was on track to finish by the end of the school year.

A niggling thought kept popping up in my brain, though. Why was Tina always talking about Jackson? I've never seen her date anyone, but that didn't mean she wasn't pretty; quite the opposite, in fact. I'd seen Tina turn down boy after boy asking her to go out with him. She had some creative ways of saying no. If she thought the boy interesting and wouldn't mind if he were a friend, she would say, "I think we need to build our friendship before deciding whether we're meant to be together." If the boy were a Christian, she'd say, "I don't think God is wanting us to be together right now," or "Let me pray about it." Of course, she'd pray and feel as if they weren't supposed to go out. And lastly, if she weren't interested in the boy at all and thought him a stalker, she'd say, "In your dreams!" and walk away.

When I asked her why she didn't just tell the guys she didn't want to date until she was 16, she said that it was more interesting this way. I thought it was a bit sad, to give the poor boys hope before they realized she wasn't going to go out with them. She told me that if there were a guy who asked her out whom she did like, she'd ask him to wait until she was 16. If he were the right one, he'd wait; but if not, then she didn't need him. It was a test she devised. Her parents allowed her to date, but she just didn't want to date around and figured that if a guy was willing to wait until she was 16, then he was definitely a possible future husband.

I thought that was a good plan. I was allowed to date (since no one in my family cared who I dated except for Jackson), but I didn't want to. First of all, I hadn't found any guy I wanted to date. Second, dating in middle school was stupid! I remembered countless times my friends were crying at school because their boyfriend did or said something, and then they'd break up for about two weeks before they "gave one another a second chance." That was for the lucky ones. The ones who didn't make up stayed mad at one another forever. To this day I know people who hate each other after they broke up, just because of bitterness and jealousy.

I've decided to wait until high school—maybe even college—before dating. There's not quite as much drama, and you're actually dating people to find your future spouse, not just for fun. Who knows? I may stay single and end up being "the crazy old cat lady living in the giant mansion."

I stopped my little mind train before it headed too far off the tracks and realized that I was standing in the nearly deserted hallway with Tina in front of me, snapping her fingers in my face.

"Hello? Is anybody home? Late bell just rang. You're going to be late for your last class!"

I snapped out of my trance and started running down the hallway. I made it into the classroom just in time. I slipped into my seat, hoping that the teacher wouldn't say anything. Other than giving me a look over the top of her glasses, she didn't say anything. I breathed a sigh of relief as I opened my book.

After school, I walked outside and waited for Jackson. I used to ride the bus, but now that I had a caring brother, I didn't have to. He came every day to pick me up. He only worked morning shifts at Cracker Barrel, so he was always free to come and get me. Then we'd go do something together, like getting frozen yogurt, taking a walk, or going to thrift shops. Today I had an idea. I had told Tina to ask her mom if she could hang out with me after school. She didn't know that Jackson picked me up everyday, so she probably thought my grandmother would be driving us. I knew, however, that once she knew that Jackson was going to be there, she'd brighten up considerably.

I spotted Tina coming out of the school.

"Tina! Over here!"

She saw me and waved and then jogged on over. "Hey. So what're we doing?"

I noticed my ride pulling up to the curb and that Jackson was rolling the passenger window down. "Why don't you ask him?"

She turned to where I was pointing and smiled. Widely. She waved. "Hey, Jackson!"

He leaned over to the open window and grinned. Cheesily. He waved. "Hey, Tina!"

I groaned. What had I done? There was enough sugar here to outrival a gallon of Sweet n' Low. I was going to be third wheeling the whole time! But I was still happy. Look at me, the little matchmaker. We walked over to the car and I ushered Tina into the backseat before sitting beside Jackson. He pulled away from the curb and out of the parking lot.

As we drove down the road, Jackson looked at Tina in the rearview mirror. "So, what do you want to do?"

She shrugged, her glowing eyes never leaving his. "I'm good with anything you want."

He frowned playfully. "Now, I need you to choose."

She grinned. "My statement remains the same."

I cut in to their conversation before I threw up. "Why don't we do something really fun? Why don't we drive down to Georgia?"

Jackson looked surprised. "Why Georgia?"

"Well, everything around here is pretty boring right now, and if we went to Georgia we'd be able to go to a nature park down there that I've heard about. It is supposed to be super pretty, with trails, park benches, swings, and flowers. I think it will be a nice change of scenery."

He considered it. Then, his eyes lit up. "That will work out great because I just called a woman who's moving and put an ad on the Internet to sell her car. It's a good car—a red Chrysler Sebring convertible—for a great price, and I wanted to check it out. I have been wanting to buy my own car so I wouldn't have to keep using the family car. I wanted to see it but didn't know when I'd be able to drive down to Georgia. I'll call Marj and see if I could come by today. You guys up for that?" By guys, he meant Tina. He knew I'd be fine with anything.

Tina, of course, nodded until I thought her head would pop off.

"Sure!"

I flinched. Her voice was up in dog whistle range. Jackson beamed. He literally beamed. "Okay, then. I guess Georgia it is."

Tina got a funny look on her face. "Wait, what's the last name of the woman you're buying the car from?"

"Marj Farris."

Her eyes grew wide. "My mom knows her! What a small world!"

While he called Marj, Tina texted her mom and asked her if she could go down to visit Marj with us. Her mom said it was fine as long as she got her homework done. Apparently, her mom had already met Jackson and "really appreciated meeting a man of such good character." When Tina had taken him to meet her parents I don't know. I just knew that Jackson could be taking us to Spain, and her mom would probably be fine with it.

Once he received word from Marj that he could see the car today, he drove to the bank, extracted some money, and then headed to the interstate, where we began the trip down. Tina and I pulled out our homework from our backpacks and began doing it to kill time. Tina, however, wasn't fully concentrating on her homework. Every now and then I'd glance back, and she'd be staring off into space, doodling on her paper, or gazing at the back of Jackson's head. I looked at Jackson. I supposed he could be handsome, if I weren't his sister. He has dark, wavy hair and brown eyes, same as me, and he was pretty tall, unlike me. I was about 5'6 and he was over six feet tall. His teeth were straight, due to the braces he had in middle school, and he didn't wear glasses. But I still couldn't figure out why Tina was so enchanted with him.

I shrugged. Oh, well. I guess I'll never know.

We were almost to our exit, so I put up my homework. I had gotten almost all of it done, and I wanted to take a break. Propping my foot up on the dashboard, I leaned back in my seat and closed my eyes.

I was awakened 20 minutes later by Jackson telling me to get up and Tina poking me with her pencil.

"We're here," Tina said.

I yawned and sat up. Power naps were my speciality. I sleepily looked around, taking in the woman's nice, two-story, house. We climbed out of the car and went to the front door. Jackson knocked while Tina and I stayed in the background. A few moments later, a woman with graying hair and glasses opened up the door. She smiled.

"Come in! Are you here to look at my car?"

"Yes, ma'am, I am," Jackson said, walking in. He motioned for us to follow him.

She led us into the living room. "Take a seat." Then, she saw Tina. "Oh my goodness! Tina! How are you doing?"

Tina smiled. "Wonderful. How have you been?"

"Not too bad." Marj and Tina spent the next few minutes catching up, asking about this person and that person.

Marj then looked at Jackson and me. "Are these your friends?"

She nodded. "Yes, ma'am, they are."

We introduced ourselves to her. We made some small talk, and I found out that she was a Christian. An idea immediately sprung to my mind, and I looked at Tina, who appeared to be having the same idea. She nodded. I looked at Marj.

"I'm doing a challenge where I meet with a different godly woman each week. I haven't met with one this week. Would you be interested in spending a bit of time with me and sharing your stories?"

Her eyes lit up. "I'd love that!"

I looked at Jackson. "Once you decide on whether you're buying the car or not, you and Tina can go ahead to the park. When I'm done, I'll give you a call."

Marj interjected. "I can take you to the park when we're done, if you want."

I smiled. "Thanks! That'd be great."

Tina, of course, was absolutely thrilled with the idea, though she tried not to show it. Emphasis on tried. Jackson and Marj walked outside to look at the car. Tina looked everywhere but at me.

I laughed. "Hey, I was the one to suggest it. I'm not going to get mad or anything. You can have Jackson all to yourself."

She seemed relieved. "He's a good friend." She sighed dreamily. "And a handsome one, at that."

"Alright, alright, enough of the sappy stuff. Just have fun." I frowned. "But not too much fun." Then I smiled to let her know I was joking.

Jackson came back inside. "I love the car, and I'm going to buy it. Because I have cash, she gave me a great price on it. I'm going to have to drive down later this week with one of my buddies to pick it up, though, since neither of you can drive."

I feigned astonishment. "Didn't you hear? I turned 34 last week."

He laughed. "Enough." To Tina, he said, "Let's get out of here. Have fun, Sis."

Marj walked in just then. "Don't worry, we will." She sat down next to me. "So what am I supposed to do?"

"You can just tell me about yourself, some lessons you've learned, and I'll ask a few questions now and then."

She began. "Well, I used to work as a teacher, and then I worked in management systems in the engineering field." She paused. "A roadblock in my career was my boss, who was Korean. His culture did not place women in leadership positions and that carried over to how he treated me. I was unable to move up the corporate ladder because of his viewpoints. I'm not being racist; that's just the way he was."

I nodded. That'd be a struggle if you had to constantly fight with that sort of treatment.

"My dream has always been to retire at 55 and do something meaningful for God. I believe that dream is coming true. You see, God wanted me to leave the business world, so I did it without knowing why. He led me to join Operation Mobilization, which is basically an organization of missionaries which, among other things, creates jobs in almost every country. When you partner with them, you can find a job in a country and then tell people about Jesus. I'm going to Thailand."

I sat up straight. "Whoa. That's super cool. How did you decide on that country?" It wasn't exactly your typical place to visit.

"Awhile ago I went on a personal retreat at the beach so I could get away and have some meditation and prayer. While there, God told me, 'I want you to open a bed and breakfast guesthouse. It will be for profit, and the employees will be restored victims of human trafficking.' I went to church the next day wondering how I was going to do this. Imagine my surprise when the sermon was on how Abraham almost sacrificed Isaac and how God provided a ram for him. I returned home from the beach, and when I went to church, a woman who had just come back from Thailand was in my small group. The woman had been praying for a place called Tamar's Center. It was a place where bar girls were given a chance to start over. Tamar's Center was in a shady part of the city. It had a hair salon, a house of prayer, a house of peace, a restaurant, a craft room, and a counseling center. I was hooked. I visited Thailand this past October, and I will be going to Thailand this spring. I won't be working at Tamar's Center right away, though. I'll be taking language classes for a while. All in all, I'll be there for 3-5 years."

My jaw dropped. "That long?" She nodded. I could understand a month or two, but years? I guess that it would take years to learn a language and begin making a difference in a country, like helping bar girls. Sometimes those girls do that kind of work because they have no choice. It's not fair that they get more condemnation than help, especially from Christians. Hate the sin, not the sinner, that's what I've always heard.

Marj continued. "This is what I want to do, and it's not like I have anything tying me here." She got up from the couch and began pulling on her shoes. "Let's head on over to the park."

"But what about family?"

She shook her head. "I'm single." She stopped tying her laces. "More accurately, I'm divorced." She sighed as she pulled on the other shoe. "It was one of the biggest challenges in my life. My husband and I were married for 22 years. When we met, he told me he was a Christian, but he wasn't. After he cheated on me several times, I divorced him."

I frowned in sympathy. "I'm so sorry. He didn't deserve you."

She smiled. "Thank you. Now that I don't have a husband, Jesus takes that role. He's the only one I can always rely on. I've learned to wait on Him through the years to tell me my next steps. But waiting does not mean inactivity."

I stood up with her, and we walked out the door. "So what you're saying is that if I'm waiting for God to show me my next move, I don't sit around doing nothing, but I also don't take action to go down a road before God tells me to."

Nodding her head, she said, "Correct."

I was still confused. "What do I do then? How can I be active and yet still wait on God?"

"That's a good question, and answers may vary based on whom you ask. One way is to prepare for whatever God may tell you to do. It's like the tale of two farmers. They both prayed for rain, but only the second one prepared his fields for rain. The first guy was waiting without action. The second one was waiting but also preparing for the answer to his prayer. Whether God had sent the rain then or days later, his fields would still have been ready. The farmer who prepared his fields took action but still waited for God to show up."

It suddenly became clear to me, and yet I still had a concern. I climbed into her truck. "How do I know if God's talking to me or not?" Something had recently been brought to my attention that I didn't know the voice of God well enough to know whether a voice in my head was God or myself.

She started up the truck and pulled out of the driveway, heading down the road. "Find a place where you can shut the door and pray. Shutting the door symbolizes you mean business. God will meet you there." She turned to me as we stopped at a red light. "Prayer is a huge thing. In fact, I believe it's one of the qualities of a godly woman."

I looked at her. "What are some other qualities of a godly woman?"

Tapping the steering wheel thoughtfully, she continued, "To be focused on worship, to live your life according to the Bible, to exhibit the gifts and fruits of the Spirit in whatever circumstance God puts you in, to take the passions God gives you and use them for Him, and lastly, to rely on God through the good and the bad."

I leaned back in my seat. "Wow. That's a lot to take in."

As we pulled into the parking lot for the park, I said, "One last question: what's your favorite scripture?"

She smiled. "That's an easy one. My favorite verse is Colossians 3:16, which says, 'Let the word of Christ dwell in you richly in all wisdom, teaching and admonishing one another in psalms and hymns and spiritual songs, singing with grace in your hearts to the Lord.'"

I spotted Jackson and Tina starting to walk one of the trails. I leaned over and gave Marj a hug. "Thank you so much for sharing your stories! I hope your trip to Thailand goes well."

She smiled. "You're welcome! I'm glad I got to meet you."

I clambered out of the car and waved to her as I walked toward Tina and Jackson. They hadn't seen me yet, so I decided to surreptitiously see what they would do. After a couple of minutes, I realized that they were just walking and talking, so I got ready to catch up with them when I stopped. Did my eyes fail me, or was Jackson's hand getting closer to Tina's? I peered intently at him, wondering what he'd do. His hand brushed hers, and she looked at him, smiling. Ever so slowly, Jackson's hand reached for Tina's, and their fingers laced together. I gaped. No. Stinking. Way. Jackson was holding Tina's hand! I decided that things were becoming a little too much for my stomach. I snuck up behind them. Breaking through their joined hands, I put an arm around each of their shoulders.

"Hey, guys!" I said, my voice bright and chipper. "What've you been up to? Are you guys having fun? Together? Just the two of you?" With each question, I glanced between them. Jackson's face looked as if he'd forgotten to apply sunscreen. Tina's matched his. "Did you both forget how to talk, or have you recently contracted laryngitis?

Jackson spoke first. Well, spoke is an overstatement. More like stuttered. "Uhhhh, we've had f-fun, haven't we, Tina?"

She nodded. "Y-yeah, we have." Her eyes were large and her voice was squeaky.

I smiled. "Good. I'd hate for things to get out of hand." I raised my eyebrows. "But I know you guys have handled things pretty well while I've been gone. I have to hand it to you guys; you're both really mature people."

By this time, Jackson was turning purple, and Tina looked as if she wanted to disappear. I smirked as they squirmed. "Now, then, let's enjoy the fresh air, shall we?"

We walked some more trails and saw a variety of plants and flowers. After about half an hour, we decided to head back home. As we climbed into the car, I let Tina have the front seat. I decided I could keep an eye on them better if I were in the back. On the trip back, I finished up my homework, as did Tina, but I doubt she'll be making any stellar grades for this batch. She was a bit preoccupied. I smiled. It seemed as if my matchmaking plans were working out just as planned.

Chapter Thirty-Eight

I scrunched my eyebrows together in concentration. I knew I was close. I had to be. Perhaps if I came at it from a different angle, I might be able to find the right answer. Just then, I had a breakthrough.

"Yes!" I cried. I had it. I was just about to scribble down the answer when a noise broke through my train track of thought. I ignored it and tried to remember what I was going to write down; however, it was that one noise that completely overturned the train, and the answer flew out the window. I grabbed my hair.

"Nooooooooo!" Completely frustrated, I yanked my phone off the charger. Whoever just texted me would receive my wrath. I unlocked it, and when I saw who had just texted me, I rolled my eyes. Of course it was Tina. I called her.

"Why in the world would you text me?"

There was a pause on the other end of the line. "Uhhhh, because I wanted to contact you. What would you rather me do? E-mail you? No? Then maybe I could cut down a tree and make it into paper, then pluck a chicken, fill the feather with ink I made from berries, and then write you the letter which I would deliver by walking over to your house and presenting it to you in person?"

I'm pretty sure she was the queen of sarcasm. "No, I'm sorry. I'm just really upset because I was doing a super hard Sudoku puzzle, and I almost got the answer. Then you texted me, and it interrupted my thoughts."

"Sorry." She sounded anything but sorry. She continued on in an excited voice. "Did you read my text?"

I chuffed out a breath. "No, I wasn't exactly thinking clearly. Why don't you just tell me?"

I could feel her smiling through the phone. "I got us tickets!"

I was very confused. "To what?"

"You really didn't read that text, did you?" She didn't wait for me to answer. "Winter Jam!"

I gasped. Winter Jam was a huge annual concert of Christian music artists. I knew there were going to be some pretty famous singers and bands there, but I also knew the cost was more than I wanted to spend. "How much is it going to cost me?"

She squealed. "That's the best part! I know the people who put it on every year, and our families have been friends for, like, forever, so they always make sure that we get tickets every year. My parents aren't going to be able to go this year, so I wanted to know if you and Jackson would want to come?"

I was stunned. "This is amazing! Jackson will be so jazzed! Thank you so much!"

"There's just one thing, and you don't have to say yes."

"Go on," I said.

"The woman's name is Reba Kunselman, and she's a Christian. It's her brother who's over most of it, but she and her husband are over the money side of things. When I was talking with her, I was telling her about you, and she was really intrigued with your challenge. Would you be interested in meeting with her? You'd be backstage with her the whole show and would get to see what goes on back there."

I thought about it. It'd be fun to be able to watch the concert, but I didn't know the next time I'd be able to be backstage for a concert. "Sure, I'll meet with her."

She squealed again. I honestly thought she knew the guinea pig language. "Great! You won't regret it."

Well, she'd said that before, and she's always been right, so I figured I might as well trust her on this one, too. I told Tina goodbye and then went downstairs to find Jackson. He was in the kitchen on the computer. When he saw me, he motioned me over.

"Look, Sis! All my favorite artists are going to be at Winter Jam this year! I really wish I could go."

I frowned sympathetically. "I'm sorry. What can I say to make you feel better? What about this: Tina got us free tickets to go see it with her."

His jaw dropped. "You're joking."

I shook my head, a grin breaking through on my face. "Nope. She has connections, and we're all going for free."

He laughed out loud and then stood up, grabbed me, and spun me around. "Yes! That's amazing! I'll have to thank Tina when I see her."

Just as I was leaving the room, I turned around. "One more thing. I'll be meeting with a godly woman while there, so it'll just be you and Tina in the audience." I narrowed my eyes. "I hope I can trust you two to keep your eyes on the stage. Deal?"

He colored. "Yep. You made that clear. Very, very clear."

I could barely hold back a smile. "Good," I said, raising an eyebrow instead. With that, I flounced out of the room and went back to my bedroom. Sinking into my chair, I took a look at Thunder. He looked so peaceful sitting in the sun that I just wanted to hold him. I didn't, though, knowing that he turned into a grumpy cat whenever he didn't get enough sleep, which was a solid 19 hours every day. Any less and he'd be upset. I snorted. I wish I had his problem.

The following day, Tina called again. Lucky for her, I wasn't in the middle of a Sudoku puzzle, so I didn't scream in her ear again.

"I'm so excited about the concert tomorrow! Jackson's going to love it. As will you, too, of course," she said hastily.

I squinted. "So what's going on between you two anyway?"

"Nothing!" she said, in a voice only Chihuahuas could hear. She cleared her throat. "We're just friends. Anyway, I honestly don't even know how I'll sleep tonight."

I smiled, thinking of an idea. "Would you sleep better if I told you that Jackson won't be able to come?"

Even Thunder heard her distressed gasp, and he abruptly awoke and glared at me, as if it were my fault. "What? Why? Oh, that's awful. I'm sure he was looking forward to it." With every word, her tone escalated until she sounded as if she were wringing her hands.

I smirked. "As were you, I can tell. To tell you the truth, he is coming. I just wanted to confirm something."

I could feel the heat of her glare through the phone. "You liar. Confirm what?"

I chuckled. "Oh, nothing. I guess you'll find out one day."

She made an exasperated sound. "You're impossible."

"Tsk, tsk, Tina. Nothing is impossible with God." That I really believed. Even though it seemed like there were walls closing in around me at times, I knew that God was with me and could change the situation. Just like how Kelsey just happened to stop by our table during lunch and ended up becoming a Christian. Like how I'm serving the God I had once thought never existed.

I stood up from the chair and began gathering the clothes I would wear to the concert: jeans, a black T-shirt, and tennis shoes. It was getting late, so I pulled on sweats and a tank top and went to brush my teeth. As I climbed into bed, I yawned. I always loved Fridays. I could finally relax after a long week of school. Normally I would stay up late on Friday nights, but I needed my sleep for the concert tomorrow. From what I heard from Tina, we wouldn't get to bed until about one o'clock in the morning because we would be staying late at the concert, and then it would take an hour to get home. Turning off my whirring brain for the night, I drifted off to sleep within a few minutes.

At about 10:30 the next morning, I decided to arise from my slumber. More accurately, I was awakened at that time by Jackson coming into my room.

"Wake up. You need to eat breakfast," he said, shaking my shoulder.

As I munched on an apple, Tina texted me that we could get there as early as 4:00, which was much earlier than when the doors opened for the public. Reba would meet us at the doors and open them for us. I relayed this information to Jackson.

"Alright. I think that we need to leave for the concert at about 2:30, which means we'll pick Tina up at about 2:45. Are you ready for today?" Apparently he was, if the excitement in his voice was any indication.

"Yeah! I can't wait to meet this mysterious Reba Kunselman. I bet I'll have a blast with her."

The day progressed quickly, and I soon found myself getting ready to leave for the concert. As I braided my hair, I gazed at my reflection. Just a couple of months ago I was completely different from what I am today. You couldn't tell from the outside, really, but I knew it was very evident on the inside. I brushed the wispies of my brown hair unconsciously. What would it be like to have blond hair like Tina? To have it cascade down my back in a shimmering waterfall? I shook my head. I guess not everyone can be as pretty as Tina Lankford. I had no incredulity about why Jackson liked her so much. She was gorgeous, smart, fun to be around, and a godly person. What more could a guy ask for in a girl? Nothing.

What do I have to offer anyone? I mean, I guess I could be considered pretty, but only if you were looking for it. I have the kind of beauty that takes time to notice. I definitely wouldn't consider myself as pretty as Tina. As for personality, I'm pretty good at noticing when people are down and then trying to cheer them up. I guess that would make me caring. Christianity wise, well, I'm still a work in progress.

I sighed. I was probably going to end up being the crazy, old, spinster cat lady. As I grabbed my bag and made my way downstairs, I decided that it didn't really matter to me whether I married or not. I had Jesus and Thunder, and that's all I needed.

Jackson plugged his phone into the auxiliary cord as soon as I climbed into the car.

"Let's jam out on the way to the concert."

He started playing a new song by a Christian rapper. I bobbed my head to the beat as it played, but I had no clue what the words were, so I wasn't really getting anything out of it. When we picked Tina up from her house, however, she gasped as soon as she heard the song.

"Oh my goodness! I love this song!" She immediately climbed in the backseat and began rapping. I was impressed. I had no clue she had it in her.

Jackson pulled onto the interstate, and we began the trip. I mostly half-listened to the songs. I knew none of them, and I didn't think Jackson and Tina, who knew every word and were jamming out together, would appreciate me making up words to fit to the songs.

As a result of the lively atmosphere in the car, the hour passed quickly, and we were soon paying for parking outside of McKenzie Arena. Tina was visibly growing more excited with each passing minute.

After circling the building multiple times to figure out which one of the many entrances we were supposed to enter, we found the right one and were met at the door by an older woman who was wearing a big smile.

"Hello, Tina! It's so good to see you! And are these your friends you told me about?"

Tina nodded after giving her a big hug. "Yes, they are."

I smiled at her. "I can't wait to hang out with you tonight!"

"Me, too."

She then led us inside. I was immediately shocked by how many people were in the building already, and the doors hadn't even opened yet. The noise was pretty loud; I had to shout to say goodbye to Jackson and Tina as they went to pick out seats and get settled in. I then turned around to see where Reba had gone. I found her at a table ripping apart paper bracelets. I went over and began helping her.

She smiled at me as she handed me a sticker that had the Winter Jam emblem on it. "This sticker will let you go to and from the money room and the arena. I'm going to be honest with you; we probably won't have a lot of time to talk today. It will be pretty chaotic, with people talking and with us running around everywhere and having to count money."

I shrugged. "As long as it's what you normally do at this sort of thing, I'm fine with it; however, I do have some questions for you when we have time. There are only a couple, so it'll be quick."

"Sounds good. Could you ask them now? I think this will be one of the least busy times all night."

I nodded. "Sure! My first question is this: what are the qualities of a godly woman?"

"I believe the qualities of a godly woman are to have godly friends and to be in the Word every day."

I thought about that. Godly friends? Tina. Check. In the Bible every day? Well... I try, but normally it's about every other day. Still, that's more than I was doing a few weeks ago. I'll say it's a check.

"What's a verse that you love?"

She gave a little laugh. "Wow, that's a hard one. I guess my favorite verse would have to be Psalm 46:10, which says, 'He says, "Be still, and know that I am God; I will be exalted among the nations, I will be exalted in the earth."'"

I let that verse sink in. Rarely do I remember that I should be still and let God take care of me. I guess I'm a control freak, always wanting to know what's going on and making sure it fits my plans. I have a hard time trusting people, and to trust God is even harder since I can't see Him. I'm trying to do better, though.

"What has been the biggest challenge in your life?"

"Parenting my children. They're grown now, but I still have to parent them sometimes." She laughed, but then quickly replaced the laugh with a worried look on her face as she looked at her watch. "Oh no, I've got to go meet with someone right now. Please put your questions on hold for a second."

"Sure," I said. We walked to another table, one that had t-shirts on it.

"These are t-shirts for the volunteers tonight. I'm supposed to meet two of the volunteers here and tell them what they're supposed to do." Said volunteers, a man and a woman, were heading her way at that moment. She smiled. "There you guys are. Are you ready for tonight?"

Both nodded enthusiastically. The man spoke. "Where do you want us tonight?"

"I need help down in the money room."

They nodded at each other and then looked at her. "Okay, we're on it."

"We'd better go downstairs and get ready because the doors for the pre-show are about to open."

We all rode the elevator down to the last floor, where Reba led us into a room that had a large table in the middle and three smaller tables along the walls. She pointed to the large table.

"That's where all the money will be dumped to be sorted out. The other tables are for snacks, computers, and the money-counting machine."

"When does the money come down, and what are we doing with it?" I inquired.

"We have someone who will go to the doors and bring back the money, a sack at a time. When he brings it in, we'll sort it out into stacks. Then two people will be feeding the money into the money-counting machine. After all the money from the doors has been counted, we will sort and count the money from the offering, which will happen later tonight." She paused. "Basically, we'll be counting money all night."

I rubbed my hands together. It was going to be a fun night. I put my sling bag in a corner and grabbed the water bottle that Reba offered me. Two police officers, a man and a woman, entered the room and greeted Reba. She was apparently expecting them, which was a good idea, seeing how there would be all that money in one room at one time. I immediately felt safer with their presence in the room.

Reba introduced me to two other people: her husband, Don, and her good friend Daniel. They both greeted me warmly, and I liked them at once. I grabbed a seat at the large table and sat there drinking my water while I waited for the money to come in. Reba joined me.

"Can I ask you a couple more questions while we have a break?"

She checked her watch. "Sure. The doors for the pre-show have already opened, and the pre-show should be starting now, so we have a short break before the money comes in."

"Who are some mentors who have affected your life?"

"One mentor was my Sunday school teacher from the fourth grade through the sixth grade. Another mentor was a woman who taught me to look at the Word before making decisions. Lastly, there was a woman with lymphoma. Even though she still has it, she has blessed so many people in spite of it."

Just like Jeni Turner, whose story has affected me. "What has been the biggest struggle in your life?"

"The biggest struggle I've had is with worry and fear. It's a big issue in my life. Don't let worry or fear ever control you."

I nodded earnestly. I needed to definitely be on the lookout for worry and fear sneaking up on me because I fall into the pattern of anxiousness and paranoia very easily, which leaves me distraught, depressed, and dead inside. Worry and fear are very good at worming into people's lives and then attacking them when they're most vulnerable.

Right then, a college-aged guy walked in with a sack. I assumed it was the money, since I didn't think anyone had ordered bagels. Sure enough, when the bag was dumped, green bills spilled onto the table. Immediately, Reba got up from her chair and began sorting. I figured I should probably do the same, so I did just that, as did the couple who had come down with us.

I decided to start collecting the twenty-dollar bills. With one hand, I would quickly rummage through the pile of green bills looking for Andrew Jackson and then put him in my other hand. Once I had a large stack, I would set it on the table and then continue my search.

A while later, we finally had sorted all the bills into their respective stacks. I sank into a chair, grateful for the respite. I was drinking my water when the guy returned, carrying another bag. My eyes bugged out. More? It had taken so long for the first bag, and this one was even fuller. I was determined to get ahead of the rolling ball, so I got up again and began sorting, a little quicker this time.

I did ten-dollar bills this time. Once I had a stack of fifty or so, I would rubber band it and hand it to Daniel and Don, who were counting the bills with the money-counting machine.

"Thanks," they'd say and then return to counting the money.

When the money was almost completely sorted, the guy returned with a third sack. I groaned inwardly. I didn't mind handling thousands of dollars, but it would be nice to get a little break. However, this bag was pretty empty, so we sorted it rather quickly.

By this time, the actual concert had started. We had finished sorting for now, so I looked around for something to do. The table that Daniel and Don were at was pretty messy, so I began to organize it. After it was completely organized, I turned and took a drink of water. When I turned around again, the table was almost as messy as before. I looked at them accusingly.

They grinned sheepishly and shrugged. I glared at them and then cleared it off again. Keeping a wary eye on them, I reached back for my water. With a mischievous grin on his face, Don reached out one finger and knocked over the bag of rubber bands. I scowled and set it back up. He knocked it over again. The process went on for a while until I set it out of his reach and rolled my eyes.

"Honestly. Can't you keep it clean for two seconds?"

Another round of money was brought in again, and we all went back to work. I kept switching between five-dollar and one-dollar bills. Finally, we were told that the bag on the table was the last bag of money from the doors.

Reba smiled. "Great." To the rest of us, she said, "You guys are welcome to go out into the audience and listen to part of the concert for a little bit, if you want. It'll be about 30 minutes before the offering takes place, and then we'll really have to put it in full gear to get that done; it's mostly small change, so it's not as easy to count."

I decided to go out into the audience and see who was singing. When I walked out, I was shocked at how full it was. The place was completely packed. I couldn't find Jackson and Tina, but I knew they were probably having a great time together.

Kari Jobe was onstage, and she was singing "Forever," one of her best songs in my opinion. I listened to her until she finished her set of songs, and then I returned backstage, where Reba led me into a room where people were eating.

"You need to eat, and this is a good time."

We both got in line and began selecting food from the buffet. Once seated, she prayed, and we dug in. I hadn't realized how hungry I was until I began eating. It was like my stomach had been on mute this whole time. Not any more. About ten minutes later, we went back to the money room and sat around waiting for the offering money to come in. We didn't have to wait long. Five minutes later, they came in. Buckets upon buckets came in. Now, some of them didn't have any money in them, and others had little, but there were some that had some cash in it. I was confused. Surely with all those people, there would be a large offering. Reba saw my confusion and explained.

"The average gift people make in these offerings is a little over a dollar. While we appreciate it, it's sad to think that's what people are averaging when they're asked to give for a purpose that helps the Kingdom of God."

Out of all the money on the table, the majority of it was change. I began sorting it out, and kept sorting it out until it was all ready to be put through the money-counting machine.

Finally, after many hours of hard work, the money was completely counted and sorted. I put hand sanitizer on and breathed a sigh of relief.

Then, my phone dinged. Jackson let me know that the concert was over, and he and Tina were making their way to the exit. I told Reba, and she gave me a hug.

"Thank you so much for your help today!"

I smiled. "No problem. It's not every day I get the opportunity to handle thousands of dollars."

She laughed. "That's for sure."

With one last wave, I left the room and got into the elevator. When I made it to the exit, I found Jackson and Tina waiting for me.

Jackson smiled. "There you are. How was it?"

"Great! What about you guys? Did you two have fun?" I said it as innocently as possible, but they both quirked their eyebrows in unison.

Tina spoke first. "I thought it was awesome! I love Winter Jam!"

We walked out the doors and into the night. When we reached the parking lot, we climbed into the car. I chose the backseat again because I needed sleep.

Tina grinned at me from the front. "Looks like you're worn out."

I nodded, slowly slipping into dreamland. The last thing I remembered before falling fast asleep was Tina smiling up at Jackson.

Chapter Thirty-Nine

I threw up my hands in the air and let out a deep breath. Finally. School was out for spring break, and I was more than ready for a vacation. But how was I to get one? My mom wasn't going to stay sober long enough to drive me anywhere on a vacation, my grandmother didn't like driving long distances, and Kimberly likely had plans here with her friends. Lucky her. That left only one person: Jackson.

I found him outside, sitting next to a tree. I sat down next to him and pretended nonchalance. He gave me a strange look.

"Ok, what do you want from me?"

I frowned. Apparently I wasn't very good at pretending nonchalance. Well, I might as well get down to the point since my cover was blown. "What're you doing for spring break?"

He thought about that, propping an elbow on his knee. "I don't think I'm doing anything. Why?"

"Well, how would you feel about taking me someplace far, far away for spring break? Like, I don't know, Florida? You know that Grandmother owns a house down there that she can't bring herself to sell, so why don't we use it while it's available?"

He contemplated my suggestion. "I don't know. I would love to, but I'd have to take a lot of days off work."

I could tell he was starting to say no, and I wanted to go so badly. "We don't have to go for the whole week, and I would wash your car for a month!" I clasped my hands together and dramatically bent low to the ground. "Please, dearest brother, I beseech thee. Let me not be under the horrendous burden of staying in our house for a whole week knowing I could instead be on the beach."

He rolled his eyes. "Drama queen. All right, you win. I'll drive you down for a couple of days. But you have to promise me that you won't tease me about Tina while we're down there, ok?"

I smiled and launched myself into his arms. "Thank you, thank you, thank you! You won't regret this, I promise! And I won't tease you about Tina, at least while we're down there." He had said nothing about no teasing when we got back.

He laughed. "Great. Let's go tell Grandmother and start packing. We'll probably head down two days from now so we can prepare. Also, have you met with a godly woman this week?"

I shook my head, confused. "No."

"Alright. Just asking."

I gave him one last squeeze. "Thank you again!" I ran back to the house and skipped upstairs. As I began packing, Kimberly walked into my room. I put on a faux stern face. "Kimberly Ray Thompson, what right do you think you have strolling into my room without knocking?"

She rolled her eyes. "I have all the right in the world. What are you doing?"

I gestured to my open suitcase. "Packing." Duh.

She looked surprised. "Where are you going?"

"Jackson and I are going to Florida."

At this, her eyes lit up; but then a mask slipped over them, and she looked only sad. "Oh. Well, have fun."

That sounded genuine. I wondered why she'd be so upset. "What are you doing for spring break?"

She slowly started moving towards the door. "Nothing, really. Almost everyone is leaving for vacation."

Oh. I hadn't thought that she wouldn't be with her friends all break. Then, as if a hand was moving my mouth, I blurted, "Do you want to come with us?"

She turned around abruptly with a completely shocked expression. "What?"

I swallowed. It was too late to take the words back. "Do you want to come to Florida with Jackson and me? It's not like you're doing anything here."

A grin broke out on her face. "I would love that." Then, the grin was replaced with a guarded expression. "Why are you being so nice to me?"

I shrugged. "It's part of being a Christian. We're supposed to be nice to people." I didn't tell her that the verse which mentioned that was specifically talking about our enemies.

She sort of nodded. "Ok. As long as you're not doing it so you can make fun of me or anything, then I'll go. When are you guys leaving?"

"Day after tomorrow."

After she left, I told Jackson that she was coming with us. I was expecting him to be surprised, but I wasn't expecting him to be happy about it.

"Really?" A smile lit up his face. "That's amazing! I've been praying that our relationship with Kim would get better. This is our chance to reach out to her and show her the love of Jesus."

I hadn't thought of that. I guess I was so caught up in the fact that she'd been so mean to me for so many years that I didn't realize that I should love her and reach out to her.

Two days later, Jackson, Kimberly, and I all woke up before dawn and headed out to Jackson's convertible. Ever since he bought it from Marj, he loved driving it, and I loved riding in it, even though there wasn't exactly a plethora of legroom. Kimberly yawned as she slid into the backseat.

"I want to sleep. You can have shotgun—at least for now."

I was happy with her choice. I wanted to ride up front but didn't want to seem rude if I took it instead of Kim. "Thanks."

Jackson put all our bags in the trunk, made sure we had everything, and then pulled out of the driveway. We were off.

It wasn't until we were actually on the interstate heading south that it really sank in that we were actually going to Florida. A sense of adventure filled me, and I grinned. I hadn't been on a long trip in a while, and this was going to be a lot of fun.

Two hours later, I woke Kimberly up. "Time for breakfast. I have juice, cups, plates, napkins, and muffins in the bag next to you." I had packed breakfast, lunch, and even a snack in case we were hungry before arriving at our destination. The house was just outside of Orlando, so it was going to be about a nine-hour trip. I figured that since we left at 6:00 a.m., we should get there around 3:30, counting stops for gas.

Kim reached for the bag and handed out the food to us. I bit into the muffin and took a swig of juice. I was still feeling tired, but the apple juice was waking me up. Years ago, I had read that apple juice wakes you up more than coffee; and after I had experimented to see if it were true, I came to the conclusion that it was correct. Since then, I've been drinking apple juice every time I feel tired in the morning, and it has really helped me since I'm not a morning person.

I helped Jackson with his food while he drove. In fifteen minutes, the muffins were gone, and everyone was satisfied. Kimberly went back to sleep, and I turned on the radio to a classical music station. I had also read that classical music improves your IQ.

"Are you excited?" Jackson asked as he wiped his mouth with a napkin.

"No, I'm bored to death," I said sarcastically. "Are you kidding? I can't wait! What's going to be our schedule while we are down there?"

He ran a hand through his hair as he thought about it. "I'm not completely sure. I'm positive that you want to go to the beach. Also, there are a bunch of thrift stores down there that we could visit. And then, there's that one person..." He trailed off and abruptly turned the radio up.

I narrowed my eyes. "What 'one person'?"

Ignoring me completely, Jackson changed lanes to get in front of a minivan that was going 60 miles an hour in the left lane. He calmly slid back in front of them and kept going. Jackson never got angry with people on the road; he thought that they had just as much right to drive on it as he did, and just because they weren't as fast as he was didn't mean he should waste energy becoming mad.

Pretty soon, I let his slip-up go. If he thought it was worth telling me, he'd tell me. If he didn't, I shouldn't worry about it.

We rode on for another hour, which consisted mostly of me reading, resting, and texting Tina. Her family had decided to go to Arizona to visit the Grand Canyon. Her dad, Peter, was an electrician, and her mom, Jenny, was an E.R. nurse, so they could afford it. Sometimes I envied her because she was an only child, her family had a lot of money, and both parents loved her. Yet I knew that I loved my siblings and that I'd be lonely if I didn't have them.

Speaking of siblings, Kimberly was awake once again and was sitting in the backseat not saying anything. I decided to try and start a conversation with her.

"So how's school been going for you?"

She wrinkled her nose. "As well as school can go, I guess."

Ok, so she didn't want to talk about school. "What about life in general?"

She squinted her eyes at me. "Good, I suppose. Why all the questions? I didn't come on this trip for the Spanish Inquisition."

"I'm just trying to get to know you better."

She seemed puzzled. "Why? I haven't exactly been nice to you. Like, ever."

I shrugged. "We're still sisters, and I want to build our relationship."

She shook her head. "Ok. Life stinks. I hate how I always have to be perfect for Mom and Grandmother. I hate how I'm always so mean. I hate how I have to keep getting straight A's or else I'll lose popularity. I hate how Dad died. I hate how Mom doesn't care about any of us, and I hate myself!" She burst into tears. "You two are so nice to everyone, and I don't know why. You have every reason to hate everything in life, but you don't. Why?"

Jackson and I looked at each other. We had not expected all that. Taking a deep breath, I began. "Jesus."

When she glared at me, I rushed on before she could interrupt. "I know you probably hate God right now too—although He wasn't on the list you just gave—and you think He doesn't care for you whatsoever. I know because I've been in your position. After Dad died, I was left bitter and hopeless. I had no peace in my life, and I was always angry. But God found me. He opened my eyes, even though it took years. He forgave me, and He can forgive you. All you have to do is ask."

She shook her head. "No. I knew I shouldn't have come on this trip. I knew you two would try to evangelize me. That little speech may work on others, but not on me. God's not real. If He were, He would've done something, anything, to help us out. But no. He ignored us." She lay back in her seat and closed her eyes.

The next couple of hours were tense. I passed out lunch when we got hungry, but other than that, few words were spoken. I offered Kimberly the front seat, but she declined; so I lay back in my seat and drifted off to sleep. Jackson woke me up at 2:30. "We have a little less than an hour to go. I'm going to get gas."

I looked into the backseat. Kimberly was still asleep. I was amazed that she was so tired. When I glanced back at Jackson, he gave me a sad smile.

"She's just another lost sheep. I wish she were more open."

I nodded. "She just needs time. Look at me! It took me over 5 months of talking with Christians to even accept the fact that God might be real. Don't worry, Jackson. Trust God. He'll work on her in His timing."

He laughed. "You have more faith than I do, sis. I should be the one telling you that, not the other way around."

He pulled into the gas station and got out. I did so as well so I could stretch my legs. I woke up Kimberly to see if she needed to go to the bathroom. She didn't, but she did want to stretch. I started washing the windows while Jackson finished filling the car with gas.

We were all awake the last little bit, the excitement growing as we neared our destination. Then, finally, after many long hours and some unexpected tension, we arrived.

We unloaded the car and put everything next to the door while Jackson unlocked the little house. As we set our separate bags into our bedrooms, one for each of us, I began to relax. Even though it was still a little awkward after the conversation with Kimberly, I knew that we would soon forget about it if no one mentioned it again.

If there was one thing we could agree on, it was food. We were all hungry, and we all had the same tastes, so it was easy to agree on pizza. Jackson went out to pick it up while Kimberly and I unpacked. Kimberly came into my room.

"Sorry for blowing up earlier. It's just a very touchy subject, and I'd prefer it to be left alone."

I nodded. "Ok, I can respect that. I was the same way."

She gave me a small smile. "Thank you. I don't want to fight with you guys, and I do want to get to know you both better. Hopefully we can do that while we're here."

"Yes, that's what I'm hoping for."

Jackson returned shortly, and we ate the cheese pizza, saving the leftovers for breakfast the next morning. We were all pretty beat, so we popped a movie into the TV and sat down to watch it before going to bed.

As I looked in the mirror while brushing my teeth before bed, I thought about how sad it was that our family wasn't united. A family was supposed to be the place where a person felt loved and accepted, but I felt like I didn't belong. Not only did I not look like anyone in my family but Jackson, my mom constantly reminded me of how much like my father I was. Did she think I was going to turn into a druggie like him? Probably.

The next morning, we all got up and ate breakfast. It was around 8:30, and we felt refreshed after our long sleep.

I was super pumped. "What do you guys want to do today?"

Kimberly shrugged. "I'm not sure. Anything but school sounds fun."

Jackson gave me a funny look and cleared his throat. "Well, I sort of had something planned for you."

I was puzzled. "What?"

He gave me a sheepish grin. "You see, I arranged for you to meet with a godly woman while in Orlando." He gauged my reaction before continuing. "Her name is Lori Jean Smith, and she's a professional violinist. In fact, she's played her violin in 45 of the 50 states. I wanted you to meet a couple of famous people while doing this challenge, and when I emailed her a few days ago, she agreed to meet with you for a little bit. I hope you're not mad."

I smiled. "Not at all. This saves me from worrying about meeting with someone, and I'm touched that you went to all this trouble for me. Yes, I'll meet with her! What time?"

"She said she'd be free from 11:00 until 1:00 and that Kimberly and I could join you guys for lunch at 12:30."

"That would be great!" I said enthusiastically.

"Are you fine with that, Kim?" Jackson asked, turning towards her. But Kimberly just stood there, with a puzzled look on her face.

"What challenge?" she asked.

Oh snap. I had forgotten that she didn't know what I was doing. Choosing my words carefully, since I didn't know how she would react, I explained to her the general idea of it, without going into too much detail.

She gave me a long look. "Fine. I'll go along. I can't control what you do with your time, even though I wouldn't recommend wasting the precious little time we have in Florida with a Christian."

We decided to go thrift shopping until I met with Lori, so we piled in the convertible and headed to Goodwill.

Two hours and lots of purchases later, Jackson dropped me off at a park where I was to meet Lori. I hadn't been there thirty seconds before a woman walked up to me, grace oozing from every pore. She took off her sunglasses and extended her hand.

"Hi! I'm Lori. Are you Jackson's sister Brie?"

I nodded, smiling. "Yes, ma'am, I am."

"Great! Do you like walking?"

"I do."

She beamed. "Wonderful. Let's walk down this trail to a picnic table farther on down where we can talk before heading to the restaurant."

We set off walking at a leisurely pace. I told her a little about myself and filled her in on what I normally did when I met with women for my challenge. She said to ask her questions anytime, so I began with my standard question: "What are the qualities of a godly woman?"

Without pausing, she answered me. "To pursue God, know God, follow God, and obey God. Obedience is very important, including obedience to your parents, but even if you disobey sometimes, God's always going to have grace for you because no matter what, God is always there for you." She picked up her pace a little. "I know that every time I feel as if there isn't grace for me, I keep going back to the Bible and reminding myself that if there was grace then, there's grace now."

Obey my parent? That can be a struggle when the parent I have to obey is someone like my mom. Lori's tidbit of knowledge made me want to know more of what she thought about the Bible. "What's your favorite scripture?" I asked.

"Psalm 32:6-7, which says, 'For this cause everyone who is godly shall pray to You in a time when You may be found; surely in a flood of great waters they shall not come near him. You are my hiding place; you shall preserve me from trouble; you shall surround me with songs of deliverance.'"

I thought about that for a moment before asking, "Speaking of songs, what song do you like playing the most on your violin?"

She groaned. "Oh, no. That's a hard one." She thought about it for a solid minute while we walked. Then, her eyes lit up and she spoke. "I've got it. A song I love to perform is "Indescribable." If I had to pick only one to play at a concert, I would choose that one."

"Why did you start playing violin? Is being a professional violinist something you've always wanted to do?"

She laughed. "Not really. I started playing piano at the age of 5, and I played for two years. I then decided to move to the violin. Why, you ask? I'll tell you. My grandmother had a violin, and I had an older sister with whom I was super competitive."

I could relate to that.

"I knew that if I didn't claim the violin, my sister would probably get it, so I told my grandmother I wanted to start taking lessons just so I could have the violin." We came to the picnic table and sat down. "I took lessons for 4 years and then stopped when I moved to Florida. While in Florida, I began practicing for a state-wide violin contest, which I won. I then went on to Nationals, where I earned second place—and this was all without a teacher. The next year I went to Nationals but didn't win anything; however, I wasn't discouraged and kept playing my violin. God turned my spur-of-the-moment decision to enter a violin contest into a profession."

"The competitiveness between you and your sister sounds like something that would happen between my sister and me," I said, sighing. "I have a hard time loving her sometimes. She isn't a Christian, and she hates God because of how we grew up and because of our circumstances right now. I was an atheist until two months ago, and I too wanted nothing to do with any God—real or make-believe."

She nodded sympathetically. "I'm glad that your eyes were opened. You can't look at your circumstances and judge who God is from them. Just because you're having an awful week, everything's been going wrong, and you don't know what to do, that doesn't mean that God is punishing you or is insensitive to you. It's easy to say that 'God is good all the time, and all the time God is good' when you've been having the time of your life and you're moving up in the world. But to be able to say that when you've just gotten hit by the 'struggle bus' shows faith that God will get you through it and that He'll always be right there next to you for the ride."

"I believe that. I just wish my sister would, too."

She shifted on the bench. "When adversity comes, the first thing I do is pray. Normally, people's first response is to feel upset or seek help from their friends; however, it's imperative that your first response is prayer. Another thing people do that isn't healthy for them is picking up burdens they don't need to carry. If it's someone else's problem, don't worry about it! Most of the time, you can't even do anything about it, so don't stay up late at night trying to figure out a solution."

I grimaced. That was something I did all the time. I hadn't seen it as picking up other people's burdens; I just thought that I was "helping them out." I guess I've been lying to myself.

"But what if those burdens affect you? My mom has a lot of problems, and her bitterness affects all of us kids."

She looked at me compassionately. "I'm sorry. It sounds as if things aren't great between you and your mom, but if you've ever been forgiven in your life, then you are responsible to turn around and forgive others. Even if that specific person doesn't forgive you, you still need to forgive them no matter what they've done. If you don't, you'll become bitter, and bitterness causes alienation, which then leads to you being bitter towards everyone around you, including the people who haven't wronged you."

I felt defensive. "Even if that person treats you like trash?"

She nodded sadly. "Yes. It's hard, but it's what Jesus wants."

I sat there, eyes closed. I didn't want to forgive my mom. I knew she didn't deserve it. But God forgave me, and if He could forgive someone who hated Him, then I should be able to forgive my mom who acts like she hates me. While sitting at a metal picnic table, surrounded by God's nature, I gave my mom to God. I gave up fighting with her and always having to have the last say. I gave up judging her and comparing her to myself and acting as if she would never be anything more than a drunk. And I gave up holding onto old grudges and constantly bringing up the past. I forgave her. It was as if weights dropped off my back. I smiled at Lori. "Thank you. I needed that."

"You're very welcome," she said softly. "We'd better head back to my car so we can meet your siblings at the restaurant in time."

I texted Jackson the location of the restaurant PDQ, which Lori said had great food. As we walked back to the car, I asked Lori what has been the biggest challenge in her life.

She got a sad look on her face. "Probably marriage. It's hard to prioritize my profession, my family, and myself. Not being able to prioritize correctly brings strife into my family."

We climbed into her car. She pulled out of the parking lot and headed over to the restaurant.

I decided to ask my last question. "What's the most exciting adventure you've every had?" I figured it would probably be good, seeing how she was a famous violinist.

She smiled, remembering. "The most exciting adventure I've ever had was when I went to Russia for three weeks right after the Cold War ended and was able to tell people there about Jesus."

"That's so cool!" I couldn't wait until I was allowed to go overseas, or at least somewhere in America all by myself.

We arrived at PDQ and walked inside, choosing a table. Within minutes, Jackson and Kimberly arrived, and I introduced everybody. Jackson gave Lori a large grin and a handshake, while Kimberly only waved, a small smile on her face. I figured she was still a little shocked about my challenge. We ordered hamburgers and shakes and talked while we ate. Kimberly soon relaxed and even laughed occasionally.

Too soon, though, Lori had to leave to go to an appointment. I stood and gave her a hug. "It was so good to meet you. I hope we'll meet again."

She smiled. "Me too. You were a joy to be around."

She said goodbye to Jackson and Kimberly and left the restaurant. Once we were finished with our shakes, Jackson, Kimberly, and I got into Jackson's car and headed back to the house. Once inside, we grabbed our swimsuits and towels. We all wanted to go to the beach, even though the nearest beach was an hour away.

The trip to the beach was very fun. Jackson turned on the radio, and we jammed out, excited for some salt water. Thankfully, the water was pretty warm, although Kim didn't stay in long because she wanted to "work on her tan." She wasn't quite as cold to us as normal, but I knew that we weren't suddenly best friends. She still had her own opinions and still didn't want to talk about God, but I knew that the best thing I could do for her was to be her sister and support her even though we didn't agree on most things. As I bathed in the sun later that day, I thought about Lori. She was so full of life and good lessons. Her laugh was contagious, and I didn't think that there was a single person in the world who could possibly not be happy while around her. She was something special, that's for sure. She made me realize that I was just as bitter as my mom, and she helped me change that. I owed her a lot. Hopefully, when I returned to Cleveland in a few days, I'd be able to start bridging the gap between my mom and me.

Chapter Forty

I felt so sad returning to school. I wished that the Florida vacation could've lasted forever! Sadly, though, the school demanded my presence, so I began to get back into its monotonous schedule once again. The only bright day in my week was Wednesday night youth group. I had been attending the youth group at Tina's church for a while, and I loved it. I felt at home there.

Thursday morning, I ran into Tina at school.

"Hey!" She called, glancing around sneakily before looking back at me. In a lower voice, she said, "Did you like youth group last night?"

I rolled my eyes. "Tina, I don't care if you shout it for the world to hear! I'm a Christian and proud of it. And, yes, I did like youth group last night."

"Do you want to hang out after school?"

I shook my head. "I'd love to, but I can't. Jackson has to go to some bank and talk with a woman there. He wants me to come along. Maybe tomorrow?"

She nodded. "That sounds good."

After school, Jackson picked me up, and we began our drive to the bank.

I gave him a sideways glance. "Remind me again what you're doing?"

"I'm talking with the manager, a woman that our family's known for basically forever, to get her advice on some financial questions. I'd rather speak with someone I know than a stranger."

I shrugged. "Ok. Whatever floats your boat."

We arrived at the bank a few minutes later, and after Jackson parked the car, we got out and walked inside, a bell jangling overhead. A woman came around the corner to greet us. When she saw us, her eyes widened, and a smile came to her face.

"Hello! I haven't seen you two in years! How's the family?"

Jackson and I looked at each other. "Well," Jackson began, "I guess pretty well, considering our circumstances."

I vaguely recognized the woman, but I couldn't remember her name.

Seeing the blank look in my eyes, she smiled at me and said, "I'm Lynn Taggart. My husband, Jim, and your dad were good friends before your dad passed away. After that tragedy, we lost contact with your family, which is probably why you don't really remember me."

Ah. I remembered her now. When she said her husband's name, I remembered him hanging out with my dad a lot, and I used to see them at church sometimes when I was younger.

I gave her a friendly smile. "I have a bad memory when it comes to people's names."

She waved her hand. "Oh, don't worry about it." To Jackson, she said, "So, to what do I owe the pleasure of this visit?"

He explained to her his situation and asked for her advice. She agreed to help him out, and I soon found Jackson and myself seated in Lynn's office. She took her seat behind her desk and handed Jackson some papers, which he began to peruse. I was just sitting there, wondering what to say, when Lynn spoke.

"Jackson told me that you're doing some sort of challenge. What's it about?"

At last, something I was able to talk about. "It's where I meet with a different godly woman every week for a year, learning about them and learning from their experiences. It's a challenge I was talked into, but I've grown to love it."

She seemed incredibly interested in it. I felt instinct taking over, and I let it.

"Would you be interested in being the godly woman I meet with this week?"

She was blown away. "I'd be honored!" She frowned slightly. "What do I do again?"

I smiled. "I'll just ask you some questions, and you tell me about what you've learned in life."

She seemed relieved. "Great! I can do that! What are some questions you normally ask the women you meet with?"

While Jackson looked over all the pamphlets, I said, "What are the qualities of a godly woman?"

"I believe the qualities of a godly woman," she paused slightly, "are to pray, love your neighbor, and support your husband, sometimes being his voice of wisdom."

Being his voice of wisdom. Interesting. I know I'd want my husband to look to me for wisdom sometimes. That is, if I ever have a husband. "What's your favorite verse?"

"My favorite verse is Psalm 103:3, which says that God 'forgives all your iniquities and heals all your diseases.' God is a Healer, and there's no sickness or infirmity that's too small or too big for Him."

A few months ago I would've scoffed at that. But now, despite the fact that I've had someone die because of an "infirmity," I trust that God knew what He was doing when He allowed my dad to die without healing him of his addiction.

"Have you had something in your life that you needed healing from?"

"Pain from a divorce I went through in my 20's. I learned a lot from it, but God still had to heal my heart. It sure didn't help my introverted personality," she said with a sad smile. "If I could change one thing about myself, it would be that I would be more outgoing."

I have heard that from a lot of the women I've met with. It seems like many women have to deal with wanting to be more outgoing but can't. I don't think I'm introverted; I'm just not as much a social butterfly as, say, Tina. "Besides overcoming your shyness, what is another challenge you have had in your life?"

She laughed. "The biggest challenge in my life has been this job. It was very hard, especially in the beginning, because I only had three months of training."

"So why banking?" I asked, puzzled.

"I didn't choose it because I liked it. I started working part-time at a bank when I first came to Cleveland. I then came to this bank a few years later. I was persuaded to take over the managerial position, and I have been here ever since."

"How long has that been?"

"I've been working here for nine years. That's nothing, though, compared to the manager before me; she was here 28 years."

I whistled. Twenty-eight years of banking! The lady before her must have really loved her job—or hated it with a passion but felt like she had no other choice.

"Pardon my ignorance, but is this a normal bank? It looks differently from other banks I've been in."

She shook her head. "Not exactly. Here at Pathway Credit Union, we only do banking for employees at the Church of God offices, employees at Lee University, or anyone who works in a Church of God church. This bank is basically supported by Christians."

Jackson stood up then and handed her the pamphlets. "I finished these, but I have a question."

She smiled. "Ask away."

As Jackson and Lynn conversed about banking, I zoned out. I was thinking about what it would be like to explore the world without having to think about finances. I sighed. Lynn looked at me. I smiled quickly, hoping she didn't think I was sighing because of her and

Jackson. She gave me a puzzled look.

I explained. "I was just thinking about how much I'd love to travel the world."

She smiled. "It's fun, I can tell you that. I've been to numerous countries and have experienced many things. I hope you do get to travel one day."

"What's the best adventure you've had overseas?" I asked.

"The best adventure I've had was going to Europe. I've been to a lot of countries, but being in Europe was such a wonderful experience."

I was intrigued. "What countries have you been to?"

"Well, I was born in Japan; and I've been to Mexico, England, France, Belgium, Amsterdam, and Canada. I've even lived in Germany for a time."

"Why were you born in Japan? You don't look like your parents were Japanese."

"No. My mom was Russian, and my dad was an American. My dad was in the military and then went to Japan, where he met my mom. After I was born, we moved to the United States. None of my family was a Christian until my dad got saved and became a minister. That's when the rest of us got saved."

Just then, Jackson stood up. "I hate to interrupt your meeting, but I have to get home. I just realized that I forgot I have a get-together with some friends tonight." He gave Lynn a hug. "I'm glad we were able to reconnect."

She smiled, returning the hug. "So am I!"

Following Jackson's example, I gave Lynn a hug, as well. "Thank you for agreeing to be a part of my challenge!"

"You're very welcome. It was a pleasure."

Waving goodbye, Jackson and I exited the bank and headed to the car. Sliding into the convertible, I smiled. I still thought his car was amazing. As he drove home, I asked him what get-together he was talking about. He glanced at me, puzzled.

"I thought I told you. You're invited. It's a birthday party for one of my friends, and he wanted you to come."

I made a face. "What? Who in their right mind would invite me to a party?"

He laughed. "Kody, that's who."

I was surprised. Kody Parker was two years younger than Jackson, but still good friends with him. I didn't think that Kody knew I existed. I knew he existed. As the soccer star at Rainier High School, the high school Tina and I would attend, he was super popular. I liked soccer and had considered trying out for it when I went to high school, but I knew I probably wouldn't make the team; I didn't think I was that good. So the fact that Kody Parker wanted me to come to his party, even as "Jackson's little sister" was pretty strange. I wanted to go, though.

"I guess I'll go, if I have nothing better to do." I made an exaggerated silly face, and we both laughed.

Once at home, I ran to my room. I had absolutely no clue what to wear. This was a party with high schoolers, and I was a middle schooler! At only 14, I didn't know a lot about fashion. Tina always had the cutest outfits, though, and I bet she could give me some advice. Sending a quick text, I opened the door of my closet. Rummaging through my clothes, I realized that most of what I owned was either too small, or too out-of-style. Now, I'm not really picky on clothes, seeing how I don't have money for any item over five bucks, and most of what I get is at thrift stores, but I know when something's out of style. Shouldn't everyone? I mean, if you haven't seen someone wearing a certain clothing look in at least 7 months, it's probably not the "hot item" right now. Especially when people give you strange looks and snicker behind their fingers.

Tina sent a text right then, saying that she also would be at the party, and suggested several things I could wear. She said it would be a casual affair, so I didn't need to wear a dress, unless it was a sundress. She suggested jeans and a nice top with a necklace. I ran to my dresser. Yes! I had jeans! I ran to my closet. Yes! I had a nice top! I knew I had a necklace, so I quickly got dressed and selected one from my jewelry box. Slipping on some flats, I wondered whether I was supposed to bring a gift, since it was going to be a birthday party.

I asked Jackson the question as I braided my hair.

"I already have him something, so you can just pretend we bought it together."

I smiled. Not having to spend money but still getting credit for something nice? I'm in.

We hopped into Jackson's convertible, top already down. I felt stylish, riding down the road, the wispies around my face blowing in the wind. It was almost six, and my stomach was growling, but Jackson assured me that there would be food at the party. I hoped he was right—for his sake. I get grumpy when I don't have food. When we pulled into the driveway of what I presumed to be Kody's house, I felt excited. No matter what happened, I knew that I'd have fun tonight. I assumed that everyone here would be Christians, so it wouldn't be a drinking party. The only person drinking and driving tonight would be Jackson, who was finishing his mineral water.

I slid out of the car and walked with Jackson to the front door. Kody answered it. He grinned as he ran a hand through his blond hair.

"Hey, you two. Come on in! Not everyone's here yet, but the pizza is, so obviously the party's started."

I shared a smile with Jackson. Apparently Kody loved food just as much as we did. We walked into the kitchen, where Jackson and I grabbed pizza and soda, and then we followed Kody into the living room.

Tina was sitting on a couch but immediately sprung up when she saw us.

"Hi!" she said, bouncing over to us and giving us hugs. I tried not to snicker when Tina hugged Jackson for twice as long as she hugged me. Some things were just meant to be.

I recognized a couple of people in the room but didn't really know them. I did, however, spot Kimberly. She looked surprised to see me. I felt just as surprised before I realized that she and Kody were in the same grade and probably knew each other well. What I didn't understand was how she got here, so I walked over and asked her.

She rolled her eyes. "You never listen to anything I say, do you? I told you that I was going to a friend's house after school before the party. In fact, I told you about it two days ago!"

I frowned in concentration. I vaguely remembered talking to her about something, but I didn't really remember her saying all of that. I shrugged. "Oh, well. You're here now."

"Yeah, I am. The question is, why are you here?" She didn't say it as if I were an annoying bug like she normally does but rather out of pure curiosity. I didn't blame her; I was confused myself.

"Apparently Kody wanted me to come."

She raised her eyebrows, obviously skeptical of my answer. I rolled my eyes.

"It's the truth! Jackson said so. Ask him!"

She marched over to Jackson and asked him, rather loudly, if what I was saying were true. I wanted to disappear. Then to make it more awkward, Kody heard her question and walked over to answer it personally.

"I did. I figured it was high time I get to know the little sister you both tell me so much about." He looked at me mischievously, and I wondered if he was telling the truth—as did Jackson and Kimberly.

Kimberly spoke first. "I don't talk about her. At all."

Even though that hurt, I at least commended her for telling the truth. Jackson was a different story.

"Wowww. Kimberly Ray! That was nice." To me, he said, "I do talk about you." As an afterthought, he said, "Well, sometimes."

I felt so loved. "Wow, guys, you're just the best siblings I could ever have." I rolled my eyes. "I don't know what to do with all this attention."

Kody laughed and gave me a thumbs up. "Nice. Way to tell 'em."

Tina chose that moment to come over. "What's so funny?" She was confused that Kody and I were laughing, but Jackson was red from embarrassment, and Kimberly looked... Well, I couldn't put a word to what was on her face. Maybe anger, maybe embarrassment—or was that jealousy? Why would she be jealous unless... Ah. She liked Kody. But why would she be upset with me being here? I'm just the little sister that everyone forgets, so it's not like I'm going to steal her limelight.

The party continued until 9:00, and then most of the people left, likely because they needed to finish their homework for school the next day. Tina gave me a hug before getting into her car.

"Bye! I'll see you at school tomorrow."

I waved as she left and then went back inside the house to find Jackson. He was in the kitchen talking with Kody. They looked to be in a serious discussion, so I didn't want to walk in. What they were talking about, though, intrigued me to the point that I started unintentionally to eavesdrop.

Jackson was talking. "I don't know what to do, man. I mean, I don't know if I'm ready for a relationship right now, and I don't think she is, either, but I have to make a decision about college, and it all hinges on whether we're serious about each other or not."

I could only assume that the "she" was Tina. I knew it wasn't me, and Jackson hadn't been hanging out with any other girl that I knew of.

Kody spoke, voice laced with concern. I could almost picture his blue eyes piercing Jackson through. "Have you prayed about it?"

Jackson groaned. "I've been doing nothing but praying ever since I realized I liked her. I come from such an awful background that I don't deserve her."

Kody snorted. "If there is anyone who comes close to deserving her, it'd be you, bud. Have you considered just talking with Tina? Getting your feelings out in the open and explaining your situation?"

So it is Tina. I knew it!

I heard Jackson sigh. "I don't know, man. It's scary to get your feelings out there."

Kody laughed. "As if I don't know. It was hard enough just working up the courage to talk to your sister. I don't know what I'd do if I had to tell her how I felt."

I flattened myself against the wall. I sincerely hoped he meant Kimberly. If he didn't, Kim would actually kill me. I knew I couldn't walk in at this point. If I did, it would look like I was eavesdropping, which I was, and everyone would be embarrassed. No, it would be better for everyone if I stayed right where I was.

Just then, Jackson scraped his chair against the floor as he stood up.

"I'd better get my sisters and head home. Thanks for the talk, man."

"Anytime."

Maybe it wasn't best for everyone if I stayed right where I was. I scurried down the hall as quietly as I could and into the living room, slowly sitting on a chair and trying to catch my breath as inconspicuously as I could.

Jackson walked into the room moments later, Kody on his heels. Jackson smiled at me.

"Ready to go?" At my nod, he said, "Where's Kim?"

I shrugged. I had lost my ability to talk after practically sprinting into the living room.

Jackson left the room in search of Kimberly, which left just Kody. And me. He sat down in the chair opposite me.

"So," he began, "how's school going?"

I cleared my throat. "Great! I'm looking forward to high school."

He smiled. "So am I." Then, realizing what he said, he corrected himself—or at least tried to. "I mean, I'm looking forward to you looking forward to high school." His face flamed. "Sorry, I lose all ability to speak like a normal human after 8:30."

I laughed, which seemed to make him relax a bit. "Have you had a good birthday?"

He smiled. "Absolutely! I'm glad you were able to make it."

"So am I."

Jackson entered the room, Kimberly behind him, with a look on her face like a panther stalking its prey. Kody and I both stood up at the same time, and we all walked out to the car. Waving to Kody, I got in the front seat, earning a scowl from Kimberly.

Jackson came to the car after he gave Kody a bro hug and called, "Thanks again for inviting us!"

Kody smiled as he went back inside. "Anytime."

When Jackson slid into the car, he gave me a funny look. "How come you were breathing so hard when I came into the living room?"

Flustered, I said the first thing that came into my brain. "I was exercising and didn't want Kody to know I was on his carpet doing leg workouts."

Half of his mouth twitched. "Exercising."

I nodded, eyes as innocent as could be. "Yes."

He chuckled. "I know you were eavesdropping, Sis. You can admit it. In fact, I knew you were there from the minute you stopped in the hall to the minute you turned and left."

I was mad at being caught. "How? Last I checked, you don't have X-ray vision!"

He full out laughed. "There was a mirror on the wall opposite you. All I had to do was glance in it, and there you were."

I gulped. I hoped that Kody hadn't seen me eavesdropping. It would be awkward if he had.

As if reading my thoughts, Jackson shook his head. "No, I was the only one who knew you were there."

Kimberly, who hadn't said anything up to this point, interrupted our conversation. "Are you going to pull out of his driveway, or what?"

Jackson and I both laughed as we realized he hadn't even turned on the engine. He soon remedied that, and we were on our way home. As we drove, I realized that the banquet for New Hope Pregnancy Center was the following week. I had been talking with Tracie about it, but with everything going on lately, I had forgotten. When I mentioned it to Jackson, he said he wanted to volunteer as well. I was glad that I was going to be able to help out.

Chapter Forty-One

The following Wednesday after school, Jackson was just pulling on his coat and about to leave the house when I stopped him at the door, a confused look on my face.

"Where are you going?"

He grabbed his car keys. "I'm going to pay a visit to the Coelhos."

I couldn't place the name. "Who?"

He chuckled. "You really do have an awful memory. The Coelhos have known our family for years. Marianna Coelho used to sing me a little song when I was little. All of their kids are grown, but I have chatted with them a few times since coming back into town; and I wanted to say hi to her and Carlos before they head back to Cambodia. They're currently on furlough." Pausing, he said, "You should come, too. I bet Marianna will be surprised at how big you've gotten."

I was beginning to remember who he was talking about. "Ok, I'll come. Just let me grab my coat."

I ran up the stairs, grabbed my coat from my closet, and sped back down the stairs, taking them two at a time. Jackson was already out the door, so I dashed outside and got into his car.

"Do they know we're coming?" I asked.

He nodded. "Yes, I spoke with Marianna, and she said she'd love to have me. She also said to bring whoever else in the family wanted to come."

We rode in silence until we came to the Coelho's house. Jackson gave me a sideways glance. "Something you should know about Marianna; she's very godly, and she's free for at least two hours."

I ruminated on that. He was obviously hinting at me meeting with her, and I wasn't opposed to it; I was just a little dejected that I couldn't find women to meet with on my own anymore. Jackson and Tina had been setting up most of my meetings recently. I resolved that for the next woman I met with after Marianna, I would find her on my own, no help required.

Jackson got out of the car once he had parked it in their steep driveway and walked to the front door. Following him, I pulled my coat a little tighter. Even in the middle of March, it was still freezing cold. As Jackson knocked on the wooden door, I wondered when I should ask Marianna about the meeting. I wasn't able to think about that long, however, for she opened the door and ushered us in, giving us both warm hugs.

"Sit down, sit down!" She gave us both a tender smile. "Oh my goodness, you two look so much like your mother. How is the family?"

Jackson spoke first. "We're managing."

She nodded. "I know it can be rough. I'm sorry. How's Kimberly doing?"

I shrugged. "She's at the top of her class academically and is very popular at school."

She smiled. "She always was a social butterfly."

Marianna invited us to sit down. "What's been happening in your lives recently?"

Jackson smiled. "Not much for me, but this girl here," he clapped a hand on my shoulder, "has been doing an awesome challenge! Tell her about it."

I silently thanked Jackson for leading the conversation in the right direction. "It all started when a friend at school dared me, as an atheist, to really give God a chance to prove Himself to me. The challenge is basically to meet with a different godly woman each week for a year. I've been doing it for about 9 months now, and I got saved a couple of months ago. I'll be sorry when it ends in June." Pretending as if the idea had just hit me, I smiled at her. "Would you be interested in participating in it as a godly woman I could meet with?"

Clasping a hand to her heart, she gasped. "Would I? Oh, I'd love to!"

Jackson gave me a secret smile and asked Marianna if he could talk with Carlos while we chatted. She directed him to the study and then came back and sat down across from me.

"So what do I do?"

I had heard this question so many times that my response automatically came. "You simply tell me about life lessons you've learned, and I ask you questions."

"Sounds good! Why don't I get us something to drink before we start?"

I requested water, and she hurried off to the kitchen. When she returned, she was carrying two glasses of water. I thanked her and took a satisfying sip. She gave me a smile.

"Now, what do you want to ask me?"

I pondered that. Normally I would start out asking about the qualities of a godly woman, but I wanted to start it out differently this time. "Tell me about Cambodia. What inspired you to go?"

She thought hard. "I guess it was God."

I tilted my head. "Could you explain?"

She nodded. "After Carlos and I had been married for 9 years, God called us to be missionaries. We went to Chile for 10 years and planted a church there. Then God told us to go to Cambodia, where we planted a church and opened a coffee shop. We also had a classroom there where we taught math, science, and other subjects, including the Bible, which was done undercover. We were in Cambodia for 5 years before going to Albania, a Muslim country, to teach English. After we left Albania, we went back to Chile for another 5 years."

I blew out a breath. "Whew! That's a lot of traveling! No wonder you're on furlough!"

She laughed. "Yes, it is tiring physically, but I love the people we encounter. Through it all, we have had to live out my favorite verse, Proverbs 3:5-6, which says, 'Trust in the Lord with all your heart and lean not on your own understanding. In all your ways acknowledge Him, and He shall direct your paths.' If God tells you something, it will come to pass in His timing, and His timing is perfect. You just have to trust Him while you're waiting for it to happen. We'll be going back to Cambodia soon, when God tells us the timing is right."

"Why do you feel the need to go back?" I asked. "You already ministered there, so why not go to a country you've never been to?" I knew if I did missions in a country for a while, I'd probably want to change countries to see more of the world.

She took a sip of water. "We're going back to Cambodia because the children we had ministered to previously are now grown, and they want to learn how to minister to others. Carlos and I will be going so we can mentor them."

That made sense. I had forgotten that people grow and move on with life.

She smiled fondly. "The best adventure I've ever had was ministering to those kids in Cambodia. There was definitely never a dull moment with them around. They are now successful people in the world, but they want to use their positions of power for God's glory. It's amazing!"

She took me over to the computer where she showed me some pictures of the people from Cambodia. She told me their occupations and what they had loved doing as kids.

I was moved by her obvious love for these people and her passion for the work there. "What are some more stories you can tell me about Cambodia?"

She thought for a moment. "One day we returned to the city after ministering in a village to take a three-day break. Every night we ate at the same restaurant. On the third night, our waiter, the same one who'd served us for the past three nights, stopped our conversation. 'Why are you so different?' he inquired. We told him that we were Americans. He said, 'No, you're different in another way.' We knew he was talking about our faith, even though he didn't realize that was what it was. Even though we weren't technically allowed to speak in public about our faith, we told the waiter about God. He believed and we prayed with him. After praying, his countenance completely changed, and he kept saying, 'I'm a happy man!'"

I could understand the change in countenance. Becoming a Christian had changed everything about me.

She continued. "Oh! I thought of another one. While working in Cambodia, there were two high school girls who became Christians and went back to their village in the jungle and started teaching all the kids and adults there about Jesus. They came to me one day and asked if we would come and minister to their village. When my husband and I arrived, we found that the girls had already been ministering without knowing it. They didn't know how much they had already influenced their friends and neighbors."

I wished that would happen in my life. I had influenced one of my friends because of my conversion, Kelsey, but I still hadn't affected my family—or at least, not to my knowledge. Kimberly wasn't quite as sour to me the other day, but that could just be because she had forgotten to suck on her lemon for the day.

I suddenly thought of a really good question. "What was the strangest food you had to eat while being a missionary?" Cambodians don't exactly eat hamburgers and fries.

She smiled slyly, saying, "The strangest food I've ever had was tarantula."

I grimaced, aghast. "Gross! I would never eat that!"

She laughed. "Actually I kind of liked it. It tasted a little like salty popcorn; however, I only had the legs. My husband was the brave one who actually ate all of it."

I pretended to throw up. "Nasty." I shuddered. To imagine those furry legs going down my throat was too much. I needed to change the subject before I puked. "So, what are the qualities of a godly woman?"

Knitting her brow, she said, "The qualities of a godly woman are to be humble, to be sensitive to the Holy Spirit, to have a knowledge of the Word, and to express joy and a mother's heart. I have a mother's heart for the orphanages in Cambodia."

Obviously, or else she wouldn't have risked her health by eating that hairy spider!

Jackson walked into the living room, interrupting our chat. He looked sheepish.

"I'm really sorry, Sis, but we have church in half an hour, and we need to get back to the house so we can get ready."

I was shocked. I had completely forgotten it was Wednesday. In fact, I had forgotten most everything as I talked with Marianna. She was a very engaging speaker. I stood up, sad to leave so soon. I gave her a hug and smiled at her.

"Thank you so much for talking with me! I learned a lot and enjoyed spending time with you."

She walked us to the door. "I enjoyed spending time with you, too. You've grown up so much."

As Jackson drove away from the Coelho's house, I wondered what it'd be like to go to a different country and do the things that they did—except for the eating tarantulas part. Yet, even though I loved talking with Marianna, what she'd said when we first saw her was confusing. She said that Jackson and I looked like our mother, which was impossible. My mom had blond hair and green eyes like Kim, and Jackson and I had brown hair and brown eyes, like our dad. In fact, my mom and I didn't look alike at all. It was Kim that was the look-alike. Maybe Marianna just hadn't seen our mom in a long time and had forgotten what she looked like.

We arrived back at the house, and I quickly changed into jeans and a nice shirt, the outfit similar to what I'd worn to the party last Thursday. Once I was ready, I went to find Jackson. He was a quick changer, and we were soon on our way to church.

Once there, I walked through the doors of the church and was grabbed by Tina.

"Hey! How've you been?"

I stifled a smile. "Tina, it's literally been about 3 hours since we saw each other. I'm pretty much the same, other than the fact that I had another meeting today."

She grinned, pleased. "Great! Did you like it?"

I nodded. "I had a lot of fun with her, and it made me think about a lot of things." Like what if the tarantula wasn't actually dead while you ate it, and it bit you while going down your throat before crawling back up out of your throat and out your mouth. Then you'd get a throat infection and die of spider poisoning. Yeah, Marianna definitely made me think about a lot of things.

Service was about to start, so Tina and I went into the main room. I saw Kody playing guitar for the worship band, and he smiled at me. I smiled back, surprised that he remembered me. I was glad Kim wasn't around to shoot daggers into my back. During the service, I felt God's presence and was once again amazed at the fact that He'd want me back, even though I ran away for so long. I guess that book Vanessa Broxbern gave me was right: no gone is ever too far gone.

Chapter Forty-Two

This was it. This was going to be the week I, not Jackson or Tina, arranged a meeting. I had done it before with family members, but I wanted to do it with someone not related to me, someone whom I barely knew or didn't know at all. The only question was who? I prayed that God would give me wisdom on my choice, and His timing was perfect, as always.

I was at church Sunday morning listening to the pastor when I felt the need to glance around the sanctuary. Confused, I did so. Halfway through my scan, I noticed an older woman sitting near the back. I passed over her with my glance when something caught my eye. The lady in the grey coat was sitting two seats away from her. I was stunned. Then, the lady looked at the older woman sitting next to her, and I followed her gaze back to the woman I'd passed over earlier. I felt God say, "That's who you should meet with." I blinked. That was easy.

After church, I immediately scurried to the back and stopped the older woman from leaving.

"Excuse me, but I have a strange proposition for you."

She smiled kindly. "Go ahead."

"I'm doing a challenge where I meet with a godly woman each week for a year. I was wondering if you'd like to meet with me for this challenge?"

Eyes widening, she nodded. "I felt the Lord tell me today that someone was going to ask me something strange, and that I was to say yes. So, yes! Where do you want to meet? I could always take you back to my house and we could have lunch together. Would that work?"

I bobbed my head enthusiastically. "That's great!"

I was about to walk over to Jackson to let him know where I was going when I remembered something.

"By the way, what's your name?"

She chuckled. "Edna Frazier."

I then found Jackson and told him what was going on. He smiled at me. "You're doing great with this challenge, Brie. It's made you a lot more confident. A year ago you wouldn't have gone near a stranger, much less talked to her."

I pondered his words. He was definitely right. This challenge has changed me for the better in so many ways. Giving him a parting hug, I walked to where Edna stood talking with what I assumed to be her husband. I was right.

"I'd like you to meet my dear husband, Lloyd."

Shaking his hand, I noticed out of the corner of my eye that I was being watched. When I turned, I found Tina staring at me with an odd smile on her face. She widened it until it was a grin and walked away. I shook my head. I'll never understand her.

I then remembered something from earlier. I asked Edna, "Who was the woman sitting next to you?"

She stared at me in confusion. "There was no woman sitting next to me. My husband and I were the only ones on the back row."

"But there was a lady wearing a grey raincoat a few seats away from you."

She shook her head. "Maybe you saw someone in front of me. There wasn't anyone wearing a grey raincoat next to me."

I was confused. Did the lady leave church early and Edna truly didn't see her, or did Edna just not remember? I knew I had seen her.

Shaking off my puzzling thoughts, I followed Edna and Lloyd to their car and climbed in. On the trip to their house, I thought about the strange woman. Why did no one else see her? She's always showed up when I needed to hear or see something important, and today was no exception. It was freaky. I shook my head, clearing my thoughts. Edna gave me a curious glance, obviously wondering why I was randomly shaking my head.

We soon arrived at their one-story house, climbed out of the car, and walked through the door. Offering me a seat in the living room, Edna went into the kitchen, returning with two glasses of tea. She sat down and handed me the tea.

"What would you like to talk about?"

I shrugged. "Why don't you tell me about yourself."

She tilted her head. "Well, to start off, I was a missionary to Haiti for over 22 years."

I gaped. "That's amazing! Did you like it?"

"Yes! A word of advice, though. When you go to do mission work in another country, learn their culture, even if there are some things in it you disagree with. Find something in their culture that you admire and focus on that and not the things you don't agree with."

That would be smart. If I went to a different country and I didn't like something that they did, knowing me, I'd fixate my mind on that one thing.

She continued. "Also, when you travel to other countries, especially as a missionary, don't try to make them Americans. If their customs don't contradict the Bible, don't try and change their ways. For example, the people in Haiti don't cross their legs; they cross their ankles. It's an insult to show the bottom of your foot. The Bible says nothing about how to cross your legs, so I tried to respect their custom and sit with my ankles crossed."

I surreptitiously uncrossed my legs. I wondered if she, having lived in Haiti for so long would think I was insulting her by crossing my legs. I settled back in the chair, ankles crossed.

If she noticed, she didn't say anything. "Traveling to other countries is a lot of fun. Tiring, but fun, especially doing mission work."

I leaned forward. "What countries have you been to?"

"I've been to Guatemala, Panama, Haiti, Dominican Republic, Puerto Rico, Germany, Switzerland, France, Ghana, and all the countries in Central America."

I blinked. "That's a lot."

She laughed. "Yes, but I loved Haiti a lot. There are so many stories I could tell you."

I sat forward in my chair eagerly. "Can you?"

She looked surprised. "If you want to hear them, I'd love to." When I nodded confirmation, she spoke. "One day, we were going to an early morning church service. When my husband and I got home, the car stopped working. My husband pushed the car into the shade, and then we went into the house before trying to find another car to jumpstart ours. At that moment, two men came out of the woods."

I widened my eyes. This sounded interesting.

"They put handcuffs on us and pushed us up against the wall. They then put a gun to Lloyd's head and said that they would kill him."

I gasped.

"Lloyd, instead of begging for mercy or crying like some people probably would, began to sing 'Blessed be Your Name.' We were both praying, and I was speaking in tongues. The men slapped me and told me to stop, but the power of the Lord was on us. I was calm the whole time because of Jesus. The men decided that they weren't going to kill us but instead were going to rob us. I gave them all the money I had in Haitian currency, the

240

total adding up to $1,000 American dollars. They slapped me again and said they wanted American money. Now, I had just gotten the money from the church, but I didn't want to give it to them; however, they wouldn't let up until I told them where it was. Instead of being satisfied with all the money, they demanded more, still not letting us go."

The greedy jerks! I wished I could've given them a piece of my mind.

"I told them that if there was any more money, it would be in my purse in the car. They left in order to find it. As soon as they were out of the house, I locked the door. We came back to America shortly after that traumatizing incident."

I shook my head slowly. "Wow. I would, too, if that happened to me. That's awful!"

She nodded. "Yes, but at least they didn't harm us or kill us. The Lord was looking after us and keeping us safe, just like He did for Lloyd on another trip to Haiti."

Intrigued, I motioned for her to go on. "What happened?"

"Lloyd went back to Haiti by himself because I had just had knee surgery and couldn't go. Right after he arrived in Haiti, there was a 7.0 earthquake. I was so scared when I heard that because I didn't know if Lloyd was okay. He called me shortly afterwards and told me what had happened. When the earthquake happened, a giant concrete wall fell on the car he and some other people were in. One man died because of it, but Lloyd was fine thanks to God."

"Another time God protected my children and me. Lloyd had to teach a Bible class in a different village for a month. We lived in an apartment at the time—an apartment that had very noisy neighbors. While he was gone, I was at home with my two kids and was really scared. Thieves broke into apartments around us all the time, and I didn't want that to happen to us, especially since we were very defenseless. I prayed that the Lord would protect the kids and me, but I also made a plan: I would put the kids to bed and then stay up all night to watch and make sure no one broke in. I would then sleep while the kids were at school. But my plan wasn't God's plan. Even though I wanted to stay up because I was scared, God put me to sleep every night for 30 days, protecting us through the night."

"That's amazing!" I said.

"There was another time when Lloyd had a really bad temperature. I couldn't make it come down, so I prayed. I told God, 'I can't take it anymore! Please help me!' Instantly, Lloyd cooled down right underneath my hand. That's when I knew God would never give us more than we could take."

Edna stood up suddenly. "Oh, my, I completely forgot about lunch!" She looked at me. "Do you have any allergies?"

"Just to cilantro."

She shook her head. "What a shame. Cilantro tastes very wonderful. Why don't we go get a pizza?"

I was good with that, so Edna and I climbed into her car once again and headed for Papa John's.

Once there, we ordered a multiple cheese pizza. On the way back to her house, I sighed in delight, smelling the magnificent wafts of pizza.

When we arrived at her home, I placed it on the table as Edna got cups and plates out. I told Lloyd it was time to eat, and he got up from his chair and came to the table. I sat down as Edna finished putting the last thing on the table. They asked me to bless the food, and I, after a little hesitation, did so. I was very proud of myself for doing so. I had never prayed out loud in front of people before. Whenever I was at lunch at school, Tina always prayed.

Thankful to be able to dig in, I took a bite and gave a deep sigh of pleasure. Edna and Lloyd seemed to love it, as well. Edna smiled at Lloyd.

"At least this stuff is edible," she commented, "and easy for me to hold down, unlike that one drink we had in Haiti."

"What drink?" I asked.

She grimaced. "There was only thing I couldn't eat in Haiti. It was a drink made out of something similar to an olive. The Haitians would mash it up and put water in it. When it was first offered to me, I took one sip and knew I'd never be able to stomach it. Thankfully, my son, bless his heart, noticed that I couldn't drink it without throwing up and drank it for me."

That was so sweet of him. I don't know how I'd be able to drink that if Edna couldn't, but at least it wasn't a tarantula!

Then Edna began sharing something rather personal. "While doing missions, I felt as if I wasn't doing anything for God because I was just Lloyd's secretary. But God told me one day, 'Whatever your hand finds to do, do it, for you are working for Me.' From then on, I did any job, from the smelly to the easy, because I knew I was doing it for God."

I took a sip of tea. "That really gives a new perspective on how to view what we do. Is there another different perspective that you have on life?"

"Well, people always want to know what's going to happen. My view of it is that we really don't need to know what's going to happen. If we knew, we might stop being faithful to what God has called us to."

Lloyd was finished with his pizza, so he stood up and walked into the other room. I continued the conversation. "What do you think are the qualities of a godly woman?"

She pursed her lips. "Now, that's a harder question than the others you've asked." She thought for a minute before replying. "I think some of the qualities that godly women should have are to love the Lord, be hospitable, be yourself at all times, and live your life in a way that people see Jesus through you—because you may be the only Bible they ever read."

"Speaking of the Bible, what's your favorite verse?"

"I think one of my favorite verses in all the Bible is Philippians 4:19, which says, 'And my God shall supply all your need according to His riches in glory by Christ Jesus.'"

That's definitely a good verse, especially for someone like me, who needs money all the time yet always seems to get it at the right time—God's timing. Speaking of timing, Jackson texted me just as I was about to get up from the table. He said that he was coming to get me and would be there shortly. I passed the information along to Edna, and she nodded.

"Just like there's a time to sow and a time to reap, there's also a time to come and a time to leave."

I laughed. Leave it to her to use the Bible to say goodbye. As I grabbed my coat, she placed a hand on my arm.

"Before you go, I want to say this one thing to you. Don't be afraid if God calls you to do something. He's not going to call you to go where He won't be with you."

With that, she gave me a hug and walked me to the door.

As I climbed into Jackson's car, my head spun with her words. What did they mean? Obviously I knew what she was saying, but why did she say them right before I left? Maybe to save the best for last? I didn't know.

As we drove the short distance to our house, Jackson sensed that I was unusually quiet. "Everything okay?"

"I was just thinking. Have you ever felt as if there was a big piece of your life missing and all you can see is a jumble of pieces that don't make any sense without that one piece?" He nodded. "Well, recently I feel as if I'm so close to finding that one piece but can't quite grasp it, and it's frustrating."

He smiled sympathetically as he parked the car in our driveway. "I'm sorry. Do you want me to pray for you?"

I bobbed my head. "Please."

As we had a tear-jerking brother and sister prayer, I realized that God won't lead me to a place where He won't go. He won't give me a puzzle just to never give me the final piece. He is the Master of timing. The One who knows all and sees all. The One who won't look at my mess from a distance and not do anything about it but will instead sit beside me in my mess and grieve with me, biding His time until it is right for Him to step in and turn the shattered pieces of my life into a beautiful masterpiece.

Chapter Forty-Three

Tina, who was sitting in front of me during Beta Club, handed me a sheet of paper. I glanced at it. It was a permission slip to give to my grandmother. Apparently the Beta Club students were going to an elementary school to job-shadow the teachers there. I thought it was pretty interesting. A day off from normal school to hang out with little kids? Count me in.

After class, Tina grabbed my sleeve and tugged me aside.

"Are you going?"

I nodded. "I think it'll be fun."

She smiled. "Great! I've job-shadowed before, and it's a lot of fun. You'll definitely enjoy it."

When the long school day was finished, I waited outside for Jackson to pick me up. On our way home, I told him about what the Beta Club students were going to do in two days. He seemed happy for me and encouraged me to do it.

With his words boosting my confidence, I strode through the doorway of the house and walked into Grandmother's room. Sure enough, Grandmother was sitting there concentrating on a Sudoku puzzle. Upon closer examination, I noticed that it was the same Sudoku book I had flung out of my room because I couldn't finish that one puzzle that Tina interrupted. I was never able to remember the breakthrough, thus spiraling me into a state of depression. Well, not that bad, but close. I had vowed to stay away from Sudoku puzzles for at least a month, and just being near the book gave me an unexplainable wariness. She glanced up.

"What do you need?"

Since her tone wasn't harsh and condemning, I became even more confident. "I have a slip for you to sign. Beta Club students are going to an elementary school in two days to job-shadow some teachers there. Can I go?"

She blinked. "It's 'may I,' and yes, you may. I'm glad you're finally breaking out of your shell."

That had me blinking. She was glad about something that I did? Well, I guess it really was a good day. I smiled and gave her an impulsive hug. Stunned, she drew a quick breath and then adjusted the blanket on her lap, frowning.

"Now, don't get all mushy on me."

I simply laughed and skipped up to my room. When Kimberly asked why I was laughing, I grinned.

"Grandmother finally doesn't hate me!"

She scrunched her eyebrows together. "Why would you think that she hates you?"

I rolled my eyes. "Oh, I don't know. Maybe because she complains about everything I do, nitpicks on everything I say, favors you more, and curls her lip in distaste every time I walk into the room? Other than that, we get along just dandy."

She wrinkled her nose at me. "You don't have to be so sassy. You're just like how Dad used to be. He was sassy before he got all serious and gloomy."

Serious and gloomy. Yep, that pretty much described how my dad was the last few years before he died. Probably because he was snorting drugs all the time. That would do it.

"Do you ever miss Dad?" I asked.

She shrugged. "Sometimes, yeah. Other times I remember how sad I'd get when he wouldn't pay attention to what any of us kids did and how he and Mom would fight all the time, but other than that I don't have a lot of young childhood memories of him." She scrunched her eyebrows together. "I guess I just have a bad memory." She shook her head and walked into her room.

A bad memory was what I kept blaming these days when I felt like something important was missing. Some detail that could radically change my life. I had no clue what it was, but I knew there was something not right.

As I stood there ruminating, I realized that I needed to do homework, so I dejectedly walked to my room and heaved my twenty-ton backpack on the bed. It sank in the middle and I'm sure I heard the mattress groan. I sighed and grabbed a pencil and got the first part of the 7,382 pages of homework I had to finish by tomorrow.

Two days later, I was on the bus headed for Black Fox Elementary. Tina sat beside me, full of excitement.

"It's going to be so great!"

I thought so, too. Not many students were going, though. One girl, Olivia, caught the flu so she couldn't come, plus Beta Club wasn't exactly huge, so there were only 9 students going, Tina and me included. The other seven were five guys and two girls. The first girl's name was Elyse. She was really nice to both Tina and me, and after Tina's version of twenty questions, we found out that she was a Christian as well. Tina and she really hit it off, but I didn't enter the conversation much. I had broken out of my shell some, but I wasn't about to share my social security number with someone I barely knew. The other girl was Zoe, an agnostic who kept to herself and seemed pretty snooty.

The five guys were Samuel, Ryan, Adam, Carter, and Herbert. Samuel was a smart guy, but an atheist. He used his smartness to try and defend his beliefs. I could understand where he was coming from, but I was afraid to reach out to him. What if he thought I was just another girl trying to give him the "Christian spiel"? Ryan was the opposite. He was not as smart as the other guys in Beta Club, and he was a Christian—at least, I thought he was. He wasn't very outspoken about his faith. Adam was super smart and was at the top of every class I had with him. He was a Christian and just as outspoken about it as Tina. He tried every day to get her attention but to no avail. She didn't care for anyone but Jackson. Carter was a nice guy, I guess. He didn't talk a lot. I've seen him and Adam at Tina's church every week, but Ryan only comes every now and then. Lastly, there was Herbert, who was a complete nerd and proud of it. I wasn't sure what his beliefs were, but I knew that if there were a religion called Mathianity, that would be what he believed in.

I leaned back in my seat. It wasn't a long drive to the school, so I couldn't sleep—sadly—but I could at least block out the large amount of noise on the bus. I sat like that for a few minutes before we arrived at Black Fox.

Once there, our teacher handed us each a sheet of paper. On it was the name of the teacher we were assigned to. Since there were an odd number of us, two people were assigned to each teacher except me. The pairs were Tina and Elyse, Ryan and Herbert, Carter and Zoe, and Samuel and Adam. The last two didn't seem happy at the pair-up, since they were both very outspoken about their very opposite beliefs, but I knew that they'd get over it soon enough. I don't know why I was chosen to be the loner, but I believed that God would do something great because of it.

The class tromped inside the school and then split up to go to our separate classrooms. I was left alone, trying to find a Denise Jones, 4th grade teacher. Finally, I came across the classroom with her name next to the door. I quietly opened the door and gingerly peered inside. At least 15 pairs of eyes stared back at me. With a start, I realized that they were having class, and I was interrupting. I was just about to close the door when a woman walked over.

"Are you from Keaton Middle School? The student who will be job-shadowing me today?"

I nodded, thankful she at least knew what I was there for.

She ushered me in and pointed for me to sit beside her desk in the back of the room while she walked back up in front of the class and began teaching again. I sat down in a chair next to her desk and watched her. She was very interactive as she taught. I looked at my surroundings. On her desk were the typical things for a teacher: stapler, tape, mug with pens, and the like. But the one thing that surprised me was a Bible verse taped to the corner of her desk. It said, "Whenever I'm afraid, I will trust in You." I was stunned. I hadn't expected to be paired up with a Christian teacher. I wondered if I could make her a part of my challenge.

After she finished teaching and the kids were walking out the door, she came over to me.

"Hey, I'm Denise Jones."

I smiled. "Nice to meet you." I hesitated, unsure of whether to ask her about the verse, but then pressed on. I decided it couldn't hurt. "Are you a Christian?"

She nodded. "That I am. Are you?"

"Yes, ma'am, only recently. I have an odd request for you."

"Shoot," she said.

I licked my lips. "I'm doing a challenge where each week for a year I meet with a different godly woman. I basically learn about their life and their struggles and how they overcome them, getting to know them better. Would you be interested in being the woman I meet with this week?"

She tapped her finger against her chin. "I think I may be able to do that, although we wouldn't have a ton of time. I have some free time during the day, so we could talk then. What time is your class leaving?"

"We'll be staying until 2:00. Then we head back to KMS."

She smiled. "Wonderful!"

The next group of students came in, and Denise went around the room greeting each one. I stayed in the back and watched her interact with the students. She was amazing at what she did; I took notes as she taught the class in case I ever wanted to become a teacher. Once the class was over, she walked to the back of the room and sat down.

"I have my free period now. Do you want to talk now?

I nodded. "Sure! How long have you been a teacher?"

"I've taught for 30 years."

My jaw dropped. "That's a long time! You must really love it."

"I do. I love taking difficult things and breaking them apart to make them easier for young kids to understand. The Lord put the love for teaching in me, and I want to use it for Him. The kids are like sponges at this age, and I am able to influence what they soak in, making sure it's healthy. The responsibility and weight of teaching them can be frightening at times, but then I remember my favorite verse, Psalm 56:3."

"The verse on the corner of your desk!"

She nodded. "That's right. I'm glad you noticed it. And my hope is that all my students will read it and that it will help them when they face obstacles and challenges in their lives."

"What has been a challenge you've had to face?"

"The biggest challenge I've had to face was raising my daughters and keeping a strong marriage."

Both good things to fight for. I wished my mom had fought for a strong marriage. Maybe

246

then my dad wouldn't have killed himself. I wished that she would pay attention to her kids every now and then. I also wished that a million dollars would fall from the sky into my lap, but just like the rest of my wishes, I knew it wasn't going to happen.

She scrunched her eyebrows together. "But I think that even though I've had to face some big challenges, it's when you're facing the big hardships that you can find peace and see the good God is doing in your life, if you're looking for it."

"How?" I asked, with a confused look.

"It's during the tough times that we see the miracles. People usually don't notice all the good God does when everything's right in their lives. It's when things are rough when they miss the good."

Ah. Now I understand. It was very true. I don't notice my big toe all that often, but if it were chopped off, I'd miss it in a big way and wonder why something so awful would've happened to me. I wouldn't realize that the same big toe had been there for a very long time, thanks to God, and I should instead be thanking Him for giving it to me for that long.

She looked at her watch. "We have a little bit more time. Let's walk around and I'll show you the school."

"Alright. Lead the way!"

We walked out of her classroom and began going down the hall. When we passed by some classrooms, she let me peek in and then told me all about the teacher. She appeared to be good friends with all the teachers there. At one point, we passed by a classroom that had a Bible verse on the door.

Puzzled, I asked, "Why doesn't the principal take that verse down? I thought schools had policies that won't allow that."

Denise shook her head, smiling. "Not this school. We're so blessed. Many of the teachers here are Christians, and the school board even allows Christians to come in at the beginning of the school year and pray over the classrooms."

"That's really cool." I wondered why KMS didn't do that. If they were more lenient with faith policies, Christians—like me—might feel freer to step out and profess their faith without feeling embarrassed.

She sighed. "Yes, it is. But it's also sad that so many other schools don't allow it and the kids there are afraid to speak about their faith. There's so much fear that tries to keep us from having faith."

Whoa. Did she, like, read my mind or something? That had to be God telling me not to be afraid. I was stunned. That was super cool.

She then glanced at her watch and began briskly walking back to the classroom. "I need to head back because my class is about to start. We can still talk on the way back, though."

Picking up my pace to match hers, I asked, "What're the qualities of a godly woman?"

"To me, the qualities of a godly woman are to be the first to say sorry and to live in a way where people don't have to ask if you're a Christian because it's so obvious."

I knew a lot of people wouldn't be able to pick me out of a crowd and say, "She's definitely a Christian." I need to work on that.

We made it back to the classroom right before the students did. I resumed my seat in the back of the room and watched as Denise taught another class full of students. It flew by quickly, and after the students left, Denise motioned for me to come to the front.

"It's ten minutes until lunch. Should we head over to the cafeteria?"

I nodded. My stomach had just rumbled and food sounded wonderful.

On our way to the cafeteria, Denise took me down a hallway.

"I had to show you this first."

I looked around me and realized that we were standing in front of a wall covered in art.

Denise smiled at me.

"We're having an art competition right now with the individual grades."

I looked around and only saw imitations of Van Gogh's The Starry Night.

"The kids all imitate Van Gogh's work, and the judges pick out the best one based on uniqueness and talent."

Making our way toward the cafeteria, we passed some classrooms, where I saw some of my fellow students from Beta Club. Tina and Elyse seemed to be having a blast, but Samuel and Adam weren't looking very happy with each other. It appeared they had just had a theological debate. I chuckled inwardly. They were like oil and vinegar; they rarely mixed.

Once we reached the cafeteria, Denise led me into the line. My mouth watered. At KMS, I had to pack a lunch because the food was so nasty. This, however, was a blessing. Chicken, rolls, and steamed carrots were in trays, as well as some other food. I piled it on my divider and grabbed a cup of sweet tea. Denise did the same except she got coffee. We walked out of the line and went to the teachers' lunchroom. I felt special—I was eating with teachers! I spotted Tina through the glass window that separated us from the cafeteria. She waved, a curious smile on her face. I would explain everything to her later, but now I was going to eat! Denise said a prayer, and we dug in. A few other teachers had joined us in the room.

Denise turned to me. "So what interests do you have?"

I shrugged. "I play the piano, have a cat, and do various sports for fun, but that's about it." I sighed. "I used to really love to sing and wanted to be a professional singer, but my mom didn't like the noise and told me I had a horrible voice, so I stopped. When I was forced into joining choir at my school, I met with a woman who gave me a voice lesson and helped me improve enough that I realized I didn't have 'a horrible voice.' Nonetheless, I dropped out of choir as soon as I could. I had lost my passion to sing because of my mom." I stopped to nibble some chicken.

She frowned. "I'm so sorry. If I could tell you anything to help you out, it'd be this: you shouldn't stop doing something you like just because someone else doesn't like it. Don't let what other people say about you stop you from doing what God has given you a passion for." She paused to let that sink in. "Have you ever read the story of David and Goliath?"

I nodded. Multiple times. I leaned back in my seat and sipped my tea, wondering what she'd say.

"You have to slay the giants who try to make you feel like you're small and insignificant. But it's not just realizing that. Whenever I read Bible stories, I ask myself if they apply to my life and see if I really believe them. It's easy to listen to a story without really believing that what is being said is true."

I had changed my behavior based on my mom's opinion of my singing, and I still change who I am because of her opinions. That needed to stop, starting now. I made a change inwardly to no longer shrink away from her hurtful words. I wouldn't be disrespectful; I just wouldn't let her push me around with her words and control what I liked and didn't like.

We were finished with lunch, so Denise and I threw away our trash and headed back to her classroom. When we arrived, Denise readied herself for another class, as did I. I really enjoyed watching Denise come alive as she spoke with the students and helped them learn. Soon after the class, I realized I should probably go to the principal's office because it was almost 2:00. I gave Denise a hug and then walked down the hall.

When I made it to the office, all the students were already there, and we headed out to the bus together. Everybody wanted to talk at the same time about their time with the teachers, so I just stayed quiet most of the ride home while everyone had their say. Tina noticed my silence and asked about it. I told her how I met Denise and made her a part of my challenge.

"I'm so proud of you!" She gave me a hug. "Denise is a good woman. She goes to our church, so I know all about her, and I'm glad you were paired up with her so you had this opportunity to learn from her."

I agreed. She was fun to be around and really seemed to love the kids in her classroom. I thought about what she had said about not listening to what my mom had said about my voice. I decided that the next day I would begin doing voice exercises at home and then sign up for choir in high school. I wanted to show my mom that she couldn't manipulate my decisions based on her opinions. I was about to slay one giant who had been towering over me for way too long.

Chapter Forty-Four

I couldn't believe it. I was a little over two months away from being finished—more specifically, nine more meetings away. I was sad that it was almost over, but I was also stunned to realize that once this challenge was over, I would no longer have something to look forward to every week. I didn't know how I would grow spiritually. I mean, meeting with these women had convinced a cold-hearted atheist that God is real. These women have helped me grow and believe that I could be more than just "Penny and Jared's daughter," the daughter who wasn't as good as her siblings and who would never accomplish anything in life. Instead, these women showed me that I was loved, strong, worthy, and enough. I am afraid that not having a constant flow of encouragement in my life will make me sink back into the hole I had been in for most of my life.

I wondered how Christians were able to live without that kind of encouragement. Take Kelsey, for example. She was a new Christian and didn't know a lot about God. Just like in the story of the sower sowing seed, the seed that fell on her heart sprung up quickly but would it be scorched just as quickly, when the troubles and persecution of the world come upon her? I wanted her to be grounded in the Word; I just didn't know what to do to accomplish that. I could always have a Bible study, but there's only so much a person can learn in a Bible study when the teacher doesn't know much more about Christianity than the students do.

Not being able to think this through fully, I did what I always did when I couldn't think: I paced. As I trod on the well-worn carpet in my bedroom, I began to think up ideas of what I could do to help Christians—not just new Christians but also those who had been Christians practically from birth but didn't really live out their faith. People like Ryan. This challenge has helped me so much already that I have a passion to share it with others. I suddenly felt as if this is part of God's calling for my life. I needed to figure out, though, how I would do this. Maybe I could speak with all the women I'd met with and see if they would be willing to meet again—not with me but with whoever was interested in increasing their spiritual growth, people who were willing to let mentors into their lives to learn from their experiences. I could speak with people who were new Christians or people who I felt weren't connecting with God to see if they'd even be interested.

I halted on the carpet. There were a few things that needed to happen before any of this could take place. I needed to finish my own challenge, I needed to figure out how many people were actually interested, and I needed to see if I would have the endurance to set people up for meetings. That would be very stressful, and I didn't want stress. My brow furrowed. I could feel an idea coming. Suddenly, I had it! I could set up the first, say, 5 people for one person. Then, the person doing the challenge would be required to set up the rest on their own. They'd be able to get my advice, but I wouldn't be responsible for keeping them on track with the schedule every week.

Yes! That was it! I shot a thank-you prayer up to God right then and there. He was always faithful with giving me the ideas I needed at just the right time. I snorted. When does God ever not have the right timing?

I was so excited about the idea, I texted Tina. She responded practically the instant I hit send.

Her message: "OH MY GOODNESS, THAT'S AMAZING!!!"

My message: "Uhhhh... thanks. It wasn't me, it was all God."

That was the truth. I could take credit for nothing I did. It was all God. The A I got on my test? All God. Being able to overcome my fears? All God. The fact that Thunder actually pooped in his litter box instead of on the carpet? Definitely all God.

The key thing I needed to do before I could start this new challenge was to finish my challenge. I wondered whom I could meet with this week. I could meet with someone from Tina's church—well, now my church, since it was becoming my home. I didn't know whom, though. I wasn't exactly buddy-buddy with everyone there, and I definitely wasn't social enough to go around introducing myself to everyone. Edna Frazier was a big step for me. I couldn't think of anyone immediately, so I decided to eat something while I waited for inspiration. It was nearing 5:30 on a Thursday, and I was hungry. While I grabbed a banana, I scanned my brain for any woman whom I'd be able to meet with. I couldn't think, and I was confused. Normally, God would give me an idea when I thought. I didn't know why He didn't now.

I shook my head. What was I doing? I was doubting God's timing, and that wasn't smart. So, instead of worrying that God had left me because I couldn't hear Him at that moment, I ate my banana, knowing perfectly well that worrying would get me nowhere. In fact, I had just read a verse about that early that morning. Psalm 37:7-8 said, "Rest in the Lord, and wait patiently for Him; do not fret because of him who prospers in his way because of the man who brings wicked schemes to pass. Cease from anger, and forsake wrath; do not fret—it only causes harm."

I thought that really applied to my everyday life. I was always fretting, and I needed to realize that it got me nowhere. I decided that, until God dropped a woman into my lap, I wouldn't worry about it and instead do something with my life. I decided to do something fun and reckless: go swimming in April. Now, I know that's not as reckless as swimming in January, but I hadn't felt the same urge then. The air temperature outside was cold enough, so I had a feeling the pool temperature wouldn't be like a sauna.

I ran upstairs and got my swimsuit on. I don't know why I felt so reckless; I normally waited until at least June before even sticking my feet into the big body of water screaming at me to jump in. Kimberly was different; she loved swimming at all times of the year except November through February. She was on the swim team at school, so it made sense why she'd be swimming every chance she got. In fact, she was the reason we always opened our pool early in the year and closed it up late. I wondered if she'd want to join me. She had just got home from swim practice, so it was possible, but she also might be super tired. I decided to throw caution to the wind and ask her. I walked back inside and upstairs into her room.

"Yes?"

I smiled. "Wanna go swimming with me?"

She lifted her eyebrows. "You're going swimming in April? Are you sick?"

I laughed. "Nope, just reckless."

Snorting, she replied, "Reckless. Ha. I've been swimming since early March, in temperatures that are way colder than what you're about to experience."

She had a point. "So do you want to or not?"

She shrugged. "I'm already wet. Why not?"

I went back downstairs, grabbing a towel on the way, and walked outside. Sticking a foot into the pool, I wondered if I was making the right decision. No chance of turning back, though. Kimberly would hound me about it for weeks if I didn't. She'd call me a cold-footed chicken and never let me forget about it. Nope, I wasn't going to back out of it.

Kim came out in a few minutes. She cocked an eyebrow. "Ready?"

I cocked one back at her. "As I'll ever be."

She motioned for me to follow her to the deep end of the pool. "On the count of three, we'll jump in together. Deal?"

I nodded. Sounded fair enough. Kimberly counted. "One, two, three!"

I jumped. She didn't. That was the last thing I saw before I hit the water. The very cold water. The water that made me wish I wasn't so incredibly impulsive. The water that surrounded me and gave me a sick feeling to my stomach as I realized that it was very, very cold, and I was only wearing a swimsuit. Spluttering, I swam to the surface. I tried glaring at Kimberly, who was doubled over in laughter, but I couldn't because the water had frozen my eyes in a wide-eyed shocked look. She only laughed harder. My limbs were currently stiffening to the point where I was counting on the fact that it was a saline pool so I could stay afloat enough to breathe every now and then. I felt like a piece of driftwood. I struggled to stay afloat.

"Really? This is what you do to thank me for extending my invitation to you to go swimming? I'm touched," I spouted sarcastically. "Now I'll really want to invite you to do stuff with me again! NOT!"

She was still laughing, the jerk. I decided two could play at this game. I half floated, half swam to the edge of the pool and held my hand up. "Help me out of here before I drown."

Completely unsuspecting, she grabbed my hand. As soon as she had latched onto me firmly, I pulled. With a yelp, she came tumbling head over heels into the pool next to me. She was spluttering too when she came to the surface. Fury radiated from her eyes.

"How could you?"

I laughed, nearly drowning myself in the process, since laughing requires oxygen, and I wasn't getting very much of that at the present. "Don't even bother being mad. After what you did, it's only fair that you get a taste of your own medicine."

A full second passed, then she burst out laughing. I joined her, relieved she wasn't going to drown me. She swam to the side and pulled herself out. Due to my lack of muscles in my upper body, I swam for the ladder. When we had both dried off, we went inside to the kitchen for some hot tea. While I boiled the water, she prepared the cups and tea bags. Ten minutes later, we sat at the table drinking tea together. I thought it was very nice; I hadn't had quality time with my sister in a while, and I missed it. Even though she was a pain in the neck and looked nothing like me, we were still sisters, and I loved her.

I checked my phone and frowned as I looked at the notifications. A number that wasn't in my contacts had texted me. The message read, "Hi, my name is Nikki DeLong. I own The Clayful Artist. Your friend Tina, whom I'm good friends with, came in the other day to paint. We got to talking, and I realized that you were the one who was meeting with all the godly women. While you were at my shop doing several of your meetings, I wanted to know more about it but didn't know if I should approach you while you were in your meeting. Tina gave me your number. Would you be interested in coming by the studio and talking to me about it? I know some people who could benefit from this type of mentoring, and I'd love to see if you could talk with them about it and explain what the challenge is."

I was completely floored. God literally dropped a woman into my lap. She was interested, texted me about it, and knows people whom she thinks would want to do this! This answered all my prayers. God is so good! I quickly responded, asking what time would be best for me to come by. We agreed on the next day after school. I was so excited I did a happy dance there in the middle of the kitchen, much to the bewilderment of Kimberly.

Friday after school I told Jackson where to drop me off and that I would text him when we were almost finished.

Getting out of the car, I walked into the studio, bell jangling to alert my presence. I recognized the woman who came out of the back with a smile on her face.

"Hi, are you Nikki?"

She nodded. "Yes, I am. You're Tina's friend, right? The one doing the challenge?"

Bobbing my head, I smiled. "I have an odd request. Since I'm telling you about the challenge anyway, would you mind if you were a part of the challenge? Then you could really know how it works."

"I'd love that!" Her enthusiasm was contagious.

She led me to a different room connected to the main studio. In it were a couple of chairs and two tables. We sat down and I began.

"I'm going to ask you questions, and you can answer them to whatever length you want."

"Okay, go ahead."

"What're the qualities of a godly woman?"

"The qualities of a godly woman are respect and fear for the Lord, humility, patience, discipline, and a strong sense of self-worth."

A strong sense of self-worth is very important, especially for someone like me, who doubts her abilities and worthiness. "What's the biggest challenge you've had to go through?"

"The biggest challenge I've had to face is forgiving myself. I'm very self-critical, and I don't like giving myself grace. I can give it to other people easy peasy, but not to myself."

Same! Years after my dad's death, I still blamed myself for it. After our fight, he died. To a girl my age, it was more than just a coincidence. I thought I was the straw that had broken the proverbial camel's back, the straw that pushed my dad to his decision of suicide. Even now, I believed that. He was very influential in the shaping of my childhood, and I hated to see him gone. Speaking of which, I asked, "Who was the most influential person in your life?"

She rested her head on her hand. "My grandmother. She was the most consistent thing in my life."

I wish I had that. My paternal grandmother has been consistent ever since I met with her and broke the invisible line between Mom's family and Dad's family, but she wasn't in my life for most of my childhood. My maternal grandmother was a whole different story. She was in my childhood a lot but never acted as if she liked me, always favoring Kimberly, so I never really developed a good relationship with her. That has changed a little bit, though. Ever since I gave my life to Jesus a few months back, she has seemed subdued. She even began going to church again, which she hadn't been doing because she preferred "her alone time with God better." Anyway, I decided I'd better say something before Nikki thought I was deaf. "What's your favorite Bible verse?"

"My favorite verse is Psalm 43:5. It says, 'Why are you cast down, O my soul? And why are you disquieted within me? Hope in God; for I shall yet praise Him, the help of my countenance and my God.' You might try reading it in The Message version."

"That's so true! Whenever I feel sad, I count on God to help me get out of my funk, and He always does." I shifted my position in my chair and looked around. "Why did you open this studio? Has it been a childhood dream?"

"Yes. It was a childhood dream to open an art studio. When I turned twenty-one, God told me it was time, and I took the risk. It's only by the grace of God that I was able to. Come this August, it will have been opened four years. I never really had access to art while I was growing up, so I wanted to open a place where people could come and experience art."

"I love all the pieces in this studio. What has been your favorite piece of art that you've done?"

She laughed. "What's my favorite art piece? Probably the last thing I painted. It always changes based on what I just did."

"Was opening this studio the most exciting thing you've done?"

She tilted her head in thought. "Yes, but I also was able to spend two months in England by myself, and that was also a big adventure in my life."

My interest was piqued. "Have you been to any other countries?"

She nodded. "Yes."

"What countries?"

"Let's see. I've been to Germany, Mexico, Ecuador, Brazil, South Korea, Cambodia, Vietnam, England, Wales, Scotland, France, Denmark, Italy, Switzerland, Puerto Rico, Myanmar, Poland, Ireland, Belgium, Austria, Peru, and Columbia."

I gaped. "That's a lot."

She laughed. "Yes, but it was a lot of fun."

Just then, a customer walked in. Nikki excused herself and went to help the customer. I listened to her being so cheerful and wondered if I'd ever be able to be that happy all the time. I hadn't seen her frown since I walked in. Looking at the time, I realized that we'd been talking for a while, and I needed to get home. I texted Jackson to come and get me and then grabbed my backpack.

I peered around the corner and waited until Nikki was done talking with the customer before speaking. "I need to get home."

"Alright. Thank you for spending your time with me! I will text you later with some people's numbers who I think will be interested in this mentoring experience."

"That sounds great! Thank you!" With a parting hug, I exited the shop and sat on the curb for a few minutes until Jackson pulled up to the studio in his car. I climbed in, and he headed home. Eight women left before I was done. I couldn't believe it. No longer did it seem like work to meet with these women. It was a lot of fun, and I benefited greatly from the meetings. Now I wanted other people to get the chance to have the same experience.

Chapter Forty-Five

One of the contacts Nikki texted me was a guy whose name I vaguely recognized. When I asked Tina if she knew him, she said that he was one of the youth pastors at Westmore.

"Ah," I said, everything clicking into place. I guess Nikki wanted me to suggest my challenge to him to see if he knew any kids who would be interested. That would be very smart.

I texted him and asked him if he knew kids who might be interested in learning more about God through mentors. Within two minutes, I received a response. "Let me think on that today and I'll have a list for you at church tomorrow morning. By the way, are you still meeting with godly women? If so, I know someone who is a very godly woman and a prayer warrior. If you're interested, I could see if she's available."

I replied with an enthusiastic, "Yes!"

Later that day, he sent me her contact information. "She told me she's willing to meet anytime this next week. You can talk with her directly and decide on a good time. By the way, it's my mother-in-law, Iris Ray."

Iris Ray, huh? I had never heard of her, but I was willing to meet with just about anyone. I shot her a text about when we could meet. While I waited for her response, I sat down and made a list of kids I could ask about the challenge. Kelsey was at the top, of course. Then I added a couple of people from school, like students from Beta Club, and then I added some from church. I've been trying to branch out and get to know the kids in youth group better. Tina has also been trying to help me branch out—so much so that I'm beginning to mix everyone's name up. I'm surprised I haven't forgotten Tina's name, or my own name, for that matter.

When I felt like I had written enough, I stood up and walked downstairs. Passing by the photos on the wall, I wondered again about what our family would've been like if Dad hadn't killed himself. I might still be an atheist, or we could all be one happy, Christian, loving family. I snorted. Yeah, and maybe I would sprout wings and fly off to Togo where I could be made a tribal chief with my own private teepee.

I kept walking. Tina didn't know how lucky she was to have a family with two stable parents who loved her more than life, a nice home, a good environment, the whole package! She could never fully understand how blessed she was. Speaking of Tina, she wanted me to hang out at her place tonight. She said something about a party. I was totally fine with that. Saturday night and no homework—except for that one assignment I'd been putting off for three weeks. I couldn't wait.

I couldn't decide on what to wear, so I eventually just grabbed a pair of jeans and a sweater. I ran a brush through my hair and then skipped downstairs to ask Jackson for a ride. Apparently, he was going to the party, as well. I should have known Tina would invite him. Not that I minded. He was the best brother ever.

We hopped into his car, and he pulled out of the driveway. Since the weather had warmed all the way to 60 degrees, Jackson decided to put the top down. The wind blew my hair every which way as we rode along. When we pulled up to Tina's house, I ran a hand through it and hoped it didn't look too much like a rat's nest. Jackson and I walked up to the front door, and I let him knock. I noticed there were a bunch of cars I didn't recognize, but I knew that Tina was super popular, so I wasn't surprised. When Tina opened the door, she smiled.

"Hey, you two! Come on in!"

She hugged us and then led us into the living room, where several people were already seated. I recognized most of them from school. Kelsey and Elyse were in the group, as well as Ryan, Benjamin, and Carter. The rest were high schoolers of varying ages, which explained the cars. I sat down next to Kelsey while Jackson went into the kitchen with Tina to help her with the food. I noticed that there were only two seniors, and both of them were girls, so Jackson didn't have any friends close to his age. Obviously, Tina liked him enough to invite him to a party when she didn't have to.

I tuned into the conversation around me. The guys were controlling the conversation, talking about how the KMS basketball team wasn't doing so well, but the wrestling team was amazing. I honestly didn't care. The girls were talking about who was going with whom for the spring dance coming up. I also didn't care. After sixth grade when I figured out that nobody was ever going to ask me to any dance whatsoever, I decided to never care about it. If I never got my hopes up, then they could never be crushed. It was a safe tactic but also a depressing one. I had been very depressed after the Valentine's Day dance. I didn't go, to save myself the heartache, but Tina did, as well as a bunch of her friends, so they were talking about it for weeks afterward. I promised myself that I wouldn't let a dance be so important in my life that I was as silly as those girls. Not Tina, but her friends. They all were goo-goo-eyed over some boy and then they were all angry-eyed at each other for all wanting to go to the dance with said boy. In the end, there was so much drama I just stopped hanging out with them until weeks after the dance, when they finally all became friends again. Tina tried to be a peacemaker between them all, but it was stressing her out how rude they were to each other.

Now, hearing about another dance coming up, I groaned silently—or so I thought. It actually turned out to be an audible groan, and everybody stopped talking and looked at me. I could feel my cheeks heating up faster than a room with no air conditioning in the middle of summer. I smiled sheepishly.

"Sorry, folks. Just a little stomach problem." That was true to some level. All this talk was making me sick.

They gave me quizzical looks but returned to their conversations. I gratefully stood and began walking down the hallway towards the kitchen before freezing in my tracks. There, next to the sink, were Jackson and Tina. And they were holding hands again! Jackson was talking to Tina in a low voice, and they looked to be having a serious conversation. I slowly backed out of the doorway and wondered what to do. If I walked in, it would be awkward for them, and they might lose whatever vibe they had going on in there. However, if I didn't walk in, I'd have to either go back to the living room and listen to all those kids talk about boring middle school problems, or just wait here until they were done and risk being caught.

With a devilish grin, I decided on the latter. At least I'd be able to hear at least parts of their conversation. I pressed my ear against the wall and closed my eyes, straining to hear what they were saying but failing. I scrunched my eyes even tighter and tried to concentrate. Surely they couldn't be that quiet. After a moment, I realized that they had stopped talking. In a moment of truth, I realized that they were probably about to leave the kitchen and find me with my ear pressed against the wall. My eyes sprung open, and I found myself staring into two faces. I groaned.

"It's not what it looks like, guys, I promise! I just got here and didn't want to ruin the moment. Please continue. I'll be so silent you won't even know I'm here. I'm good at being invisible. In fact, it comes naturally." I gave them a too-cheery smile.

They didn't smile back, but they didn't look angry. In fact, they looked… embarrassed?

Why were they embarrassed? I had seen them holding hands before, so it wasn't like they were committing a felony. Maybe they thought I had heard what they'd said to each other, which I didn't. I reassured them with that fact. "I didn't hear a word you said. Seriously, guys. You should stop sneaking around corners and just be open with the fact that you two like each other. It's not like anyone's going to judge you."

Jackson spoke as he shook his head. "Sis, please stop. Tina and I were just talking. That's all."

I was going to say more, but the doorbell rang, and a very relieved Tina ran to answer it. I turned to Jackson. "Listen, bud, Tina is my friend, and I don't want to see her get hurt. If you're going to ask her out, just do it! If not, stop leading her on! You're my brother, and I love you, but Tina was my first real friend, and I don't want to see that end because you can't make up your mind."

He gave me a pleading look. "Stop. Please? I have to make some really big decisions regarding college, and Tina knows that if I leave to go to college out of state, then I won't see her for years. By that time, she'll have moved on, and I shouldn't expect her to wait for me when she could be having the time of her life. I really like her, but I need to figure out my life before trying to figure out our relationship."

I smiled. "As long as you both understand where the other person stands, then my work is done." I struck a pose like James Bond. "For now." Blowing imaginary smoke off the top of my imaginary gun, I strutted away. I could hear Jackson chuckling behind me. I ignored him and kept going. I wondered whom Tina had answered the door for, so I went back into the living room. Imagine my surprise when there, in the middle of the room, stood Kody. He turned around when I entered and shot me a grin.

"Hey! How've you been since we last talked?"

I shrugged. "Ok, I guess." I wasn't okay. I so wasn't okay. Why in the world did Tina invite him? Sure, their families were really good friends, but she could've at least told me! I felt betrayed. Didn't she realize that Kimberly probably likes Kody, and every minute I spent around him made her angrier and angrier? This is my life that's on the line, people. Kimberly is not somebody you mess around with. She knows where I sleep!

Ok, so maybe I was being a bit dramatic. I took a deep breath. "What about you?"

He tilted his head. "So, so. School's exhausting, and everybody's getting ready for the spring dance that's coming up. I find it all boring."

I perked up at that. "No kidding. Me, too! I detest having to listen to all my friends go on and on about the dance."

He laughed. "Really? I wouldn't have ever guessed it."

Nodding, I allowed myself to smile, since Kim wasn't within a ten-mile range and couldn't do bodily damage to me—right now, that is. "There's a lot about me that people just assume is true. Most of it's wrong, though."

"In that case, you're like an onion."

I squinted my eyes. I think I was just insulted. "Excuse me?"

He shook his head. "That sounded weird. Sorry. Have you ever seen Shrek?"

I nodded, still not knowing what he was talking about.

"Well, you know the part where Shrek is telling Donkey about how ogres are like onions?"

I understood then, remembering the scene.

"You're like an onion. People have to really get to know you to even begin to see the first layer, and then they find out you have a lot more layers underneath."

I smiled. "Thank you—I think. I was worried there for a second because that's something girls say when they're breaking up with someone. The girl says to the guy, 'You're like an onion: you're bald, you smell funny, and you make me cry.' Then she breaks up with him, and that's the end of the story. I was hoping that you weren't calling me bald, stinky, and cruel."

He died laughing. "Not at all."

The rest of the night went very well. Kody and I hung out for much of it, but I didn't really mind it. We talked about all sorts of stuff, including my challenge. He was really intrigued with it. I was glad he was there. Not only was he good company but also I needed to have someone to talk to so I would leave Tina and Jackson alone. I frowned. Maybe that was why Tina invited Kody. Hmm... I decided to find them, realizing that almost everyone had left except for Jackson, Kody, and me, and we all had church in the morning.

I went into the kitchen, but they weren't in there. Puzzled, I wondered where they could be. I began searching the house and eventually found them out on the back porch sitting at the table. They were in another deep conversation, but I wasn't about to repeat my earlier mistake and try to listen. They both had the hearing ability of a bat. Walking out onto the porch, I cleared my throat.

"Jackson, everyone has left except for us and Kody. We'd better leave so we can get a good rest before church tomorrow."

He looked surprised as he checked his watch. "Sorry, Sis, I had no clue it was so late." He looked at Tina. "Thanks for the party. I loved talking with you."

She smiled, but she looked a little reserved, so either she was dead tired and not able to pull out a cheerleader-worthy grin, or they had been talking about some sort of serious topic. Like death. She stood and gave us both a hug, and then we all walked back inside. Kody was pulling on his coat in the living room. He gave Tina a hug and thanked her for the party. Then, he pulled Jackson into a hug.

"Good luck with your college search, man."

Jackson thanked him.

Then, Kody did something I never would have expected. He leaned over and gave me a hug, too. "You know, you're not as bad as Kimberly always made you out to be. I'm glad I got to talk with you tonight."

Stunned, I nodded. "Me too," I said, barely able to form a coherent sentence.

Half-dazed, I sort of stumbled down the steps like a drunkard and made it to the car—barely. As Jackson turned on the ignition and pulled out of the driveway, I thought about what Kody had just said. Kimberly had been talking to him about me? And saying bad stuff? I mean, it's not like that's a big shocker coming from her, but I don't know why she would even bother talking about me unless she thought I was some sort of threat to her make-believe relationship with Kody, which was stupid. Kody didn't even like me. I was only interested in one relationship, and that was between Jackson and Tina. Maybe I should give them a cute couple name, like Tackson. I shook my head; too strange. Jackstina, maybe? I shook my head again. Absolutely not. Suddenly, I had it. Jina! That was it. It was so adorable, and I felt so proud of myself for thinking of it.

When we arrived home, it was eleven thirty, and I was pooped. I wasn't used to being around so many people. I walked inside and into my room. Plopping down in my chair, I pulled out my phone and checked my messages. Iris had texted me back and had said that Monday after school would work best for her. I made a reminder to text her the next morning.

I was very pleased with the outcome of the events of the day. I had a great time at the party, set up another meeting, and found out that there was a whole lot more to Kody Matthew Parker than I had thought. I don't know how I knew his middle name. I frowned, trying to remember. Then, I realized that I had seen his name written on the inside of a girl's locker at school. I had no clue whose locker it was at the time, but it made me laugh. That girl must've been very infatuated with him to write his name in her locker! I would never waste my time thinking about someone who could break my heart. I fell asleep quickly, knowing that morning would come sooner than I wanted.

At church the next morning, Jackson and I decided to sit up front where the youth always sit. I found myself squished between Tina and about two inches of space before the end of the row. We still had four minutes and thirty-five seconds before service began (thank you, countdown), so I tried to get comfortable. Jackson was sitting on Tina's right, so they were talking. I felt so happy that they were sitting next to each other, and that if they said anything, I'd be close enough to hear it! Third wheeling is amazing! I pulled my phone out and realized I still needed to text Iris. I quickly did so and let her know I was good with that. A minute later, she responded and said that she would meet me at Panera. When I looked up again, there were twenty-five seconds left, so I put my phone away. When the minister of music, Laura Allen's husband, stood up and greeted us all, I felt like I could finally relax, stretching slightly as I stood. A week of school had taken its toll on me, and it was good to be able to be in the presence of God and just breathe. I was breathing deeply, eyes closed, body relaxed, and I wasn't really tuned in to what was happening around me. Then I felt a poke on my shoulder as a person came to stand next to me in those two inches of space.

"Are you asleep?"

It wasn't Tina's voice or Jackson's voice, but I recognized it, which meant... My eyes sprung open. Sure enough, Kody was grinning at me. I moved to my right to make more room for him. Tina and Jackson started shuffling until there were a few more inches for Kody to call his own. I answered his question, rolling my eyes. "No, I wasn't asleep. I was just relaxing."

He narrowed his eyes. "Sure, sure. That's what they all say. You can admit that last night was tiring. I know it was very tiring for me. I got home and fell asleep as soon as my head hit the pillow."

Raising my eyebrows, I realized that the music was starting up. "I wouldn't have thought that you tired so easily. Aren't you a party boy?"

He laughed. "Absolutely not. I sleep like a baby at night, and I normally prefer going to bed at ten-thirty, eleven on weekends."

I laughed with him as we began to sing the first song. Service continued, and I tried to concentrate—which was hard, since I was squished next to a guy my sister probably wanted to date, a guy that infatuated her so much that she would kill me if she thought I was a threat. I couldn't understand it. Why in the world would you harbor anger and malice against your own sister just because of a boy? Argh! Life was so complicated. At least he smelled nice.

Out of paranoia, I stayed away from Kimberly for the rest of the day, thinking that she might have spies who informed her about my morning at church. Or she might have planted a camera on me without my knowledge, and she could be planning my death at the very moment. Yeah, 98% of it was my vivid imagination, but there was still that 2% that said that she might actually kill me.

The next day, I told Tina about my upcoming meeting with Iris. Tina squealed. "No way! I love her so much!"

I felt happy that Tina knew of her and was happy that I was meeting with her. I began looking forward to meeting with Iris.

After school, Jackson took me out for ice cream.

"How are you able to spend so much money?" I asked, as we sat and ate our ice cream cones. "You seem to have an unending flow of cash. I mean, soon after you came home, you bought a car."

He smiled. "God provided the money for my car. You remember the family I was staying with for over a year before coming home?"

I nodded. I didn't know them personally, but Jackson had told me about them.

He continued. "Before I left, the dad, Shane, gave me an envelope and told me to open it when I had a big need. Well, when I needed to buy a car, I debated whether or not to open it. I told God that if He wanted me to buy a car, then whatever was in the envelope would be the exact amount I needed. And it was."

I gaped. "That's incredible!"

"Yep, I was pretty amazed myself." He frowned, shaking his head. "But it was just so strange. Whenever I was with that family, there seemed to be something about them that was almost familiar." He shook his head again. "The mom reminded me of someone, but I can't put my finger on who. I can't stand it when that happens!"

I nodded. "Me too. It always takes me days of agony before I forget about it." Satisfied that Jackson hadn't robbed a bank, I enjoyed my double scoop of chocolate ice cream. Once we were done, we left and went back to the house so I could get ready for my meeting with Iris. After going into my room, I pulled on a sweatshirt and tried doing some homework before it was time for Jackson to drive me over to Panera.

When I arrived at the restaurant, I scanned it quickly, searching for anyone who looked like an Iris. Seeing no one but teenagers and a group of old men, I decided that she probably hadn't arrived yet, which was fine since I was early. I simply moved out of the doorway and to a table, where I waited. A minute later, a woman walked into the restaurant and, after scanning the crowd, came to my table.

"Hello, I'm Iris Ray. Are you Brie?"

I nodded. "Yes, ma'am."

We went over to the counter and waited in line. She told me to order whatever I wanted, so when it was our turn, I ordered a soup and salad. She ordered the same thing, and we went to pick out our table while we waited for the food. After sitting down, she placed her purse underneath her chair and asked, "So what questions do you want to ask me today?"

I was mildly surprised that she knew what we'd be doing. Most women didn't, but I guessed that her son-in-law had told her beforehand. "The questions will mainly be about your life."

"Sounds good. Go ahead and start asking while we wait for our order."

"What's your favorite verse?"

"I love Psalm 123:1, which says, 'Unto You I lift up my eyes, O You who dwell in the heavens.'"

She knew that right away. I liked that. I knew if someone asked me, I probably wouldn't be able to give them one immediately. "What are the qualities of a godly woman?"

"The qualities of a godly woman are to love Jesus and love people. If you do those two things, then all the other many qualities of a godly woman will naturally fall into place."

"Does it come easily to you to love people?"

She smiled. "I'd like to think so, but if I could change one thing about myself, it would be that I would be more outgoing. It makes it harder to love people with a large amount of exuberance when you're naturally an introvert." She shook her head. "But I've had to learn an important lesson in my life: God is in constant control. I shouldn't worry about speaking to people and stepping out of my comfort zone. There's nothing we have to worry about. As long as we give Him control, He's in control. We may have to go through difficult seasons, but it's all in the big picture for His glory and His eternal purpose for us.

The people who have hard lives are the ones who have been fighting God, even if they didn't know it."

At that moment, our order number was called, so Iris and I went up to the counter and retrieved our food. Once we sat down again, Iris prayed over the food. Listening to her pray, I realized that what my youth pastor said about her was true: she really was a prayer warrior. After the prayer, I asked her how praying came so easily for her.

"My dad was a person of prayer. It came naturally for him. I grew up in a quiet family, which allowed me to seek God while I was alone—which was a lot."

I ate my soup and thought about that. My dad definitely hadn't been a man of prayer, but hopefully I could reach the point where people thought I was a prayer warrior, too.

She looked at me after she had taken a drink of water. "What are your aspirations in life?"

I shrugged. "I really don't know. I haven't thought much about it because my life has changed a lot in the past few months, and I'm trying to figure out what my life will be like without my brother. He left the family three years ago, and now he's back; but he'll be leaving again in the fall for college." I stopped. "Well, he might. He's not sure yet. He might just be a missionary."

Her eyebrows lifted in interest at that. "Where to?"

Shrugging again, I said, "I'm not sure."

"I've been thinking about missions recently, and I realized that there are more Christians in China than in America. One third of the world is Christian. Most people think that you have to leave your country to be a 'missionary.' That's not the case. America needs help, and while it's still important to go to other countries to spread the gospel, you can be just as effective right here in America."

Finishing up my salad, I smiled. "I'll tell him that. I've never thought of that."

She held up a hand. "However, if that's not his calling, then he shouldn't feel pressured into staying in America just because I mentioned it. He needs to follow God's purpose for his life and not give into the demands and wishes of others who—either knowingly or unknowingly—try to keep him from God's plan. If we try and do God's purpose for our life, He will meet our needs so we can accomplish it. He will always be ready to meet our needs."

Spooning the last bit of soup into my mouth, I checked my phone. Seeing thirteen missed calls from Jackson, I frowned. Looking at Iris, I said, "Can you excuse me for a moment? My brother is trying to reach me, and something might be wrong."

She nodded. "Of course. Take all the time you need."

I stood up and moved to a quiet corner in the restaurant. I had barely heard the phone ring before Jackson picked up.

"Brie! Thank goodness you called."

I was worried. "What's wrong?"

I heard a frustrated sigh in the background. "It's Mom."

"What about her?"

"She's gone."

I froze. "Wait, what?" I couldn't actually believe that. "Jackson, are you sure she's just not at the bar?"

"Yes, I'm positive. She just up and left, and I've been all over town, calling her cell but not getting any answer."

"What happened?"

I could hear him moving, as if he were pacing. Like brother, like sister. I was doing the same thing. "I saw her in the living room and wanted to talk with her about where I had been for the past couple of years. As soon as I mentioned the name of the family I had stayed with, she grew pale and stiffened. I couldn't understand it, Brie. One minute she was fine—well fine for her—and the next minute she was acting as if I said Dad were still alive."

I couldn't understand it, either. "So you have no clue where she went?"

"All she left was a note, but I can't understand it. It just says, 'With Rita.'"

"That shouldn't be too hard to understand, though, right? It means that she's staying with a friend named Rita."

He groaned. "I don't know who Rita is; that's the problem! And Grandmother isn't saying anything. She's holed up in her room and won't come out. I feel so responsible for making her leave, Sis."

I tried to process all of this. "Jackson, come pick me up, and then we can figure this out together at home with Kimberly and maybe Grandmother, if she'll come out of her room." I wasn't sure if she would. Eileen Morgan was one stubborn woman, that was for sure.

Walking quickly back to Iris, I told her that I had a family emergency and had to leave. She was very understanding and told me she'd be praying. I thanked her and gave her a hug. "Sorry we had to cut our meeting short," I said. "I loved spending time with you!"

I only had to wait a couple of minutes out by the curb before Jackson showed up. We didn't talk much on the way home. Once home, we all gathered in the living room, except for Grandmother. I felt like she held a crucial piece of information that would help us in our search for Mom, but who knew? She could just have a stomachache. I shook off thoughts of Grandmother as Jackson, Kimberly, and I began brainstorming about where in the world our mother could be hiding. And what was she hiding from?

Chapter Forty-Six

Hours later, Kimberly decided to head to bed because she had a big test the next day and didn't want to be drowsy. I looked at the clock and realized with a start that it was already 11:00. I gave Jackson a frustrated look.

"It's been hours, and we still have no clue where Mom has gone. My question is, why do we care? It's not like she's ever been there for us."

He sadly shook his head. "You need to let go of your bitterness, Sis. I feel so guilty that she left because of something I said, and as the man of the house, I should have taken better care of her. You wouldn't understand. You're just a kid."

I stood up angrily. "Just a kid? Well, I guess I'm too young and immature to help you find Mom. Have fun trying to bring that drunkard home." I stomped up the stairs and into my room, furious. I could hear Jackson's voice, telling me he didn't mean it like that. I wouldn't listen to him. Slamming the door, I collapsed in my chair. Why did life have to be so frustrating? A tiny part of me regretted having acted that way to Jackson, but he was the one who instigated it by calling me a kid and saying I wouldn't understand. He was right about one thing: I didn't understand. Mom was never there for any of us when we needed her, and all she does now is use up our money on booze. And now, when she disappears, Jackson feels like he needs to run after her? Nope. Good riddance is what I say. We can make it fine on our own.

Even though I knew what I had said was true, I still felt a twinge of regret over what I said about my mom, but I shook those feelings off. If God wanted me to help find my mother, then He would have to give me a sign. A big sign. I wasn't going to waste my time trying to find someone who didn't even want to be here.

For the rest of the week, I awoke every morning with a bitter taste in my mouth. Even after eating breakfast and brushing my teeth, I still tasted it. Every time Jackson drove me to school, he dropped me off without a word. I felt like I needed to apologize, but I didn't know what for. I didn't say anything wrong, right? Everything I said was the truth. The bitter taste grew stronger. All through my classes, I tried to focus but couldn't, as my angry words from Monday night played over and over again in my head. They taunted me, mocked me, and made me feel like an awful person. I couldn't concentrate during church on Sunday, and by lunch on Monday, I was sick.

As soon as Tina sat down next to me at the lunch table, a line appeared on her forehead. "What's wrong?"

I shook my head. "Nothing." Then, I buried my face in my hands. "Everything."

Bewildered, Tina set her hand on my back. "Want to talk about it?"

"No, but I will probably end up telling you anyway. Mom's gone."

She gasped.

"Jackson was talking to her last Monday," I said, "and she just left and hasn't returned. She left a note, saying she was with Rita, but we have no clue who Rita is, and my grandmother won't say a word about any of this, and Jackson feels like he needs to find my mom, but I don't think he should because she's not a good mom, and then we had a fight, and now I feel so awful!" I ended the enormous sentence and took a huge breath. "I don't feel better. In fact, now that I've told you, I feel worse because now you're going to hate me for yelling at Jackson."

She held up a hand. "Before you tell me what I'm going to do, let me speak. First off, I think you have a right to be upset with your mom; however, I don't think that you should be so angry with her that you give her up for lost. People can change. You of all people should know that, and if you don't have any hope for your mom, then how is she going to have hope for herself? As for your fight with Jackson, just apologize to him and make everything right. It's not like you insulted him, but you still yelled at him, and he's probably not feeling too well right now, especially if he said something mean to you, too. Am I right?"

I nodded. "Why aren't you our school counselor?"

She laughed. "They haven't asked me. I would love to go into counseling when I'm older, though. Maybe do it at a church."

After Tina's words of wisdom, I realized that the bitter taste was gone from my mouth. Apparently all I needed was to be able to forgive, and I had done so. Well, that wasn't completely true. I had forgiven Jackson, but I hadn't forgiven my mom, and I still didn't know if I would try and find her or not. I was still waiting for that big sign from God, telling me to find my mom.

When school was over, Jackson picked me up and began the drive home. I immediately started my apology to him, but halfway through, he waved his hand.

"Listen, I really appreciate your apology, and I forgive you, but it doesn't change what you said. You can apologize a million times, but unless you change your heart, this will happen again in the future. I'm sorry for what I said, but I'm still going to search for Mom, with or without your help."

I was silent the rest of the trip home, thinking on what he said. He was right. Even if I was sorry, it would still happen in the future until I truly forgave Mom.

Once we were home, I went for a walk around the neighborhood. After five minutes of walking, I felt someone watching me. Turning around, I gasped. It was the lady in the grey coat again. She walked towards me, still wearing that serene smile.

Opening her mouth, she spoke. "If you continue to hold your mother's faults against her, your heart will become so bitter that you won't be able to move on in life; therefore, you won't be able to completely fulfill God's purpose for your life. Let it go. Don't judge her because you think her faults are greater than yours. Sin is sin in God's eyes; it's not for you to decide whose sin is greater. Jesus came for everyone. Read Luke 5:32."

With that, she turned and walked away. I stared at her retreating back, mouth open. This lady was creepy in the sense that she knew everything about me, but her words hit home. Then I realized, with a start, I still had no clue who she was.

"Wait!" I said, running after her. By the time I came to the place where she had turned onto a different street, she was gone. I slapped my forehead, muttering under my breath. "Every time. When will I ever remember?"

As I began walking home, I looked up the verse she mentioned, Luke 5:32. It read, "I have not come to call the righteous, but sinners to repentance." I felt chills run down my arms. I realized everything she had said was so right. I had been judging my mom, thinking I was a better person than she because I had accepted Christ. Instead, I should have been helping her realize that there was forgiveness for her, too. I shook my head. I had been such a jerk. I wanted to make things right, but I didn't know if it was too late or not. I had to find her first. Suddenly, I knew that the lady in the grey coat was my big sign from God.

When I walked inside, I looked around for Jackson until I found him.

"I've had a change of heart. I want to find Mom so we can try and fix our relationship."

He gave me a skeptical look. "Are you sure? I don't want us to find Mom, and then you two get in a fight."

I nodded. "I probably would've done that, but now I feel differently, and I know I want to bring her home. I shouldn't have judged her for her sins when mine were just covered."

He smiled and pulled me into a hug. "That's great! What are we waiting for? Let's get to work."

We sat down at the dining room table, and Jackson pulled out his computer. It was a laptop he had recently won in a drawing. Some people call it luck. I call it a blessing from God. He had already begun searching people named Rita on the Internet, but hadn't found anything yet. I decided to pull out an old wedding scrapbook I had found in Mom's room and began flipping through it. An hour later, I was only halfway through the book. I kept stopping when I remembered times with my dad (and to discreetly wipe away the tears). Despite my slow progress, I finally found what I was looking for.

"Jackson, look!" I excitedly pointed at a picture in the scrapbook. "Under this photo it says, 'Rita and Hector Carrion.' This could be the Rita Mom's with!"

He quickly searched the full name on the Internet. Immediately, websites popped up, one of them with information on a book entitled My Adventures With God. Once I saw a picture of her on the website, I knew this was the person we were looking for. With a little more research, we found out she lived in Ringgold, Georgia.

Jackson and I high-fived. "We did it!" I exclaimed. Kimberly walked into the house right then, home from her volleyball practice. It was something new she decided to try this past semester, and she was good at it.

After taking a swig of water, she asked, "What's up, guys? What did you guys find?"

I quickly filled her in, watching as a smile lit up her face. "Great!" She said. "Are you guys going to drive down there?"

Jackson and I exchanged glances. "Well," I began, "we don't know exactly where Rita lives. We only know she's in Ringgold."

"I know where she lives." We all turned, surprised, as my grandmother finally emerged from her room.

"Where?" Jackson queried. "I thought you didn't want to help us."

My grandmother shook her head. "I was doing what I thought was best, but I finally prayed about it, and I feel like you all deserve the truth."

Confusion was on all of our faces. I hesitantly voiced the question all of us were wondering. "The truth about what?"

Forty minutes later, packed in Jackson's convertible, all four of us finally arrived at Rita's beautiful house. Grandmother rang the doorbell while Jackson, Kimberly, and I stood there nervously, not knowing what to expect. I was very confused. My mom had left, supposedly hiding from something, but I had no clue what she was hiding from!

A woman opened the door. I recognized her face from the picture in the scrapbook. She smiled wide. "Eileen Morgan? I can't think of the last time I saw you!" Then, she turned to my siblings. "Jackson? Oh my goodness, you were just a toddler the last I saw you, and Kimberly! How you have changed!" Then she saw me. "Are you really Hazel? So tall and matured? The last time I saw you, you were a baby!"

I nodded. I was surprised when she used my given name. Since everyone called me Brie, I had accepted it as my name, but I guessed that since I didn't know her, and apparently the last time she saw me was when I was a baby, that was before everyone started calling me Brie.

Rita ushered us inside and told us to sit down in the living room while she brought in some water for us. Jackson, Kimberly, and I all glanced at one another, not sure what was happening. Soon, Rita came back with our water and sat down.

"What have all of you been doing recently?"

Jackson gave her a rundown of himself, adding in how he was looking to do mission work overseas. She seemed happy at that. Kimberly went next, telling her a bit about volleyball, but then we all fell silent and looked around uncomfortably. Was Mom even here?

She seemed to read our minds. "I'm going to assume you're all here for Penny, is that correct?"

We all nodded. I spoke first. "Is she here?"

Rita held up a hand. "First I want to know why you're looking for her."

"We want her to come home," Jackson said. "I feel so bad that I made her run off, and I want her to know that even if she has some faults in her life, we still love her and won't abandon her."

Rita smiled and then angled her head toward a hallway. "It's safe, Penny. You can come out now."

We all whipped our heads around as she walked out of a bedroom, a confused expression on her face. She looked at each of us in turn. "Why do you all feel this way when I've been such a horrible mother?"

"You're our mother, and that's all that matters, no matter what you've done," I said, my voice strong and confident. Jackson and Kimberly nodded their agreement. Grandmother simply cleared her throat, and my mother dropped her head.

"What did I say wrong?"

Rita smiled. "You didn't say anything wrong, dear. It's just...well, never mind." She stood. "Anyone up for something to eat?"

Since I hadn't eaten since lunch, and it was nearing dinner, I nodded. "I'd love something, as long as it's not Brie cheese." Jackson and Kimberly laughed and told Rita the story. When she heard it, she laughed, too.

I went into the kitchen with Rita to help her get some food out. Before leaving, I saw my mom tentatively sit down on the couch and Jackson beginning to talk with her. I hoped he would be able to get the answer from her about why she ran away.

Rita must have noticed my frown. "What have you been doing lately with your life?"

I told her a little bit about my backstory and then about my challenge. She seemed impressed.

"That's amazing! I'm a Christian, too, but I haven't always been one, and changing from one lifestyle to the other is pretty difficult."

Sensing a story, I asked, "How did you become a Christian?"

"I was living with a guy for 11 years. We weren't married. I wondered at one point what it would be like to be married to a minister. One day, my friend called me and said that God had told her to burn her tarot cards. She bought a Bible and began reading it. Later, she was talking with me and told me that the Bible says a person is either for God or against God. I figured that since I wasn't exactly against God, I was for Him."

I hadn't heard that until I became a Christian. Either way, I probably wouldn't have listened to that, anyway.

"The next day, my friend called again and said that she read that you're either hot or cold for the Lord. It's like coffee. If you're cold, then God's not going to want to drink you, but if you're hot, then He'll really be able to use you to build His kingdom. After hearing her say that, I turned on the TV and there was a preacher on it. He said, 'You, yes, you.' Then he listed 13 sins I was doing. He said, 'Get on your knees.' I got on my knees. He led me through renouncing every one of the 13 things. Then he led me to the Lord. I felt pure. God told me to clean out my bedroom closet. I did so and found an astrology book. I threw it away. I did a bunch of spiritual house cleaning. My boyfriend was not in the house when I got saved. I called him and said that he had to move out of the house. Once I became a Christian, everything in my life changed."

"Yet, even as a sinner, God was looking out for me. Once, I was at a party, and the cops showed up and started searching people. Unbeknownst to me, someone had snuck pills into my pocketbook, and the cops found them. I told them they weren't mine, but they had heard that a million times before, so they didn't believe me. I had to go to court and fill out paperwork. One of the questions they asked me was to draw a tree, so I drew a tree, including the roots. When the judge saw my drawing, he asked why I drew the roots. I said that I was told to draw a tree, not half a tree. The judge allowed me to go home that day. Even then, God had a plan for my life. I have some incredible stories of my adventures with God."

"Didn't you write a book with that title?" I asked, as I remembered our Internet search.

She nodded. "Yes. Have you read it?" I shook my head. "Well, I can just tell you some of the stories myself while we have the time, if that is okay?"

"Better than okay. I'd love that!"

Rita and I grabbed some plates of food and went out to the back porch to eat chicken salad and talk while everyone else was inside.

"Where do I start? Hmm, let me see." Rita cleared her throat. "I was a hairstylist for a good part of my life. I was working one day at the salon when I heard a customer using God's name in vain. I felt like a knife went through my heart. I said, 'God, what is it?' He said, 'That's what it feels like when people use My name in vain.' I was about to tell the woman what God said when the devil whispered that if I did, I'd lose all my customers. I did it anyway. The woman was so mad that she yanked the rollers out of her hair and walked out of the salon. The next week she came back and said, 'I used the Lord's name in vain at least 100 times this week.' I just stared at her. The woman then said, 'But I heard myself every time I said it. I no longer use His name in vain.' You see, if I hadn't spoken to that woman, she'd still be using God's name in vain. Hearing His voice and obeying it is the key. If you simply listen to Him but don't obey, then what's the point of Him even talking? You have to obey if you want to see big things happen."

I shook my head. I've heard kids at school misusing God's name all the time. I had gotten to the point where I didn't notice it because I was so used to hearing it. Now I knew that I wouldn't be able to listen to people say stuff like that without remembering this story. Even Christians at the school misused His name.

"But obedience isn't always fun and easy," she said, after taking a drink of water. "One day, my husband kept asking me to do things that he could've easily done. After he asked for coffee when the coffeepot was five feet away, I felt like slamming the cup down on the table. Right before I was about to do it, God said to me, 'As you do to your husband, you do to Me.' I calmed down and gave him his coffee. It was hard not to pour it on his shirt, but worth it to keep my calm and be a servant of God, obeying what He wanted me to do. I believe that a married woman who is godly should put her husband right under God and let him be the head of the house—although as I just related," she said, laughing, "it is not always easy to do."

"Speaking of obedience, here's another story about doing what God tells you. In my old house, I had a cross on the wall of my master bedroom, and the carpet was blood red. I wasn't too sure how I felt about the carpet color; however, God gave me a dream that the cross was dripping blood onto the rug. I knew then that I couldn't change the color. Instead, I ended up painting 13 drops on the wall from the cross to the carpet. 13 means sin and atonement. Then, I happened to mention the room in a conversation with an unsaved friend. When the friend saw my room, she sat by the cross and wept. She was saved that day. If I hadn't painted it like Jesus showed me in the dream, there's a good chance she wouldn't be saved right now."

"Are you an artist?" I asked.

She nodded. "Yes, I am. In fact, I have created a ton of paintings and sketches. Do you want to see some of them?"

"Sure!"

We walked back inside, passing the family eating at the kitchen table. Rita led me into a back bedroom where she opened the closet to reveal dozens of paintings. I was amazed. They were all fantastic, and I hadn't even seen all of them. Rita began to pull them out of the closet, showing them to me. With each one, I was more and more enthralled. Finally, after all of the paintings were out, she turned to me.

"Pick one out."

I gaped. "Really?"

She nodded. "Take whichever one you want."

Hesitantly, I began going through them, too excited to believe it was true. I've never owned a piece of artwork before. After much contemplation, I chose a gorgeous painting of a sunset on the beach with the silhouette of a child in the foreground and the words "Be still and know I am God" on the sunset.

Rita remarked, "Those words are from Psalm 46:10, which is probably my favorite Bible verse. You must wait and watch for the Lord. If you just wait, you won't be looking for Him."

Seeming pleased with my choice, Rita led me back outside. Once we were seated in our chairs, I commented, "You seem to be in tune with God. Does He often answer your prayers?"

"Yes, He does. Would you like to hear about some He has answered?"

"I would love to!"

"One summer, I felt dry spiritually, so I asked God what I was supposed to do. He told me to wake up at 5 a.m. every morning all summer. I made a prayer closet with the names of God written on all the walls. I wrote down the Lord's Prayer and expounded on it. Then I expounded on the names of God, but I skipped over His name El. Now, listen. God wants you to be specific in your prayers because then when your prayers get answered you know that it's Him. I had prayed for flowers that were too old to sell but too beautiful to throw away—a very specific prayer. I forgot my prayer. Later, two people who were staying at my house came home from a florist shop with a bouquet of yellow roses—31 in all. The florist had said he had roses that were too old to sell but too beautiful to throw away, so they decided to take the roses and give them to me. Thirty-one means El, the one name of God I skipped over when writing my list. God is so good!"

I nodded in agreement and munched on some more chicken salad. The sandwich was incredible, but her stories were even better.

"I had just recently gotten saved," she said, starting another story, "and wanted a locket in the shape of a Bible with scriptures written inside. I truly believe that a godly woman should honor the Word of God as truth. Well, I prayed about my desire, and one day God told me to go to a flea market. I went to a jewelry table and asked for that specific piece. The woman said she had been putting that specific locket out for the past ten years, until she no longer set it out because no one would buy it. That was a very specific prayer that God answered."

"Another time we needed a couch. The one we wanted was $4,000. We didn't have that kind of money for a couch; however, we found out that the furniture store was having a drawing where customers picked a number out of a basket. If it was a certain number, they could get almost anything 50% off. Before picking, I prayed that God would direct my fingers to the right number. It was. The woman who was holding the basket was dumbfounded. She said that I was the first person to pick from the basket, and I had found the right number—and there was only one 'right number' in the whole basket."

I gaped. The chances of her picking the right number were—if my calculations were correct—slim.

"Despite the fact that we picked the right number, we found out from the salesman that the couch we wanted wasn't a part of the sale. I told the salesman that I had prayed about it. Now, he wasn't a Christian, but he still told the manager what I requested. When the salesman came back, he was mad because the manager said that we could buy it with the discount. I asked for it to be delivered that day. It was Christmas Eve, and the chances of them delivering that day were very slim. But God doesn't work based on chance, and it was delivered that day."

What an amazing saying! I'm taping that to my mirror. "God doesn't work based on chance."

"God has not only answered many of my prayers but He has also given me dreams."

"Like Daniel?"

She nodded. "I once had a dream I was in heaven. I was in the library in heaven. I was reading a book and felt as though I were about to wake up. I began repeating a phrase over and over so I could remember it. When I woke up, I wrote it down. It said, 'We work well together. The drinking glass and the formula.' It was talking about how no matter how puffed up you get in life, you're only a drinking glass. It's what's inside that really matters."

"Another day I was at the salon, doing the hair of a woman who had been a customer for 10 years. Her name was Doris, and she never chatted, but it was always the same routine. One day, Doris didn't show up. I was a bit puzzled because she never missed appointments. That night, I had a dream that I went to the hospital, and Doris was in a hospital bed. I witnessed to her and she accepted Christ. The next morning in the salon, a man walked in and said he was Doris' husband. He asked me if I were Rita. When I told him I was, he said that Doris had died the night before."

I gasped. That was horrible!

"I felt so awful that I hadn't had time to go to the hospital and talk to Doris, but then he said something that was strange. He thanked me for coming to the hospital the night before and leading his wife to the Lord. He said that he too was now a Christian. I was so awestruck. I knew that I hadn't gone to the hospital in person, but he and his wife had seen me that night, and what he said was what my dream had been about."

I'm pretty sure my jaw clattered onto my lap. She had teleported? That was like something from a movie! God works in mysterious ways, for sure. I never thought that could have been possible, but I'm beginning to learn that with God, nothing is impossible.

"In another dream, I saw a table with two objects on it, and several demons around it. One demon said to the other, 'If the humans ever got ahold of these two objects, it would be all over for us.' I saw a harp on the table, which symbolized worship. I couldn't see what the other object was, so I walked closer to the table. When I got near enough, I grabbed the object, a mass of material that was all wound up. The demons started chasing me, trying to get it back. I released part of the material and it began to unwind, revealing what it said: 'Holiness unto the Lord.' I told a prophet at my church about the dream, and she shared about a dream she had had where she saw a cloth falling from heaven that read, 'Holiness unto the Lord.' I wanted to make a banner like it, but God wouldn't let me until nine years had gone by. When I finally made the banner, the letters were out of chipped mirror."

I was amazed with her stories. She was talking about things that I had never thought about and I didn't even know were possible. She had showed me a whole new part of

God, that God wants me to pray specific prayers and that God can make the supposed impossible possible.

"This is the last story I'm going to share because I can see your family getting ready to leave. God wanted me to start a Bible study. I didn't even know the Bible that well, but I obeyed. Every week, God told me what to teach, and people got saved. One man at the study was a demonologist who worked for the courts. If a criminal stated, 'The devil made me do it' as their excuse for breaking the law, he would be called in to investigate whether it was true or not. One day he got a call to investigate a certain man. When he arrived at the house, the man threw himself against the wall, so the demonologist realized that the man was definitely demon-possessed. Well, the demonologist didn't know what to do next, so he called my husband and me. We went to this house and walked inside. What we saw was pretty freaky. There was furniture floating around the house, and there was an upside down cross in blood on the man."

I felt a chill run down the back of my spine. It was as if I were watching a horror movie.

"His wife and two kids were hiding in a different part of the house. Hector and I talked to the wife and led her to the Lord, as well as her daughter. Her other child was just a baby. We then had a short Bible study with her. The woman, who was previously Catholic, immediately threw away all of her Catholic statues. I then went into the man's bedroom. It was very cold, unnaturally cold. I bound the devil in Jesus' name and was able to lead the man to the Lord. That wasn't all, though. God wanted the man to be filled with the Holy Spirit; however, every time we tried to tell the man about the Holy Spirit, he went into a trance. I prayed for angels to show up in that room to fight off all the demons. Immediately, I felt crowded, like angels were on all sides. Then we started praying in tongues. The man was thrown across the room and hit the bathroom sink, but when he arose, he was free from the demons. He told us that he had had a pain in his stomach for 20 years, and now that pain—the demons—was gone."

I was floored. "That's so incredible!" I couldn't quite wrap my mind around all of this. I felt goose bumps on my arms. I would have loved to see God's power at work in that room, to be able to feel His presence and know that no power in hell could stand against the awesome glory of God.

We rose from our chairs and went inside. Rita first handed me the painting I had picked out and then gave everyone a hug.

Turning to my mom, she said, "I'm glad you came down. Even if you didn't mean for it to turn into a family visit, it did, and I'm grateful to have had the chance to reconnect with all of you. Penny, don't forget what I told you. Eileen, make sure you don't go crazy with all of these munchkins." Everyone laughed. "Hazel, or should I say Brie, never give up hope! Keep up with your studies so you can excel in your work. Kimberly, don't twist anything in volleyball. And Jackson, I hope you find the perfect country in which to share the gospel. I'll be praying for you."

I deflated at that. I had gotten used to the idea of Jackson possibly going somewhere for only a little while to do mission work, but with Rita praying for him to find the perfect place, I knew God would answer her prayer, and then Jackson would never want to come home! On the way out of the house, Rita pulled me aside.

"Everything okay?"

I told her how I felt about Jackson leaving.

She nodded sympathetically. "Here's some advice. If you have someone you love, let them go. If you want what's best for them, let them go because if you try and hold on to them forever, then when they do leave, it'll be heartbreaking."

I lifted my chin. "Thank you." I gave her a hug and then walked out to join the rest of my family. Grandmother wanted to ride home with Mom in the van, so Jackson, Kimberly, and I piled into Jackson's convertible again for the trip home. All during the ride, I thought about Rita's words of wisdom. She was one in a million, that's for sure. Just then, I slapped my forehead. It hit me that I had just met with another godly woman! And I didn't even set it up or ask her the standard questions! So that is what mentoring is all about: not just setting up meetings and checking them off a list but spending time with people and listening to their stories and their experiences from life.

I laughed out loud, which drew some glances from Jackson and Kimberly. Speaking of Jackson, I remembered what Rita had said about him. I knew it wasn't going to be easy to let Jackson go, but it would be better for Jackson if I did so. That way, he wouldn't constantly feel awful for leaving when I selfishly tried to hold on to him.

But as I thought about my time at Rita's, I remembered one small detail I had forgotten: I still didn't know why Mom had left in the first place.

"Jackson, when I was with Rita, did you guys talk to Mom about why she left?"

He nodded. "I tried, but Mom and Grandmother kept changing the subject every time it came around, so I eventually stopped mentioning it. I can't believe it was random, though. I don't know what happened to make her run away like that." He looked at me in the rearview mirror, determination glinting in his eyes. "But I intend to find out."

Chapter Forty-Seven

The week flew by. Church on Sunday was great, as usual, but it was even better when Grandmother attended with Jackson and me. She didn't sit with the youth, of course, but she was there all the same and told us afterwards that she liked it. Mom had been in her bedroom all weekend, but when I would quietly tiptoe in there occasionally, I didn't see any empty bottles, so maybe, just maybe, she was changing. All throughout the school week, I kept praying. Mom would leave for work, but she never came home with alcohol; and she came home on time, so I knew she hadn't been to a bar. By Friday, it had officially been a week and four days since we had found Mom. Despite that fact, I hadn't seen much of her. Grandmother went into her room every evening, but we kids never ventured in—partly because we didn't know what to say but mostly because Grandmother "advised against it."

I had just finished the last homework assignment and was about to head down to the kitchen to grab a snack when I realized that I had been so focused on my mom this week that I hadn't met with anyone for my challenge! I groaned. I only had six more women to meet with, so with forty-six meetings under my belt, it was getting harder to find women.

I did the only thing I could think of that sounded reasonable: I prayed. I told God that I didn't have the motivation to find someone to meet with, so could He please drop someone in my lap? Feeling a lot better, I went downstairs to grab the snack I needed.

Munching on a Pop-Tart, I was scrolling through my text messages when Jackson walked into the kitchen.

"Hey, are you interested in hanging out with me tomorrow morning?"

I stuck the last bit of Pop-Tart in my mouth. "Of course! What do you want to do?"

"I was thinking about going to eat at Cracker Barrel. I get to serve food there, but I never get to eat it, and I want a chance to finally sit down and just eat their amazing food."

"I'm cool with that. What time do you want to leave?"

"Around 9:00 in the morning."

"Great. I'll be ready by then."

Saturday morning, I woke up earlier than I normally did and got dressed. Jackson was waiting for me when I came downstairs. We hopped into his car and began the drive to Cracker Barrel.

Once there, many people greeted Jackson, and he introduced me to them. We were seated quickly, and I began perusing the menu to figure out what I wanted to eat. I finally decided on their pancake breakfast. It was a lot, but I was pretty hungry. Jackson got the same. Our food came shortly, and we prayed and then dug in. Halfway through my second pancake, I felt like someone was looking at me. I turned around in my seat and scanned the restaurant. A person sitting in a far booth waved at me. With wide eyes, I waved back. It was Kody, with his mom and dad, and his ten-year-old identical twin brothers, Alex and Chris. I could never tell them apart because they both had blond hair and green eyes, they both played soccer, and their mom, Ivy Parker, loved dressing them in matching outfits. I only knew them because Kelsey's little brother was on their soccer team. Most of the time when I hung out with Kelsey, they would have a soccer game that we would attend. Kelsey's family sat with Kody's family, as would I whenever I was there.

Kody waved me over. "How are you doing?"

"Pretty great. Jackson and I came here for breakfast. What about you guys?"

"We're here for some family time. Normally there's always some sort of soccer game or event on Saturdays, but not today; so we decided to spend some time together."

"Cool!" I looked at Jackson, who was still eating. "Well, I'd better go back to my food."

I walked to my table again. Jackson, when he saw who I had been talking with, waved to the Parkers. I thought about them as I finished breakfast. They were so much fun to be around, especially the mom, Ivy. I had called her Mrs. Parker when I first met her, but both she and her husband insisted I just call them Ivy and Devan. She had black hair—naturally blond—and green eyes, while Devan had blond hair and blue eyes. Ivy and I were a lot alike in our personalities.

Once Jackson and I finished our breakfast, he walked over to say hi to the Parkers. Out of the blue, Ivy invited Jackson and me to come over for dinner Sunday afternoon. We were more than happy to accept.

On our way out of the restaurant, we passed a table with an older woman sitting by herself. Completely oblivious to my surroundings, I walked a little too close to the table and accidentally bumped her cup. Almost in slow motion, coffee sloshed over the sides and all over the table. I gasped in horror.

"I am so sorry, ma'am." I grabbed a wad of napkins and began wiping up the mess. I chanced a look at her, hoping she wasn't too mad.

To my utter surprise, she began laughing. "My cup truly runs over."

Jackson joined her in her laughter, and soon I was even chuckling a bit, even though I still felt awful.

She held out her hand. "My name's Gail Lemmert."

As I shook it, I realized that some people at church had referred me to her for counseling. "My name's Brie, and this is my brother Jackson. I love the Bible verse you just said. I had never thought about applying it a situation like this, though."

Her eyebrows went up as a pleasantly surprised expression lit her face. "You're a Christian, too? That's amazing! How long have you been saved?"

Seeing an opportunity, I told her how I was an atheist for most of my life and how God brought me to Himself about 4 months ago through a mentoring challenge I was doing. I then went on to explain a little bit about the challenge. Suddenly, I realized that she could be the answer to my prayer. Quickly, I asked if she had a couple of hours to spare today to meet with me.

"I would love to do that," she said enthusiastically.

"Perfect!"

Jackson gave me a hug. "See you later, Brie."

She led me out to her car, where we climbed in. "Would you like to go to my house to chat? Whenever you get hungry, I can fix you a sandwich or something."

"That'll be great!" I said.

During the drive to her house, I asked her about herself. I found out that she used to be a counselor at Lee University. After giving me a brief synopsis of her life, she then turned the question around to me.

"What about you? What do you like doing?"

"I don't play any sports at my school, but I like to play tennis, and I play the piano. I have two siblings, but my dad died three years ago."

She patted my hand sympathetically, looking at me briefly before continuing to drive. "I'm so sorry. I understand loss. Four years ago, my only daughter died of cancer. A mass on her appendix and colon had traveled to her liver."

"Oh, no. That's awful."

Nodding, she said, "I've experienced a lot of loss in my life. I divorced my husband after being married to him for 16 years. I found out he had been having an affair for five years with another woman. He told me that he loved both of us, so I said he had to make a choice. He moved in with the other woman. I eventually remarried, but that was a painful experience to go through."

We arrived at her house. Walking inside, she led me onto a patio where we sat down on a swing. She continued talking. "The divorce affected me more than I would have thought. One day, soon after my divorce, I was out driving, and I saw an 18-wheeler coming towards me. A voice in my head told me that if I swerved just a little bit, I wouldn't have to worry about the divorce anymore; but then I felt like God said to me that the divorce wasn't the end of God's plan for me and that He had a good plan for my life."

I could relate. I had had my own doubts about whether I should live or not, but now I viewed life differently. It took time for me to believe that God actually had prepared a plan for me, that I wasn't just put on the earth for no reason.

"I almost lost my current husband, too."

I leaned forward in my seat. "How?"

"One and a half years ago, I went to a restaurant with my husband, Al. It was pretty windy, and when Al tried to open the door, the wind caught the door and hit him, knocking him flat on the ground. When I ran to him, there was a pool of blood on the ground already. A nurse was near the area and came rushing over. While she was staunching the blood flow, she noticed blood on his shoe. Confused, she rolled up his pant leg. There was a bone sticking completely out of his leg. He's still trying to heal from that injury."

I gasped. "That's awful!" I shook my head, grimacing. "I hate pain. Even thinking about other people in pain gives me pain."

"Even though pain hurts, pain causes you to learn lessons you won't learn otherwise. For example, I don't think I would have done what I've done with my life if I hadn't experienced pain. I felt a calling on my life when I was a little girl. I didn't know what to do, however, because there weren't a lot of women's ministries I could get involved in. I finally found my niche in counseling. I have a heart for people because of the pain I've been through. I can now understand pain better and relate to people better because of what's happened to me."

She was right. If I hadn't known the feeling of loneliness, I couldn't relate to so many people at my school when I talked to them. Normally, if I see someone crying in the hall, I stop to talk with them and see what's wrong. When they learn I'm a Christian, they brush me off, thinking I could never relate to their problems. That's when I tell them about my family situation and what I've been through. Once they realize we have a lot in common, they open up, and I'm able to share with them some about Jesus. My once non-existent friend group has been expanding more than I could have ever hoped.

A pensive look came upon her face. "We only really come to know God when we go through hard times. You don't fully believe God is Provider until He provides for you. That's when you have more faith."

She stopped talking suddenly as she looked at her watch. "Oh, my. Are you hungry? It's nearly two o'clock."

I was shocked. "Yes, I am, but I didn't realize how long we had been talking!"

As she began making grilled cheese sandwiches, I asked her what she thought the qualities of a godly woman were.

"I believe the qualities of a godly woman are to have honesty, truthfulness, a servant's heart, and to be a woman of the Word."

There's that servant's heart again. "What's your favorite Bible verse?"

"My favorite verse is John 10:10, which says, 'The thief does not come except to steal, and to kill, and to destroy. I have come that they may have life, and that they may have it more abundantly.' I know that sounds like a strange pick for a favorite verse, but I love how it doesn't just stop with how the thief comes. It ends the verse with Jesus promising us to give us life more abundantly."

I had to admit, I never thought that would've been anyone's top pick. That verse is quoted when people are talking about how evil Satan is, but I realized that everyone just seems to forget that there's a second part to that verse, one that gives hope.

"What's an adventure you've had in your lifetime?"

She thought about that. "When I went to Indonesia to speak at a women's conference. Some of the women who came had just faced horror: a group of Muslims had come into their village and beheaded many of their husbands. When they sang at the conference, it was so mournful. Their pain was so evident in their singing."

If I had been there, I would have cried. Just seeing people who have gone through something like that would have felt like a kick in my gut; but, as Gail said, pain can help you relate to people better. Maybe God wants those women to be able to share their story of how they kept serving God even after tragedy happened to them.

The sandwiches were finished, so Gail set them on the table, and we dug in. Soon after lunch, I texted Jackson where I was so he could pick me up. While we waited for Jackson, Gail and I went on a walk down the block. The day was beautiful, with no clouds and the perfect temperature. We walked for at least fifteen minutes before returning to her house. By that time, Jackson was just pulling into her driveway. I gave her a hug as I said goodbye.

"Thank you for your time and for the sandwiches!"

She laughed. "You are most welcome. Anytime, my dear."

On the way home, I told Jackson how the meeting went. He seemed pretty happy that I had a good time. Speaking of having a good time, I couldn't wait to spend tomorrow afternoon with the Parkers. What a great day it had been. Not only had I met with a godly woman and learned a lot from her but I had also been invited over to the house of an amazing guy!

Chapter Forty-Eight

Sunday morning I was getting ready for church when I received a text from Kody. He wanted to know if I had scheduled anyone to meet with me for my challenge yet. I told him no. He told me that his maternal grandparents were in town, and his grandmother was a very godly woman. I could see where he was going with this. I said that I would love to meet with her.

Later, when I saw him at church, he gave me the details. "She will be leaving this evening, so she's only free this afternoon. You can back out if you want to."

I thought about it. If I accepted, I wouldn't be able to have dinner with the Parkers, but I would be able to meet with a woman for the week. If I declined, I could have dinner with them, but I wouldn't have any one-on-one time with his grandmother. I furrowed my brow. "I think I'll still meet with her."

He nodded. "Okay. My grandmother said that she would take you out for dinner after church. Whenever you are done with your meeting, she'll bring you back to our house, and we can play some games before heading to church tonight. Jackson is still welcome to come over for dinner, though. By the way, my grandmother's name is Diane Lytle."

"Alright. Thanks, Kody."

"No problem. We'll have to compensate for the dinner you won't be able to have with us by having you over another Sunday."

I laughed. He was so sweet. Church began then, and Kody and I stopped talking. After service, Kody took me to the back of the church, where his parents normally sat. Next to them were his grandparents. I walked over to his grandmother, and as soon as she realized I was the girl she was meeting with, she gave me a hug.

"My grandson has told me all about you, dear. I can't wait to get to know you better!"

I smiled. Kody had talked to his grandmother about me? Strange... I shook my fantasy thoughts away. Of course, he would talk to her about me so she would know something about me. We all walked outside, with Jackson and Kody talking, Ivy and Devan talking, Alex and Chris talking, and Kody's grandparents talking. That left me walking by myself and talking to myself.

Once we arrived at where our cars were parked, relatively close to one another, we figured out seating arrangements. Jackson would drive his car over to the Parker residence, Kody would take his car, Ivy, Devan, and Ivy's dad would ride together, and I would ride in Diane's vehicle so we could head over to the restaurant. As I climbed into Diane's van, I marveled at how large it was. There was so much legroom! Jackson's car had its perks, but its legroom was equivalent to what you got on an airplane. She pulled out of the parking lot and began driving.

Looking over at me, she said, "Do you have a preference of where you want to eat today?"

I shook my head. "I'm fine with anything."

"We'll eat at Golden Corral, then. It's just a few minutes until we're there."

Once we had arrived at the restaurant, Diane and I walked inside where she paid and we got our drinks. As I grabbed a plate, I walked around the restaurant, wondering what I should eat first. I quickly decided on sweet potatoes with chicken as a starter. Diane had also gotten a plate of food, so we found a table and sat down to eat. She asked me to pray, so I did. Afterwards, as I dug in, I sighed in pleasure.

"This is amazing!"

She agreed with me. "I love coming here. I don't come here often, but when I do, it's a treat."

After swallowing my mouthful of chicken, I said, "I'm going to ask you some questions, if that's okay."

"That's perfectly fine. Ask away."

"What do you think the qualities of a godly woman are?"

"I believe the qualities of a godly woman are to help others, attend church, have good endurance, pray, and not throw a temper tantrum when things don't go your way."

"What's your favorite Bible verse?"

"Proverbs 3:5-7. It says, 'Trust in the Lord with all your heart, and lean not on your own understanding. In all your ways acknowledge Him, and He shall direct your paths. Do not be wise in your own eyes; fear the Lord and depart from evil.'"

That was one of my favorites, as well. I drank some water as I pondered what my next question would be. "If you could change one thing about yourself, what would it be?"

She answered immediately. "Nothing. I think people should be fully content with who they are."

I was amazed. Out of all the women I'd asked that to, she was the only one who had said that she wouldn't change a thing. My eyes were opened to the realization that I should—and could—be content with who I am and not constantly wish to be someone else.

"What's an enjoyable adventure that you've had?"

"One of my favorite adventures was when my husband and I drove along the Pacific coastline in California."

I sighed. "I've always wanted to go to California." I hoped to one day visit all 50 states and do something fun in each one of them.

We were both done with our meals by now, so it was time to hit the dessert bar. I selected many goodies, and after eating them, I was stuffed to the max. I managed to waddle out of the restaurant and heave myself up into the van. After buckling in, I asked my last question.

"What's a life lesson you've learned?"

She began pulling the van out of the parking space as she responded. "A life lesson I would want to give you is this: stay on the right path and don't venture off. But if you do venture off of it, make sure you immediately get right back on it."

As I thought about what she said, we drove down the road a little ways, and then unexpectedly she pulled into the parking lot at Lowe's. She led me into the store to the back, where the wood was kept. Turning to me, she asked, "What do you see?"

I scrunched my eyebrows together. Wasn't it obvious? "Wood."

She tilted her head. "Maybe technically speaking, but I see the making of a house."

We left the store and got back into her van. She then drove to Aldi. I was confused at what she had said back at Lowe's. I had never thought about wood in that way. Once we were in the store, she looked at me.

"What do you see?"

I felt like "food" wasn't the answer she was looking for, so I thought a little harder. "The opportunity to feed people?"

"The making of a body."

I was beginning to see a theme. She then drove us to our next stop, a church, and I felt like I might have a better chance at getting the answer right.

"What do you see?"

I thought hard. "The making of a world-wide phenomenon?"

"You're getting closer. The making of a soul for a free trip to heaven."

Lastly, she drove to Lee University. "What do you see?"

"The making of a brain?"

She smiled widely. "Close. The making of a mind."

Feeling much better about myself when I realized I had practically gotten it right, I was in much better spirits when we pulled into the Walmart parking lot. We entered the store and she bought a bouquet of roses.

Once we had climbed back into the van, she said. "We are like a rose. God wants us to fully bloom in His timing; but we have a tendency to think that He needs assistance in helping us bloom, so we try to bloom early." She began pulling at the petals, trying to get the flowers to open up. Every time she pulled at the petals, however, the petals broke off until there weren't any petals left on the rose, just the stem. "When we try to get ahead of God, all that we're left with is thorny trouble."

I stopped for a minute to think about that. I was guilty of that. Trying to get ahead of God is almost second nature for me, especially since I had done everything on my own for years before I became a Christian. I was still ruminating on what she had said as we climbed once more into her van so we could head to the Parker home.

As we walked into the house, Kody came out from the living room and gave me a hug. "How was it?"

I smiled at him. "Amazing. Diane is full of deep truths!"

"Well, that's why I wanted you to meet with her. I've been learning from her all my life!"

We walked into the living room together. Jackson and the rest of the Parker family were playing Scattergories, and it seemed like they were almost finished.

Kody spoke up. "Guess who's here, guys?"

They all said hello, and then Kody offered me a chair before sitting back down into his chair. The game lasted for another three minutes. Apparently they had been playing for at least half an hour, so they added up all their points from the multiple games they had played. Devan won, with Jackson coming in a close second. The twins both had pretty low scores, and Kody and his mom tied. They decided to play a different game next. We all agreed that we should pick an easier game for the twins' sake, so Mad Uno was chosen. Due to the length of the twins' arms, we all sat on the floor. Kody plopped down next to me, and Jackson sat down on my other side.

After ten minutes, the game was finished when I laid down my last card. Victorious, I stood up and raised both hands. "Boom!"

They all laughed. As Devan checked his watch, he slowly stood.

"Sorry to leave so soon after you got here, Brie, but I need to head to the church because I have a leadership meeting."

I gave him a hug. "No worries. I understand." Devan was one of the small group leaders for the youth at Westmore, as well as Ivy, but she didn't have to be at the meeting today. Once he left, the twins got bored of the games, so they went out into the backyard to jump on the trampoline. Kody asked if we were up for a movie, and both Jackson and I agreed. Ivy went into the kitchen to get some snacks, and Jackson and I sat down on the sofa as Kody popped the DVD in. He came back over and sat down next to me, which made Jackson look over at Kody with a quizzical expression on his face before facing forward again as The Fellowship of the Ring started. Kody was forever and a day quoting The Lord of the Rings, but Jackson and I had never watched any of the movies, so we were always confused. Kody had said that we should all watch it together sometime, but I didn't expect it to actually happen. I guess since people in my life always made empty promises, I never really trusted that someone would actually do what was promised.

Ivy came in just a few seconds later, popcorn and drinks in hand. I reached for the bowl of popcorn and dug in. This was absolutely perfect.

Three hours, and forty-eight minutes later—including two trips to the kitchen to grab more popcorn—the movie was over. I stretched my legs.

"That was a great movie! No wonder you love The Lord of the Rings so much!"

He nodded. "Yup. And that's only the first movie."

I stared at him. "There are more?"

He laughed. "There are still two more movies of almost equal lengths to this one. This was just the backstory and introduction." Upon seeing my gaping mouth, he laughed again. "But don't worry. We're not watching them all today. Besides, we have to get to church."

I breathed out a sigh of relief. I didn't think I could sit still for almost twelve hours of movie watching. I guess that meant we'd have to get together again to watch the two remaining movies. I smiled to myself. What a shame, I thought sarcastically. Spend hours on end with the Parkers? That would just be awful.

Jackson and I helped clean up the living room. Kody asked if I would be going to church that night. I shrugged. Normally I only went on Sunday mornings and Wednesday nights, but I could do something different for a change.

"Sure!"

He seemed a bit surprised. "Really?"

"Yeah, why not? I've never done it before, and I need to try new things in life."

Jackson looked at me. "Do I need to take you?"

Kody interrupted him. "I can take her, if that would make it easier for you." Then he turned to me. "And if that's okay with you."

I shrugged, seemingly unaffected, when really I was freaking out inwardly. "I'm fine with it, if Jackson is. Jackson?"

"Sure, as long as you let me know when to pick you up."

Jackson left soon afterwards, giving hugs to all. Once I had all my stuff, Kody and I went out to his car, and we climbed in. Ivy and the twins were leaving at the same time we were, but they were going to the main church for the adult and little kid classes. The youth had their own separate building where they had all their services. Kody pulled out of the driveway and headed down the road.

"Is it okay if I put on some music?"

I nodded. "I don't mind at all." In fact, I was sort of glad. I didn't want to have to think of things to say to fill the silence. Once he turned the radio on, I was pleased to find that a popular Christian song I knew was playing. I didn't want to have to pretend to sing to something I didn't know the words to. I was able to sing along with Kody as we drove down the road. We arrived at the church in under ten minutes. Getting out, I felt a bit strange. Once Tina saw me, she'd be all over me with questions like a flea on a dog. Not only had I come to Sunday night church but I had also arrived with Kody. She'd be suspicious.

I walked through the doors of the church and counted to seven in my head. Sure enough, as soon as I mentally reached seven, Tina came from out of nowhere and grabbed me by the arm as she dragged me to the girls' restroom. As soon as we were inside, she narrowed her eyes.

"So what are you not telling me?"

I tried going for the innocent look. "What do you mean?"

Rolling her baby blues, she stuck her hands on her hips. "You know exactly what. Why are you here, and with Kody?"

"I met with his grandmother today for my challenge, and their family had invited us over for lunch anyway, so when I was done with my meeting, Jackson and I just hung around and watched a movie with them. Then Kody brought me to church because Jackson wanted to go home. There. Are you satisfied?"

She squealed. "Oh my goodness, that's so cool!"

I squinted my eyes. She was so strange sometimes. With her curiosity satisfied, she let me leave the bathroom. Church was great, and I really enjoyed how it was a lot more laid back than Wednesday night. It was basically just a recap of the Sunday morning service, and there were snacks, which were really good. Jackson picked me up that night, and as we rode home, he asked how it went.

"Great! I loved it a lot," I said as I took a sip of the soda I had gotten from church.

His face grew pensive, and I sensed he was about to ask a question that I wouldn't want to answer. "What's going on between you and Kody?"

I was right. I didn't want to answer that. I shrugged. "Don't ask me." That was a solid answer. I didn't lie, nor did I tell him the truth. It was vague. Very smooth.

Undaunted, he looked at me. "Oh, come on. You have to have noticed the fact that you two have been getting a lot closer these past few weeks."

I got real. "Listen, no matter what happens, please don't say anything in front of Kim, okay?"

"Ahhh," he said. "Now I understand. It's a love triangle."

I immediately spit out the soda in my mouth. Thankfully, it all went into my cup. "What? No! We're just friends."

Jackson narrowed his gaze. "I'm skeptical. That I don't believe."

I sighed exasperatedly. "Can you please drop the subject? If you don't, I'll start grilling you about Tina."

He immediately turned bright red. "Okay, I'll drop it."

"Thank you." I turned my focus to the road and watched the scenery pass by until we got home. Kody was a nice guy, but when you have a crazy sister who likes said guy, some things just weren't meant to be.

Chapter Forty-Nine

The week passed quickly. I did rather well in my schoolwork, even though most of the time I was thinking of my time on Sunday. That was the highlight of my week, the thing that kept me going when I wanted to force feed my homework to Thunder so I wouldn't have to do it. Thunder refused to even touch it, though. He was smart. I did my homework, despite the fact that I wanted to burn it all, and received fairly high scores on my tests later in the week. I was looking forward to Sunday and watching the second movie of The Lord of the Rings with Kody, but that excitement quickly plummeted when Kody texted me and said that his family was going out of town for the weekend. I sank into a mood, even though it was Friday, normally my favorite day. Jackson noticed and asked me about it.

"Why are you so sad all of a sudden? You've been so positive since the beginning of the week, but now that it's the weekend, you're all upset."

"It's nothing. I'm fine."

He crossed his arms. "You don't look fine."

My jaw ticked. "I said I'm fine."

He frowned. "I'm pretty sure you're not fine."

"I said I'm FINE!" I stomped upstairs, away from Jackson. Once I was in my room, I plopped down into my green chair. I could hear Jackson talking to himself downstairs.

"She's definitely not fine," he muttered.

I felt bad that I had lashed out at Jackson, but I didn't want to tell him that I was pouting because the Parkers were out of town. A few minutes later, Jackson came upstairs with a chocolate bar.

"You can talk about it with me, if you want. I'm not going to make fun of you. Besides, I'm pretty sure I know what this is all about."

I swallowed nervously. "You do?"

He nodded. "Yup. You're mad that you haven't seen a certain someone since Wednesday and won't see him again until next Wednesday. Am I right?"

How was he so perceptive? I sighed. "You're right. I didn't want to tell you because I thought you'd think I was being silly." I gave him a warning look. "Now don't get any ideas, mind you. We're just friends."

He rolled his eyes. "Yeah, and I was raised in a treehouse, joined a circus when I was seven, and shot a moose the other day while blindfolded."

I laughed. "Stop it. I'm serious."

Cocking an eyebrow, he said, "And I'm not?" He shook his head. "Brie, you need to stop denying it."

"I could say the same thing about you and Tina," I said, giving him a look.

"Well, that relationship is complicated."

I scowled. "As if mine is easy? Do you know what Kim would do if she ever got wind about Kody and me?" I shrugged. "Some things aren't meant to be," I said, thinking of what I had thought almost a week ago.

Jackson waved a hand in front of my face. "Do you even hear yourself? So you're saying that you guys are," he pulled out the quotation mark fingers, "just friends?"

I nodded.

He groaned. "Listen, you need to get your mind off of him for a little bit. It's Friday! You don't have anything planned, so we're going to have some fun together. Forget about Kody for the weekend."

I swatted at him. "Only if you forget about Tina."

He avoided eye contact. "Sure, sure. Whatever you say."

"What are we going to be doing?"

"I can't tell you. Just get some clothes on. I'm going to make a few calls while you pack."

"Pack for what? For how long?"

He was already walking out of my room. "For the weekend."

"Where are we going?"

"Can't tell you."

I hated it when I didn't know everything going on. "Jackson, you know I don't like surprises."

He smiled smugly. "Until it happens, and then you always say, 'Now I know why you kept this a surprise.'"

Jackson was right. I did say that. A lot. Sighing, I grabbed a backpack from my closet. Opening my dresser drawers, I began putting random items of clothing into the bag, hoping it would be enough. Once I felt as if I were sufficiently packed, I sank into my chair and pulled out my phone. Scrolling through my photos, I began deleting ones that were fuzzy, since I had nothing better to do. Thirty minutes later, Jackson called me from downstairs.

"Bring your stuff and put it in my car. Everything's ready for us to go."

I tried to be patient with him. He was giving me no hints whatsoever, and it was very frustrating. "Jackson, can you at least give me one hint?"

"Absolutely!"

I grinned.

"Not."

I frowned. "If this isn't a good surprise, you'll pay for it."

He simply lifted one side of his mouth. "Believe me, it's worth it. You're going to think I'm the best brother ever after you find out where we're going."

I huffed out a breath. "We'll see about that."

Still grumbling, I loaded my stuff in his tiny little trunk. He already had a backpack in there, so it was a tight wedge with both of our bags in there. I had brought a pillow for the ride, since I had no clue how long we would be in the car. Jackson had brought us both water bottles and had a bag of food in the backseat. Once we had all of our stuff in, he climbed into the driver's seat and turned the key.

With a rumble, the car pulled out of the driveway, and we headed down the road.

"One hint?"

Smiling, he said, "Nope. You'll just stress about it if you knew where we're going. Just relax! It's just until Sunday afternoon, and I want you to have a good time!"

"Did you tell Grandmother?"

He nodded. "I told her that I was spending some sibling time with you this weekend and that we'll be home by Sunday. She was fine with it, of course."

I was a little less stressed. As long as Jackson thought it was going to be fun, I could trust him and relax. Leaning my chair back, I laid on my pillow and pulled out my phone. I texted Tina and told her what Jackson and I were doing for the weekend. She thought it was hilarious that Jackson wouldn't tell me anything, and for some reason, I had a feeling he had probably told her—and not me—where we were going.

Half an hour later, Jackson told me to retrieve the bag of food from off the backseat. Well, I wouldn't call it food, really. He had put in two small packs of pre-made peanut butter and crackers, a bag of chips, a carton of cookies from the pantry, and some Pop-Tarts. I think the word junk needed to be placed in front of food. Opening the bag of chips,

I offered some to Jackson. He grabbed a handful and put them in his mouth. I noticed that he had forgotten plates, not to mention napkins. Oh well. At least he packed something to eat. We finished half the bag quickly, and I then pulled out the cookies.

"What a healthy meal," I said sarcastically.

Jackson pretended to be hurt. "You don't like what I brought? Well, it doesn't really matter because we'll be having dinner when we get there."

Aha! A hint. Since we had left at about 4:30, that means that we'll get there before eight, since most people don't have dinner that late. It was almost 5:30, so we should be there in under two and a half hours. "Should I keep eating, then?"

He shrugged. "It's up to you. We'll be there in an hour and a half, so as long as you snack lightly, it shouldn't affect your appetite too much." Then he scowled at me. "Hey, no tricking me into giving you hints."

I laughed. It wasn't really a hint. All I knew now was that we'd be arriving somewhere at seven. I was happy that we weren't going to be driving all night, though. I like long trips, but not when I don't know where I'm going.

For the remainder of the trip, I ate more cookies and a Pop-Tart, drank most of my water, listened to the radio, and took a power nap. Jackson shoved my shoulder at 6:50.

"Wake up. We're almost there, and you're going to want to be awake for tonight."

Yawning, I raised the seat up and began rubbing my eyes. I brushed cookie crumbs off my pants and put all the food away. Taking a swig of water, I popped my neck. Then I looked out the window. I couldn't see much more than trees. It appeared we were going up some sort of mountain. Every now and then the trees lessened, and I got a glimpse of the view. We were pretty high up and still going. I still didn't have a clue of where our final destination was.

A couple of minutes later, the road began to level off, and I noticed campers parked here and there, and a few tents off by themselves. Suddenly, I had a very good idea of where our final destination was. Then we passed a sign that confirmed my suspicions. Gatlinburg Cabins. There was an arrow pointing straight ahead. I looked at Jackson.

"Why are we here? Did you rent a cabin for us?"

Jackson shook his head. "Nope."

He was crazy. "We don't have a tent or a camper. Where will we stay?"

Raising a hand, he pointed. "There."

I turned my head. Up ahead was a cabin that looked beautiful, with a great view, and a nice outdoor fireplace. The problem was, there were people already by that house, and they were coming straight towards us. I immediately recognized them and nearly fainted.

"We're staying with the Parkers?"

He smiled as if he were the best person in the world. "Yes, isn't it great? You see, they own this cabin and have for years. They always come up here a couple of times a year, and rent it most of the rest of the year. Devan had asked if I wanted to come up with them, and I asked if you could come along, too. No one had a problem with it—especially Kody—so I decided you deserved a weekend away up in the mountains."

I just stared at him.

Brow furrowed, he said, "Do you not want to? I can take you home if you want."

I shook my head. "No, this is great! I'm just surprised." And a little mad Jackson hadn't told me what to pack. I didn't even know what clothes I had packed, and they could be all old and unfashionable. Jackson parked the car, and we both got out. Grabbing our stuff from the back, we were greeted by the family.

Ivy gave me a hug. She brushed some of her black hair out of her eyes. "I'm so glad you could come! As the only girl in the family, the boys always do boy things off by themselves, and it'll be nice to have some girl time for a change."

I smiled. I looked forward to hanging out with her. Kody took my bag. "It's good to see you again, Brie."

"You too," I said. Alex and Chris were next. They each hugged a side of my waist and took turns barraging me with questions about what sort of games we could play. Devan, laughing, came and detached them from me.

"Now boys, let her get her stuff in and settled before you scare her away!"

I walked inside the cabin. It was beautiful. Ivy gave me the full tour, green eyes sparkling as she did so. There was a medium-sized kitchen that was connected to a dining room that had a cedar table and matching chairs. Then, in the living room, there was a television mounted above a fireplace. A long couch had two recliners next to it, and there were deer heads and bearskins all over the walls. Next were the three bedrooms and the two bathrooms. One of the bedrooms even had a bunk bed in it! Everything was amazing and very rustic, and I absolutely loved it. On the second story, there was a walkout deck with two chairs and a small table.

Ivy smiled once we had been through the whole house. "Kody and Jackson will be in the bunk bed, and the twins will be on an air mattress on the floor. You'll get the smaller room across the hall."

I was relieved. "Thank you!" I didn't want to share a room with Jackson. He snored. I went into the room and found that my backpack was already next to the bed. I unpacked my clothes and placed them into the dresser that was next to the bed, relieved that I had packed decent-looking clothes. As I looked around my room, I marveled again at how nice the cabin was. Devan's job as a lawyer must really pay well. Ivy worked as a counselor, but I knew she didn't make as much as Devan. Either way, their family was very well off.

Once my stuff was organized, I went downstairs. Devan, Jackson, and Kody had already turned the television on, and they were watching some sort of sport. Ivy was in the kitchen making dinner. I went to help her. We were having hotdogs and macaroni and cheese for dinner, which was perfectly fine by me. I loved easy meals. I set the table and then went to tell Alex and Chris, who were outside, that it was time to eat. I then relayed the same message to the guys in the living room. They tramped into the dining room and plopped around the table. I helped Ivy put the food on the table and then sat down myself. I was positioned right between the twins.

Dinner was great, and everyone paid their compliments to the chef. I helped Ivy wash the dishes afterwards, and then everyone gathered in the living room to play some games for the remainder of the evening.

I went to bed at 10:00 because I was pretty wiped out. Ivy sent the twins to bed then, as well. As I got ready for bed, I realized that Jackson had been right. I ran downstairs. He had stepped into the kitchen to grab a glass of water. I threw my arms around him.

"You were right. You are the best brother in the world!"

He laughed. "You're only just now realizing that?"

I swatted at him. "Oh, be quiet."

He was still laughing when I ran back upstairs and hopped into bed. Yawning, I recapped the day. It had definitely been full of surprises, that was for sure. I felt myself drifting to sleep, and I smiled, wondering what tomorrow would hold.

Saturday passed quickly. It was very laid back and relaxing. The boys went for a hike in the woods while Ivy and I watched a movie. Halfway through the beginning of Up, I was already reaching for the tissues, as was Ivy. By the time the guys got back, we had gone through a whole box of tissues, and both of our eyes were red. They were concerned at first, but once they found out what movie it was, they laughed at us.

Indignant, Ivy and I marched out of the living room and went to the kitchen. We decided that I would make a dessert while Ivy made dinner. I didn't have much experience with cooking, so I had to keep checking with Ivy to make sure I was doing it right. I was just making chocolate chip cookies, but it felt like I was making a three-tiered wedding cake, it was so hard. But it was soon done, and they smelled amazing.

Dinner was spaghetti and garlic bread with the cookies for dessert. Everyone complimented not only Ivy but me also. I was surprised because no one had ever told me I was a good cook. Afterwards, we tried to figure out what we should do for the evening. Then, Kody had an idea.

"What if we watch the second movie of The Lord of the Rings?"

I perked up. "Sounds fun!"

Jackson agreed, as did Devan and Ivy, so we decided we would make popcorn and then gather in the living room to watch it while we ate the remainder of the cookies.

Later, after the movie, I was eating the remaining kernels of popcorn in the kitchen when Kody walked in. He looked startled.

"Oh, sorry, I didn't know you were in here. I'm just going to get some water."

I thought it was funny that he was apologizing for being in his own house. "It's fine. I don't mind the company."

He came to stand next to me, glass of water in hand. "Are you enjoying being up here?"

I nodded vigorously. "Yes, it's been a blast! You're lucky to have a place to go where you can escape the world."

His eyes crinkled sympathetically. "I'm sorry you have to deal with everything at your house. If I could make it better for you, I would."

"Thanks, Kody. I don't know how to make it better. I can't wait until I get out of the house. Once I turn eighteen, I'm out of there."

"Will you stay in the state for college?"

I shrugged. "I'm not sure. It depends on whether my friends do or not. I don't want to lose connection with everyone I've gotten to know for the past few years." I sighed. "Sometimes I wonder what I'm supposed to do for God. How am I supposed to witness to people if I can't even convert my family?"

He frowned. "That's a tough question, one I don't have the answer to. Don't lose hope, though. You changed Kelsey's life forever, and I know she won't be the only one. You're something special, that's for sure."

My heart warmed. "Thanks, Kody."

I felt lighter as I went to bed. Even though I didn't have all the answers, I trusted that God would use me in whatever way He wanted to.

Sunday morning, Devan called us all into the living room. He opened his Bible and began reading a chapter in Galatians. When he was done, he put on some worship music, and we all prayed together. I prayed that God would give me hope to believe that He was going to use me, and that despite my circumstances at home, I would be able to trust that He would make good come out of it, somehow.

We left after lunch. Packing all our stuff up, I went around giving hugs and saying goodbye. Ivy was her normal perky self.

"I'm so happy you got to come! We should definitely do this again!"

Devan smiled at me and said basically the same thing, but in his own words. I tried not to cry when he hugged me. He was literally the dad I never had. Devan was always caring about me and asking how I was feeling. My dad was never that attentive. My dad loved me, and we did have a special connection; but he's gone, and obviously our connection wasn't enough of a reason for him to keep living. Devan filled that empty spot that craved a father's love. Yes, I know that when I became a Christian, God ultimately filled that spot, but it was different when I could feel someone's arms around me. Devan filled the place of my earthly father, while God was my heavenly Father.

Alex and Chris almost knocked me over when they said goodbye. Honestly, I had no clue how they could have so much energy. Then, I went over to Kody. He was sticking my bag in the back of Jackson's car.

"Thanks for everything this weekend, Kody. I had a lot of fun!"

"Me too! I want to do something like this again sometime!" He pulled me into a hug. "We still need to watch the last movie of The Lord of the Rings."

I loved excuses to hang out with people. "Yeah, I have to know what happens to Frodo and Sam!"

We all got into our respective vehicles and began the drive back to Cleveland. Jackson and I jammed out to music most of the trip, and we finished off the snacks Jackson had brought. Once home, I lugged my bag upstairs and unpacked. It had been a fun weekend, and I was relaxed and ready to face the week. Sinking into my chair, I tried to remember if there was anything specific I had to do this week. Sitting straight up, I realized I needed to schedule a meeting with a godly woman. I had completely forgotten about it over the weekend, but I had a week to find someone, so it wasn't too stressful. All the same, I thought about who I wanted to meet with. Maybe meet with a woman at her workplace? I hadn't met with someone at work in a while.

Texting Tina, I asked her if she knew anyone whom I could hang out with at work for my weekly meeting. She responded with several women's names and phone numbers. I chose one at random, Anita Hughes, and then contacted her.

Later that evening, she responded and said that she would be willing to meet with me the next morning, if that was fine with me. I agreed, and then asked where to meet her. She said she worked across the street from the Church of God International Offices at The Center for Ministerial Care. I didn't know where that was, but I was sure my phone would find it somehow. I didn't have to go to school the next day because it was supposed to snow.

Monday morning I woke up at 9:30, rested and ready for the day. I wasn't supposed to meet with Anita until 10:15, so I wasn't in a rush to get ready. I moseyed down to the kitchen and ate a bowl of cereal while I watched it snow. Then, I realized that Jackson was at work and wouldn't be able to take me to my meeting. That meant I had to ask either Kimberly or Grandmother to take me, and I didn't want to do either; but Grandmother would probably do it without saying anything, so I opted to ask her.

"Good morning, Grandmother," I said, entering into her room.

She glanced up from Little Women. "Oh, good morning. Why aren't you at school?"

"We don't have school today because of the snow; however, I was wondering if you'd be able to take me somewhere this morning. I am supposed to meet with someone this morning, but Jackson can't take me because he's working. Could you do it?"

"Where to?"

"It's near the Church of God International Offices. I have to be there by 10:15."

She shrugged. "I guess I could."

"Thanks!"

I skipped out of the room and upstairs. I hadn't expected her to just agree to it. Normally she grills me when she has to take me somewhere. I finished getting ready until it was time to leave. I climbed into the car, and Grandmother pulled out of the driveway and onto the road. We drove for a little bit until we were there. I had already figured out where it was according to the map on my phone, so I was able to tell her where to turn and such.

She dropped me off at 10:13, so I walked into the reception area and sat down, pleased I wasn't late. Within moments, a woman with a short brown bob walked into the room.

"Hello there. I'm Anita Hughes. Are you Brie?"

I stood up. "Yes, I am. It's nice to meet you."

She smiled. "Nice to meet you, too. Will you come to my office with me?"

Nodding, I followed her back around a corner and down a long hallway until we had reached her office. She offered me a seat.

"Tell me a little bit more about this challenge of yours," she began. "Am I able to take you out for lunch?"

I nodded. "Normally I ask questions of the woman I'm meeting with, and she tells me about what she's learned in life. Where we go and what we do depends on the woman."

She gave a decided nod. "Very well, then. You may ask me questions until we leave for lunch. Then you may continue asking until you run out of questions," she added with a smile.

I grinned back. I liked how she made decisions very easily. Settling back in my chair, I said, "Tell me a bit about your job. What exactly do you do here?"

"At The Center for Ministerial Care, we counsel all types of ministers in the Church of God. As the General Executive Assistant, I counsel two people a week on average, and I've been here 20 years. Basically, I'm a counselor for ministers and their families. Also, as part of my job, if the income for retired ministers or widows or widowers of ministers is below the poverty level, my department sends them money each month to help them."

"That's really neat." I had thought about going into counseling when I grew up, but I had doubted my abilities—if I couldn't fix my own problems, then how was I supposed to help others fix theirs?

"What's an adventure you've had in your life?"

She thought about that, tilting her head as she did so. "Traveling throughout the Holy Land. I loved walking where Jesus had walked and being able to see the places where he had taught, lived, and died."

I envied her. "I've always wanted to travel. I hope to go to Israel one day."

She smiled at me kindly. "Well, I believe you can make that dream come true if you put your mind to it. It really is a beautiful place."

"Who has been the most influential person in your life?"

She sucked in a breath. "That's going to be a toss up between my mom, my dad, and my grandmother. My mom because she would pray all day long. She would pray while doing the dishes or any other household chore. She was a prayer warrior. My grandmother because whatever she made up her mind to do, she did it, even though she didn't even have a high school education. And, lastly, my dad because whenever I would have trials and would start crying and praying at the church, my dad would come up next to me and pray with me. I love my family."

I couldn't say the same about mine. She was lucky to have such amazing parents. "Has it always been so loving in your family?"

She looked at me. "Well, the biggest challenge I've had to face was getting married at the age of 21 and immediately becoming a mother. My husband already had three kids aged 4, 5, and 6. The marriage didn't last, though. I don't believe in divorce, but, through no fault of mine, we divorced. I then lived alone for four years. Then I met a man named Ray Hughes, the man I've been married to for 28 years now. He also had been through a divorce and had two boys. So, it hasn't always been easy family-wise, but God has seen me through." She paused for a second. "Even if you're a Christian, you're not immune to the struggles and hurts of the world."

Then, she glanced at her watch. "Oh my goodness; it's time to go to lunch!" Standing up, she said, "Do you like Olive Garden?"

I nodded enthusiastically. "I love it!"

"Great!"

Walking outside of the building, we climbed into her car and began heading to the restaurant. I texted Jackson to let him know where I was. He would be off work in an hour, and I would probably be done with the meeting by that time, so I asked him if he could pick me up from Olive Garden before he went home.

Once we arrived at Olive Garden, we were seated near the back. As I looked at the menu, I decided on chicken gnocchi soup and a salad. Our server came to our table and asked us what we wanted, being very helpful and jovial. As I told her, I couldn't help but notice the multiple piercings and tattoos she had. I had considered getting my ears pierced a few months back, but I had never found the time to do it. When she left, I resumed our conversation.

"What is your favorite Bible verse?" I asked Anita.

She thought about it for only a moment. "My favorite verse is Romans 8:38-39. It says, 'For I am persuaded that neither death nor life, nor angels nor principalities nor powers, nor things present nor things to come, nor height nor depth, nor any other created thing, shall be able to separate us from the love of God which is in Christ Jesus our Lord.'"

A very good verse, indeed. "Is there a life lesson you've learned that you would be willing to share with me?"

"Some parts of my life I don't like remembering, but they remind me of God's grace in my life. My pastor says that God can take your mess and turn it into a message. Even if you hate remembering how vulnerable or selfish or wicked you've been in the past, it's good to be reminded of what God has brought you out of and what He can lead you through."

I leaned back in my chair, ruminating on that for a second. I didn't like thinking about how I'd snubbed God over and over again, how I was a selfish little brat that always wanted to get her way, or how I didn't act right to my siblings; but that has all changed. It was good to remember the past so hopefully it would be an incentive to not do those things again.

"Last question. What are the qualities of a godly woman?"

"I believe the qualities of a godly woman are to love God first, love your family second, and to set a good example for your husband and children."

Our server was back with our food by then. She was very polite and very happy. When she left, Anita smiled at me.

"You can't judge people's hearts by their outward appearance. I've never been a fan of tattoos and multiple piercings, but she has been the best server I have ever had."

I agreed. "Don't judge a book by its cover" is definitely a true statement.

As we finished our meal, we carried on a light conversation. I told her a little about myself and found out that we both went to the same church. Apparently she was even in the choir. I would have to look for her on Sunday. Soon after I finished scraping my bowl, Jackson texted me, saying he had just pulled into the parking lot. I rose and thanked Anita for the meal and for her time. She gave me a hug.

"Have a wonderful week, my dear, and I look forward to seeing you on Sunday!"

I left the restaurant full, both physically and spiritually. She had taught me some lessons I wasn't going to forget. As I climbed into Jackson's car, I told him about my day. He listened attentively, popping in questions as I talked. I loved him so much. He really was the best brother ever.

Chapter Fifty

Over the next week, I really thought about the last few people I would meet with for my challenge. I had three more meetings to schedule, and I really wanted to make sure I chose carefully. I called Tina over the weekend to see if she would recommend someone.

"I think that it would be cool if you met with a family member, it doesn't matter whom, for your very last one. You started this challenge by meeting with a family member, and I think coming full circle would be very neat. I do have an idea for one person you could meet with, if she would be free. If you like, I can make a phone call, and I'll get back to you as soon as I find something out."

"Sounds awesome," I said. "Should I go ahead and plan for a meeting this next week?"

She made a humming sound. "Yes, but keep the plans open. Most likely, the woman I'm thinking of won't be able to meet this coming week, so yes."

After we hung up, I got right to work. I pulled out a notebook and a pen and began some serious contemplation. After ten minutes, I had an idea. I had been thinking about all the women I had met with, and I remembered that during my meeting with Patricia Kinston, I had met the manager of the warehouse, Sheila McElhaney. In fact, I remember Patricia saying that Sheila attended Westmore. I don't really socialize after church on Sundays, so I don't see that many people other than the youth. This Sunday, however, I would try to find Sheila and ask her if she would be willing to meet with me.

That settled, I spent the rest of the evening with Jackson watching Mary Poppins. He was a big fan of Julie Andrews, and we had all of her movies as a result. We had watched the Sound of Music the night before, and Jackson had been humming "Do-Re-Mi" ever since.

The next morning, I set a reminder on my phone scheduled for after church so that I would remember to try and find Sheila. Right after church, I began to walk around, hoping to find her. Tina noticed I didn't automatically leave, so she asked what I was up to.

"I'm looking for Sheila McElhaney. Do you know where she is?"

She grabbed my arm. "Follow me."

She led me closer to the front, and then I saw Sheila coming down from the choir loft. I slapped my head. She was in the choir the whole time, and I hadn't seen her? Tina smiled at me and headed in the opposite direction as I went to talk with Sheila.

"Hi, I'm Brie. You're Sheila McElhaney, right?"

She nodded. "That's right. Don't I know you from somewhere?"

"I came to The Caring Place to help out a couple of months ago. I met you there, but we didn't really get to talk much. I was with Patricia Kinston for the day."

A look of recognition flashed across her face. "Ah, yes. I remember now. Did you have a question for me?"

"Actually, I do. When I met with Patricia, it was for a challenge. Basically, I'm supposed to meet with a different godly woman each week for a whole year. The year is almost over, but I still have a few more women to meet with. I was wondering if you would be interested in meeting with me?"

She smiled at me. "I would love that! What am I supposed to do?"

I shrugged. "Every meeting is different. I might meet with women at their workplaces, in their homes, or at restaurants. It's all up to the woman to decide. I would be interested in helping out at The Caring Place again, though, if that's okay."

"That'll work! Are you free tomorrow morning?"

I wasn't sure. "I have school, but I may be able to get a pass since it would be for service hours. What time would I need to be there?"

"Probably about 9 or 10. I will take you to my house for lunch afterwards, if that's okay."

"Perfect! I'll contact my teacher and ask if I can get a pass for the morning." I said goodbye and went to find Jackson.

Back at home, I texted my teacher about the pass, and she said as long as it was for service hours and Sheila signed my paper, it was fine. She was a really flexible teacher.

The next morning, I went downstairs to ask Grandmother for a ride to The Caring Place.

"Why there?" she asked. "Don't you have school today?"

I shrugged. "I technically do have school today, but I got permission from my teacher to get out of school this morning to do service hours at The Caring Place."

She squinted at me and crossed her arms. "How do I know you're not just playing hooky?"

I sighed and showed her the text from my teacher. "It says right here, okay?"

"Fine, I'll take you; but if you are skipping school, I won't take any responsibility for your actions."

"I don't expect you to." I ate a quick breakfast and headed out to the car.

When we finally arrived at The Caring Place, I hopped out of the car and went around to the side entrance. When I opened it up, Sheila was sitting at her desk working on the computer. When she saw me, she stood up.

"Hi! I'm so glad you've come!"

I smiled. "Put me right to work!"

She led me over to the main table in the center of the warehouse. There were about three people already there. They were taking packages of waffles and stacking them in boxes.

"You can help them with that. We have a lot of waffle packages that need to be stacked."

I grabbed an empty box and plopped it next to a large pile of waffle packages. I looked at all the other boxes to see which way to stack them and then began. I introduced myself to the other people there. They were all older folks, and they greeted me warmly. Thirty minutes and an innumerable amount of waffle packages later, we were done. Sheila then put me to work organizing egg cartons. She had been a flurry of activity all morning, going from one job to the next, constantly doing something. I was very impressed; however, I was confused about something.

"Aren't you giving bags to people today?" I asked her, after I had finished all the egg cartons.

She shook her head. "No. On Mondays we aren't open to the public. We set up on Mondays and do all the work that needs to be done for the week."

I understood. "Is that why Patricia isn't here?"

"Yes, she only works on Thursdays."

I went back to work. Sheila had informed me at the beginning that it would be best if I didn't ask my questions until we ate at her house. There, she would be able to think about her answers. For my next job, I began taping cartons of baby formula together. Before I knew it, the morning had disappeared and two of the workers had left, leaving just Sheila, one last worker, and me. I sat down at a table and began to do my last job: pull apart plastic bags, fluff them into a bag shape, then mash them up into a ball so they could be stuck into a bag. It was an enormous task because there were a ton of bags.

Finally, we were finished with the bags, and I realized that it was time to go. Sheila went around locking up and making sure everything was in order. Once she had all her ducks in a row, we left the building. As I climbed into her car, I blew out a breath.

"I don't know how you do this all the time. That was exhausting!"

She laughed. "Sometimes I don't know either. What do you want for lunch?"

"I'm not sure. It doesn't matter to me one bit. I don't have any allergies other than cilantro."

"Great! I'll make some soup and sandwiches."

When we arrived at her house, she turned on the stove and began making grilled cheese while the soup started to heat up. Seeing an opportunity to learn more about Sheila, I began the conversation.

"What's been a life lesson you've learned?"

She paused as she flipped a sandwich and then answered. "Worry won't give you anything but anxiousness. You have to give it to God and trust Him to help you through whatever situation you're in." She tilted her head. "In the easy times in our lives, we normally don't learn a lot of lessons from God. It's in the hard times that we really learn. You see, the best decision I've ever made was putting the Lord first. Yet, it wasn't until I had cancer that I really started doing that."

I gasped. "You had cancer?"

She nodded. "It was when my kids were young. I worried a lot that I would never be able to see them grow up." She sighed. "That cancer has been the biggest challenge I've had to face. I did chemotherapy and six radiation treatments. To this day, I still have side effects because of the chemotherapy. It was a hard struggle, but I'm still here and thankful for it."

She stopped talking momentarily as she began to set the table, and then she looked at me. "You know, I'm glad that I didn't turn away from God during that hard time. I knew of a man who had a tragedy happen. He blamed God and told God to get away from him. Immediately, peace, assurance, and God's presence left him, and he was completely empty and alone. He was so scared and upset that he immediately apologized to God and asked Him to come back. God did."

I was amazed. The man must have felt awful to know what it felt like to be with God and then to suddenly be without Him.

"It was especially during that difficult time," Sheila continued, "that I learned the true meaning of my favorite Bible verse, 1 Peter 5:7, which says, 'Casting all your care upon Him, for He cares for you.'"

She prayed for our meal, and then we began eating. Between mouthfuls of sandwich, I asked, "What do you think the qualities of a godly woman are?"

"I believe the qualities of a godly woman are to consider others and to love."

"Who have been the most influential people in your life?"

"My mom and dad. They taught me what it meant to be a Christian. They also told me that I didn't know what anyone else was going through, so I shouldn't judge them."

That's a good motto. I should remember that for the future. It's so easy for me to judge people that I forget that Jesus loves us all equally. I shouldn't compare myself to others and point out their shortcomings, even if I know they're in the wrong. It still isn't okay to talk about them behind their back and justify it by saying that you're just venting.

Sheila had already finished her tomato soup and sandwich, and I was almost done. She looked at me as she began to clear the table. "Another life lesson I've learned is this: if the enemy thinks that you're going to bite into the lies he gives you, then he'll keep lying to you. Don't allow yourself to bite into whatever he's cooked up for you. It's only a pot full of lies, and you shouldn't listen to them."

Wise words, indeed. I put my plate in the sink and sent a quick text to my grandmother, letting her know where I was, and asking if she could pick me up. She said she could, but she needed an address. I asked Sheila, and she provided it. After I finished texting my grandmother, Sheila led me into a room and showed me her rock collection. She had been to many countries and had brought rocks back from all over. Her collection was very impressive, and I was amazed at the variation of rocks she had found. They were all beautiful. Soon, though, my grandmother arrived, and I gave Sheila a hug.

"Thank you so much for spending your morning with me. I had a wonderful time!"

She smiled. "As did I."

She quickly signed my paper for service hours and led me out the front door. I climbed into the car as I waved goodbye. Grandmother didn't say much on the way to school, which I was fine with. I had brought my backpack with me, so I was all set. Once at school, I went first to my teacher and gave her the signed sheet of paper. Then I went to my class. Tina was happy to see me.

"How did your meeting go?"

"Great," I said. "I can't believe I haven't seen Sheila in the choir for the past couple of months! How did I miss seeing her?"

She laughed. "That's true. I could've just told you if I had known. By the way, I made that call and the woman says that you can come next week on Tuesday."

I smiled. "Wonderful! What's her name?"

"Her name's Mary Perdue."

"Cool!" I paused. "Who's that?"

"Mary Perdue is the wife of the former governor of Georgia, who is now the Secretary of Agriculture over the whole United States!"

I was flabbergasted. "How do you know her?"

"My mom met her once and they became friends. I wasn't sure if she'd be free, though. Thankfully, she is; however, you'll need to drive a few hours down to Georgia to meet with her."

"Alright, I'm fine with that." I shook my head. "I can't believe I'm going to meet her!"

Tina smiled. "It looks like this challenge wasn't such a bad idea, after all, was it?"

"You're right, as usual." I rolled my eyes as she laughed. We walked together to our next class. For the rest of the day I thought about how much the challenge had changed me for the better. I was very happy Tina had kept after me to do it. She was an amazing friend, even if she did get on my nerves sometimes.

Chapter Fifty-One

A week later, Tina sent me a text, reminding me that I would be meeting with Mary Perdue the next day. I was glad she had reminded me because I would have forgotten otherwise. I was never good at remembering things, especially now that school had just let out the Friday before, and I had turned into a lazy mess. I went downstairs to ask Jackson what he was doing the next day.

"I don't have anything scheduled, really, except for work. Why?"

"Will you drive me down to Georgia for another meeting?"

He shrugged. "I guess so."

"Thank you! Let me get the exact address. It's a few hours away, though. What time do you have to be back for work?" He had quit his job at Cracker Barrel and was now working at Longhorn Steakhouse.

"I work from 1 until 6."

I grimaced. That wouldn't give me enough time to drive down, meet with Mary, and then drive back.

Seeing my expression, he said, "I can call my manager to see if I could work a later shift tomorrow night."

I grabbed him in a bear hug. "Thank you, thank you, thank you! You're the best brother ever!"

He laughed. "You're welcome."

Tina sent me the address later that night. I couldn't wait to finally meet Mary Perdue. I quickly fell asleep, dreaming of what she would be like.

The next morning, Jackson and I left at 7 o'clock, taking breakfast with us. It was a long drive, so I had brought car bingo to keep me occupied. Jackson turned on some music, and we were set for the rest of the morning. At around 9 o'clock, we arrived at a large house. Jackson parked, and then we climbed out of the car.

As I rang the doorbell, I remembered that Tina said it wouldn't be like a normal meeting. She wouldn't say anything else, though. I figured that I shouldn't worry too much because none of my meetings were "normal." They were all unique in their own way.

A few moments later, a woman answered the door. She looked to be in her mid-thirties. I was a bit confused because Tina had said Mary was a grandmother, but I held out my hand anyway.

"Hi, I'm Brie, and this is my brother Jackson."

She squinted at us. "Who?"

I was feeling a bit strange. "Brie Thompson, the girl you were going to meet with today."

She scratched her head. "I don't know anybody by that name."

"Do you know a Tina Lankford?"

She shook her head. "Nope."

I felt awful. "I'm sorry. There must have been a mix up with the address we were given. Does a Mary Perdue live nearby?"

At this she smiled broadly. "Yes, she does. Right down there." She pointed at the house farther down the road.

"Thank you! Sorry for the mistake."

She waved at us as we got back into our car. "No problem!"

Once inside the car, I slapped my forehead. "What in the world?" I checked the address one more time and then groaned. I had written the house number down on a sheet of paper, but I had been looking at it upside down! The house number we were supposed to go to was 90016, not 91006.

We quickly drove down the road until we came to the actual house. This time, when the door swung open, an older woman greeted us.

"Hello," she said, "you must be Brie!"

I nodded. "Yes, I am, and this is my brother, Jackson."

She ushered us in. "It's so nice to meet you both!"

She brought us into the living room, where I was startled to see over ten kids, ranging from 7 to 18 years old, playing games. Mary introduced them all, one by one.

"These are my grandchildren. Every year I hold something special for them: Nana Camp. They come for a couple of days during the summer without their parents to hang out here. We do crafts and activities, and they love to go swimming in the lake."

I wished I had a lot of cousins that I could hang out with. "That sounds like so much fun!"

Mary smiled. "It is. The plan for today is just to hang out and have fun. Tina told me that you normally have some questions to ask, so I figured we could probably do that over lunch. Is that okay?"

I nodded. "Absolutely!"

Mary turned to Jackson. "You're welcome to join us, if you want."

"If it's alright with you, I need to work on my computer if I can hook up to your Wi-Fi."

"Sure! There's an outlet for your power supply next to that table."

He smiled. "Thanks." He pulled out his computer and power supply from his backpack while she told him the Wi-Fi password. I knew he would probably be doing some research on colleges since he was now a high school graduate. I was hoping that he would go to a nearby college so I would be able to see him regularly. I didn't know what I would do if I had to go back to dealing with Kimberly, Mom, and Grandmother without Jackson's support and kindness.

Mary told all the kids that it was craft time, and they all began to go out to the garage. When I walked out there, I noticed a table set up with paint. While the kids put oversized t-shirts over their clothes, Mary quickly explained what they were going to do. I watched them as they began to paint. I once again wished I had a large extended family I was close to. Within twenty minutes, most of them were done. We went back inside, and a lot of the kids went back to playing games. The two oldest grandchildren were doing a puzzle of a town in the dining room. When I went to look at it, I was amazed. It had at least 1,000 pieces.

After the grandchildren played for a little while longer, Mary brought them all together to read Psalm 23. Apparently her theme for this year was based off that chapter. I was impressed with how many kids knew the chapter. Even the youngest girl quoted it from memory!

Every now and then I glanced over at Jackson, who was deep in thought, brow furrowed. I wished he didn't have to go to college. I wasn't even sure what he wanted to do for a living. There was so much I didn't know about my brother, and I wanted to change that. My thoughts were interrupted as one of the young girls pulled me aside to play a game with her. She taught me how to play it and then proceeded to destroy me; however, I soon improved at the game and even won a game against her.

Before long, the kids grew restless and asked Mary if they could go swimming. She frowned as she looked at the sky.

"I don't know."

They all turned on their charm. "Please, Nana? It won't be for long, and we really want to go!"

"Well, only for a little bit."

Cheers went up amongst the kids.

She wagged a finger at them. "But if it starts storming, you're getting out immediately, understand?"

They agreed. Mary and I grabbed two chairs and went outside, putting the chairs under the deck. We watched as they ran down to the water and began splashing each other. Mary turned to me.

"Since we have a moment of peace, do you want to ask me some of your questions?"

I nodded. "Of course. What do you think the qualities of a godly woman are?"

She propped a hand under her chin as she thought. "I think a godly woman is someone who has the Lord in her heart and someone who seeks to live each day to please Him— which involves intimacy with Him, prayer, reading the Word, and listening to the Spirit."

"Do you have a favorite scripture?"

Smiling, she said, "Yes. My favorite verse is Psalm 119:165, which says, 'Great peace have those who love Your law, and nothing causes them to stumble.'"

"What's the biggest challenge you've been through?"

"The biggest challenge I've had to face was when my daughter was in an abusive marriage. It was hard to keep her safe and give her godly wisdom."

That's awful. I can almost imagine how hard it would be. I face verbal and emotional abuse from my Mom every time I see her. After the incident where Mom disappeared, we thought that maybe she would change, even a little bit; but after the first few weeks, she went back to her old life of being "the dragon" and drinking herself silly. I shook my head to get my mind off of her and back to the present.

"If you could change one thing about something you've done, what would it be?"

"Looking back, I think it would have been when I was a governor's wife. I wish I had been a little more astute and not as trusting."

"Was it fun being a governor's wife?"

She nodded. "Very much so."

"What was your favorite thing about it?"

"My favorite thing was the opportunities. I never would've gotten those opportunities otherwise. We were able to show God's love and spread His Word."

Just then, it started raining hard. Mary looked up at the sky and noticed how dark the clouds had gotten. Immediately, she called the kids in. They were out of the water in a flash, and not a moment too soon. Lightning cracked in the sky, closely followed by a magnificent roll of thunder. Mary herded the kids inside, where they changed out of their swimsuits and went to play more games. She motioned me over to the stove.

"I'm going to start lunch. Will you help me?"

I nodded. "Of course! What are we having?"

"Grilled cheese sandwiches."

I set to work buttering bread while she got the skillet ready. The kids, seeing that lunch was being made, grew excited and began to get plates and cups out. They lined up youngest to oldest and began to put grilled cheese sandwiches on their plates. Mary stopped them and prayed, then let the rest go through the line. Once they had all gotten food, Mary and I grabbed some food and then went to sit at the table. I tapped Jackson on the shoulder.

"There's an extra sandwich over there if you want it."

"Yeah, thanks!" He stood up and went to eat.

Mary took a bite of her sandwich. I did the same and then drank some juice before asking, "What is an adventure you've had?"

"The biggest adventure I've had in my life so far is being married to my husband. There's never a dull moment," she said with a smile.

"Who has been a mentor in your life?"

She paused for a moment to swallow. "One mentor in my life was my mother-in-law. She passed away too soon. I was closer to her than my own mom. She was a good, godly woman. I learned how to be a godly woman and wife because of her."

"What's a life lesson you've learned?"

"I don't take offense to what people say about me because I know that God has a plan, and nothing anyone can say can change that."

I should memorize that and remember it whenever people say things that make me automatically defensive.

"Also, I learned to trust that God will always work things out in the end. I moved from Nashville to Atlanta in 8th grade. I was really involved in dance and piano. It wasn't that hard to leave all of my friends behind, but it was still challenging. Looking back, I realize that if I hadn't moved, I wouldn't have gone to the University of Georgia, and I wouldn't have met my husband. If I hadn't met him, I wouldn't have done all the things I've been able to do because of my position. God always lines things up in the end. You just have to stick around to see it happen."

I was absorbing all of her words, making sure I would remember them later on. Jackson broke my focus by tapping me on the shoulder.

"I'm sorry to break up the party, but I have to get back so I can work. I was only able to get a two-hour extension."

I nodded. "Okay."

Mary gave me a hug. "I'm really glad I got to meet you! Next time you see Tina, tell her I said hello!"

I smiled. "I will."

Jackson and I grabbed our bags and headed out to the car. He pulled out of the driveway and headed down the road. I rummaged around the floorboard until I found my sheet of car bingo and resumed my game.

Hours later, Jackson dropped me off at home and then left to go to work. Before he left, I gave him another hug.

"Thanks again for taking me! I don't know how I would've been able to go down there without you."

He smiled. "No problem. That's what big brothers are for."

Jackson pulled out of the driveway and headed down the road. I went back inside the house and up to my bedroom. Plopping down onto my bed, I released a sigh. With summer finally here, I was free from homework and early mornings. I could do practically anything, and I was so happy. As I began to relax, I received a text from Tina.

It read, "Do you want to spend the night with me tonight?"

I told her yes, with at least three exclamation points. Tina responded and said that her mom would come and pick me up in three hours. I packed a bag and then decided to take a nap.

Two hours later, I awoke to the alarm I had set so I would wake up before Tina's mom arrived. I brushed my hair and slipped on some shoes. Within a few minutes, Tina's mom pulled into the driveway. I ran downstairs and told Grandmother I would be spending the night with Tina. She waved a hand at me and told me to have a good time and then went back to her knitting.

When I slid into the passenger's seat of the car, Jenny Lankford smiled at me.

"How are you doing this evening?"

"Wonderful. What about you?"

She headed down the road. "Pretty great, actually. I didn't have that many patients today."

Jenny Lankford worked as an E.R. nurse. Tina said that her mom enjoyed it, unlike Tina, who couldn't tolerate blood. Tina much preferred her dad's job as an electrician; electrical wires didn't make her queasy.

Once we arrived at their house, I went inside. I found Tina in the kitchen making bean dip. I set my bag in her room and then went into the kitchen to help her. Soon the dish was in the oven, and Tina and I set the table while we waited for it to cook. When it was done, her parents came in and sat down. Peter blessed the food, and we all dug in.

"This is great," Peter said.

Jenny agreed. "Thanks for making it, girls."

After dinner, Tina and I went into her room and sat on her bed. Tina pulled a leg up under herself and then looked at me. "How are you feeling about your challenge almost being over?"

I sighed and propped my chin on my hand. "I'm not sure. Part of me is sad because it's been so much fun, but the other part is glad to not stress over deciding whom to meet with. I guess I'll feel better whenever I have another person set up to do this mentoring experience. It'll give me something to concentrate on."

Tina nodded. "Yes, I can't wait until that happens."

We chatted for a little while longer before watching a movie and going to bed. Sleepovers with Tina were always fun except for one thing: she wasn't a night owl by a long shot. If she were tired, she would fall asleep and not try to stay up. I'd had multiple occasions where I'd been talking, and she would fall asleep when I was in the middle of a sentence. I tried to never take it personally. Most of the time.

Chapter Fifty-Two

I couldn't believe it. I had one more meeting, and then I was completely done with the challenge. It was the last week I would ever do this. With so many emotions coursing through my mind, I didn't know how to feel. Sadness was mixed with relief, happiness, and anxiety. I just took a moment and looked back at where I was a year ago. Alone, shattered, confused, and hurting. I thought I knew everything, when in actuality I couldn't see the truth right in front of my face. I was blind to what I didn't want to see, to what I didn't want to accept. If it were not for Tina's push towards finding the truth, I would still be in the same place I was 52 weeks ago.

I shook my head. She was a blessing sent straight from the Lord. Before I went too far down memory lane, though, I needed to think about what family member I should meet with for my last meeting.

Even though it was my last meeting, I wasn't super stressed about scheduling a meeting. I trusted that God would help me find the one I needed to meet with. Using an old address book, I wrote down a list of extended family members and then crossed out the ones I'd already met with. One caught my eye. I didn't remember a lot about cousin Kelly, but I knew that she always loved playing with me when I was younger. I quickly texted my paternal grandmother to see if she could send me Kelly's number. Soon, she responded with the contact information I needed, and I was able to text Kelly, explaining about the challenge. While I waited for her response, I cleaned my room—a monotonous yet necessary task.

I didn't have to wait long. She texted back within a few minutes with an enthusiastic, "Of course!" I smiled. God always provided.

We settled on a Saturday meeting, and I went back to cleaning my room, glad the scheduling was finished. I was about to walk downstairs when Kimberly called me into her room.

I went in. "What's up?"

She said, "Have you noticed anything strange about Grandmother recently?"

I shook my head. "No. Have you?"

"Yeah. She keeps staring off into space and doesn't finish her sentences."

A funny feeling crept into my stomach. "What do you think is wrong with her?"

"I'm not sure. It could be nothing, but I just wanted to see if you had picked up on any of it."

"I'll keep my eyes open, and I'll talk to Jackson." I left her room with a sinking heart. I had never actually thought about what would happen if something were wrong with Grandmother. She was the reason I could go on school trips, and she occasionally drove me around town.

When I walked into the living room, I sat down next to Jackson and talked to him about Grandmother. He said he hadn't noticed anything strange either, but he would also keep an eye on her. I felt better knowing that all three of us were going to be looking out for her, but I was still a bit worried.

To get my mind off anxious thoughts, I carried a puzzle into the kitchen and dumped it on the table. I began the laborious task of turning the pieces over and hoped that concentrating on something challenging would get my mind off my problems.

A little while later, Tina contacted me.

"Hey, I'm having a party tonight. You free? It starts at 5."

I quickly responded that I would be there. Her parties were always a blast, but I knew I wouldn't be able to stay too late at this one because I had to meet with Kelly the next day. I felt bad that Jackson wouldn't be at the party, since he had to work, but he was considering changing jobs again, so he might not have to work in the evenings anymore.

Looking at the clock, I realized with a shock that I only had an hour before the party started. I ran upstairs and began to get ready. Then I walked into Kimberly's room to ask for a ride to the party. I was surprised to find her dressed and putting on makeup.

"Where are you going?" I asked.

She barely looked at me. "To a party."

"I need a ride to Tina's. Can you take me?"

That's when she actually looked at me. "Wait, you're going, too?

"Too?" I said, astonished. Did that mean she'd been invited to Tina's party? "Are you going to Tina's?"

She nodded. "Tina invited a ton of people from KMS and from RHS."

RHS stood for Rainier High School, the enormous school Kimberly went to and the one I would be attending in the fall. This was apparently going to be a bigger party than I had realized. "Regardless, can you take me?"

Sighing, she paused, mascara in hand. "Fine; but don't expect me to do any more favors for you anytime soon."

I rolled my eyes. She never did favors for me anyway, and she wasn't even going out of her way to do anything. I clumped back into my room and decided to put a little more effort into my outfit. I thought it was going to be a small party, but now that I had other information, I swapped my t-shirt for a nicer shirt, and French braided my hair.

Once Kim was finally ready, we got in the car and left. She didn't say a word the whole time we were in the car. I wondered what I'd done to make her mad. I thought we were on better terms after the incident with Mom, but, then again, I thought Mom was going to get better after said incident.

As we came to Tina's house, I was stunned at the number of cars in the driveway and lined along the road. Kimberly found a place behind a green Honda, and we began walking toward the house. Knocking on the door, I heard lots of people talking and laughing. Tina opened it a few moments later.

"Hey! Come on in!"

I gave her a hug. When I saw how many kids were packed in her house, I raised my eyebrows. "I had no clue you knew this many people."

She laughed. "It's a small world. I wanted to celebrate summer, and I basically sent out text after text. I forgot that there was such a thing as too many people, but it's fine. It's only for one night, and my parents told me they were fine with it as long as I cleaned up afterwards."

I walked towards the kitchen. Food always was a first priority in my book. On the way there, several people said hi to me. When I finally squeezed through all the people standing in front of the counter of food, I grabbed a slice of pizza and two cookies and stuck them on a plate. Swiping a soda from the cooler, I went to find a place to sit down.

Tina had—very conveniently, I might add—opened the French doors leading to the porch, so I decided to head outdoors to sit since fewer people were out there. Halfway through my slice of pizza, someone walked over and put a plate down. I looked up to see who it was and grinned.

Kody smiled back. "Mind if I sit here?"

I shrugged. "Nope." That is, I didn't mind unless Kimberly saw me. Then I would be dead meat. Perhaps, I'd better not hang around him too much tonight, or Kim might see us.

He sat down and dug into his pizza. "Are you enjoying your summer so far?"

I nodded. "It's been great!"

"Your last meeting is this week, right?"

I drank my soda. "Yes, it's tomorrow. I'm meeting with my cousin."

"Cool!" He said. "After that, what are your plans this summer?"

"Well, I haven't thought about that yet. I normally lounge around at home, but I may try and see if there's something a little more productive that I could do. Who knows? My grandmother might decide that we need a vacation, and we could spend the whole summer in Italy!"

We both laughed, knowing that would never happen. Not only would it be too expensive but also my family would tear each other apart if we were together all summer, having "quality time."

Just then, Tina walked over and put down a plate full of food. "How are you guys doing?"

I answered first. "Pretty good. Your parties are always a blast!"

She smiled. "Thanks."

"Yeah, I love coming to them," Kody said.

As we were talking, I sensed someone watching me. I slowly turned my head and spotted a girl sitting at the table in the house. She was staring at me oddly. Uncomfortable, I turned to Tina.

"Who's that girl over there?"

Tina leaned her head to see where I was subtly motioning, and then her eyes lit up. "That's Amanda Rockwood. She's in our grade and goes to KMS."

I was confused. "Why haven't I seen her before, then?"

"Well, she told me that she just transferred here about four months ago and that it's been hard making new friends."

I decided to help this Amanda out. I stood up and walked inside. Going over to the table she sat at, I smiled at her. "Hi. I'm Hazel, but all my friends call me Brie. Can I sit down?"

She nodded, surprised. "I'm Amanda Rockwood." She then paused, as if debating whether or not to ask a question. "Where did you get the nickname Brie from a name like Hazel?"

I laughed. "It's an old story, one from my childhood. Basically I was hungry one night and went into the kitchen to get a snack. The only thing I could reach was some Brie cheese, and when my parents walked in to see what the noise was, they found a little girl eating a huge rind of Brie. The name just sort of stuck."

She smiled. "I understand now," she said.

"Have I met you before?" I asked. "Your last name seems familiar."

She gave me a quick glance as she brushed back a strand of her short black hair behind her ear. "No."

"Okay," I said, but I still thought I had at least met someone related to her. I was sure I used to know someone named Rockwood. Who, I could not remember. "What do you like doing?"

Puzzled, she said, "What do you mean?"

"Do you have any hobbies?"

She nodded. "I play the violin, and I was on the swim team at my old school. I'm hoping to try out for the swim team at RHS next semester."

"That's cool!"

She smiled. "I think so, too."

"Where did you grow up?"

She stiffened. "A lot of places. I move all the time with my uncle. I'm never in one place for long, although my uncle has promised me that we will settle down soon."

I noticed that she rather cleverly avoided the question. Strange, indeed. I smiled as if I didn't distrust her completely. "It was nice meeting you. I'm going to go say hi to some of my friends."

"Nice meeting you too, Brie."

I stood up and walked away, feeling rather strange. Then, I felt bad. Just because she didn't like talking about her childhood didn't mean she was some sort of serial killer. I know I didn't like talking about my childhood. I shook my head. Amanda needed a friend, not someone who mistrusted her based on feelings. I decided to try and be nice to her, just like Tina was nice to me.

I went to talk to Elyse and Kelsey. They said they were having a good time, as well. I told them a little about Amanda and encouraged them to talk to her so she wouldn't feel alone.

Sooner than I wanted, the party ended, and Kimberly took me home. On the ride home, she didn't say much to me, as usual. I didn't mind, though. I just wanted to go home and go to bed; however I wasn't able to do that quite as quickly as I would've liked. I remembered that Jackson would be meeting a friend in Knoxville and wouldn't be able to take me to see Kelly. When I asked Kimberly to take me, she said she had plans with her friends and wouldn't be able to. That left me with two options: Mom or Grandmother. The first one was completely unwise and the second wasn't very appealing. I had to ask one of them, though, so I chose to ask Grandmother.

"Why are you wanting to see Kelly?" she said, as she looked up from her knitting.

"It's for a project I'm doing." I left it vague on purpose. I didn't want to explain my whole challenge right when I was about to finish it.

She nodded at me nonchalantly. "Alright, I'll take you."

"Thank you! I need to be there by 12:30 tomorrow." I went to bed more relaxed, knowing that I had a ride.

The next morning, I awoke and went downstairs to eat breakfast. I wondered what it would be like to actually have a good breakfast in the morning, rather than cereal and Pop-Tarts. I bit into my Pop-Tart glumly. There were so many "what ifs" in my life it wasn't even funny.

A little bit later, Grandmother came to get me from my room. "I think we should leave soon if you want to get there by 12:30."

I agreed and followed her out to the car. Pulling out a Sudoku book, I began a puzzle. By the time I solved the puzzle we were there. I climbed out of the car and went to knock on the door. A woman opened it a few moments later.

"Hey, come on in!"

I gave Kelly a hug. "It's good to see you! It has been too long."

"I agree." She led me inside the apartment. Sitting on the couch was her husband, Zach. He waved.

"Hey, Brie."

I hadn't met him yet, but I had heard some about him from my paternal grandmother when I called her every now and then to check in with her. Kelly showed me around and then asked what kinds of food I liked to eat.

"It doesn't matter. All food is wonderful to me."

She smiled. "Great! I want to take you out for lunch at Tony's. Are you ready to go now?"

I nodded. "Yes!"

We hopped into her car, and she began driving to the restaurant. Zach was going to eat at the apartment so we could have some girl time together.

"Have you ever been kayaking before?" Kelly asked as we pulled into the restaurant's parking lot.

"I have, but it was a long time ago." I haven't been kayaking since Dad died. He was always the one to take us kids on outdoor activities, like hiking and skiing and kayaking.

"I have two kayaks, and I was hoping that we could go today. There's a river not too far from my apartment, and I often kayak on it. What do you say?"

"I say yes! I'd love to!"

Walking into Tony's, we were soon seated and given menus. Within five minutes, we had decided and given the server our order. She ordered pasta, and I requested chicken tetrazzini. While we waited, Kelly and I began to catch up.

"Are you doing any sports right now?" Kelly asked.

I shook my head. "No. Where are you working?"

She took a deep breath. "I have a lot of different places I work at, but the main thing I do is teach. During the summer, I teach online with Lindamood-Bell Learning Processes for reading and reading comprehension. They make reading easier for kids with learning disabilities. Both Harvard University and Massachusetts Institute for Technology did MRI scans on students before and after the process. When looking at the scans, it showed that the makeup of their brains had actually changed after going through the process."

I gaped. That was incredible!

"I also teach full-time online with V.I.P. Kids, tutoring Chinese kids in English. I have to get up at 4:30 a.m. because of the twelve-hour time difference. I also tutor at Chattanooga Christian School in all subjects except for calculus and physics. Finally, I market for Rodan and Fields skin care."

"That's a lot of jobs!" I said. "How do you make time for it all?"

She laughed. "It's hard, believe me."

Our food came right after she said that, and I nearly fell out of my chair in delight. The chicken tetrazzini looked absolutely scrumptious with the alfredo sauce poured on the top. Kelly prayed, and then we began to eat. My food was as delicious as it looked. After I had taken a few bites, I asked Kelly another question. "Did you always dream of finding Mr. Right before you met and eventually married Zach?"

She shook her head. "I never wanted to date around, and I always thought I was going to be a single missionary. Obviously," she said with a laugh, "that's not the case."

"How did you know he was the one?"

"When I met Zach, I prayed about him, and God gave me peace that very day. I knew that whatever happened, everything would turn out according to God's plan."

"Do you always feel peace when you pray?" I know I didn't. Sometimes I just felt confused.

"If I don't, I keep praying until I have peace. God will always hear you, so don't think that He's not listening. Even if it's not the answer you want or expect, don't let it steal your peace. You see, the theme of my life has been having doors slammed in my face and then windows being opened. Those doors shutting were confusing because I thought I was supposed to walk through them, but God always knew the best plan for me."

I took a drink of root beer as I thought about that. "Are there any exciting window-opening experiences you would like to share?"

She smiled. "I had a very exciting experience while studying abroad in Switzerland. Another experience I've had recently is doing yoga. I was having back pain, and the doctor discovered that my vertebrae weren't straight, were inflamed, and contained lots of liquid. The doctor recommended yoga, so I did it for many weeks until finally the pain left; and I've been doing it ever since."

Since we were finished with our meal, we left the restaurant and went back to her apartment to get ready to hit the river, while Zach strapped the kayaks to the top of the car. He was going to drive us to the river and then come back later to pick us up. Climbing into the backseat, I began to grow extremely excited. I hadn't been kayaking in forever, but I still remembered that I loved it.

The drive wasn't that long, and we were soon there. Kelly and I strapped on life vests before she gave me a quick review of how to kayak. Then Zach pushed us out onto the river and we were off! I was pretty uncoordinated at first but soon got the hang of it and was able to keep up with Kelly pretty well.

As we paddled side by side, Kelly looked at me, squinting a bit in the sun, and asked, "Do you want to ask me any more questions for your challenge?"

I nodded. "Sure. What qualities should a godly woman have?"

She paddled a bit before answering. "She should have patience, discernment, and a servant's heart. She should be attuned to the Holy Spirit, trusting and malleable, and consistent in the insignificant."

Consistent in the insignificant. I liked that. I normally tried to be consistent in the big things, but she just reminded me that little things are important, too. "What's your favorite Bible verse?"

"It would have to be Proverbs 3:5-7, which I'm sure you already know."

Of course I did. I had read it so many times I could say it in my sleep. "'Trust in the Lord with all your heart and lean not on your own understanding; in all your ways acknowledge Him, and He shall direct your paths. Do not be wise in your own eyes; fear the Lord and depart from evil,'" I said, taking a deep breath.

She smiled. "That's the one!"

We slowly passed an impressively large house, one of the many on the river. "Why that verse?"

"It's a really good reminder, especially through hard times."

"What has been the hardest time in your life?"

"Probably my parents' divorce, and then later when they found new spouses."

Family problems are definitely some of the hardest to deal with. I knew from experience. We came upon a small cove, and Kelly began to paddle towards it. Once we had entered the cove, I smiled at her.

"It's so peaceful."

She nodded. "Yes, it is."

The noise from the boats on the river wasn't quite as prominent here. The only noise I really heard was the smooth dips of our paddles. The sun was glistening off the water, and there was hardly any current in the cove. I set the paddle down and just relaxed. Kelly pulled out her phone from a Ziploc bag.

"Let's take a picture," she said.

I smiled for the camera. She took the picture and then sent it to my phone.

"Thanks," I said.

After resting for a bit, we began heading back. We had already been paddling for quite a long time, and my arms were reminding me how I never exercised them regularly. On the way back, I noticed lots of floating debris and six dead fish, which I paddled far away from. As our destination came into view, I spotted movement along the riverbank. I pointed it out to Kelly.

"What is that?"

She gasped. "No way! That's a raccoon!"

My jaw dropped as I got a closer look. It was, in fact, a raccoon on the riverbank in the middle of the day. How strange was that! I brushed some hair out of my face as we paddled closer to where Zach was standing on the shore. "What's a life lesson you can tell me about?"

"Life is never what you expect; but it's okay because God will always be in it. So have a plan for your life, but trust God and let Him lead."

With that, our kayaks bumped up on the bank, and we climbed out of them. We dumped the water out of the kayaks and then helped Zach strap them to the top of the car. As I opened the car door, I noticed a milkshake on the seat.

"I got milkshakes for you guys while I was out," Zach said.

"Thanks!" I exclaimed. "I love milkshakes a lot."

Kelly looked up from her phone. "Apparently we kayaked two miles today!"

I was surprised. It hadn't felt that long time-wise, but my arms felt like it had been six miles. I really needed to work out more. On the way back to the apartment, I texted Grandmother to see if she could come and pick me up. She had told me she would be at a bookstore near Kelly's apartment for the morning, so whenever I was ready, I was to text her.

By the time we arrived at the apartment, Grandmother had just pulled into the driveway. I gave Kelly and Zach a hug.

"Thank you so much for spending time with me today! I had a blast, and it was a lot of fun catching up!"

"You're welcome," Kelly said. "I had a lot of fun, too!"

I climbed into Grandmother's car and she pulled onto the main road. "Did you have a nice time?"

I nodded. "I did. I haven't been kayaking in forever!" We rode the rest of the way in silence. Grandmother never liked talking while driving because it "broke her concentration too much."

Once I arrived home, I climbed the stairs to my bedroom and was about to flop onto the bed when I received a text from Tina.

"Hey, I know you just came over yesterday, but I was wondering if you would want to come over again tonight for a sleepover? I can take you to church in the morning, if you want."

I quickly responded. "Of course!" Going to Tina's house never got old. Tina told me that her mom would swing by to pick me up because she was in the area doing errands. I packed a bag of clothes for the sleepover, which only took a few minutes, and then I ran downstairs to grab a drink of water from the kitchen while I waited for Jenny.

I was just about to walk out of the house to wait for Jenny on the front porch when Mom, who had been lying on the couch with a bottle in her hand, stopped me.

"Where do you think you're going?" she said, her words slightly slurred.

I was surprised she could even form a coherent sentence. "A friend's house. Why do you care?"

She glared at me. "Don't give me that attitude. You're not supposed to disrespect your parents." She waved her bottle in my face.

I'd had enough. "Yeah, a fine parent you turned out to be!" I yelled, motioning to the bottle. "Can't you just give it up?"

"Give what up?" she said, a scowl on her face.

"Getting drunk, not caring for us kids, spending all your money on alcohol, and acting like a child!" I grew more enraged with each word.

She stood up, fire shooting out of her eyes. "Stop talking! You don't know what you're talking about." She winced as she held her head. "Oh, my head."

A knock sounded on the door, but I ignored it as I scoffed. "Oh, I don't? When was the last time you asked me how I was doing? When was the last time you gave me a hug? When was the last time you told me you loved me?" my voice broke, but I kept going. "You don't care. You go work your pathetic little job every day and then get drunk. When will it ever end? When will you wake up and realize that you've messed up? When will you finally realize that you will never be the parent Dad was?"

She slapped me across the face. "Shut up! Your father didn't have enough self-control to stay alive. He died because of you! It was your fight with him that was the last straw. If you had just simply listened to him and accepted what he said instead of arguing, he never would've killed himself. He would still be here!"

I was stunned as I shook my head. "What kind of a mother blames a person's death on her own daughter?"

She narrowed her eyes and shoved me away, taking a few unsteady steps backwards as she held her temple in pain. "Get out of my house," she shouted, her words beginning to slur. "I don't care where you go. I don't care who you see. I don't care what filthy hole you end up in. Why should I care? You're not even my daughter."

Everything, including the air, seemed to freeze. Time stood still. "What did you say?" I asked in a whisper, barely believing what I had just heard.

She turned white as she realized what she had just said; then, as if in slow motion, crumpled to the floor.

Epilogue

I rushed to her side. "Mom? Can you hear me?"

Her only response was silence. I started screaming for the family. The front door burst open and Jenny ran into the house.

"I heard a lot of what happened," she said, as she bent down to check my mom.

I felt tears welling up in my eyes. I was thankful Jenny was an E.R. nurse. She would know what to do. After twenty seconds, Jenny looked up at me, face grim.

"It's not good. You need to call 911 right now."

I gasped. "Oh no! Do you know what's wrong with her?"

She put her lips together. "I'd rather not say until we get her to the hospital. Has she had any headaches lately?"

"Right before she collapsed she said something about her head."

"This isn't good. Call 911 immediately."

I pulled out my phone and punched in those three ominous numbers. By this time, Grandmother had heard the commotion and came in to see what was happening. When she saw Mom, her hand flew to her mouth.

"What happened?"

Jenny stood up and gave her the details she knew while I talked with the 911 emergency dispatcher. Kimberly, hearing shouting, rushed into the living room. Upon seeing Mom lying on the floor, she almost fell over. Jenny reached out a hand and steadied her.

Very soon, the wailing of a siren was heard, and an ambulance pulled into the driveway. A couple of EMTs rushed into the house with a stretcher. I watched in silence as they put my mom on it and then took her out to the ambulance. Jenny was talking with them in low voices about what happened. They nodded and then left in a hurry for the hospital. The rest of us climbed into our car and followed. Kimberly was driving because Grandmother was an emotional wreck. On the way there, I called Jackson.

He answered. "Hey, Sis! Can I call you back? I have to work right now."

"No! Listen!" I said. "Mom just collapsed, and the ambulance is taking her to the hospital."

He gasped. "What? I'll go talk to my boss right away and then drive to the hospital as soon as I can!"

"Okay, Jackson," I said. "We've just arrived at the hospital. Try and be here as soon as you can."

As we rushed into the hospital, we were instructed to wait while they did some tests on Mom to figure out what was wrong with her. I paced in the waiting room. I knew if I sat still, I would overthink the situation and panic; however, that didn't stop the guilt from wiggling in. I had a fight with my dad, and he died right after. Now I had a fight with my mom, and she might die. Why did I always let my anger get the best of me? Mom would still be perfectly fine at home right now if I hadn't kept arguing with her. I kept pacing, trying to suppress the guilt that fought to surface. Jackson arrived five minutes later.

"How is she?" he said, rushing to me.

I shook my head. "I don't know. They haven't told us anything except that they're doing some tests right now."

"What happened?"

"Mom and I were fighting, and then she collapsed. Jenny had come to pick me up to go to Tina's and was there to assess the situation and to help me stay calm." I left out what

Mom had said right before she collapsed. I still had no idea what to make of it. If what Mom said were true, then my whole life would be turned upside down. If it wasn't true, then I had to deal with a Mom who hated me and didn't care where I ended up.

Hours later, a doctor finally came into the room. She gave us a grim smile. "I'm Dr. Stanton. Are you the family of Penny Thompson?"

We all nodded, anxious to find out what the results of the tests were. The doctor pointed to some chairs. "You all might want to sit down while I say this."

Grandmother, Jackson, and Kimberly sat down, but I stayed standing. I couldn't stay still.

Dr. Stanton began. "I'm afraid I have some very bad news for you. Penny has atrial fibrillation, a type of irregular heartbeat. Atrial fibrillation increases your risk of stroke by five times because it can cause blood clots to form in the heart. If these clots move up into the brain, it can lead to an ischemic stroke."

I was trying to process all this information. "Are you saying she had a stroke?"

Dr. Stanton nodded. "Nurse Lankford says that Penny held her head in pain before collapsing, correct?"

"Yes, that's right." I said.

"That is a common occurrence in patients before they have a stroke."

Jackson spoke up. "How long will it take for her to recover? Can we see her?"

She shook her head. "Not yet. We still need to run a few more tests. As for recovery, I'm not sure yet. It all depends on the patient. Some recover in 3 to 4 months. Others take the rest of their lives to get back to normal. Penny may have some lasting effects from this stroke: memory loss, problems with speech, and even issues with mobility."

I was struggling to comprehend all of this. "She won't die, right?"

"I'm not going to promise anything. The risk of having another stroke is highest right after having a stroke, but we're doing our best to prevent that."

I sank into a chair. I could no longer support myself. "How long will she be in the hospital?"

"Again, I can't say anything for sure, but I doubt she will be leaving soon. My advice is to go home and get some rest. You probably won't be able to see her tonight."

Jackson stood up. "Alright. Thank you, Dr. Stanton." When she had left, he ran his hands through his hair. "So what are we going to do? Just go home?"

Grandmother nodded. "You three go ahead. I'm going to stay here in case I'm allowed to see Penny."

Jackson began to protest. "But this hospital doesn't have anywhere for you to get a good night's rest. I'll stay. You go home with them."

Grandmother sighed wearily. "If you think that's best." The three of us went outside to climb into the car, Kimberly sliding behind the wheel. The ride home was very gloomy and silent. When we arrived home, Grandmother disappeared and Kim ran upstairs. I was left in the living room all alone. I collapsed on the couch. Millions of emotions and thoughts were swirling through my head. I put my head in my hands.

"Please help me, Jesus." I said, "I don't know what to do."

I decided to try and make sense of it all. What did Mom mean by her little statement? Is she really not my mother? I wanted answers. I needed answers. I went to the only place where I knew the past would be: the trunk in Dad's closet.

Their bedroom was designed so both Mom and Dad had their own closet. Tentatively, I walked into the closet, realizing I hadn't been in it since Dad had died. Nothing had been touched. I saw the trunk hidden behind his clothes. As I slowly opened it, I saw two photo albums lying at the top. I recognized them as the ones I had overheard, as a child, Mom asking Dad to get rid of. When she left the house, I peeked into his room and watched him hide the albums in the trunk, and she never found out.

I pulled out them both and sat down on the floor. I took a deep breath and then opened the first one, dated before I was born. The first picture was of my dad by Niagara Falls surrounded by his friends; he looked happy. The next few pages were more of my dad with his friends. Then, I flipped one more page and saw a photo that rocked my world. It was Dad at his wedding. But the woman he was marrying wasn't Mom. I tugged the photo out of the page protector and turned it over. On the back, someone had written, "Melody Greer and Jared Thompson. May your love be stronger than your fears."

I gaped. Who in the world was Melody, and why did I not know who she was? I kept looking at the photos. More wedding photos, vacation photos, and photos of them at their house. Too soon, I had looked through all the photos in that book. Hoping for more clues to help me bring to light this long-kept secret, I opened the second photo album. The first picture was of Melody at the hospital, holding a baby boy. I flipped the photo over and read, "Jackson Eric enters the family."

The next twenty photos were of Jackson getting older. Then, I saw another picture of Melody in the hospital, holding a baby girl this time. Looking at the back, I gasped. "Hazel Marielle, a beautiful gift from God."

I watched myself grow up. Then, the book ended. Why wasn't there a picture of Kimberly with Melody? I was even more confused. Apparently, Jackson and I have a mom no one told us about. There was still no closure, though. Why did no one tell us? What happened to Melody? I opened the first book again and pulled out the picture of Melody and Dad at their wedding. Setting it aside, I stood up and reverently put the albums back into the trunk and quietly closed it. I then picked up the picture off the floor and walked out of the bedroom, going back into the living room.

I didn't know what to do. If I told Kim and Jackson what I had just found, it would cause even more tension among us, and we didn't need that right now, especially after Mom just had a stroke. I shook my head and slid the picture into my pocket. This was one secret I would have to keep to myself. Lifting my chin, I whispered, "Even if I have to spend years unearthing the truth, I will find it and finally get some closure."

I considered all my options. I knew that I couldn't just go back to my old life and pretend like nothing happened. Finally deciding on what I was going to do, I snuck upstairs and packed a backpack full of everything I knew I would need. As I called for a taxi, I wrote a long letter to Grandmother and told her what I had found out and why I was leaving. After thinking about it, I also left a note for Jackson, not saying much, but letting him know not to worry. I knew that if he found out the truth, then he wouldn't feel as pressed to take care of Mom, well, Penny. I would rather him try and mend things between him and Penny before I tell him this and it shatters everything. Then, after taking $300 from Grandmother's moneybag, I ran outside. As I waited for the taxi, I debated whether my decision was rational or not. I had no time to fully think about it, though. The taxi pulled up our driveway, right on time. I stared at the vehicle as I prepared myself for whatever was to come and then climbed in. I was going to find some answers.

A Note For You

And now it's your turn. You get to finish the story in your life. What has changed in the story beneath the cover of your book? Will you take the step to accept Christ and experience life-changing events, or will you deny more and more, until you are consumed by the doubts and fears that reside on your pages? There's an ending to every story. We may not agree with the author's views or how they decided to write the ending out, but there will always be some sort of finality. It's the same in your story. You are the main character; you have the ability to make decisions to change how the story plays out; however, there is only one Author. You can try to change your ending based on your choices chapter after chapter, but there will be an ending. And if you don't surrender your story to Him, it will not have reached its full potential. God wrote a story for you, that you now have the privilege of playing out, but because of free will, the story can be changed. Even if not by much, it can be enough to ruin your life.

God is not a dictator in some great abyss. He loves you enough to give you freedom with the most important tool used in this world: your choice. You can choose decisions that will lengthen your story into a series, or cut it short. He provides a simple escape from the weightiness of having to decide everything by yourself, though. As Proverbs 16:33 says, "The lot is cast into the lap, but its every decision is from the Lord." God has the answers and solutions for every problem you are facing. Sometimes our pride can get in the way of asking for help, though. We have this strange notion that our way is better than God's way, and we don't like accepting the fact that we don't know everything. God can always see things we can't, and He tries to protect us from hurting ourselves and losing our way.

So once again, I ask you, will you take the step? Will you let Jesus into your life so He can help you live your life to the fullest, keep you from unnecessary hurt, and be the Author of your book? You will never regret it if you do. I won't deceive you and say that it's easy, but it's simple, and it's worth it. As 2 Corinthians 4:17 says, "For our light and momentary troubles are achieving for us an eternal glory that far outweighs them all." We need to remember that no matter what we face on earth, it will be worth the prize we receive at the end. So what journey will you choose? Who will write your story? And what will your book look like once finished? Will it be filled with chapter after chapter of denial and anger until you come to a very different ending than what God had originally wanted, or will it have tale after tale of victory in Jesus against the devil and the wickedness of this world?

God is waiting. What will your answer be?

Acknowledgements

First off, I would like to say that there is absolutely no way I could have written, edited, and published this book by myself. Not only would it have come out months later than it has because of procrastination but it would also be filled with grammar mistakes. A rousing thank you to my beautiful mom, who spent many, many late hours tediously editing each and every chapter. I couldn't have done it without her. Next, I would like to thank my dad who set up this program and gave me this wonderful gift. He was also a key factor in much of my brainstorming. I would also like to thank my family and friends for their support and ideas, and ennifer Walker who answered all my medical questions. And a huge thank you to all the women I met with! If it were not for them, this book would never have been written.

I believe that a title is what draws the readers in, and without my dear sister Anna, this book would have had a very uncomfortable, cringy title. Here are a few examples of what I had written down as possible titles for this book: *Band-Aids, Nothing but a Backpack, No Place to go Except Taco Bell, Putting the Extra Into Ordinary,* and lastly, *Have I Been Holding the Map Upside Down?* I thank her for being honest about those titles, and many, many more like them. And most importantly, I would like to thank Jesus, who brought me through many a day when all my creative juices had dried up and I was left with brain-dead ideas. All glory to Him forever and ever.

About the Author

Petra Thompson is a fun-loving fourteen-year-old who enjoys many things, one of which is writing. She's homeschooled and runs her own bread business called Rock House Bakery. She loves to read, sing, and dance. Petra is fond of photography and will also never pass up an opportunity to go hiking. One of her aspirations in life is to backpack across Europe and to travel to all seven continents (three of which she has already visited). She loves her friends, her family, and is always wearing a smile.

You may contact her via Thompson Publishers at PO Box 2605 / Cleveland TN 37320-2605 or online at ThompsonPublishers.com.

Comments

Did you enjoy this book? If so, we would really enjoy hearing from you. To share a comment on this book or a story about how it helped you, send us a note at: shatteredbook@walkwithgod.com.

Please visit us on the Internet at thompsonpublishers.com where you can find more resources.

Errata

A list of corrected errata is maintained at:

https://www.thompsonpublishers.com/shatteredbook

The publisher requests that any additional errata be sent via the form on that page.

COMING SOON

If you enjoyed Shattered, stay tuned for the next chapter in Brie's story: Gathered. To receive updates about this book as well as interesting notes from the author, send an e-mail to gatheredbook@thompsonpublishers.com.